GHOST GUM
VALLEY

JOHANNA
NICHOLLS

GHOST GUM VALLEY

SIMON & SCHUSTER
AUSTRALIA
A CBS COMPANY

GHOST GUM VALLEY

First published in Australia in 2012 by
Simon & Schuster (Australia) Pty Limited
Suite 19A, Level 1, 450 Miller Street, Cammeray, NSW 2062
This edition published in 2013

A CBS Company
Sydney New York London Toronto New Delhi
Visit our website at www.simonandschuster.com.au

National Library of Australia Cataloguing-in-Publication entry
Author: Nicholls, Johanna.
Title: Ghost gum valley/Johanna Nicholls.
ISBN: 9781922052209 (pbk.)
Subjects: Penal colonies–New South Wales–Fiction.
           New South Wales–Social life and customs–Fiction.
Dewey Number: A823.4

Editor: Jody Lee
Cover design: Blue Cork Design
Internal design and typesetting: Midland Typesetters, Australia
Printed and bound in Australia by Griffin Press

The paper used to produce this book is a natural, recyclable product made from wood
grown in sustainable plantation forests. The manufacturing processes conform to the
environmental regulations in the country of origin.

Sydney, New South Wales, January 1836

The whole community is rancorously divided into parties on almost every subject. Among those, who from their station in life ought to be the best, many live in such open profligacy that respectable people cannot associate with them...there is much jealousy between the children of the rich Emancipist; the former being pleased to consider honest men as interlopers. The whole population, rich and poor, are bent on acquiring wealth...

Charles Darwin
His 1836 reflections on the Penal Colony of New South Wales during the fourth of his five years as Naturalist on a survey voyage around the globe on HMS *Beagle*.

In honour of the creativity and courage of Actors, Actresses and Comedians throughout the ages.

With special tribute to the First Fleet convicts and marines who performed the first play on Australian soil, Farquhar's *The Recruiting Officer*, January 4, 1789.

And in memory of the quixotic 'Father of Australian Theatre', Barnett Levey.

Book One
The Liaison

A mistress should be like a little country retreat near the town,
Not to dwell in constantly, but only for a night and away.
William Wycherley, 1675, *The Country Wife, Act I*

CHAPTER 1

Sydney Town, Penal Colony of New South Wales,
December 1832

Marmaduke Gamble felt a surge of something akin to love for the bawdy mistress of his native land.

You'll never be a lady, Sydney. But you're my kind of woman. Lusty, voluptuous, gutsy, mercenary – but dead honest for all that.

The marine blue of Port Jackson's giant harbour, busy with convict transports and trading ships under sail, reflected the electric blue of a summer sky so high, so cloudless that Marmaduke was shocked to realise the truth. It had taken four years travelling the northern hemisphere for him to forget the magic of an Australian sky.

He stood on the rooftop of the new luxurious Princess Alexandrina Hotel with the stiff harbour breeze buffeting his long hair and silk dressing-robe. Sydney Town lay at his feet waiting for him to rediscover her. When he had set sail for England as a naïve youth of twenty, humiliated and vowing never to return, the Sydney he left in his wake was dismissed by many as the Whore of Oceania – like some lush, raucous street harlot who was forced to bed all-comers. He now saw Sydney with fresh eyes, transformed like a woman who has risen from the gutter to become a beautiful courtesan and could demand tribute from all her admirers – convicts, free settlers, military officers and men of Quality right up to the new Anglo-Irish Governor Sir Richard Bourke.

Below him lay the panorama of Sydney Town, its northern foreshores dense with species of eucalypts. South of the harbour the wild contrast in architecture seemed to be locked in a battle for supremacy. Impressive mellow sandstone public buildings and church spires that would not disgrace Georgian London stood at close quarters with the infamous Rocks area, packed with rows of hovels and strings of shanties that were an unwelcome reminder of how his Emancipist father Garnet Gamble had begun to amass his fortune.

Sydney's tallest building, completed during his absence, was the extraordinary five-storey complex that comprised a huge warehouse, topped by a mill and windmill and, fronting George Street, the façade of the grand Royal Hotel that housed the Theatre Royal.

Marmaduke gave a hoot of delight. *My God! Barnett Levey actually did it! Against all odds he's achieved his dream. Built our first professional theatre!*

He remembered his excitement as a youth, that June day in 1827, a witness to the celebration that drew an even larger crowd than a public hanging – the laying of the foundation stone for Barnett Levey's entrepreneurial vision, a lavish 1000-seat theatre.

Today, Marmaduke saw the windmill on the top of Sydney's tallest building as a symbol of the penal colony's growing wealth and culture. He knew Sydney's first purpose-built theatre was only flourishing due to the liberal policies of Governor Bourke, who had overturned his autocratic predecessor's veto of Levey's theatrical licence. Hungry for culture, all levels of Sydney society rejoiced in the young actor-manager's victory. But it had come at great cost to Levey's health and finances.

Thank God the convict class can now enjoy Shakespeare under the same roof as the Quality, no longer segregated by Darling's ban on social contact between bond and free. I reckon the Bard of Avon must be smiling in Heaven to see his groundlings in the pit booing Richard III *and weeping over* Romeo and Juliet.

Marmaduke decided he would support the new theatre by hiring a private box for the season. But he reminded himself he had not returned to the Colony merely to continue his pursuit of pleasure and adventure.

He hurried down to his chambers to change into appropriate clothing to launch himself into Colonial Society. Today was a red-letter day. The prime reason for his return to New South Wales was to lay claim to the inheritance his father had withheld from him.

Checking his appearance in the full-length mirror Marmaduke was pleased by the immaculate cut of his Savile Row tailcoat and trousers but frustrated by his usual battle – the art of keeping the wings of his shirt collar high enough to be fashionable yet just low enough to be free to turn his head.

What a bloody stupid fashion. I'd ring Beau Brummel's neck if he hadn't long gone to God!

He tied back his long, dark mane of hair in a ponytail that made him look like an eighteenth century pirate – a style that had intensely irritated his father and was reason enough for Marmaduke to refuse to have it shorn off in order to become a 'real man' in his father's eyes. His Currency-style long hair was an indelible part of his identity.

You failed in your quest to make a man of me in your own image, Father, but I'm my own man now. A hybrid. The outward appearance of an English gentleman, thanks to London tailors, but I've retained the native-born Currency traits you tried to eliminate.

Marmaduke surveyed his reflection critically as he assumed a rapid series of poses impersonating different types of Englishmen – an effete Regency dandy, a pompous government official, a fiery Whig orator making his maiden speech, a jaded libertine confident of his prowess of seduction, finally assuming to the cocksure stance of a Currency Lad.

In Europe he had had no need to impersonate an English gentleman. Arriving as a naive Colonial, he had camouflaged his embarrassing status of virginity by a reverse show of confidence, making no attempt to disguise his Australian accent and swaggering like an adventurer into the drawing rooms of the gentry. To his great surprise he discovered that delightful English trait – the acceptance of eccentricity. Wherever he went he was feted as something of a novelty, like a rare Antipodean plant plucked from a hothouse in Kew Gardens. When invited to house parties on country estates, he rode and hunted with gentlemen, was careful to avoid young virgins but charmed older matrons and widows, discreetly entering Society via the bedroom door.

A flock of sulphur-crested cockatoos alighted on the balcony, railing and squawked in chorus. Marmaduke had a vivid memory of his beautiful mother's wicked smile as she taught her tame cockatoo, Amaru, the phrases designed to infuriate Garnet.

Marmaduke smiled at this rare happy childhood image as he grabbed his top hat, gloves and cane and made for the door, intent on visiting the only two real friends he had in the whole colony. One was Josiah Mendoza, the elderly watchmaker who had found him distraught and broke after fleeing the Gamble mansion, Bloodwood Hall, and had given him bed and board and taught him some tricks of the jewellery trade.

Thank God for the lucky night at the gaming tables that enabled me to become his silent partner in our jewellery store.

Marmaduke's other old friend, Edwin Bentleigh, despite being a member of the two species Marmaduke distrusted most – a barrister and an Englishman – was a man he would entrust with his life.

With good reason. Edwin's already saved me from the gallows.

George Street was swarming with all levels of society. Elegant carriages fought for access between lumbering bullock-drays, chaises and carts loaded with farm produce. As Marmaduke crossed the road to gain a closer look at the exterior of the Royal Hotel, his passage was blocked by the crowd drawn to a procession. Marching behind a red-coated military band, by whose uniforms he recognised as the 17th Leicestershire Regiment, was a body of Freemasons dressed in full regalia complete with gold braid, medallions and painted Masonic aprons. But the true catalyst for the carnival mood of the crowd was an open landau carriage drawn by white horses.

The sole woman passenger waved her gloved hand like some Hanoverian queen acknowledging the motley throng of subjects running beside her carriage, shouting out their adulation and raining her with rose petals.

Who is she? Some European aristocrat dethroned by a revolution? Who knows? I've been isolated from world news for near three months at sea.

The answer became clear when Marmaduke caught individual cries of 'Bravo!', and a bold Cockney voice that demanded, 'Sing for us, darlin'!'

Marmaduke pushed his way closer to her carriage when it stalled in the crowd. He focused on her face and the impressive pale bosom decked with jewels, startled by the exotic, dark beauty of the woman who was a legendary singer and courtesan.

Josepha St John. The Irish-American Nightingale! It must have cost Barnett Levey an arm and a leg to entice her to the Colony. At last I'll see her perform in the flesh. And with a bit of luck – perhaps even closer.

Marmaduke had never been in the right country at the right time to see her perform. But he had greatly admired the controversial portrait of her as the goddess Juno, a painting refused by London's National Gallery due to the notoriety of its subject. Amongst a group of wealthy London gentlemen who had flocked to the artist's Hampstead studio, he had been transfixed by her lush beauty but the painting was not for sale. The artist was clearly enamoured by the diva who, it was said, had rejected him as a lover in favour of a British duke and a European prince warring for her attention. Marmaduke had seen the diva scandalously portrayed with them both in a series of ribald caricatures that sold like wildfire on the streets of London.

Marmaduke managed to catch the diva's eye as she alighted from the landau and entered the Royal Hotel.

We'll meet again, sweet lady – either on stage or off.

When Marmaduke tried to flag down a hansom cab to take him to Edwin's legal chambers, he was blocked by a flash new carriage from which the liveried driver jumped down and accosted him.

'You'd be Mr Marmaduke Gamble, right? I been trying to catch up with you. I'm your driver, sir, instructed to take you anywhere you require, night or day.'

'Instructed? There's some mistake. I didn't order any carriage.'

'No mistake, sir, if you're my master Garnet Gamble's son. This here carriage is your father's 'omecoming gift.'

Marmaduke barely managed to contain his rage. Since the day he had galloped away from Bloodwood Hall, shattered by his bride's rejection and threatening never to return, he had refused to accept the allowance from his father's bank. He had lived solely by his own resources, his travels sustained by his share of the quarterly profits from Mendoza's store.

Garnet's assumption that I'd accept this ridiculously expensive carriage is typical of Father's ego – a calculated gesture of manipulation. Nothing has changed!

Marmaduke was on the point of rejecting the gift when he noted the driver's anxiety.

'I'm Thomas, begging your pardon. If you don't accept it, Mr Gamble, I'll be out of a job.'

No point in cutting off my nose to spite my face. I'm in a dead hurry to have Mingaletta's deeds changed to my name. When that's legally square, I'll return this carriage to Garnet. His bloody hide, to think he can buy my forgiveness with a carriage and pair.

Despite his anger, Marmaduke could not help admiring the stream-lined bodywork, luxurious upholstery and the beautifully matched pair of greys.

'Any flashier and it'd put Governor Bourke's vice-regal carriage to shame.'

Thomas looked anxious. 'The team ain't to your taste, sir?'

The man's gold-braided livery, knee-breeches, buckled shoes, tricorn hat, everything was in mint condition – except his face. Judging by the beaten cast of features that looked prematurely aged, Marmaduke decided he was an old lag who'd done it hard.

'The coach is more my father's taste but I congratulate whoever chose the horses.'

Thomas's mouth split in a grin of surprise. 'I thank ye, sir. The master said you was an excellent judge of horseflesh, so I was to choose the best team money could buy.'

Marmaduke was surprised by this rare, second-hand compliment from Garnet, but he was more curious about the coachman's back-ground.

'Your face seems familiar. Your full name?'

'Thomas Thomas, sir.' He hesitated. 'I come out on the *Fortune.*'

Marmaduke knew this was the convict ship that had transported Garnet to the colony in 1806, so he tried to put the man at ease. 'Ah, yes, my father's shipmate. He said you tended his wounds after the ship's master had him flogged.'

The coachman looked startled when Marmaduke offered his handshake.

'No doubt you'll hear tales about my lurid past, Thomas. Most of them are true. But I'm not one of those Emancipists' sons who ape the English and are ashamed of the men who helped build this Colony. I'm native born and proud of it.'

With a sense of resignation that he had been out-manoeuvred by Garnet, Marmaduke took a seat in the carriage.

'But despite Father's orders, Thomas. Be a good fellow and save the "sirs" for him. I prefer Marmaduke.'

'Yes, sir – Marmaduke!' Thomas leapt up onto the driver's seat and took the team at a smart trot across town to where most of Sydney Town's legal fraternity had their chambers.

The carriage swung around the elegant square in front of the fashionable church of St James, designed by Governor Macquarie's once-favoured architect, Francis Greenway, the Emancipist who had been granted a pardon in the same year as Garnet. Greenway had fallen from grace during the subsequent Governor's regime and was now living in obscurity.

A typical Colonial pattern. The faster they rise, the harder they fall.

Edwin Bentleigh's legal chambers were two flights up in a convict-brick building that had been built early in the Colony's history.

Ushered into the inner office Marmaduke enveloped his friend in an extravagant hug, causing the diffident Englishman to turn pink with embarrassment.

'Edwin, how glad I am to see you. Time and again I wished you'd been sharing my adventures, mate!'

Edwin mumbled his pleasure at his friend's return and ordered tea but Marmaduke was struck by the barrister's careworn appearance, an even more marked contrast between his powerful courtroom persona and his reticent private face. Edwin's looks were ordinary, being thin of frame, gaunt of face with a sandy, receding hairline. But in the courtroom galvanised by oratory and his belief in the innocence of his client he was transformed into a figure of Shakespearean grandeur, fighting to uphold the spirit of British law.

Marmaduke knew he defended many convicts trapped in that nebulous zone between guilt and innocence and unable to pay him, yet Edwin fought for them with the same zeal he would bring to the defence of his sovereign, King William IV.

Outside the court Edwin shrank into a shy, perennial bachelor resigned to living under the thumb of his widowed mother in a Wool-loomooloo Hill cottage. Marmaduke had never seen him in the social company of a woman and wasn't sure whether this was due to lack of courage or inclination.

They laughed and jousted for half an hour, filling in the gaps between four years of letters, Edwin quietly enjoying Marmaduke's stories of his lost innocence abroad.

'You appear to have created quite a stir at Home, old chap.'

'Odd thing is, mate, I had to go to the Old World to feel really accepted as a native-born Australian. But back on my own home turf being a Gamble is the kiss of death. Garnet may be the second richest man in the Colony, able to buy and sell the Quality in business, but you know as well as I do, no Emancipist's son can ever break the class barrier or marry into their mob. This penal colony's invented more levels of society in forty-five years than Europe chalked up in ten centuries.'

Slipping into legal questioning mode, Edwin made seemingly casual enquiries about whether Marmaduke had returned to the Colony 'heart whole'.

'While you were away were you never tempted to ask for a lady's hand in marriage?'

'Hey, what do you take me for – a prize idiot?' Marmaduke said lightly. 'Once was more than enough. Being left high and dry at the altar at nineteen was the only chance any female will ever get to trap me in matrimony.'

Edwin said quietly, 'The bride wasn't worth a broken heart, old chap. I hope you realise that now.'

'I had a lucky escape,' Marmaduke said a shade too quickly. 'You were the best possible best man, mate. But there's no chance we'll front up for a repeat performance.'

'I trust you haven't foresworn the fair sex,' Edwin asked anxiously.

'Not a snowflake's chance in hell. I'm no misogynist. But maybe because I'm totally discreet I enjoy my fair share of "women of a certain age" as the gallant French say. Virgins are safe around me, mate. Voltaire said it in a nutshell. "It's one of the superstitions of the human mind to have imagined that virginity could be a virtue." I'll second that!'

'But you are young, Marmaduke, one day you may want to have children.'

Marmaduke sliced his hand through the air with the finality of a guillotine.

'Hold your horses, Edwin. You're so anxious to see me settled you'd marry me off to a bearded lady in a circus. Let me make it clear. There's no way I'm ever going to breed, Edwin. The Gamble dynasty began with Garnet and *ends with me*!'

Clearly troubled, Edwin gave a sigh of resignation best suited to an old man.

Marmaduke added casually, 'While we're on the subject, has Father's mental imbalance increased in my absence?'

'He's still in control of his empire, axing financial advisors in his customary style. He's expended large sums of money – with no known objective.'

Marmaduke shrugged and turned to the subject uppermost on his mind. 'Let's get down to brass tacks. Taking rightful possession of Mother's land means more to me than inheriting a gold mountain. I'll honour the promise I made when I was sixteen.' The words said in anguish on his mother's deathbed were now quoted coolly. '"I give you my solemn oath, Mother. I shall reclaim your land, become master of Mingaletta. And make Garnet Gamble pay for everything he did to you".'

Marmaduke's stare was intended as a silent challenge.

Edwin returned his gaze. 'I see. Miranda Gamble's Will did more than bequeath you her property. She left you a legacy of revenge against your father.'

Marmaduke shrugged. 'I've discovered that hatred is an emotion easier to sustain than love. Where do I sign my name to the transfer deeds, mate?'

'I regret to say, Marmaduke, it's not quite as simple as that. It is only in recent weeks that your father agreed to hand over your Mother's last Will and Testament. There is an irregularity. Please read it then we shall discuss ways to deal with it.'

The document was written on parchment yellowed with age. Marmaduke read it quickly the first time then evaluated every word on the second reading.

'It's as clear as a bell. I am to take possession of Mingaletta on my marriage or my twenty-fifth birthday, whichever comes first. Mother left several items of family jewellery and a sum of money to my childhood nanny, Queenie, whom she describes here as "my faithful friend and servant whom I love as my sister". She left nothing to Garnet, except Amaru, her sulphur-crested cockatoo that drove father nuts.

Mother's insult reminds me of Shakespeare's Will – leaving to his estranged wife, Anne Hathaway, his second-best bed.'

Marmaduke tossed the document on the desk. 'So what's the problem, mate?'

Edwin sighed. 'This Will isn't *signed*, Marmaduke.'

'But I heard her dictate it. We'll demand Garnet hand over the original copy.'

'This *is* the original. It was immediately written up by Garnet's manager and returned within the hour for her signature. But your mother had died minutes earlier.'

Marmaduke's voice rose in frustration. 'But I was *there*. So was Garnet – he was drunk at the time – in one of his manic moods. He'd brought an Irish fiddler to the house to play jolly Irish jigs to cheer up my dying mother, for God's sake. But Garnet's had ten years to remember that night and honour Mother's wishes!'

'I regret I must act as the legal servant to two masters, Marmaduke. But you can count on me as your friend. Your father insists on sticking to the letter of the law. Challenge him in court if you will but I believe every barrister in Sydney will give you the same advice. Garnet Gamble has the law firmly on his side.'

'You mean the bastard never intends to hand over Mother's estate to me?'

'He will…on condition you return to Bloodwood Hall to sign the deeds face to face.'

'Face to face? I'd rather kill the conniving bastard!'

Edwin thumped the table in an uncharacteristic display of aggression. 'Don't be a damned fool, Marmaduke. You are his only son and heir. You stand to inherit his whole empire – given you don't lose your head and sign your own death warrant!'

'If I killed Garnet Gamble in a duel half of Sydney would applaud me!'

'I managed to get you off one murder charge for killing a man in a duel because you were a wet-nosed youth of sixteen. But don't count on me or the law to prevent you swinging on Green the Finisher's rope if you murder your own father!'

Marmaduke quietly digested those words until his mood turned to icy calm.

'I thought I'd felt the full gamut of hatred. For my father and that villain I killed. But I see now there's no end to Garnet's manipulation and no end to my hatred.'

Edwin ran his fingers through his hair and seemed to have aged in the past hour. Marmaduke felt a sting of pity for his friend and hastily assumed a cavalier manner.

'Forgive me for shooting the messenger, mate. I can see it's a helluva role playing lawyer to both father and son. Don't worry. I'll return to Bloodwood tomorrow and play Garnet at his own game. I'll *talk* him into his grave.'

Marmaduke grabbed Edwin's hat and jammed it on his friend's head.

'That's enough real-life *sturm und drang* for one night. You and I are off to enjoy the French chef's cuisine at the Princess Alexandrina. My treat to celebrate my homecoming. And after we've drunk our fill of the new Hunter Valley wines I've read about, We're off to the box I've taken at the Theatre Royal. No arguments. They're giving us scenes from *Hamlet* tonight.'

He steered a mildly protesting Edwin out the door and bundled him into the carriage, quoting lightly, '"The play's the thing to catch the conscience of the King!"'

Beneath the surface of his changed mood, Marmaduke examined his options.

Unlike the Prince of Denmark I'm not indecisive. If push comes to shove I won't baulk at murder. They say the second time a man kills is so much easier than the first.

CHAPTER 2

De Rolland Park, Gloucestershire, England,
December 1832

'Do I *really* have to wear this awful corset, Agnes?' Isabel groaned, holding onto the bedpost as Agnes laced her so tight she could hardly breathe. 'It's not as if I need this. I'm built like a boy. I wonder if I shall ever have any curves.'

'Keep still, lamb, and I'll have you all trussed up in a minute. You're seventeen – you can't run around like a tomboy, it ain't seemly.'

'What's the point? I'm not allowed to go into the village nor attend church. Nobody ever sets eyes on me except you, the other servants and occasionally the family. I haven't even been allowed upstairs to visit Cousin Martha in her sickbed. I might as well be in Newgate Prison.'

'Don't say such things, even in jest,' Agnes said quickly. 'You must not dwell on the past. Your sleepwalking sickness was to blame, not you, dearie.'

Isabel sighed, '"What's done is done and cannot be undone."' Her hand flew to her face in horror. 'My God, I just quoted from *The Scottish Play* – that's bad luck!'

Realising she had broken the theatrical taboo against quoting from *Macbeth* in a dressing-room, Isabel flung a shawl around her shoulders and broke free from the bedchamber she had been forced to share with Agnes for the past three years. She bolted along the long, winding corridors with Agnes racing after her, begging her to stop.

On reaching the kitchen herb garden she turned around three times and spat into the garden, watched in horror by Agnes.

'Have you gone out of your mind, Isabel?'

'No, that's what actors must do to reverse their bad luck if they quote lines from Shakespeare's *The Scottish Play*. You see they call it that to avoid saying its true title.'

Agnes looked thunderstruck. 'But you're not an actress! You're a born lady, a de Rolland!'

'Yes, unfortunately. But I would far rather be an actress. And I don't want to tempt fate to bring me any more bad luck than it has already wished on me.' Her mood was suddenly serious but she pushed past images from her mind.

'Come indoors, lamb, or you'll catch your death of cold,' Agnes said, gently shepherding her inside. 'Your guardian wants to see you at three o'clock sharp and we must have you looking presentable.'

Back in the chamber, Isabel sat impatiently while Agnes dressed her hair with side curls. A pretty blue ribbon was small compensation for her scuffed shoes and the hand-me-down jacket and skirt that she had outgrown over the past two years and now needed to tug down to cover her ankles. New clothes never came Isabel's way – one small sign of the severely straightened circumstances into which the grand de Rolland ancestral home had been sinking for several years, sucked down by the quicksand of extravagance and gambling.

With an hour to spare before her encounter with her guardian, Godfrey de Rolland, Isabel insisted they go to the library, the one communal room in the great house that she was free to enter. She had continued her studies there alone following the departure of her governess – another luxury the family no longer chose to afford.

Isabel knew exactly how she would spend this precious hour. For years Cousin Silas had forbidden her access to their ancestral family tree, claiming it was for her own protection. Why? What was the dark secret involving her? This question had gnawed at her curiosity until yesterday during Silas's absence in London. She had chanced on a rare encounter with her guardian, as he paused on the landing of the staircase, frowning as he read some papers that she recognised by their red seal as legal documents.

Seizing her chance Isabel had made a hasty curtsey. 'You know how much I love history, Uncle Godfrey. Is there any reason why Cousin Silas says I may not study our de Rolland family tree?'

Godfrey de Rolland peered at her over the rim of his pince-nez as if weighing his words. 'Silas considers himself the Keeper of the Seal. Like his father, Silas sees darkness and evil where others do not. In medieval Spain my brother Henri would have gloried in the role of

Inquisitor. I think, Isabel, you are now sensible enough to understand that all old families have their share of secrets. Heroes or villains, none of us is perfect. You have my permission to peruse the document but remember it is ancient and fragile. Handle with care, what?'

'Indeed I shall, Uncle. Thank you...'

Now as she waited to be summoned Isabel tried to dismiss her unease about her guardian's opinion of her. *Would Uncle Godfrey consider me sensible if he knew that I was born with the gift – or curse – of being able to see 'the Other', the presence of departed souls who no one can see but me – and that Silas says is born in witches.*

With a feeling of suppressed excitement mixed with trepidation Isabel slipped on the white cotton gloves that must be worn on pain of death when handling rare manuscripts and carefully removed the ancient vellum scroll from the safe.

'This family tree should prove whether or not I was born on the wrong side of the blanket, Agnes,' Isabel added under her breath, 'yet another Plantagenet bastard.'

She carefully unfurled it. The de Rolland family tree traced the generations of her ancestors back to 1154 and down to the births, deaths and marriages of the living generations of Uncle Godfrey, his nephew and heir, Silas, married to Martha, and Isabel – the poor relation that Uncle Godfrey had made his ward after the death of her young parents. But did it record the details of her father Walter de Rolland's youthful marriage to Alizon – the mysterious girl no one wanted to remember?

Isabel vividly remembered the first day she had been brought to this Gothic mansion as a five-year-old orphan and was made to watch as the name Alizon de Rolland was struck from the list of family names written in the ancient bible.

Isabel looked across at the faithful old servant who was gazing in awe at the document, even though she was unable to read a word.

'What's the big secret about my birth? Was I born five months before my parents' marriage – or five months after? Did I miraculously survive a premature birth? Or I was conceived by lovers who couldn't wait for the priest's blessing?'

Agnes looked flustered but Isabel rather liked the idea of a wicked liaison.

'In or out of wedlock, at least *someone* in this cold-blooded family was conceived in love.' She began at the top of the tree. 'For generations every de Rolland except my father Walter wedded their cousins to keep the fortune in the family. Even Silas did – although Martha was the heiress when he married her. He was hoisted on his own petard!'

Agnes hid a giggle behind her mittens. 'Isabel, you do have a naughty tongue!'

The clock in the corridor outside the library chimed the hour, reminding Isabel that, as fond as she was of Agnes, she valued these golden hours of freedom.

Ever since that terrible day three years earlier when she was found wandering in the woods, unable to remember the two missing weeks in her life, Isabel had been forced to eat, walk and sleep with Agnes, a condition laid down by her guardian to avoid the dishonour the public revelation of her crime would bring to the family name.

Even in bed I have no freedom to dream without Agnes spying on me.

Isabel paused as honesty forced her to face the unpalatable truth. *I can hardly blame her for my sleepwalking illness. Agnes is paid to protect me – from myself!* She ran her finger down the scroll, hoping it would reveal the family secrets. *Nobody tells me anything. I'm forced to indulge in subterfuge – or go to my grave dying of curiosity.*

The yellowed parchment revealed the complex pattern of genealogical branches that sprang from their founding ancestor, King Henry II, the son of Geoffrey V of Anjou, who established the House of Plantagenet, until in 1399 it split into two branches represented by the White Rose of York and the rival Red Rose of Lancaster, who for generations battled in the War of the Roses for lands and titles stretching from Ireland to Jerusalem. Reverently Isabel touched the name of the last Plantagenet king, Richard III.

'Shakespeare's play *Richard III* is great drama but it made poor Richard notorious. I never believed he murdered the two little Princes in the Tower of London. I'm sure it was Henry Tudor's dirty work but historians made poor Richard go down in history as the villain – to bolster the Tudors' claim to the throne.'

Agnes nodded sagely. 'I always thought so, too.'

By the time Isabel reached the present de Rolland generation, she was convinced that, despite Silas's claim to the contrary, their link to the Plantagenet bloodline was indeed via a cadet branch 'on the wrong side of the blanket'.

'Do the servants think I'm illegitimate too, Agnes? Is that why I'm treated like the poor relative?'

Agnes looked discomforted so Isabel added, 'Never mind, I'll soon find out.'

The current generation seemed like a last withered branch on the tree. It confirmed that Uncle Godfrey, her guardian and head of the family, had married his cousin. No issue. His only sister Elisabeth had been banished in disgrace after her elopement with a mariner. No issue. The middle brother, Henri, had contracted a marriage with the elder of two Lancastrian sisters who was mistakenly believed to be an heiress. This unhappy union had produced Godfrey's heir, Silas. Godfrey's youngest brother, Isabel's father Walter, had married the younger sister, Alizon, under mysterious circumstances. The date showed he had died of consumption in 1816, the year after Isabel's birth.

Agnes said guardedly, 'When your father Walter fell in love with Alizon, the more beautiful of the two sisters, his jealous brother Henri tried to block their marriage.'

'I see. So two de Rolland brothers fathered children to two sisters – which makes Cousin Silas my 'double cousin', the closest relationship to brother and sister. But what is the awful mystery about *my* birth?'

Isabel grabbed the magnifying glass and read the words in the margin, 'See Notes' and an arrow pointed to the reverse side. With care she turned the document over.

'It says Henri accused my mother of killing her sister – by witchcraft.'

Agnes evaded her eyes, a sure sign she knew the story. Isabel was stunned. The date of the Not Proven entry was followed by the date of her parents' wedding. She realised Godfrey de Rolland must have relented and given his consent in time to legitimise her birth. She was born on 8 November 1815 – five months after their marriage.

'Agnes! That's the mystery no one would tell me. Mother was accused of witchcraft! Cousin Silas said she was descended from one of the Lancastrian witches burned at the stake. Silas is right! **I am** cursed!'

Isabel felt the library walls spinning rapidly around her. Sick with panic and, overcome by nausea, she felt herself falling into a black whirlpool. Agnes ran to her side.

'I'm not a bastard, Agnes,' she mumbled, dazed, 'but I am a witch.'

'Hush, no more talk of witches. Your mother was a pretty young thing. All she did was give her sister herbal physic when she was ill. Alizon would nay hurt a fly.'

Isabel realised she owed her guardian a threefold debt of gratitude – allowing her to be born legitimate, making her his ward and then standing by her in her own disgrace.

I can't change my ancestors or my own shameful past. But I shall do my utmost to prove to Uncle I'm worthy to bear the de Rolland name.

At the sound of an approaching carriage Isabel hurried with Agnes to the window, where a new phaeton charged down the snow-covered carriageway. Isabel recognised the man's elegant cape and high-crowned hat.

'How on earth can Cousin Silas afford new carriages and fashion-able clothes when we're on the brink of bankruptcy? Only months ago the servants said Uncle Godfrey was so deeply in debt he was about to be carted off to live under The Rules!'

Isabel was horrified by the paradox of the special debtor's prison. It was reserved for gentlemen who lived under guard in a degree of comfort, their food, clothing and rent supplied by friends, but they were unable to leave The Rules until their debts were paid. Had Cousin Silas finally reversed his losses at the gaming table?

'That's the way of the world, lamb. We servants ain't been paid in two years but fine folk always find money for luxuries.'

When the clock struck three Isabel hastily checked her appearance and flew down the corridor. Outside her guardian's doors she turned to Agnes for reassurance.

'Uncle hasn't summoned me here since the day they found me in the woods. What have I done wrong? Have I been walking in my sleep again?'

'No, lamb. You sleep like a babe. Go in with a smile. All will be well.'

This grand room was an oasis of calm. Light streamed through the windows, forming a misty prism that held wisps of cigar smoke.

She made a quick curtsey to Uncle Godfrey, who was seated at his desk, his quill scratching across a letter. He acknowledged her presence with a faint smile.

'One moment, m'dear. This must be delivered to London today.'

Isabel studied the portraits of five generations of de Rollands that lined the walls. Despite the costumes of different eras, their features appeared to be cut from the same genetic pattern. The male faces were aquiline in youth, chiselled like white marble, becoming veined in middle age. Each face was stamped with the distinctive de Rolland mouth, the lips full and sensual, suggesting they were more venal than passionate, if Isabel could believe the legends about them. Generations of intermarriage gave them such a strong resemblance Isabel thought they could be mistaken for brothers and sisters who were dressed in period costumes for a fancy dress ball.

Isabel felt like the cuckoo in the de Rolland nest. Although she bore a marked resemblance to them in her golden brown hair and green, hooded eyes, her face was heart-shaped and she was forever marked as 'an outsider' because of her nose. She ran her finger down the bridge in the faint hope that, like 'water dripping on stone', she could alter its shape over time. The nose she had inherited from Alizon was far from aristocratic, so tip-tilted not even the French translation *retroussé* could comfort her. Feeling a sudden wave of guilt as she sat under the noses of her ancestors, she mentally challenged them.

Many of you weren't shining examples of morality. Our fortune was built by privateers, rebels and slave traders. You didn't come by this mansion by growing potatoes and grazing sheep. Don't dare look down your aristocratic noses at me!

The silence was broken only by the scratching of her uncle's quill until Isabel could bear the suspense no longer and cleared her throat.

'You wished to see me, Uncle Godfrey?'

'What? Oh yes, indeed, Isabel. Quite some time since we talked about your progress. I take it there's been no recent recurrence of – your illness?'

'Thank you, no. The only walking I do these days is when I am wide awake in tandem with Agnes.'

'Quite.' He looked embarrassed. 'And I take it you have diligently continued your studies alone since your last governess departed?'

Departed? Mademoiselle's dismissal was one of the economic measures you took so that Cousin Silas could keep up appearances.

'Indeed yes, Uncle, I practise my French, Italian and Latin each day. And the pianoforte. But my German is growing rusty. Agnes told me that the wife of the Prussian clockmaker in the village heard I was learning German and invited me take tea with her. May I have your permission to accept and practise my German conversation? She is by all accounts a most respectable lady.'

Uncle Godfrey looked discomforted. 'No doubt she is. But you have not been seen in the village for the past three years. We don't want to risk arousing fresh speculation as to the reason a girl your age has not yet come out in Society.'

Will it never end? I might as well have served time in Prison!

'May I at least attend church services, Uncle?' she asked with studied sweetness. 'I don't care which religion, your Church of England, Cousin Martha's Catholic Mass or Agnes's Methodist Chapel – anywhere I can sing and ask God's forgiveness.' At his startled expression, she added quickly, 'In private, of course. No confession to a priest!'

Uncle Godfrey rang the bell rope then, when a footman appeared, handed the letter to him. He silently withdrew.

'I am not unmindful of how confined your life has been, Isabel. I do not want to revive memories painful to you. But I want you to know that I have never blamed you for the actions you committed during the periods our physician diagnosed as amnesia. You are not responsible for the sleepwalking illness God visited on you – nor its tragic consequences. But I face difficult decisions that affect every member of this family. Do you understand me, child?'

Isabel felt her face draining of colour and her tongue cleave to the roof of her mouth. *He means he's in danger of living under The Rules.*

'Uncle, I have studied hard in the hope I could take up some employment and no longer be a burden to you, to repay your great kindness to me.'

'Burden? Repay me? You are not to think of it!' He looked distressed. 'I am not a man given to displays of emotion, Isabel, but from the moment you first entered this bleak old house as a child you brought the sunlight indoors. You were so alive. So eager to learn. Yes, yes, headstrong at times, but quick to apologise and loyal to a fault. Loyalty is not a quality readily found amongst our de Rolland clan. I fancy you inherited that trait from Alizon.'

Isabel felt her chest tighten with emotion to hear this belated compliment to her mother but she knew it was impossible for her to cry. Cousin Silas had told her as a child that witches can never cry.

At that moment her eyes were drawn to the looking glass and the reflection of the handsome face of the man she had adored as a child. Cousin Silas. The image smiled at her. How long had Silas been standing there?

Isabel felt torn by contradictory emotions as Silas advanced into the room, dressed in a fashionable plum-coloured waisted frockcoat over buff trousers and a richly brocaded waistcoat of oriental design. His shining golden-brown hair curled around his face in a poetic Byronic mode, the heart-shaped chin held high by the immaculately starched, pointed folds of his collar and the snow-white stock tied with great artifice. His face was a male version of hers.

He sauntered across the room and used his height to full advantage, looking down at her with that oddly amused expression that always unsettled her.

Something is very wrong in this room. I can feel invisible currents between them. They know my fate. I'm in the dark.

Silas bowed to them. 'Is this the welcome I receive after weeks in France?'

'No doubt you found ample distractions to amuse you?' Uncle Godfrey said crisply.

'None to compare with artless English beauty,' Silas said.

As Isabel curtseyed to him he ran his eye over every detail of her shabby appearance.

How I detest being born a woman! Always at the mercy of men.

Why wasn't I born a man? To fight duels, go to war. I'd pay them back in kind. Take no prisoners!

Isabel found her voice and said sweetly, 'I trust you attended the Comédie-Française? Did you see the work of the new dramatist Victor Hugo they're calling the leader of the French Romantic movement? *Marie Tudor* or *Lucrèce Borgia?*'

Silas was amused by her eagerness. 'Shall give you my critique later. Enough to say that Hugo's work shows melodramatic brilliance and erudition but his characters tend to perform like puppets against their historical backgrounds. Talma was brilliant in his day but I've yet to see another French actor equal Edmund Kean. The actress who played Lucrèce Borgia was charming, but her voice failed to move me half as much as yours when reading Juliet, *ma petite cousine.*'

Isabel blushed when she realised Uncle Godfrey was observing them sharply.

'Enough of your Froggy court manners, Silas. May I remind you you're back on English soil? A country founded on roast beef, common sense and plain speaking.'

Silas's voice held a hint of mockery. 'I await the disclosure of your plain speaking with interest, Uncle. I trust that I will be given a voice in the decision?'

'My plans are governed by a necessity not of *my* making. As well you know.'

Isabel saw her cousin's full mouth tighten to a hard line. The sudden flash of his eyes made her shiver as he warned softly, 'Be careful, Uncle.'

Uncle Godfrey frowned over the top of his pince-nez. 'If you wish to remain, let it be on the understanding the one person entitled to voice an opinion is my ward!'

Isabel was so nervous her words came out in a rush. 'When I know what the subject is, Uncle, I shall be pleased to do so.'

'Marriage, m'dear. You are seventeen. High time to decide your future.'

Oh Lord, here it comes. How can I tell him it makes me sick to think of a man climbing into my bed? But I must stay calm.

'I have no wish to marry, Uncle, now or ever. Please don't make me do what is...repugnant to me.'

The old man held up a hand to halt her. 'My dear child, I am not an ogre. This is almost 1833, not the Dark Ages. But the preservation of family honour is at stake here – yours and mine. I do not enjoy raking up the past. But face facts, we must. It is common knowledge our ancestral estate is under dire threat of being lost to future de Rolland generations. We three are the last of our bloodline. There are no wealthy family members to come to our rescue.'

Silas broke across his uncle's words with barely restrained anger. 'May I remind you, Uncle, I married a wealthy de Rolland cousin. It's not my fault Martha's senile father remarried and produced sons who've replaced her as his heirs!'

'Leave your wife out of this! An invalid has enough to contend with!'

Isabel was overcome by guilt that she had failed to defend Martha.

Silas stood with folded arms as if prepared for combat.

Uncle Godfrey turned to Isabel. 'The question being asked around the county is why we keep you sheltered without any evidence of suitors on the horizon?' He added tentatively, 'One solution would be a respectable marriage to a wealthy older gentleman who would take care of you.'

Isabel fought down her panic. 'I am most mindful of the fine education you have given me. I beg you to allow me to take up a position as a governess in another county. That would bring an end to unwanted gossip. And I would most willingly turn my wages over to you as a small gesture of my gratitude.'

'No, m'dear. I will not countenance the idea of a de Rolland being trapped in a downward spiral of genteel poverty as a governess. I ask you to consider the advantages of marriage to a kindly older man who would dote on you.'

Silas seized on the idea. 'In a few short years you would be a widow, young enough to marry again and bear children. You could return to me – to *us.*'

Godfrey lost his temper. 'Silas! I will not allow Isabel to be cajoled against her wishes, no matter what fate is to befall me!'

Isabel's voice rose. 'Uncle, I could not stand by and see you live under The Rules!'

Silas's sudden loss of control caused Isabel's stomach to knot in fear, reminding her of that terrible moment as a child she had seen him transformed into the face of a stranger. His silky voice was more dangerous than if he had shouted in rage.

'We would not be faced with this threat, Uncle, if you'd allowed me to marry Isabel years ago. I'd have living heirs by now, instead of a wife who's a permanent invalid!'

Uncle Godfrey's face turned ruddy. 'You know perfectly well the reasons why I had to refuse. Consanguinity. Your blood is *too close!*'

Double cousins can legally marry. What other reason? Why am I always left in the dark? I have a right to know. 'Uncle, the *future* is all that matters. I would appreciate knowing your plans.'

'Quite so,' her guardian said wearily. 'You have seen so little of the world. I thought perhaps you'd welcome a journey to London to visit art galleries, attend plays. You fancy all that theatrical stuff, I take it?'

Isabel almost laughed with relief. 'Yes! It's long been my dream to see the great Edmund Kean. Lord Byron was said to have been so terrified by Kean's convincing rages on stage that he suffered a fit of apoplexy. They say Kean's *Richard III* holds audiences enthralled.'

'Not surprising, really. Richard was a Plantagenet after all. We are none of us exactly famous for our cool tempers,' he added, casting a meaningful glance at Silas before returning his gaze to Isabel. 'I shall arrange for you to attend a play in our box at the Theatre Royâl Drury Lane, His Majesty's own company of players.'

Isabel wanted to fly across the room and hug him but decided on a more demure response. 'Thank you indeed, Uncle!'

He scratched the long de Rolland nose, a sure sign he was nervous.

'Actually I wasn't merely thinking of London, m'dear. I thought perhaps a sea voyage might be beneficial for your health, as you have been confined so long indoors.'

'A sea voyage? To France? Oh Uncle, that would be wonderful!'

He appeared flustered, 'Very well, a visit to Paris. But I had in mind a slightly longer voyage to further your education.' He rose to signal her release.

Isabel felt confused by her guardian's sudden dismissal before she had time to ask questions. Was the subject of marriage to be delayed until her return from London and Paris? Would she have a right to veto the choice of suitors?

Closing the doors behind her, she checked the corridor to make sure she was alone before she peered through the keyhole, straining to piece together their broken phrases. Uncle Godfrey sounded defeated.

'I refuse to force the girl...she'll do the right thing by the family in the end.'

Isabel caught Silas's rising inflection. 'You're old...don't know what love is!'

'No? But I know what love is *not!* You think I don't know where your tastes really lie? Poor Martha. I've just had to pay off a tenant farmer to prevent gossip about your interest in his daughter.'

'More fool you, Uncle. I simply gave the lass a half sovereign for watering my horse...this wretched village breeds gossip faster than it breeds bastards...can't wait to return to London...'

Isabel felt a sudden chill at Silas's careless words. Unable to decipher their conversation as they moved out of range, she felt confused by the half-truths and innuendo of their meeting. Only one thing was clear. At last she was going to have some say in her future. She suddenly felt light of heart, drunk on hope.

I'm going to see Edmund Kean and sail across the English Channel to buy myself a Paris bonnet!

Unable to contain her happiness she gave herself up to the arms of an imaginary partner, waltzing in a dizzying spiral pattern down the corridor.

Men are only good for one thing. To lead us in the waltz!

CHAPTER 3

Bloodwood Hall, New South Wales, December 1832

In no man's language could this be called a 'homecoming'.

The giant wrought-iron gates appeared through the early morning mist as Marmaduke rode towards Bloodwood Hall. The grandiose entrance with its central carriage gates and side pedestrian gates was designed in the style favoured by Napoleon Bonaparte. Instead of the N at the heart of the iron olive wreath was the double G, a reminder that Garnet Gamble had created himself a mercantile prince of New South Wales.

Beyond these gates the avenue that stretched for a quarter-mile to the house was guarded on either side by a row of eucalypts that had doubled in height since the night Marmaduke had galloped down this carriageway blinded by rage, vowing never to return. The sight of these Bloodwood trees and their heady eucalyptus smell triggered a memory of himself as a small boy, standing at his mother's knee on the front terrace.

Her beautiful face was lit by the glow of battle. 'I told you, Garnet, I do not want English elms!'

Marmaduke saw his father's face darken and, as usual, he took out his anger on whoever was close at hand. Today, the target was his surly overseer, Fordham the Flogger, who Marmaduke instinctively knew was trying to keep face in front of their assigned men.

'You heard the lady, Fordham. What are you waiting for, man? Get 'em to rip out those elms. So what if you did plant 'em last week? Replace them with those damned Bloodwood trees. By nightfall!'

Garnet tossed his parting words over his shoulder. 'That make you happy, Miranda? Is that Australian enough for you? As if we haven't got enough gum trees in this damned colony!'

Marmaduke's heart grew a notch lighter at the memory of one of his mother's rare victories. At least her beloved trees had survived.

Before he had time to open the gates a figure stumbled out of the darkness, a convict blanket clutched around his shoulders, rubbing sleep from his eyes. The lad hastily touched his forelock, pulled the bolt then swung on the gate to open it.

'Sorry, sir, just nodded off, I did. No need to tell me overseer? Won't happen again.'

'Rest easy, lad,' Marmaduke said lightly. 'But why didn't you ask my name? I might have been a bushranger come to overhaul the place. Plenty of bolters in this locality, I hear.'

'I knew you was the master's son. For weeks past we've all been told to expect a fine English gentleman like yourself, sir.'

'The clothes are English but make no mistake, I'm Currency born and proud of it.'

Marmaduke asked the lad's name then tossed him a coin.

'Can I stable your horse for you, sir?' the boy asked as he trotted alongside him.

'Not yet, Davey. I have a call to make before I announce myself to my father,' he said, knowing full well that Garnet would be aware of his presence the moment he set foot on the estate.

At the end of the avenue Marmaduke saw the dark Gothic outline of the house was just as he remembered it. The double-storey mansion with its side wings and strange cross-bred style of architecture had been designed and built to his father's exact orders.

All the conflicting emotions Marmaduke had felt since childhood returned with a force that surprised him – hatred for this mansion but love for the surrounding land. He rode to the rear of the house to what was in effect a village – rows of assigned men's whitewashed cabins, a blacksmith's forge, dairy, storehouses and the overseer's cottage. In the English rose garden stood the wrought-iron dome of the aviary where his mother had kept her beloved multi-coloured budgerigars, the tiny prisoners Garnet had ordered his assigned men to capture from the bush for her, and where their tiny feathered descendants continued to live.

The delicate sound of a fountain playing reminded Marmaduke of his first visit to Paris three years before. Standing by a fountain at the edge of a crowd, alone and awkward. Until that magical moment when an older woman, dressed in full evening regalia and a white wig, smiled at him with her eyes. Without a word she slipped her arm through his and led him to her bedchamber. The lady spoke no

English. His French was fluent enough to appreciate the subtleties of Molière and Voltaire but when spoken his Australian accent drew a tolerant smile and a Gallic shrug. He never did know her name. But the delicate lines of her face and the erotic suggestions she whispered in the dark schooled him in a night of love he would remember all his life. *Every youth should be initiated by an older woman who is mistress of the love arts.*

Marmaduke followed the old familiar track towards Mingaletta. Before he faced his father at Bloodwood Hall, Marmaduke needed to reclaim two precious links with his childhood. First to visit his mother's land, Mingaletta, then take a short detour to see Queenie, the nanny he counted as his second mother.

The track to Mingaletta had always been open to the sky but during his absence the bush had reclaimed it. Ahead of him lay the ridge that formed the invisible western boundary between his father's estate, Bloodwood Hall, and the ruins of Mingaletta, his mother's dowry and his imminent inheritance.

To Marmaduke, this boundary was far more than a geographical line on a map. It marked the delineation between his past and his future.

His pulse quickened at the thought of his first ride down this track. A memory that brought with it the taste of a child's pleasure – and fear.

Today was his fourth birthday. At the sight of his father's gift he was overcome by awe. The dark colt was led by the new groom who Marmaduke recognised by his worn, bleached clothing as one of that other race of people – the convicts.

His father turned to his mother. 'What do you think of the boy's birthday gift, eh, Miranda?'

Marmaduke saw his mother's hands outstretched in denial. 'You can't be serious, Garnet! He's a brumby, half wild by the look of him. It isn't safe for a child.'

'It's time to put them both to the test.' Garnet ordered the groom, 'Proceed.'

Marmaduke felt a surge of importance, suddenly airborne as the groom swung him up into the saddle. His short legs trembled in anticipation as his mother cried out.

'No, Garnet! Don't do this to me. Don't use him to punish me!'

Garnet drowned out her protest. 'Control yourself, madam. Your days of pampering the boy are over. He's mine now. I'll make a true Gamble out of him or one of us will die in the attempt.'

Marmaduke looked into his father's eyes, shocked to realise the man was suddenly a stranger, his face as blank as the faces in the portrait gallery upstairs.

With a gesture of great deliberation Garnet cracked his whip across the colt's rump.

Marmaduke's breath was torn from him in painful gasps as he crouched desperately in the saddle, his feet unable to retain their hold of the stirrups, his hands clinging to the horse's mane. Every moment he expected to hear Garnet's laughter when the colt bucked him to the ground. Yet somehow he did not fall. He clung on to the bolting horse, sensing that what lay ahead of him was that unseen wild valley where the brumbies ran free. Mingaletta.

Blind terror was splintered by a new emotion, a magical flash of triumph. This brumby was now part of his own body – they were joined together to become one animal. He was born to ride!

That day Marmaduke had discovered the truth. He could trust horses. But never again would he trust his father.

Now when he reached the crown of the ridge he drew his cloak around his shoulders as the wind whipped his hair. The open grassland in the valley below stretched for miles towards the folds of the mountain range.

He smiled at the sound of horses' hooves galloping wild and free. The brumbies. Black, brown, piebald, though their leader was as white as a unicorn. He led his mob down the length of the valley. Marmaduke let out a whoop of exuberance as the brumby king headed straight towards the tall chimney and the stone cellar walls – all that remained of his mother's homestead. The brumbies charged through the grassy corridor between the ruined walls and bolted towards the mountains.

'I've come home to honour my promise, Mother.' He spoke the words aloud, half addressed to her, half to the land itself.

Queenie's whitewashed two-room cabin was some distance from the other buildings on his father's estate and was the oldest building, the first dwelling Garnet had built for himself on his initial land grant. It was exactly as Marmaduke remembered it, still surrounded by Queenie's cottage garden, smelling of Indian herbs and English flowers.

'Did you think you could sneak back home without me knowing?' Queenie asked in that familiar tart tone he knew was her camouflage for deep emotion.

The moment he saw her Marmaduke tried to mask his shock. Her dark eyes were young and luminous but her classic Indian features were now haggard with age.

Her tiny frame was lost in his silent bear hug then he held her at arm's length. 'My God, Queenie, you've found the secret of eternal youth. You don't look a day older than when you spanked me for telling lies.'

'Don't think you're too old – though now your lies are called flattery. Come in and get a proper breakfast into you. You look half starved.'

'I will, Queenie, the minute I've confronted Garnet. You know why I'm home. Mother wanted you to share in Mingaletta. Just as soon as he signs over the deeds to me I'll rebuild the homestead and build you a little place of your own close by me. You were my second mother. Now it's my turn to take care of you. You'll never have to live here in Garnet's grace-and-favour cottage again.' Marmaduke tried to make his question casual. 'How is the old boy? Edwin Bentleigh says Sydney's hot with rumours that Garnet's spending money like a drunken sailor.'

'Who knows? I've hardly spoken to the old reprobate since you deserted the ship.'

Marmaduke gently pressed for an answer. 'But does he seem pretty normal to you?'

'Well, he still rides around the estate bellowing out orders and throwing wild fits of temper. But Magistrate Summerhayes and the bank manager dine here regularly, so there's not much hope of him being locked up in a lunatic asylum just yet.'

Marmaduke gave a grim nod. When he kissed her goodbye, Queenie caught his arm to detain him. 'No matter what fool thing Garnet says, just hold that hot temper of yours in check. Remember, Miranda will be watching every move you make!'

On his return Marmaduke led his horse to the stables and turned him over to Davey's care. Watched by assigned men at work, who each acknowledged him with a surly nod, he strode to the front of the house ready to make his entrance.

His eye was caught by a movement of the curtains at the upper windows of his mother's chambers, the room where he had watched her die in childbirth. For a split second he imagined the shadowy figure was his mother's ghost. Then he realised it was no wraith. It was Elise. Who else had that arsenic-white flesh, that flowing mane of auburn hair? When she covered her mouth Marmaduke realised she had also recognised him.

So my father's whore is still in residence. Usurping Mother's role, sleeping in her bed. No doubt wearing Mother's jewellery.

The front door was opened by a sassy young servant with wild curly hair and an Irish accent. Her bold glance clearly placed her as being assigned. No English servant would have dared look him over from head to foot.

'I am Bridget. To be sure ye are being the Prodigal Son.'

Marmaduke brushed past her. 'No need to announce me to your master.'

Outside Garnet's library, he squared his shoulders and muttered, 'Here goes, Mother.'

Garnet Gamble was seated at his desk. His mane of white hair, unblinking stare and bared teeth gave him an uncanny resemblance to the lion's head trophy mounted on the wall.

Marmaduke stood poised in the doorway and gave his father a deep, theatrical bow.

Garnet's voice was as strong and scathing as ever. 'Ah-ha! The Prodigal Son returns at long last, his tail between his legs.'

That was enough. Marmaduke's cool resolve instantly vanished.

'The rotten apple never falls far from the tree, Garnet.'

CHAPTER 4

For the first time in more than four years Marmaduke was face to face with his father. A swift glance around Garnet Gamble's domain reminded him how curious it was for an illiterate man to surround himself with books in three languages.

The firearms and duelling pistols in the glass cabinet were placed side by side with an Aboriginal bark shield, a lethal-looking woomera and a hunting boomerang that had belonged to the tribal elders he remembered as a child. Marmaduke felt the bitter irony.

Symbols of the unequal struggle between us and the tribes we dispossessed.

But the two trophies most prized by Garnet hung framed on the wall. The certificate of conditional pardon signed by Governor Macquarie in 1810 was the proof of his freedom. The document that proclaimed his initiation as a Freemason into the Australian Social Lodge No 260 on 3 March 1823 was the proof of his social acceptance.

Marmaduke flung himself into the winged leather chair facing Garnet's mahogany desk. To Marmaduke this chair was a witness box for the accused. From the time his legs were too short to reach the ground, he had endured paternal tirades of abuse about his behaviour.

Today he felt a sense of grim satisfaction. Against all odds his father had failed to break him. Today the tables would be turned. He promised himself that no matter how much his father raged, he would control his temper and refuse to be sidetracked.

At first glance Garnet appeared to be undiminished by time. The aura of power and his sheer vitality were written in every line of his face and body. The arched bridge of his eyebrows was still black in contrast to the premature white of his hair.

Marmaduke was reminded that although they were violently opposed in temperament, they were separated by only twenty years.

The old bastard's forty-five but he's aged visibly since we last crossed swords.

Garnet's voice had lost none of its vitriol. 'Damned well took your time in coming. No doubt Edwin Bentleigh informed you that you remain my sole heir?'

Marmaduke toyed with his Indian ruby ring, a ploy to mask his odd sense of relief.

So the mistress has not succeeded in breeding. Garnet's not fool enough to wed her until she's great with child.

'Marry again by all means, Garnet, breed a parcel of sons. I have no desire to inherit a penny from *your* estate. I've only returned to claim what belongs to me. Edwin tells me the Will is legally invalid but I promised Mother on her deathbed I'd never sell Mingaletta or let the banks claim it. Perhaps you don't remember, being in your cups at the time.'

'Drunk? I was half mad with grief!' The bait taken, Garnet hurtled out of his chair and paced the room. 'My hair turned white overnight!'

Marmaduke was on guard, holding the whip hand against an old but still dangerous lion. 'You wanted to see me – here I am. Now it's time to produce the deeds. We'll sign them before a witness and the past will be dead and buried.'

'It isn't about the past, damn you. It's the future. Why do you think I sacrificed twenty-five years of my life to build an empire? Clawed my way up tooth and nail to become the Colony's most successful entrepreneur, second to none but Sam Terry.'

Marmaduke had heard this litany for years. 'Yeah, yeah, Garnet. Pipped at the post by your fellow Emancipist for the title of wealthiest man in the Colony.'

'Old Macarthur and Wentworth may own more land and Sam Terry holds more mortgages than the Bank of New South Wales. But me, I hold more power in this colony than all your high and mighty Macarthurs and their ilk. Do you think I achieved all that just to take my fortune to the grave? No! To prove to your mother that, although she'd married beneath her, I was the man who succeeded in giving her beloved son *everything*. A fine education, a life of luxury and your rightful place in society as an English gentleman.'

Marmaduke made a self-deprecating gesture. 'Instead all you got was *me.*'

Garnet's glance took in everything from Marmaduke's long,

tangled hair to his mud-splattered riding boots then lingered on the flamboyant ruby ring set in Florentine gold. His summary was surprisingly calm. 'Is it too much to ask you to conduct yourself as befits an English gentleman?'

Marmaduke gave a mock show of surprise. 'Why should you be disappointed, Garnet? I've done my best to live up to your expectations of how the sons of the Quality live. I've done the Grand Tour of Europe, been a house guest at hunting parties at some of England's great rural estates, explored India by elephant and bagged the odd tiger or two, lost and won a fortune over the gaming tables and I've drunk the Seine dry. In short, I have become the very portrait of an idle wastrel.'

'Do you think I didn't know every move you made? You were hell bent on proving the first generation creates the fortune for the second generation to squander.'

Marmaduke flipped open his snuffbox but returned it to his pocket, determined to remain cool in the face of his father's contempt.

'Your wish, not mine. The very day I completed my studies I asked your permission to be trained in the management of one of your estates. Or learn the ropes in some aspect of your business affairs. I had no wish to sponge off your fortune. I always wanted to be financially independent. You know I did!'

Garnet, on the defensive, shouted back. 'You were a naïve boy, planning to marry a silly girl who was far beneath you. I saved you from a life of certain disaster!'

Marmaduke refused to take the bait. 'You held Mingaletta over my head. Wanted me to abstain from work on the grounds that being labelled with the stigma of "trade" would close society's doors to me.'

Garnet thumped the desk. 'I don't make the rules. I just *bend* them!'

'Indeed, you're past master of that game, Garnet. But I'm one of the new breed of Currency Lads. Born free but forced to carry the taint of being a convict's son—'

'I am an *Emancipist*, damn you! Everyone in the Colony knows Governor Macquarie granted me that pardon,' he said, waving angrily at the framed document.

'Only a *conditional* pardon,' Marmaduke corrected. 'Forbidden to return to England. Banished for life. No amount of power, fortune, your status as a Mason or public generosity to charities, nothing can ever buy you – or me – acceptance by the Quality.'

'Money can buy anything in this colony.'

Marmaduke was determined he would steer the conversation back to Mingaletta. 'Don't you remember what happened when I was sixteen and you tried to launch me into Society? You sent me to a dancing class for children of the Quality. Georgina, the daughter of one of the Top Thirteen families, invited me to be her partner at her mother's fancy dress ball. We planned to wear Indian costumes, Georgina as an Indian dancer, me as a Maharajah. Queenie supervised my costume. I arrived splendidly dressed in brocade with a jewelled turban, invitation in hand. To be met by my hostess, Georgina's mother. She told me I didn't *know my place*. No Emancipist's son would be invited as a guest. But my costume was useful. She put me behind the bar to serve her guests.'

Garnet's face was taut, a noticeable pulse on his temple. 'I had not forgotten.'

'Nothing's changed. No Emancipist's son is allowed to marry into their hallowed ranks! I defy you, Garnet. *Name just one.*'

Garnet banged his fist for emphasis, sending a whisky glass flying. 'You will be the first – or one of us will die in the attempt!'

Marmaduke responded calmly. 'When are you going to accept the truth, Garnet? I don't give a damn what your precious Quality thinks of me. But they've got *you* by the balls because you're the one who *cares!*'

Garnet's response was to ring the servant's bell. The two men glowered at each other in silence until Black Mary, a timid little Aboriginal girl, scampered across the Persian carpet and removed the shards of broken glass.

'Let's get back to the question of Mingaletta, Garnet.'

The glint in his father's pale blue eyes showed him that Garnet was not to be deterred.

'I have it on authority you've shown no inclination to court respectable young ladies.'

Marmaduke shrugged. 'Unlike you, I conduct my liaisons with discretion.'

'It seems you are more attracted to unsavoury company. Prize-fighters, actors, jockeys and drinking companions who've never married and are devoted to their mothers. Like that radical firebrand who's always in court involved in one libel suit after another.'

Marmaduke forced himself to keep his tone light. 'Rupert Grantham? Clever fellow. A most entertaining host. It takes all kinds to make the world go around, Garnet.'

'So it's true?' Garnet asked sharply. 'You intend to be a *perennial bachelor* like our lawyer Edwin Bentleigh?' The innuendo was obvious.

'Leave Edwin out of this! He's a true friend and the most ethical lawyer in Sydney. He's devoted to his invalid mother. And so involved in trying to save his impoverished clients from the gallows he hasn't got time to court any girl!'

Garnet shrugged. 'If I doubted his quality as a lawyer I'd have fired him years back.'

Marmaduke needed to even the score. 'You pay your informants. But you forget that Sydney Town is a rumour mill. Most are patently false. Remember? Rumour even had it that Mother married you for *love.*'

The barb thrust as deep as he intended. Garnet jumped to his feet bellowing.

'I forbid you to take your mother's name in vain! We shared a depth of love and loyalty totally beyond your comprehension. You're incapable of love!'

Marmaduke almost smiled. For the moment he knew he had gained the upper hand.

'We agree on that one point, Garnet. I shall *never marry.* Now hand over the deeds to Mingaletta and let's end this farce once and for all.'

Garnet's anger evaporated like smoke. 'I fully intended to do so when you proved yourself mature, a gentleman of substance. But I can't wait any longer for that miracle. I have decided it is time to marry.'

Marmaduke was thrown off kilter. 'So, you intend to marry Elise and instal her here officially as my stepmother?'

Garnet made him wait for his answer. 'I'm not such an old fool I'd confer respectability on a mistress whose favours are so easily bought.'

Marmaduke's curiosity forced his question. 'Then who's the lucky bride?'

'A young woman of impeccable virtue and bloodline, the daughter of an aristocratic family.' He removed a miniature portrait from a desk drawer and offered it with a flourish.

'It's taken two years of protracted legal negotiations with this young lady's guardian. I took the precaution of having this commissioned. I'm assured it is a true likeness. This girl is the key to our total acceptance in the Colony. A de Rolland will be welcome to dine at His Excellency Governor Sir Richard Bourke's table.'

Marmaduke pretended to study her image with mild interest. It was painted in chocolate box mode with bland, insipid features. But he was well aware that his father's second marriage to a *young* woman was likely to provide another heir. Would this marriage wreck his chances of claiming Mingaletta?

Garnet was eyeing him keenly. 'What do you think of her?'

'Hard to tell. She looks like a mere child. The face is bovine. The flesh suggests she's on the bony side. A flat bosom. Consumptive perhaps? I take it she comes from good breeding stock? Unlikely to die on the voyage out before you get your money's worth?'

'My London lawyers have investigated every detail. The girl is young, healthy, above average in education. Her virtue is beyond question. Kept under lock and key since puberty.'

'Then she must be weak in the head. Why else would this noble family send their paragon of virtue thirteen thousand miles to wed a *nouveau riche* colonial?

'Her guardian was on the brink of debtor's prison. My offer was the family's salvation. The girl's in no position to be anything but tractable. She'll give us no trouble.'

'Give *us* no trouble? Why should I worry? She'll play no part in *my* life once you marry her. Just sign over the deeds to Mingaletta and you'll be quit of me. I'm happy to sign anything as proof I'll make no claim on your estate against any of my future half siblings.'

Garnet's smile was so confident that Marmaduke felt distinctly uneasy.

'On the contrary, Marmaduke. I have not negotiated for this noble young lady to be my bride – she is *yours!*'

'You jest, sir!' Marmaduke leapt to his feet and thrust the portrait across the desk.

'Dead serious. Follow my plan to the letter. Marry the bride I've chosen. Then you take full possession of Mingaletta. It's a fair trade. Your de Rolland bride will bring you stability. Blot out your tarnished status in the eyes of Colonial Society. The killing of a man in a duel does not endear men to Governor Bourke – he's frightfully moral. '

Marmaduke now knew the truth. He had kept his temper but lost Mingaletta.

'I'll be damned if I'll be a pawn in your game. I'm going straight to Edwin. We'll take immediate steps to break off this absurd liaison before the poor benighted girl sets sail.'

Garnet looked confident. 'Too late. The contracts are all signed, the money's transferred. In a couple of months her ship will arrive in Port Jackson. You will be there to welcome her. Unless you wish to dishonour the deathbed promise you made to your mother?'

Marmaduke was so appalled he almost laughed. 'My God. This is infamous even for you. It's like a deal between Faust and the Devil.

'Use your head, boy. This way we both get what we want. I have reserved a suite of rooms for her at my new hotel, the Princess Alexandrina.'

Marmaduke was jolted. 'So that's *yours*? I should have guessed, it's so ostentatious.'

Garnet ignored the insult. 'No doubt the bride will arrive with a mountain of trunks. In addition to the contract, I sent a handsome gift of money for a lady's maid to accompany her and to order her a Paris trousseau that will bedazzle every lady of Quality in the Colony.'

Marmaduke saw that Garnet was unstoppable, his eyes unnaturally bright as he rattled off the details of the wedding to be performed at St James's Church, the new organ he would donate, the guest list drawn from the cream of colonial society.

Garnet delivered the final *coup de grâce*. 'The deeds to Mingaletta are here in my safe. They await my signature after you consummate the marriage.'

Inwardly seething with rage but outwardly calm, Marmaduke rose to take his leave.

'You seem to have everything signed, sealed and delivered, Garnet. Except for one small point. You don't have *my* consent.'

Mounted on the ebony stallion ready to return to Sydney Town, Marmaduke turned to take a final look at the house of his childhood that was haunted by so many dark secrets.

The front doors flew open and Elise hurried down the steps. Running to his side she grabbed hold of his reins to detain him.

Marmaduke tried not to look at her. But as much as he held his father's mistress in contempt it was difficult to ignore her beauty – and her distress.

Her words came in broken phrases. 'Marmaduke. You're leaving without saying goodbye? I need to talk to you. Alone. Only you can help me. Your father's mental state grows worse. I'm desperate.' She lowered her eyes. 'I don't know how much longer I can do what he wants of me.'

As he unwound the fingers of the pale hand clinging to his reins he flinched to see the emerald ring his mother had worn for her portrait. It gave him no pleasure to see Elise's unnaturally pale complexion flush and her eyes fill with tears.

'You'll manage, Elise. You're well trained for the role. He pays you handsomely, no doubt.'

Remaining in the saddle, Marmaduke swept his hat from his head and bowed low in imitation of the flamboyant flourish he had seen an actor perform on stage at the Comédie Française. Elise responded as she would to royalty with a curtsey so deep it revealed the curve of her breasts, a gesture he suspected was by design.

It would be almost worth bringing home that blue-blooded bride, just to see Elise's face when she realises she's been usurped as mistress of Bloodwood Hall.

CHAPTER 5

De Rolland Park, Gloucestershire, England, February 1833

Isabel pulled the old overcoat around her shoulders as she stood shivering on the castellated walkway on the roof of her ancestral home. Below her lay the expanse of countryside, bathed in a pale, uncertain light. She shivered at the sight of the ice on the lake that was beginning to thaw. That lake had nearly drowned her. She cut off the images, sounds, and the fear of water that she had learnt to push back into the dark recesses of her memory.

I'm alive. That's all that matters.

Isabel felt an odd unease. The temperature had dropped dramatically in the space of a few seconds. She was on the point of turning to the only exit on the roof when there was a loud metallic crash. The door was forced open as if by a powerful gust of wind.

She was no longer alone, but in the presence of a stranger. Isabel shrank back and concealed herself behind a stone pediment. The man at the far end of the narrow walkway stood with his back to her, unaware of her presence. Tall and heavily built, his age was uncertain because his head was covered by an elaborate periwig.

He took a commanding stance, legs planted wide, arms stretched out as if to encompass the entire countryside. His fine clothing proclaimed him a gentleman: an immaculately tailored dark green velvet tail coat worn over knee breeches, white silk stockings and silver buckled shoes. When he turned his head in profile the only jarring note was the crumpled neck linen that lay open at the throat.

The cold seemed of little concern to him. After removing a silver flask from a pocket he tossed the jacket aside to fall in a crumpled heap. She saw the glint of sunlight on the flask as he raised it high in a flamboyant toast.

'To King and Country! Devil take them both!' His words echoed in her head as he drained the contents then wiped his fleshy lips with the back of his shirtsleeve, leaving a trace of wine like a bloodstain.

He was so close to her that Isabel could see the dark stubble on his jawline and despite his fine clothing he had the smell of a man who had been too busy carousing to bathe.

Isabel felt trapped, unable to reach the sole exit because the stranger had turned to face her and now stood blocking her flight. There was something strangely familiar about his smile and the odd expression in his eyes chilled her even more than the cold. Was this man one of Uncle Godfrey's wealthy, eccentric neighbours come to dine with her guardian in a return of hospitality?

She was appalled by her second thought. *Oh Lord, please don't tell me he's that older gentleman Uncle has invited here as a prospective suitor. This man is clearly in his cups! How I abhor drunkards.*

Isabel cleared her throat and forced herself to address him. 'Excuse me, sir, the cold is biting. I must return inside.'

The gentleman stood his ground. Isabel felt her throat tighten as she watched him in unwilling fascination. He turned his head towards a sun struggling to emerge from the grey mass of clouds – and let out an unnerving cry of ecstasy.

Isabel felt the hair prickle on the back of her neck. His blue eyes were unnaturally bright. His air of nobility disintegrated as he pressed his fingers to his lips in a childlike gesture of secrecy before chanting words in an alien tongue she could not recognise.

His sudden move caught her off guard. To her horror he was charging straight towards her, his arms extended sideways in the caricature of an embrace! His body passed so close to her she could smell the musty aroma of incense. She was overwhelmed by an impression of pure evil as he stepped up onto the edge of the parapet, laughing wildly into the face of the sun. Flapping his arms like the wings of a bird he chanted, 'The Gods are with me. Watch me fly! I am immortal!'

Laughing, he leapt out into space.

Isabel struggled against the vertigo that terrified her as she tried to peer over the edge of the parapet. She heard the echo of his laughter end in a heavy thud out of sight below. She was almost overcome by an acute wave of nausea but knew she must not lose consciousness in case by some miracle he had survived the fall.

She struggled to wrench open the metal door and ran down the stairs in search of someone, yelling that there had been an accident.

Charging headlong into Baker, an old family retainer, Isabel was almost incoherent but took the old man's hand and dragged him outside to the stretch of garden that lay directly beneath the line of the victim's fall.

She froze at the sight that lay before her. The pristine bed of rose bushes and shrubbery was intact. There was no sign of his body. Not a blade of grass seemed out of place.

Isabel pointed up in confusion to the exact stone from which the stranger had taken his swallow dive. 'He can't have survived that fall. No one could.'

She was suddenly aware of the frown that creased Baker's face.

'Is this some kind of a jest, miss? Like April Fools' Day?'

'Of course not. I tell you I saw him jump. He was as close to me as you are right now.'

Isabel tugged at his sleeve to detain him, as she blurted out the stranger's description, remembering the mock beauty spot on his cheek.

'If you say so, miss,' Baker said warily. 'I best go back to my duties.'

Isabel closed her eyes to blot out the realisation. *Oh dear God, that gentleman must have been 'the Other'.*

Disregarding the servants' startled reactions, she raced up the staircase to the portrait gallery, her hair flying, her skirts bunched up so as not to impede her progress, to search the portraits in pursuit of one particular face she remembered – the one that bore no name.

Short of breath, she halted before the portrait of a young man dressed in extravagant Georgian style who bore a distinct resemblance to the older man she had just seen leap to his death.

'That's you, isn't it?' she said aloud to the portrait in an attempt to restore a sense of reality to counter the vision she had been forced to witness.

'I take it you've *seen* him, have you, Isabel?'

The voice behind her spoke in a tone somewhere between pacifying and mild mockery. She spun around to confront Cousin Silas.

'Don't play with me, Cousin. Who is he?'

'Don't you recognise the resemblance to us both? My father, Henri, painted in his youth. Before he married my mother and later became enchanted by *your* mother, Alizon – the witch.'

Isabel chose to ignore the accusation. 'He's not buried in the de Rolland family vault. How did he die?'

'Suicide, a drunken accident or what you will. Father began meddling in the black arts. Came to believe he was greater than Icarus. Leapt off the parapet to prove *he* could fly and survive.' Silas shrugged. 'He did *not*.'

Isabel felt the blood drain from her face. *Henri de Rolland – the man who accused my mother of being a witch. Yet he himself had met his own death – through practising witchcraft.*

She had a sudden flash of insight but she baulked at the word 'ghost'. 'You have seen him yourself, haven't you?'

'He repeats his final folly periodically.' His hand curved gracefully downwards in illustration of a swallow dive. 'You see? We share the same gift, *my petite cousine.*'

Despite her protective instincts about her dead mother's reputation, Isabel could not hold back the words. 'But Henri was your father. Can you feel no pity for him?'

'Father was an amateur who dabbled in what he could not control. Where as I have *mastered* the black arts.' He reached out and stroked her hair. 'That's why I am the one man who can protect you from yourself – my little witch.'

His smile was tender, but Isabel found herself trembling as she avoided his hand, dropped a curtsey and hurried away to her bedchamber.

Something inside her mind had changed irrevocably. Since childhood she had glimpsed misty, fragmentary visions of the Other in this house. Never before had she seen one who appeared to her to be the embodiment of a living person. The significance of that idea terrified her. She could no longer be sure. What was real and what was not? *It's true. I am a witch. I am cursed.*

Needing to regain her grip on reality, she searched for old Agnes, who always had a calming effect on her. But she decided not to confide in the servant about her encounter with the 'Icarus' ghost. Agnes would panic, believing it to be a sign of her returning illness.

*

Later that morning, as Isabel came back downstairs, she felt a new pulse of vitality inside the great house – as if it was a giant in a fairy-tale being roused from centuries of sleep. Isabel could feel the fresh surge of hope that filtered through to her from Agnes and the network of lives in service who were dependent on the fate of the de Rolland family.

But is my life being changed for better or for worse?

Through the windows she looked down on the carriageway. The old family carriage, its doors emblazoned with the ancient crest, stood waiting before the front portico in readiness for the master's imminent departure for London. It was whispered Uncle Godfrey had important business with the family lawyers that would put an end to the long threat of debtors' prison. Cousin Silas's new phaeton stood nearby, its beautiful white horses pawing the gravel as if eager to charge off to some neighbouring estate.

Winter was drawing to a close and Isabel had still not been given the date for her promised journey to London. As her most reliable source of information was eavesdropping, she managed to give Agnes the slip and planted herself in the garden. It was so chilly no one would think of looking for her there. One of the French windows was slightly ajar so Uncle Godfrey's King Charles spaniel could come and go at will and it now allowed her to hear her guardian's conversation with Cousin Silas.

It was soon clear to her that Silas was using every facet of persuasion to bring the old man around to his way of thinking.

'There's no need to panic, Uncle. We must go on as if nothing untoward has happened. The local constable hasn't even bothered to call. Why should he? There's no reason to link Isabel with this grim discovery. Her weeks of amnesia and discovery in the woods all happened three years ago. She's been closeted so closely since then half the villagers wouldn't even be able to describe her.'

Uncle Godfrey's voice was so hushed Isabel strained to hear it. 'But the infant's corpse has evidently been buried for some time. What if the child was hers? She's never denied the fact that she remembers smothering it the moment it was born. She wasn't responsible for her actions. It was her sleeping sickness, of course. It could hardly be called infanticide in the true sense. A fourteen-year-old girl of good family would never have been gaoled under the circumstances. But it would only take one malicious gossip in that God-forsaken village to make our long negotiated marriage contract null and void.'

'Indeed, Uncle, I admit that George Gamble's stipulation of a healthy young de Rolland bride of immaculate virtue and breeding would hardly fit Isabel at the best of times. But now, with the possibility of a babe's corpse linked to her name...?'

Isabel bit hard on her hand to prevent herself from crying out in fright. She felt as if her whole world had come to an end, without time to pray for redemption or reach out to farewell the few people she loved. She had totally lost control of her life.

'The final documents have yet to be signed, sealed and delivered. I don't trust those damned Colonial lawyers – they talk mighty big, but despite their fake British accents and Bond Street tailors, God only knows how many of them were spawned from convict stock. It sticks in my craw to think George Gamble—'

'Who cares how that convicted thief made his fortune? All is not lost, Uncle, if we leave for London immediately and sign the final contract confirming Isabel's date of departure. Then on our return we announce her engagement to an Australian gentleman – if there is such an animal. And have Isabel packed off to London to stay in our townhouse until her ship sails.'

Uncle Godfrey sighed. 'What choice is there? Half the debts have been paid but you've been spending the money as if you'd won shares in a gold mine. We simply can't return Gamble's money, even if we wanted to. We have to deliver the goods!'

Isabel closed her eyes, imagining the winning smile on Silas's face as he replied, 'Dear Uncle, as a child you taught me that those of us with royal Plantagenet blood must live like princes. Now we shall once again. That convict rogue's money has changed everything.'

'Wretched fellow. If only salvation had come from any hands but *his*. What's the world coming to? God allows a convict to triumph yet sends a de Rolland to a god-forsaken place like New South Wales!'

Isabel suddenly opened her eyes. *They mean me!*

'Calm yourself, Uncle. Tomorrow, when you've signed the final contract, we need never mention his name again.'

Isabel's confusion grew when the silence was broken by her uncle's anxious voice.

'I'm not looking forward to breaking the news to the sacrificial lamb. I promised her a say in the decision. The child will do her duty by the family, of course, but women's tears are the very devil.'

'No chance of that, Uncle. She's never been known to cry.' Silas added lightly, 'One of the proven signs of a witch, they say.'

'Medieval poppycock, Silas—' The sound of their voices was cut off by the closing of a door. Isabel sank to her knees, shivering violently. It was only when she saw the red spot of blood on her hand that she realised a thorn had pierced her finger. The bare stem of a *Rose Alba* bush.

The full horror of the situation washed over her. She saw a series of disordered, fragmented pictures in her mind – the lake, the woods, the old Romani woman's gentle hands stroking her body, a child's grave, a globe in the schoolroom with her finger pointing at the tiny pink island of England, then the globe spinning on its axis so the whole world became blurred.

I've been sold in marriage. Why did they let me believe I had a choice? That I was going to London and Paris. The truth is I'll be buried in that penal colony in the South Seas. And who is this 'wretched fellow'? Why didn't anyone warn me?

The answer came to her with such a jolt she felt sick in the stomach.

Killing two birds with one stone! The family fortunes are restored and they rid themselves of the greatest threat to family honour – me! My God, it isn't just the dregs of British society who are transported. Now it's my turn! And marriage is a life sentence!

Isabel's head throbbed with confusion and frustration. She knew she would have no chance to speak to Uncle Godfrey before his departure. Farewells were something he always avoided. She took up her customary spying position in the basement.

Through the bars of the window just above ground level that gave her a glimpse of the carriageway, Isabel caught a glimpse of her guardian's buckled shoes, white stockings and breeches as he was assisted by a footman into his carriage. The sound of a whip cracking was followed by the crunch of wheels on gravel. She stifled a cry of despair. The only people who knew about her fate were gone – unless Cousin Martha was privy to the plan?

Isabel picked up her skirts and ran for the stairs, determined to evade Agnes and go to Cousin Martha's bedside, where the surgeon was again in attendance.

Please God, don't let him bleed Martha again. She grows weaker after his every visit. I don't care how many medical degrees he claims. The man's little better than a vampire.'

Breathless when she reached Martha's bedchamber, she gave a perfunctory knock and entered. Feeling her gorge rise, she tried not to gag at the sight before her. The elderly physician, be-wigged and dressed in sober black like a cleric or an undertaker, gave her a dismissive wave, his hand stained with blood.

Martha's weak voice made a heart-rending plea, 'No! Please, doctor, bid her remain. Young Isabel's presence is the best medicine I could have.'

Irritated to have his orders counteracted but unable to refuse his patient, the doctor waved Isabel towards the far corner of the room.

She sank down on the sofa, her legs trembling so violently she was forced to disguise it in the manner of a schoolgirl, hugging her knees to her chest. She forced a smile in an attempt to give both herself and Martha false confidence as she took in the ghastly scene.

Isabel was shocked by the sight of Martha's deterioration. On the bedside table was a glass jar which Isabel recognised with a shiver of dread held a supply of leeches. Martha was scarcely thirty years old yet her whole frame seemed to have shrunk to the dimensions of a child's body since Isabel last saw her. Was it only two weeks ago?

Dressed in a white nightgown so plain it looked like a shroud, Martha gave Isabel a smile free of any trace of fear. Her pale oval face seemed pinched from within, the sweating flesh stretched taut across the cheekbones. Her gentle grey eyes shone with unnatural brightness from the dark hollows of the eye sockets.

One thin arm stretched across the counterpane as if in a feeble attempt to reach Isabel's hand to comfort her. The other arm, with its sleeve rolled up to her bony shoulder, hung over the bleeding bowl held by the physician.

Isabel tried to prevent her false smile from fading, sickened by the smell and sight of the fluid that dripped continuously from Martha's open vein as if eager to satisfy the doctor's quota of bright red blood. Already it filled half the bowl. Isabel hated herself for her involuntary recall of the lurid images in *Vampyre,* the novella written by Lord Byron's young physician John Polidori. The story's mysterious vampire, Lord Ruthven, had so haunted her imagination that Isabel felt he was right here in the room to claim Martha.

Isabel wanted to scream out the words, 'Stop, you butcher! Look how fragile she is. Do you want every last drop before you're satisfied?'

She dug her fingers into her arms in the hope self-inflicted pain would prevent her from fainting. *God knows if I passed out, the old leech would start draining my blood too.*

Just at the point she was ready to charge at him the physician ended the ordeal and bandaged Martha's arm.

Once his task was completed he cast a severe look at Isabel. 'You've strict instructions not to tire my patient. You may stay two minutes, no more.' He turned to Martha. 'I shall return tomorrow to check your progress. Continue with the laudanum doses I prescribed. Is your husband at home? The Master?'

When Martha looked uncertain, Isabel jumped to her feet. 'They are both expected to return very soon.'

'Meanwhile I shall deliver my instructions to the housekeeper. They are to be followed to the letter.'

The moment the door closed behind him Martha patted the counterpane and Isabel flew to her side to stroke the hair back from her forehead and kiss her cheek.

'Forgive me, Martha. I wanted to come sooner but Cousin Silas gave instructions you were not to be disturbed.'

'Dear man. He's overly protective. Doesn't he realise that you bring a breath of spring into my sickroom every time you visit me?'

Isabel was shocked to see that the claw-like hand that gripped hers wore a wedding ring that was now two sizes too large for her. Isabel felt her throat constrict at this visible proof that Martha was wasting away within her own body.

'Tell me, are the tulips in bloom yet?'

Isabel was startled to realise her cousin had been confined so long in this sick room that she had lost all sense of the changing seasons.

Isabel carefully chose her words to describe imaginary flowers as if they were now in bloom. 'We have such a wild profusion of colours that Netherlands are jealous we'll steal their title as the tulip capital of Europe!'

Martha gave a little laugh, eager to catch her mood. 'How young and vibrant you look, sweetheart. Tell me, what have you been reading? Love stories? Novels? Sir Walter Scott or that clever Miss Austen's work?'

'I'll read *Sense and Sensibility* to you tomorrow when you've had a good night's sleep.'

'Lovely. But first I want to know everything about your world.'

My world? We've both been locked in our own private prisons. Mine is to be exchanged for a marital prison in the Antipodes. But I must raise her spirits, not upset her.

'Uncle Godfrey is sending me to have my first taste of London society. Imagine! Plays at Drury Lane and Covent Garden. And I'll practise my French conversation in Paris.'

'London, Paris. How wonderful. I'm even kept in the dark about happy news!'

Isabel was stung by the plaintive note in her voice, the first time Martha had sounded like a fretful invalid. Isabel made an instant decision.

'But I'm not going anywhere, dear Martha, until you are fully recovered.'

Martha shook her head with a weary smile. 'No, no. You must write me about the plays. And dance and flirt with those charming young French officers – their uniforms are so elegant it's a shame to send them into battle. And please describe the latest Paris modes.'

'Better still I'll buy you a beautiful shawl and your favourite French perfume.'

Martha squeezed her hand and whispered like a schoolgirl, 'Don't forget the *demi-monde*. I hear their courtesans are the most exquisite creatures in the world. Even the ladies of Louis-Phillipe's court follow the fashions they set.' She sighed happily. 'You see? I will see Paris through your fresh young eyes!'

Isabel forced herself to say firmly, 'Just until *you* are well enough to visit Paris with your husband.'

Martha's face creased in a funny little smile. 'All in good time, m'dear.' Her breath caught and she was overtaken by a wracking cough.

Disturbed Isabel said quickly, 'I fear I am tiring you.'

'No!' Martha regained control with great effort. 'Stay! Tomorrow they might pull up the drawbridge against your visits.' She paused. 'Promise me you'll make sure Silas doesn't suffer from melancholia. I know how much he enjoys your company.'

Isabel nodded, unable to meet the pale eyes until she found the courage to say the words. 'Martha, I want you to know how much I love you. But I have a confession to make. Remember that first time we met when you came here as Silas's bride? There was a ball held in your honour. I was only a child so I watched you from the bottom of the stairs. You were the most beautiful bride and when you danced with Silas and looked up into his eyes, I was struck by the thought. '*So this is what love is!* But I confess I also felt a little jealous. Martha, you are always so gentle with me. I don't deserve you. Can you forgive me? Do you understand? You were everything *I* wanted to be!'

Martha gently stroked Isabel's cheek. 'Now the tables are turned, my dove. *You* are everything *I* want to be.'

She's telling me she's going to die. Isabel felt her heart was breaking. She wanted to cry but knew the tears were forever trapped inside her.

'You wouldn't want to be me, Martha. If only you knew how evil I am.'

Martha reached up and held her face with a hand so strong that Isabel felt the sharp outline of her bones. 'Evil? Nonsense. I can see inside your very soul. I wish with all my heart that Silas and I had been blessed to have you as our daughter.'

Daughter. Isabel buried her face in the warmth of Martha's neck. The bed linen's odour was a rank mixture of laudanum and sweat but Isabel never wanted to pull free from that refuge.

It was Martha who broke the spell. 'Do something for me, little dove. You'll find a small velvet drawstring purse in that drawer over there. Bring it to me.'

Isabel tried to hand it to her but Martha waved it away. 'My pin money is little enough – the contents diminish without my knowledge. Buy yourself a gift in Paris.'

Isabel gasped at the contents. 'I can't! It's all you have.'

'Take it to please me. And wear my grey travelling ensemble to London. It is two years old but I've scarcely worn it. And, Isabel, I want you to remember something. One day in the future you will fall in love with a man—'

'Never, I *promise* you. I hate—' Isabel stopped short of saying 'Silas' just in time to replace it with, 'the whole idea of marriage.' Although the words were said in panic she did not doubt they were true. 'But Uncle Godfrey has arranged a marriage for me. There's no love in it. Just duty. It's my chance to atone for the crime I committed.'

'I see.' Martha grew quiet but held Isabel's hand as if searching for the right words.

'The de Rollands consider that romance is quite separate from the marriage contract. Falling in love is exciting, Isabel, but *learning* to love a man is far richer. It takes time and courage.'

Martha's breathing sounded like a clock that was winding down. 'One day you *will* have the courage to love a man of your own. When you open your heart to him, remember I shall be with you. Like a guardian angel watching over you.'

'Stop it! You're going to be well again. But Silas must order that stupid quack to stop bleeding you. Look how poor Lord Byron's physicians killed him in Greece with constant bleeding. Martha, you only need rest, fresh air, healthy food and time to grow strong again.'

Martha's short laugh turned into a hacking cough.

Isabel's voice rose in desperation. 'An old Romani gypsy's caravan is back in the woods. Her herbal magic cures everything. I'll go to her. I *will* make you well again! I will!'

Martha's smile was tolerant, close to angelic. 'That's why I love you, Isabel. I simply accept whatever life brings me. But you have the courage to defy God's will!'

A few minutes later Martha closed her eyes and the rhythm of her breathing indicated she had fallen into a deep sleep.

*

From the foot of the stairs Isabel heard Agnes anxiously calling her name. To avoid her she ran in the opposite direction, to the kitchen pantry. Unnoticed she filled a wicker basket with a freshly baked loaf, a fine ball of cheese and a large kipper. No doubt Cook would accuse some innocent kitchen maid of theft but Isabel chose to block the thought.

There's only so much guilt I can carry. I'm weighed down with it already.

She added herbs from the kitchen garden and, taking care not to be observed, headed for the woods, clutching her basket. Reaching the drystone wall, she hitched up her skirt and clambered over the stile. The woods soon swallowed the house from sight and she could breathe more easily.

Isabel closed her mind to the memory of that night she had come as a stranger to the gypsy's caravan and had received solace in the old healer's hands. There was no sight of the Romani encampment. This year their caravans must have moved on early. Disappointed that she was unable to gain help for Martha, she crossed the fields that led to the isolated hamlet.

Arriving at the old stone cottage Isabel found the woman seated by the back door, patching linen and resignedly shooing random hens from her vegetable patch. Isabel knew she was not yet fifty but her grey-streaked hair and worn face had aged her since last autumn.

During her rare, clandestine visits Isabel never ceased to be saddened that the widow was reduced to eking out a pitiful existence by taking in washing and mending. She bore little resemblance to the portrait of young Elisabeth de Rolland stored in the basement of de Rolland Park, banished from sight along with its subject, who in the eyes of her family had betrayed her class by running off to marry a common mariner. Even after he died young at sea, Elisabeth remained ostracised.

Isabel handed her the basket of little luxuries and apologised for her long absence.

'You know how they keep me closeted, Aunt.'

'The de Rollands fear history will repeat itself.' At Isabel's startled look, she added quickly, 'I refer to my own wayward past. May I offer you tea, my dear?'

'There isn't time, Aunt. I came to say goodbye. I must leave for London tomorrow.'

'I wish you a safe journey. How goes my brother?' Elisabeth asked stiffly. 'Not that I expect he'd acknowledge my existence after all these years. But rumours reach me even in this hamlet. I hear that he's a hair's breadth from debtors' prison.'

'Rest assured Uncle Godfrey is well and the family fortunes restored. I cannot stay long. I only came to tell you he has arranged for me to marry into the family of a wealthy Emancipist in New South Wales.'

Elisabeth was shocked. 'The Penal Colony!'

'Yes. I don't know how this will affect my financial situation.' Isabel raised her hand. 'But I swear by hook or by crook I'll find some way to take care of you!'

'I'll survive. You can only do what is possible. To be born a woman is to be born powerless.' She reached out and clasped Isabel's hand. 'But New South Wales is the other side of the world. Promise you'll write to me!'

'Do you think I could leave you behind? You must follow me later. Meanwhile...'

Isabel handed her the money purse but despite her aunt's surprise at the weight of it, she was once and always a gentlewoman so did not count the contents.

'I shall send you my address and money for your passage as soon as I'm able. But, of course, the colonial family must never know about my past.'

Elisabeth's tone was wistful. 'No doubt your marriage is for the best. There was no future for you here. But I can't imagine what it must be like to leave England forever!'

Isabel summoned up her courage to ask the question she trusted no one else to answer. 'You know that since childhood I have sometimes caught glimpses of the Other. Those beings who seem to talk to me in my head – and then dissolve like smoke in front of my eyes. Well, now everything's changed. I saw a real flesh and blood man leap to his death from the parapet. But he wasn't real. It was a ghost.'

Elisabeth's hands flew to her mouth. 'Oh God, my brother Henri!'

'Yes. I'm sorry to shock you, Aunt. Cousin Silas has seen him, too. Silas believes his mother and mine, two sisters, came from a line of witches. I've just discovered a document stating Mother was accused of witchcraft and murder. Is that true?'

'A scurrilous lie. Alizon and her sister used herbs to heal illness. I never saw signs of any attraction to the black arts – except from Henri – and Silas.' She hastily turned the subject to her beloved lost garden. 'I suppose the roses were beautiful this year?'

'Old Fletcher is bent double with ague but he tends your knot garden with great care. Especially your white roses.' Isabel hesitated. 'How is our own Rose Alba?'

'Growing more beautiful each year. Come, see for yourself.'

Isabel rose on the edge of panic. 'No! I must return. Or I'll be missed.'

There is only so much pain I can bear. I feel that I'm leaving my heart behind.

Aunt Elisabeth took her firmly by the hand and drew her to the room in which she slept. The little girl lay asleep in her cot, her heart-shaped face framed by a circle of blonde curls, her eyelashes like tiny fans on her pale cheeks.

Isabel caught her breath. 'She reminds me of what that ancient Pope Gregory said when he saw blonde Anglo-Saxon children in a slave market. "Not Angles, but Angels."'

'An angel, indeed, sweet of nature. But it's *au revoir*, not goodbye,' Aunt Elisabeth said firmly to banish her own tears. 'Now hurry back.'

Dry-eyed Isabel kissed her Aunt's tear-stained cheek and heavy of heart hurriedly retraced her steps through the fields.

Isabel found Agnes busily packing her freshly laundered clothing and airing Martha's grey travelling ensemble to remove the smell of the lavender that kept moths at bay.

'Where have you been, lamb? I've been looking all over for you. The coach for London passes early in the morning. I'm to accompany you to the Master's townhouse and stay with you until your ship sails. That's something, eh?'

'I regret if I have made life difficult for you, Agnes. Please don't worry that I'll run away. I must say goodbye to Cousin Martha, despite the ban on my visits.'

Too late. The drawbridge to the sickroom was already raised. Isabel reached the door of Martha's room only to be blocked by the emerging figure of Cousin Silas. He gently assured Isabel she could see Martha on her return from London and Paris.

Isabel was tired of all the deceitful family games. 'When did you plan to tell me that Paris is now in New South Wales, Cousin? And that the marriage contract is already signed.'

Silas spun around, his face the mask of a stranger. Would his eyes take on that strange expression that had frightened her as a child? She felt so anxious she almost forgot to breathe. But when Silas spoke she was surprised by the tenderness in his voice.

'Do you honestly believe I was party to this plan? Have you forgotten how I forgave you for your disgrace? *Ma petite cousine*, don't you know that I love you as no other man will ever love you?'

'You must not speak to me like this. It isn't right,' she stammered.

His expression was more sad than angry. 'How strange to hear you take the high moral ground – after the heinous crime you committed. My silence made me your partner in crime. Must I lie to protect you again?'

'What do you mean?'

'You can tell *me* the truth, Isabel. An infant's corpse has been found buried in the woods. Was it the bastard of some drudge who gave birth there? Or was it *your* bastard?'

Isabel's mouth dried fear. Would this unexpected discovery cause Silas to probe deeper into her self-confessed crime of infanticide?

Which lie is the safest? How can I protect Rose Alba's fate from the family's control?

Despite her fear of the powerful aura that surrounded Silas, she met his eyes.

'Mine. What's more I'd do it again.'

Silas gave a sigh of resignation. 'May God forgive you, Isabel.'

'God might. But I shall never forgive *him*, whoever he was.'

'You depart at dawn for London,' he said. 'Uncle Godfrey insists I remain at Martha's bedside. So this is the last time we'll be alone.'

Silas moved towards her. Isabel felt drawn to him as surely as if a magnet linked her soul to his. With a great effort of will she made a swift curtsey then backed towards the door.

'Don't worry, Cousin,' she stammered. 'Family honour has been preserved – in public. In a few weeks you'll be free of me forever.'

'No, Isabel. We will never be free of each other. That is your destiny.'

CHAPTER 6

Sydney Town, Penal Colony of New South Wales,
February 1833

'Will Shakespeare was right. Parting is such sweet sorrow – when *you* are the lover I must leave, my sweet lady.'

Marmaduke said the words gently. Naked and damp with sweat he looked down at her as she lay like a full-blown rose, her plump body creamy pale in the moonlight that filtered through the milky screen of the roof of the glasshouse. When she stirred and looked up at him with that soft dreamy expression of fulfilment, he felt rewarded for his patience during the weeks of their liaison. He had awakened her to her true nature.

'You are a special man, my dear. I shall never forget you. But as this is our last time, can't you stay a little longer?' She almost said his name but Marmaduke's warning look reminded her it was taboo.

'I know. No names. You're quite right. I agreed to your rules for the sake of discretion. And you did warn me we would share great pleasure with no love involved.'

'You are *worthy* of great love, sweet lady. But it is not in my nature to love any woman. And you know I can't stay until dawn. I must protect your good name.'

Marmaduke avoided her eyes, knowing this was a half truth. It was his ironclad rule never to be discovered in a lover's bed at breakfast. A condition designed to create for each lady a memorably erotic experience – a romantic illusion that would be shattered by his early morning raspy voice, unshaven jaw and the headache that made him uncivilised until after two cups of coffee. This agreement for him to depart from a lover's bed under cover of darkness was established at the beginning of each liaison. Marmaduke knew he was valued for his discretion – it had opened a surprising number of bedchamber doors for him.

'*Please* stay, my dear,' she pleaded. 'You know I have always loved my husband but I was a great disappointment to him. I believed

I was cold by nature until you showed me who I really am. Each night you have always been the giver. This last time please allow me to be the lover who gives more. I want you to remember the woman you set free.'

Marmaduke hesitated. This latest 'sweet lady', whose name he never used but knew to be Mrs Cagney, was not like any other woman he had bedded. Modest and faithful during her marriage to the husband who had rejected her, she had been in despair when Marmaduke first met her. She had long ago lost her husband's love but Marmaduke had introduced her to the world of the senses. Now she was a very different woman. Her pale blue eyes expressed the passion of a young girl in the delicately lined face of a thirty-five-year-old woman.

Marmaduke had only intended to kiss her lips in farewell but he discovered he had taught her too well. Her hands caressed him with gentle urgency, stroking his face, his chest, his thighs, drawing him to her with the courtesans' tricks that he had shown her. Her mouth covered his body with passionate, demanding kisses, gently biting him. She grew in confidence as he responded to her seduction, murmuring his pleasure to encourage and excite her. He knew it was now too late to make his planned exit. He must allow her to use his body, departing in the knowledge that she now possessed all the love arts she needed to win back her husband.

Marmaduke stroked the long Nordic blonde hair with its delicate grey streaks, kissed her neck and guided her tentative hands in the ultimate caresses she needed to make him break his last taboo.

'Please,' she whispered, 'you have driven me crazy with delight but you've never once lost control. How do I know if I can succeed *without* you, unless—'

'Hush, sweet lady. You must remember the thing you want most – a babe with your husband. There must be no doubt of that. Every child deserves to know its true father. And you know I've vowed never to risk fathering children.'

She clasped her hands around his waist, dug her fingernails into his back and, in a rising peak of passion, entwined her legs around him to hold him captive.

'Let me love you completely. I shall never see you again. The shield you use to keep a woman safe, I beg you, use it again!'

Marmaduke tried to calm her with kisses. 'Safe, sweet lady, but not infallible! Nothing is. Forgive me, I can't risk it.'

Marmaduke held her in his arms while wrestling with his personal code of ethics. When they first came together he did so knowing she had been publicly and privately humiliated by her philandering husband Sean Cagney. Marmaduke had decided she deserved every bedroom art he could teach her. But now it was no longer a simple question of keeping to their original arrangement to explore everything, teach her everything.

Marmaduke knew that all Sydney Town gossiped about her rival. This lusty young former convict had Sean Cagney so infatuated she drove around in his carriage flashily dressed, determined to replace his wife.

Marmaduke realised that for once he had lost control of the game. He did not have the heart to deny this sweet lady's desperate need to prove her powers of seduction.

God willing my luck holds and the damned shield will protect us both.

He held her face between his hands, kissed her with a well-judged measure of 'uncontrolled' passion and cried out in fervour.

'My God, you're so beautiful. I can't resist you!'

The lady's joyous cry of triumph was his reward.

Marmaduke awoke at dawn feeling distinctly uneasy but unable to pinpoint the reason. It was not until he heard the mocking sound of a kookaburra's laughter and his eyes focused on the shadow play of sunlight on the rows of exotic plants around him that he remembered where he was – lying on the floor of the glasshouse on Sean Cagney's estate. Cagney's naked wife lay asleep with her head on his shoulder. The fine age lines of her face were erased except for her sleepy smile. Her body was as supple and relaxed as a cat. He felt a flash of satisfaction followed by anger at himself for breaking his arch rule – *never stay till dawn.*

Marmaduke gave a wry smile at the sight of the fall of false hair that had parted company with her own and lay across the bedroll like an exhausted lap dog.

'Wake up, my sweet lady.'

He kissed her cheek like an absent-minded friend, helped her to dress and secured the bedroll out of sight.

Mrs Cagney reached out to stroke his cheek. 'I'll *never* forget you.'

'Nor I you! But you must return to the house right now! Take some flowers with you in case you are spotted in the garden. *My* reputation is of no consequence. Yours is precious. Remember your husband is returning from Van Diemen's Land next week!'

She sighed with resignation. 'Yes, but with his young mistress. He intends to pack me off on the next ship to England and instal her in my place.'

Marmaduke hid his growing agitation. 'For your own sake, please leave me now.'

As he watched her saunter dreamily back to the house with a bunch of flowers in her arms, he hastily dressed, slung his coat over his shoulder and headed for the tradesmen's gate. He congratulated himself on his narrow escape too soon and was confronted by the sight of a carriage approaching along the carriageway towards the villa. Marmaduke knew his luck had run out when he identified the carriage by the coachman's livery.

It's Sean Cagney! Just for once, God, I'm asking you to save my skin, not for my sake but to protect that sweet lady.

He had seconds to decide. Flee or face the consequences? Salvation came in the form of an abandoned garden hoe. He ditched his coat jacket, rubbed soil on his face and shirtsleeves and began diligently hoeing the rose garden.

When Cagney ordered the carriage to draw level with him, Marmaduke wore the hang-dog expression common to many assigned men. The older man's gravelly voice sounded as if he had just smoked a box of Cuban cigars. His thick crop of greying red hair and heavy Irish jaw suggested he could be a jovial singing drunk one minute and a fighting drunk the next. Right now he had the look of a husband who had been rogering his mistress and has come home half satiated, half guilty.

Sean Cagney addressed Marmaduke in the arch tone of master to servant. 'This rose garden is a damned disgrace.'

Marmaduke quickly ran through his options. *I haven't a hope in hell of fooling an Irishman with a fake Irish accent. I'd better try a Geordie one.*

He mumbled a reply so thickly accented it was undecipherable. But Sean Cagney cut across his words.

'Hang on! Haven't I been seeing you before? Who are you? No Government man sports a ridiculous head of hair like yours!'

Marmaduke answered with real pride. 'I'm a free man. Earnt me ticket-of-leave, I did. Hired to landscape your garden!' For a moment Marmaduke wasn't sure if the cuckold had bought his story.

Cagney seemed to waver. 'Well, if this is being the best example of your work, you ain't worth your salt. Get back to work!'

Before Marmaduke had time to mask his relief at his reprieve, Cagney ordered his coachman to proceed to the villa.

Marmaduke whistled, light of heart, as he jogged along the new road being built by the convict labour of an iron-gang shackled together. He sent up a vote of thanks to Aphrodite, goddess of love and other related matters, that Cagney had not noticed his flash new landau when driving past it. Thomas had stationed it in a spot discreetly screened by the bush. As Marmaduke approached it the driver was slumped asleep on his box seat but woke up startled and apologetic.

'Shall I return you to the Princess Alexandrina, Marmaduke?'

'A short drive around the harbour foreshores, Thomas. I'm in need of fresh air.'

On arriving at the curve of a bay where a sliver of golden sand was sucked by the incoming tide, Marmaduke felt drawn to the water.

'Drop me down here, Thomas. Order yourself a decent breakfast at the new inn down the road. Come back for me in, say, an hour,' he said, handing him money to cover the meal.

Marmaduke removed his brandy flask and one of the books he kept on board then strode down to the water's edge.

Relieved to find this serene little cove deserted, Marmaduke sank down on the grassy verge that sloped down to the beach. Despite its pristine beauty his mood suddenly plummeted and he gazed disconsolately at the tranquil scene. Not a soul in sight. The only signs of life were seagulls. Close at hand, two fat specimens squawked in a high-pitched argument as they struggled to gain a share of their prize – a fish, flapping in its death throes.

These raucous birds seemed to symbolise what his life had become – a string of clandestine, meaningless liaisons. Women he called 'sweet lady' but never by name. Each one brought him intense but transitory sensual gratification. He did not include Cagney's wife on this list but his other fleeting affairs had left him in a place somewhere between irony and emptiness. He performed so well that these ladies of Quality would do anything to please him in bed; however none would ever risk her place in Society by publicly acknowledging one of the 'untouchables' – the son of an Emancipist.

His control over the hypocrisy of the game gave Marmaduke an odd sense of pleasure. But was this all there was to life? He flipped the pages over to his place in his well-worn copy of *The Sorrows of Young Werther*. Goethe's first novel continued to draw him back at intervals in search of fresh meaning. He was fascinated by the brilliant portrait of the gifted but melancholic young man so obsessed by his passionate love for a married woman that he blew out his brains rather than live with the truth that he could never be more than her friend.

Werther's sorrows had haunted Marmaduke for years.

How can any man be fool enough to destroy himself for love? Romantic love is a fine tool for poets, but in real life it's a ridiculous illusion to be avoided like the plague. Passion is nothing more than Lust sailing under false colours – like a pirate ship that lowers its Jolly Roger to trick the ship it intends to plunder.

Momentarily satisfied he had mastered the truth that eluded so many romantic fools, Marmaduke was forced to concede that at nineteen he had been one of them, standing humiliated at the altar waiting for the bride who never came. That memory drew him towards the grey danger zone of that no man's land – melancholia.

Intent on shaking free from it, he downed another mouthful of brandy then wandered across to a tiny stream, cupping his hands to drink the deliciously cold fresh water before it drained into the harbour.

Yet he was haunted by the unwanted memory of a night some weeks earlier, the faces of two cousins whose husbands neglected them in pursuit of their convict mistresses. These cousins were on the guest list of every polite assembly, yet in private they had vied for Marmaduke's attention until they agreed with each other to share him on the same night. He hadn't desired either of them. Marmaduke tried to shrug off his tawdry role in the game but the memory persisted and overcame him with a sense of his own degradation.

I give women pleasure. No one gets hurt. But what in hell lies ahead of me? Nothing of value now I've lost Mingaletta.

On impulse, he stripped off his clothes. In need of the shock of cold water to lift his jaded spirits, he walked into the harbour until the waves covered his shoulders. No doubt any passers-by would gain the impression he was hell-bent on suicide, but in tough old Sydney Town few would bother to prevent it. As low-spirited as he felt Marmaduke had always dismissed suicide as the option of a coward.

If young Werther had chosen to go on living he would have found a dozen pretty women who wanted him. He'd have forgotten his Lotte in a trice.

A line of Werther's leapt to mind. 'Our happiness and misery depends very much on the objects and persons around us. On this account, nothing is more dangerous than solitude.' He was overcome by a primitive desire to cleanse himself of his decadent memories.

Submerging himself under the waves of the incoming tide, he swam the length of the beach close to the shoreline, reminded that Aborigines seemed devoid of fear of shark attack. But when he had examined sharks strung up by the tail, their eyes and jagged rows of teeth, ghastly in death, he felt a strong desire to avoid them.

Drawing his clothes on over his wet body, he was suddenly cheered by the thought that today, after his weekly visit to his partner Mendoza's store to discuss the latest shipload of English jewellery of dubious legal provenance, he had arranged to take Edwin to lunch.

How pleasant it is to get drunk with a fellow bachelor. Who the hell would be tempted to fall in love on a beautiful Sydney day like today?

The Sign of the Red Cross was one of an ever-diminishing number of inns owned by Garnet's rival landlords. It wasn't frequented by the Quality but the Hunter Valley wines *were* top quality. Marmaduke had it in mind to buy shares in a winery.

As he paused by the entrance, he was confronted by the sight of a bedraggled woman with blood seeping from her skull, being dragged along in the custody of a police constable in the direction of the George Street Watch House.

Marmaduke idly wondered how many of the Colony's victims – men, women, children, bond, free or Aboriginal – were denied basic British justice?

Edwin spends his life fighting for the rights of outcasts and underdogs. I'm a parasite living for the pleasure of the moment. I wonder why Edwin puts up with me?

In the private room he had booked he found his friend's head bent over a pile of legal papers, his spectacles teetering on the edge of his nose. His lawyer's wig lay slumped on a vacant chair. The crown of Edwin's head revealed a bald patch like a monk's tonsure surrounded by wisps of sandy hair. Although Edwin was past thirty and had an air of entrenched middle age, Marmaduke felt as protective of him as he would a younger brother.

He placed his arm around Edwin's shoulder. 'Is there never an hour of the day you free yourself from saving the world, mate? Today you're my guest. Here to take lunch with me and, God willing, get drunk with me. Legal work is taboo!'

'Ah, yes. Good idea in theory. But I was just combing through documents that concern *you*. They bear Godfrey de Rolland's signature. Your esteemed father finally released copies of the documents from his London lawyers to enable me to study your dilemma. I must say it's a most intriguingly explicit marriage contract.'

'Not to *me*, mate. It feels more like a bloody noose around my neck.'

Over their first bottle of a new label claret Marmaduke gave full attention to the legal scenario and waited for Edwin's verdict.

'There you have it. You appear outraged by what you consider your father's manipulation, my friend, but I must confess myself a little surprised by your naiveté. There are three points you need to consider.

'One: it has long been common practice in England for marriages between upper-class families to be arranged to their mutual advantage. Two: your father's an Englishman and despite the grudge he bears the British System for his unplanned departure—'

'Transported. Fourteen years for theft,' Marmaduke corrected mildly. 'We're both adults, mate. No need to hide behind euphemisms like half the Colony does.'

'Quite. But despite Garnet Gamble's status as an Emancipist, or indeed because of it, he is hungry to embrace all things granted to the English Quality – I suspect, to prove he is not only their equal, but a better man than many who Came Free.'

Edwin paused. 'And Three. There is the problem of *you*!'

Marmaduke agreed. 'Ah, there's the rub!'

'Leave Shakespeare out of it for once,' Edwin said crisply. 'Your father has spent a quarter of a century building his empire and made every attempt to educate his son to be a gentleman who is more English than the English.'

'Fat chance of that!' Marmaduke said as he signalled their waitress to replace their empty bottle of wine. He raised a toast to Young Werther, the colt he'd entered in the next Hawkesbury race meeting but Edwin was like a dog with a bone.

'Marmaduke, are you blind? Garnet's conditional pardon means he can never return to England. Yet the upper echelons of Colonial Society are too rigid, too insular for him to be able to live down his youthful crime. His fortune has failed to buy him the two things he craves. Respectability and acceptance. You alone can achieve that for him if you, forgive my choice of words, agree to *marry up.*'

Feeling betrayed Marmaduke raised his voice. 'I thought you were my friend! Why are you pushing me to tie the knot with some boring English virgin whose sole redeeming feature is her long pedigree? You want me to cave in to my social-climbing father so that I can inherit my mother's land which is rightfully *mine*!'

'Morally, yes. Legally, no. You forget her Will wasn't signed,' Edwin said calmly. 'I strongly advise you to meet Isabel de Rolland before you decide categorically to jilt her. This marriage contract is so watertight the Devil himself could have drawn it up. It boils down to this. If your fiancée sues you for breach of promise your father stands to forfeit a huge sum in addition to the fortune he's already paid out. This would wipe out your father's Bloodwood Hall estate—'

'No tragedy to me. I hate the bloody place.'

'But also swallow up your Mingaletta estate. Is that what you want?'

Marmaduke sat back in his chair, stunned by the full import of the contract.

'Shit! It sounds like those bloody aristocrats are just as determined to see this marriage proceed as Garnet is. What's wrong with her? Has she got two heads?'

'Family honour is at stake, Marmaduke. Their honour, not yours.'

'You know what drives Garnet crazy? For years he's been paying informers to report on my movements. I've never consorted with a marriageable girl since I was jilted and I'm totally discreet about my liaisons with older women. Garnet suspects I'm what Saint Paul called blokes who "loveth their own kind".'

Edwin was angry. 'That's no joke. The death penalty for sodomy remains on the Colony's statute books and it only takes two men to *swear falsely* as witnesses and The Finisher's in business to string you up!'

'Don't worry, mate. I've got a great lawyer. Let's drink to women, God bless 'em!'

Edwin sounded faintly envious. 'Your life is fun and games but no responsibilities.'

'Dead right. I've proved how easily married women are open to seduction once they've got a wedding ring. I'd trust 'em as far as I'd trust a Caribbean pirate.'

Edwin eyed him thoughtfully. 'I don't know whether to envy you or pity you.'

'I'm more interested in laying hands on Mingaletta than a shipload of *pirates in petticoats*!'

They were both startled by the sultry voice of the black-haired serving maid who leant over to place a huge platter of roast beef and Yorkshire pudding between them.

'No pirates in petticoats on the menu today, gentlemen!'

Marmaduke noticed the girl wasn't exactly young, maybe twenty-five, but she was magnificently buxom, had a naughty smile and was every bit as beddable as she was Irish.

He quickly recovered enough to ask her name, which Maeve supplied in a lilting accent that suggested it was a favour rarely given to gentlemen.

The provocative way she leant across the table granted Marmaduke a fine view of the globes of breasts pressed against her low-cut bodice, barely inches from Edwin's face.

'Enjoy your dinner, gentlemen. And if there is any rare vintage you fancy,' she added over her shoulder, 'you have only to ask.'

They observed in silent appreciation her hip-swinging departure.

'Now that's a *real* woman. She clearly fancies you, Edwin. I can recognise an invitation in a woman's eyes when I see one.'

'Let's stick to business, shall we?' Edwin carved the beef and they washed it down with another bottle of Hunter Valley claret.

'Third bottle's always the best,' Marmaduke pronounced sagely.

Edwin lay down his knife and fork. 'Care to hear my suggestion for ridding yourself of a de Rolland bride without depleting the Gamble fortune in a breach of promise case?'

'Try me!' Marmaduke paid strict attention as Edwin outlined his recommended plan.

'Trust you to come up with something dodgy but legal, mate. Will it work?'

'Play your cards right, but one false move and you'll be caught in your own trap.'

Marmaduke gave a dismissive wave of the hand. 'For that folly to happen a bloke would need to fall in love. Physicians can immunise people against small pox. Me, I'm totally immunised against *love!*'

CHAPTER 7

London, March 1833

The great proscenium arch curved over the Covent Garden stage like the portal to a world of dreams that Isabel had been waiting to enter since she was a small child.

From the pit below and from the tiers of giant horseshow-shaped galleries above her came the buzzing sound, pierced by raucous laughter, of an audience restless for the red velvet curtain to rise and begin tonight's performance.

Waves of excitement ran through the audience. Isabel felt that she was the only person present who waited in tense silence. Tonight was an experience she wanted to savour to the full. In her first ever visit to a London theatre she was seated close to the stage in the dress-circle box used by generations of the de Rolland family. She clenched the stem of her fan, folded in contrast to the sea of painted and feathered fans fluttering to counteract the heat and smell generated by the crowd of perfumed and unwashed bodies.

Isabel blocked from her mind the inevitable departure of the *Susan*, scheduled to sail in a few days from the Port of London. Cousin Silas's assurance that the Calcutta-built vessel was seaworthy and speedy and would take the more unusual Madeira route to New South Wales hardly mattered to her.

Tonight one half of her childhood dream would be fulfilled. She would witness the legendary magic of Edmund Kean. The other half of her dream remained a secret she hugged inside herself – to be an actress who played Desdemona to Kean's Othello, Lady Anne to his Richard III, Juliet to his Romeo, Ophelia to his Hamlet. An impossible dream all the more beautiful because it hurt no one.

Seated all around her were high-born ladies dressed in evening finery, bedecked with feathers and jewels. She admired rather than envied their fashions but draped Martha's cashmere shawl around her shoulders to disguise the grey worsted travelling ensemble that was her only decent outfit until she took delivery of the bridal trousseau from Paris. Reassured that her hair at least was *á la mode,* she patted one of the long side curls that escaped artlessly over each cheek. Old Agnes had worked all afternoon to dress her hair in the current style copied from a fashion paper.

Isabel glanced at her hands, naked of rings. She owned no jewellery and her heart sank at the ironic thought that when her ship sailed into the Penal Colony at Port Jackson, she would be forced to wear the hated gold wedding band of servitude.

She was excited by the wild fancy that the *Susan* might be wrecked before it cleared the English Channel, washing her ashore in France or Portugal where under the pretence of amnesia she could begin a new life under a new identity.

Now there's a plot worthy of Will Shakespeare. But tonight is mine! I'm witness to an event in theatrical history – the first ever performance of Othello *by the Keans, father and son. The master's legendary Othello opposite the Iago of his son Charles.*

Isabel suddenly felt anxious. What was causing the delay? The performance had been scheduled to commence at half past the hour. Isabel felt her heart beat uncomfortably fast, catching the throb of anxiety in an audience that had also braved the night's storm. Were they here out of loyalty or cynicism – to see the great Edmund Kean return to the stage in triumph or to watch him suffer another disastrous failure?

At age forty-six he should be at the pinnacle of his illustrious career but all newspaper reports in recent years showed that England's greatest tragedian was plagued by scandal, ill-health and drunkenness. During his second American tour some volatile audiences had worshipped him as a hero. Others had pelted him with tomatoes.

She whispered in prayer, 'Please God take pity on him tonight.'

'Is your prayer offered up for me, *ma petite cousine?*'

Isabel was startled from her reverie, so caught between the waves of excitement and anxiety that she had forgotten the presence of her escort, who had rejoined her after smoking in the gentlemen's saloon. Against Uncle Godfrey's orders Silas had arrived at the family's townhouse that morning to farewell her.

Isabel forced herself to answer politely. 'I doubt you have need of my prayers, Cousin. I asked the gods to smile on Kean.'

Silas made a languid gesture towards the uppermost gallery where a rowdy crowd was sandwiched in rows of the cheapest seats in the house.

'The Children of the Gods are Kean's most fervent supporters. They cheer him whether he arrives drunk, sober or carted on in a wheelbarrow.'

'Why do you mock him? You know it has long been my dream to see him.'

'Perhaps I'm just a little jealous,' he said gently. Then, as if to restore himself in her favour, he assumed a note of greater respect.

'I can't bear to see your disappointment when the thespian fails to appear. It's said Kean's been cursed with the greatest terror that can befall an actor – the loss of his memory. When he opened in some new role especially written for him—'

'*Ben Nazir*,' she prompted.

'Indeed. He not only forgot his lines but the plot of the whole play. He's now confined to the roles he made famous in his youth.'

'Richard III,' she said, 'Othello, Macbeth, Shylock and the mad villain Sir Giles Overreach in *A New Way to Play Old Debts*.'

Silas smiled. 'I forgot you devoured as gospel every word written about the fellow.'

'I *read* every word,' she corrected. 'But I never believed that scurrilous gossip about him in the broadsheet rags and lampoons.'

'Despite your loyalty, I'm afraid there was evidence aplenty in the Kean versus Cox trial to prove him guilty of adultery. Kean's no gentleman. His hilariously passionate love letters to Alderman Cox's wife, when read out at his trial, kept London amused for months.'

'Mr Kean was gentleman enough to refuse to allow his lawyer to use Charlotte Cox's love letters to *him* as evidence in his defence,' she snapped.

'As I suspected, you're one those young girls who are attracted to scoundrels.'

The teasing note in Silas's voice held an undercurrent that made her eager to change the subject. The audience in both gallery and pit were now chanting Kean's name.

'How restless they are. Mr Kean is late but I don't doubt he'll give us his Othello.'

'Don't doubt he shall if he's seduced by enough money to keep the bailiffs at bay.'

Isabel barely kept her anger in check. 'If that were the case our family should have sympathy for him. We've only just escaped the spectre of poverty ourselves, Cousin.'

Silas's reply was soft but equally dangerous. 'What makes you so sure Kean won't drink himself senseless to escape his fear of failure? Money is all that thespians understand.'

'No. Mr Kean will play tonight. Even more than he needs money, his son needs *him*.'

'What touching faith you have in drunken actors, m'dear.'

Isabel turned to face him. 'Perhaps I'd be wiser to put my faith in actors than in my kinsmen.'

Silas whispered in her ear. 'You forget yourself, Isabel. If I had not lied to protect you, you might have been transported to the Colony. The minimum sentence is seven years.'

Isabel withdrew her hand, disguising her gesture of rejection by joining the wild applause that greeted The Great Kean's entrance.

Edmund Kean brought his son forward to acknowledge the audience. Standing beside the taller figure of young Charles, the elder Kean seemed at first glance frail, almost shy, but was suddenly heartened by the warmth of their reception. Isabel felt a delicious tremor at the illusion that Edmund Kean looked directly up at her box. Those amazingly eloquent dark eyes blazed out from the Moor's black countenance and seemed to speak to her alone.

At last the play began. In Isabel's eyes the actors were transformed into living Venetians. Charles Kean's Iago was indeed the double-faced Janus whose jealousy of his commander Othello caused him to hatch the plot to destroy the Moor, while presenting himself as a bluff, honest soldier and Othello's friend.

The magic of Shakespeare's dialogue held Isabel captive. Her lips moved in silent communion with Othello and Desdemona's speeches she knew by heart. It seemed as if the flimsy barrier of oil lamps between stage and audience dissolved and she offered up her heart to the *real* world being created for her. Nothing else existed. Othello the Moor and Edmund Kean had fused to become one soul.

The first acts kept Isabel so entranced she refused to break the spell by leaving her seat at interval to take the champagne refreshment Silas offered her. But by the Third Act she grew tense, unable to block out the truth. Her hero was engaged in a life and death struggle to continue to perform. She willed him to draw strength from her own body, became one with the house in total silence, hanging on Othello's tortured words after he was duped by Iago's poisonous lie that his beloved Desdemona had betrayed him with a lover.

The agony in Edmund Kean's voice pierced Isabel's very body as he said the words: 'What sense had I, in her stolen hours of lust? I saw it not, thought it not; it harmed not me. I slept the next night well, was free and merry; I found not Cassio's kisses on her lips...'

But midway through his next speech Kean faltered. Isabel almost cried aloud to give him the cue. His eyes filled with black confusion.

Is this Othello's agony? No. God help him, it is Edmund Kean's!

Horrified, Isabel's mind blotted out his words until suddenly aware of the dual significance of his speech.

The great actor paused as if fighting for breath but gave to Othello's words a world of sadness, 'Farewell! Othello's occupation's gone!'

Isabel covered her mouth to silence her cry. *My God, this is not merely part of the play. This is real!'*

Like an automaton Isabel joined in the audience's warm applause at the end of this speech but although his son Charles silently acknowledged the compliment to his father, Edmund Kean stood as if abandoned, marooned on stage, his eyes downcast. After the last shouts of 'bravo' the silence was drawn out too long to be intentionally dramatic. An uneasy murmur spread throughout the theatre.

Isabel felt the actor son's own quiet desperation seep through Iago's line to Othello, 'Is't possible, my lord?'

Cracked words were torn from Othello's lips. 'Villain, be sure thou prove my love a whore—'

Isabel felt faint with fear. Othello did not complete this speech nor step forwards as she knew the scene demanded for him to seize Iago by the throat and throttle him.

Instead Kean broke into a desperate fit of weeping as he fell on his son's neck and cried out to him, 'Oh God, I am dying – speak to them for me!'

Charles Kean caught his father as he slumped unconscious in his arms.

The whole house rose as one with loud cries of encouragement as the great Othello was carried from the stage. Isabel did not know how long she sat there, isolated from everything around her, until Silas drew her into his arms, softly assuring her.

'I am here, Isabel. Another actor is to take Othello's place.'

Isabel was ignited by anger. 'No one can *ever* take Edmund Kean's place!'

The de Rolland townhouse faced a central park that was kept locked for the sole use by the residents of the terraced villas that surrounded it. Isabel desperately wanted to sit there alone with her thoughts but Silas dismissed the idea as absurd.

The oil lamps were alight in the entrance hall both the butler and old Agnes waited to attend to their needs. Silas ushered Isabel into an elegant small room in which supper had been prepared for them. He dismissed the butler then told Agnes that her mistress had no further need of her. But stubborn Agnes acknowledged no authority except Godfrey de Rolland and looked to Isabel to take her cue.

Isabel countered Silas's order. 'Please prepare yourself for bed, Agnes. I will be up in a moment. You can *be sure* I'll call in to say good night.'

Left alone with Silas, Isabel watched him intently as he closed the door then poured champagne for them. She drank in silence, trying to divorce herself from the tragic final image of Edmund Kean's face.

I must not appear vulnerable, tonight of all nights.

Silas took the chair close to her and looked searchingly at her before speaking.

'I would not have had this unhappy ending occur for the world, Isabel.'

She was instantly on guard. She drained her glass to give herself courage but chose her words with care. 'Are you referring to Edmund Kean's temporary exit from the stage? Or my permanent departure from England?'

Silas's eyes narrowed as if he was for once unsure how to gauge her true feelings. 'The actor's debauched history has brought about his own downfall, whereas—'

'Mine has not?' she said quickly. 'Come, Cousin, I may be young and naive but I am not entirely stupid. This arranged marriage is an act of Divine providence. It restored the family coffers and settled that awkward question, "What on earth do we do with poor Isabel?"'

'You surprise me, Isabel. You sound bitter. Yet you showed no emotion when the offer of marriage was put to you.'

'What choice did I have? The decision was *fait accompli*. New carriages, lavish entertainment, your Grand Tour of Europe. Don't lie to me! The marriage contracts were already signed by you and Uncle Godfrey, weren't they?'

Silas didn't flinch from her anger but leant closer and held her arms fast to restrain her. 'If you want the truth you must hear the *whole* truth.'

Isabel was thrown off guard by his expression of tenderness. She had a sudden rush of memory of the night she had seen Silas for the first time, when she was nine years old and sitting in her nightdress, hidden at the top of the marble staircase awaiting the return of the family hero.

Cousin Silas entered the hall, tall, blond and handsome, resplendent in his cavalry officer's uniform. He handed his cloak to the butler.

Isabel felt her breath sucked from her body, awed by the god-like creature who fixed his eyes on her as he sprang up the stairs and sat on a lower step to bring their eyes level.

'So you are my little orphan Isabel come to live with us. I am your kinsman, Silas. I had great affection for your mother, Alizon. I promise to love and protect you like a brother.'

Isabel nodded, unable to speak. His gaze held her as he bent over her hand and kissed the fingertips just as if she were a grown lady.

'I shall be your champion. Always. But one day when you are all grown up I shall ask you to marry me.'

She gasped with surprise when he whispered, 'Will your answer be "yes", ma petite cousine?'

The magic of the moment was shattered when Isabel turned to see the figure in evening dress standing in the doorway of the assembly room. Uncle Godfrey frowned, an uncertain expression on his face as he curtly reminded Silas their guests were waiting.

Isabel closed her eyes to blot out that memory but was shaken by Silas's perception. He had always been able to read her thoughts.

'I pressured Godfrey for your hand in marriage before you reached the age of consent. He refused. Claimed our blood was too close. I would have defied him and waited for you but your fall from grace and your crime of infanticide made that impossible. Even then I forgave you. Surely you must know I have always loved you, Isabel.'

'Stop! You must not speak of such things. Cousin Martha—'

'She is dying. Everyone knows it – even Martha.'

'No!'

'The physician predicts she won't outlive the spring.' Silas's expression frightened her. 'Look at me, Isabel. This arranged marriage isn't the end of the world. Do this for the family – for me. Go through with this wedding to that convict's son. It will only be for one year. When your marriage fails, as it must, those Colonial rascals will have no chance to reclaim the money in the contract. When I'm free I'll come to the Colony to claim you.'

Free? He means when Martha dies.

'I can't believe you're saying this!'

'There's method in my madness. I'll rescue you, bring you home to England. We'll have the world at our feet. A life of luxury. And you will at last belong to me. *Only* to me.'

'Aren't you forgetting something?' Isabel said coldly. 'No doubt my husband will expect me to bear him a child.'

Silas watched her reaction as he toyed idly with a cushion. 'There's a solution to every problem. A pillow can snuff out a life in seconds. Shakespeare made it seem so easy.'

Isabel felt her blood run cold. *He means Othello smothered Desdemona.*

'Why does that idea shock you, Isabel? You've already solved that little problem once before.' The statement was calmly delivered.

That little problem. Please God keep him believing I killed the babe.

Isabel made a rush for the door but Silas blocked her flight. His hands reached out and folded around her throat in a sign of possession, forcing her to look into his eyes. She saw it, that flash of something akin to madness. Was it also inside her?

Unable to speak she felt that familiar surge of fear mixed with guilt and desire.

'You see?' Silas said calmly. 'You know it, too. I am the one man on earth who is strong enough to possess you, little witch. You will destroy any man who loves you – except me! I'm your kinsman. Double cousins, only a heartbeat away from being brother and sister. We share the same Plantagenet bloodline, the same ancestors on both sides. You shall become flesh of my flesh, as it was always meant to be.'

Silas's mood altered so suddenly Isabel was shocked at how easily his voice resumed a business-like tone. 'Now off to bed with you. We must deliver you to the *Susan* by three of the clock tomorrow afternoon.'

From the doorway she managed to ask, as if nothing was wrong. 'What of my Paris trousseau? I understand the Gamble lawyers agreed to pay—'

'All is in hand. Your trunks are already on board ship. Everything's arranged with the ship's master. No need for us to suffer a farewell scene, *ma petite cousine*. My new manservant will drive with you to the dock. He was a prize-fighter trained in his youth by Daniel Mendoza, but my man Cooper lives by a different code. He has no scruples about being heavy-handed with women, so don't have any fancy ideas about missing the boat.'

'I know my duty,' Isabel said coldly. 'But what of Agnes: isn't she to sail with me?'

'Only to see you on board for the sake of appearances.'

Isabel turned to gain what she hoped was her last ever sight of Silas. He stood before the fireplace, one foot on the fender, wine-glass in hand. His smile was so conspiratorial it made her flesh creep.

'No doubt Agnes will shed buckets of tears at the wharf as you sail away. But *you'll* be dry eyed. Witches never cry.'

He raised a hand to halt her. 'One final question. Uncle Godfrey says you never changed your story. You did not identify your partner in crime. But you know you can trust *me*, Cousin.'

Isabel's mouth dried. She took her time, knowing that three lives depended on her answer. 'He was just a boy, a traveller passing through the village. I never knew his name.'

'Thought as much,' he said idly. 'Oh well, that's ancient history now.'

Isabel closed the door behind her and ascended the stairs, feeling dazed and curiously empty. In her bedroom she discovered Agnes asleep on the sofa alongside her bed. A small coin purse lay on Isabel's pillow. The accompanying note was reasonably legible so must have been dictated.

My dear little Lamb,

I know you'll be making a fine Marriage when you gets to Botany Bay. But it don't bear thinking about you sailing so far from Mother England without a penny to bless yourself. Your Guardian give me this money as a Reward for keeping you safe. But I ask you, what's an old servant like me need with money?

Try and be happy, my good girl. They say Marriages are made in Heaven. I pray you're going to a decent man who won't beat you like my rotter did me.

I hopes you'll forgive old Agnes for being cranky. I would have been glad to sail with you and look out for you. Mr Silas said there weren't no money to waste on my Passage.

Ever your Faithful Agnes

Beside her name was a neat cross where Agnes had made her mark.

Isabel lay awake, clutching the purse inside her nightgown, marvelling at how strange life was. *My family believe they are now rid of one unwanted de Rolland. They're mistaken.*

For the first time in her life Isabel felt the bittersweet taste of triumph. She had outwitted her de Rolland kinsmen. In time her guardian's disgraced sister Elisabeth would be free to follow her to New South Wales.

And Cousin Silas will never know the truth about my 'confession' of infanticide. Or that the de Rolland family has another heir, my little Rose Alba.

CHAPTER 8

Bloodwood Hall, New South Wales, March 1833

'Shut your mouth, you stupid bird. You're lucky I didn't wring your neck years back.'

Seated on the front terrace in his Indian planter's chair, shaded by the network of purple wisteria that wound its way around the verandah columns, Garnet Gamble found a ready target for his fury in Amaru. The cockatoo responded with his own brand of anger. His sulphur-coloured crest fanned out to its full range as he strutted on his exercise bar.

'Shame on you! Shame on you!' Amaru kept repeating in the aggressive squawk that Garnet knew from experience would take time to cool. Miranda had spent endless months teaching her 'clever bird' to speak and he fancied he could hear the intonation of her voice in the bird's words. It irritated him intensely to realise that this accursed bird would be spouting Miranda's provoking words long after he was dead and buried.

He cast a steely glance at Elise, who was seated on a nearby sofa, her face shaded by a Leghorn hat adorned with too many flowers, her milk-white bosom flouting far more décolletage than any real lady would deign to reveal in daylight hours. He knew Elise was doing her best to imitate an English gentlewoman, working threads into a tapestry frame that she had laboured over for the past three years. Garnet suspected the floral design was decorated with more pinpricks of her blood than flowers.

We both know she'd never pass the test of behaving like a lady. Why doesn't she give up? Stick to what she was born to do – being paid to perform in my bed.

Garnet was glad to be distracted by the sound of a horse's hooves and the clang of the wrought-iron gates at the end of the avenue. Was this Marmaduke returning home with news of the bride's arrival?

He hooked his spectacles in place. Not that they were the slightest use except on those occasions he pretended to read documents requiring his signature. Spectacles proved a useful foil against those who suspected his illiteracy and tried to take advantage to cheat him of his fortune. He had recently dismissed his previous secretary.

No bastard's going to get one over me! But there's no one in the world I can trust.

When the horseman rode into his line of vision, Garnet felt a jolt of disappointment. The rider was not Marmaduke, just a scrawny messenger that Garnet's instinct told him was an old lag who had done it hard to complete his time. Prison left an invisible brand on a felon's face that no subsequent amount of freedom could entirely erase. Garnet saw that same mark in the face that looked out of his bedroom mirror.

He jerked his head in Elise's direction. 'See what this bloke wants.'

Elise's fashionably pale face was instantly flushed with a pink dot on each cheek.

'Surely that's a servant's role, Garnet dear.'

'The only difference between you and my assigned servants is you get *paid* to do my bidding.'

He ignored her emotional sniffs. Elise tossed down her sewing, wrapped the shawl across her bosom to protect her from the sun and the horror of freckled flesh. She assumed a haughty duchess air as she descended the steps to ask the man his business.

'Thank you, ma'am, but I've strict instructions to be handing over this letter into the hands of none but Mr Garnet Gamble himself.'

The Irishman doffed his hat to Elise but inclined his head at Garnet. 'Would that gentleman be yourself, sir?'

'Here, give it over.'

Garnet placed the large envelope on the footstool as if there was no urgency involved.

'You've ridden your horse into quite a lather.'

'Mr Bentleigh's instructions were to deliver this to you post haste, sir.'

'A horse deserves better treatment. Take him to the stables and get the ostler to see to him. Go to the rear of the house and ask for

Cook. Tell her I said you're to be well fed before you hit the road again.'

The Irishman mumbled his thanks but hesitated about leaving.

'What are you waiting for, man? Your master pays you, don't he?'

The courier took the horse's reins and skulked off with a hangdog expression.

'These old lags must think a man's made of money,' Garnet snapped at Elise.

She was overcome by curiosity. 'It must be urgent. It could be from Marmaduke. Aren't you going to open it?'

Garnet knew the answer to his question before he asked it. 'Why don't *you* read it to me seeing as you're so dead keen?'

Elise quickly gathered up her sewing in an attempt to cover her humiliation about the illiteracy she believed was hers alone. 'I must instruct Cook about tonight's menu in honour of the new magistrate. Mr Summerhayes is a real gentleman.'

The moment she was out of sight Garnet grabbed the envelope and tore open Bentleigh's familiar wax seal. The letter was written in a copperplate hand and Garnet could only recognise his name peppered across it.

Who in hell could he trust to read it? Perhaps he had packed his thieving secretary off to the magistrate too soon. Until a replacement arrived he was left high and dry. The only solution went against the grain.

The old bitch hates my guts but Marmaduke's the light of her life so no matter what Bentleigh's letter says she won't spread gossip about him.

Amaru began to squawk and he turned on the bird.

'Shut up, Amaru! Oh, all right, come along with me.'

The bird perched on his shoulder and Garnet crossed the landscaped oriental garden at the rear of the house, only half aware of the beauty of the scene. On reaching the wings of the convicts' cabins he was conscious there were no assigned labourers in sight. The familiar rhythm of the lash sounded close at hand, followed by the grunts that reminded him of a dog in pain. Fordham the Flogger was performing his favourite exercise, stepping into the role of scourger to mete out some felon's punishment rather than wait for the new circuit magistrate to pass judgment.

Time had hardened Garnet to this ritual. The prisoner tied to the crossbeam was young in years but old in terms of The System. His exposed back was bloody from fresh cuts of Fordham's lash that cross-hatched the raw scars of previous floggings – what the felons called the Red Shirt.

Garnet recognised the face that turned to fix him with a baleful stare. Paddy Whickett. No mistaking that red hair. The lad's skin was stretched taut across the cheekbones, the bloodshot eyes bulged, the teeth clenched against each flaying of the lash. Whickett had been assigned to him several years back but rebelled so often his sentence never grew shorter.

'What's he done this time?' Garnet demanded of Fordham.

'Insubordination, blasphemy on the Sabbath, stealing Government stores from the cooling house. You name it, he's done it.'

'Right, well don't go overboard. Make sure he's fit to work tomorrow.'

Garnet recognised in Whickett's eyes the same fire of revenge he had felt himself as a young transportee. On impulse he halted Fordham.

'He's already copped enough stripes for insubordination and blasphemy.' He turned to the prisoner. 'Why did you steal Government stores? To barter?'

'To eat! Ye don't know what it's like being forced to work on half rations.'

'Don't I just,' Garnet said under his breath before he addressed the men. 'Understand this, you lot. Government stores are supplied to feed you. Some of you were transported for stealing food. I'm not here to punish you twice for hunger. I'll pack you off to the magistrate and see you hanged if the crime warrants it, but no man goes hungry while I'm Master here.'

Garnet kept his face expressionless. To undercut his overseer's authority in front of convicts was an invitation to mutiny. But he ordered Fordham to cut the prisoner loose.

'Your choice, Whickett. You can continue to work here or be returned to the convict barracks in Sydney and take your chances on being assigned to a new master or an iron-gang. Which is it?'

Paddy Whickett turned his head in the direction of the house and Garnet followed his gaze to the Irish girl standing alone with her fists clenched. Bridget.

So that's the attraction. I don't like the lad's chances. She's more woman than any one man could tame – except me.

Whickett eyed her as he gave his answer. 'I'll be taking my chances with the Devil I know.'

Garnet turned to Fordham. 'This dog's young enough to learn new tricks. Give him time for his stripes to heal. He's off the work lists as of now.'

As he passed his overseer Garnet lowered his voice. 'Understand me. If you cut their rations again, Fordham, I'll have your balls for breakfast!'

He continued down the winding track to the whitewashed two-room stone cottage that held long memories. He had built it himself as a twenty-year-old, dreaming of how he would lay the foundations of his empire when Governor Macquarie granted him a pardon. The cottage aroused images of Miranda so strong that Garnet could not erase the pain of them, yet never wanted to relinquish a single one.

Garnet walked from his cottage to watch the spectacular sunset from the boundary of his Bloodwood grant. The adjacent estate had been granted to a British Army officer as a reward for his years of service in India. Colonel McAlpine looked straight past Garnet's cart whenever he passed him on the road to Sydney Town, leaving his daughter in the care of her Indian servant girl.

The ritual of sunset was Garnet's daily hope of gaining a glimpse of his new neighbour's daughter, a young lady of Quality. A few hundred yards beyond the slip rail boundary fence was McAlpine's Indian bungalow, Mingaletta.

Since her father's departure the girl had also made it her habit to watch the sunset. Today for the first time she acknowledged Garnet with a wave and beckoned him.

He hesitated then leapt over the fence and hurried down the hill, his heart thumping in his chest. She wore a filmy white dress. Her hair and eyes were dark, a vivid contrast to her flawless English complexion.

He made her an awkward bow. 'George Gamble at your service, miss. But I answer to Garnet.'

Miranda curtsied but her eyes teased him with laughter. 'I know who you are. Garnet Gamble, our only neighbour. It's so lonely here. You and I are the only two young people within miles.'

'We're the only two people within miles, miss,' he stammered.

'Father's very strict. We haven't been properly introduced. But we are neighbours. So would you care to dine with us?'

'Aye, miss. But perhaps another time when your father returns?'

'You'll be quite safe. Queenie will chaperone us.'

Miranda teasingly gestured to the Indian servant, who wore an orange sari and was eyeing Garnet with barely concealed distrust.

Right at that moment Garnet knew Miranda was the girl who would haunt him all the days of his life. Her beauty was breathtaking and her voice soft and musical, a cross between her father's Scottish heritage and the lilting Hindi cadences of her childhood.

Queenie served them but left them alone at Miranda's request and the girl slipped into using the name Garnet as easily as if she had known him for years.

'The Governor's ball at Parramatta was so boring. The young officers looked as if they've been stamped out of the same mould. Much more fun to talk to the shy young man who is always watching me.'

'Forgive me, miss,' Garnet stammered.

She tilted her head to one side to consider him. 'You don't look too dangerous for a transportee. Father forbade me to talk to you. But we are neighbours.'

Were Miranda's eyes innocent or flirtatious or both? Whatever, she was a creature of impulse. 'I want to hear all about your adventures in the Colony. And how did you come by the name Garnet?'

'I was transported on a charge of stealing a lady's garnet ring. I know every convict says they were innocent, but I was.'

'Don't worry, Garnet,' she whispered. 'I'm a thief myself. But I only steal men's hearts.'

Garnet was jolted back to the present. Miranda had indeed stolen his heart. He had lain with her for three glorious nights. On the Colonel's return Miranda was forbidden to speak to him, until she discovered she was with child. The Colonel had finally given in to her tears and tantrums and gave his consent to their marriage.

At Garnet's knock the cabin door flew open to reveal Queenie. The dark-skinned old woman who had been Miranda's faithful servant was now his implacable enemy. She had grown up in India sharing Miranda's lessons with a governess. It riled Garnet to know that this cranky servant was fully literate whereas he could barely sign his name.

Queenie scowled. 'Who gave you permission to come here?'

'You live in this cottage due to my generosity!'

'I won't be here much longer now Marmaduke's coming home to Mingaletta.'

Garnet forced himself to batten down his temper. 'I need your help. Not on my account but because of your affection for the lad. I want you to read a letter from his lawyer. Can you bury your hatred of me long enough to do that, woman?'

Queenie begrudgingly gestured for him to enter. Inside the cabin that now seemed too small to hold him, he handed her the letter but remained standing. She had not given him permission to be seated. *How ridiculous this is. I can strike terror into the hearts of half the men and women in the Colony – except this old witch.*

She placed the letter on the table and stared at him with narrowed eyes. 'So you're up to your old tricks again, manipulating people's lives.'

'It's for the best.'

'Judges say that when they sentence prisoners to transportation. It's for the good of Society!'

'Damn you, Queenie, I didn't come here to be lectured on The System. What does the letter *say*?'

'Edwin Bentleigh acknowledges the deeds you hold to Mingaletta, which you agreed to sign over to Marmaduke when he marries his fiancée.' She raised her voice in anger. 'No one told *me* about this. Who is she?'

'Go on, for pity's sake, Queenie!'

'This letter states that it is Marmaduke's final offer.'

Garnet grew suspicious at the sight of Queenie's faint smile. 'Out with it!'

'Marmaduke, confirms he relinquishes all future claims on your properties and fortune. On condition you sign over Mingaletta, release him from this unwanted engagement and abstain from any future involvement in his affairs.'

'Insolent puppy! He hasn't given way a damned inch!'

'Hold your horses. There's more,' she added with a gleam in her eye. 'He insists on paying Miss de Rolland's expenses in the Colony and her fare to England on the grounds that "this proposed marriage is no fault of hers." Furthermore as your *neighbour* at Mingaletta, he undertakes full responsibility for any future *medical expenses* you may require to enable you to remain in residence at Bloodwood Hall.'

Garnet exploded with rage. 'Lock me up, a prisoner in my own house? I'll be damned if he will.'

'No! Face the facts! It's his promise to keep you out of a lunatic asylum.'

Garnet changed tack to blot out the spectre of madness. 'The fool's cutting off his nose to spite me. I haven't worked my guts out to leave my fortune to a string of grasping charities. Marmaduke is my sole hope to forge a Gamble dynasty.'

'You should have thought of that when you prevented him marrying his first love.'

'He was wet behind the ears. I saved him from certain disaster – you know that.'

'Yes, but ruined both your lives in the process. Your son hates you. You failed to make him in your image. He isn't greedy like you. You've picked the eyes out of the whole country. All Marmaduke wants is Mingaletta, to honour his promise to Miranda. I was there when she made him swear on the Bible, remember?'

Garnet was forced to relive the moment of her death. He said the words softly in defeat. 'Do you think I can ever forget my shame?'

'That's the punishment you deserve. Miranda comes to me every full moon. She'll hate you 'til your dying day!'

As Garnet strode from the cottage Queenie's derisive cackle rang in his ears.

The old bitch's hatred of me is the one thing that keeps her alive. But no one could ever hate me as much as I hate myself.

*

Garnet hurried up the marble staircase, overcome by the need to see Miranda's face before he lost all sense of time and place.

He felt compelled to visit her before it took hold of him again: the malevolent thing growing inside him, the return of the mania that unleashed the furies that spun him out of control. He could feel it building in intensity – the rush of fear that no other human being had ever been able to arouse in him. The fear of himself.

In the portrait gallery he halted, breathless, in front of his quarry – the portrait of Miranda. Impossibly seductive, timeless, she smiled down on him, eternally sure of her elusive power over him.

'You know the truth. If I could love any other woman, *I would*. But you won't let go of me.' He heard his voice cry out, 'All the others are just bodies I use to escape *you!*'

He froze at the sound of the soft female cry behind him. Would her ghost at last make itself visible to him? No. His impotent rage boiled over at the realisation it was only Elise.

'You're not well, Garnet. Please don't fight it – come to bed and I will comfort you.'

'I give the orders. Unlock the door, damn you.'

'Please, Garnet, don't put me through this again.'

He propelled her down the passage to the door of the secret room that remained locked, lying in readiness for nights such as this. Elise took the key from its hiding place behind the panel and unlocked the door. Before them the narrow stairs ascended into darkness.

CHAPTER 9

At the stroke of six Marmaduke's carriage turned into the open road that led to Woolloomooloo Hill. The cool southerly breeze off the harbour was welcomed by the whole of Sydney Town at the end of a humid day.

Marmaduke felt a pleasant sense of anticipation. Thanks to Edwin's invitation, the evening promised to bring him one step closer to his goal – an assignation with the legendary opera singer whom he had admired since he first sighted her on the day of his return to the Colony. After each of her performances at Barnett Levey's Theatre Royal he had sent her a bouquet conveying his coded message via the language of flowers. Each was delivered with his calling card, the same words handwritten on the back: 'With great respect and admiration. I look forward to our first meeting. Marmaduke Gamble.' He hoped to arouse the diva's curiosity about his identity because although his flowers kept arriving, he had never tried to contact her.

Aware of his interest in Josepha St John, Edwin had invited him to the kind of social event from which Marmaduke was ordinarily excluded. A select assembly of some fifty members of the Quality was to attend a private performance at the impressive Woolloomooloo Hill mansion of a wealthy banker, said to be so besotted by Madame St John he had sent a special ship for her return from a season in Van Diemen's Land. Tonight the Top Thirteen families would be introduced to the diva whose fame and notoriety made her the most talked-about woman in Sydney Town.

Everyone knew that Josepha St John's career spanned two decades across the Americas, Europe and India. Her fabled collection of jewels were the tributes of princes, potentates and presidents. The *Sydney Herald* claimed her legendary diamond ring was the gift of an Indian Maharajah so desperate to win her love that her departure caused him to take a lethal dose of poison. Marmaduke wondered if the young man's suicide was another in the cult inspired by Goethe's tragic hero in *The Sorrows of Young Werther*. The novel had crossed cultural boundaries across the globe and was said to have triggered the suicide of a number of young men suffering from acute romantic melancholia.

Tonight Marmaduke had dressed with particular care, choosing a dark blue velvet waisted jacket over an understated waistcoat, tight buff-coloured breeches, silk stockings and silver buckled evening shoes. He had spent an excessive amount of time, swearing in the process, as he tried to create the intended waterfall of linen folds at his neck. His long hair was tied back with a black ribbon in the romantic style of a pre-Revolutionary French courtier.

He had hesitated about whether or not to wear his spectacular ruby ring, only too aware that any attempt to upstage an actress is an unforgiveable sin and he should take care not to outshine her jewels. But he also wanted to establish himself as a man of wealth and mystery and the ruby was his signature piece.

Thomas halted the carriage in front of Edwin's charming cottage on the foreshores of Woolloomooloo Bay. The house was surrounded by an English cottage garden studded with orange and peach trees, alive with a boisterous choir of birds. Tempering the Anglo-Celtic quality of the garden were flowering native shrubs and lush cabbage tree palms, the species that had begun the Colony's craze for woven cabbage-tree hats.

Marmaduke rapped the doorknocker, hoping that tonight Edwin's bedridden mother would not throw one of the predictable fits of hypochondria that prevented her son from attending social functions if she sensed the danger of his meeting eligible young women. Marmaduke was well aware that his mate's devotion might prevent him seeking marriage until the end of his mother's mortal term.

I'd love to see Edwin happily bedded, if not wedded – an unlikely prospect given Mrs B's antecedents were famed for their longevity.

Edwin's weary welcome and philosophical air of disappointment came as no surprise to Marmaduke.

'You don't have to tell me, mate. Your esteemed mother has taken a turn for the worst. But I'm selfish enough to want you to get me to the starting post tonight not just for the pleasure of *your* company but for the advancement of my own plans.'

'I suppose the prospect of an imminent marriage makes your final fling as a bachelor all the more urgent. Not that I'm ever likely to enjoy either experience.' Edwin added dolefully, 'Mother is convinced she will not survive through the night.'

'Mate, I'd put money on the fact she *will* let you off the chain tonight.' Marmaduke took the stairs two at a time and halted on the landing to add, 'What are you waiting for, Edwin? Change into something a bit more flash than a lawyer's garb.'

When Marmaduke closed her door a half hour later, he descended the stairs to find Edwin attired in full evening dress, his hair neatly groomed, looking bemused.

'What on earth did you do to Mother? I heard her laughing!'

'I simply delivered all the gossip I learnt last week dining with Rupert Grantham – stories so libellous even The Australian doesn't dare print them. I also told your mother you're taking me to my first Masonic dinner, so of course no females. Don't look so shocked, Edwin – it was my lie, not yours. Now, let's hit the road. We can't keep a legend like Josepha St John waiting!'

The semi-circular driveway of the Georgian villa was crowded with carriages delivering formally attired members of the Quality. Inside the ornate assembly room Marmaduke shepherded Edwin to a pair of chairs ideally placed to offer a fine view of the performance.

Marmaduke listened intently to Edwin's account of the true story of The Convict They Couldn't Hang, who on the day of his execution stood on the scaffold and was hanged. But the rope broke. They tried again. When it broke for the third time it was considered an act of God. The condemned man was set free.

'Good luck to him,' Marmaduke said absently. He had spotted Mrs Cagney walking towards him. Her husband had paused to speak to one of the guests. Uncertain of the correct Colonial etiquette for greeting a former 'sweet lady', he gave a discreet nod of the head. She stared right through him as if he were invisible.

'You know Sean Cagney's wife, do you?' Edwin asked in surprise.

'A case of mistaken identity.' Marmaduke felt stung but shrugged off the memory of her parting words. 'I'll never forget you, my dear.'

Cagney didn't send her back to England so I must have done the right thing by her.

The babble of voices grew hushed when the grey-bearded host delivered a introduction to 'the artiste Terpsichore blessed with the operatic voice of the century'.

Marmaduke said from the corner of his mouth, 'I suspect he means Apollo. Not the goddess of *dance*. But who knows? Maybe Madame plans to sing an aria *en pointe*.'

Josepha St John entered the room on the arm of her short, handsome young Italian accompanist, Federico. Marmaduke sprang to his feet to initiate applause that was enthusiastically taken up by the audience. As he intended his move caught the singer's eye.

Marmaduke doubted if all the legends were true but, now he had time to study her without the barrier of footlights, he was convinced there was nothing overstated about Josepha St John's allure. She was the total embodiment of his kind of woman. Dark-haired, full-bosomed, a lush beauty Goya might have chosen to paint – preferably bare-breasted.

Her speaking voice with its Irish hint of an American accent smouldered with promise. In contrast her singing voice revealed clues to the countries she had travelled on her road to fame. Although Marmaduke had not fully mastered Italian, French or German he had an acute ear for accents and pinpointed traces of an Italian accent when she sang Heinrich Heine's romantic lyrics, but a Prussian edge to her Italian arias and a charming French accent when she sang in English. These tiny imperfections charmed him rather than diminished her performance.

The gestures of her pale ring-laden hands were as delicate as the fluttering wings of a dove and there were sighs from the audience when during one passionate love song she laid her hand on her breast. Her eyes were pools of dark magic. Under the soft light of oil lamps her complexion glowed with health. The illusion she projected was of a beauty time could not confine to any age.

To Marmaduke she was a fascinating rogue of a woman, a lover worth possessing – for however long the demands her world-travelled career allowed.

At the completion of three encores Josepha St John threw her arms wide to offer a theatrical embrace to her audience. This simultaneously afforded gentlemen a view of her deep décolletage and gave the ladies a chance to admire the magnificent, glittering spider-web necklace said to be worth a king's ransom.

Bowing her head in a deep curtsey to acknowledge the ardent applause, Josepha St John departed the room on the arm of her pianist, pausing in the archway to give a sad little wave as if forced to take leave of a lover.

I feel I know you already, lady. Any audience that pays full tribute to your gifts will always be closer to your heart than any man you choose to take to your bed.

Marmaduke exchanged an urgent word with Edwin. 'I must seize my chance to meet the lady, mate. Come on, come with me.'

Edwin begged off on the excuse of tomorrow's interview with a client in the cells.

'For you the law always comes first, eh? Well, in that case Thomas will drive you home and return for me later.'

Edwin replied dryly, 'I'd say the best of British luck. But something tells me you don't need it. I fancy when Madame sang that final *lieder* her gaze kept returning to you.'

After Marmaduke escorted Edwin to his carriage he returned to the villa, determined not to seek a formal introduction and risk her refusal. His height and an assumed air of authority allowed him to bypass the Quality who crammed the corridor.

He bowed as he handed his card to her dresser. 'Madame is expecting me,' he lied.

Josepha St John was seated before a large mirror, ready to hold court in an elegant room that served as her dressing-room. The door was ajar. Without waiting to be admitted Marmaduke entered with outstretched arms as if throwing himself on the diva's mercy.

'I beg your forgiveness, Madame St John, I was not strong enough to wait for our host to introduce us.' He bowed low and in kissing her hand could not fail to notice the fabled diamond, set in a Florentine gold ring. It was indeed very beautiful and very large. Only an expert would recognise it was a fake.

'I am your servant, Madame. Marmaduke Gamble.'

'Ah, so *you* are the Gamble gentleman,' she said with a curve of her lips. He followed her glance to the flowers he had sent her. The language of flowers had no exact way to convey his coded message,

I will die if you don't take me to your bed. But Marmaduke saw by the look in those dark eyes she had interpreted it correctly.

Marmaduke's praise was genuine. 'You held me spellbound tonight and, indeed, every performance I have seen since your arrival in the Colony. I've no gift for words, Madame, but your fame failed to do justice to the magical reality of your presence in the flesh.'

Josepha St John inclined her head in the manner of a queen accepting a courtier's tribute. 'For one who claims no gift for words, young man, you use your tongue with surprising eloquence.'

Marmaduke fancied he caught a slight inflection on the word 'tongue'. He pretended innocence. 'I confess I'm disappointed by one thing. If you'll give me leave to say it?'

'Granted,' she said coolly but he saw the wary glint in her eyes.

'Your fabled diamond ring is unequal to the truth and beauty of your performance, Madame.'

Her eyes flashed a warning. He bent on one knee and held her hand with a playful smile he hoped would sustain the delicate balance between flirtation and sincerity. 'Your secret dies with me. But I beg you not to harden your heart. You have the power to sentence me to the grave. Unless you promise this first meeting will not be our last – and next time we shall be alone.'

Josepha tilted her head to reveal the beautiful line of her neck. The laugh she had no doubt mastered for the stage was nonetheless enchanting. 'You are either very bold or else a young man who can happily predict the future. Perhaps we shall meet again, Mr Gamble, who knows?'

Marmaduke interpreted the promise in her eyes as she turned away to be feted by a trio of gentlemen, including the bearded banker who was their host. Marmaduke backed from the room smiling, holding her eyes as he made his exit.

Moments later in the corridor the dresser discreetly handed him a card. 'My lady says you may call on her tomorrow morning at eleven at this address.'

So mine host doesn't yet have the lady 'in keeping'. But I must move with care. He instantly recognised a rival for her favours. His advantage is he's president of the Colony's wealthiest bank. I have two advantages.

He felt sure Josepha trusted him to keep her secret that her legendary diamonds were paste. His other advantage he had learnt from a story about Giacomo Casanova – that one of the secrets of success in getting a woman into bed was to make her laugh. And Marmaduke had already made her laugh.

He had no sooner pocketed the lady's card when he was caught off guard. He found himself being hurled bodily through a doorway by an unseen force that left him sprawled on the floor. His wild-eyed aggressor slammed the door, placed his foot on Marmaduke's chest and held a knife blade at his throat.

'G'd evening, Mr Cagney. There seems to be some mistake,' Marmaduke said politely.

'I know what you did to my wife!'

'Whatever your good lady has said, you must accept her word over mine but—'

'Don't lie! I caught you skulking in my garden!'

Marmaduke smothered a nervous laugh. The man was so enraged that one false move and the knife could pierce his windpipe. 'What exactly do you mean, sir?'

'My wife is with child!'

'I see.' Marmaduke said carefully. He was genuinely pleased but felt that any congratulations might incriminate him. There were no rules of etiquette for a scene like this.

Sean Cagney was shaking with rage. 'I should kill you!'

'If you kill me, the best you can hope for is a one-way ticket to Norfolk Island. That would be a tragic mistake for you and Mrs Cagney because then you'd never be free to watch your wife's forthcoming child grow up to be the *spitting image of you.*'

'What?'

'I didn't father the babe. I admit that during your absence in Van Diemen's Land on your own *private* business – I did spend time with your wife. She was distraught at the thought of losing you to your mistress. I did my best to comfort her, took tea with her and admired the rare plants in your summerhouse. Mrs Cagney kept telling me how much she loved you and only you.'

Marmaduke caught the uncertainty in Cagney's eyes. 'After your wife gives birth the whole world will know the babe was fathered by you a full *nine months* after your return from Van Diemen's Land. If I'm lying, by all means challenge me to a duel *then*.'

'Fight a duel with you? That satisfaction is reserved for gentlemen. Not the spawn of an Emancipist.'

Marmaduke quietly weighed the insult. 'Yes, it's true I am no gentleman. But equally correct to say *you* are the true father of your wife's babe. I wish you well, sir.'

Cagney strode from the room leaving Marmaduke lying on the floor.

How ironical to think I might have been murdered for the one unselfish act of adultery I have ever committed. God willing the Cagney babe does not come early. And that it does *resemble Cagney.*

As Marmaduke climbed into his carriage he checked the time on his gold pocket watch. Only a few hours of sleep remained before his first assignation with Josepha St John. He knew the lady had no performance scheduled for tomorrow night. Monday was her traditional day of rest. But Marmaduke promised himself she would have little rest with him in her bed.

How wonderful to find a woman who knows the rules of the game.

CHAPTER 10

Isabel realised she had been duped by her kinsman the moment she saw the *Susan* lying at anchor in the Thames. There was nothing wrong with the 572-ton ship itself. A massive, strongly built teak vessel that for the past twenty-one years had been an active Indian country trader, she lived up to Calcutta's fine ship-building reputation that rivalled Britain's East Indiamen ships. The *Susan* also had a reputable master and surgeon.

Isabel's shock lay in the discovery that she was one of only two passengers on board. An even greater shock was the nature of the *Susan's* cargo. The ship was making her first voyage to New South Wales as a convict transport with three hundred male prisoners!

For the first week of the voyage Isabel had clung to her cabin, overcome by the knowledge that yet again her life had been manipulated and she had been left in the dark about the details. Gradually, out of curiosity she had become absorbed by the dramatic sights and sounds of a convict transport. She was delighted to discover her sole fellow passenger was Murray Robertson, a gentle Scottish lad a year or two older, who was also a book lover and no more experienced in the ways of the world than she was. He, too, had been booked on the *Susan* because the fare was cheaper than regular passenger ships.

The voyage via the Madeira route had not been without drama. Eight convicts had died before the surgeon was also struck down with fever and was replaced by at the next port.

Today promised to be the final day in a seventeen-week voyage that she was assured had been speedy under the circumstances.

Isabel felt a sense of pride that she had mastered her fear of the ocean and had not been prey to the seasickness that had dogged many of the prisoners on board. Despite her sense of trepidation about facing an unknown bridegroom at journey's end, she was excited by the prospect of her first sighting of the great headlands at the entrance to Port Jackson.

The copies of ancient maps she had studied in de Rolland Park's library had shown the imagined shapes of the mysterious, giant continent represented in fragments on the charts of Spanish, Portuguese and Dutch navigators over the centuries and variously called The Great South Land, New Holland, and Terra Australis Incognita. None of these explorers had laid claim to it until that Yorkshireman, Captain James Cook, had mapped the entire eastern coast fewer than fifty years earlier. In 1788 Governor Arthur Phillip arrived with the First Fleet filled with convicts and raised the flag to claim the land for the British Crown. Isabel had no illusions about the chief attraction it held for the British.

Nothing more than a useful dumping ground for our convicts after poor old George III lost our American colonies. Now it's my life sentence.

Through the porthole she glimpsed the rain lashing at the starboard side in wild, turbulent sheets as the mighty waves of the Pacific Ocean rocked the *Susan* like a defenceless baby's cradle.

Wrapped in an oilskin as a shield against the tempest, she paused before going up on deck to look back at Cousin Martha's gift of the grey travelling ensemble swaying wildly on a clothes hanger ready to wear when she disembarked. Her Paris trousseau was safely locked in the hold to be explored on arrival. She would wear Martha's gown ashore as a loving link with her and to give herself courage when making her entrance in the Colony.

Isabel could almost taste the bitter irony of the idea of being welcomed but the sense of despair must be much worse for the two hundred and ninety surviving prisoners who had been transported for crimes ranging from from picking pockets to trade union demonstrations. But there were no murderers on board – they evaded transportation by being hanged.

My name is officially listed as Came Free in the records but no doubt in God's eyes I'm no better than the convicts on board.

Braving the deck she found Murray Robertson waiting for her. Their friendship had begun after he had discovered her memorising Rosalind's role in *As You Like It*. Their mutual admiration for Shakespeare and Sir Walter Scott had forged a bond.

The Scottish lad clung to the ship's railing, leaning against the wind. He wore a caped greatcoat and one of the colourful caps he had sported throughout the voyage. He gave Isabel a wide grin of welcome and pointed to the sole visible sign of civilisation, the white lighthouse on South Head, casting its reassuring beam across the water.

'So *this* is New South Wales. Seems a good place for a Penal Colony,' she said wryly.

'Aye, miss. It was not my idea to be sent here, either.'

The fifth son in a large family of Highlanders, Murray had been packed off to 'the Colonies' armed with a pocket watch from his father and a letter of introduction to a distant member of his clan, a wealthy landholder Murray described as a 'squatter'. To Isabel the term sounded dubious, almost illegal.

'I'll be out in the bush to gain what they call 'Colonial experience'. I imagine I'll be riding around the estate to check that all the farm labourers aren't slacking on the job. Problem is I dinna have much experience in riding a horse.'

'Your kin are lucky to have a hard-working, loyal lad like yourself to help them.'

Murray blinked at the compliment. 'And what about yourself, Miss Isabel? Forgive my curiosity about your fiancé, but are his letters kindly?'

'He never wrote any. Neither did I. Our marriage was arranged.'

'Aye,' he said carefully. 'Do ye have any plans? Apart from the wedding, of course.'

'I don't suppose one could find a theatre in a Penal Colony?' she asked hopefully.

'I read that in the early years the convicts and the military produced plays for a convict theatre. But the last governor – Darling – vetoed theatrical licences to prevent the convict class socialising with free settlers.'

'What a Philistine!' Isabel cried into the face of the wind. 'No theatres? No Shakespeare? Just my bad luck. For the first time in my life I'll have enough money to go to the theatre and the governor banned it to *protect* people like me!'

'Dinna distress yourself, lassie. They tell me the new governor's an Irishman with liberal ideas – he even fights for the equality of Catholics and Protestants. It's said he's related to the great Edmund Burke.'

Isabel was wary. 'Didn't Edmund Burke make speeches in Parliament defending America's fight for Independence? And wasn't he in sympathy with the French Revolution?'

'Aye, he's a champion of human rights. But he dinna approve the excesses of the French Revolution, guillotining the aristocrats.'

Isabel touched her own neck, wondering how the French felt about Plantagenets. And what was the attitude of those born free in the Colony, like her future husband?

'Are the rumours true? Are there factions here who hold the same Republican ideas that caused the French Revolution and the Reign of Terror?'

'I fancy the Colonists are more in line with the American way of doing business. First pressure the British to change the laws. If that fails fight for independence as a last resort.'

Isabel gasped. 'Good Heavens, Murray, you sound in sympathy with the rebel Yankees. Would you have fought on their side against our Redcoats?'

Murray gave a rueful smile. 'I am a Highlander. We have quite a history of fighting the English for our rights.'

At the thought of her own impossible pursuit of independence Isabel sent a silent blasphemous message up to God.

You made a big mistake trapping me inside this body. I should have been born a man!

The sliver of land lying between sky and ocean grew in height as they approached the headlands guarding the mouth of the harbour. The storm clouds suddenly vanished to reveal the intense blue of the sky. Isabel returned to her cabin, intent on preparing to face whatever lay on the far side of The Heads.

Isabel struggled to free herself from the drenched cotton dress that clung to her skin. She replaced it with her last remaining petticoat and bodice. She had left London on a cold March day that was nominally spring but the Colony's reversed seasons meant that this was mid-winter and she only had one decent gown. Would the worsted wool make her perspire?

She stared at her image in the sole fragment of mirror to survive the storms of the voyage. The cracked triangle reflected a pinched white face that she had sheltered from the sun for seventeen weeks. Her taut features were dominated by blue-green eyes ringed with shadows and the tip-tilted nose she would never learn to live with. She remembered Cousin Martha's prediction, 'You will blossom into a beauty, Isabel, when you least expect it.'

Meanwhile, here I am, trapped inside this tall, bony frame better suited to house a boy. To think that as a child I was foolish enough to dream of love and marriage.

What was it Uncle Godfrey had once said? 'No de Rolland can ever expect to experience in tandem the opposing states of love and marriage.'

Isabel instinctively ran her hand down her flat chest, remembering that extraordinary moment when a man's hands had first touched her skin and fingered the tiny buds of her breasts. In her mind she heard his soft, urgent whisper, 'You were made for me, Isabel. No other man will ever love you as I do.'

Isabel blocked the voice from her head. She decided to lift her spirits by examining the contents of the large metal trunk that until today had been kept in the hold for the entire voyage so that her Paris trousseau would remain pristine for her arrival. Neatly painted on the lid were the words, *Miss I. de Rolland. London to N.S.W. 1833.*

Unlocking the lid of the trunk for the first time she sat immobilised by the contents.

So this is what I can expect from George Gamble. Like all men's promises – worthless.

Not a single article was new. All had been worn by her for years past and she had outgrown most of them. She had confined herself to wearing two old dresses on the voyage to save herself for this!

Rummaging down to the false bottom of the trunk she rescued her treasures. The Bible and *The Complete Works of William Shakespeare* each bore the handwritten name Walter de Rolland on a bookplate in the flyleaf. These volumes were her last tangible link with her father and England. She held to her breast the memory book in which she had carefully pasted every review of Edmund Kean's performances, even the cuttings from the trial brought against him by the husband of his lover Charlotte Cox. *Poor Edmund.*

Opening the cover she discovered an envelope addressed 'To My

Beloved Cousin Isabel' and gave an involuntary shudder at the sight of Silas's strangely distorted, spider-web handwriting. As she had been cheated of her promised Paris trousseau, she felt certain it would not contain money. So why had Silas taken such pains to hide this letter? She struggled silently about whether or not to open it.

He wants to continue playing his secret game. If I open this I'll go on being his frightened little mouse. No Silas! I don't want to feel any more pain.

With trembling hands she finally found the strength to replace the envelope in the trunk and quickly covered it with the pile of worn clothing before locking the padlock.

Placing the key in the carpetbag that now contained her three treasured books and a few items of underclothing, she hurriedly dressed in the travelling ensemble.

Examining her face in the mirror again she pinched her cheeks to give them colour, tidied her hair and tied her bonnet strings firmly under her chin. She knew her miniature portrait had flattered her. Her fiancé was likely to be disappointed.

What manner of man was he? At worst she pictured Marmaduke Gamble as an uncouth Colonial peasant who would keep her barefoot and pregnant in some hut in the wilderness. When common sense prevailed she decided she might expect a tolerable degree of comfort as the wife of a landed Emancipist's son.

But his conversation will probably be limited to wool and cattle prices.

It irritated her that Gamble Senior had refused to supply a miniature portrait of his son. What on earth was wrong with him? The lawyers dismissed him in a few words as 'Native-born'. What did this mean? Could he in fact speak English? Or was some Aboriginal language his mother tongue? Isabel felt sick at the thought of the unknown alien male who awaited her. A body she must suffer in bed for the rest of her life!

I have no rights. No money. No escape.

When she saw the shadow of fear in her eyes she gave her reflection a false smile. *What am I worried about? The current generation of de Rollands may be scoundrels but my ancestral tree will be impressive to a family with the convict stain. No doubt they expect me to make this Marmaduke Gamble fit to dine at the Governor's table. But how on earth can I turn a Colonial sow's ear into a silk purse? I'm a de Rolland. Not a miracle worker!*

Grabbing her carpetbag she raced up on deck. The impact of the sheer beauty and size of the harbour took her breath away. But before she had time to absorb the details she was stunned by the sight of a man who seemed to be walking on water!

He was positioned close to the shore, poised motionless on a sliver of boat that looked like the shell of a floating tree trunk. He had a lean, dark-skinned body with long, straight limbs and a handsome head that showed a flash of white teeth. One arm was raised above his head holding a spear until, in a lightning flash, the spear hurtled into the water to find its target in a large fish.

It was only then that Isabel realised the youth was entirely naked except for a skimpy fold of cloth the size of a handkerchief that hung between his thighs. She hastily covered her face but was tempted to peer through her fingers. This was the first naked male body she had ever seen. She was shocked by the beauty of it.

Isabel seized the moment when she saw the approaching figure of an elderly seaman with whom she had occasionally exchanged words. She approached him with what she hoped was a show of confidence befitting a lady of her class.

'Sir, there is a worthless old trunk in my cabin. It is of no value to me or anyone else. Would you be kind enough to throw it overboard in the harbour at the first available opportunity? I thank you for your trouble.'

Isabel extended her gloved hand and offered him a coin. She hoped its value was neither insultingly small nor large enough to be extravagant. She had seldom had the opportunity to handle money. In every port of call she had been determined to conserve the alarmingly few coins in her purse. She had no idea what was socially acceptable.

The old salt had bright blue eyes in a weathered face and his mouth creased in a smile as he waved away her proffered coin.

'No need, young lady. I'll toss the trunk overboard afore we drop anchor.' As he turned in the direction of the forecastle, he added over his shoulder. 'Don't you go believing all the tall tales you hear about the Colony, miss. It's Heaven or Hell, depending on whose eyes are doing the looking. You'll fare well, you will.'

Gazing across at the cluster of stone buildings that formed a frieze on the southern foreshores of Sydney Town, Isabel was startled by the unexpected evidence of fine Georgian architecture, a sight so indicative of civilisation that she felt her spirits rise. She removed from her reticule the key to her trunk and held it in the palm of her hand.

This is the key to my past life.

With her arm stretched behind her the way she had seen demon bowlers begin to hurl a ball down a cricket pitch, Isabel flung the key as far as she could and watched the arc of its flight before it sank with a splash in water so clear and deep it appeared to be fathomless.

She remembered the words of *Farewell to All Judges and Juries* – the old song that had been printed on broadsides under different names and lyrics, all sung with bravado by Britain's convicts as they were being transported here to the land still popularly known as Botany Bay. No doubt the well-known Old Bailey had passed sentence on many of these prisoners.

Her eyes traced their faces. For the most part blank, listless, some mere boys were marked by a wild glimmer of hope.

She quoted the words under her breath. 'They left their country for their country's good.' Reminded that her own 'judge and jury' were her kinsmen, on impulse she sang the opening lines in a clear voice that carried on the wind.

'Here's adieu to all judges and juries,

Justice and Old Bailey...too'

One by one the prisoners' voices joined in the song...

Isabel sat on King's Wharf clutching her carpetbag on her lap. Rivulets of perspiration rolled down her back and chest but there was no relief from the heat. Her jacket was fastened to the neck to preserve her modesty. Beneath it was nothing but her flimsy petticoat bodice.

Murray had sat stoically by her side during the three hours since they had disembarked from the *Susan*. Even their lively discussions about Shakespeare's plays and Murray's insights into the colourful life and poetry of Robbie Burns had finally run dry.

Finally Murray broke the silence. 'Miss Isabel, I dinna want to cause ye any embarrassment but it must be said for the sake of your safety, lass. The night after we left King George Sound I was strolling on deck in the wee small hours to escape the heat. I was surprised to see ye walking towards me, barefoot in your nightgown. When I asked if ye were unwell, ye looked me in the eye but walked straight past me. Next morning you said you'd been reading a Jane Austen novel all night and hadna slept a wink.' Murray looked discomforted. 'Until I see ye safely in the hands of your fiancé I canna leave ye here alone.'

Oh dear God, no. It's started again. I had no idea.

Isabel tried to sound confident. 'Please don't worry. I walk in my sleep occasionally. It's not a problem but I promise you I'll tell my fiancé. I was given instructions he'd meet my ship.' She tried not to sound too hopeful. 'Perhaps some terrible accident has befallen him?'

'I pray naught. But surely a servant will soon arrive to assist ye?'

'Oh yes, his family have scores of servants and many grand houses,' she said airily. 'I'll be perfectly safe here. But you must go or you'll miss your coach to Moreton Bay.'

Murray glanced at his pocket watch. 'I willna leave ye alone, Miss Isabel. I could cancel my seat and take another coach later.'

'No, I wouldn't hear of it. But you did offer to help me if I were ever in need.'

'Aye, name it.'

'I have a rather unusual request. 'Could you spare me one of your tartan caps?'

Murray blinked but she knew he was too much the gentleman to comment as he opened his valise and began fishing around in the contents.

Isabel thanked him for the cap then tried to sound matter of fact. 'And Murray, there's another small favour I have to ask you...'

Her whispered words sounded so garbled to her own ears it was hardly surprising that Murray's jaw dropped.

He recovered quickly enough to assure her, 'Aye, it's no trouble at all, Miss Isabel.'

CHAPTER 11

There were scores of euphemistic terms for copulation that Marmaduke knew were in currency at different levels of society. They ranged from the genteel 'to have connection' and 'to comfort', to earthy sailors' slang and thieves' cant such as 'rogered', 'launched', 'pinned', 'scored' and 'nailed'. The old biblical standby, 'Adam *knew* Eve', satisfied the churchgoers. But in Marmaduke's eyes the so-called shocking Anglo-Saxon four-letter word that required smelling salts if overheard by a lady had for him the cheerful connotations of the name of the mischievous Puck in *A Midsummer Night's Dream.*

Marmaduke dismissed all these definitions as inadequate when evaluating the nights and afternoons he spent in bed with Josepha St John. None of those terms even hinted at the exotic range of pleasures they exchanged. Freed from his bout of melancholia, Marmaduke found he had discovered a Junoesque woman of the world who met him on his terms – a liaison based on adventurous exploration, abandonment to the senses and total honesty.

He had made it clear from the first passionate kiss, which led her to bed, that to him love was a debased currency. He was incapable of feeling it, giving it or accepting it. And Josepha must understand that while he was her 'silent partner' in public, in private there would only be one master. Him. Until such time as they parted as friends. Josepha accepted these conditions and his role as her lover and played her own role to the hilt. Marmaduke met and surpassed her demands, teasing her and making her beg before he led her to the wildest heights of ecstasy.

Lying satiated in his arms, only once had she expressed a faint reservation about his performance, saying dreamily, 'Darling, you know exactly how to make me surrender but *you* never lose control.'

'And I never will. That's my secret, sweet lady.' He said it teasingly to disguise that it was the truth.

Marmaduke's time now revolved around two aspects of performance. He regularly attended the Theatre Royal, where Barnett Levey's amazing presentations ranged from Shakespeare to melodrama, opera and ballet and changed several times each week. These nights were in juxtaposition with Marmaduke's private performances with Josepha in one of the changing venues he arranged to keep their liaison secret from the Colonial press. He took particular care to avoid her name in Rupert Grantham's company so that any leak would not be his doing.

But this morning when Marmaduke awoke in bed at the Princess Alexandrina he had a champagne hangover and the uneasy feeling he had forgotten something. He had. Yesterday had been the first time in weeks he had failed to check the shipping arrivals.

Foregoing breakfast except for a cup of whisky-laced coffee, he had Thomas drive him to the shipping office. To his horror he learnt that although no passenger ship had arrived, the convict transport *Susan* had dropped anchor the previous afternoon and had listed two passengers – I. de Rolland and M. Robertson. No doubt Isabel and her lady's maid.

At King's Wharf, where he found the *Susan* moored, Marmaduke looked around in agitation. From the milling crowd came a babble of voices in which the English tongue was peppered by diverse foreign languages and racial features and costumes indicating far-flung corners of the British Empire, except for one group, who had clearly gained their independence. These officers wore the distinctive, smartly tailored uniforms of the United States Navy and to Marmaduke's ears spoke a nasal form of English remarkable for its powers of projection. In contrast to them, His Majesty's Marines and Redcoats stood apart, stiffly 'at ease' and issuing brisk orders to turbaned Indians engaged in unloading an East Indiaman's cargo. Female faces, always a minority presence in the Colony, still covered a wide social spectrum from genteel ladies who sheltered under parasols to retain their fashionable English pallor to bawdy wenches touting for custom in accents that ranged from Cockney to Currency.

Along the fringe of the wharves, Aboriginal figures stood like dark shadows in the sun, their eyes seemingly fixed on a different, distant horizon. Most of them, their women included, smoked pipes. All wore an odd assortment of brightly coloured European attire that seemed to be chosen for novelty value rather than modesty.

Marmaduke admired the confidence of one proud tribal warrior who stalked down the length of the wharf, nonchalantly wearing a discarded British officer's short red coatee over a body stark naked except for the sheath covering his penis. He was amused by the stir he created. English ladies spun their parasols to shield him from their sight.

Wincing in the sunlight that aggravated his splitting headache, Marmaduke searched with Thomas for a girl bearing any resemblance to the bland miniature he had rejected and left behind in Garnet's hands. How useful it would prove right now.

If I hadn't been so involved in the pursuit of my own pleasure I'd have met this wretched girl's ship on time yesterday and had the whole mess under control. Now I've put myself at a disadvantage.

Perhaps the girl was marooned in her cabin in a state of hysteria, supplied with smelling salts by the lady's maid Garnet had paid to accompany her. No English girl of Isabel's station would disembark alone in an alien land or have the initiative to organise transport. Did she even know the Princess Alexandrina was her destination?

Marmaduke strode up to a ship's officer and stated his business.

The response was cool. 'Our sole two passengers disembarked yesterday afternoon.'

'You must be mistaken. My fiancée was travelling with her maid and a heap of cabin trunks, her trousseau.'

The officer gave Marmaduke a condescending smile as his gloved hand gestured to a pathetic-looking trunk abandoned on the deck.

Marmaduke saw it was no joke. '*That's it*? Miss de Rolland's entire baggage?'

'It appears the lady instructed a crew member to toss it in the harbour. It was such an odd request he decided to leave it here in case someone came to collect it.' The officer added smugly, 'and indeed, here you *are*, sir.'

There was no porter in sight so Thomas tested its weight. 'Light as a feather, sir.'

'Take it back to my chambers, Thomas, *not* the suite reserved for Miss de Rolland and her servant. Meanwhile I'll search for them. They can't have gone far.'

Last night's marathon performance with Josepha and the champagne that followed had left Marmaduke ill-equipped to handle this bizarre turn of events. It was one thing to be hell-bent on jilting an unwanted fiancée, quite another to have her disappear off the face of the earth. What had gone wrong? Garnet had also paid for her maid's passage and ample storage room for the family antiques and memorabilia any lady of her rank considered essential to begin married life in the Penal Colony.

Marmaduke strode up to the watchman's sentry box, described Isabel as best he could. 'If you know where she was heading, I'll make it worth your while.'

The watchman shook his head. 'After the *Susan* berthed there was a free-for-all barney here on the wharf. Some Yankee whalers fought a young lad over a girl, a prostitute most like. The traps carted the whole bang lot of 'em off to the lock-up.'

Marmaduke thrust coins in the man's palm then hurried to lower George Street.

As he sprang up the entrance stairs of the Watch House the full absurdity of the situation struck him. Within hours of her arrival this aristocratic bride of 'impeccable virtue', whom Garnet had imported from England to facilitate the Gambles' entrée into Society, had been involved in a waterfront brawl with a whore and drunken whalers.

'The stupid girl must have the brains of a seagull!' he muttered.

The constable on duty appeared to be one of the minority of police officers who had come free and had a degree of literacy. Marmaduke outlined the facts.

'Perhaps she used the name Gamble?' he asked in desperation.

'Them whores all got aliases, mate.'

Marmaduke drew himself up to his full height. 'Look, constable, my fiancée is a born lady, a damned English aristocrat in fact.'

The policeman gave him a squint-eyed stare. 'Yeah? Then what's she doing *here*?'

Marmaduke's anger was on the brink. 'Do you recognise her description or not?'

'No such lady on my watch but we might have a relative of hers in the cells.'

'A relative? Probably her servant. What's the charge?'

'Causing a public nuisance. I locked this obstreperous person in the laundry closet to keep the other prisoners from *doing what they do best*, if you take my meaning.'

Marmaduke was appalled. He presumed this referred to sexual connection either in the context of rape or consent. 'Why protect her from other females?'

The constable pursed his lips. 'Well, sir. Some would say this prisoner's birth was an act of God, sir.'

Jesus. I knew I shouldn't have drunk that third bottle of champagne.

Marmaduke gritted his teeth. 'Please speak plainly, Constable.'

'We come across this type in the cells, sir. More to be pitied than condemned. A half and half. Neither one thing nor t'other.' He added on a note of pride, 'What us educated men call a homofrogdite, sir.'

Shit. He means hermaphrodite! She can't be. Or can she? Maybe this explains why the de Rollands were so eager to foist Isabel off on us.

'What name is recorded on the charge sheet, constable?'

'A blank, sir. Wouldn't tell me nothing. But it fought like a tomcat to hang on to this here carpetbag.'

Marmaduke discovered the contents were a grey lady's garment and three books. A quick examination revealed one was a scrapbook of Edmund Kean's career. The inside covers of the Bible and *The Complete Works of Shakespeare* contained bookplates in the name of Walter de Rolland.

'That's her father's name. The person in the cells must be connected to her. I'll pay the fine to prevent this poor creature facing court and I'm happy to cover the costs of *your* inconvenience.'

Marmaduke had no doubt the sum of money he placed on the constable's desk was large enough to open the cell door for him. He was immediately conducted to a windowless room in the basement. When the door was closed behind him Marmaduke stood with folded arms but his decision to employ firm confrontation wavered at the sight of the pathetic figure huddled on a pile of dirty laundry.

'Stand up and let's see you, eh, lad?'

The boy slowly rose to his feet. He was dressed in a loose woollen jerkin over a pair of skin-tight breeches, torn stockings and buckled shoes. A floppy tartan hunting cap covered his hair and ears. The pinched white face was dirty and the full lips swollen and stained with dried blood. But it was the eyes that startled Marmaduke. One was so badly swollen it looked like a rotten egg resting on a purple bruise. The other hooded eye was of a startling blue-green colour and filled with such fear that Marmaduke immediately softened his tone.

'Well, lad, I give you my word I'll pay your fine and get you out of here and properly fed. On condition you explain who and why you are here.'

'Who's asking? Are you a policeman?' the deep gravelly voice snapped back at him.

Marmaduke gave a snort halfway between amusement and irritation. 'The hide of you! No, I'm no trap. As it happens, I'm Marmaduke Gamble.'

'Then God help you.' The deep voice cracked. 'What's wrong with you, can't you recognise a lady when you see one?'

The tartan cap was whipped off to reveal a head piled up with jagged, spiky hair that resembled the dirty spokes of a wheel. She smelt as bad as a wet, mangy dog.

Marmaduke looked her over and said in a tone of faint distaste. 'So it *is* you! Jesus Christ!'

'Wrong again. The name is Isabel de Rolland.'

She stood swaying on her heels and when her face suddenly drained to a deathly white she pitched backwards in a dead faint. Marmaduke leapt forwards just in time to break her fall before her head hit the flagstones.

Slumped unconscious at his feet, Isabel's jerkin fell open to reveal two small buds of breasts pressed against the male under-vest. The breeches were as tight as a second skin but the 'cod piece' of padding she'd evidently put in place to suggest a penis had slipped askew.

She's only got one redeeming feature. Those legs were born to strut the stage in breeches roles.

'Now let's be getting you to the hotel,' Marmaduke said, amused despite himself.

Isabel stirred and groaned faintly. 'Is there food there? I'm so hungry I could die.'

She passed out cold before Marmaduke could answer, so he

scooped her up in his arms, surprised at how light she was even when unconscious and a dead weight.

As he carried her into the sunlight she struggled and cried out in alarm, 'My books!'

After Marmaduke retrieved the carpetbag she cradled it in her arms like a lost baby and once inside the carriage fell asleep, exhausted.

Marmaduke climbed up on the seat beside Thomas, who despite his bemused expression said nothing.

'Your restraint is admirable, Thomas. Yes, this *is* my aristocratic fiancée.' He suddenly laughed out loud. 'For once in my life I wish Garnet was here. I'd love to have seen the look on his face when he saw his prized English rose!'

Marmaduke carefully avoided the scrutiny of the housemaids and carried Isabel upstairs to her suite undetected. Normally he would have called a female servant to undress the girl, but the story of how the de Rolland bride had met her fiancé wearing boy's clothing, sporting a black eye and straight from a night in gaol would be circulated around Sydney by sundown.

So he undressed Isabel himself, preserving what little modesty she had left by rolling her onto her stomach to shake her free of her male breeches. The rear view of her naked body caused a wry smile.

Her face is on a par with a Madagascar ape but her bum is delightfully female.

Rolling her naked body beneath the bedcovers he locked the door behind him and slipped down the back stairs to the kitchen. He tried out a few sentences of French on Emile the chef who looked bemused by the Australian accent flattening his mother tongue but insisted on assembling platters of food.

After placing a tray by Isabel's bedside with cheeses, *petit choux*, tropical fruit and a decanter of red wine, Marmaduke hung a sign scrawled with 'Do not disturb' from her door handle. Back in his own chambers, he was confronted by the forgotten cabin trunk. Within minutes he had expertly unpicked the padlock, a trick learnt during his own brief sojourn in prison. His examination of the pitiful contents shocked him. He sank a glass of wine then strode around the room, venting his anger in a monologue before an invisible audience.

'The de Rollands are an honourable family, eh? Garnet provided generous funds for a fashionable trousseau. Those aristocratic bastards must have pocketed every penny. Why did they humiliate her? Sent her down here with wretched clothes no self-respecting pawnbroker would flog. No wonder she wanted this junked overboard.'

Marmaduke deliberated on whether to open the letter sealed in red wax. Isabel had clearly chosen not to read it, a fact that intrigued him. He had so few clues about her he decided to grab whatever came his way. He tore it open. The handwriting was idiosyncratic. Letters sloped crazily left and right and were embroidered with capital letters. His study of graphology made him distinctly biased against the writer.

Ma petite Cousine,

I cannot convey what conflicting emotions your Departure aroused in me. Take comfort that in marrying into that Barbaric Gamble family you've saved our Uncle from debtor's prison and secured our Ancestral estate for my Inheritance.

I swear on the Royal graves of our Plantagenet Ancestors that within the year I will come to New South Wales to reclaim you. The love that binds us can never be broken. Remember the Curse you carry. You will Destroy any man who loves you. Only a man of your own Blood is strong enough to withstand that Curse. You are Flesh of my Flesh. Think of this Marriage as your Act of Penance – to your Beloved Cousin.

Marmaduke tried to imagine the faceless writer of this letter standing before him.

'So Isabel de Rolland is flesh of your flesh, is she? You sold her in marriage to us *barbaric Gambles* to pay off your debts, yet you didn't even have the common decency to clothe her in the French wardrobe we paid for!' He tossed the letter aside as if it was contaminated. 'What a goddamned ego! Now this beloved cousin Silas is planning to do the poor girl a big favour. Sail down here to reclaim her, will he? Well he can bloody well think again. First he'll have to get his royal Plantagenet body past this Currency Lad!'

CHAPTER 12

Isabel woke up as a stranger in a strange room. She was alarmed by the thought she may have been sleepwalking again. Unwanted memories flashed through her mind.

One minute I was seated on the wharf, a perfect lady, even if I was dressed as a boy. All I did was try to stop two drunken mariners molesting a young girl. Then one said something odd – 'Put your dukes up, ya queer'. The next moment he punched me in the eye.

Isabel gingerly fingered the puffy flesh around her eye, overcome by the shame of being frog-marched to the Watch House by two hefty constables with the Yankee whalers and the girl she now knew to be a prostitute. Afraid her voice would betray her gender she had refused to answer questions. She smiled at the thought of the policeman's odd expression on finding lady's unmentionables in her carpetbag.

Being dressed as a boy gave me a wonderful sense of freedom. If I lived as a boy then I'd be safe from men. I'd never have to marry!

Sitting upright in bed she was horrified to discover she was naked.

'Who undressed me? Please God, tell me I didn't spend the night with *him*?'

She had only one clear impression of Marmaduke Gamble. Arrogance! She felt humiliated by the way his nose had twitched in distaste at the rank smell of her and the memory now made her desperate to bathe. But how?

The elegance of this unknown room surprised her. The Regency fabrics and furniture would not have looked out of place in Uncle Godfrey's London villa. But there was no sign of a washbasin and jug. *How uncivilised: don't these Colonials ever wash?*

Isabel sprang from bed to discover her carpetbag was missing. So where were her clothes?

Tentatively peering around the door to an adjoining room, she squealed with delight – a bathroom with splendid modern plumbing and elegant brass fittings! She shied away from the mirror to avoid the reflection of her beaten face, but immediately ran a bath, exclaiming in ecstasy over the bars of perfumed soap, the first since the *Susan* set sail.

What luxury! She washed her hair twice to free it from the matted combination of sweat, grime and saltwater accumulated during the voyage. After ducking beneath her bathwater like one of the playful dolphins that had raced beside the *Susan,* she scrubbed her body until her skin glowed pink. She now felt courageous enough to examine her bruised face in the mirror.

Maybe it wouldn't be such fun to be a boy. I'd always be on the wrong end of a fight.

She carefully washed the dried blood from her lips and bathed her swollen eye in cold water until she could *almost* peer out of the slit.

Clean, shining hair restored a degree of dignity. To be dirty was the most demoralising thing in the world. *How degraded women prisoners must feel being unable to bathe for months on a convict vessel.*

With no clothes to wear she improvised by pulling a sheet from the bed and winding it around her body in a makeshift sari. Examining a brand new silver-backed hand mirror, brush and comb set, she discovered they were engraved with the initials I.A.G. Beside them was a card that read, *Welcome to Australia. Forgive me jumping the gun in adding the G for Gamble. I trust you are comfortable in my new hotel.* It was signed *Garnet Gamble* in a different hand from that of the rest of the note.

At least Marmaduke's father has some kindly instincts, 'Colonial barbarian' or not.

Now she felt ready to tackle breakfast from the tray that must have been left for her while she slept. A wine decanter was an odd substitute for a water jug but the warmth of the wine coursed through her body to give her Dutch courage.

These Colonials must drink wine as liberally as the French. But I have a raging thirst so who am I to quibble?

Startled by the heavy knock at the door she hastily secured her 'sari', seated herself on a winged armchair and hastily swallowed the last mouthful of breakfast.

The key turned in the lock and Marmaduke Gamble strode into the room.

No longer diminished by fear or hunger and fortified by fine wine, Isabel had her first chance to evaluate by daylight the man to whom she had been sold.

The reality of Marmaduke Gamble totally appalled her. There he stood nominally English, but clearly a hybrid version. One of the new species called Currency Lads, he did not fit into *any* of the categories of the English class system she had known all her life.

It took her only ten seconds to reach her verdict of him and feel insulted. He had not made the slightest attempt to create a good impression on his English bride. Tall and long-limbed, he stood planted in the centre of the room wearing moleskin trousers tucked into mud-stained thigh-high boots. In place of a gentleman's stock was a crumpled neckerchief. The width of his shoulders was accentuated by a red shirt open at the throat, revealing the hair on his chest. He wore a suede waistcoat and a flashy silver-buckled belt. His coat jacket was hooked by one finger and slung over his shoulder. She noted his flamboyant ruby ring. And the final insult – he did not bother to remove his broad-brimmed hat.

Piercing dark eyes stared back at her from a rugged face tanned by the sun and when he turned his head Isabel was startled by the long mane of hair that hung like a horse's tail halfway down his back – wavy dark brown hair that caught the light.

Damn him, his hair's more luxuriant than any woman's.

She was shocked by his hands. *He's clearly never done a day's work in his life. And that ruby ring belongs in an Indian bazaar. His manners are uncouth. He didn't even bother to say good morning. I'll be damned if I'll curtsey to him in this bed sheet.*

Isabel refused to be intimidated by the direct, challenging stare that no English gentleman would ever direct at a lady.

When at last he spoke his deep voice had an odd accent, like a lazy version of their common mother tongue.

'So that's the *real* colour of your hair,' he said. 'Quite an improvement. I see you've discovered the bathroom. I didn't want to disturb you by sending up a housemaid to help you dress.' He gestured to the sheet. 'That the latest Paris mode, is it?'

Her tone was icy. 'What did you expect? My carpetbag and clothes were stolen.'

'Nah, don't panic. I've got your books in safe-keeping. But you won't need that grey outfit. It's far too heavy for our July.'

'Must I wait for *your* winter before I can appear in public?'

'This *is* our winter.'

'I knew that. I just forgot,' she said, lying to conceal her humiliation. 'All my trunks went missing at sea.'

'Yeah? Sorry to hear it. You must feel pretty riled about the crooks who stole your Paris trousseau and no doubt all your antique stuff from home, eh?'

Isabel wasn't sure if she detected irony or disbelief but she continued the pretence. 'Indeed. My guardian gifted me with heirlooms that had been in our family since the reign of Richard III.' She added on a note of challenge, 'God rest his soul.'

'Yeah, I forgot Dick the Hunchback was one of your mob. He murdered his nephews, the two little princes in his Tower of London, didn't he? Or did Shakespeare get it wrong?'

Isabel could hardly restrain her anger. 'Clearly your knowledge of English history has been confined to biased Tudor historians and sycophants.'

'You must put me straight some time, Miss de Rolland,' he said.

Isabel was infuriated by the trace of laughter in his eyes but she could not resist rising to the defence of a royal Plantagenet king.

'To begin with King Richard was *not* a hunchback. At his coronation many witnesses were present when he was stripped to the waist for the traditional ritual anointing. There are no contemporary accounts of Richard having any deformity! Do you think all those nobles would not have noticed?'

'I stand corrected.' Marmaduke made a mocking bow. 'I regret I failed to welcome you properly to our fair Antipodean shores.'

He's insufferable. Anyone would think he's doing me a favour entering this benighted marriage contract.

Isabel responded coolly. 'I'd been warned not to expect the manners of an English gentleman.'

'Then I won't disappoint you, Miss de Rolland. That's the last thing you'll ever get from me.'

'I regret I cannot offer you tea, Mr Gamble,' she said quickly in the hope of disguising the rumbling in her belly.

'I only drink billy tea in the bush. And you can drop the Mr Gamble tag. That's my father's title. I answer to nothing but Marmaduke.'

He still hasn't removed his hat! Infuriated by his confidence she was determined to force him to make the running.

'You can rest easy,' he said. 'I've had the name Walter de Rolland removed from your charge sheet. I notice you didn't use our Gamble name to get yourself off the hook.'

'I have no wish to attract scandal to your father's name. The man has done me no harm.' She gestured to the silver dressing-table set. 'Please thank him for his gift.'

Marmaduke raised one eyebrow. 'How very sensitive. Quite unlike Father, but then *he* is the one who's impressed by your family tree.'

Isabel seized her chance. 'I take it my episode in prison gives you the perfect excuse to break off our engagement?' She hoped her voice had not betrayed her. *You've no idea just how much I want that but I can't appear too eager.*

Marmaduke's expression was unreadable but he avoided her question. 'Did your mob give you the chance to decline my father's offer? Or did they twist your arm to accept me?'

Furious to be cornered into this humiliating position, Isabel tried evasive tactics. 'Surely your father kept you informed? Both our lawyers examined the fine print for two years past.'

'The first I heard of your existence was a few months back. To be frank I hadn't the slightest desire to marry you or any woman, certainly not an upper-class Pommie.'

'Are all Colonials as forthright as you? You are about as blunt as a rusty nail.'

He looked pleased he had drawn blood. 'Yeah, I like to think we are. The truth cuts through a lot of polite social crap. What's to be gained from pussy-footing around at this late stage of the game? We both know why we're here and the brass it cost my father to pay up your guardian's debts and keep him out of the nick.'

Isabel was equally shocked by his blatant reference to her family's financial plight and by his vulgar underworld cant. She rose with what dignity she could salvage.

'I will have you know I do not appreciate being regarded as some prize ewe imported for breeding purposes. Like those Spanish merinos

John Macarthur brought down here to improve the poor quality of his sheep.'

Marmaduke's expression told her nothing. Was his voice insultingly polite or amused? 'I see you've done your homework. I hadn't reckoned on a girl of your *exalted breeding* being interested in Australian rural life, except maybe a tapestry of our landscape.'

Exalted breeding? If only he knew the truth about me.

Isabel was at a loss to know how to talk to him. None of the rules of etiquette learned during her sheltered county existence were applicable. Fighting off a wave of panic she rapidly considered her options. What hope did she have of extricating herself from this mess? *I did sign that marriage contract. I can never return to England. If I became a governess I'd need to work for a hundred years to repay the money. I have only one chance. Somehow I must force* him *to jilt* me.

Aware that Marmaduke was observing her bare feet, she tucked them under the chair.

'I don't shock easily, Isabel. If you want to pad around barefoot, feel free. Our heat plays havoc with English complexions and swells your feet. I'm used to seeing English heads grow too big for their hats. But that's a national trait. Can't blame our heat for that, huh?'

'You are insufferably rude!'

Knowing she had totally lost control she bombarded him with questions. 'If you consider we British are so inferior, why was your father so desperate to marry you off to a girl from an English Old Family? I'm not even an heiress. Now *that* would have made sense to a Colonial mind like yours, would it not? Money breeds money. It can buy anything or any*one*, isn't that what you think? Tell me, wasn't there a Currency Lass brave enough to walk down the aisle with you? Or was your avoidance of marriage due to the fact you prefer *your own kind?*'

Isabel stopped, suddenly aghast that she had sunk to the level of a fishwife.

The lines around Marmaduke's mouth tightened but his quiet response was more effective than rage.

'To borrow a boxing term I see the gloves are now off. So let's get things straight. I'm a bachelor by choice – some would say a dedicated libertine. I have not the slightest intention of giving up that pleasure, married or otherwise.'

The intensity of his gaze caused her to flinch when he continued. 'No doubt my interest in gemstones triggered your assumption about my masculinity. I'm not a man to sit in judgement on other men's sexual practice if it involves adults. But for the record I've never had the inclination to sleep with any man.'

Isabel leant forwards and looked him straight in the eye. 'Neither have I. You'd best know the reason. *I hate all men*!'

For a moment Marmaduke looked slightly taken aback then fixed her with an unblinking stare. 'How interesting. So it's not just *me* you can't stand a bar of?'

Isabel stammered. 'I hate the whole male race – you're just part of it!'

Marmaduke studied her so long that the silence made her nervous. 'Is that the truth? Can no man tempt you with romantic words and promises?'

'There isn't a man born of woman who could seduce me!' She took a deep breath and played the desperate last card she hoped would prove to be her ace. 'And it's only fair to tell you that your father has...what is the vulgar expression? "Bought himself a pup".'

Marmaduke's eyes narrowed. 'Perhaps you'd care to enlighten me?'

'He demanded two things. A de Rolland bride of impeccable lineage and virtue. My legitimate birth is on record and my Plantagenet ancestry dates back seven centuries so I meet your father's requirements on that score, but...'

Marmaduke eyed her speculatively, twisting the ruby on his wedding finger.

Isabel took a deep breath to control the tremor in her voice. 'But it is only fair to tell you the truth. I am no virgin. So if you wish to break our engagement I will, of course, agree to disappear from your life and cause your family no further trouble.'

Marmaduke said the words softly. 'Did the man to whom you gave that privilege inspire your hatred of the entire male race? Or was it other men?'

Isabel felt her cheeks burn. 'There is no need to treat me like a wanton tavern wench.'

'That's not what I meant,' he said quickly.

'I've told you the truth. My shame has forever placed me outside the pale of God's forgiveness. But it is of no importance to me what you or any man thinks of me.'

Isabel turned away to avoid the contempt she expected to see in his face. The silence was unbearable. Would he never set her free?

Marmaduke's response was unexpected. 'I admire your honesty, Isabel. That's a quality rarely encountered in women. But decadent as my life is, no one can ever call me a hypocrite. I'm the last man on earth to demand virginity from any woman.'

Oh God, I've failed! She felt a sickening sense of nausea as the room began to spin.

Marmaduke grasped her by the shoulders. 'You're as pale as a ghost. You might be going down with ship's fever. That's deadly, I'll call a doctor.'

'No! I'm not used to wine at breakfast. I only need a drink of water.'

Instead Marmaduke whipped a silver flask from his coat pocket and held it to her lips.

'Here, get this into you. Down the hatch.'

The liquid hit her throat causing a burning sensation. Isabel pushed it away.

'Don't worry. Brandy. I always carry it for *medicinal* purposes.' He guided the flask back to her lips and added, 'And if you believe *that,* you'll believe anything!'

The warmth that diffused through her body brought a marked degree of pleasure.

Marmaduke leapt to his feet. 'It's my fault you're getting a poor impression of Colonial hospitality. You must be half starved. I wouldn't insult my horse by feeding him that prison muck.' He grinned. 'Yeah, I had a taste of gaol myself – after a duel.'

He was halfway out the door before he added, 'Rest easy. I've ordered a fine meal to be sent up to you. Meanwhile I have something for you. Wait here, don't move.'

He returned bearing a stack of boxes tied with ribbon. 'Just a few things I bought this morning while you slept. They'll do to go on with. I'll take you to a mantle maker and dressmaker to replace your lost trousseau. So if you decide to leave the Colony you'll be all decked out to marry a gentleman of *your own class.*'

Isabel let the jibe pass. She tried to sound nonchalant. 'How did you know my size?'

'A typically female question. Australian men are nothing if not practical – the key to survival in this country. I took your grey dress to show the storekeepers your size.'

'How clever. I'll have something to wear when I face the magistrate this afternoon.'

Marmaduke shook his head. 'I've taken care of that. You'll soon learn the way things work here. There's nothing and no one that can't be bought, if you know the ropes.' He hesitated. 'Rest up today. Tomorrow I'll show you a typical Saturday in Sydney Town. The kind of life you can expect as Mrs Gamble. I'll pick you up at nine sharp in the morning.'

He was gone. Despite the frustration of her intitial failure to break their engagement, Isabel was overcome by curiosity. She flung herself on the floor among the boxes, exclaiming with pleasure over exquisite lace-trimmed silk undergarments, silk stockings, a parasol and two dresses with fashionable belled sleeves, striped in Regency wallpaper patterns with peonies and violets. An Indian silk shawl was threaded with silver, a bonnet sprigged with flowers. The shoes slipped on like the fabled glass slipper that was lost then found by Cinderella's Prince.

The clothes fitted to perfection. *Marmaduke Gamble certainly knows his way around a woman's body. I suppose that's not surprising for a libertine.*

Admiring her mirror image Isabel felt so excited she almost forgot the legacy of her fight: her egg-sized swollen eye. But Marmaduke had thought of everything. A small package contained a domino-checked silver and gold Venetian eye mask.

What manner of man am I dealing with? He's as far from an English gentleman as the North Pole is from the South. He's blatantly arrogant, ill-mannered, insensitive, devious and insulting. It sounds as if he breaks the Ten Commandments as casually as other men break open a box of cigars. He dislikes me and every English settler he considers has invaded his country. I hated him on sight – and that's the one thing we have in common.

Isabel covered her eyes with the Venetian mask and asked her reflection. 'But a man who buys a lady a mask to save her public embarrassment can't be all bad, can he?'

The moment that this thought found a voice Isabel was suspicious. Marmaduke's gifts might look like the act of a generous heart but she had proved the truth to her great cost. A man's charm and kindness simply concealed the weapons of his cruelty and manipulation.

Isabel sighed as she repeated the line from *Romeo and Juliet*: 'There's no trust, no faith, no honesty in men.'

CHAPTER 13

The following morning Isabel dressed in one of the becoming new gowns Marmaduke had bought her, carefully placed her Venetian mask to avoid flattening her side curls and waited in the Gamble hotel suite, clutching her furled parasol like a weapon.

She had no idea where the barbarian planned to take her but his reminder that this was winter in the Colony prepared her for the day to be warmer than an English spring.

Marmaduke sauntered into her chambers on the stroke of nine. Isabel took one look at his dress and was appalled. Bareheaded, he wore the slop shirt and trousers she recognised as typical convict garb, plus a red neckerchief tied around his throat and a second spotted handkerchief knotted around his skull like a pirate.

Yet as if he considered himself an arbiter of fashion he cast a critical eye over her.

'What's wrong?' she asked defensively.

'You'll pass muster. But you'll need a sun bonnet unless you want to cop a heap of freckles. That parasol's only good for flirting. Bring a shawl and a fan. And change into outdoor shoes. You'll be sitting outside all day by yourself.'

'Where will *you* be?'

'Don't worry. You'll have your eye on me all the time. My mates and I have been issued with a challenge. War games against twelve desperadoes.'

Isabel refused to take the bait. 'Really?' she asked coolly. 'Are you likely to be mortally wounded?'

Marmaduke raised one eyebrow in amusement. 'I reckon that'd solve both our problems, right?'

Without waiting for an answer he took her elbow and hurried her downstairs to where Thomas was waiting beside a closed Gamble family carriage.

Driving in silence to their unknown destination Isabel was torn between catching tantalising glimpses of the town's scenery – a prisoner in the stocks being pelted by boys with rotten fruit and an altercation between a humble 'shay' cart and a bullock train – and sidelong glances at the man who was a total enigma to her.

Despite her disdain of Marmaduke's boorish Colonial manners she found herself observing him as keenly as a schoolboy studying an alien bug under a microscope. She was disconcerted to discover the reverse was also true. The bug was examining *her*.

He finds me as unpalatable as I find him. But what can I do? If I jilt him George Gamble would be justified in demanding the return of all his money and Uncle Godfrey would be forced to live under The Rules.

Isabel felt like an inexperienced female in a de Rolland–Gamble chess game being played by powerful men.

How can a pawn like me hope to challenge the opposing King and deliver the check mate to win the game?

She concealed her surprise when Thomas halted the carriage in front of iron gates in the high stone wall of the George Street Military Barracks. Marmaduke identified himself to the guard on duty and added laconically, 'Colonel Despard's expecting us.'

'Right you are, sir,' the guard replied in a clipped English accent, 'may the best men win.' And like open sesame the gates swung open for Thomas to drive the carriage through.

Isabel was startled by the bold notice attached to the gate: *Citizens Must Keep Off The Grass – by Order of Colonel Despard.*

The barracks were vast, like a military village behind the massive stone walls. Two long double-storey buildings stretched endlessly on either side of the impressive central headquarters. The total barracks must have covered four town blocks, capable of housing any or all of the four regiments stationed in the Colony, together with their horses, weaponry, ammunition, stores and the small army of convicts assigned to serve the soldiers' needs.

After halting by a green sward in front of the Officers' Mess, Marmaduke hurriedly escorted Isabel to a shady bench under a tree on the edge of what appeared to be a drilling square covered by grass.

'This should be safe enough. It's out of the line of fire,' he added enigmatically before disappearing inside one of the buildings.

Feeling as if she were the last woman alive in a world of men,

Isabel waited for the war games to begin. But instead of the expected appearance of armed military officers in the traditional uniform of British red coatee and shako helmet, the line of men who marched onto the field were formally dressed gentlemen wearing tall black silk 'bell-topper' hats and spiked boots. They planted wicket stumps at either end of what she now saw was a worn strip on the grass.

'My God, it's a cricket match!' she said aloud, suddenly aware that two ladies, likely officers' wives by their accents, had taken their seats behind her and were animatedly discussing the latest French fashion papers to arrive from a ship that had recently dropped anchor in Port Jackson. They broke off to glance at the men on the field.

'Naturally, m'dear,' said one matron condescendingly, 'the pity of it is we don't have enough officers available to make up two teams. So we were forced to invite a Currency team – scratched together so you can imagine how rough they'll be. No doubt the visitors will all be bowled out by the tea break, thank Heavens.'

Soldiers of the lower ranks had assembled around the edge of the field and there was a warm round of applause from the team of officers and the soldier spectators when the team of Currency Lads filed out onto the field, led by their captain – Marmaduke.

Isabel gave a sharp intake of breath at the contrast between the top-hatted formality of the Officers and Marmaduke's Currency team – none of whom had changed into the traditional cricket uniform of cream shirt and trousers. All twelve men wore casual slop clothing, their heads covered by a rag-bag assortment of knotted scarves or battered cabbage tree hats. Two were in their stocking feet. The rest of the team, including Marmaduke, were intent on playing barefoot.

Isabel caught the horrified female whispers behind her.

'The Currency captain is the son of Gamble, that *nouveau riche* Emancipist. What else can you expect from convict stock? They simply don't know how to behave. '

'Colonial barbarians, *n'est-ce pas?*'

Isabel flushed with anger but decided to ignore them.

The captain of the English military team won the toss and sent his team in to bat.

Marmaduke was the first to bowl. Isabel felt an odd flash of pride at the sight of him hurtling barefoot towards the pitch as he sent down the opening ball at a speed that flew past the batsman's wildly swinging bat, narrowly missed the wicket and was caught by the wicket-keeper crouched behind it. The fact their captain was almost bowled out for a duck on the first ball of the match drew a murmur of surprised approval from the soldier spectators.

Two runs later when the same bell-topper batsman was again facing him, Marmaduke bowled him out on the last ball of the over. There was a roar of delight from every Currency Lad on the field and a jubilant cry of ''Owzat?' Several lads leapt like frogs at Marmaduke and slapped him on the back exuberantly, one tugging his long hair in a gesture of triumph.

Isabel turned to the officers' wives and said politely, 'That demon bowler is my fiancé. Not bad cricket for a Colonial barbarian, *n'est-ce pas?*'

Their haughty reaction to Isabel's face reminded her she wore a carnival mask – an unthinkable fashion for a lady by day.

I must appear to be a woman of the demi-monde.

That idea was quite appealing.

The match was clearly not going to be won without a fight. Bold cricket was played by both teams, but Isabel could see that the high-energy tactics of the Currency team, their irrepressible humour, risk-taking, extraordinary feats of barefoot running and athletic leaps in the air to take impossible catches, combined to swung victory within their sights by the time they broke for tea.

Rather than risk being snubbed again by the officers' wives, Isabel declined to take tea and crossed to join Thomas, who was standing beside the carriage.

'He's not bad, is he!' she admitted.

'That's nothing. I reckon you're in for a rare treat,' Thomas said proudly.

When the Currency Lads went in to bat Marmaduke proved Thomas's prediction correct. Isabel grew increasingly excited as Marmaduke swung his bat wildly and sent balls regularly flying to the boundary for fours or over the heads of the spectator soldiers for sixes.

Victory was now clearly in the grasp of the Currency team. At stumps the military officers, true gentleman one and all, warmly shook hands with them. They had never questioned one decision given against them by the umpire – their fellow officer.

'God, I've got a raging thirst.' Marmaduke turned to his team as they climbed back into the saddle to ride home. 'Anyone care to join us for a few ales? I'm headed for the Parramatta road turn-off and the Surry Hills.'

Two of the team who had arrived on foot climbed up beside Thomas on the box seat to get a lift to the other end of town. Even before they had passed through the barrack gates they 'rubbed salt in the wound' by singing the 'doggerel' lyrics of a song to celebrate their triumph.

Isabel had no trouble picking out the refrain at the end of each verse when Marmaduke lustily joined them to sing, '*Keep Off the Grass says Corporal Desperado!*'

When his two teammates climbed down off the carriage at the end of George Street before the Toll Gate and headed off to a shanty, Marmaduke turned to Isabel with that infuriating half-smile she had learnt to distrust.

He thinks he's so clever. As if he's just laid a trap for me.

'If you're as thirsty as I am, care to try a watering hole that stocks the best grog in Sydney Town? You can bet your sweet life you don't have anything like this where you come from.' He added casually, 'That's if you're game to try it?'

'Anything you can do, Marmaduke, I can do,' Isabel said coolly. Her mouth was so dry she was ready to cross the Blue Mountains on foot if there was something to drink on the other side.

After they by-passed the gothic Toll Gate the road veered into a wide track that took on a new name – the Parramatta road. A milestone marked the miles to Parramatta, the village Marmaduke explained had grown the crops that saved the little Colony from starvation in its first years after the arrival of the First Fleet.

'Parramatta's now a prosperous community. Our second Government House is the governor's summer residence and favoured far more than the original one in Sydney.'

'Parramatta. What a lovely word. Aboriginal, I presume?'

'Yeah. The translation I like best is "The Place Where Eels Sit Down" – where eels breed.' He added slyly, 'Ever eaten eel?'

Isabel stopped herself in time from a derogatory reference to eels being considered a delicacy by the lower orders. She was relieved that they were approaching their destination. A painted sign swung over the doorway of an inn, showing a black dog standing on three legs, his lame leg curled under him.

'The Sign of the Lame Dog. Step inside those doors tonight, Isabel, and you'll be making history,' Marmaduke said enigmatically.

As Thomas swung the carriage around, a bearded drunk wearing a cabbage-tree hat weaved into the direct path of the horses, hurling abuse at Thomas who desperately swerved the horses to avoid running him down.

Marmaduke helped Isabel alight and told Thomas to wait.

The moment she passed through the doors of the noisy, smoke-filled tavern Isabel felt she had been set down on the far side of the moon. They were surrounded by densely packed bodies fighting their way to the bar, each man cursing and jostling to gain a wide enough berth to avoid spilling his grog.

To Isabel these rough-hewn faces were like caricatures in a lampoon. Their pugnacious features, shaggy hair and matted beards made them look as if they had all sprung from the same tribe. The women ranged from bedraggled drudges to flashily dressed girls in gaudy colours with wild flowing tresses. Not a bonnet or glove in sight; and every man kept his hat or cap fixed on his head.

'I'll get us a drink. Stay put and don't wander off!' Marmaduke warned as he shouldered his way through the crowd.

Isabel flattened herself against the wall, trying to look as if she was a regular customer but was soon aware that she was the object of hostility from two bosomy young girls. One had flaming red hair that matched her dress and the other, a strong-jawed brunette, was decked with strings of baubles.

A brutish man, wearing a top hat shaped like a concertina and a waistcoat over his bare tattooed chest, gave Isabel an encouraging leer of approval.

'Ain't seen you here before, sweetheart,' he said to Isabel and the words instantly enflamed the two women staring at her.

Isabel was relieved when Marmaduke manoeuvred his way back

to her and handed her a mug that she immediately drank down to quench her thirst.

'Here have mine, too,' he said dryly. 'I had a quick one at the bar. It isn't vintage wine but at least it's wet. What do you think of the place?'

The heat and smell of unwashed bodies made her feel faint but she was determined not to buckle. *This is Marmaduke's idea of a test. But what on earth is he trying to prove?*

'Quite interesting. Do you come here often?'

'Regular as clockwork. It's one of Garnet Gamble's shanties, so at least I know the grog isn't lethal moonshine. During his climb to fame my father cheated drunks but now he's hell-bent on respectability his grog's the real stuff. That's why this shanty's packed to the rafters.'

Isabel felt uneasy when the tattooed man drew Marmaduke aside and locked him in a confidential chat.

On Marmaduke's return to her side, she asked, 'What did that awful creature want?'

'Don't worry, he just wanted to buy you. Doggo is a small-time pander, a whoremonger. He used to train fighting dogs, now he runs a couple of street girls. He mistook me for your procurer. Wanted to add you to his team. I told him you were my "wife for the night",' Marmaduke added nonchalantly, 'but to come back here tomorrow night and try his luck.'

Isabel was glad her Venetian mask concealed her horror. She forced herself to sound equally offhand. 'How much should I charge him?'

Marmaduke raised one eyebrow. 'Same as you charge me.'

Aware that Doggo and his two girls were moving towards them with intent, Marmaduke hooked his arm around Isabel's waist and steered her through the crowd, giving a shrill whistle to Thomas as a signal to keep them in sight.

Shepherded through a network of paths in the Surry Hills, Isabel found herself swallowed up in a colourful kaleidoscope of Saturday night action. No matter how ragged the spectators, they all seemed to find money to wager on the contests engaged all around them. Even children had farthing and ha'penny coins to bet. She shuddered at the brutality of the fights between bloodied bare-knuckle pugilists, local fighters pitted against the celebrated Hawkesbury champions. But at least men had a choice. Isabel flinched with horror at the cruel 'mills', the contests between animals. Cock-fighting drew raucous cheers from the spectators as the trained roosters fitted with deadly spurs fought to the death. When a large bulldog almost devoured a brave little kelpie in the ring, the crowd booed even though most had wagered on the bulldog.

'That's typical Currency sportsmanship,' Marmaduke explained. 'As competitors we play dirty to win, but when it comes to spectator sports we tend to root for the underdog.'

The wine made Isabel bold enough to ask, 'Did *you* play dirty when you fought your duel?'

He threw her a sharp look. 'Gentlemen duelists play by a code of honour. I'm no gentleman.'

I wish I hadn't said that. If he killed a man in a duel, my flippant words must have felt like stabbing a finger in a wound that never heals.

There was no time to temper her manner. Isabel saw they were now closely tailed by Doggo and his flash girls. The tattooed bruiser pushed his fist into Marmaduke's chest, spoiling for a fight.

The flaming redhead issued Isabel an open challenge. 'Keep your paws off our Doggo. Go tout your business down at The Rocks, where ye belong!'

The lantern-jawed brunette made a vain grab for Isabel's mask at the same moment the redhead gave Isabel a shove that sent her tottering backwards. Regaining her poise, Isabel pointed at the tattooed Doggo and summoned up the most vulgar phrase she knew.

'*Him?* I wouldn't touch him with a barge pole!'

Insulted, both girls roared and lunged at Isabel. Marmaduke and the pander broke off their negotiations and stepped in to block them.

Isabel had never heard language as virulent as the obscenities the two girls yelled in her face. She tried to stand her ground, but was relieved when Marmaduke exchanged words with Doggo and they nodded agreement.

The pander jerked his thumb at his girls and they backed off.

Marmaduke casually informed her, 'This is his territory. Don't worry, there's an easy way to allow him to save face. Gambling is the Colony's religion. I've staked you to race against Doggo's working girl.'

'You're crazy. I couldn't run five yards in these slippers!'

'You won't have to. Turn around. Quick smart.'

Confused, Isabel turned her back on him but looked warily over her shoulder. 'Why?'

'Shut up and open your legs.'

'I'll do no such thing!'

'Open your legs, soldier, that's an order!' Marmaduke roared.

Isabel was all ready to swing around and slap him when she felt an appalling sensation, as though some hairy dog was pushing between her legs. She was airborne! Her skirts were hiked up to her thighs, her legs flew out in front of her and her vision rocked sideways. Hoisted up in the air she was mounted astride Marmaduke's shoulders above the heads of the crowd. Marmaduke grabbed hold of her left ankle and her right hand to steady her balance.

Isabel saw that the busty redhead was now locked in argument with her tattooed pander. The brunette was the lightweight of the two girls so when Doggo chose her to be his jockey she scrambled up onto his shoulders and yelled in triumph.

A young bloke in a red shirt, the self-appointed referee, announced that the starting point of the race was a barrow of cabbages, the route twice around the block to finish at the cabbage starting point. They were fast drawing a fresh crowd and a street urchin was quick to cash in on a way to make money.

'Place your bets! Who's gunna win, our whore Maggie or the Pommie whore?'

Isabel hissed in Marmaduke's ear, 'Does he mean *me*?'

'Yeah, soldier, but only for tonight. Tomorrow you'll be respectable again.'

The red-shirted referee stuck two fingers in his mouth and gave a shrill whistle.

The race was on. Marmaduke was first off the starting line but Doggo ran close at his heels. The crowd scrambled behind them, cheering, booing – and cat-calling when Marmaduke half-stumbled, causing Isabel to tilt dangerously close to toppling over. On instinct she grabbed his hair like the reins of a horse.

Appalled by the public display of her bare legs, Isabel was equally disconcerted by the warmth of Marmaduke's neck between her thighs – it felt like riding bareback on a two-legged horse. Marmaduke kept up a sharp pace but as they passed the brick walls of the Albion brewery his words came in a series of laboured grunts.

'I've put money on you, soldier. Are they gaining on us?'

Isabel looked back. Doggo and his jockey, Maggie, were fast gaining ground.

'Faster, faster!' She rode Marmaduke's shoulders in a surge of excitement.

The two 'horses' drew level fifty yards short of the finishing line. The brunette jockey screamed out a gaol-house oath and swung her beads like a lasso at her target – Isabel's head. Isabel had no chance to duck the blow.

'Shame on you! That's not cricket!' Isabel's English County accent rang out in outrage and the crowd roared approval. In sight of the cabbage cart at the finishing line, Isabel urged Marmaduke onwards.

'Come on! *Faster*! We can beat those cheats, I know we can!'

With a final spurt of energy Marmaduke pulled ahead to win by ten yards.

Isabel was furious at her rival's lack of British fair play but to her surprise she saw Maggie the whore was hugging her pander and laughing. The crowd seemed to be applauding all four of them. There were no losers.

The redheaded whore descended on Isabel and threw her arms around her.

'You're all right, girl. Come and have a grog with us.'

The two whores linked arms with Isabel and were heading her gaily in the direction of the Sign of the Lame Dog, when Marmaduke came to the rescue.

He folded an arm around each whore's waist and explained he had booked the Pommie girl for the night, a transaction they understood and accepted.

Isabel was relieved to see Thomas manoeuvring the carriage to reach them.

Marmaduke acknowledged the crowd's whistles with a royal wave of the hand then bundled Isabel into the carriage. Slumped on the opposite seat, he eyed her curiously.

'What do you think of a Colonial Saturday's entertainment? Pretty uncouth, eh?'

So that's his game. He's trying to force me to jilt him! *Two can play at that!*

'Your Currency cricket team won fair and square – even if playing barefoot is not the done thing. But you would not have won tonight's race without *me*!' She added coolly, 'How much money did you win on me?'

Marmaduke raised one eyebrow but she saw the laughter in his eyes.

She pulled off her mask and confronted him, black eye and all.

'Well, did I pass your test?'

Marmaduke gave a slow nod of approval. 'You came through with flying colours, soldier.'

CHAPTER 14

The morning sunlight made Marmaduke wince as he approached the Sign of the Red Cross Inn, where he had hired a private room to take luncheon with Edwin. He was also irritated by the raucous sounds from the saloon where drunken voices bellowed out a sea shanty in conflicting keys.

Marmaduke needed his friend's cool legal mind to balance his own confusion about the events of the past few days, including Isabel's honest revelation about her lost virtue. Marmaduke prided himself that being jilted as a youth had armed him against falling for any female's lies. He was confident Isabel had told him the truth, yet instinct warned him there was more to her story.

He was distracted by the arrival of Maeve carrying a tray bearing the inn's best wineglasses and the bottle of Hunter River claret he had ordered.

'This will be fine, Maeve. I'm pleased the publican is supporting the Colony's fledgling wine industry.'

'Thank ye, sir. I take it you'll be dining with your friend – the barrister gentleman?'

'Edwin Bentleigh, yes indeed, Maeve. But frankly, I'm pleased to have arrived ahead of him. There's something I wish to say to you in confidence. My friend greatly respects and admires you but he is exceeding shy by nature. I know he has it in mind to ask you...'

Maeve's smile did not falter but he saw from the subtle way her eyelashes fluttered it was a sign of wariness not flirtation. He pressed on quickly to put her at ease.

'My friend would like to get to know you better.'

Maeve stood with arms akimbo, eyes blazing. 'So, you're asking me to take him to bed, are ye? Well I'll be giving it to ye straight, Mister Gamble. I'm here to serve your meal, not to *service* you, your mate or any other fine gentlemen, no matter what the publican might have been telling ye. The old pimp's been pressuring me to make myself available to gentlemen after closing time and pocket his cut.

I have to dress like a tart to keep me place working here but I'm pretty damned choosey about the man I take to me bed!'

Marmaduke was appalled that his attempt to act as go-between had misfired so badly.

'Please, Maeve, you've mistaken my meaning! I know Edwin *so well*—'

'What on earth's going on here, Marmaduke?'

Edwin stood in the doorway. Framed in a shaft of sunlight from the window he assumed an heroic stature.

Marmaduke collapsed in his chair. 'God help me, I should never have got out of bed this morning. I swear on my life, Edwin, I simply tried to convey to Maeve that you admire her but that you're a bit shy. I swear I had nothing but good intentions.'

'With which your particular road to Hell is well paved!' Edwin said crisply. He turned to Maeve and bowed to her. 'I came here today with the express purpose of requesting your permission to escort you next Sunday to whichever is the church of your persuasion.'

Maeve's mouth softened. She turned to Edwin and resumed her professional manner. 'I'd be recommending the beef bourguignon today, sir, followed by the apple fool.'

'Perfect,' Edwin said, 'my friend will have the same. He's a harmless lad when you get to know him. All talk.'

Maeve was clearly dubious on that score but paused in the doorway to give Edwin an uncertain little smile. 'If you were serious, sir, my preference is for the local Catholic Church – if you can tolerate a bit of Popery.'

Edwin bowed. 'I shall be honoured.'

When Maeve left the room Marmaduke poured their drinks with a sense of relief.

Edwin mopped his brow. 'I'd rather fight a lion in court than go through that again.' He gave a shy smile of triumph. 'But it worked a treat, eh? Now, down to business.'

He drew a letter from his briefcase. 'Your father is nothing if not blunt. He hasn't disinherited you but refuses to hand over Mingaletta until you've wedded and bedded Miss de Rolland. We are back to taws, my friend. Unless you've succeeded in alienating your fiancée so effectively that she's desperate to jilt you and sail home on the next tide?'

'Mate, I've been so uncouth you'd have been proud of me.'

'So the plan worked? She dislikes you?'

'Despises me! But the game isn't over yet. I can't betray a lady's confidence, of course. Let's just say I need to up the ante tonight to get me off the hook.'

'What is she like? Pretty, innocent, malleable, a fool?'

Marmaduke rolled his eyes. 'None of those. She's no beauty. As flat-chested as a boy. Prickly as a hedgehog. And so arrogant I suspect she believes the English rather than the Jews were God's chosen people.'

'Good Lord, doesn't she have a single redeeming feature?'

Marmaduke considered the question. 'Well, she does have *one* pretty green eye.'

Edwin choked on his wine. '*One*? What happened to the other?'

'It's hidden under a black eye she copped in a brawl with Yankee whalers in The Rocks.'

Edwin was speechless until Marmaduke told him the whole Isabel saga except for one point. He worked his way around the hole in his narrative to avoid Isabel's confession of her lost virginity.

'And last night when I took her to the Surry Hills to the Sign of the Lame Dog—'

'You did *what*?'

'All part of the plan, mate. I threw her in at the deep end of the seamy side of Sydney life to convince her I'm such an irredeemable libertine she has no option but to jilt me.'

'Surely that must have worked.'

'Not *quite*. There's the rub, mate. Isabel's got the worst English traits – arrogant superiority and a sarcastic tongue as sharp as a cut-throat razor. But the odd thing is she's also got the *best* English qualities. She's quite intrepid, even brave. Any other female would have turned on the waterworks after what she's copped since she landed here. But Isabel hasn't so much as shed a tear. And she has a surprising sense of adventure. There's something about her that intrigues me, mate. I can't put my finger on it. But it's possible she's the only female I've ever met who's dead honest – and *real*.'

Edwin digested that carefully. 'I see. So how do you plan to proceed with the jilting?'

'I'll dine with her this evening in Garnet's private suite. I'll give her such a graphic account of my murderous duel it will shake her to the core.'

He paused to refill their glasses and kept his tone light. 'Then after dinner I'll leave Isabel to cool her heels. I'm off to the Theatre Royal. This evening's star attraction is Josepha St John.' He added carelessly, 'I'm taking her to supper after the performance.'

Edwin was ever cautious. 'Does your actress friend know you have a fiancée?'

'Of course. But the marriage farce will be broken off before sunset.'

Edwin looked dubious. 'Good luck, my friend. Should I say, on both counts?'

'Luck has nothing to do with it, mate. Strategic planning is everything. What's that British boast? "The English lose every battle – except the last."'

'In that case you'd better be on your guard, Marmaduke. *You* are a Currency Lad. *Isabel* is the one who is English!'

CHAPTER 15

Marmaduke felt buoyed by the prospect of the long, lusty night ahead of him – in bed with his mistress. It would be his reward after his final confrontation with his fiancée.

But just because I'll force the girl to jilt me tonight, there's no call to starve the poor thing – she's already as scrawny as a kitten.

Back at the Princess Alexandrina Hotel he headed straight for the kitchen to discuss with Emile the details for the dinner *á deux* he ordered to be sent up to Miss de Rolland's suite on the stroke of six.

'That sounds perfect, Emile. And include a platter of your delicious *choux* pastries.'

In his chambers Marmaduke bathed and dressed in evening clothes cut in the latest London mode then went through his usual tussle to get his neck linen to sit right.

He had his schedule planned to the last minute. His decisive conversation with Isabel over dinner would still allow him ample time to depart for the Theatre Royal and his night with Josepha. But now for some odd reason his mind kept harking back to the pathetic image of Isabel wrapped in a bed sheet and trying to look dignified with one black eye. He was annoyed to feel an unaccustomed sense of responsibility.

At the door of Isabel's chambers he gave a perfunctory knock, turned the key and entered. And there she was, waiting for him, masked as if for a carnival.

Marmaduke was quite taken aback by the transformation. Isabel sat in a chair facing the door. The bodice of the sprigged muslin gown he had chosen fitted to perfection and although it pressed her boyish chest even flatter than Nature had endowed, he noted the demure curve of her breasts above the décolletage. Satin slippers peeped out beneath the belled skirt that revealed inches of lace petticoat, and her ankles. He realised this was not the action of a coquette. The length of her gown simply proved that she was several inches taller than the average English girl. How had all this escaped his notice last night?

Her hair was carefully coiled on the crown of her head but a careless lock escaped down one cheek. Her single undamaged eye glinted behind the domino-checked Italian mask but the camouflage only succeeded in drawing his eye to her funny little tip-tilted nose. And he was struck by the pretty curve of her mouth.

Her lips are naturally full. But just look at the poor chick! She's as nervous as hell. Keeps licking her lips with the tip of her tongue. God, how young she is.

Despite his intention to continue his boorish Colonial performance, Marmaduke found himself saying, 'How charming you look. I trust you're quite recovered from our race last night? I reckon you're the best jockey who's ever ridden me.'

Shit! She thinks that was deliberate innuendo.

Feeling himself beginning to sweat, he draped his jacket casually over the chair back.

'I've ordered a number of dishes. English food or, if you're feeling adventurous, the French cuisine our chef hopes will tempt you.'

'*Tempt* me? I'm hungry enough to eat—' Isabel clearly stopped short of the word horse and added, 'whatever you've chosen. Your father's hotel is very elegant and modern.'

'One of many he's collected in the years since he was transported.' He seized on this Heaven-sent cue to blacken the Gamble name. 'Father made his reputation in the Colony as a swindling publican. Whenever cockies – that's our name for settlers from the backblocks – came to Sydney Town to blow their hard-earned pay, Father enticed them to bed down at his shanties and tote up their drinks on tab. After a few weeks of grog fever the cockies had run up bills they couldn't pay. The only way to avoid prison was to sign over the deeds to their bush properties. That's how Father began to amass his Gamble empire.'

Marmaduke waited for her horrified reaction. The mask did not betray her.

'These days Garnet Gamble lives on the largest of his rural estates, Bloodwood Hall, leaving his business affairs in the hands of a team of administrators. He's always hiring and firing them, accusing them of fraud – which is pretty ironic coming from him!'

'Do you help your father in his business?' Isabel asked.

Marmaduke raised one eyebrow. 'I thought you ladies of Quality looked down your noses at us inferior *nouveau riche* who engage in trade.'

'My de Rolland ancestors made their fortune from the slave trade, which the current generation lost in gambling and high living. *Your* father traded on human weakness. *My* ancestors traded in human flesh. Who are the greater villains?'

Despite himself, Marmaduke's respect for her shifted a notch higher. 'You have a sharp tongue, Miss de Rolland, but I see you're also a realist. To answer your question, I refused to be financially dependent on my father. So my own financial activities are of a diverse, covert nature. I have a share in a cargo ship that trades with New Zealand and I'm the silent partner of an old Hebrew Emancipist – Josiah Mendoza.

'He's an excellent watchmaker. Jos buys up quality second-hand jewellery and we don't ask awkward questions about the provenance. He taught me a lot about gemstones so I sometimes redesign pieces of dubious origin. It's taken for granted in Sydney that antiques and jewellery stolen in England find their way here. More easily disposed of because it's difficult to trace their origins.' He asked hopefully, 'Does that shock you?'

Isabel gestured to his ruby ring. 'No. But it does explain your interest in displaying your merchandise.'

'Touché,' Marmaduke admitted.

Damn, just when I think I've got her stumped she hits me for six. She's not the silly little goose she seemed at first glance.

A door knock was followed by the entrance of two assigned housemaids, who set up a trolley of food on a white cloth on the table before they departed giggling and bobbing.

As Marmaduke lit the candles he registered the way Isabel licked her lips, betraying her hunger at the bounty of gourmet food. He felt an odd jolt of pity.

Poor little duck, I've never in my life known what it is to be hungry.

'Allow me to serve you small portions of everything so that you can decide which dishes you prefer,' he said. He filled the wine glasses then raised his own in a toast. 'To the land we live in.'

After he had placed several dishes before her, he attacked his own plate with gusto but paused, aware he was under observation.

'Is something wrong, Isabel? You haven't touched a thing.'

'I was wondering. Don't you say grace in a penal colony?'

Marmaduke dropped his knife and fork, annoyed to be reprimanded like a schoolboy.

'I'm known to be an agnostic and a Philistine. But feel free to give the bearded Old Gentleman Upstairs a vote of thanks, if it pleases you.'

Isabel lowered her head and said softly, 'Thank you, Lord, for the blessing of your bounty and for bringing me safely across all the oceans to this land of plenty.'

Marmaduke growled a hurried, 'Amen.' *I'll keep the wine flowing not for the usual seduction but to discover her Achilles heel.*

By the time Isabel had devoured three *choux* pastries they had also sunk the first bottle of champagne. Marmaduke saw that her pale cheeks were now flushed and her posture relaxed. The wine had freed her tongue. This was the perfect time to seize his chance.

'Tell me frankly, Isabel, what's your first impression of the Colony?'

'I thought there would be some semblance of English manners. I expected the worst and I've not been disappointed. But perhaps it's not fair to judge everyone by you, the first Colonial man I've met.'

Marmaduke felt a confused mixture of pleasure at her intense dislike of him and a jolt of irritation. 'In what way have we failed to live up to your English standards of etiquette?'

She airily waved a hand as if there were far too many to count. 'No English gentleman would remove his jacket or keep his hat on in a lady's presence. Or use vulgar terms that presumably belong to the convict class. And your table manners, well, the best I can say is you eat with more gusto than finesse. You could never hope to pass yourself off as an English gentleman.'

Despite the success of his performance Marmaduke felt unaccountably disconcerted, but he responded in an off-hand manner.

'I asked for your opinion of my *country* but it seems I must personally stand trial. During my years based in London I had no wish to pass myself off as a counterfeit Englishman. It was more amusing to be what I am – a Colonial observer of the English class system.

I found English rural folk down-to-earth and hospitable – Nature's gentlemen. And the very best English aristocrats have such perfect, unaffected manners that they make everyone at all levels of Society feel at ease in their company.'

He refilled her glass and added casually, 'I was impressed that no true English lady would embarrass a person of inferior rank by drawing attention to his social *faux pas*.'

Isabel turned bright pink. It was a long time since he had seen a woman blush.

She lowered her eyes. 'You are clearly better qualified than I am to judge good manners, sir. I regret I have given you offence.'

'As I do myself if I have hurt you,' he added quickly. 'Now let's get to know the best and worst of each other, shall we? You've a right to know the dark side of my character. No doubt our London lawyers successfully hid the truth from your family's legal advisors.'

Marmaduke shepherded her to the sofa and placed the champagne within easy reach.

'This morning you asked me in anger was there no girl in the Colony brave enough to walk down the aisle with me? A not unreasonable question that struck close to home.'

He crossed to the window as if to enjoy the breeze off the harbour but, in fact, to use the shadowy alcove to prevent her from reading his expression while he studied her.

'When I was nineteen and had just completed my studies I became engaged to a young girl. To my inexperienced eyes she was a great beauty who had been transported for a crime sadly all too common. I knew she was a fallen woman but I treated her with full respect. To me she was an innocent victim of Society. My father thought otherwise. He forbade our marriage. When I threatened to elope with her, he signed permission for me to marry but refused to attend the ceremony. I waited at the altar for three hours. My bride never arrived. I was a mere schoolboy in love with the idea of love. But that absurd misalliance forever cured me of the *illusion* of love.'

Marmaduke waited. *Damn that mask. I can't read her expression.*

He was surprised when she said the words softly, 'Does she still cause you pain?' He replaced his jacket as if donning a suit of armour that made him invincible.

'Good God, no! That young girl freed me to see the world as it really is. Since then I've been incapable of confining my life to one woman. Married or not, I intend to live as a bachelor taking my pleasures where I choose. I'm immune to tender feelings. Of course, I'm kind to horses and dogs but when it comes to the fair sex I promise you, I have *no heart*.'

Marmaduke resumed his seat and said in a friendly tone, 'So you see, Isabel, this gives you the perfect excuse to renege on our arranged marriage.' He felt suddenly curious. 'Forgive me if this sounds like male vanity but the miniature portrait of me my father sent to you – it did not deter you from the prospect of marriage?'

'What portrait? I never saw any.'

'Our London lawyers delivered it to a kinsman of yours. A certain Silas de Rolland.'

He expected her to be shocked by the proof of duplicity he did not doubt was caused by the 'beloved cousin'. But whatever her true feelings, Isabel shrugged it off.

'I'd have come here to marry an ape. I know my duty to my family. No doubt they considered banishment to the Colonies adequate punishment for my heinous sin.'

Marmaduke waved his hand in a gesture of dismissal. 'Come, now. It's hardly a heinous sin for an innocent young girl to fall into the arms of her lover. If that were the case, half the world's female population would be in prison.'

He glanced at his pocket watch. Time was running out. He must tackle the von Starbold business now. 'There's something else you have the right to know about me. A deed far worse than you could imagine.'

He poured himself another glass of champagne in preparation for recounting the event for the first time since that day he stood in the witness box at his trial – a gauche sixteen-year-old boy desperate to appear a man of honour. He remembered how calm his voice had sounded in contrast to the way his knees trembled when Edwin, his defence counsellor, had asked him the question that was the key to his innocence or guilt, 'Tell me in your own words, the cause of your quarrel with your deceased tutor, Klaus von Starbold.'

The past came back with the force of white heat.

The sun was fast setting as Marmaduke rode through the bush in search of his mother, who had not returned at the accustomed time from her daily walk with Queenie. His father had sent out a party of assigned men to their planned destination, Scavengers Creek, where they swam. But on impulse Marmaduke rode in the opposite direction. Mingaletta.

The setting sun outlined the chimney of the ruined homestead. The only room that remained intact was the empty wine cellar. Marmaduke felt sure he'd find her there listening to Queenie's stories of their childhood in India.

The door swung open at his touch. Two figures were dimly outlined in the shaft of light that fell through the grill of the window. When his eyes grew accustomed to the darkness he was riveted by shock. A naked man lay on top of a woman, pinning her arms above her head as he penetrated her in a wild frantic rhythm. His mother's voice cried out, 'No!' but the man stopped her mouth with a savage kiss as if to devour her.

The man turned his head revealing the old duelling scar on his cheek.

Now as Marmaduke looked across at the masked girl watching him intently, he selected his words with care.

'Klaus von Starbold was my tutor. He raped my mother,' he said without emotion.

'I had two choices. I was my mother's witness. I could have him charged with rape and see him hanged. Or meet him on the duelling field to avenge mother's honour. Von Starbold vowed that if he survived he would leave the Colony never to return. He told me this choice was my test of manhood. Would I see my mother's good name dragged through the court and lampooned in the Colony? Or face him on the duelling field?'

Isabel was wide-eyed but silent.

'Next morning at dawn I faced von Starbold on the cricket pitch out of sight of the house. My tutor was so damned correct he continued to give me instructions in the duelling code. At the count of twenty we turned. I fired first and shot von Starbold in the stomach. He looked at me in surprise. Aimed the pistol directly at my head to make me sweat. Then deliberately fired his pistol into the ground.'

Isabel gasped. 'He never intended to kill you. What happened to him?'

'A bullet wound in the gut is fatal. He asked me to stand by him so he wouldn't die alone. I told him I would stay to watch him die. He gave me an odd smile and said, "I taught you well. Next time we meet aim at my heart, it's quicker that way." I saw his eyes glaze over. The last words he said were, "You were right to protect your mother against me. I'm proud of you, young man."'

Marmaduke felt drained but aware that Isabel was watching him intently. He took the snuff case from his pocket and inhaled a pinch to cover the fact his hands were shaking.

'He died in Queenie's cabin a few hours later. Edwin Bentleigh, my then barrister and now my friend, succeeded in getting the military jury to return a verdict of Not Guilty. The true reason for the duel was concealed to protect Mother's name. But it probably helped my case that my Emancipist father was the second wealthiest man in the Colony. Men in high places were in his pocket. Perhaps some sat on the jury, who knows?'

'Your mother must have been proud of you.'

'She never spoke of it again. She died some months later. The truth is, Isabel, I marched on to that duelling field with murder in my heart. I had every intention of killing him. Do you understand? I really was *guilty of murder!*'

Isabel was breathing so heavily he wondered if she was about to faint. Marmaduke was totally unprepared for what came next.

Her voice cracked with the strain of her words, 'So am *I!*'

Marmaduke was so surprised he actually laughed. He crossed the room to pat her shoulder as if to reassure a wayward child that all was forgiven.

'My dear Isabel, if you are so intent on breaking our engagement, you have only to say so. I am more than ready to compensate you for your journey and place you on the next ship bound for Home. You don't need to outrank me in villainy.'

Isabel stammered out the words. 'I am far worse than you. I never stood trial. My family succeeded in concealing my crime – murder.'

Intrigued, Marmaduke drew a chair close to her side. 'A man?' he prompted.

She shook her head. 'I wish it had been. Then I would feel no guilt. No. I have a medical condition. Sleepwalking. In that state I can't remember what I've done or where I've been.' She was blushing. 'When I was thirteen I had not yet become a woman. You understand?'

'Menstruation is a simple fact of life, Isabel, no need to shy from the word.'

'I can't believe you said that out loud! No one in polite society dares speak of it.'

'You're not in polite society. You're with me – an Australian.'

'I'm not likely to forget that,' she said angrily. 'Look, this might be amusing to you, but it is very painful for me.'

Marmaduke quickly assured her, 'I'm truly sorry. Please continue.'

'My sleepwalking grew worse. I disappeared for seven days. They found me wandering in the woods – without any memory of the time lapse. On my return I was kept under lock and key. Too late.' The words came in a rush. 'I had never *bled* so I did not realise until months later. I was with child.'

Marmaduke reached for the champagne. *Jesus Christ, what's coming next?*

'My guardian said I was not responsible for my sleepwalking illness, but I must be kept closely confined to conceal the truth. I discovered their plan. The babe was to be placed in an orphan asylum in Scotland, never to be seen again.'

Marmaduke knelt beside her chair. 'My God, what you've been through.'

'The birthing came early. I escaped from the servant who guarded me. Ran off into the woods where the gypsy travellers camped every spring. There was an old Romani healer famous for her herbal remedies. I begged her to help me. She delivered the babe. Next morning I left her camp to avoid bringing trouble down on her head from my family.'

Marmaduke chafed her hands to warm them. He said gently, 'Please go on.'

'Cousin Silas found me wandering in the grounds of our estate. I shall never forget the look on his face when I confessed I'd smothered the babe. Buried its body in the woods.' Isabel added defiantly, 'I told him it was better off dead!'

Her voice was bleak with despair. 'The bible tells us "the truth will set you free". It never does. My crime of infanticide will haunt me the rest of my life.'

Marmaduke reached out to touch her but she pulled away from his hand.

She added coolly, 'So, now *you* are free. What are you waiting for? Go ahead. Break our engagement. I can't sue you for breach of promise. I can never return to England. I'll never marry. What man wants a wife who murdered her own child?'

Marmaduke realised there were no adequate words to cover her experience. He had no idea what to say until he heard his voice answering her in a quiet, deliberate measure.

'Understand me, Isabel, There's only one thing I want – Mingaletta. I don't want to marry you. It's nothing personal. I don't want a wife, I want an *ally*. A woman who'll be my accomplice. Like a paid mercenary. Marry me. Give me your unquestioning loyalty *in public*. And in private I'll grant you complete freedom to speak your mind – as you do only too well!'

She gasped. 'Are you insane? After what I just confessed?'

'You and I are two of a kind. We can never shock each other by how low we have sunk. We've both committed murder. We're a perfect match. You hate men and I enjoy women too much to confine myself to any one female. You see? We're ideally suited to living in an arranged marriage. Strictly as brother and sister, of course!'

Isabel pulled off her mask and stared at him for a full minute as if his crazy idea was firing her imagination. 'What exactly would you expect from me as your ally?'

He briefly ran through the history of his promise to his mother and his long struggle with Garnet. 'I'm sorry to be blunt but this is the only reason I'd consider marrying you or anyone else. But it isn't a life sentence. In a year or so when Mingaletta is mine I'll set you free to live your own life.'

'You *are* mad!'

'No. To quote Hamlet, there is *method* in my madness. If you agree to my proposition, you are free to state your terms.'

'Two things,' Isabel said promptly. 'Money. Paid quarterly. Secondly, you must never again question me about my crime or my past life in England.'

Marmaduke was surprised by the speed and nature of her conditions but he did not quibble. 'Fine. Agreed on both counts. I'll have Edwin draw up a private contract. When the terms are fulfilled you'll be free to leave as a financially independent young woman.'

He offered his hand in the manner of two men sealing a pact. 'It's a pleasure to do business with you, Isabel de Rolland. We have a busy few days ahead of us so I'll leave you to your beauty sleep. I'm off to the theatre.' He paused in the doorway. 'Tomorrow I'll take you to the finest dressmaker in Sydney Town to fit you for your wedding gown.'

The distant church clock chimed the ninth hour as Marmaduke hurried down the hotel steps towards his carriage, where Thomas nodded asleep on the box seat.

Marmaduke was annoyed that tonight he would be guilty of the one breach of good manners that mattered to him – his late arrival at the theatre. He hoped he would be in time to hear the aria that had made Josepha St John famous or at least to catch her final encore so he could genuinely rave about her performance at their late supper.

He felt unsettled by the extraordinary scene he had played out with Isabel. His description of his mother's rape and the murder he'd committed under the guise of a duel would have shattered his engagement to any girl in the British Isles. But not Isabel de Rolland. She had immediately topped his story with her own bizarre crime.

It wasn't the act of infanticide that shocked him, a not uncommon remedy for women of the lower orders to dispose of an unwanted babe at birth. The law often dealt leniently with what was considered a misdemeanour rather than a crime. But he was angered by the imbalance of the scales – justice without mercy. To pick a gentleman's pocket and relieve him of his handkerchief meant transportation. A prostitute who rolled a drunken customer and stole a few paltry coins earned seven years in New South Wales – in reality a life sentence. Few convicts ever returned home.

What truly saddened Marmaduke about Isabel's story was the manner of her babe's conception. No star-crossed love affair, no single night of pleasure. Isabel clearly had no memory of how she had come by the child. Did amnesia conceal a traumatic experience? He recalled the venom in her words, 'I told him it was better off dead!'

Marmaduke realised with a sense of shock that although Isabel was technically a fallen woman, in terms of her sexual experience she was indeed, though he baulked at the word, a virgin.

On the point of climbing into his carriage and prodding Thomas awake, Marmaduke paused to look up at the second-storey window of Isabel's chambers.

The curtain was drawn back. Her pinched little face, free of its mask, was looking directly at him. He flipped back his cape, doffed his top hat and made a deep bow.

Isabel responded with a timid wave of the hand and an expression so wistful Marmaduke felt a pang of guilt.

She loves theatre so much she was distraught at the memory of Edmund Kean's last performance on stage. I must take her to the Theatre Royal one night.

He felt loath to depart while Isabel remained watching him. 'She keeps saying she hates men. But "the lady doth protest *too* much, methinks".'

Thomas sat bolt upright, embarrassed to be caught napping. 'What's that, sir – Marmaduke?'

'Nothing, Thomas. Just thinking out loud. It's off to the Theatre Royal and I'll need you to return for me later. Expect a very long night, Thomas.'

'He's like a chameleon,' Isabel said to herself as she watched Marmaduke depart in his fine carriage. One day he looked and acted like a Colonial yokel with *nouveau riche* pretensions. Tonight he cut such a handsome figure she suspected he would not look out of place among the crème of London society. *Not that I've had much experience of that!*

Resting her head against the window frame she admired the extraordinary expanse of star-filled sky above the row of new buildings lining the street, beyond it the impressive church towers and sandstone public buildings. It hardly seemed credible that Sydney

Town had grown to this state of Georgian elegance since the First Fleet arrived less than half a century earlier.

Isabel patted her stomach, grateful for the unaccustomed pleasure of a belly filled with fine food. She enjoyed the champagne's magical transformation of her mind and body. Unused to drinking alcohol, she had imbibed more in the past twenty-four hours than she had during the rest of her life. The sensation gave her an idea as to why some men indulged in the practice to the point of ruin.

Relieved to be free to sleep alone in her luxurious chambers she blew out the candles, shed her fine new clothes and crawled under the bedcovers. She was so emotionally exhausted that she waved aside her customary prayers. 'Sorry, Lord, I'll say twice as many tomorrow.'

On the point of giving herself up to the pleasant haze of sleep she heard her slurred voice holding a dual conversation with herself as if with a trusted old friend.

'You realise what you've done, don't you, Isabel? You've agreed to marry a man who is totally insane.'

'Yes, I know. But it's only for a year or so. And at least I'll have money to keep Aunt Elisabeth safe when she arrives...and my little Rose Alba will never go barefoot again...'

CHAPTER 16

Garnet Gamble rode towards the plains that stretched to the mountains on the western horizon. This wasn't legally his land according to the documents that defined the boundaries of Bloodwood and Mingaletta but he would brook no arguments from any man or the law. This was all his land by right of occupation. He knew to the headcount how many of his cattle and sheep grazed there. Heaven help any duffers who tried to steal them. Despite the law he had ordered his ticket-of-leave boundary-riders to carry firearms and be ready to fire at any bolter on sight.

Today, armed as usual, Garnet surveyed his realm and the endless expanse of blue sky above him with an ambiguous sense of pleasure. His ultimate plan for his empire was about to come to fruition but he was still in the dark about the exact details thanks to Marmaduke's bloody-mindedness.

In recent months he had been preoccupied with thoughts about the God whom he had divorced from his mind since the day of Miranda's funeral. Was this an omen that his days on earth were numbered? He had begun to suspect he was not immortal.

Hell, I'm only five-and-forty. I've got another thirty years or more. The world's my oyster now I've got that profligate son of mine cornered to breed the next generation of Gambles. The boy will thank me one day. All the riches in the world can't replace a son. But I'll be damned if I let Marmaduke know that, the ungrateful whelp.

He stiffened at sight of the lone horseman galloping towards him across the plain. Garnet's hand moved to the pistol in his belt. The rider waved his hat with both hands to signal he wasn't armed but drew rein just out of range of Garnet's pistol and hollered.

'It's me, Hooley, sir. The mail rider's horse went lame. Here's your mail.'

Garnet didn't recognise Hooley's face but then he would be hard pressed to identify every man jack on his estate. 'Right, give 'em over. Back to work with you.'

Garnet turned his horse's head for home. He saw the ecclesiastical seal on one letter. A son's wedding day gave a man a fresh lease of life – it promised grandsons.

He remembered the words of a fellow convict on the *Fortune*. Chained together at night they had made an odd couple, he a rugged sixteen-year-old and Josiah Mendoza, a haggard old Hebrew who feared the ship's bullies but kept a fatherly eye on him. They never discussed their sentences, guilt or innocence but Garnet called to mind Josiah's words one night when the old man was in philosophical mood.

'I am descended from a long line of respected merchants but I regret I failed to live up to the good name I inherited.'

'At least you know who your ancestors were.' Garnet added quickly, *'No shame of my Mam's, but I don't know for sure who my father was.'*

The old Jew nodded sagely. *'Our Talmud describes men like me who fail to build on the merits of our ancestors. We're called Vinegar Son from Wine. The reverse is a man who has improved on the record of his ancestors. He's called Wine Son from Vinegar.'*

'Too late for me to change. Transportation has marked me for life.'

Josiah shook his head. *'You have youth on your side. There's time to turn your life around. You can become Wine Son from Vinegar.'*

Josiah Mendoza. Thanks to one of his paid informants Garnet knew that Marmaduke had been Mendoza's silent partner in his jewellery store ever since the boy had bolted. But Garnet kept that knowledge to himself. He had failed with Marmaduke. But when he got his hands on a Gamble grandson he would make damned sure he'd grow up to be Wine Son from Vinegar.

The sight of Bloodwood Hall in the distance gave Garnet an upsurge of spirits. Few men in the Colony possessed a grander English country residence and he prided himself he had planned every corner. His knowledge of the interiors of English country houses was limited so to furnish it he had relied on that London arbiter of good taste, Rudolph Ackerman, in the copies of the lavishly illustrated *Repository of the Arts*. With these as his guide and Miranda's fine eye for quality he had imported expensive pieces and outbid competitors at

Sam Lyons's Antique Auctions. All Bloodwood Hall needed now was an aristocratic mistress.

On his arrival home Bridget informed him 'The Welshman' was waiting for him. Garnet hurried to his library, gave the nervous young man a cursory glance and seated himself behind his desk. Rhys Powell was in his mid-twenties and had the square, manly features, dark hair, grey eyes and stocky build common to the Welsh. His plain tailored jacket had seen better days.

Garnet referred to Father Sibley's previous letter of introduction. 'It says your guardian gave you a decent education at a church board school where you had two years' experience as a teacher of maths, English and music. On your arrival in the Colony you were reduced to the post of tutor from which you were dismissed.'

The young man stammered, 'My employment ended by mutual consent not disgrace.'

'How so?' Garnet demanded.

'I am a gentleman, sir. My employer treated me as a lower servant. I was forced to eat in the kitchen with his assigned servants. Father Sibley was sensitive to my discomfort and drew my attention to your need for a trusted secretary to help manage your affairs, sir. So here you find me, ready and willing to serve you if you so choose.'

Quiet as he is, this young Taffy is not without balls.

Garnet stared him out. 'Right. You'll do. If you prove an asset at the end of three months I'll double your quarterly salary. Agreed?'

'You're most generous, sir.'

'No, I'm not! You'll earn every penny, Powell. I'm known to be irascible, hot-tempered and nothing if not moody. But I never fire a man without good reason. Above all I demand honesty and loyalty, two commodities that are in damned short supply in this Colony – at all levels of Society.' He tossed the unopened letters across the desk. 'Enough of this chit-chat. I've mislaid my spectacles. You can begin by reading these to me.'

The letter from Reverend Richard Hill informed him that Marmaduke had cancelled Garnet's booking for the wedding at St James's Church. Garnet was further irritated when Powell baulked at a letter addressed to Marmaduke.

'My son and heir. Open it.'

'But Mr Gamble, I cannot in all conscience open another gentleman's mail.'

'What's the matter with you? Are you a bible-bashing Methodist or what?'

'I'm a bible-*reading* Wesleyan, sir. That does not entitle me to open another's mail.'

'Huh! I've no such scruples.' Garnet grabbed the silver letter opener and sliced it open. 'Now the crime is *mine*. Read it or I'll send you packing without a written character.'

Rhys Powell read it in silence before he spoke. 'It is of an intensely personal nature, sir. Are you sure you wish me to proceed?'

'Of course I bloody well do!'

'To Marmaduke Gamble. By now you will have under your protection my Niece Isabel de Rolland. I can safely presume this Marriage will soon take place because this letter was carried on the Susan *which brought her to New South Wales.*

I address this letter to you, her Future Husband, on the understanding that you will fully Respect the confidence of my disclosure and refrain from sharing the contents with your Father, George Gamble with whom I have no wish to have further contact.'

Garnet thumped his desk in rage. 'The arrogant bastard! I saved his whole damned family from ruin and he's got the colossal hide to dismiss me as garbage.'

Rhys Powell looked anxious. 'Would you prefer me to desist, sir?'

'No! Get to the meat of the sandwich!'

'The letter continues.'

'I am not a man designed by Nature to reveal my feelings therefore my Niece may be unaware of the degree of my affection for her. Far from trading her in Marriage as some may interpret our Contract, I chose to send her as far from harm's way as the geographical limits of the Planet allow.

Isabel is a loving child and loyal to a fault. For her own

protection you, as the new Master of her fate, need to know
that she suffers periodically from the malady of sleepwalking.
Her Physician considers the cause may be repressed memories
of an experience for which she is in no way to blame.

For reasons I am not at liberty to disclose, her life in
England held no hope for her future happiness. I trust you
will treat her with kindness and the proper respect due to
her rank and that you will do all in your power to protect
her from the criminal influences surrounding her in the last
outpost of the British Empire.

'It is signed *Godfrey de Rolland, Esquire.*'

Garnet suppressed his rage while he considered the facts. He
decided to withhold this letter from Marmaduke until he knew what
was going on. The wedding had been cancelled, yet according to an
informant's letter just read to him, Marmaduke and Isabel were both
living at his Princess Alexandrina Hotel, which posed a risk to the
bride's immaculate reputation given Marmaduke's bad name.

'The wedding will now take place here in my chapel,' Garnet
said firmly. 'Prepare wedding invitations ready to mail to all on this
list. They are the cream of the Quality, the Top Thirteen families
in the Colony. The Colonial-Secretary Alexander McLeay may have
to decline and Governor Bourke's still in mourning after the death
of his wife. But these invitations will let the whole of Sydney Town
know that the illustrious de Rolland name is forever linked to Garnet
Gamble. Even the most uppity snobs won't dare ostracise *her*.'

Rhys Powell cleared his throat. 'I notice this list includes a well-
known Emancipist and his wife. Is that a mistake or your intention,
sir?'

Garnet glared at him. 'I don't make mistakes! Samuel Terry is the
Worshipful Master of my Masonic Lodge.'

His decision to invite his rival had been a battle. For years Sam
Terry had surpassed him, acknowledged as the wealthiest man in the
Colony, a status far above even the landed Exclusives. Despite his
affluence Terry continued to live and work with his wife in a modest
dwelling in Sydney Town.

'Although the man is a benefactor to every charity, holds a seat on the Board of the Bank of New South Wales and mixes in business daily with the top gentlemen of the Colony, Terry's never invited to their homes. None of his offspring has 'married up' into their ranks.'

Isabel de Rolland was Garnet's trump card. At last he had out-flanked his arch-rival.

Garnet dictated a sharp set of directions to Marmaduke at the Princess Alexandrina, demanding his son's immediate return with Isabel to Bloodwood Hall to be married.

His secretary jumped to attention when Garnet strode off to the dining room.

Elise was waiting for him in her accustomed place. Garnet took his seat at the head of the table and frowned in response to Bridget's overly familiar attitude as she served him. In contrast the servant's manner to Elise was barely civil.

Elise knew better than to chatter when he was in one of his moods but her curiosity finally overcame her better judgement. Her pretty pout came into full play.

'I'm always left in the dark, Garnet. Has the *bride* ship arrived yet?'

'Safe and sound. And my future daughter is very beautiful,' Garnet said, convinced this was the case by her miniature portrait. 'It's time you climbed down off your high horse, madam. Isabel will soon be mistress of this house!'

'As if I could forget,' she sighed.

When Bridget served him from the tureen of vegetables she bent so close to his shoulder her ripe breasts were an obvious invitation.

Just because I've tumbled the girl there's no call for her to forget her place.

Elise looked petulant as she picked at the roast mutton on her plate. 'Is the bride going to wear Miranda's wedding gown?'

'No. One from Paris. I sent her family a small fortune to cover her trousseau. I want Isabel to turn the ladies of Quality green with envy. Just like you fare right now, Elise!'

His mistress squirmed in her chair, embarrassed by the smirk on Bridget's face.

'Could we talk alone, please, Garnet?'

'We *are* alone.'

Elise jerked her head in Bridget's direction. Garnet took his cue and gave Bridget a dismissive wave. 'I'll ring if I want anything.'

'Certainly, sir. Whenever you *need* me.' The Irish girl cast a glance of triumph at Elise before she closed the door behind her.

Elise sniffed into her handkerchief, a habit Garnet found tiresome.

'How can you humiliate me in front of the servants, Garnet? I only wanted to ask if you'll allow me to choose a fashionable new gown for the wedding. I don't want to be put in the shade by Marmaduke's bride as if I were some poor relative.'

'You're not even *that*, girl. Besides, you've got plenty of gowns you've never even worn. While we're on the subject, brush up on your etiquette. You'll be playing hostess at the wedding banquet to introduce Marmaduke's bride to the very best people in the county. We'll entertain 'em here – right after the ceremony in my chapel.'

'Is that wise, Garnet? You surely know how sensitive poor Marmaduke would be about that chapel.'

'My son has no choice. If he wants Mingaletta bad enough he'll do it my way.'

He lit a cigar without bothering to withdraw to the smoking room.

'You'd best realise, Elise. Life's going to change on every level when Isabel Gamble is mistress of Bloodwood Hall. You are going to have to play second fiddle.'

'You promised me you'd marry me when I'm with child. I'll hold you to that!'

Garnet gave a curt laugh. 'You've been threatening to fall for years. God knows I've done my part to deliver the goods. Produce a babe and I'll have you churched.'

'How cruel you are. I don't know why I put up with you.'

Garnet leant across the table and lowered his voice to a harsh whisper. 'Because I pay you far better than you deserve to play your part whenever I am *in need*.'

Elise's sudden spark of fire surprised him. 'How is Marmaduke's high-born bride going to react to your dark little secret?'

'She'll never know. Because I pay you for your discretion, remember?'

Elise's voice rose in anger. 'Well, don't ask me to protect *her* if

157

she's one of those who claim they can see the resident ghost. I have never.'

Garnet seized the chance to bait her. 'No, but she's seen *you*. I've seen her standing at the foot of the bed in her nightgown, pointing at you lying in *her* bed. Take care, m'dear. Miranda never forgives anyone.'

Elise burst into tears and fled from the room.

Garnet called after her. 'No point in locking your door against her, Elise. Ghosts don't recognise man-made boundaries. They walk through walls!'

He listened to Elise's footsteps retreating to the east wing. The slammed door of Miranda's bed chamber cut off the sound of Elise's sobs. Garnet felt a small twinge of guilt. *Why did I lie? Miranda's shade has never shown herself to me – if only she would.*

Restless now that he no longer had anyone around on whom to vent his anger, Garnet stubbed out his cigar. Elise would sulk for the rest of the night.

He pulled the bellrope for Bridget.

CHAPTER 17

Fear swamped Isabel, covering her, blinding her, paralysing her. Fear blocked all other emotions, hate, love, everything except one primitive instinct – the will to survive. The lake was her enemy, sucking at her skirts and petticoats, turning them to leaden weights as it began to drag her down to its depths. She flayed her arms in a desperate attempt to break its power.

Forcing her head above the surface she took frantic gulps of air before the lake drew her down to its dark depths. *No! Guilty. Innocent. I don't care. I want to live!*

She sank again, clawing at the water. Any moment her mouth would be forced open to swallow water.

Where is God? She looked up towards the fragile shimmer of light on the surface and saw the distorted reflection of a man's face. *His face?*

Isabel awoke drenched in sweat. For one moment she believed she was dead. Then the dream images dissolved as the room took shape and forced her back to reality.

I'm here! Alive! The lake rejected me. Silas, all of them, are thousands of miles away. I'm safe.

Isabel hurtled naked from the bed and stumbled to the bathroom. She slathered cool water over her face to banish the images of the nightmare. She ran a warm bath and soaped her body with a sea sponge, taking comfort from the sensual pleasure of water and perfumed soap – until sharply reminded that poor Greek boys risked drowning, diving to sell these sponges for a pittance to foreign tourists. *Drowning. Will the memory ever leave me?*

After emerging from the bathroom, she began to dress herself in a fresh set of lawn underclothes. A pair of assigned housemaids who looked about twelve years old entered the room. The girl who had the complexion of a speckled brown egg spoke with an accent that married Cockney with what Isabel's ear already identified as a Currency drawl. The other girl's brogue was so heavy it needed an interpreter.

Isabel smiled her thanks for the breakfast they brought her but declined their offer to assist her with dressing. After years of being laced into a constricting corset by old Agnes Isabel felt genuinely free fastening her new day dresses down the front in contrast to the back-laced gowns worn by upper-class ladies as visual proof they had a maid to dress them.

The housemaids chirped like sparrows as they opened the curtains, sending streams of sunlight flooding the room. As they left Isabel caught the Cockney's aside to the other girl.

'I reckon she don't get much shut-eye with young Master Gamble in her bed!'

Little do they know! Isabel attacked the food with relish, relieved she had no need to disguise her hunger with the required public display of table manners.

The fruit was so colourful and exotic it might have been plucked from the Garden of Eden. She was reminded of Adam and Eve's easy life before The Fall, when fruit had dropped at their feet, before they ate from the Tree of Knowledge and God banished them.

'Reminds me of my own fall.' She added wistfully, 'I only wish I had some romantic memory of what I'd done to deserve it.'

In the days since Marmaduke's extraordinary proposal he had not abandoned her. He regularly brought her books on loan from the new Gentleman's Reading Room, which denied membership to the lower classes and women of all ranks. Each day she devoured the novels of Jane Austen and Sir Walter Scott and was absorbed in reading about the Quaker Elizabeth Fry's work to reform the conditions of English prisons, hospitals and lunatic asylums.

Every afternoon Thomas drove her with Marmaduke in the landau to different parts of the town. Isabel was fascinated by the amazing variations in the exotic scenery and the unique Australian flora and fauna that she had only seen illustrated in botanical books. Her favour-ite drive provided breathtaking views of the harbour along each curve in the winding road that led to the white lighthouse at South Head, where she watched the arrival and departure of ships from or bound for England, the British Empire and the rest of the world.

Isabel loved the golden sandy beaches in the coves along the harbour foreshores. Angered that people were forbidden to swim there for most hours of the day, she saw it was a law blissfully ignored by dark, laughing Aboriginal children, who were expert swimmers from an early age.

Whenever they drove past the massive Prisoners' Barracks near Hyde Park, Isabel was struck by the contrast between the impressive Georgian Greek Revival sandstone architecture and the dejected lines of felons who filed from it in leg-irons, guarded by red-coated soldiers.

Today as she waited for Marmaduke to call for her, she wondered if he would ever take her to a performance at the Theatre Royal – it seemed to be his second home. The night before, when leaving for the theatre, he had told her to be ready this morning by half eight.

Now as she checked her appearance in the full-length mirror Isabel was pleased to see her eye had healed sufficiently to make the Venetian mask unnecessary. She had bathed it several times a day with the tea tree oil 'bush medicine' Marmaduke assured her was an effective treatment known to Aborigines – 'far better than quacks' patent medicines'.

Dressed to her satisfaction Isabel discovered that the dainty reticule Marmaduke had bought her yesterday contained a number of odd foreign coins used to supplement the English sterling currency stamped with Britannia on one side and backed by profiles of several generations of King Georges. The Hanoverian Royal Family had occupied the British throne for so long that Isabel no longer thought of them as foreign, but she looked with disapproval at the profile of the reigning monarch, His Majesty King William IV. Before he ascended the throne the Duke of Clarence had lived in domestic bliss with his mistress, the actress Dorothy Jordan, and their ten children – until he and all his brothers had been pressured to produce a legitimate heir to the throne. He had given up Mrs Jordan to marry the German princess, his consort Queen Adelaide.

Isabel forced herself to be honest. *I've no right to judge our poor old Sailor King. He was required to do his duty by his family – just as I was. And he did ennoble his illegitimate children, which is more than many of my Plantagenet ancestors did.*

When a distant town clock struck nine, past the appointed time Marmaduke was meant to collect her, Isabel marched down the corridor and knocked on his door. A passing housemaid casually informed her, 'The young Master ain't returned home yet, miss.'

That sounded as if Marmaduke's all night stop-outs came as no surprise to anyone. Isabel felt suddenly liberated, free to explore Sydney Town alone and on foot.

She passed through the foyer twirling her parasol and hurried towards the harbour.

No business of mine what Marmaduke's been up to all night. Just so long as he keeps the money flowing into my purse – and his body out of my bed.

The parasol was token protection against the warmth of the winter sun. The colour of the cloudless sky reminded her of de Rolland Park that day as a child when Cousin Silas had held a delphinium to her face and told her, 'Your eyes are even more beautiful than Nature, *ma petite cousine.*'

Isabel felt her throat constrict in anger. Would all these conflicting images from Heaven and Hell never cease to haunt her? She prayed God would keep Martha alive, not only because she loved her, but because Uncle Godfrey would never allow Silas to leave England while his wife was alive.

God never seemed available to listen to *her.* But as the bold sunshine, the swirl of bright colours, foreign accents and sheer vitality of this strange alien land all meshed together, Isabel was enchanted. She gave a little skip of pleasure as she began her solo adventure.

Maybe freedom is all in the mind.

George Street was alive with activity, crowded with carriages and pedestrians of every description. The cries of hawkers included an exotic one she'd never heard at home, 'Ho, all fat Oysters, all fine O!' mingled with foul-mouthed oaths from bullock drivers cracking their long whips in the air.

She swivelled around at the guttural cry, 'Stop that thief!' coming from a constable giving chase, a command that was foiled by a street urchin who blocked the path of the law and allowed the thief to escape before he evaded capture himself.

Drawn by curiosity to a milling crowd, Isabel found herself sandwiched at the core of a phalanx of men, unable to escape the rank smell of their unwashed bodies. She clutched her furled parasol as a defence weapon.

At the sight of ragged children clinging to lamp posts and trees like monkeys to gain a better view, she realised with a sense of horror where she was. Trapped. A witness at a public execution on Hangman's Hill.

The raised gallows seemed like a bizarre altar built to sacrifice criminals.

The raucous crowd parted to allow red-coated soldiers to frogmarch the young prisoner up the steps of the gallows. The ritual procession was followed by a rough timber coffin which was placed in front of the him to remind him of his fate.

Isabel was overcome by a wave of nausea but was unable to avert her gaze from the condemned man. Eyes the colour of periwinkle blue stared from his haggard face. A priest said a few quiet words to him then made the sign of the cross over his bowed head.

A female voice called out something in Gaelic which caused the condemned youth to acknowledge her.

'My thanks to ye, missus. Light a candle to Saint Patrick for me if ye will, to help me soul on its way.'

Isabel was stunned. *My God, he doesn't seem afraid. Almost relieved. Does he hold his life so cheaply?*

Many voices in the crowd booed and catcalled the thick-set figure of the man in charge, dressed in shabby black frock coat, a battered top hat tilted drunkenly over matted flaxen hair that framed a face truly as ugly as sin.

So this is Alexander Green, the hangman, who Marmaduke called The Finisher and Jack Ketch. The most despised man in Sydney Town.

Unable to break free Isabel was forced to watch Green staggering, obviously drunk, as he bound the prisoner's arms, trussing him up like a chicken before forcing the white hood over the lad's head. After testing the noose The Finisher threw his arms wide with a flourish as if he were a magician – and pulled the lever.

Isabel muttered a prayer, her eyes fixed on the lad's body strangling on the rope, his legs and bare feet writhing in a macabre St Vitus dance. The spectators, incensed by Green's bungling of the execution, hurled abuse at him.

She pushed her way through the crowd, aware that an executed body must hang for a full two minutes before the witnessing surgeon legally pronounced it dead.

On reaching the edge of the crowd, Isabel looked back to see the corpse being pushed into his coffin. The lid was nailed down. The carnival atmosphere over, the spectators at last began to disperse.

Isabel froze at the sight of the lone figure of The Finisher. He was shuffling directly towards her, brushing dust from his top hat. Distracted, he looked over his shoulder at a man steadily pursuing him with measured steps.

She backed away in horror, mesmerised by the expression on the chalk white face now peering over Green's shoulder...his eyes rolled to the sky...showing nothing but the whites of his eyes...around his neck...*a piece of rope.*

Oh my God! No matter where I go I can never escape them. Why do they come to me? I can no longer tell who is alive – or dead!

Afraid to look behind her Isabel dodged blindly through street after street, unaware of which direction she was taking.

A distant clocked chimed the hour. Exhausted, she paused for breath, hesitating about crossing a road but suddenly relieved to recognise a familiar landmark on the opposite side. *Thank God! I'm near the Princess Alexandrina hotel.*

Stepping off the curb she found herself whirled into the heart of chaos. Men's voices shouted in warning, brakes screeched, horses reared up from two carriages and she was sailing through the air, feet flying out in front of her, a man's arm pinioned her waist so tightly she gasped for breath.

Dumped unceremoniously on the footpath Isabel turned to accuse the ruffian who was shaking her by the shoulders and found herself face to face with Marmaduke.

'What the hell do you think you're up to, you stupid girl?' he yelled.

Isabel was shaken but assumed a haughty tone. 'Do I need your permission to take a walk?'

Marmaduke was so enraged he didn't draw breath. 'Yeah, you do! I told you to wait for me. You're like a damned jack-in-the-box.

No sooner do you take it into your head to do something and you're up and off. This town isn't some sleepy English hamlet. You were heading for The Rocks – it's not called the cesspool of the South Pacific for nothing. You could have been snaffled up by some slave trader or brothel-keeper, never to see the light of day again. If you can't use your own brains, have the decency to allow me to protect you!'

Realising she was at fault she stammered out an apology. 'I'm sorry. A housemaid told me you hadn't come home all night so I—'

'If you believe servants' gossip, more fool you. The truth is I went out *again* early this morning to attend to business involving you. Like it or not, you're my responsibility.' Only slightly mollified he offered her his arm. 'For Heaven's sake behave yourself.'

He bundled Isabel into the carriage, jumped in beside her then gave Thomas the order to drive to Macquarie Street.

Isabel had learnt as a child that a man's rage can only be cooled by two things. Tears or silence. As witches were incapable of tears, she had no choice but to remain silent.

But her spirits began to lift when the carriage drew up in front of a familiar building. The sign read, 'Madame Hortense, Mantua Maker and Dressmaker. Late of Paris.' Marmaduke had previously brought her here on a flying visit to be measured for her wedding gown.

Isabel scarcely had time to take note of it before Marmaduke whisked her down a narrow, cobblestone lane where a drunken man weaved along, singing a sea shanty.

'Never cut through here without me. This is a shortcut to Edwin Bentleigh's legal chambers to discuss our personal contract. Nothing shocks him, except injustice meted out under the law.'

At the foot of the staircase Marmaduke paused to look down at her. 'Edwin is my friend, better than I deserve. I won't be at all annoyed if you reveal to him your intense dislike of me. But Father has to believe we have a genuine marriage. From now on in public you are to look at me with utter adoration. As if you believe the sun rises and sets in me. Can you manage that?'

Isabel was equally cool. 'Perfectly. I always wanted to be an actress.'

Marmaduke gave a cynical laugh. 'Believe me your acting ability will be severely put to the test at Bloodwood Hall. If you think I'm an ogre, just wait till you meet my father!'

He paused before knocking at the door beside Edwin's brass plaque.

'Our future relationship depends on mutual trust. If you chose to sabotage my chances of gaining Mingaletta you could do so just like this.' He snapped his fingers.

'Don't worry, our family motto is "Faithful Unto Death". I'll be your faithful mercenary as long as you don't trick me.'

'I'd be nuts to do that. I am indeed a very *bad* man, Isabel, but not even my worst enemies claim that I'm a madman.'

Isabel stiffened when he suddenly reached out and held her face in his hands, his mouth so close she thought he was going to kiss her.

'What do you think you're doing?'

He gently touched her eye with one finger. 'You have a tiny smudge under your eye.' He whipped out a white handkerchief and ordered her, 'Keep still. Lick it.'

Marmaduke gently rubbed the spot then continued to hold her chin. 'I thought it was a speck of dirt but it's a natural beauty spot. Charming.'

She was unnerved by his unblinking stare inches from her face. 'What's wrong now?'

'I was trying to decide if your eyes are blue or green.'

'They turn green when I'm angry, so watch out!'

He almost smiled. 'Come, we mustn't keep Edwin waiting.'

Isabel felt wary of all lawyers. While Marmaduke described last night's performance at the Theatre Royal, the barrister cast surreptitious glances in her direction as if she were a living specimen on a microscopic slide.

He's not what I expected of Marmaduke's best friend. They're chalk and cheese. He looks too shy to be a lawyer. No doubt he'll show his true devious colours soon enough.

Edwin handed each of them a copy of the contract and explained it could be finetuned like a piano if the future Mrs Gamble had any reservations.

Isabel read her copy with care. Marmaduke merely gave his a cursory glance.

Edwin opened the discussion. 'I should make it quite clear, Miss de Rolland. Despite protracted negotiations between both sets of lawyers representing the two parties involved in the marriage contract you signed in England, there remain these clauses of a confidential nature that my client,' he gestured to Marmaduke, 'wishes you both to sign. I trust you agree this is a wise move to avoid any possible future misunderstanding. Do you understand your fiancé's reasons for this?'

Isabel did not hesitate. 'Perfectly. We don't trust each other.'

Marmaduke's mouth twitched. 'Told you she was nothing if not forthright, mate.'

'Forthright and most sensible.' Edwin turned to Isabel. 'I see you are a lady who values the art of getting straight to the point, an admirable trait in dealing with an unusual contract of this nature.'

Isabel was quick to answer. 'Nothing personal, Mr Bentleigh, but I have good reason to distrust the legal profession. I was promised a sum of money by Mr Garnet Gamble for my trousseau. It was never delivered.'

She turned to Marmaduke. 'I lied to you. There never was a Paris trousseau lost on board the *Susan*.'

'An understandable white lie,' he said quietly.

Edwin watched the exchange between them. 'Miss de Rolland, there is something you should know in fairness to Mr Gamble Senior. Your family nominated a sum for that express purpose. Garnet Gamble doubled it. Here is proof that this transaction took place and was received by a Mr Silas de Rolland,' he said, handing her a file.

Isabel felt herself blushing as she read it. 'My apologies. I was mistaken.'

Marmaduke covered her embarrassment by addressing Edwin. 'There's no need for Father to learn of Silas de Rolland's *oversight*. A new trousseau is already in hand. Madame Hortense is most clever at adapting the latest Paris modes to suit our climate.'

Isabel felt her heart leap but was determined not to reveal her feelings.

Edwin gave her his full attention. 'Do all the points in this contract meet with your approval? Should you desire a future judicial separation it will be granted, without question, a twelfth month *after* the deeds to Mingaletta have been signed over to your husband. The nominated allowance would enable you to live independently in the degree of comfort appropriate to your place in Society. A quite generous allowance, do you not agree?'

Isabel nodded. 'Except for one missing clause. The quarterly sum I am to be paid from the date of the wedding. No questions asked as to how I dispose of it.'

Marmaduke cut in. 'Forgot to tell you, mate, I agreed. Tack it on by all means.'

Isabel was afraid this rider would cause the lawyer to advise Marmaduke against it, so she added quickly, 'I am confident you will add this clause. I'm happy to sign it now.'

Edwin shook his head. 'My advice to you is never sign any legal document before all clauses are in place. I will rectify that matter right this instant.'

Taking up his pen he wrote in a clear copperplate hand the final clause on both documents. Marmaduke signed without bothering to read it but Isabel checked the additional lines with care. The future welfare of Rose Alba and Aunt Elisabeth depended on its accuracy. She was conscious this was the last time she would sign her maiden name.

If only I could bury my past as easily as I can ditch the de Rolland name.

Isabel hoped the interview was over but Marmaduke went off on another tack.

'Edwin has done me the honour of standing up for me as my best man. I thought I had everything in hand until it came to booking a priest. I realised we'd never enquired as to your religious persuasion. Are the de Rollands Anglicans, Catholics or something else? It makes no difference to yours truly. I'm an agnostic.'

Isabel answered coolly. 'It doesn't matter. It isn't a real marriage. My de Rolland ancestors regularly changed their coats right down through the centuries. Catholics or Protestants depending on which faction was in power. It was safer to be Catholics in the reign of Bloody Mary and some of the Stuarts. Advisable to be Protestants during others, such as Henry VIII and Oliver Cromwell's Civil War. We have a hidden priest hole in our manor house that's been occupied in different eras. My guardian is an Anglican, but Cousin Martha is a Catholic and her husband, my Cousin Silas, turned his coat to marry her.'

The corner of Marmaduke's mouth twitched. 'So which do you prefer?'

'I believe in God but I'd be a hypocrite to choose one path to Him over the others. I was never christened because my mother was a practising pagan. I'm told her ancestress was burned at the stake for witchcraft.'

Isabel had not intended for all this family history to pour out of her but she was mentally depleted by the events of the morning and by the contract's legal jargon and just wanted the business to be completed.

Marmaduke and Edwin exchanged a long, unblinking look that appeared to be more amused than angry.

Marmaduke broke the silence. 'In that case I'll take whoever I can get.'

Edwin bowed to Isabel at the door. 'I am at your service, now or in the future.'

Seated in the carriage, Isabel was surprised when Thomas took the opposite direction to the Princess Alexandrina Hotel.

'Where are we going now?'

'You'll see,' Marmaduke said casually.

Isabel recognised the building that seemed an amalgamation of one and two-storey structures that had been expanded to meet the growing demands of the Colony. It was set amidst lovely parkland that married specimen trees from England with native pines and shrubs right down to the harbour foreshores.

'That's Government House, isn't it? It's exactly like Augustus Earle's lithograph of the painting. So this is the residence of the governor, Sir Richard Bourke?'

Marmaduke sounded disinterested. 'It's where he conducts his business when in Sydney Town. But like many of his predecessors he prefers the other Government House, a quite elegant building at Parramatta, his summer residence.'

'I can see a gardener pulling a roller to flatten the gravel carriage-way. But where are the kangaroos grazing on the lawn? They looked so charming in the print.'

'The 'roos might be artistic licence. But if you want to see kanga-roos we have a few tame ones at Bloodwood Hall – if the convicts haven't eaten them.'

Isabel gasped in shock. Was he teasing? It was impossible to tell.

She twisted in her seat to catch her last sight of it. 'What is the interior like?'

'Why ask me? I'm *persona non grata*. The son of an Emancipist, remember? Only a few of the liberal governors, like Lachlan Mac-quarie, invited Emancipists to dine at their table.' He turned to look at her with the expression that always unnerved her. 'But thanks to your illustrious forebears, soldier, I may well be invited inside the place even if only to hold the train of your ballgown.'

Isabel felt the edge to his sardonic laugh. *Soldier,* his nickname for her, his paid mercenary. Thomas had explained nicknames were common in the Colony and they ranged from mateship to denigration.

She now knew that Garnet Gamble's true name was George, his nickname a reference to his being transported for his theft of a garnet ring. She was intrigued by the prospect of meeting the man and learning the reasons for the deep father-and-son enmity.

'What plans do you have for us tomorrow?'

'Nothing much of interest to either of us, soldier,' he said casually. 'Tomorrow is our wedding day.'

CHAPTER 18

Marmaduke glanced at his pocket watch. It was only midday but already he felt in need of cracking open a bottle of champagne. He congratulated himself that he had every detail of tomorrow's wedding farce under control. Madame Hortense's seamstresses had completed Isabel's wedding gown. He had eliminated the need for three weeks of church banns by obtaining a special marriage licence. A strategically placed cash envelope had ensured its speedy passage. And he had chosen an unusual venue that did not require a church booking.

But disaster struck when a messenger informed him that the priest he had booked had been knocked down by a bolting stallion and was hospitalised with three limbs in plaster. No other church or clergy of any persuasion would be available at such short notice, so Marmaduke hastened back to his best friend's chambers.

Edwin listened patiently to Marmaduke's desperate story and suggested there was a long-shot possibility. James Backhouse. The English Quaker missionary renowned for his humanitarian work was based in Van Diemen's Land but was currently on a short trip to Sydney to look into the future establishment of a Quaker Meeting House.

Edwin immediately began writing a letter.

'I can't promise he'll agree but this letter will serve as an introduction.' Edwin shrugged. 'Perhaps as a favour to me...?'

'Wonderful! Where will I find him?'

Edwin looked over the top of his spectacles. 'In the death cell.'

Marmaduke hurried back to the hotel and changed into his most conservative grey frockcoat. After stopping off at a hatter's to buy a grey top hat, Marmaduke armed himself with Edwin's letter and the relevant legal documents required for his wedding and tracked down James Backhouse inside the prison, where the minister was inspecting the conditions of condemned prisoners as part of a report for governor Bourke.

Marmaduke soon discovered that the dissenter was a man cut from very different material from most other 'men of the cloth'. He was dressed in the plainest suit of clothes, the same Quaker grey as his beard. His Northern English accent was studded with thee's and thou's as if he'd stepped straight out of the pages of the King James Bible. He had the gentlest eyes Marmaduke had ever seen in a man.

Marmaduke knew he was treading a very thin line between fudging the truth and an outright pack of lies, but he suddenly felt determined that the wedding would proceed without delay.

The Quaker listened sympathetically to Marmaduke's story of how anxious he was for him to perform a Quaker commitment ceremony for Isabel's sake. How he wanted to take his bride home to meet his father, but could not travel with her unless they were married. Not wanting to sail under false colours, Marmaduke admitted he was not a committed Quaker because there was not yet a Friends Meeting House in the Colony.

He held his breath. Would this be an impediment?

'We believe that no man has the power to marry a man and woman. Only the Lord has that power. As a minister I act as witness to their vows of commitment. But no doubt thy Quaker friend has instructed thee about our beliefs?'

Marmaduke smiled vaguely. *What Quaker friend? How do I get myself out of this?*

'Brother Edwin Bentleigh?' the minister prompted gently.

'Oh, *Edwin*, yes of course, he's been a truly great influence on my life.'

Why the hell didn't Edwin tell me he became a Quaker in England?

Marmaduke's hands were sweating but he felt relieved he could genuinely sing Edwin's praises, his tireless work in helping impoverished prisoners and how he had saved many men from the hell of secondary transportation to Norfolk Island and Moreton Bay.

'Brother Edwin tells me thou hast played a kindly role in assisting prisoners to begin a new life in New Zealand.'

Marmaduke's embarrassment was genuine. No doubt Edwin had failed to mention his assistance came in the form of illegal escape plans.

'Is thy English bride a Quaker, brother?' James Backhouse asked gently.

Marmaduke chose his words with care, knowing how far he was stretching the truth.

'Not *yet*, sir, but Isabel says the Friends' beliefs are the closest to her heart. Her heroine is one of your mob, Elizabeth Fry. Isabel's read about all her wonderful work in prison and hospital reform in England.'

James Backhouse gave a silent nod of acknowledgement. Marmaduke pressed on in desperation.

'Mr Backhouse, this wedding might *look* rushed, but it's been planned for two years. Here's all the paperwork, Isabel's guardian's permission for her to marry me and the legal correspondence showing my father's efforts to make the marriage happen. I know it doesn't quite fit the Friends' rules but I really want to make Isabel happy and it was sheer luck you were passing through Sydney Town on your way back to Van Diemen's Land.'

Marmaduke paused for breath and played his final card. 'Edwin told me that you and your fellow missionary, George Washington Walker, plan to return to New South Wales to write reports for the governor on the condition of our prisons, Aborigines and lunatic asylums. We'd be most honoured if you'd be our guests at Bloodwood Hall. My father built his own chapel, available for all denominations. You'd be most welcome to use it for your meetings of the Friends.'

James Backhouse's eyes were smiling. 'I thank thee, brother, for thy kind invitation. It is true this is a most unusual circumstance, but I feel it would be unkind to disappoint thy bride who has travelled so far and waited so long to marry thee. I will explain to thee the Quaker commitment procedure to put thee and thy friends at ease.'

Marmaduke listened with respect. Tomorrow James Backhouse would witness the commitment ceremony. The venue would come as a total surprise to Isabel.

The dawn of his wedding day was ominous. Marmaduke had slept late and the shadows around his eyes were proof of the night before. He dressed in haste and hurried past Isabel's door on his way downstairs to the waiting landau.

'First drop me off at Mendoza's store, Thomas, then wait for me. We've got a tight schedule to plow through before the main event this afternoon.'

Thomas flicked his whip in the air to give the horses the message.

'Great weather, sir – Marmaduke. When the sun smiles on a bride on her wedding day it's a good omen.'

'You surprise me, Thomas. You're a romantic. Did the sun shine for you?'

'It poured cats and dogs.' Thomas added morosely, 'I should have seen it was a rotten sign and done a bunk while I had me chance. Only managed to get rid of the shrew when the magistrate transported me here. But he did me a good turn. Being as I was marked down on the convict shipping lists as married, no woman's got a hope of trapping me again!'

'Good man!'

Marmaduke dismissed omens of any kind but found himself checking the weather. Judged by the sun's position and the bushman's method of calculating time, Marmaduke reckoned it was around ten o'clock. A glance at his pocket watch confirmed it. He was disconcerted to realise that at three o'clock he must front up to tie the knot – a slip-knot designed to set him free from Isabel a year from today.

The landau drew up in front of the window of Mendoza's Jewellery Store and Marmaduke hurried inside to find his grey-bearded partner seated at his workbench.

Marmaduke was annoyed that his voice betrayed his nerves. 'G'day, Jos. How's business? Can't stop. Just on my way to deliver the rings to my best man. No need to inscribe them if you're too busy.'

Mendoza removed the jeweller's magnifying eye-glass from under a shaggy eyebrow.

'Would I be too busy for your bride? I thought I must be buried and turned to dust before you got enough sense in your head to take a good wife. Here!'

Marmaduke opened the velvet box and read the inscriptions inside the pair of gold bands artistically engraved with the names Isabel and Marmaduke and the wedding date.

'You've done a beautiful job – as always, Jos.'

Mendoza gave him a quizzical look. 'Your father, he is attending your wedding?'

'Not unless he's got wind of it on the grapevine!' Marmaduke said firmly.

Mendoza rocked his head in disapproval. 'Oya veh! A son should show his father respect. Garnet Gamble is a good man. When we were shipmates on the *Fortune* every bully on board beat me up because I bear the same name as the champion pugilist Daniel Mendoza of Blessed Memory. Your father was only a lad but he fought them off to protect me. I accept your wish to remain my *silent* partner but I hope one day to pay my respects to your father.'

Marmaduke was discomfited by Garnet's social snobbery about his son being 'in trade', but even more by the knowledge of Garnet's youthful valour.

'Hey, Jos, I invited *you* to the wedding but you said you needed to work right up to the beginning of your Sabbath.' At Mendoza's nod he added, 'Did you also find time to alter my ruby ring to fit a lady's hand?'

When Mendoza offered it for inspection, Marmaduke expressed his pleasure at the delicate setting. He was about to take his leave when his partner handed him a small box.

'My own betrothal gift for your bride.' Mendoza said impatiently, 'Open it, open it!' The old man's mouth was hidden by his beard, but his eyes were smiling.

Marmaduke did not have the heart to destroy Mendoza's illusion that it was a love match. The box held a gold pendant in the shape of a miniature house with a ruby door.

'Jesus, Jos. You've surpassed yourself. This is exquisite workmanship.'

Mendoza shrugged with pleasure. 'My people have a saying along the lines that a man's true home is his *wife*. So may you be blessed in your new "home".'

Marmaduke reached across the counter and gripped Mendoza's shoulders. 'I don't know what to say, Jos, except Isabel will love it!'

'Be off with you. I must work to keep our doors open or we'll both end up in bankruptcy court.'

Marmaduke departed, grateful that fate had led him to be

Mendoza's partner. Their store was closed from sundown Friday and all Saturday to enable the old man to celebrate his Shabbat and was also closed on Sundays along with the rest of Sydney. He felt guilty that Mendoza worked long hours the rest of the week to ensure the success of their business.

Back in the carriage Marmaduke gave Thomas the order to return to the hotel. On the carriage seat was the box with the wedding gown made by Madame Hortense's seamstresses.

Aware these apprentices earned a mere pittance, Marmaduke had paid them generously to work around the clock to finish it on time. He had designed the gown to do double duty as a ballgown, white being the accepted colour worn by a bride during her first year of marriage.

Marmaduke's instructions to Madame Hortense had been blunt. 'Give her the illusion of a bosom, right? I've seen broom handles with more curves than God gave the poor girl.'

It gave him satisfaction to know that today he would sabotage his father's plans.

Did the bastard really believe I'd consent to be married in the same chapel where I was publicly jilted?

The memory of that earlier disastrous wedding day triggered unwanted images.

Standing before the altar...nervous perspiration was running down the inside of Marmaduke's winged collar. His darling girl was habitually late. Edwin had hurried back to the house to check. What was taking her so long?

The convict organist had played his repertoire four times over. The faces in the congregation were mostly assigned men. Queenie wore her best purple sari but her face was unsmiling.

Any moment he would see his sweet bride enter, her bridesmaid holding the train of his mother's wedding gown. If only Mother had lived to witness his happiness.

His heart raced at the sight of Edwin's strained expression as he hurried towards him...

Marmaduke repeated Edwin's words out loud. 'The bride has had a change of heart!'

At Thomas's shocked expression Marmaduke recovered himself

quickly. 'A change of plans, mate. Drive us to Edwin's place, post-haste, eh?'

The front door of the Bentleigh home opened and Marmaduke stepped back in surprise at the sight of this latest housekeeper in the procession of drunken assigned servants that the invalid Mrs B had packed back to The Female Factory at Parramatta. This candidate was dressed sedately in black with starched white collar and cuffs, her hair drawn back in a chignon.

'Maeve! You look wonderful. How long has this been going on?'

Mindful of her new role Maeve made a demure bob but her accent was as Irish as ever.

'Since that rat of a publican tossed me into the street. Edwin said I was meant for better things. I could work for his mother if I could survive the changes in the *weather*.' She rolled her eyes to the ceiling in the direction of Mrs Bentleigh's bedchamber.

'You're just what the doctor ordered. Edwin's lucky to have you here.'

Maeve led him into the study. 'He'll be glad of the excuse to escape for the day.'

'You *are* still free to attend my wedding? I wanted to ask if you would help Isabel dress and calm her nerves? You and Edwin are my witnesses. In fact you're the whole congregation. No church, so not even any church mice.'

Maeve cast him a wicked glance. 'Would I be missing the chance to see some lovely young girl putting a ball and chain on ye, Mr Gamble? The Pope himself wouldn't stop me!'

She was gone with a swish of petticoats. Despite Edwin's undoubtedly honourable intentions, Marmaduke would lay money on Maeve's ability to break the barrier of his best man's shyness.

Edwin greeted him relaxed and smiling. 'How's the bridegroom bearing up? I've cleared the decks of all legal commitments. I'm at your service all day.'

Marmaduke tried to sound nonchalant. 'Just another day in the week to me, mate. But I couldn't have a better best man. Here are the rings. Maybe this time we'll get to use 'em. I must say you're a sly dog having Maeve under your roof.'

Edwin stammered. 'I assure you it's all above board, Marmaduke!'

'Yeah, mate, that's what I was afraid you'd say.'

When Maeve re-entered the room she was dressed in her Sunday best.

'When exactly will you be wanting me to attend Miss de Rolland?'

'Would now be too soon?' Marmaduke asked quickly, 'I could drive you to the hotel to check that the wedding gown fits. Just make sure *this* bride turns up on time.'

Edwin's eyes followed her as she climbed into the landau.

Marmaduke laid a hand on his shoulder and said quietly, 'You're home and hosed, mate. She thinks the world of you.'

Edwin gritted his teeth. 'Another crass word and I'll flatten you, wedding day or not!'

'Righto! I get the message, mate. Just don't forget to collect James Backhouse. Thanks to your reference he's agreed to witness our marriage.' Marmaduke felt uneasy. 'He's a great bloke. I hated being a bit dodgy with a Quaker, mate, but – well, y'know that letter of permission from Isabel's Uncle Godfrey? I sort of – wrote it myself.'

'Forged it, you mean,' Edwin said with a sigh. 'Why should that surprise me?'

'Well, I must say I was rather surprised to know you were a Quaker, mate. You've been keeping that dark.'

'You never asked me,' Edwin said enigmatically.

Marmaduke looked up at the sky. 'Don't forget to bring a couple of umbrellas. The sky looks dirty. I'll meet you there well before three. First, I've got an appointment at the Theatre Royal I simply can't break.'

CHAPTER 19

For Isabel her mock-wedding day dawned with an overcast sky but her spirits lifted in anticipation of the arrival of the boxes marked with Madame Hortense's label.

Isabel gasped at the wedding gown. It was love at first sight.

If I wasn't a witch I'd be crying tears of joy. But at least I can enjoy a thing of beauty.

With a racing heart she shed her morning dress, reverently slipped into the magnificent ivory silk wedding gown and gazed at her image in the mirror, dry-eyed with admiration.

Unable to lace up the back unaided, she clenched the two sections together with one hand. The beauty of the gown transformed her. She knew that it was based on an illustration of a Paris creation that Marmaduke had re-designed to suit the Colony's climate. In wonderment she touched the daring curve of her breasts above the padded bodice.

'My goodness, for the first time in my life I look like a real woman!'

Everything fitted to perfection, though the white satin slippers were a size too small. She checked the shoemaker's name on the box, relieved that the address was close to the hotel. Hurriedly changing back into her morning dress she hugged the wedding shoes in her arms as she headed for Blunt the Shoemaker's store in George Street.

Outside the shoemaker's window she hesitated to look across the road at the grandiose edifice of the Royal Hotel which she knew held in its heart the one-thousand-seat theatre that was the culmination of Barnett Levey's dream, the Theatre Royal. When she spotted the billboard announcing tonight's performance was *The Merchant of Venice,* she longed to be free to attend it but knew her duty to play the loving bride at her own wedding made that impossible. She felt the magnetic pull of the theatre and decided that as soon as she had exchanged her shoes she could at least try to have a peek at the empty auditorium. She felt a delicious sense of freedom as she hurried inside the shoemaker's store.

I'm not married yet. I'm still my own woman until three o'clock.

*

It was noon when Marmaduke alighted from his carriage. The five-storey façade of the Royal Hotel complex combined Greek architectural elements with the promise of theatrical grandeur.

Standing at the rear of the empty theatre Marmaduke almost felt as if he was inside a living, breathing creature; he was delighted by the smell of greasepaint that had already seeped into the theatre's pores during its first months of legitimate theatrical life. Greasepaint sent his pulses racing with a feeling of anticipation, excitement, a promise of magic with a dash of danger at its heart.

Making his way down the aisle of the empty auditorium he marvelled at the size and splendour of the architecture and embellishments. Built on a scale that rivalled many an English theatre, it was an extraordinary tribute to Barnett Levey.

Since his return to Sydney, Marmaduke had joined the small band of the man's allies, buying shares in Barnett's company, which now rented the theatre because crippling financial problems had forced him to sell the building he had built. Marmaduke openly championed the entrepreneur, telling anyone prepared to listen, 'Barnett Levey staked his business empire, creativity and passion on bringing Shakespeare, melodrama, opera, ballet to every class of society in the Colony. One day this whole continent will acknowledge him as the true Father of the Australian Theatre.'

Now as Marmaduke looked up at the tiers of galleries his eyes rested on the box he had taken for the season and where tonight he would attend a Benefit Performance for an elderly actor whose memory was now so governed by alcohol he tended to break into Polonius's speech to his son in *Hamlet*, regardless of the play in which he had been cast.

The moment Marmaduke spotted the lone figure standing rigid in the wings, he knew that despite her legendary reputation Josepha St John was terrified. Tonight she must step aside from the security of her American Nightingale legend to face her baptism as a dramatic actress. It was no small challenge to play the leading female role of Portia in *The Merchant of Venice*.

There was no one else in sight so Marmaduke sprang up onto the stage with the agility of a born horseman leaping into the saddle. He crossed to the wings and drew Josepha by the hand to centre stage. She clasped a shawl around her shoulders like a shield but he saw she had not forgotten to wear the diamond necklace that was part of her legend – the fake diamonds glittered against her ivory flesh. Her lush hourglass figure was his idea of womanhood but today she seemed drained of confidence. Recognising the depth of fear in her dark eyes, he smiled to reassure her and kissed her hand.

'I came early in the hope of catching you before your rehearsal – I have Barnett's permission of course. You have never looked more beautiful, Josepha. All Sydney Town will be at your feet tonight and every newspaper will sing your praises.'

'What if the booy me? You know how volatile these Colonials are. They can turn on you like vipers. Look at how my country-men treated poor darling Edmund Kean in America. And *he* was the world's greatest tragedian at the height of his powers. I'm just a novice attempting Shakespeare.' Her voice broke with a sob. 'Marmaduke, I can't go on. I can't face them!'

Marmaduke dismissed her words with a flourish. 'First night nerves, nothing more. I'd be worried if you didn't have them. *You* are already adored in this town – you can't put a foot wrong.'

'As an opera singer, yes. But Shakespeare!' She turned as if to flee.

Marmaduke held her face between his hands and spoke sooth-ingly as if to a child. 'Don't let that word terrify you. Shakespeare was an actor himself. He understood actors, body and soul. If you had been born in his Elizabethan era he would have written the role of Portia especially for you – if women had been allowed to play female roles then.'

Conscious that actors had begun to filter to the rear of the stage and were chatting in small groups, Marmaduke placed his arm around Josepha's shoulders and drew her down-stage, determined to restore her confidence without being overheard.

'This play isn't pure tragedy although it has some electric, tragic moments thanks to Edmund Kean's revolutionary interpretation. Earlier, Shylock was played as a grotesque Hebrew in a clown's red wig. Kean refused the wig and made audiences see inside Shylock the man and his years of suffering humiliation at the hands of the Venetian nobles.'

Josepha hung on his every word, so he pressed on. 'Portia is Shakespeare's first and most triumphant heroine – a courageous woman who disguises herself as a male judge to save a man's life. Portia is everything *you* are, Josepha, brave, sunny of nature, beautiful, wise, witty, a real woman. Remember how Bassanio describes her?' Marmaduke quoted the speech in the tones of a lover's admiration. '"She is fair and fairer than that word. Of wondrous virtues. Sometimes from her eyes I did receive fair speechless messages. Her name is Portia."'

He saw the hunger in Josepha's dark eyes, now a vulnerable child seeking the reassurance of praise. She reached out and grasped the lapels of his coat.

'You *really* think I can do it, Marmaduke?'

'Josepha St John, you won't merely *play*, Portia, you'll *be* Portia!'

She gave a nervous laugh. 'I want to believe you.'

'Have I ever lied to you, my sweet lady?'

She was suddenly serious. 'No. You were even honest about your fiancée.'

'The wedding is a mere formality for both parties. But much as I desire you, you've always known I'm a man who's incapable of love.'

'*Yet*,' she said slyly, glancing up at the box he had taken for the season. 'You *will* come tonight, won't you? I know it's your wedding day but I *need* you tonight.'

He kissed her hand, freeing it gently from his lapel. 'I have every intention of witnessing your triumph. But do not look for me, I may be forced to arrive late. That's why I ask you to do me the honour of wearing this ring on stage tonight. I designed the Venetian setting to suit the plot, the ring trickery Portia initiates.'

Josepha gasped as she placed the ruby ring on her wedding finger.

'You darling! It's perfect for Portia's ring! It's so large – and beautiful.' She extended her hand to admire the effect. 'Look how it catches the light, it looks so *real*.'

Marmaduke hid a smile. 'This ring is not simply for Portia – it's a token of my huge admiration for your gifts. Don't grow careless and discard it amongst the theatre props. It *is* a genuine Indian ruby.'

She laughed in delight. 'I should have guessed.'

Alerted by the stage manager's impatient call to the cast, Marmaduke said softly, 'I must bid you *adieu*, my Portia.'

'My offer is serious, my love. We can travel the world together. You as my manager to guide my career and whatever private roles you desire me to play.'

There was no mistaking the innuendo in her words. Marmaduke was saved from the need to respond by the stage manager's strident call of panic.

'Christ! Will someone go and drag Shylock out of the dunny? How the hell can we stage *The Merchant* without the Jew?'

Marmaduke bowed a hasty farewell to Josepha as the irate stage manager called out to a figure lurking in the shadows of the back stalls. 'Hey, you! No auditions today. If you want to try out, join the queue in Barnett Levey's office!'

The shadow disappeared. As Marmaduke hurried down the aisle he looked back at Josepha, now the central figure in a tableau of actors all charged with nervous energy like thoroughbred horses before a race. Josepha stood centre stage, every inch the actress, the star. He saw she had already stepped into the role of Portia and, for the moment, forgotten him.

As Thomas drove him back to the Princess Alexandrina to change, Marmaduke vividly recalled the London performance of this play, when he had been spellbound by Edmund Kean's Shylock. The poet and critic Samuel Taylor Coleridge's description of Kean's genius was no exaggeration. Kean had indeed revealed Shakespeare through flashes of lightning.

Marmaduke had been tactful not to remind Josepha of the Portia he'd seen play opposite Kean in London. Young Fanny Kemble was a London favourite who had saved her theatre manager father from bankruptcy. Josepha was a woman long past youth. He reassured himself that Sydney Town was hungry for culture and Barnett Levey was giving it to them – no matter how ragged the birth pangs.

I'd put money on Josepha's triumph tonight. But Barnett's sailing close to the wind financially. I only hope to God his heroic dream doesn't end in his own bankruptcy.

The town clock's second chime drew a sigh of resignation from Marmaduke. His own performance as a counterfeit husband lay one hour in the future – a role he must play to the hilt if he were to convince Garnett Gamble he had fulfilled his half of the bargain.

Mingaletta will soon be mine, Mother.

Marmaduke closed his eyes, seeing the wild brumbies racing through Ghost Gum Valley. He could smell the rain on the eucalypts, the golden blossoms of the wattle trees dancing in the wind. How strange that his senses were excited by two such diverse sensations – the Australian bush and greasepaint.

Dark grey clouds were massing to conceal the cloudless blue of morning. Marmaduke knew the signs. The air was growing thick with tropical tension. There would be an electrical thunderstorm before the night was out.

CHAPTER 20

Marmaduke checked his pocket watch for the third time in ten minutes. He dismounted and freed his horse to graze, knowing he was a half hour early and relieved to be the first to arrive. The bush was alive with birds. A mob of sulphur-crested cockatoos swooped in a chaotic pattern to squabble for residency on the branches of a Forest Red Gum. The range of their screeched falsetto notes reminded Marmaduke of a choir of schoolboys excited at their release from school at the beginning of the Christmas holidays.

He had envied other boys who experienced the camaraderie of school life, who went on bivouacs in the bush and formed lifelong friendships. In contrast he had been incarcerated with a progression of tutors of various nationalities and degrees of competency. They ranged from elderly remittance men to former clerics of different religious persuasions. One tutor daily slashed his ruler across Marmaduke's knuckles to correct his Latin grammar until the night he awoke to find Marmaduke had planted a snake inside his periwig.

Marmaduke's final tutor, Klaus von Starbold, was a teacher like no other. The Hessian had fostered his love of Shakespeare, Goethe, Voltaire and Moliere, had entertained him with tales of his adventures as a soldier and hinted at a procession of *amours* with the advice that, 'Women are the very devil, young man. But only a saint or a fool abstains from the greatest pleasure known to man – taking a woman to bed.'

This admired tutor had fired up Marmaduke's own sense of adventure – until he betrayed him and died at his hands.

Marmaduke returned the gold watch to his waistcoat pocket. The hour of the wedding was fast approaching. He checked the location he had chosen: a grassy open space backed by a rocky cliff with a cave large enough to give shelter in the event of rain.

A rough walking track skirted the foreshores in the direction of Farm Cove, site of the first farm established after the arrival of Governor Arthur Phillips' First Fleet. Marmaduke found it difficult to believe that rag-tag fleet of convict ships had sailed into this harbour only twenty years before his birth.

Every Currency Lad knew the story. The soil on the these fore-shores was so poor and the majority of the convicts so ignorant of farming methods that when English vegetable seeds were planted in seasons diametrically opposed to the Southern Hemisphere, not surprisingly the crops failed. The First and Second Fleeters lived on the edge of starvation. Convicts and even soldiers were publicly hanged for stealing food. To his credit Governor Phillip had placed himself and his officers on half rations. Food was so short that when his officers and rare female guests such as Elizabeth Macarthur, wife of the free settler John Macarthur, were invited to dine at Government House, the invitation was understood to include bringing their own bread rolls.

What an amazing reversal. Today Emancipists like Garnet and Sam Terry are the wealthiest men in the Colony and I dine on gourmet food cooked by our own French chef.

Marmaduke re-checked his pocket watch and surveyed the idyllic scene he had chosen to avoid the risk of a second humiliation at the altar. Now that the Colony's crops flourished on the rich farming land west of Sydney Town, this foreshore had returned to its original untamed state – an Antipodean Garden of Eden.

Marmaduke felt his European dress was inappropriate for this setting – the stiff winged collar, tailcoat, boldly striped waistcoat, his long hair tied back like a Regency fop's. His choice of trousers in place of the older fashion of breeches reminded him of the tale told in London about the heroic Duke of Wellington, until a few years earlier Britain's Prime Minister, who was once refused admittance at Almack's by the club's formidable aristocratic hostess because he dared to wear trousers instead of breeches.

As the minutes passed Marmaduke grew increasingly edgy. He felt he could count on the Quaker minister's arrival but would Isabel change her mind?

Marmaduke heard the sound of the first carriage and went to greet it, relieved by Edwin's wave of reassurance as he shepherded James Backhouse towards him. The minister was again dressed in the plainest possible Quaker grey. The eyes under the shaggy black eyebrows were friendly and mildly amused. Marmaduke escorted them to the cave to sort out the Quaker commitment procedure, including the marriage certificate to be signed and dated.

James Backhouse looked around the scene in admiration. 'Thou hast chosen a fine place for a meeting house, Brother Gamble. I trust it will find favour in the eyes of thy bride.'

When the hour of three passed without the arrival of the landau and other wedding carriages, Marmaduke began to suspect history was repeating itself. Had Isabel reneged on the deal despite their contract? He strode off down the track anxious to catch sight of the approaching bridal carriage he had ordered to be hung with garlands of flowers.

Instead, he was confronted by a man emerging from the bush. Barefoot, clothed only in ragged slop trousers with a neckerchief tied around his neck, the sunburnt face looked tough at first glance but as he drew nearer Marmaduke looked into the lad's eyes and felt the impact of his youth, hunger and fear.

The bolter brandished a hatchet but seemed to have little strength left to attack. Marmaduke saw the reason – one of his leg irons trailed a chain that he must have hacked free from his other bloodstained ankle.

The Irish lad's voice rasped out in desperation. 'Hand over your watch and money. If ye think I'll stop short of killing ye, you're a dead man.'

Marmaduke answered quietly but remained on the alert for any movement of the hatchet. The lad looked crazed enough to kill.

'No need to fear me, mate. I ain't armed. And that bloke over there's a Quaker. He's as gentle as Jesus. So how about you put that thing down and have a grog with me? It's my wedding day and I could do with a drink. How about you?'

The bolter swayed on his feet on the verge of passing out. 'Why should I be trusting a ruddy English ponce?'

'I'm Currency, mate. What's more I'm your ticket of escape from the Colony.'

Marmaduke pointed to the top masts of a sailing ship anchored beyond the curve of the next headland. 'That's the *Kythera*. I've got a cargo of rum on board her, no questions asked. The ship's master,

Michaelis, is a Greek mate of mine. I guarantee you'll sail on her on tomorrow's tide. I'll see you're clothed, fed, with enough cash in your pocket to see you right when the *Kythera* drops you off in Auckland as a free man.'

The Irish lad grunted in disbelief. 'What do ye take me for, an eejit?'

'I reckon you're a bloke ready to change your name, stay out of trouble and begin a new life in New Zealand.' Marmaduke held out his hand, 'Name's Marmaduke.'

The lad clung dazedly to his weapon so Marmaduke carefully reached inside his pocket and withdrew a silver flask.

'You look like you could use a nip of brandy.'

The bolter gulped the contents down in one spluttering draught then, still gripping tightly to the hatchet, reeled forwards and collapsed into Marmaduke's arms.

Lights out, mate. Best thing for both of us.

Drawing the lad's arm across his shoulder Marmaduke dragged him to the edge of the clearing, watched at a distance by Edwin and James Backhouse. He removed his own coat and rolled the boy over to place his arms in the sleeves, freeing his hold on the hatchet.

Propped up against a tree the bolter stirred. 'Where's me hatchet?'

Marmaduke saw the approach of Thomas driving the flower-bedecked landau and knew he had to act fast.

'Listen mate, you can have all the grog you can drink. But first I have to get married. Just sit quietly in the shade while the Quaker does his job. Then I'll drive you to Cockle Bay and see you safe on board the *Kythera*. Right?'

The bolter looked bemused. 'Will I be getting another grog?'

'You can bet your life on it, mate.'

Edwin crossed to greet the wedding carriage then rejoined Marmaduke.

'What possessed you to give that bolter your tailcoat? Now you'll have to be married in your shirtsleeves!'

'It beats getting married with a hatchet in my skull, mate.'

It was a wedding like no other. It began with utter silence. No music.

Maeve held Isabel's long train as the bride approached on Thomas's arm, taking small measured steps that suggested she was playing *The Wedding March* in her head.

Marmaduke was surprised to feel his throat constrict. *Jesus. Is this the same girl?*

Madame Hortense's apprentices must have worked themselves ragged for days. The ivory satin gown and the veil floating in the breeze transformed Isabel from a tomboy into a delicate creature, half dryad. The gown moulded her tiny waist and enhanced the delicate curve of a bosom Marmaduke had thought non-existent. Her crown of orange blossoms and the veil framing her face gave her an ethereal quality, like a vision out of *A Midsummer Night's Dream*. Her luminous green eyes were the colour of an Irish field. He noted her long delicate hands were trembling as they held the bouquet of white roses.

Marmaduke was suddenly anxious. Had he ordered the wrong roses? He knew the Plantagenets had broken into two warring factions, their emblems the White Rose of York and the Red Rose of Lancaster.

Shit! Which side is Isabel on? Red or white? Oh hell, what does it matter? This whole marriage thing will be over in a year.

When she reached his side Marmaduke whispered without any trace of sarcasm, 'Thanks for coming, Isabel.'

His bride's resigned expression reminded Marmaduke of a painting of Mary Queen of Scots minutes before she laid her pretty neck on the chopping block.

James Backhouse broke the silence by quoting the words of the first Quaker, George Fox. 'The right of joining of marriage is the work of the Lord only and not the priests or magistrates, for it is God's ordinance, not man's and therefore Friends cannot consent they should join them together – for we marry none, it is the Lord's work and we are but witnesses.'

He explained how a Quaker meeting would be conducted in a spirit of worship based on silence in which anyone present who was moved to speak could feel free to do so.

The only sound to break the silence was the delicate snoring from the Irish bolter under the tree.

A few minutes later Edwin was moved to speak. 'I am witness this day to the decision of two very special people who have joined together after difficult journeys in life. May they always find in each other their true friend.'

Marmaduke found himself casting sidelong glances at Isabel now that she had lifted the front layer of the veil to reveal her face and Maeve had taken custody of the bridal bouquet. Marmaduke knew the ropes. James Backhouse had given him a copy of the words to read but Marmaduke had learnt them by heart. He took hold of Isabel's hand and chose to be the first to make the marriage declaration.

'Friends, in the presence of God and this assembly, I take this my friend, Isabel Alizon de Rolland, to be my life partner, trusting with divine assistance to be loving and faithful as long as we both on earth shall live.'

Those simple, beautiful words had seemed so easy on paper. Words that Isabel deserved to hear from a man who truly loved her.

I'm the last man in the world fit to say them. What would James Backhouse think if he knew that I'll be spending my wedding night in Josepha St John's bed?

It was now Isabel's turn to make the same declaration. Her profile with its little tip-tilted nose looked as delicate as a piece of porcelain. Marmaduke noticed for the first time the way her eyelashes curled as her eyes fixed intently on James Backhouse's face. The soft chin of her heart-shaped face trembled on reaching the words 'as long as we both on earth shall live'.

Marmaduke felt like yelling out loud. *It's only for a year. I'm not an ogre!*

But the next moment when she touched Mendoza's gift of the house-shaped pendant as if to draw comfort from the symbol, he wanted to reassure her.

I won't hurt you, girl. I'm not your so-called beloved cousin.

Suddenly conscious of the intensity of his stare, Isabel turned her eyes to him as if to read his thoughts. His smile died on his lips when she whispered crossly, 'What's wrong *now*?'

He said through gritted teeth, 'Smile. We're in love, remember?'

James Backhouse read out the details of the marriage document, the names of their parents living and dead. Edwin was prompted to hand across the wedding rings.

Marmaduke felt Isabel's hand trembling as he placed the wedding band on her finger.

The romantic illusion was shattered when Isabel placed the man's ring on his finger and said under her breath, 'I'm surprised you were willing to give up your ruby!'

Marmaduke felt confused. How the hell did she know?

He had forgotten to ask the minister if and when he was supposed to kiss the bride, so he took matters into his own hands by quietly asked Isabel's permission. 'May I?'

Isabel obediently tilted her face for his kiss but closed her eyes tightly and clenched her mouth in a hard little line. That was the final straw. Enough was enough.

Well, soldier, this is a kiss you're never going to forget.

He executed the movement with a rapid flourish, pulled the veil forwards to screen them from sight and held her face between his hands. With the tip of his tongue he touched her lips and when they parted in surprise, Marmaduke kissed her, a kiss a beloved bride should receive in the privacy of her wedding chamber.

Marmaduke did not break from the kiss until he felt her body melt in his arms.

Then with a casual flourish he replaced the veil and whispered in her ear. 'There, Mrs Gamble. I will never do that again. Until you beg me.'

From the look in her eyes he thought Isabel intended to strike him but realised she would never do that in the presence of a pacifist Quaker. She gently touched the flower in his buttonhole and smiled sweetly at him for the benefit of those present.

Only Marmaduke heard her words. 'I'll die first!'

He hooked Isabel's hand through his arm and led her to the cave to sign the wedding certificate. Isabel's bouquet was caught by Maeve. Edwin organised a carriage to deliver James Backhouse to his lodgings. Marmaduke placed his bride inside the flower-decked bridal carriage and closed the door after her.

'I'll join you in an hour, soldier. First I've got to get my Irish mate on board ship.'

As Isabel was driven away she peered back at him in total disbelief.

Edwin was resigned to the worst. 'You could be convicted for aiding a bolter escape!'

'I reckon everyone deserves a second chance. You gave me mine when you got me off a murder charge scott-free. I'm just passing on my good luck to this poor lad.'

Thomas whipped the horses in the direction of Cockle Bay. Marmaduke propped the bolter upright beside him, trying to sort out his feelings about the girl who had turned into a chameleon in front of his eyes. He knew Isabel had only married him for his money. But now that she was bought and paid for, she was his responsibility. He assured himself that tonight he would enjoy committing passionate adultery with Josepha. So why this confusion?

Discreet adultery is fine. Isabel expects it. But I'll be damned if I'll allow my bride to be publicly humiliated. She's copped enough of that from her cousin Silas.

By the time Marmaduke boarded the *Kythera*, the Irish bolter had passed out cold so he lumbered him over his shoulder like a sack of potatoes down to the cabin and let his inert body slide to the floor. Captain Michaelis tilted his cap back on his head and gave a cursory glance at the bolter's Bond Street tailcoat, frayed trousers, bare feet and iron shackles.

'*Yasou*, my friend. I see you've brought me another human cargo for New Zealand.'

'Yeah, mate. Tote up his fare on my account. I'll have a grog with you next time you're in port. Must fly. Got to be in two places at once tonight – it's my wedding night.'

CHAPTER 21

The French chef had surpassed Marmaduke's instructions by creating a small but superb wedding banquet fit for a royal princess. Set up in Marmaduke's chambers it was an intimate affair shared with their witnesses, Edwin and Maeve.

Marmaduke had also invited his sometime dinner companion, Rupert Grantham, to join them but his friend had sent an apologetic note by courier to explain his absence. He had another libel suit pending, *that could blow one of the most respected men in the Colony out of the water!*

Accompanying his letter was a gift wrapped in Indian silk: a coromandel box inlaid with mother-of-pearl containing a beautiful pair of silver loving cups. The card was inscribed, *To the new Mrs Gamble. May your bridegroom, my friend, bring you to dine at Waratah Waters one Sunday very soon. I look forward to riding with you to show you over my Petersham estate – my oasis.* It was signed *Rupert Grantham, Esquire.*

Throughout the banquet Marmaduke was an attentive host. Having dispensed with servants in order to create an informal mood, he paid chivalrous attention to Isabel and Maeve. He tempted them all to try the various exotic dishes and kept both the champagne and the conversation flowing, amusing them with anecdotes about the Colony's most colourful rogues. He took care to present Edwin in an heroic light as the legal champion of the underdog and was rewarded by seeing his mate so uncharacteristically relaxed that he placed his arm around Maeve's shoulders.

Isabel looked pale and fragile. Marmaduke caught her gazing at him from time to time with a look of feigned adoration. In response to his romantic, intimate gesture when he hand-fed her chocolate-coated strawberries she coloured prettily. He hoped he was the only one to notice the flash of anger in those green eyes and the way she almost bit his finger.

To his surprise Isabel seemed to have genuinely warmed to Maeve, who in Irish Republican style acknowledged no social barriers and treated Isabel like a little sister who needed her advice about the wicked ways of the Colony.

Reminded of his need to depart for the Theatre Royal, Marmaduke tried to avoid looking at the clock but he was inwardly relieved when Maeve suggested to Edwin none too subtly, 'It's time to leave the bride and groom to entertain themselves.'

Edwin jumped to his feet, full of apologies. They all exchanged warm hugs then Marmaduke escorted them downstairs for Thomas to drive them home to Woolloomooloo.

On his return Marmaduke felt unaccountably awkward alone with Isabel.

'I've arranged for a housemaid to help you undress. I hope you're not afraid of electrical thunderstorms. There's a real beauty about to burst. We do things on a grand scale down here.'

'Thank you for your concern. I'm not a child afraid of the dark,' she said firmly but Marmaduke did not believe her.

Isabel added hastily. 'I prefer to undress myself but that's not a complaint. It is the most beautiful gown I've ever seen. I thank you.'

'Glad you like it.' He backed towards the door. 'It's late. I must hurry.'

'Yes, it's bad manners to be late for the theatre. Don't let me detain you.' She added with quiet dignity, 'I trust the audience will be kind to Mr Levey's new Portia. She looked so nervous.'

Marmaduke was thrown off guard. 'How did you know that?'

'The wedding shoes you chose were lovely but a size too small. When I slipped out to exchange them I couldn't resist having a look at the new theatre from the back of the stalls.' She added politely, 'Your sweet lady is very beautiful.'

Marmaduke was shocked by her cool acceptance of his adultery. She must have heard everything. Seen him kiss Josepha. Feeling defensive he floundered for the right words.

Isabel cut him short. 'No need to explain. You are free to do as you please as per our contract. Now if you'll excuse me I must get some sleep. What time do you want us to depart tomorrow for Bloodwood Hall?'

'You look tired. Sleep late. Later this week will do.'

Isabel nodded. 'Fine. I forgot to thank you for remembering my family's emblem. The white roses were beautiful. You went to a great deal of trouble to make the day perfect. Just like a real wedding.'

Marmaduke felt wary. Was this polite English sarcasm? 'You didn't mind missing out on the traditional big social affair in church?'

'It was the most idyllic place I've ever seen. The Quaker ceremony was so beautiful. Imagine what those words would mean to two people who really did love each other.'

Marmaduke was annoyed to feel a touch of guilt. He wanted to keep the mood light.

'Did you see those wallabies hop out of the bush and watch the ceremony? It took me weeks to train them to stand to attention.'

Isabel gave a sidelong smile. 'Is that what you call an Australian tall story?'

Marmaduke assumed a look of mock outrage. 'Really, Isabel. Would I lie to you?'

She shrugged. 'You're a man, aren't you?'

Jolted by the underlying note of bitter acceptance he wanted to leave her on a positive note. 'A good commander never lies to his allies. Good night, soldier, sleep well.'

Making a hasty bow Marmaduke returned to his own chambers to bathe and change into evening clothes. If he was in luck he would time his arrival to catch the last act of *The Merchant of Venice* and Portia's famous 'quality of mercy' speech. Josepha would be none the wiser. He knew the play by heart but was it Colley Cibber's modern adaptation tonight or Shakespeare's original text?

The Bard was a genius but Cibber was a crowd-pleaser. If I were King I'd forbid anyone to rewrite Shakespeare. Goethe's translations are more faithful to Will's plays in German than Cibber's are in English.

A half hour later, dressed in immaculate evening dress and opera cape Marmaduke was satisfied he passed muster except for his usual cock-eyed attempt to tie his neck linen. He hesitated in passing Isabel's room. The door was ajar.

A loud clap of thunder followed by flashes of forked lightning revealed a candle burning beside her bed. The rooms were empty. Marmaduke fought down his frustration. Had the silly girl bolted again in fear of the storm? Or was it fear of him?

He strode off in search of her. Through the window at the end of the corridor rapid flashes of sheet lightning slashed the darkness. He heard the sound before he saw the source of it. The low moaning of a voice that sounded more ghostly than real. A flash of lightning revealed a misty, wraith-like figure at the far end. The hair on his arms bristled. He stood perfectly still as it moved towards him.

It was then he saw its face. *Isabel.* She was moaning softly and making repeated movements as if in the act of washing her hands. Reminded of Lady Macbeth's sleepwalking scene he realised with a start how close this was to the truth. He was chilled by the expression in Isabel's eyes. The pupils were dilated but she appeared to be locked in another world, oblivious to his existence even when she passed directly in front of him.

Marmaduke tried to decide fast. He had read somewhere that it could be dangerous to awaken a sleepwalker suddenly. He pressed himself into the shadows of the wall and gently pushed open the door of her room. A wedge of light fell across the carpet. As if drawn to the light Isabel entered her room, continuing to wring her hands and muttering broken phrases.

He caught the words 'Silas' and 'Martha' then the stream of words became clearer as she sank to her knees by the bedside and appeared to be holding an unseen bundle in her arms. Marmaduke pressed himself against the wall out of range of her line of vision in case she woke suddenly from her nightmare.

Her voice became clearer but the words made little sense. Was this purely a dream or was she replaying a scene from her past?

'God forgive me, if Thou canst find it in Thy heart to forgive a witch?' She looked down at her hands and said quite clearly, 'So beautiful. How can something so innocent come out of such evil?'

Every muscle in his body was taut as he studied her every gesture and expression, sensing she was unknowingly offering clues to the cause of her tormented soul. Her eyes were wide open but blind to everything outside her dream world. Like a fragile insect trapped inside a piece of amber.

What was it she believed she concealed in her hands? He felt the transference of her terror as she cowered and looked around her.

Then she smiled at her empty hands and with a look that stunned him by its tenderness, she untied the drawstring of her nightgown and, slipping her hand inside it, she bent over and offered her child-like breast with a gesture of such sweetness Marmaduke caught his breath.

'There, there little one. Don't cry. Mama will take care of you. I'll find a safe place to hide you, I promise. Cousin Silas will never hurt *you*.'

She gently rocked the imaginary bundle, softly singing snatches of a lullaby.

Shocked by the painful intimacy of the scene Marmaduke was unable to avert his eyes from her face. He felt like an intruder yet was grateful to witness the source of her pain.

When she climbed into bed she rested the invisible bundle beside her and closed her eyes. He waited until her breathing became so regular he was convinced she had fallen into a normal pattern of sleep. Safe to emerge from the shadows, he moved to her bedside.

Isabel's face was now peaceful. Marmaduke sat on the side of her bed, aware that his plans for the night were in chaos. There was no possible way to send Josepha a message to explain his absence on the night she needed him most. He dared not leave Isabel alone in this state. The glorious night of lust he had planned had been turned on its head.

Marmaduke had no desire to relinquish his freedom as a bachelor yet he was overcome by a strange sense of disorientation.

I feel as if I've just stepped out of my body and into another man's life.

CHAPTER 22

'God damn it, where the hell is everyone? Not a lazy bastard in sight.' Garnet raised his voice. 'I've got a bloody good mind to boot out the lot of you, send you back to the gutter where you belong!'

Standing at the foot of the staircase Garnet's bellow of rage reverberated around the marble entrance hall, a sound quickly followed by shattering china after his angry gesture sent the giant Ming dynasty vase flying off its pedestal to disintegrate in all directions. Hundreds of years old, it now lay in shards at his feet.

'Never liked the bloody thing, Chinese junk covered with cracks. I'm damned if I know why they cost a fortune,' he mumbled then resumed his roar. 'Powell! Elise! Bridget! Red Mary, Black Mary, whatever your names are. Get here on the double! That's an order!'

Running footsteps approached from all directions, upstairs and down. Much to his surprise and chagrin the first to arrive was Queenie, who wasn't even his to command.

She tossed one end of her sari over her shoulder and her penetrating coal-black eyes eyed him with silent contempt.

'What are *you* doing here, old woman?' he demanded. 'I didn't send for *you.*'

'Who else isn't afraid to tell you the unpalatable truth?'

Suddenly curious, Garnet lowered his voice, 'What do you mean? What do you know that my informants don't?'

'That young Marmaduke has refused to marry at St James's Church the bride you imported for him. He's left Sydney Town.'

'You know nothing!' he said bluffing. 'My informants have kept tabs on every move that boy's made since his return to the Colony. All of them. My coachman Thomas, that Froggy dressmaker Madame Hortense, my Sydney accountant, Princess Alexandrina's housekeeper and a shipmate who's now high up in the police force.'

Queenie smiled knowingly at the euphemism 'shipmate'. Everyone knew that old lags who kept their noses clean were often appointed police constables and were usually no more corrupt than men who came free.

Garnet blustered on. 'The only one I can't pay to inform on Marmaduke is Edwin Bentleigh. I'd sack the bastard for disloyalty to *me* if he wasn't the only honest advocate in town.' He finally conceded defeat. 'All right, who was *your* source?'

Queenie narrowed her eyes in triumph. '*Miranda*. She told me Marmaduke's on his way back here with Isabel.'

Garnet felt his gut wrench. 'So Miranda came to you again, did she? Not to me. You won't be happy until you dance on my grave, will you, old woman?'

Queenie did not deny it.

Garnet tried to save face. 'Anyway, I knew all that. I was just going to announce my change of plans. The wedding will be here in my chapel. I'm putting you in charge of the ceremony. I want the chapel perfect, polished to a shine. Make sure the blacksmith fixes that damned bell. And tell the priest he's to wear robes fit for a coronation.'

Queenie had the final word as she turned to leave. 'You're deluding yourself if you think Marmaduke will toe the line and marry there. If you want the chapel restored, get your mistress to do it. She must be good at *something*.'

Garnet knew the insult was deliberately timed because Elise had just appeared in the doorway beside Rhys Powell.

Several assigned servant girls hung at the fringe of the vestibule but Bridget was the only one who openly smirked at Queenie's barbed comment.

Garnet's secretary hurried to his side, carrying an armful of books, with a flushed and anxious Elise at his heels. Garnet was uncomfortably aware of the way his mistress watched him like a hawk, afraid he was building up to another manic episode. Although this surveillance was one of her paid duties, the anxiety in her eyes irritated him.

Anyone would think the bitch cared about me.

'Where the hell have you been, Powell? I gave you instructions to teach Elise the alphabet and write her name, not to read the bible from cover to cover.'

Elise looked so stricken Garnet instantly regretted humiliating her in front of the servants. It was his secretary who jumped to her rescue.

'Miss Elise is an avid pupil, sir. I am delighted by her progress and feel sure you will take pride in her accomplishments.'

Refusing to be mollified Garnet turned his anger on his servants. 'What are you gawking at? Back to your duties the lot of you. This house must be in perfect condition from top to bottom for my son's return. Every man Jack of you who falls down on the job gets shunted back to the Female Factory or the Prisoners' Barracks.'

He pointed at little Spotty Mary, who was quacking in her boots. 'You! Clean up this broken china.'

As Elise passed him at the foot of the stairs she tentatively touched his shoulder and said softly, 'I'll wait for you in my chamber, Garnet, dear. I must speak with you about a new gown for the wedding. I've nothing *á la mode* for such an important occasion.'

Garnet cut her short. 'Your job is to transform Miranda's chambers into the bridal suite.'

Elise coloured in embarrassment and lowered her voice. 'Miranda's room? But that's *my* room, Garnet.'

'*Was*. Miranda and I spent our honeymoon in that bed. So will Marmaduke. Clear out all your stuff.'

He turned to Powell. 'You. In my library. There's a fresh pile of mail. One has the Governor's seal. I knew there was no way the powers that be would ignore the arrival of a de Rolland in the Colony.'

Seated behind his desk Garnet weighed the envelope addressed to Miss Isabel de Rolland with a mixture of pleasure and frustration.

'No doubt it's an invitation, eh? I don't suppose there's any way you can open it without breaking the seal?'

Rhys Powell said stiffly, 'That's what a wax seal is designed to prevent, sir. To preserve state secrets and communications of a highly personal nature.'

'I know that!' Garnet snapped. 'All right. Read the rest of them.'

Edwin Bentleigh had written a polite reminder of Garnet's promise to concede the deeds of Mingaletta on his marriage.

'The man writes like the proverbial iron fist in the velvet glove,' Garnet grumbled. 'He continues to refuse to hand over the new papers before I've signed the deeds.'

'Why not, sir?'

'Because the man's no fool. He doesn't trust me!'

Rhys Powell looked taken aback. 'I see. Then how do you wish me to respond, sir?'

'Tell him he's to get himself down here for the banquet I'm giving for the best people in the county to meet our new bride. God knows Bentleigh's the only respectable friend Marmaduke has. I can't have the whole damned county thinking my son only hobnobs with gamblers, jockeys, libertines, actors and low life.'

The secretary coughed discreetly. 'Excuse me, sir, but what is the wedding date?'

'I haven't decided that yet. What's next?'

Rhys Powell read out a number of what Garnet derisively called 'begging letters' – requests from charities and institutions to which Garnet gave regular generous donations and a few on whose committees Garnet held a seat. He gave the nod to the Quaker Australian School Society.

'That big-noting philanthropist Sam Terry was elected to their committee so there's no bar to Emancipists there. Double his donation. Let's see if that draws an invitation.'

Garnet didn't hesitate to throw his weight behind plans for the new Sydney College.

'Keep an eye out for any newspaper reports. I won't support it unless it sticks to its charter to admit lads from poor families who've got the brains to make a go of education. Terry says the shareholders are flooded with applications, some from men who are in a position to *give* charity rather than claim a free education for their sons! Mean bastards!'

Rhys Powell tried to distract him. 'What a coincidence, sir. Here's a letter to you signed by the Worshipful Master of Lodge 260 – Samuel Terry no less.'

Garnet looked wary. 'What's he want?'

'To advise you he'll be pleased to nominate Marmaduke as a member of your lodge.'

'He will, will he? Write and thank him. In that case you'd best invite him and Rosetta to the banquet as well. They probably won't come, too hell-bent on making money, but it won't lower the tone to have the odd Emancipist amongst the gentry.'

Catching sight of his secretary's expression, Garnet said crisply, 'Next?'

'I'm the bearer of bad news, I'm afraid. A death in the family.'

'Not my lot. They're all long gone.'

'It's from a Mr Claude Appleby, one of your London lawyers.'

'An Emancipist's son. Tricky as hell, thank God. So who's snuffed it? If there's any justice it'll be Godfrey de Rolland.'

'Mr Appleby begs to inform you of the death of Martha de Rolland, Isabel's aunt who it seems was also her cousin.'

'Not surprising. They're so inbred they look like brothers and sisters. Marmaduke's the first fresh blood in their family for generations. They should pay *me* for his stud rights!'

'Mr Appleby states that the widower, Silas de Rolland, is in correspondence with His Excellency Governor Bourke's secretary, Mr Deas Thompson. The widower plans to visit this Colony at the end of his mourning period.'

Garnet was suddenly quiet. 'Hasn't taken the grasping bastard long to make his move. His wife is hardly cold.'

'I take it you know him well, sir?'

'Only too well. He was the manipulator that held up the marriage contract, kept demanding more money. Silas de Rolland was born with two faces. He loads the cannon for his uncle Godfrey to fire. I wouldn't trust him to put his big toe in the Pacific Ocean without trying to steal it.'

The secretary ventured a question. 'I take it your condolences are not required, sir?'

'Not likely! Instruct Appleby I want details of that man's every move. Silas is the rotten apple in the de Rolland barrel. Old Godfrey is the head of the clan and full of born-to-rule arrogance. But he has his own code of honour – his letter about Isabel's sleepwalking sickness proved his concern for her.'

Rhys Powell looked discomforted. 'Excuse me, sir, but I must remind you that is a letter that *you have not actually read.*'

Garnet was quick to respond. 'Quite right. You managed to reseal it?'

'I copied his handwriting on a fresh envelope.' Rhys confessed.

'Good man, you're getting the idea! We must keep one step ahead of those tricksters.' Garnet paused in the act of leaving the room to clap his secretary on the shoulder. 'You're not doing such a bad job, Powell.'

The young man quickly jumped to his feet, clearly unable to decide whether this was his master's lukewarm praise or a veiled insult.

Garnet remembered overhearing Powell say in bemusement to Elise, 'Australians have a strange way of distorting the English language.' It amused Garnet to leave the young man feeling unsettled.

You've got a lot to learn about us, boyo.

Garnet took the back stairs and, with Amaru the cockatoo perched on his shoulder, strode down the length of the picture gallery past the rigid faces of the ancestral portraits. All stared back expressionless. It was only Miranda who came vividly to life each time he gazed at her picture. Amaru was suddenly quiet as if he recognised the woman who taught him to speak.

'My beauty!' Garnet said under his breath. 'I don't believe you're gone. You're just out of sight, teasing me with the sound of your footsteps, the smell of your perfume. Well, your dream is at last coming true. Your beloved son will soon be home wedded and bedded with his bride. Time to relinquish your title, m'dear. Isabel will be the new mistress of Bloodwood Hall. I trust you'll make her feel welcome and not frighten the lass.'

He was distracted by strange sounds coming from the far end of the corridor.

Miranda's room.

Garnet pushed open the bedroom door, his breath tight in his chest, hoping to catch a trace of roses, proof that Miranda had just left the room. He saw a wisp of bridal veil in the mirror and thanked the God he had ceased to acknowledge since the hour of her death.

Miranda, you've come back to me at last.

The image grew clearer. His heart sank. Elise turned to face him, smiling coquettishly, her pale shoulders gleaming above the low neckline of the white satin gown, the pearl coronet pinned to the crown of her flowing auburn hair. He saw reflected in the mirror a slash of her naked back where the gown was unlaced. Beautiful, yet all wrong. He hated the sight of Elise in Miranda's bridal gown.

'What do you think you're doing?' he said quietly, his voice husky with disappointment.

'I wondered if it would still fit me? I couldn't resist trying it on.'

'You had your chance. Now it's Isabel's turn.'

'But darling, you promised I would be your bride.'

'There were conditions, remember?'

The layers of silk rustled as Elise moved towards him with intent, nestling her head against his chest, kissing his throat, her hands eager to arouse him to the state of passion she had always done, cleverly caressing his body as she began to undress him.

Garnet felt cold as he watched her. 'Are you with child?' he asked, knowing the answer.

'Not yet, I think. But the moon is with me. *Now* darling, take me now.'

Her mouth was hungry but he saw the need in her eyes was too calculating to be lust.

'Why now? Feel threatened, that Marmaduke's bride will give me the Gamble heir that you've failed to do?'

Elise bit into his shoulder in a desperate attempt to arouse him to the violent pitch of their lovemaking.

'No,' he said coolly. 'I'm not in the mood for that today.'

Her eyes flashed in anger and frustration. 'Garnet, give me a chance. How can I fall if you avoid my bed for weeks? I can do it – you know I can. I'm not barren. But you've taken to slipping downstairs to that slut Bridget. Do you think I don't know?'

Garnet didn't bother to deny it. 'That's always been my way. You knew that when you first came to my bed. I like variety. Nothing has changed. You wanted money more than any man's love. I give you what you want and take what *I* want, *wherever* I choose to find it.'

She grabbed hold of his shirt and shook him, helpless with rage. 'No other woman would do for you what I do!'

'You get well paid for it.' He pulled her hands away and pushed her off balance to fall on the bed. His question was polite. 'Are you hungry for more money now, Elise?'

'Why do you always talk of money? I come to you because I love you. I want nothing more than to give you a child.'

'To earn you a wedding ring, make you respectable,' he teased. 'All right. I've nothing better to do this afternoon. But first take off Miranda's wedding gown.' He added with a smile. 'You've grown too fat to wear it, m'dear.'

Elise's eyes widened as his words stung her with the memory they could never erase.

Garnet coldly watched her as she shed the bridal gown and left it lying in a silken heap on the floor. Then while his anger was still under his control he took her quickly, violently, without bothering to kiss or caress her. Coldly he observed the fear in her eyes, the realisation that her world was in danger of being stripped from her.

But fear aroused her lust and she swung her body up on top of him and took control, as if trying to force the essence of a child into her womb with each thrust of her body.

'Yes, yes! I will give you what you want. Another son. Better and stronger than that wastrel Marmaduke.'

His hands gripped her so hard she cried out, forced to break her rhythm.

'Don't you *dare* try to come between me and my son! My battle with Marmaduke is a private war. We may choose to fight to the death. But no woman – no slut – will ever come between us!'

Garnet was now total master and Elise cried out in pain and relief each time he mounted her.

At last he lay on his back, satiated, with Elise's limp body sprawled across him. His eyes were fixed on the closed bedroom door.

The memory would never die. That terrible look of confusion and pain in his son's eyes as Marmaduke burst through the door, crying out, 'Father, please help me, Elise has run away!' And then the dawning realisation on the lad's face as he froze in shock, standing at the foot of the bed, forced to see the whole truth – that his bride lay half-naked in Garnet's arms, wearing Miranda's wedding gown.

CHAPTER 23

'I don't believe what I'm seeing!' Isabel said in awe. Seated alone inside the carriage she moved back and forth between the open windows on either side trying to absorb the changing patterns of the bush landscape. 'This must be the way explorers feel when they discover new lands.'

There was nothing like seeing the bush *in situ*. In Sydney Town she had pored over books of botanical drawings that recorded in exquisite, microscopic detail hundreds of flowering plants, shrubs and species of native eucalypts, their leaves, blossoms, bark and seasonal changes. But nothing had prepared her for the sheer grandeur of the landscape or the magical transitions of scenery that kept unfolding like an endless giant tapestry. One moment she felt exhilarated by its beauty, the next so awed by the towering cliff faces, the impenetrable density of the bush that she felt God had reduced her to the size of an ant.

Discarding the veiling that Marmaduke had swathed around her hat to shield her from the red dust that rose from the convict-built road, Isabel thrust her head through the window and yelled into the face of the wind.

'Marmaduke! Tell Thomas to slow down. He's going too fast!'

The coach screeched to a halt so unexpectedly that Isabel was thrown to the floor.

Marmaduke stuck his head through the window. 'Get out! Be sick on the side of the road, but be quick about it!'

She jumped down onto the road unaided and brushed herself down. 'I'm not ill! Just frustrated. You've seen all this magnificent scenery before. But it's whizzing past me like a kaleidoscope!'

It was then she saw the pistol in Marmaduke's belt and the shotgun he was nursing and realised from his serious expression that the route to Bloodwood was not nearly as safe as she had been led to believe. She pointed at his firearms.

'You told me you were sitting beside Thomas to give him a spell from driving!'

'I lied,' he said. 'Hop back inside, soldier. There are reports bush-rangers are active in this locality. We need to reach the inn before sundown.'

'I don't suppose I could sit up there between you?' she asked hopefully.

'That was an order!'

Isabel barely had time to clamber back inside before Thomas cracked the whip and the team charged off again. She stretched out her legs to bolster herself against the opposite seat, reminded of Marmaduke's preoccupied mood since their departure. Was he unhappy to leave his 'sweet lady' behind in Sydney?

I could hardly blame him. Josepha St John is a fine figure of a woman.

Isabel had oddly ambiguous feelings about her wedding night. She remembered Marmaduke taking his leave before going to the theatre, no doubt to spend the night with his actress. Yet next morning Isabel had woken to find him seated by her bedside, holding her hand even in the depths of his sleep. How long had he been there? Feeling an unaccustomed sense of protection she had fallen asleep again. Next morning he had talked about the previous night's performance but in truth had he stayed by her bedside all night? And if so, why?

Isabel was relieved that Thomas was their driver on this long journey as he was unusually cheerful, glad to escape for a while from his outspoken de facto wife, a Currency Lass of whom he said, with rueful pride, 'My woman takes no lip from no one.'

Marmaduke had left his father's flashy landau behind in Sydney Town in readiness for their next visit, when it was expected Isabel would be invited to balls and assemblies at Government House.

The thought of her entrance into a world dominated by the colony's Top Thirteen families both attracted and worried her. She had never attended a ball and had little experience of the codes of Society outside the pages of Miss Austen's novels.

When they stopped at the Harp of Tyrone Isabel sank into a chair on the verandah, waving her handkerchief in a vain attempt to fan away the swarms of flies that stuck to her face as if she were a bowl of sugar.

Marmaduke idly snapped off a swatch of leaves from the branch of a eucalyptus tree and handed it to her with the laconic invitation, 'You'll find this works better.'

Isabel felt hot, tired and thirsty. 'Is it always so humid at this time of year?'

'You call *this* heat? You'd best get used to it. As Byron said, "What men call gallantry, and gods adultery, is much more common where the climate's sultry."'

Isabel recognised the quotation from *Don Juan.* 'I wonder how you libertines managed to seduce women before you had Lord Byron to quote?'

'Don't fret,' he assured her mildly. 'You're in no danger from me. If I'd had half a mind to seduce you I'd have done the deed long since.'

Isabel felt her cheeks burn with anger. 'You flatter yourself. You might prove irresistible to other men's wives, but your own wife is immune. You would be the last man in the world I would choose to take to *my* bed.'

The corner of Marmaduke's mouth twitched in that maddening half-smile. 'Methinks the lady doth protest *too* much.'

Isabel felt triumphant. 'That's a common misquotation. Queen Gertrude's actual line to Hamlet is, "The lady doth protest too much, *methinks.*" You'll find it in Act III Scene II.'

'I stand corrected,' he said amiably. 'It's nice to know we at least have one love in common – Shakespeare.'

That evening Marmaduke ordered dinner to be sent to her room but left her to her own devices. Isabel checked the door between their adjoining rooms, satisfied that the key was on her side of the lock. Marmaduke no doubt would spend the evening in the saloon drinking, talking politics with the local settlers and championing Governor Bourke's radical policies.

Isabel eyed the locked trunks in frustration – Marmaduke held the keys. Exploration of her new trousseau, made by Madame Hortense, would have to wait. She curled up on the bed to read the backlog of English newspapers, surprised by the weight of evidence that time in the Northern Hemisphere had not stood still. Wars, assassinations, revolutions, famines, royal births, deaths and marriages were covered by lurid headlines and often by a style of bombastic, jingoistic journalism far removed from normal speech. One minute Isabel felt a wave of nostalgia for Home, the next emotionally divorced from events that were some four months old by the time they arrived here and by now could well be reversed.

From the Colony's newspapers she absorbed every detail of bloodthirsty murder trials, a notice of Rupert Grantham's accusation of libel, bushrangers' bail-ups of homesteads and lone travellers and the Government *Gazette*'s accounts of Governor Bourke's battle to implement new statutes in the face of opposition from the Exclusives faction.

There were columns of advertisements for everything from China tea to thoroughbred horses, dates of auctions of newly arrived cargo that Isabel now knew was often English stolen property. She looked wistfully at the list of shipping arrivals, hoping that if her contract worked out, it would one day list a ship bearing Aunt Elisabeth and Rose Alba.

Alerted by the *Sydney Herald*'s account of the daring exploits of a bushranger active in the Bloodwood locality, Isabel hurried downstairs to the men's saloon where Marmaduke sat in his shirtsleeves, drinking with Thomas and two rough, loud-mouthed Colonials. Marmaduke looked as much at ease as if he'd known them all his life.

She was struck by the thought that though he placed heavy demands on Thomas's time he did not draw the traditional line between master and servant.

At the sight of her Marmaduke sprang up and steered her out into the corridor.

'This saloon is strictly for blokes. Not one of your sleepy English villages where the farmers have known each other since 1066. Some of these old lags haven't set eyes on a white woman in months. They're tanked up with enough grog to float the Royal Navy. When they fancy a girl they don't take "no" for an answer. Understand me?'

'Perfectly.' Isabel was inwardly shaken but thrust the newspaper at him.

'I thought your father might be in danger.'

Marmaduke frowned as he scanned the report. 'Yeah. That sounds like Paddy Whickett, the bloke who's sworn vengeance on all landowners who've brutalised their convicts. So that makes my father a likely candidate. I only hope I reach Garnet in time to get the deeds to Mingaletta signed.'

Marmaduke ignored her shocked reaction. 'I'll join you upstairs in a minute. There are things you need to know about Garnet before we hit Bloodwood.'

It was a full hour before he entered her bedchamber wearing a sheepish expression and nursing a bottle of wine. He was far from drunk but wine had made him friendly.

'I just cleaned up at cards. A Royal Flush won me a prize bull. He'll come in handy to service a mob of cows when I stock Mingaletta.'

Isabel refused his offer of wine and took the lead. 'So what's the mystery? I know next to nothing about your family. If you expect me to give a convincing performance as your adoring bride, I need to know what kind of audience I'm playing to.'

Marmaduke helped himself to a drink. 'Righto, Garnet Gamble in a nutshell. He's a born bully, seasoned womaniser, crooked businessman, feared tyrant hated by his assigned men. And, in terms of the law, he's as devious as Machiavelli.' He added wryly, 'And that's Garnet's *good* side.'

'Surely you're biased. I'm not a child. I need to know how your father will react when he realises my family cheated him, sending him tainted goods?'

Marmaduke didn't bother to offer a polite denial. 'Don't worry. To Garnet you're the genuine blue-blooded article, that's all that matters to a man desperate for acceptance by the Quality. His CP – conditional pardon – means he can never return to the Mother England that chucked him out. But didn't your family warn you about Garnet's history?'

'They told *me* nothing. Except it was my role to preserve the family honour. For Heaven's sake, Marmaduke, I have the right to know. I told you the truth about *my* shame!'

He took a swig of his wine. 'The truth is Garnet Gamble is quite mad.'

'Oh, is that all?' she said relieved. 'The British aristocracy's rife with it. Uncle Godfrey's friend is an earl whose poodles dine off gold plates at his banquet table.'

'No. Garnet's not one of your amusing eccentrics beloved by the English. He suffers periodic fits of violent insanity. If he wasn't the second richest man in the Colony, free to buy protection, he'd be carted off to a lunatic asylum and they'd throw away the key.'

Isabel felt faint. 'I don't believe you.'

'You will soon enough. Garnet's not the only entrepreneur in the Colony whose condition is tolerated. No doubt you've heard of John Macarthur? One of our most powerful "pure merinos", the man many said was responsible for Governor Bligh being removed from office. Y'know, William Bligh of the *Bounty* Mutiny fame? Macarthur's imbalance was common knowledge for years but it didn't prevent his election to the Legislative Council. Until finally Governor Bourke was pressured to remove him on the grounds that Macarthur had been "pronounced a lunatic and there was little hope of his restoration".'

Isabel was so stunned she felt her tongue cleave to the roof of her mouth.

'But I understood your father is a brilliant entrepreneur.'

Marmaduke shrugged. 'He is – between times. Why should that surprise you? Poor old George III was totally lucid between his bouts of insanity and much loved by the people, but that didn't prevent his son becoming Regent when His Maj was locked from sight.'

Isabel managed to ask, 'Exactly how ill is your poor father?'

'I don't claim Garnet's that far gone yet but there's no known cure and the quacks can't predict just how crazy he'll end up. It's said that Macarthur's insanity is the legacy of Cape fever he picked up in the port of Cape Town years ago. Maybe Garnet also copped a dose of that when he was transported. Who knows? He won't talk about his months on the *Fortune,* a hell ship from the sound of it.' With a note of bitter irony, Marmaduke added, 'So now you know why I vowed never to marry. No woman will ever give birth to a child of mine. Garnet's dynasty will die with me.'

'But you're bad, not mad,' she said without thinking. 'Forgive me. That was cruel.'

'But accurate. Madness is a matter of degree. I have some of the same symptoms – a violent temper and periodic melancholia. I'm told Garnet appeared to be perfectly sane as a young man when he married

Mother, but it's a progressive disease. I don't intend to live long enough to be locked away. Before I reach that stage...' He pointed his finger like a pistol at his temple and mimed pulling the trigger. 'Sorry to be blunt. I'll tell you what you need to know for your survival.'

Isabel asked quickly, 'Survival from your father or from you?'

'You're in no danger at *my* hands, Isabel. At least not for the brief term of our contract. So let's enjoy life while we can, eh?'

He attempted a short laugh but she saw how his hands twitched with nerves.

'I should also warn you about Bloodwood Hall. Terrible things have happened there, leaving their imprint on every stone. Some claim the place is haunted. I don't. But for me it harbours nothing but bad memories. We must stay under Garnet's roof until the deeds to Mingaletta are handed over. Not an hour longer. I hate the damned house so much if it were mine I'd burn it to the ground.' On a swift change of mood he added lightly, 'That's enough true confessions for one night. I reckon I could use another drink. Care to join me?'

This time Isabel readily agreed. When he filled her glass she lightly touched his hand.

'Marmaduke, I can't pretend to like you. But I want you to know one thing. You're in no danger of betrayal at my hands. I am your ally for as long as it takes.'

Marmaduke looked at her long and hard before he said at last, 'Thank you, soldier.'

It was late afternoon the following day when Thomas drew the horses to a halt and spoke to Isabel out of the corner of his mouth.

'The Garnet and Rose is Bloodwood's only safe inn. It's owned by Mr Gamble Senior. Rival shanties would cut your throat for a ha'penny.'

'Thanks for the reference, Thomas,' Marmaduke said dryly, 'but there's no need to scare my bride out of her wits.'

Bloodwood Village sat on a rise overlooking Scavengers Creek. Ramshackle wooden buildings had mushroomed up out of the bush along a single street that dissected the hamlet like the crooked spine of a hunchback. To Isabel, this was civilisation after hours of charging through dense eucalypt forests devoid of any sign of human habitation.

Marmaduke wagged a warning finger. 'Do me a favour. Don't wander off!'

Before Isabel had time to snap back a reply he stalked off in the direction of the Garnet and Rose. It was clear her father-in-law left his stamp on everything he touched.

Marmaduke returned holding the reins of two horses, one with a lady's sidesaddle, the other with two saddlebags.

'I want to show you Mingaletta before we confront Garnet. Thomas can stay here and bring the carriage tomorrow. Of course, if you're not up to riding a horse?'

Isabel had little experience with horses but there was no way she was going to appear a helpless female. 'Why wait? I could go on all night.'

Marmaduke helped her mount the bay mare, positioned her on the lady's side-saddle, checked her stirrups then mounted the stallion carrying their saddlebags and took the lead crossing the bridge across Scavengers Creek.

A few miles on they passed a grand house set a half mile back from the road.

'That's our nearest neigbour, Penkivil Park,' Marmaduke said laconically. 'Owner's a military officer. We often got invited there in Mother's day. Now the Gambles are *persona non grata*.'

Over the next half hour as the light faded they followed a narrow zig-zag track crowded by overhanging branches. Isabel cried out in excitement at the sight of a huge lizard she recognised from a drawing. She gasped when it opened its mouth in a ferocious leer.

'Look, isn't that a goanna?'

Marmaduke barely gave it a glance. 'Yeah, good tucker. When I was a kid the tribes who passed through Mingaletta roasted goannas under hot coals in pits. It's called lazybed cooking. The blacks took a shine to me. I shared their bush tucker, unknown to Garnet.'

'Why? Didn't he like them?'

'Who? The goannas or the blacks?' Marmaduke gave a snort. 'Neither. Garnet ran the blacks off his land. Mother couldn't prevent that but she threatened to leave him if he fired a shot at them. As for goannas, Garnet was hell-bent on raising me to be a gentleman and in his book gents don't eat bush tucker. But I'm grateful for what the blacks taught me. If I'm ever lost in the bush I'd never starve.'

He glanced at her over his shoulder. 'I'd take you camping on a bivouac, teach you how to cook snake and 'roo and eat live witchety grubs but I reckon an English girl wouldn't have the stomach for it.'

'Anything you can do, *I can do*,' Isabel snapped.

'I just might take you up on that!'

Recognising the innuendo in his voice, Isabel turned her head to conceal her blush.

They passed a drystone wall that reminded Isabel of the traditional borders of the fields beyond de Rolland Park. Here the land had clearly fallen into misuse.

Isabel was startled by the bizarre sight at the heart of it. Standing in splendid isolation against the sky was a cone-shaped tower built of variegated stones.

'Good Heavens, that looks like the sort of folly you'd find in one of Capability Browne's landscaped gardens.'

'It's a copy. That chimney over there is the ruins of an Indian bungalow built by my grandfather. He was a retired British Army colonel whose heart remained with the Raj in India. When Mother married she moved to Garnet's adjoining property but *her* heart remained on Mingaletta. The colonel survived years of warfare only to be defeated by a bank. He neglected to tell Mother her dowry, Mingaletta, was mortgaged to the hilt. When he went bankrupt he took the coward's way out. Shot himself through the heart. Father bought Mingaletta from the bank. That's how the deeds to Mother's land were swallowed up by Bloodwood Hall under Garnet's name.'

'What a tragic story. But if Heaven exists, and I believe it does, your mother will be happy to see Mingaletta back in your hands at last.'

Marmaduke's face darkened. 'Mother was *never* happy. She was married to Garnet.'

Isabel felt the force of his suppressed rage as she rode behind him towards a miniature garden fenced off by the kind of wrought-iron lace Isabel had seen on Sydney terrace houses. It was then Isabel saw it. The tombstone carved with a plump cherub. She followed in Marmaduke's footsteps to read the weathered stone inscription.

HERE LIES THE BELOVED WIFE OF GARNET GAMBLE
MIRANDA
BORN FORT WILLIAM, CALCUTTA
DIED AGE 36 AT BLOODWOOD HALL 1825
IN THE ARMS OF HER HUSBAND
ALSO
THEIR INFANT
MAY ANGELS GUARD THEIR RESTING PLACE

'In the arms of her husband – that's a joke!' Marmaduke said coldly. 'Mother only stayed with Garnet because the damned law grants custody of a child to its father. If *I*'d been born dead she would have been free to leave him.'

Isabel had no words to lance the pain she realised, with shock, had festered inside him for years.

Embarrassed by his outburst, Marmaduke's mood changed like quicksilver. 'Come, soldier,' he said lightly. 'We'll take a short cut through the Gamble family cemetery – not afraid of ghosts, are you?'

Isabel bit her lip at the sudden flood of childhood memories of the Other that had broken through the borders of reality the day she had seen the ghost of Henri de Rolland leap to his death.

She shivered at the sight of graves that perhaps were linked to the ghosts said to haunt Bloodwood Hall. Would she attract them, too? And would she even *know* they were ghosts?

Despite her anxiety she was moved by the knowledge that Miranda Gamble had not been buried here, but on her own land, Mingaletta.

The little graveyard was shielded by a windbreak of fir trees. Marmaduke halted the horses but remained in the saddle. He gestured to a mausoleum built in the style of a small Greek temple complete with pediment and Doric columns.

'Garnet controls every aspect of life and death. He's obsessed with building things bigger and flashier than anyone else. He designed this ready for his final journey, dictated his own inscription to the stone-mason. All that remains to be added is the date of his death. Even Father can't control that!'

The mausoleum made Isabel distinctly uneasy. Nightfall had

appeared like a sleight of hand. The Australian bush was eerie enough by day but terrifying by night. There was no long English twilight to soften the transition. She froze. Was it a trick of the full moon? Or was there a light shining through the door of Garnet Gamble's tomb?

Isabel's throat was so tight she could barely ask the question. 'What's that light?'

'Let's hope it's Father's ghost!' Marmaduke said lightly.

As they approached on foot, Isabel instinctively drew closer to him. Her breath came fast as if she had been running. The atmosphere felt thick with acrid emotion. She peered around Marmaduke's shoulder, shielded from sight but able to see through the aperture. Light flickered from an oil lamp that threw ghastly shadows around the burial chamber. Isabel felt the hair bristling up on the back of her neck.

Kneeling beside a stone sarcophagus was an old woman dressed in an orange sari. Her rasping chant sounded too malevolent to be a prayer. Unaware of them watching her she took the lamp and hurried off down a path where the night concealed her from sight.

'That's Queenie, my old nanny. She blames Garnet for Mother's death. She comes here to pray for *his* death.'

Isabel was shocked into silence. *I don't doubt evil things did happen here. I can sense the aura of hatred in this place.*

'I'll introduce you to Queenie tomorrow. No need to be afraid of her. She was Mother's faithful servant since they were children in India. She's as tiny as an elf, but she protected mother like a warrior. Queenie's the one person strong enough to call Garnet's bluff. I'd trust her with my life.'

Isabel was exhausted. The previous night and the past weeks had produced a chain of revelations so complex she felt too weary to make sense of them.

'Journey's end. Home, sweet home,' Marmaduke announced with undisguised sarcasm. In the distance the outline of Bloodwood Hall loomed up through a slit in the dank mist that sealed off the valley. She knew it wasn't the chill night air or the shadows cast by the full moon that caused her to shiver. It was an instinctive sense of foreboding.

When they passed through a pair of iron gates the sound of their closing left Isabel in an acute panic, as if a dungeon door had clanged shut to imprison her.

Bloodwood Hall seemed to rear out of the darkness.

The Gothic stone mansion was blanched by moonlight. For a moment she lost all sense of time and place. Was she sleepwalking in a nightmare? Was she really here in this godforsaken Colony?

Marmaduke sprang to her side. 'What's wrong? You're deathly pale.'

Her words tumbled out beyond her control. 'My God! Don't you know? This isn't *your* family home – it's *ours*! It's a replica of de Rolland Park!'

Overcome by a sickening wave of nausea Isabel reeled backwards. Marmaduke caught her in his arms.

Isabel stirred and her eyes focused on a flash of silver. Marmaduke's flask touched her lips and the brandy gave her a pleasurable burning sensation, proof she was still alive. She lay on the lawn swathed in Marmaduke's greatcoat, his arm firmly around her shoulders.

'You've had quite a shock, *déjà vu* gone crazy. This place is so bloody Gothic and English I always thought it was just a hodge-podge of Garnet's ideas of Gothic Revival. How was I to know he had recreated your ancestral home? Now his obsession makes sense. I take it this is a dead-ringer?' At Isabel's frown he translated, 'Identical.'

Isabel was still bewildered. 'It's slightly smaller in scale. Seven bays instead of nine. And the stone seems warmer in colour. But it's a remarkable copy. The same Gothic lines, chimneys, balconies, gables; the castellated widow's walk. Why would your father go to such trouble to recreate the house of a family he didn't even know?'

Marmaduke raised one eyebrow. 'Didn't your illustrious family tell you *anything*?'

'Do you mean to say he actually knew my family?'

'Knew 'em? He was their servant. Godfrey was the bloke who had him transported.'

Isabel was appalled. 'Oh my God! How your father must hate us.'

Marmaduke's head was so close to hers she could feel his breath against her cheek.

'You can't stop now, Marmaduke. Why was he transported?'

'He was a go-between, carrying love letters from Godfrey's sister to her lover—'

'Aunt Elisabeth!' Isabel was shocked at how easily the pieces fell into place. She told him how her guardian had cut his sister off without a penny after her unsuitable marriage.

Marmaduke nodded. 'That fits. When Godfrey de Rolland discovered Garnet's role in the plot he had him arrested for theft. False evidence was provided by Silas de Rolland. The magistrate accepted an aristocrat's word against his illiterate servan'st – surprise, surprise! That's how young George copped fourteen years for the "theft" of a ring he claims Elisabeth gave him as a gift of thanks. That garnet ring earned Father his Australian nickname, Garnet.'

Isabel was stunned by her family's role in Garnet Gamble's downfall.

'So why was he so determined to buy a de Rolland bride for you?'

'Don't you see? Garnet grabbed his destiny with both hands. Despite being illiterate his sharp business practices built his fortune. By hook and *definitely* by crook he recreated the world he had envied in England. You represent Garnet's sublime act of revenge. A convicted felon has saved from debtor's prison the man who had him transported. And gained a trophy – a wife for his son. Garnet triumphed. He made the de Rolland family eat dirt!'

'Yes, but my family had their own revenge by sending me!' she said bitterly.

'Nonsense. Your blood's still blue, isn't it? Let's get you ready to make your big entrance.'

Marmaduke grabbed her by the hand and ran with her to the front door. Standing before the lion's-head doorknocker, he paused to whisper his final instructions.

'Don't forget, soldier. Keep your intense dislike of me for when we're alone. In public lie through your teeth. Lay it on thick. You *adore* me!'

CHAPTER 24

The entrance to the Gamble mansion was a pair of massive timber doors surmounted by an elaborate fanlight. Marmaduke presumed this must be a replica of de Rolland Park's doorway except that it was crowned with the entwined letters *GG*. The brass doorknocker bore the head of the Royal Lion of England.

Marmaduke saw himself as a toddler in Queenie's arms playing the game in which he roared like a lion before he rapped the lion's head. Linked to the echo of Queenie's laughter, this was a rare happy memory in a house full of dark secrets.

Like a child 'whistling in the dark' to give himself courage, Marmaduke again roared like a lion. The door was opened by Bridget.

'It's you! Ye scared the living daylights out of me. We've been living in fear of bushrangers coming to overhaul us.'

Marmaduke handed her the saddlebags. 'No need to announce our arrival, Bridget. Show *Mrs Gamble* to her room and help her change. Assist her in every way she requires.'

He planted a light kiss on Isabel's cheek. 'Welcome to our *humble* home, Isabel.'

Bridget looked Isabel over before addressing Marmaduke. 'The master's in the green drawing room.'

Marmaduke crossed the marble floor of the atrium that lay between the east and west wings of the house. Glancing up at the windows of the second-storey picture gallery, he fancied that the painted ancestral faces were eyeing his progress.

The predicted storm had broken. Flashes of sheet lightning bathed everything through the domed skylight that straddled the atrium, throwing into relief the sandstone walls and indented alcoves framing Greek statues of naked Olympians and half-naked goddesses. Alternating pedestals held urns of tropical ferns with withered fronds that never thrived.

Nothing will ever enjoy health and happiness in this accursed house.

At the far end of the atrium Marmaduke squared his shoulders before throwing open the double doors. He knew exactly what lay ahead of him.

The green drawing room was exactly as Marmaduke remembered. The décor was so grandiose that Napoleon Bonaparte himself would not have looked out of place. Except that the Emperor's N was substituted by the double G emblazoned on every conceivable space – marble fireplace, tapestry backs of French Empire chairs, etched on crystal and silverware.

The powerful, broad-shouldered figure of Garnet Gamble stood poised before the fireplace, wineglass in hand.

Framed in the doorway Marmaduke announced himself in ringing tones. 'Your black sheep has returned, Garnet. I am the bearer of glad tidings that will surprise even you! My marriage to Isabel is *fait accompli.*'

'I knew that! Nothing escapes my network of informants, boyo. I presume you brought me the marriage certificate?'

Marmaduke presented it with a flourish but Garnet scowled at the unfamiliar document.

'What's this? It isn't a marriage certificate.'

'Same thing. A Quaker certificate of commitment. It's perfectly legal.'

'Quakers! They're the weird mob who practise temperance!'

'They're the mob who are respected pacifists and do great humanitarian work among the poor, in prisons,' he added, 'and lunatic asylums.'

Garnet stiffened at the reference. 'Well, where is our bride?'

Isabel stood at the top of the stairs her head held high, one lace mitten holding the balustrade. Marmaduke watched her descend in silence.

The girl who had gone upstairs travel-stained, tired and cranky now seemed to radiate sunlight. The buttercup yellow gown was trimmed with white rosebuds cleverly placed to compensate for her small bosom. The flickering light of the chandelier's oil lamps sent golden arrows darting across the silken folds and the creamy flesh of her shoulders. Her tiny waist was so inviting Marmaduke had a strong impulse to encircle it with his hands.

Her centre-parted hair gave equal balance to the side curls hanging in ringlets. Her pale face and wide green eyes held the fear she was trying valiantly to mask. She wore no jewellery except her wedding ring and Mendoza's little gold pendant. Isabel didn't need any further adornment. She took his breath away.

'Well? You designed it. Is it what you expected?' she asked.

'You'll do,' he said.

Marmaduke cupped her elbow in one hand and steered her through the double doors. Isabel's steps faltered at sight of the atrium.

'My God, your father even recreated this! There's Mercury and Diana and—'

'Never mind paying tribute to the gods. Plenty of time for a tour of inspection later.'

He paused before the closed doors that led to the green drawing room. Isabel looked so lovely, so vulnerable he felt unaccountably moved to snap at her.

'Isabel, you disobeyed my orders. I distinctly told you a woman's body must breathe. Corsets are *verboten*!'

'I – am – not – wearing – one!' she hissed at him through clenched teeth, awkwardly pulling her neckline higher.

'For God's sake *will* you stop doing that?' Marmaduke ordered. 'You're not facing the Mother Superior of a convent.' He gave her bodice a sharp tweak downwards that caused the gentle curve of her breasts to blossom above the rosebuds.

'What's wrong *now*?' she asked in annoyance. 'Why are you looking at me like that?'

'You're so pale, you look like you've seen the family ghost.'

'What did you expect? You made your father sound like a vampire.'

'You look as if you've just given your blood to one.' He touched her cheek with one finger. 'You need more colour, too late for a touch of rouge. May I?'

He took her face between both hands and kissed her mouth deeply and demandingly until he felt her body give that delightful tremor he knew was the sign of a woman caught between surprise and surrender.

Isabel broke free, flushed and very angry.

Marmaduke took a step backwards to gain the full effect.

'Yeah, that's better. You now look more like a lusty bride than a bride of Christ.'

'You insufferable pig!' she hissed.

Marmaduke dodged as her hand swung out to strike him full in the face, but right at that moment the doors were flung open by Garnet. Isabel's hand changed course, curling into a loving gesture to rearrange Marmaduke's stock.

Her eyes gazed adoringly up at him. Her voice purred, 'Marmaduke, I don't know how you ever managed to tie your stock before you married me...there! Now you are quite perfect, my darling.'

Marmaduke watched in admiration her touching portrayal of a startled faun as she faced Garnet. She sank into a deep curtsey and stretched out her hand to her father-in-law.

'I don't feel we need a formal introduction. You could be none other than the master of Bloodwood Hall, Mr Gamble. You have no idea how I have been *longing* to meet you.'

Marmaduke noted that just for once his father's smile was genuine. Garnet's expression as he bent to kiss her hand told Marmaduke all he wanted to know.

Eureka! The manipulative bastard has taken the bait!

The moment Isabel entered through the portal of the green drawing room and confronted Garnet Gamble, she knew she had irretrievably passed into another world. Another life. The wedding had been a sham. *This* was the reality. And what a reality!

Her ancestral home possessed any number of impressive chambers but ever since her fall from grace she had been virtually confined to the limited world of Agnes's quarters, the estate's gardens and Uncle Godfrey's library.

The size and grandeur of the Gamble assembly room dazzled her. It was not furnished in the exact style of the original but it had, for Isabel, one huge advantage. She would be free to enter it at will for as long as she remained under this roof. She tried to conceal her hunger to explore its treasures – the antique furniture, gilt-framed paintings, marble-topped occasional tables, sofas and chairs arranged in conversational clusters. Individually elegant French, English and Austrian Biedermeier examples were placed in juxtaposition with exotic pieces she recognised were imported from China and India, Britain's 'jewel in the crown'.

What if Garnet's style is nouveau riche? *Who cares?*

Massive mirrors on opposite sides of the room reflected them from different angles and it seemed to Isabel that these 'mirror people' watched her every move. At the far end of the room French windows opened onto a garden blackened by night. Rain fell in filmy diagonal sheets; the garden statues, were silver-etched by lightning.

Despite all its opulence it was Garnet Gamble who dominated the room. His voice lacked the deep rich timbre of Marmaduke's and in subtle ways it betrayed his lack of education. But the silver-haired Gamble was craggily handsome, virile and, although he was not as tall as Marmaduke, his posture was erect, his tailcoat immaculately tailored, *his* stock perfectly tied. The charm and power he radiated were undeniable.

'Dear boy, you did not exaggerate the treasure you brought home for me.'

The master of Bloodwood Hall embraced his son but Isabel noticed that Marmaduke's arms remained stiffly by his sides.

Garnet instantly took control. He slipped Isabel's hand through his arm and drew her down beside him on a Regency striped sofa clearly designed to be shared by two lovers.

'Marmaduke knows my preference for Garnet, the name he called me as a little chap. It amused me and became a habit. I trust you'll feel comfortable calling me Garnet, m'dear?'

'Of course, whatever pleases you…Garnet.'

'What a homecoming this is, eh? The linking of our two families under my roof. I could almost forgive my son for his impetuosity. Young blood, eh?'

Marmaduke's voice was equally silky but no less firm as he took hold of Isabel's trembling hand.

'My whirlwind courtship is in the Gamble tradition, Garnet. Isn't that how you won Mother's heart despite opposition from her father?'

Isabel noticed Garnet's rapid change of expression – veiled surprise, a flicker of suspicion and suppressed anger.

Garnet's a father who won't tolerate being outflanked by his son. But what has Marmaduke done to upset him? They speak in code.

Garnet's hollow laugh sounded ambiguous. 'Ah, so you have inherited my wild streak of passion, m'boy. But tell me, Isabel, how did you find Sydney Society?'

Marmaduke launched into a story clearly designed to forestall Isabel's answer.

'You should have seen the sensation Isabel created at a ball for the Exclusives at Henrietta Villa, surrounded by Bourke's Government officials and military officers all drawn to that rarest of Colonial treasures – a virtuous young English rose from an Old Family.'

Isabel struggled to look suitably modest. *What a bald-faced liar he is. What ball? But I must admit he's ingenious. In one sentence he's confirmed my virginity, had Sydney Town's Quality at my feet and made our grubby little contract sound like the romance of the century.*

Garnet smiled paternally. Or was there some other motivation? 'I welcome my new daughter with open arms. This house has been too long deprived of the sound of children's laughter. May you honour me with many grandsons, m'dear.'

Isabel chose her words with care. 'I hope to have many children to honour *my husband.*'

Garnet laughed in surprised approval. 'A lady born with the gift of diplomacy. Breeding tells. We have chosen wisely.'

Isabel was startled by a female voice from the doorway.

'Many children? What surprise have you in store for us this time, Marmaduke?'

'May I introduce you to my bride, Elise?' Marmaduke replied.

Isabel was startled. *Who is this woman? Where does she fit into the family picture?*

She felt a pang of envy. The lush beauty reminded her of a full-blown rose. Her bare shoulders gleamed in the candlelight that highlighted her rich auburn hair and the silken folds of her emerald gown. She appeared to be in her late twenties and had clearly spent her life avoiding the harsh Australian sunlight. Her complexion had the unnatural pallor esteemed by ladies of Quality – and the French courtesans who rubbed their complexion with arsenic.

The unknown beauty crossed gracefully to give Marmaduke a familial kiss.

Isabel watched Garnet take command of the formal introductions.

So this is my cue to exchange a curtsey with her – whoever she is. I suspect she's Garnet's lover and mistress of the house. She clearly resents me. I must watch my step.

'I am delighted to meet you, Elise,' she said, glad her thoughts were inaudible.

Elise's smile faltered but she recovered quickly. 'Welcome, my dear. Bloodwood Hall has become such a man's world in recent years I've been quite lonely for a woman's company. I trust we *shall* become warm friends.'

Garnet eyed them all as if enjoying some private pleasure.

'Isabel, I have been saving a special vintage wine in the hope of *living long enough* to celebrate my son's marriage. If you'll excuse me I will retrieve it from under lock and key.'

He had scarcely left the room when Elise broke into a lament about the inferior quality of Colonial servants. 'You can't trust assigned servants. Once a thief, always a thief. They're all lazy and disobedient and have no idea of their place.'

Since her arrival Isabel had seen evidence of the disparity between English servants born to service and convict assigned servants. It seemed to her like a form of slavery.

'I understand they work the same long hours as our paid servants in England but receive nothing for their labour except food and clothing.'

'It takes time to understand how The System works,' Elise said, then pouted prettily at Marmaduke. 'How mean you are to deny me the pleasure of arranging your wedding.'

Marmaduke's tone was dangerously polite. 'I thought weddings bored you, Elise. No doubt Garnet will find some other entertainment to amuse you.'

Isabel's head was pounding like a drum. *Doesn't anyone in this family actually say what they mean? Why is Marmaduke so hostile to Elise? Because she's usurped his mother's place?'*

Elise quickly resumed her helpless little-girl demeanour. 'I suppose I must be content to be Garnet's hostess at our banquet to introduce Isabel to the local gentry.' She turned to Isabel. 'But I imagine you find our Colonial Society quite dull after London, do you not?'

Isabel faltered. *I can hardly admit my experience of London society was confined to a theatre box at Covent Garden.*

To her relief Marmaduke came to her rescue. 'Allow me to explain the finer points of the System, Isabel. In addition to inheriting your rigid English class system we have over here Settlers who arrive on assisted passages or armed with money to invest in land. More than a third of us are transportees – a complex new" convict class" ranging from prisoners, to old lags who've done their time, to ticket-of-leave men free to work for wages. Then there are the Emancipists, those granted a full pardon at His Excellency's pleasure or like Garnet – pardoned on condition they never darken Britain's doors again.'

Isabel was relieved Marmaduke had just briefed her about her new world but the anxiety in Elise's eyes made her wonder if he had broken some conversational taboo.

Marmaduke continued on. 'Wealthy Emancipists leap-frog from class to class to do business with the Quality, join the Masonic brethren, sit on juries and even on the boards of banks. But Heaven help their sons and daughters if they try to mingle convict bloodlines with the Exclusives'. In a nutshell, Isabel, we all tend to marry – at our own level.'

Elise looked nervous. 'Goodness, Marmaduke, you'll have Isabel thinking we're all of us – free or bond – confined in a rigid class prison.'

'I'm surprised you haven't noticed, Elise. We *are*!'

Marmaduke's eyes were gentle as he slipped his arm around Isabel's waist. 'But believe me, I would have tried to win this girl's heart if she had been a kitchen maid.'

Garnet Gamble made a larger than life entrance. 'Spoken like a true gallant! I didn't know you had it in you, Marmaduke. The special wine is in hand. Dinner is ready.'

Marmaduke turned to his father. 'Perhaps we should give dinner a miss tonight, Garnet. Isabel has been on the road since dawn. We'd welcome retiring early.'

'Whenever you wish, darling,' Isabel responded with an adoring look. *Damn you Marmaduke, I'm starving!*

The Master of the house gave a knowing laugh. 'Ah! The siren call of young love! But first allow me the pleasure of your bride's company at dinner.'

At Marmaduke's nod Isabel accepted her father-in-law's arm to escort her in to the dining room.

Garnet seated the bride at his right hand and the bridegroom at this left with Elise at the foot of the table looking petulant. Garnet was a jovial host. After the first course, on a note of triumph, he announced to Isabel, 'Things move fast in the Colony, m'dear. Your arrival has already been noted in the highest circles. A letter with the vice-regal seal awaits you in my office.'

Marmaduke said languidly, 'Isabel and I plan to divide our time between Sydney Town and Mingaletta, after you find time to sign those papers, Garnet.'

The provocative words drew a heavy silence that Garnet broke. 'Patience, m'boy. Bentleigh has all that in hand. I'll make the formal announcement at the banquet. This one will be a special joy to me – a banquet to welcome our bride!'

Isabel gritted her teeth. Our *bride again! Anyone would think we were polygamists.* 'I shall gladly share your destiny wherever you choose to live, Marmaduke. As the biblical Ruth said to Naomi, "Whither thou goest, I will go also."'

Elise looked sulky. Isabel could see the wine had turned her head when she switched her attention to Marmaduke.

'You once told me that destiny was...what did you call it? A fabrication of the mind?'

'That was before I met Isabel. A pretty face is fine and dandy as our American cousins would say. But it can't compete with an intelligent mind and a faithful heart. I was lucky enough to marry the only woman I have ever met who combines all three attributes.'

Marmaduke raised his glass in silent tribute to Isabel.

Garnet's watchful gaze reminded Isabel of the falcon trained for the hunt by Cousin Silas before he grew bored with the sport and the bird suddenly died.

By the third bottle of wine Garnet was expansive. 'Tonight you and your bride will sleep in the Rose bedchamber. Miranda's four-poster bed, where you were born, lad!'

Isabel read the look of cold horror in Marmaduke's eyes. *Oh God, wasn't that also his mother's deathbed? How could Garnet be so callous?*

Marmaduke stepped in. 'We would not dream of evicting Elise from her bed, Garnet.'

'Nonsense. You will please your father on this one small point, eh, Marmaduke? I am sure your dear mother would want you to begin your life together in her bed.'

Marmaduke's face was drained of all emotion. All evening Isabel had tried to remain aloof from the undercurrent running between Garnet, his mistress and his son. Yet their emotions were so strong they felt like currents passing through her body en route to their target.

Exhausted from trying to steer clear of their tangled web she instinctively touched Garnet's hand. 'I am deeply touched by your generous welcome. I never really knew my own father, but I hope that one day you will come to look on me as your loving daughter. Tonight is very special to me – my first night under the roof of your most beautiful home. I trust you will forgive my boldness in asking a special favour of you, Garnet.'

'Name it, it is yours!' Garnet said so confidently that Isabel was reminded of King Herod's rash promise to Salome, offering her up to half of his kingdom if she would perform the dance of the seven veils, then forced to honour his promise by having John the Baptist's head delivered on a platter.

'Marmaduke has told me such wonderful stories about his child-hood here, Garnet. How you taught him to ride, to grow up to be a strong man like you.'

She saw her father-in-law was mellowed by wine, nodding at the memories.

'Garnet, nothing would delight me more than to fall asleep tonight in my husband's arms.' She held Garnet's eyes. 'In the bed in his old nursery.'

Garnet leant forwards, clearly excited by the revelation of such unladylike passion.

'Then you will please us *both* tonight. Your wish is granted!'

The footsteps of the two assigned servant girls faded down the corridor leaving Isabel thankful to be alone at last in the nursery chambers.

Dressed in her nightgown she sank gratefully across the damask cover of the bed that had been Marmaduke's as a child. The room had been sturdily furnished to suit the needs of a schoolboy, with Bloodwood timber pieces, its bookcase heavy with well-worn books. As curious as she was to explore the titles of the volumes that she knew had become his friends, this must wait until tomorrow.

She stretched out one bare foot and gently set the rocking-horse in motion, thinking of the toddler who must have felt abandoned here at the end of the west wing far from his mother's chambers. *At least his nanny slept in the dressing-room to calm him after his nightmares.*

Isabel was alerted by the sound of footsteps on the back stairs that she could already identify as Marmaduke's tread. She pretended to stir from sleep to discover Marmaduke leaning back against the door watching her. There were beads of perspiration on his forehead, the lines of his cheekbones so taut he looked gaunt.

He crossed to the window and drew back the velvet drapes to look out at the storm.

'You don't know what you've done for me tonight, soldier. Your instincts were dead right. Mother's bed has quite a history.'

She remembered his words at his mother's grave. But now his lack of emotion was all the more chilling.

'When I was sixteen Mother was with child, the first since I was born. I returned from a boundary ride to find she'd been in heavy premature labour for two days. The infant was trapped in her womb. Queenie had done everything she could but even laudanum failed to reduce her agony. I confronted Garnet downstairs, drinking and dancing to the music of an assigned Irishman's fiddle. Garnet refused to send for Doc Llewellyn, called him a charlatan and a drunk. Queenie could manage "women's business". To drown out Mother's cries Garnet made the fiddler play louder and wilder. I'll remember those Irish jigs till I die.'

Marmaduke's face glistened with sweat but he stared ahead, oblivious to everything.

'Mother dictated her Will. When she knew she was dying she begged Garnet to get the doctor to perform a caesarean. Cut her open and save the babe. Garnet refused.'

Isabel covered her mouth in horror.

'Oh, he was heartbroken at her funeral. The whole county rallied in sympathy around the grieving widower. Yet within weeks of her death Garnet slept in Mother's bed with the first of a string of servant girls.'

His eyes were bleak. Isabel felt she could drown in the depth of their sorrow.

'Garnet hates me because I'm the living reminder of the night he claims he can't remember. But I can never forget.'

Marmaduke sat with his head in his hands. Isabel felt a bewildering impulse to stroke his hair. She reached out to him but, as if he regretted his display of emotion, Marmaduke crossed the room and opened the door to Queenie's old room.

Isabel sprang from bed. 'No! You must sleep here. I'll take your nanny's bed.'

He gave a short, painful laugh. 'Loyal as a cattle dog, eh?'

Isabel stood her ground, hands on hips. 'You said you wanted a mercenary to be your ally. Well here I am! Use me! Together we will mould your father to *your* will.'

Marmaduke looked at her with weary admiration. 'You're really quite ruthless. I hope for your sake you can sustain that, soldier.' He closed the door quietly behind him.

Isabel lay listening to the raging storm that rattled the shutters and whined like a banshee.

I signed a contract. I'm Marmaduke's ally for better or worse. But it's oddly comforting to know he's asleep in the adjoining room.

This time when the recurring nightmare came to her she *knew* it was a dream from which she must struggle to wake up. She fought against the sense of sinking beneath the cold waters of the lake, struggling with bulrushes entwined in her hair. She was aware that this time there was an odd sound distorted under water.

Isabel awoke sharply. The sound muffled by her dream was close at hand. A single sharp clicking sound that seemed to come from the corridor.

Marmaduke had locked the door and taken the key. She trembled as she fumbled with the waxed matches, lit the candle and padded across the room to peer through the keyhole.

There was no longer any sound except for the blood pumping in her ears. Was this a sign of the Other? Isabel shuddered when she recognised a familiar smell that she linked to death and dying. The smell of *laudanum*.

CHAPTER 25

'My God! Have you sent me to Heaven or Hell? Or is this the Garden of Eden?'

Alone after Marmaduke's departure before she woke, Isabel surveyed her new world from outside the nursery chambers on the balcony that ran around two sides of the house. In the middle distance double folds of hills stretched towards distant mountains. At the side of the house lay an expanse of lush tropical garden.

Last night she had been disoriented by the discovery of an Antipodean replica of the de Rolland manor house. This morning she was struck by the differences. Despite the echoes of Gothic architecture and surroundings – the same splendid rose garden, vine-shaded summer house and an aviary shaped like a giant birdcage – she now saw that Bloodwood Hall was a microcosm that could belong nowhere else but in Governor Bourke's 'most peculiar Colony'.

The variety of birdlife amazed her. Swarms of exotic rosellas and rainbow lorikeets squawked in excitement as they swooped in chaotic formations, flashing their bright tropical plumage through the canopies of the eucalypt forest.

At the rear of the house was an apparent village of single- and double-storey whitewashed buildings. Smoke rose from their chimneys and the wind carried the smells of a tannery, a bakery, a timber yard. The sounds of sawyers and carpenters and a blacksmith hammering on an anvil were mingled with the guttural sounds of men's voices as they filed out of long cabins shaped like pigeonholes. These assigned men's quarters bordered three sides of a flagstone parade ground in which there was a water pump, a triangle and flogging post. A man's body was slumped in the stocks.

Isabel shuddered at the thought of what unknown depths of brutality and depravity these convicts might suffer at the hands of their master, overseer or even their own kind.

She was happily distracted by the sight of an animal at the fringe of the garden. Was it a kangaroo or a wallaby? Whatever it was Isabel was sure it was a mother. It held its head on one side as if sensing her observation. Then the little miracle happened. A baby joey stuck its head out from its mother's pouch followed by a delicate paw, like a swimmer testing the temperature before entering the water. As if satisfied all was safe in his world, the joey wriggled free of the pouch and hopped beside his protective mother. Isabel felt she had been given a gift from the gods to compensate for her fears.

Last night I panicked. My frightening sense of déjà vu, *the storm, my dream. I felt swamped by the hate and grief inside everyone – the legacy of the tragic acts that happened here. Last night the house felt on the brink of imploding.*

'And yet today the sun is shining.' Isabel tried to reassure herself that at least by contract's end, she'd have money to build a new life for the only people who mattered to her. Then she would be free of all of this.

Yet why was she haunted by the expression in Marmaduke's eyes? *I keep seeing the sad child inside him but that's a weakness I must guard against.*

Dressed in yesterday's day dress until her trunks arrived, Isabel lingered in the picture gallery before going downstairs to the breakfast room. She admired a stormy seascape she recognised was a copy showing Sir Walter Raleigh's fireships attacking Spanish Armada galleons. The others were portraits. Isabel was struck by the odd disparity of their features.

Marmaduke's ancestors obviously didn't marry their *cousins for generations. They look quite unrelated and not an ounce of humour between them.*

Two superior full-length portraits appeared to be the work of the same artist. The man was unmistakeably an earlier edition of Garnet Gamble – here the shock of white hair was dark brown. He was handsome and wore with pride his Masonic regalia, which included a beautifully detailed painted apron combining the traditional Masonic symbols of the three pillars, compass, an anchor and a stylised eye she presumed represented the eye of God – or was it an Egyptian symbol? It moved her to think that her young father Walter had also taken great pride in being a Freemason.

The other half of the diptych was a portrait of a woman dressed in a scarlet sari that was so arresting it drew Isabel to a halt. Who else could this be but Miranda McAlpine?

Despite her flawless Anglo-Saxon beauty she projected an exotic Indian quality. The colours of her sari drawn from the artist's palette were intense, the pale skin tones and dark eyes were luminous. Her jewellery was breathtakingly real. Isabel was fascinated by the necklace studded with large gems of contrasting colours that formed an intricate collar around her neck.

Despite her eastern costume Miranda was not a woman who could be overpowered by the beauty of her apparel. Her classical features were beyond mere perfection – they were *alive*. The expression in her eyes, the curve of her mouth showed confidence in her power to enchant – even from beyond the grave. Yet despite the sensuality of her face and body, she was clearly every inch a lady.

Isabel spoke the thought aloud. 'Marmaduke was right about you!'

'Really? What did Marmaduke say?'

Isabel spun around to see him propped against the wall, casually dressed in riding clothes that today made him look far more Currency than Sterling.

'You said your mother captured the heart of everyone who saw her. Or words to that effect. I can certainly see why. If she wore sackcloth and ashes she'd start a new fashion. Her beauty must have made other women green with envy.'

'*Emerald* green. Mother wasn't a woman who attracted female friends. She didn't need them. Queenie was her sole lifelong confidante.'

Marmaduke was studying her with that maddening half smile as if his painful confession last night had never occurred.

'Who is the artist? He's clearly a professional. But he didn't sign it.'

'That's quite a story. Augustus Earle was one of a family of famous American and English artists. During his world travels he became the rage here and in Van Diemen's Land. Painted wonderful landscapes and portraits, including Governor Brisbane and Darling, Captain John Piper, Mrs Blaxland – the Quality were eager to be immortalised. So naturally Garnet commissioned him to paint him in his

Masonic regalia. He even commissioned Earle to paint the designs on his actual Mason's apron to outshine Sam Terry's. I remember meeting Earle when Mother sat for her portrait in his studio. A charming man and a great storyteller, but known to live a dissolute life. Mother's portrait took so long Garnet turned up at the studio in Sydney in a jealous rage. Refused to pay him a penny. Earle was booked to sail for India. He had Mother's portrait delivered to her, unsigned, as a gift. I understand he later joined Charles Darwin's voyages on HMS *Beagle* as official artist but by then he was broken in health and was replaced by Conrad Martens. Garnet wrongly claims he had Earle kicked out of the Colony for trying to seduce Mother.'

'Your father seems a law unto himself.'

Marmaduke shrugged. 'Few would argue with that.'

'It was a shock to see Garnet's dark hair. He's rather young to have white hair.'

Marmaduke looked cynical. 'Garnet claims it turned white with grief.'

'Well, they say Queen Marie Antoinette's hair turned white overnight in prison.'

Marmaduke quickly changed the subject. 'Do you fancy Mother's jewellery? Or is it too exotic for your Anglo-Saxon sensibilities?'

'You forget I'm of half Plantagenet, half Celtic descent. But yes, her jewels are magnificent. I imagine there's a story behind them, too?'

'Yeah. The necklace is a traditional *navratan* from the Mogul period last century. The name means "nine stones". These precious and semi-precious gems represent nine deities in the Hindu pantheon. The nine gems are said to capture in microcosm the power of the heavenly bodies. To act as a storehouse of endless energy and power that enhances the life of the wearer. Maybe it worked for the Maharajah's favourite. It didn't save Mother's life.'

'Perhaps it was the key to her extraordinary powers of attraction. What are the gems?'

He identified the nine gems, the emerald, diamond, pearl, ruby, topaz, coral, sapphire, cat's eye and zircon, plus the white sapphire teardrops skirting it and the graduated pearls.

'Altogether worth a king's ransom.'

'You sound as if you could write a book on the subject.'

Marmaduke shrugged off her praise. 'Picked up stuff from Queenie – her mother was a Hindu. And Josiah Mendoza taught me a bit about gems.'

'I presume that magnificent emerald is your mother's betrothal ring.'

Marmaduke seemed restless to move on. 'By rights Mother's jewellery should come to my bride. But maybe Father's mistress has commandeered it.'

Isabel glanced up at Miranda's portrait. *He can hardly bear to say Elise's name. But I'd be honoured to wear your necklace, Miranda. I could do with with some power from the heavenly bodies myself.*

When she asked about the ancestral portraits Marmaduke's hand wiped the smile off his face to hide his amusement.

'Father was literally born a bastard. Never knew his father's identity. He bought those portraits in a job lot from Abraham Polack's auction house to give himself an instant family pedigree.'

Isabel felt a rush of pity. *Garnet's so desperate to enter upper-class English Society he even invented his family tree. No wonder he wanted a de Rolland bride to give him validity.*

They found themselves alone in the breakfast room. Marmaduke was in teasing mood. 'You peck at your food like a sparrow. Must you always be constrained by etiquette?'

'You should talk! You never cover your mouth when you yawn. You eat with your elbows on the table and fiddle with the salt and pepper as if you're playing chess.'

Marmaduke said lightly, 'What a perfect little mother you are.'

She felt herself grow pale. 'That was unforgiveable!'

He strode to her side. 'I swear I didn't mean—'

'Oh, yes you did!' she said, throwing down her table napkin, determined to flee the room.

'Don't tell me the honeymoon is over already!' Elise said sweetly.

She stood in the doorway wearing a fancy gown cut so low no lady would wear it before sundown. Her hair was fussily tied up in ringlets and anchored by little ostrich feathers. If her complexion had been one shade whiter she could have passed as a ghost.

Isabel knew there was no way to deny the scene Elise had just witnessed.

'A lover's quarrel – all my fault,' Isabel said as she rested her head against Marmaduke's shoulder. 'I'm so sorry, darling.'

Marmaduke was equal to the ploy. 'No, no. *My* fault. I didn't allow you a moment's sleep last night.' His voice was huskily intimate as he kissed the crown of her head. Isabel was pleased to see red dots of anger on Elise's cheeks.

'I must tear your bride away from you for a short while, Marmaduke, to discuss my plans for your welcome home banquet.'

'Five minutes, no more. I have plans for a bivouac in Ghost Gum Valley.'

He strode from the room without a backwards glance.

Elise appeared flustered as she showed Isabel the guest list written in Rhys Powell's hand, which Isabel realised Elise had memorised. Clearly Garnet was not the only one who was illiterate.

Elise tried to act the confident hostess. 'It's far too short notice to invite Mrs Elizabeth Macarthur, or any of the Top Thirteen. So we're confined to those close at hand. Magistrate Summerhayes, of course, and the local manager of the Bank of New South Wales – his bank would fold if Garnet withdrew his stocks and shares. Dr Llewellyn is not exactly top drawer but he's been in practice here so long he's part of the furniture. The Wesleyan pastor and his spinster daughter. Rhys Powell and Edwin Bentleigh if he isn't defending some felon or other.'

'A gentle, clever man.' *Thank Heavens I'll know one friendly face.*

'I don't suppose there's anyone you'd care to ask? You've been here so little time.'

Isabel said quickly, 'Murray Robertson, a shipmate on the *Susan*. And Queenie.'

Elise dropped all pretensions of a refined accent. 'You can't be serious! Queenie is *coloured*. An Indian servant!'

Isabel was not about to yield an inch. 'I understood Queenie was Miranda Gamble's most faithful friend. And Marmaduke would want her to be there, don't you think?'

It was a rhetorical question and Isabel glided from the room, leaving Elise open-mouthed.

*

Marmaduke swung open the picket gate of Queenie's whitewashed stone cabin and Isabel entered the small cottage garden that might have been found in any English village – except that, instead of the traditional thatch, this cottage was roofed by sheets of bark pinned down by horizontal poles cut from eucalyptus saplings. The squat stone chimney that ran up one side wall was cheerfully billowing smoke.

'Don't be put off by Queenie's manner. She's nothing if not forthright. Some people find her honesty offensive.'

'So that's where you get it from,' Isabel said. 'I thought all you Currency Lads were tarred with the same brush.'

The minute the woman opened the door Isabel knew she was in for a grilling.

Today, in place of the sari, Queenie wore a modest dark print house dress and starched Mother Hubbard pinafore. Marmaduke wrapped her in his arms and gently rocked her.

'Nanny, I want you to meet Isabel, my bride, the future mistress of Mingaletta. But I'll build you your own little house. We all know how fiercely independent you are.'

Queenie hugged Marmaduke warmly, then promptly banished him.

'I've things to say to your bride that would burn your ears. Women's business. Be off with you. Come back in an hour when I've finished with her. I've made your favourite Summer Pudding.' She gave an affectionate tug at the hair that hung down his back in a horse's tail. 'Your hair's longer than a girl's. I don't know what the world's coming to. Now be off with you.'

Isabel obediently took the seat offered her and looked around the two rooms as Queenie busied herself making tea in the skillion outside the back door. The cabin was furnished in an odd combination of bush carpentry – raw timber showed notches where branches had been lopped off – and clearly loved objects from England and India made of sandalwood, silver, brass, multi-coloured glass. Eastern embroideries glittered with semi-precious stones.

One wall held a surprising arrangement of pictures of Hindu deities and Buddhas that formed a pictorial bodyguard around a stylised painting of a very Anglo-Saxon-looking blond and blue-eyed Jesus with a group of dark children at his knee, listening intently to his stories.

Queenie placed tea and cakes on the table and gestured Isabel to begin eating, though she took nothing herself. From her rocking chair she fixed her eyes so intently on her that Isabel decided to return the stare. The woman's hair was a surprisingly glossy black, although streaked with what seemed like white stripes twisted in the shape of a tortoise shell on the nape of her neck. Her dark eyes held age-old secrets. Turquoise teardrops hung from her ears but she wore no rings on hands that were as slender and eloquent as those of a young Indian dancer.

She must have been quite a beauty in her youth. I wonder why she never married when single women in this colony were always at a premium.

Queenie took the offensive. 'So. Why *did* you agree to marry my boy? I know Garnet arranged the whole thing. I want the truth and nothing but the truth. I'm too old to be fobbed off with polite English evasion.'

Isabel decided she had no choice but to play Queenie at her own game. 'And I'm too young to bother with lies. I married Marmaduke because *he* asked me.'

That silenced Queenie for a moment. 'What's most important to you, love or money?'

'That's easy. I don't believe in love.'

Queenie gave a short. 'That's what Marmaduke claims. That makes you both fools.'

'Then we're perfectly suited. Neither of us will disappoint the other.'

'You're a liar!'

'I beg your pardon?'

'So you're a deaf liar too, are you?'

Isabel put her teacup carefully on the table, leant forwards and looked directly into Queenie's eyes. 'I know Marmaduke trusts you more than anyone on earth. And I have every reason to believe you truly love him. So exactly what is it you want from me, Queenie?'

Is that a faint glimmer of approval in Queenie's eyes?

'I want your word of honour you will never hurt Marmaduke. All his life he's been betrayed by the people he loved. Or else they've deserted and humiliated him.'

I presume she means betrayal at the hands of his lost bride, his German tutor, his father – even his mother's death must have seemed like desertion. This old servant is nobody's fool, I'd best tread Isabel *carefully.*

'I made Marmaduke a promise I will never betray him. But how can I hurt him when he's incapable of love?'

'Good Heavens, girl, can't you see through that big act of his? That he's mastered every page of the *Kama Sutra*? That he enjoys going from woman to woman, from bed to bed? He boasts he'll never be trapped by any woman because he's *clever*. Incapable of falling in love.' Queenie gave a hoot of derision. 'Can't you see the truth? He's a little boy who's afraid of the dark!'

Isabel was taken aback, as if Marmaduke's distorted image in a mirror suddenly became crystal clear for the first time. She spoke without thinking.

'But why? Marmaduke's so handsome. He could have any woman he wanted.' *Good God, I don't believe I said that, yet it's true. Why didn't I see it before?*

'Because the boy doesn't believe he's *worth* loving! His parents fought over him like two dogs with a bone. His father humiliated him. Then that bitch! It was bad enough when she left him high and dry at the altar. But when he found her in bed with his father…'

Queenie stopped in mid-sentence, aware that Isabel had sunk back in her chair.

'Elise?' Isabel asked faintly.

Queenie looked contrite. 'I thought you knew.'

'No. I'm the stupid girl everyone in the world chooses to leave in the dark.'

She rose with as much dignity as her trembling knees would allow. 'Thank you for the fine Indian tea, Queenie.'

Like a little terrier Queenie blocked her path. 'Wait, there's one important thing you need to know. Miranda left a box in my care and made me promise to hand it to Marmaduke when he had married a woman who would stick by him come Hell or high water.'

Queenie's fingernails dug into her arm. 'Tell me the truth. Are *you* that woman?'

'I don't know. But I refuse to live in the same house as the woman my husband is in love with!'

Isabel hurried out the door, picked up her skirts and stumbled blindly down a track behind the house. She hoped it led as far from Bloodwood Hall as the wind would take her.

CHAPTER 26

'Saddle up the new bay mare. Forget the lady's side-saddle, it isn't safe! My wife's not used to our rough territory.'

Marmaduke issued his orders so fast he had Davey the ostler on the run. He felt driven by the need to escape this wretched place and Garnet's manipulation but also by an urgent desire to be alone with Isabel. To try to understand her. He had slept badly last night for many reasons – all involving Isabel.

Two of Garnet's best horses were now saddled ready for departure and a packhorse loaded with stores for the bivouac. Marmaduke double-checked each detail, aware that despite her lack of complaint Isabel's pride – had been wounded by her inexperience as a rider.

She's got a lot to learn, that girl. But I must admit she's pretty intrepid. She doesn't whinge or chuck a fit of hysterics at the sight of a spider. The acid test will be her first snake!

It was time to collect Isabel from Queenie's cabin after what his nanny had called 'women's business'. But first he must brief his father, mindful of the unwritten bush law that travellers must advise their destination in case an accident or bushrangers prevented their return.

In the vestibule he caught sight of a letter on the hall table – from London. It was addressed to him but on reading it Marmaduke's suspicions were aroused by the slight difference between the hand-writing of Godfrey de Rolland's letter and that of the envelope.

This envelope is a forgery. Garnet's read my mail!

He tracked down his quarry by following the sound of the lion's roar to the library where Garnet was off-loading his frustration on Rhys Powell.

Marmaduke had hoped to find Garnet alone but he offered the young Welshman his hand and stated his preference for informality.

'My father is loath to dish out deserving praise, Rhys, but behind your back he speaks highly of your work. He's fortunate to have a man he can trust for a change. Some of your predecessors have lined their pockets at his expense.'

'Yeah, but they ended up in chains working for the infamous Commandant Patrick Logan at Moreton Bay!' Garnet warned.

Marmaduke managed to keep his anger in check. 'I received a letter this morning from Godfrey de Rolland in England, which appears to have been mislaid for some weeks. The contents are vitally important. I think we *need to discuss this now*, Garnet.'

Rhys Powell looked anxious but Garnet chose to ignore the implied accusation.

'You'll dine with us tonight, of course. My friend, Magistrate Summerhayes, is keen to meet our illustrious bride.'

'The law can wait. I'm taking Isabel on a bivouac. We won't return until Edwin arrives to witness the handover.'

Rhys Powell jumped in with alacrity. 'Mr Bentleigh sent a Government report that shows Governor Bourke wants to push through new statutes to abolish land grants and encourage free settlers to immigrate. This will affect the modus operandi of landholders.'

Garnet bellowed, 'Nonsense, Bentleigh jumps at shadows.'

Marmaduke could restrain himself no longer. 'Enough of politics. I came here to discuss Godfrey de Rolland's letter, Garnet! There have been major *repercussions*!'

After Garnet dismissed his secretary Marmaduke was free to vent his anger.

'You manipulative bastard! Reading my mail. I had the right to know about Isabel's illness for her own safety. I only discovered it by accident when I found her sleepwalking in her nightgown in the corridor of your hotel. God alone knows what would have happened if she had wandered down into The Rocks! You ought to be bloody ashamed of yourself. She's *my* wife! *My* responsibility.'

Garnet looked contrite. 'It was an oversight. I wouldn't hurt that girl for the world.'

'You won't get the chance, Garnet. We're leaving right now for Ghost Gum Valley.' As he strode from the room he flung his exit line over his shoulder.

'She'll be safer with me in the wild than she is with you in this damned house!'

*

It was only when Marmaduke led the three horses up to Queenie's cottage and saw her standing on the doorstep, her arms folded and wearing a dour expression, that he suspected his plans had begun to fall into disarray.

'Hey, what's wrong, Queenie? Where's Isabel?'

'You neglected to tell her Elise was your runaway bride. Not surprisingly Isabel's upset. She's run off.'

Marmaduke gave a resigned sigh. 'Righto. Which way was she headed?'

He sprang into the saddle and rode off down a rough dirt track that would finally peter out miles away beyond the boundary of Mingaletta. No girl could manage to walk that far in flimsy footwear.

Except Isabel. She's so damned stubborn she'd crawl on her hands and knees just to spite me.

He began to rehearse his explanation. Should his line be defensive or offensive, apologetic or a noble, hurt silence? He knew he was in the wrong. It was a delicate balance.

An hour later Marmaduke sighted her distant figure down the track. She was bareheaded, her hat slung across her back swinging from its ties. Her pace suggested she was driven by anger. Her wild gestures indicated she was having a heated debate with herself.

Within a hundred yards of her Marmaduke dismounted and led the horses at a gentle walking pace so as to give Isabel ample time to cool her anger at his approach.

He walked alongside her for a full minute before he said lazily, 'I reckon we've got good weather for it.'

Isabel turned on him a face flushed with undiluted rage. The force of her hand struck his face so heavily, he laughed in surprise.

'Whoah! I reckon you learnt the art of self-defence from Daniel Mendoza himself.'

'I'll teach you to laugh at me!'

Isabel completely lost control. She belted him with both hands and pummelled his chest, infuriated when she kept missing his face by a hair's breadth as he weaved and ducked out of range.

Finally tired of the game, Marmaduke pinioned her arms behind her back in a hold that constrained but did not hurt her. His tone was as patient as if placating a child.

'All right, that's enough. You have every right to be angry with me. I should have told you.'

'You lied to me! Why keep Elise a dark secret? You contracted me to be your ally but a soldier can't fight if he doesn't know who the enemy is! I'm not stupid. I knew Elise hated me on sight. But I thought that was because she saw me as a threat to her shaky status as Garnet's mistress. The truth is Elise is the girl who broke your heart. And you love her still. Don't deny it! I can see it written all over your face!'

'Not true! Garnet's welcome to her. I can't stand the sight of her.'

'Liar! You brought me here to live under the same roof. An act of revenge. To flaunt your blue-blooded prize, prove what a fool she was to choose Garnet over you!'

Pink in the face, Isabel tried to struggle free. 'Let go of me!'

Marmaduke answered softly, 'I will when you've heard me out.'

He sat down on a fallen tree trunk and drew her firmly onto his lap. Much needed to be said and said quickly. 'You're right and you're also *wrong*. I'm no gentleman, as you never stop reminding me. But there's one thing I never do. Talk about women I've been involved with. So I couldn't identify Elise as the girl who dumped me at the altar.'

'Everyone knew the truth but me! You envy your father his mistress. Well, don't let me stop you.' She snapped her fingers in his face. 'I don't give a damn what you do!'

'No, you don't,' Marmaduke said quietly. 'But I really wish you *did*.'

The element of surprise silenced her just as Marmaduke intended it would. He waited until her breathing slowed to a normal pattern.

'I told you the truth, Isabel. I don't believe in love. That's just a camouflage for lust. But when I was nineteen I was as green as they come. My head was filled with dead poets' sonnets and ballads. Elise was an assigned servant, the first woman who ever flirted with me. I was knocked for six. Her history meant nothing to me. I knew she was a transportee. The reason is strictly *her* business. I wrote her poems, poor imitations of the art. I even pressed flowers for her, cut silhouettes of her profile and hung them above my bed. I was obsessed with the *idea* of love. No doubt influenced by my dog-eared copy *The Sorrows of Young Werther.* You've read it?'

'Of course I have. A tragic waste of a young life.' Isabel prompted him. 'But what happened to *you?*'

'I fancied myself cast in the heroic mould, protecting Elise from the fate often suffered by female prisoners – being a concubine. I proposed marriage on the prospect of my future inheritance – Mingaletta. Father was dead against it. But clever manipulator that he is, he granted his permission on one condition. If I married Elise he'd disinherit me. I was so stupidly honourable I agreed. Elise recognised which side her bread was buttered. She believed Garnet was a sure bet for a wealthy marriage. Good luck to her. She's still waiting!'

Isabel looked contrite. 'I'm sorry she broke your heart.'

'Me? No heart to break, remember?' He paused. 'So where do we go from here, soldier? You were marching along this track like you knew where *you* were going.'

'I just wanted to get as far away from you as possible, to wherever this path leads.'

'Mind if I tag along?'

Isabel glanced wryly at the loaded packhorse. 'You seem better prepared than I am.'

'I never travel without a shotgun, a flask of brandy, a box of waxed Lucifers and a horse that can read my mind.'

'You brought me a mare with a man's saddle. I'm wearing a dress and four petticoats.'

In answer he handed her a bundle. 'This will give you better protection from any bushrangers we encounter.'

Isabel wordlessly disappeared behind a tree trunk the width of an elephant. When she emerged, she held her chin high despite her embarrassment.

Marmaduke gave a slow whistle of appreciation. His eyes followed the lines of her long slim legs encased in the tightest of breeches, her small bosom disguised by the boy's shirt and jerkin inherited from Murray Robertson. Her hair was tucked from sight under the baggy Stuart tartan hunting cap except for a silky fringe that fell over one eye and made her look more fetching than any actress he had seen on stage in 'breeches' roles.

'Yeah,' he said teasingly. 'I reckon that outfit looks better without the black eye. I could pass you off as a boy, no trouble at all.'

'I'm glad if that means I'm safe from men, including you.'

'Safe as houses,' he lied.

The sun was firmly fixed overhead when on the crest of a hill Marmaduke revealed the panoramic view below. Ghost Gum Valley was host to its namesake, the Ghost Gum eucalypts. The slender, pure white trunks and lacy canopies that shimmered in the sunlight had an ethereal quality as if one by one they might dissolve silently without trace. A creek carved through the heart of the valley in deep S-shaped curves like the body of a sleepy blue-grey snake. He heard Isabel catch her breath at the sheer beauty of it all.

'You can see why the blacks have so many legends about the Rainbow Serpent. Their stories date to their pre-historic Dreamtime and relate to natural features in the landscape. I wish I'd asked them more questions when I was a kid before Garnet ran them off our land.'

'Your land? Or theirs?' she asked.

Marmaduke gave her a sage look. 'That depends whether you live under British law or tribal law.'

He took the lead down the sharp zig-zag descent to a billabong that lay tucked like a crescent-shaped lake in the curve of the creek. They dismounted on a grassy knoll. Despite Isabel's hunger, Marmaduke only allowed her to quench her thirst from a water bottle.

'I brought you on this trip for several reasons. Survival. Do you know the two greatest killers of women in this Colony?'

'The gallows? Snakebite?'

'Nope. Childbirth and modesty. Yeah, modesty. Women have been drowned every year since settlement, especially along the banks of rivers like the Hawkesbury–Nepean. Flash floods can make our rivers rise thirty feet in ten minutes. Women drown because they are laced into corsets, weighed down with a ton of petticoats and they're too damned modest to learn how to swim. Can *you* swim?'

When she shook her head in denial Marmaduke saw the fear in her eyes.

'Right. So now it's time for Survival Lesson Number One. Strip off down to your undergarments. No arguments.'

'I will do no such thing!'

'You will if you don't want to drown.'

Her eyes widened in acute panic. 'I will *not*. I know what it *feels like to drown*. You can't make me!'

'I can and I will,' he said calmly. 'Get this straight. No wife of mine is going to die of modesty. Get your gear off or I'll strip it off you!'

Isabel glared back at him haughtily. 'You are totally uncouth. There's no need to ape Petrucchio in *The Taming of the Shrew*.'

'Yeah, well, stop behaving like the shrew.'

Isabel's blush confirmed to Marmaduke he'd won that round. He had not expected she would be easy to teach but the extent of her fear almost made him change his mind. He saw her out of the corner of his eye as she stripped down to her fine lawn bodice and drawers. In his under-breeches he entered the water at the shallow end, remembering his own fear of water as a boy when he had come to this same billabong to learn to swim.

He tried to gain Isabel's confidence by teaching her to float face up while he supported her neck with one hand, the other under her rump.

'Don't touch me there!' she snapped through chattering teeth.

Marmaduke sighed. *Her mouth is blue with cold but she still has the bite of a goanna.* 'If you think I'm taking a liberty, you're crazy. Try to relax. When you stiffen up, you sink. It's so shallow here you could stand up in it but you've got to *imagine* it's deep.'

He broke the lesson into short interludes to give her time to dry off in the sun, wrapped in a blanket, warmed and relaxed by nips of brandy. At last he judged the time was right to test if he had earned her trust.

'You're doing well. Let's have a go at floating on your own. I'll be ready to hold you, come Hell or high water.' He tried to keep his tone light. 'You can still go on hating me, Isabel – just *trust* me. I've never lost a wife yet.'

Marmaduke led her to the far end of the billabong. The deep dark water was shadowed by two giant eucalypts whose trunks arched across the water like flying buttresses in a medieval cathedral. A few yards beyond them, standing erect like a grey ghost, was the trunk of a eucalypt that had long ago been struck by lightning. He remembered it had been here when he was twelve years old, quaking in his boots, to receive instructions in the art of swimming from Klaus von Starbold.

For Marmaduke this billabong held mixed memories of the fear that had limited him to clumsy attempts to paddle like a dog and his repeated failures to swim like a man.

Now as Marmaduke looked across at the opposite bank he blinked into the face of the sun, remembering how von Starbold had stood there, expressionless, his back ramrod-straight, his greying blond hair clipped short in military mode, standing like a soldier at ease watching him.

Marmaduke was exhausted, blue with cold and ready to accept defeat. It was a battle of wills that only one of them could win. His tutor gave him no quarter. His clipped Germanic orders cut through Marmaduke's fear with quiet determination.

'You can do it, young man. I know you can.'

The high-pitched buzz of cicadas rang in his ears as if mocking his failures. Von Starbold refused to relent. Marmaduke was forced to try again. The deep cold water was his enemy as he struggled to master his fear. He struck out towards the far end of the swimming hole, knowing he would fail...then came the dawning sense of wonder, 'Maybe I can do it!'...*his pleasure and surprise when he heard the voice calling out,* 'Yes! You did it! I knew you could!'

Marmaduke's eye was drawn to the far bank of the swimming hole, to the memory of his tutor's triumphant laugh. The sun burst from behind a cloud and Marmaduke was momentarily bedazzled. For one moment he thought he saw von Starbold observing him in silence. The bank was empty. There was nothing but a mottled shadow cast by sunlight on the water.

Marmaduke looked across at Isabel and knew she hated him for driving her on, just as he had felt as a child. *If only I could make Isabel trust me.*

He dived into the billabong and trod water, fixing his eyes on Isabel's pale, pinched face, a portrait of sheer terror.

'You can do it, girl. I *know* you can!' he called out.

Marmaduke nodded encouragement and beckoned to her, a confident invitation for her to jump into the water. But she remained clutching her arms across her chest, her legs trembling. The fragile cotton of her undergarments clung to her, a wet second skin that heightened her look of a vulnerable child.

'Come to me! I'll catch you the moment you hit the water.' Still she refused to jump. He had been treading water so long his feet felt frozen. 'I need you to jump, Isabel.'

She shook her head and looked nervously at the opposite bank.

'That's an order! *Jump!*'

At the very moment Isabel hurtled her body into the air, Marmaduke realised his error. Too late he recognised an unmistakable sound often heard in the bush – the shrieking, tearing noise of falling timber that sounded almost human. He caught a flash of the giant dead trunk as it fell headlong down on them like a juggernaut. No time to drag Isabel free.

Chaos. Foam. Waves of water, dragging him under.

On instinct he dived below the body of the trunk, blinded by the swirl of water, desperate to glimpse her white limbs, any part of Isabel's body he could grasp.

Where the hell is she? Sucked downstream? Unconscious? Sunk like a stone to the bottom?

In desperation the voice in his head cried out. *Listen to me, God. Take my life not hers!*

It was at that moment that he glimpsed two pale legs floating, motionless, the toes pointing up towards the surface of the water.

He felt numb with horror. *Why is she upside down?* He struggled to peer down through the darker depths below and glimpsed her face, the eyes wide open in terror, mouth closed, trapped by the length of her hair that was pinned beneath the fallen tree trunk.

Marmaduke's eyes locked with hers. Fear met fear. *She's trapped by her hair, too tangled under the tree for me to drag her free.* He waved his hand in a futile bid to give her confidence then kicked himself up to the surface, dragged his body up the bank, grabbed his knife from its sheaf, clamped it between his teeth and dived back down to her.

When he reached her Marmaduke was overcome by waves of fury at God. Isabel's staring eyes had abandoned all hope, the last stream of bubbles from her now open mouth passed him as he gripped a rock to anchor him to the bottom of the billabong. He tore the knife from his mouth and hacked desperately at her hair. He looked into her eyes and sent her the message.

I won't leave you, soldier. We'll die together…

Marmaduke could only remember fragments: holding on to Isabel's hair, dragging her to the surface, pushing her limp body up onto the bank, desperately sucking air into his lungs.

Exhausted, he dragged himself to his knees and straddled her body, panting as he rhythmically pummelled her back with his full weight, afraid to look into her open eyes in case he saw that the black pupils had disappeared – and her life as well.

He lost all sense of time but refused to stop. He could feel no warmth in her body, so he cursed God out loud.

'You bastard! You don't exist!'

And then he felt it – or had he imagined it? A shudder in her chest, a movement he had not caused. And he saw the fingers of her hand twitch. He laughed out loud with joy as she spewed brackish water again and again, coughing and retching. A beautiful sound!

'Good girl! That's the way to do it! *That's the way to do it*!' He kept laughing at the absurd childhood memory of the words chanted by the belligerent Punch in a *Punch and Judy* puppet show, the words his mother had taught to her cockatoo Amaru.

Half drunk with triumph he continued to knead her back and chest until the water drained from her lungs in a final splutter and Isabel looked up at him. The expression in her eyes chilled him. No relief, no thanks that he had saved her.

'You're in shock,' he said firmly.

'No,' she said. 'We are alive! We cheated death!' She repeated the words like a mantra. She reached out and pulled him down on her, held his head and took his mouth in a kiss of overwhelming hunger.

'Thank God, you're alive!' Marmaduke lost control. It wasn't an act of lust or love. A brief primitive coupling that shocked him. Proving to each other that they had cheated death.

Marmaduke carried her inside the deep cave, lit a fire and gently stripped her unresisting body of its wet underclothing. He bundled her into a nightgown and his own woollen socks to warm her feet then added layers of his flannel shirt and vest, towelled her hair, rolled her in the blanket and bundled her close to the fire. He attempted to hold her in his arms to warm her, but she appeared to have withdrawn into a space where he could not follow.

Oh my God, does she remember what just happened? What do I do? How can I explain what I don't understand myself? It's all so unreal.

Marmaduke felt his throat constrict when he saw Isabel was staring at him with that strangely withdrawn expression he had seen the night she had walked in her sleep.

Is she really with me? Or somewhere else?

'They can't drown witches,' she said, then closed her eyes as if to blot out the world.

'Brandy straight,' he ordered, ready to block any resistance.

She offered none. She drank it down, only half aware of him. In the role of a gentle but firm father he coaxed her, spooning into her mouth the thick soup he heated over the fire.

'How do you feel?'

'I thought you'd left me to die. Saved yourself. I didn't blame you. I was only afraid of dying with you on my conscience. I lied to you.'

He handed her another tumbler of brandy. 'You don't owe me a thing, little one. You're alive, that's all that counts.'

'I thought I could never trust any man alive. But if I had died Rose Alba would be lost forever...'

Is she talking to me? Or in her sleep? Rose Alba. Old fashioned white roses.

Marmaduke sat near her, careful not to touch her – and waited.

Isabel stared into the fire. He listened intently to the broken phrases that reminded him of some lost child, afraid of the dark, afraid of strangers, afraid of death and afraid of life. He kept the brandy flowing, determined not to break the flow of images that might lead him to the truth. Isabel no longer acknowledged him but she was breathing, warm and alive and, for now, that was all that mattered to him.

Marmaduke controlled his urge to ask questions. Her fragmented words were divorced from sequential time and place. Instinct told him, *do nothing, say nothing. God willing she'll sense my protection. I'll never let anyone hurt you again, Isabel.*

Piece by piece he put together her dislocated story. His mind was a battlefield, torn between two conflicting emotions. His desire to protect the child-Isabel that was trapped inside her. And his hatred for the man who had scarred her life.

By nightfall Marmaduke believed he knew the truth. Isabel, the lonely little girl dominated by the kinsman she loved and trusted. How easily a man with a manipulative mind had convinced a sensitive small child she was cursed, the spawn of a witch. Isabel's child's mind believed him. That she was so evil she would destroy any man who loved her – except Silas! And this man's power over her was so strong Isabel still believed the lie.

Marmaduke had thought he was shockproof until now. Isabel's childhood fear of drowning now made horrific sense to him.

Trial by water! When she was a small child Silas put her through the same diabolical test the Inquisiters practised for centuries. An accused witch was proven innocent if she drowned, guilty if she survived! Jesus Christ, the man's a monster.

Marmaduke finally could not restrain himself. He broke the spell, reached out and held her hand.

'Listen to me! You were an innocent child – he was an adult. An evil man. You think God doesn't know that?'

Isabel seemed to be vaguely aware of him but too weary to argue. She shook her head. 'Silas was right. You know why?' Her voice dropped to a whisper as she made her confession.

Exhausted she turned her face away and fell instantly into a deep sleep. Marmaduke kept the fire stoked. He felt an unexpected jolt of tenderness mixed with rage as he watched over her, the delicate sleeping face framed by the ragged hair he had hacked to set her free.

He could not sleep, haunted by Isabel's whispered confession. The words she had said as a child when she believed she was drowning. 'I forfeited God's forgiveness forever. You see, I wanted to live so badly I prayed to *the Devil* to save me – and he *did*.'

The words made Marmaduke's blood run cold.

She believes it was Silas who saved her. The Devil in human form.

Marmaduke now knew with cold certainty what Isabel had wiped from her memory, the root cause of her sleepwalking sickness. He saw in Isabel's sleeping face the thirteen-year-old girl who had had no conscious memory of how she came by the child. She had fled to the Gypsies in the woods to give birth. Branded herself in the eyes of her family with the crime of infanticide rather than reveal the truth. That she had hidden the babe to protect it from Silas de Rolland.

The face of the beloved cousin was unknown to him but Marmaduke had formed a vivid picture of the man through Isabel's words. He imagined that Silas was now facing him at the mouth of the cave.

You stole Isabel's innocence, her childhood. But I'll die before I let you claim the rest of her life.

CHAPTER 27

'That damned Merlin's Mechanical Chair – where the hell have you hidden it?'

Garnet's voice was so loud it ricocheted off the walls right down the length of the east wing. It gave him a sense of pleasure to know that at least his voice was as strong as ever and could still trigger the response of rattled servants' footsteps that responded to him like scurrying mice.

Three of the convict 'Marys' appeared at either ends of the corridor. Black Mary, Red Mary and Spotty Mary, the girl with skin like a speckled hen – each was still young enough and newly assigned enough to panic when he bellowed his commands. In contrast, Bridget always took her time to respond, playing on her unspoken status in the relationship with her Master. But lazy as she was Garnet knew she could be counted on to boss the other assigned lasses into doing *her* share of the work. Bridget had her uses. Not least, she was the sharpest of his informers.

Bridget was last to arrive with her usual swaying of the hips. 'You called, *sir*?'

'You took your time! I'm holding you responsible for finding that damned Merlin chair before sunset. I haven't used it for a year since I broke my ankle but it must be stored somewhere. Cost me a fortune to import it. This place is falling apart. Fordham's slacking. If I don't get all the assigned men back into line nobody will. You lot! First one of you to find my Merlin wheelchair contraption gets a half day off!'

'Yes, sir,' 'Indeed, sir,' came in a flurry of accents as they fled in different directions. In contrast Bridget stood her ground.

'It's being where you left it, sir. You presented it to the Catholic priest last winter because he was suffering the gout. He's had your Irish assigned men praying for you at Mass ever since, he has.'

Embarrassed by his lapse of memory Garnet stomped off down the path with Amaru chortling on his shoulder. His eye was caught by two figures seated in the shade of a tree.

Rhys Powell and Elise sat on separate benches but their heads were close together as Rhys bent over the book in Elise's lap and underlined a phrase with one finger. She nodded like an obedient child and began to mouth the words, darting anxious looks at Rhys to seek his approval. Both were clearly unaware of being observed.

Garnet grudgingly gave a silent nod of approval. His shy young Welsh secretary was clearly doing his utmost to make his master's mistress literate but Garnet was not fool enough to show Elise open encouragement. The woman expected to be rewarded financially for every favour she did, in bed or out of it. He considered she was overpaid as it was.

On second thoughts, Garnet wondered who else could be relied on to keep his dark secret when he felt that terrible need taking hold of him, blotting out all reason, except for the desire to inflict pain. No one but Elise. Now more than ever these increasing episodes must remain their shared secret. He was determined that Isabel as the new mistress of Bloodwood Hall would not discover his secret life and be repelled by him.

He looked up at the sky and sent up a mental challenge.

If you are there, do the decent thing and grant me time to see Marmaduke and his bride settled here and my dynasty safe in their hands. Before I go the way of old Macarthur.

Fired by the sudden suspicion that Marmaduke might have played a monumental trick on him, Garnet let out a roar across the garden that caused Rhys Powell to jump to his feet and Elise to drop her primer. Garnet noted that today her gown was surprisingly demure, a modesty scarf covered the expanse of white flesh she usually flaunted in the presence of men.

He did not stop to speak but Amaru acknowledged them with a litany of cheerful encouragements. 'That's the way to do it! That's the way to do it!'

When Garnet reached Queenie's cottage she opened the door, wearing a purple sari and her traditional haughty expression.

Garnet stared her out. 'I need your help,' he said quietly. 'Your promise.'

The expression in Queenie's black eyes was instantly on guard. He realised he had finally succeeded in throwing her off balance but he took no joy in the discovery.

'What is this? Blackmail?' she asked.

'Call it a compromise. Ever since the day I married Miranda she insisted her half-sister must live here in my original old cottage under my protection. I have kept my word, even though you've shown me nothing but antagonism.'

'Mutual contempt,' she said acidly.

'In all these years you and I shared only one good thing. Our concern for Marmaduke.'

Queenie snorted in derision. 'Liar. You've put that poor lad through Hell ever since he was in swaddling clothes. Nothing he ever did was right in your eyes. You broke his heart when you caused his mother to die from your neglect. Then on his wedding day—'

'Tell me something I don't know!' he shouted. 'Don't you understand, woman, I would cut off both my legs with a hacksaw if I could change the past!'

The raw passion in his voice stunned them both. Queenie pulled the veil of her sari around her head and watched him with a new look in her eyes, as if uncertain how to evaluate the change in him.

'Don't tell me you're growing soft in your old age,' she said warily.

'No chance of that. But it's not too late for us to save the lad. Cut him free from the legacy of hate inside him that will destroy him. I want only one thing. To live long enough to see Marmaduke take his rightful place in the world. Learn to trust himself. Learn to *love*.'

'Trust? Love? Did you think you could buy all that for him? By an arranged marriage with a de Rolland bride? You must be mad.'

'Don't you see? I was desperate. For years I've kept tabs on him. Despite his wild living he refused to court young girls. He abhorred the idea of marriage.'

'After Elise jilted him,' she said sharply.

'All right! But there was never any proof he'd even slept with a woman. He never laid a hand on Elise.'

'Just proves his good taste! He's not like *you*. Bedding everything in petticoats.'

Garnet clenched his teeth, knowing his anger would not win Queenie to his cause.

'Listen, Queenie, believe one thing of me. Ever since Marmaduke was a little chap I could see what was inside him and tried to curb it. He's intelligent and gifted but also impulsive, headstrong, undisciplined, lazy. He's inherited the worst traits of his mother.' He forced himself to say the painful words. 'Yes, yes, and his father!'

The weight of the silence that hung between them was so leaden Garnet didn't know what words to choose to exact from Queenie the promise he desperately needed. She leant forwards in her chair and watched him like a hawk.

'What do you want of me, Garnet? I promise nothing, except I will hear you out. But only for Marmaduke's sake.'

'The moment I sign over Mingaletta to Marmaduke he'll turn his back on me.'

'You'll lose your control over him!'

'I'll lose *my son*! His bride is my one hope of keeping a link with him. Isabel is very young, inexperienced and charming. She appears to be devoted to him. But I have reason to believe she carries scars from her childhood. She's proved her loyalty to the de Rolland family. But I *must* know. Is she true of heart? Will she stick by my boy for better and worse? Or is she here purely out of honour? Does she have her eye on my fortune? You've talked to her. Tell me the truth. I *trust your judgement*.' He gave a sharp laugh. 'Do you know what it cost me to admit that?'

She stared at him. 'You know, I *almost* believe you.'

'Will you grant me your promise you won't wreck his life? Give those two a chance to find each other. Before you honour your promise to Miranda?'

Queenie nodded slowly. 'I agree to wait until we prove whether that girl is true blue.'

The old shrew said 'until' we prove'. I've got her on side!

Garnet hurled himself out of his chair and grasped both her hands so tightly he made her flinch. 'I have your word on that? Do you solemnly swear it on Miranda's memory?'

'I swear it.' She rose and broke free of him, crossing to the door with the veil of her purple sari fluttering behind her. Pausing in the doorway she cocked her head to one side like some strange breed of wizened Indian owl.

'I have never been sure, Garnet Gamble, if you are mad or bad. Or both. But make no mistake. If you betray Marmaduke again I'll do what I've wanted to do to you for years. Swing for your murder!'

CHAPTER 28

Isabel awoke in alarm, her heart beating rapidly at the sudden realisation she was alone in an unknown place, wrapped in a blanket.
Where was Marmaduke?

A cave! Daylight streamed through the entrance, transforming last
night's place of sinister shadows. The campfire was now reduced to a
thin spiral of smoke rising from the embers.

Last night was a jumble of memories. She remembered the wine
that warmed her body had sent her to sleep filled with uneasy dreams.
Had wine also freed her tongue?

Or was I sleepwalking again? Where the hell is Marmaduke?

Isabel sat up in her blanket roll and combed her fingers through her
hair to clear her line of vision. She brushed one long coil away from
her eyes. The other side was nothing but a tangle of short ends.

'Where's my hair gone? What's that monster done to me?'

She shed Marmaduke's outsized shirt and vest but had no idea
where Murray's clothing was stored. She was desperate to see her
reflection. No mirror. So she pounced on metal pots and pans in the
hope of gaining some rough reflection. All they offered were distorted
grimaces like gargoyles in medieval churches.

'My God, I wish I was dead!'

Death! She was suddenly halted by the memory of what had
happened yesterday. The accident at the billabong. Marmaduke had
saved her life. She was overcome by a rapid series of images. And
finally that extraordinary moment after she had cheated death, when
she had crossed the boundary of reality...lying in Marmaduke's arms,
lost to all but the blind instinct to be part of his body. A dream like
no other.

Distracted by the alarming sounds of gunfire she ran to the mouth
of the cave to hear the sharp retort of firearms being exchanged in
rapid fire.

'Bushrangers! And Marmaduke's all alone!'

She pulled on her boots and ran outside, blinking in the strong sunlight at the solitary figure in the landscape. Marmaduke stood with arms outstretched firing at his fleeing target. The thunder of galloping hooves retreated in the distance – the bolters' horses were nowhere in sight.

Isabel slithered down the incline and ran to his side, determined to hide her fear.

'Are you all right? I heard the attack. And their horses. How many were there?'

'Rough count. Twenty or more,' he said, laconically examining his pistol.

'Twenty! They might have killed you! Did you manage to shoot any down?'

'Why? They've as much right to this land as I have.'

It was then she saw that odd twitch at the corner of his mouth and felt confused.

'I must say you're mighty generous about the rights of bushrangers.'

'No bushrangers, love. Those horses were Mother's brumbies. I wasn't aiming at them. Just a bit of target practice to keep my hand in. It's quite a few years since I killed a man. Never know when I might come face to face with another villain.'

He glanced at her with an oddly embarrassed expression. 'Are you all right? Yesterday's swimming lesson was more than I'd bargained for. But all the more reason to learn to swim, right?' He avoided her eyes. 'I'm sorry if I let you down. It won't happen again.'

'I suppose it's a good idea to learn to swim.'

Looking strangely relieved by her reaction he resumed firing at a metal target tied to the trunk of a gum tree.

Isabel was startled by an unfamiliar emotion.

The sun was shining on the long fall of chestnut hair that hung down Marmaduke's back. The sleeves of his striped bush shirt were rolled back over arms that looked muscular enough to fell a forest. His pale moleskin trousers were moulded to his thighs like a second skin. His tall, broad-shouldered frame made him look strong enough to run Mingaletta single-handed.

Today there was no remaining trace of his initial persona as a counterfeit English gentleman. The young man standing before her was the pure embodiment of a Currency Lad.

Isabel felt her heartbeat quicken at the memory of that wild night in the Surry Hills when he had carried her on his shoulders in their race against Maggie the whore.

She blushed at the thought of the warmth of his hair pressed against the tops of her stockings, all modesty lost in the thrill of the chase. That was the most exciting night of her life – except for that moment yesterday on the banks of the billabong. But was *that* real?

Aware of her scrutiny Marmaduke looked her over with a teasing glint in his eye.

'Madam, you're standing with the sun shining straight through you. Your nightgown leaves nothing to the imagination. Any other bloke would take that as an open invitation.'

Isabel clenched her legs together in embarrassment. 'Any *bloke* would have to be desperate. Look what you've done to my hair!'

'Women!' He sighed in mock exasperation. 'I save your life and you complain about my hair-cutting skills.'

Her fear revived the memory of being trapped under water with Marmaduke swimming towards her, his knife clamped between his teeth.

'Thank you for my life. But it's easy for you to be so cavalier. You're blessed with beautiful hair.'

Marmaduke staggered back a step in exaggerated amazement. 'This *is* a Red Letter Day. That's the first compliment you've ever paid me. I feel as strong as Samson.'

He packed his pistols away and Isabel saw the odd, wary expression in his eyes as he swaggered towards her. *What exactly did I do last night?*

'I wouldn't be quick to ape Samson if I were you. Look what Delilah did to him. Cut off his hair so he lost all his strength and power!'

Marmaduke's tone was light. 'Is that a threat, soldier? Can I expect to wake up one morning to find you've shorn me in my sleep?'

'Easy for you to laugh. I don't dare show my face in public.'

Marmaduke studied her. 'It's not quite as bad as you imagine.'

'Oh, that's wonderful comfort! I'm expected to meet the Quality at Governor Bourke's Balls looking like a scarecrow.'

She jerked her head away from his hand as he tried to stroke her hair.

'Don't panic,' he said gently. He piled her hair on top of her head then stood at arms' length to deliver his verdict.

'Yeah. Quite fetching. Curl the short bits. I'll buy you some ostrich feathers. And the ladies of Sydney Town will think it's the latest London fashion. Before the week's out they'll all be cutting off one side of their hair in imitation of you.'

He unhooked his jacket from a tree branch and bundled her into it.

'Yesterday I taught you to swim. Today it's time for Colonial Survival Lesson Number Two. I'll teach you to shoot a pistol – straight and accurate. When the occasion demands you can cut a man down with a bullet. As you do so well with words!'

Isabel suddenly felt as if she was enfolded in the embrace of a very warm grizzly bear. Marmaduke's head was close to hers, his arms around her, guiding her hands. He gave patient directions how to grip the pistol, steady her aim and fire.

As the sun rose in the cloudless sky Isabel's confidence grew. When she managed to hit the metal target twenty yards away and send it hurtling into the bush, she crowed in triumph.

'I really did it!'

'Why are you surprised? You're a quick study. A born survivor. And I'm the man to teach you *anything*, girl – with your permission. Just name it!'

The look in his eyes made her uncomfortably suspicious there was a serious invitation lurking below the surface.

'Fishing!' she said quickly. 'I don't want to eat those beautiful kangaroos and wallabies unless we're desperate to survive. But you said tribal Aborigines have clever ways to trap fish. And I *am* hungry.'

'Right. Get dressed in your boy's gear and I'll show you how to tickle fish. And if we're lucky we'll catch a special big one the blacks taught me how to trap and cook when I was a little squirt. I've never tasted anything so good. You'll think you're in seventh heaven.'

Marmaduke gave her a light slap on the rump to send her on her way but for once she accepted the casual liberty and marched off feeling pleased with herself.

I've mastered my fear of water. I could wing a bushranger within twenty paces. And my hair's going to set a new fashion in the Colony. Maybe being stuck with Marmaduke for a whole year won't be so bad after all.

Dressed in her breeches Isabel rode with Marmaduke through the bush to another extraordinary cave screened by the white trunks of the eucalypts that gave the name to Ghost Gum Valley.

Marmaduke pointed to the black hands that covered the cave wall.

'Tribal elders brought me to this place when I was a kid. Those aren't paintings, y'know. They're real Aboriginal handprints.'

Isabel felt she was in the presence of something so lost in time that it was both a holy place and a prehistoric work of art. At the foot of a cliff beneath an overhanging ledge was a long expanse of natural rock face fringed by ferns. Like a canvas the size of the Bayeux Tapestry, this Aboriginal wall painting recorded a people who had vanished from sight. The entire expanse was covered by a pattern of black handprints, each one outlined in white like reverse cameos. At first glance it seemed a random pattern, but when Isabel held up her own hand in comparison she saw that these prints were of individual hands of different sizes. Presuming that each palm faced the wall, each print was of a left hand. On closer examination she saw that one hand had the top joint of the middle finger missing. Another hand consisted of six splayed fingers. At the heart of this sea of palm prints were two curved shapes like thick sticks.

'Hunting boomerangs,' Marmaduke explained. 'I don't know what powder they used to withstand centuries of wind and rain, but I do remember the old man known as a Clever Man, who brought me here. He mimed how it was done, blowing white powder through a thin reed pipe to outline each hand. Maybe these hands record a whole tribe. Or were added to over generations. Who knows?'

Isabel felt deeply awed. 'It reminds me of the way my ancestors recorded their names in a family tree so we will never forget we spring from royal Plantagenet blood. This Aboriginal art is beautiful – but how sad.'

'Sad? Why so?'

'Because these people can't hunt on their land any more. Garnet won't allow it. And you don't even know their tribal names. I don't understand you, Marmaduke. You studied three or four European languages – even Latin, a dead language. You have books on ancient Greeks and Romans, the Celts, Saxons and Vikings. Everyone who invaded Britain before the Norman Conquest. So why don't you Currency Lads care about the people living in your own country – before we British turned it into a penal colony?'

Marmaduke shrugged but looked uncomfortable. 'That's quite a mouthful, soldier. You've already made it perfectly clear that I'm uncouth, arrogant, vain, lazy and no gentleman. Now you reckon I'm a Philistine who doesn't give a damn about Aboriginal beliefs. Just for the record is there anything about me you *do* approve of?'

Oh God, why am I so afraid to tell him the truth? He's handsome and clever and so brave he saved my life at the risk of his own.

'Well, you *are* kind to old ladies and horses. And you have beautiful hands. I don't trust any man alive...but...but I do trust *your hands.*'

She felt herself blushing at the clumsy admission that slipped out before she had time to edit it. Marmaduke suddenly looked as vulnerable as a boy.

He examined his hands as if seeing them for the first time. 'Trust my hands, do you? I guess that's one step along the road to a libertine's redemption.'

At his whistled command her horse trotted over to them and Marmaduke caught Isabel's foot in his cupped hands and hoisted her into the saddle.

'Come on, the fish are biting.'

When they arrived at a wide, flowing creek, Marmaduke sized up their position and led her downstream to where the creek divided into two.

'Ghost Gum Creek divides like two brothers of different temperaments – one the adventurer, one the stay-at-home.'

Isabel saw it was true. The eager half of the creek sent its waters hurtling joyously onwards to join the waterfall that fell headlong from the cliff rising several hundred feet above them. This cascade of water broke into three linked falls framed between a vertical corridor of lush ferns. In contrast the placid half of the creek detoured towards a shallow crossing of smooth white river stones glistening in the sunlight.

'Come on, soldier, you've got to earn your keep if you want to eat bush tucker.'

Isabel copied his movements and pitched in as he moved rocks to form a shallow pond designed to trap fish before the current carried them downstream.

'Will this work?' she asked.

'Nothing's guaranteed in this country. But the Aborigines have been doing it for untold centuries, so that's good enough for me.'

The fish trap completed, Marmaduke retraced his steps to a quiet bank where the creek water was pristine, its mirror-like surface dappled with sunlight. Marmaduke stretched out on his belly then beckoned her to lie beside him.

'Patience is a virtue – so is silence. That's why women seldom catch fish.'

Isabel watched him as he slid his hand into the water. One pointed finger remained motionless so long that Isabel was embarrassed to hear her stomach rumbling from hunger. At last a little fish swam into his orbit, attracted by the slight flick of his finger. Its wide-eyed, silver-scaled body was within striking distance but Marmaduke's hand remained still. The fish swished closer until it finally opened its little mouth and nibbled tentatively at his finger. Still Marmaduke made no motion. The fish played with him, sucking at his finger as if with a new toy. Isabel was enchanted.

The spell was broken by Marmaduke's lightning move. He pulled the fish from the water and held its squirming body securely with a smile of triumph.

'Lunch is served, madam!'

Isabel anxiously plucked at his sleeve. 'Must you?'

'Jesus, what's wrong now?' he wanted to know.

'Please let her go – she *trusted* you!'

Marmaduke gave her a long steady look then examined the fish, eyeball to eyeball.

'The lady has spoken. You've been granted a reprieve. Go swim off and find your mates,' he said, slipping the fish back into the water.

Without a word he strode back to the fish trap but motioned her to keep her distance.

'Turn your back. If you keep striking up friendships with our dinner – we'll starve.'

Marmaduke selected several fish then whipped the knife from its sheaf and with a few speedy gestures gutted several. He kicked a hole in the fish trap to give the remaining captives' their freedom to rejoin the current.

Isabel watched him intently as he positioned small rocks to form a bush oven, built a fire inside it then swiftly knocked together a damper from flour and water ready to bury in the hot ashes. By now hunger had overcome her sympathy for the fish. She keenly observed how he skewered them on stakes ready to cook, then she followed at his heels as he strode off into the bush. They collected different coloured berries in his leaf-lined hat, as casually as if making a selection at a village store.

Suspecting she had offended Marmaduke's pride in his hunting skills by vetoing his original plan to kill and cook a kangaroo, Isabel thought it wise to remain silent while they ate. But at last she ventured a compliment.

'The fish is delicious and the damper is perfect. I can see how clever you are at living off the land.'

Marmaduke shrugged off her attempt to mollify him. She tried again.

'I *would* eat bush tucker – kangaroo and snake and anything else if I was starving. And it's perfectly natural for Aborigines to hunt them for food. But it's quite different for us, isn't it? We have a choice.'

'You didn't leave *me* much choice for today's menu,' he said wryly. 'But I've never been known to allow a lady to go unsatisfied.'

Isabel flinched at this unnerving statement. *What arrogance! He really believes he's God's gift to women. But I must turn it to my advantage. As Agnes said, honey catches more flies than vinegar.*

'I think this bivouac must be the most unusual honeymoon any bride ever had,' she said sincerely. 'I suppose being a libertine for years you gain insights into women. You know, engaging in *all that*.'

The flicker of a smile played at the corner of Marmaduke's mouth.

'*All that* is great fun, if you're careful not to fall in love. Spoils everything. Goethe was right. Just look at Young Werther. Took it too seriously and topped himself. Think of all the women he missed out on enjoying in bed.'

Isabel tried to sound polite so as not to lose ground. 'But surely you've missed the point. Young Werther only wanted *one* woman – and she loved and married someone else.'

'Any man's an idiot to kill himself over a woman.'

The sun was now high in the sky and she had a raging thirst so she gladly accepted his offer of a glass of wine.

'Tell me, Marmaduke. Do Lotharios ever fail to seduce a woman they *really* want?'

Marmaduke seemed preoccupied opening the wine bottle but finally answered. 'Casanova is said to have gained his reputation as a great lover because he never pursued any woman unless he was sure she wanted *him* to seduce *her*. So, in the eyes of the world he never failed. Clever bloke, I reckon.'

'That means Casanova's lovers chose *him*. He had no say in the matter. How sad!'

'Why do you always see the sad side of things? Most women would be shocked or excited by Casanova's career. *You* feel sorry for him.'

Isabel knew her next question was asking for trouble but she asked it anyway. 'Do you always choose your *sweet ladies*?'

'Of course. I'm no Casanova,' he said modestly.

'They say every man favours a certain type of woman. Are all your mistresses as dark and voluptuous as Josepha St John?'

Marmaduke shook a warning finger at her but his tone was gentle. 'Hey, you know better than to ask me to name names.'

'But it's true you *did* have a new mistress when we were married?' she stated as fact.

'You know I did. I never lied to you. End of story.'

Isabel gave a little sigh. 'I fancy artists like Goya painted your ideal feminine beauty.'

Marmaduke gave her an odd look. 'I won't argue with Goya's taste, but there's room for different kinds of beauty. It'd be boring if all you females came out of the same mould.'

He topped up the wine in her tin pannikin. 'Take your nose, for example.'

Isabel's instantly covered her nose. 'A snub nose is the kiss of death for any woman.'

'You're dead wrong. The most celebrated beauty of the age was Lady Emma Hamilton, the great love of Horatio Nelson's life. When she lived in Naples a local artist made cameos of her profile so beautiful that the classic Grecian profile went out of fashion. Everyone envied a retroussé nose *á la* Emma Hamilton.' He gave her a sidelong look. 'I saw Joshua Reynolds's paintings of Emma in London. Her nose was *almost* as nice as yours.'

Disconcerted, Isabel touched her nose. It sounded like a real compliment but she was not to be deterred from her line of questioning.

'Marmaduke, last night I don't know exactly what I said or did. What was reality or just a dream.'

'Don't worry. You were just in shock. I didn't take much notice.'

Isabel tried to conceal her relief. 'But I do vividly remember that moment just before the tree came crashing down on us. Why on earth didn't that man try to help us?'

Marmaduke was watching her keenly. 'There was no other man. Only us.'

'Yes, there was. Standing on the bank watching us. Tall, straight like a soldier. Piercing blue eyes.'

Isabel touched her cheekbone about to trace the line of the scar on the stranger's cheek but Marmaduke cut across her words.

'You're mistaken. Believe me, we were quite alone.'

Isabel watched him as he hurriedly doused the fire and packed their saddlebag.

Marmaduke is either lying – or else he doesn't see the Other.

CHAPTER 29

The smoky cave was quiet except for the crackling sounds of the small campfire.

Isabel lay asleep under a blanket. Marmaduke drank a pannikin of wine, trying to sort out his confusion about the events of the past weeks.

Long, lazy days of bush exploration had passed since the afternoon they had 'cheated death'. Neither had spoken of that experience on the bank of the billabong, but Marmaduke could not free himself from the images in his head. It was if the events of that whole day were divorced from time.

Isabel had never spoken again about the stranger who she believed had been watching them just before the accident. But Marmaduke did not doubt she had seen in greater detail what he believed had been a trick of sunlight and shadows – Klaus von Starbold.

Marmaduke drank deeply of his wine. He did not realise he was humming a tune under his breath until Isabel stirred.

'That's an old German love song, isn't it?'

'Yeah, very old, medieval. Can't seem to get it out of my head.'

'What do the words mean?'

'Your curiosity is insatiable.'

'Can't I ask a simple question?'

'Righto, you win. I reckon a man leaves a woman unsatisfied at his peril. My Hessian tutor – the man I murdered – used to sing that song when we were walking in the bush. Klaus von Starbold had a rich, deep voice speaking German and English. But when he sang this song there was no doubting it was a love song. His eyes took on that faraway look as if he was searching for another time, another place.'

'That almost sounds as if you liked him.'

'I did in the beginning.'

Marmaduke could see how intently Isabel observed him and wasn't surprised when she prompted him.

'How did he become your final tutor?'

'Garnet wanted to pack me off to London to be educated as an English gentleman. Mother was desperate to find a tutor to keep me at home. She wanted me to study languages, to share her love of the classics and theatre. To keep her quiet Garnet advertised in all the Colonies' newspapers. Klaus von Starbold had just arrived in Hobart looking for work and read Garnet's ad in the *Hobart Town Gazette* and *Van Diemen's Land Advertiser*. He fitted the bill perfectly so Garnet hired him.'

'Does it upset you to be reminded of him?'

'Not at all. What's done is done. No regrets on that score.'

'What was he like?'

'Oh, y'know, tall, blond, blue-eyed, athletic in the Germanic mould. Terribly correct in manners and bearing. But beneath the surface I could feel there was a wild, angry quality he barely restrained. He was about twenty years older than me. Claimed he'd been an officer in some Hessian regiment attached to the British Army. Maybe his name was Anglicised. I got the impression he'd been drummed out for challenging his commanding officer to a duel or maybe flirting with the man's wife. In my young eyes he cut a glamorous figure. One part hero, one part rogue, with a dash of mystery. A deserter? Maybe. Whatever the truth, von Starbold had clearly fallen on tough times, reduced to a post as tutor in a penal colony.'

'No doubt he was a great storyteller?'

Marmaduke gave a sharp laugh. 'How did you guess? I was hungry for excitement, fired by his adventures. Real or imaginary. I didn't care.'

He ran his finger down his cheek. 'He had a thin duelling scar right here. Told me his adversary looked far worse in his coffin.'

Isabel caught her breath. Marmaduke warmed to the memory.

'His command of English was too perfect for a born Englishman. Clearly well educated but whether aristocratic by birth or the von prefix was assumed for effect, who knows? He was an expert with swords and pistols. Taught me everything I know on that score.'

Marmaduke caught her expression and nodded sagely. 'And you're right. I didn't hesitate to use that knowledge against him when I shot him dead.'

Isabel said gently. 'I know you had good reason to kill him. But would it help you to tell me about the duel? I can bear it if you can.'

Marmaduke drank his wine, watching her bemused.

Why her? Why am I choosing to unload my guilt on this funny little girl? I've never told a soul what really happened. It never came out in court.

'After von Starbold stalked off and left us in the cellar of Mingaletta, I took Mother home. She went straight to her room and remained closeted with Queenie. I didn't sleep at all that night. Early next morning I ran to the stables and pulled a young ostler out of bed, a boy my own age. Told him he must act as my second. We headed straight for the cricket ground where von Starbold had given me lessons in the duellists' code practised by the military.

'My tutor was waiting for me in the centre of the cricket pitch. He bowed with a click of his heels. I was so blinded by rage my hands trembled, but I told him to choose his weapons. That it was immaterial to me.'

Marmaduke assumed his dead tutor's manner when he quoted his words.

'I remember he said, "I see you have inherited your father's confidence, young Gamble. But you have had little time to absorb *my* knowledge of firearms."

'Von Starbold was intent on acting the diplomat. "I appreciate your sense of honour, young man. But there is no need for us to proceed with this. I will leave the Colony today as I intended and your mother's honour will remain untarnished. You are but sixteen years. I am six-and-thirty, and a former soldier. You are clearly disadvantaged, young man."

'I remember I said something like, "Better disadvantaged than dishonourable like you! Pistols are quick and final."

'Von Starbold slowly unfastened his military jacket and flung it aside. His white shirt was open at the neck, his breeches tied with a sash around the waist. I had brought my second, where was his?

'I remember every word he said that last morning. "I have no need of a second, young master. This is a private matter to be settled between you and me.' Like an officer he ordered the young ostler to return to his bed and tell no one what he had seen.

'The next thing I remember I was standing back to back with Von Starbold. It all felt unreal, like two actors on stage in the final act of a play in which one of them must die. I heard Von Starbold giving me instructions as if this were no more than just another of our lessons. I heard the paces being counted as we walked away from each other. Turned. I heard the order to fire...'

'My hand shook as I fired. I was surprised by the red stain on his white shirt. It opened like the bud of a rose but von Starbold remained standing on his feet, smiling.'

Marmaduke refilled his pannikin and drank deeply. He knew he must soon put his confession into words for the first time.

'I was mortified when my opponent did not return fire. Then, with great deliberation, he aimed his pistol in my direction, tilted it and fired into the ground.'

'Right until that moment I had wanted to kill von Starbold but seeing him lying there bleeding, I felt sick.

'He reached up and gripped my hand. "So. Life is being full of surprises, eh, young sir?"'

'I panicked. "I'll fetch a doctor," I said.

'Von Starbold shook his head. "Stomach wound, nothing to be done. You have learnt well, my young friend, I'm proud of you. But next time, aim for the heart. Death comes quicker. Do one thing for me! You can't refuse a dying man's last request," he said.

'"Never be forgetting this. You did not take my life, I gave you yours!" His fingernails dug into my hand. "I have no son. So take this – it was my father's. Wear it for me in good health."'

Marmaduke withdrew the gold watch from his pocket and held it in his hand. He read the expression in Isabel's eyes and knew it was a mirror image of his own suppressed pain.

'I can't get his dying words out of my head. They return to haunt me when I'm caught off guard. Drunk or sober. In a crowded room or alone. I can't escape them. What the hell did it mean? That he *wanted* to die?'

Isabel said gently, 'It seems clear he respected you for protecting your mother's honour. Perhaps he wanted to leave you free from guilt.'

Marmaduke's voice was bleak. 'One night recently just at the moment I brought a woman to climax she gave a cry that shook me to the core. My mind flashed back to that terrible day I found my mother being raped. I don't know whether to blot out that memory or try to recreate in my mind the exact sound of my mother's cries.'

He saw that Isabel was holding her breath as if in denial of what might come next.

'Do you see, Isabel, why I'm haunted by the night I killed my mother's rapist? Seven months after that fatal night Mother died in childbirth, the babe trapped inside her womb. Was it Garnet's child? Or fathered by von Starbold in an act of rape? And was my tutor my mother's rapist – or her *lover*?'

There were no answers. Never would be.

Isabel reached out and touched his arm. 'I'm sorry I can't comfort you, as other women do.'

'You listened as a friend. Thank you, soldier.'

Later that night as Marmaduke fell exhausted into a deep sleep he was conscious of Isabel's gentle hands drawing a blanket over his body, putting a fresh log on the fire and the smell of his sandalwood soap on her body as she lay down and nestled against his back.

CHAPTER 30

The breeze carried into the nursery the exotic sweetness of frangipani blossoms. Isabel decided that an Australian summer needed a fresh vocabulary to define adequately its contrast with the northern summers of her childhood. Muted sounds came from the sprawling convict village beyond the house but although the air was languid it also seemed charged with some electrical current – as if nightfall promised something she had never experienced.

Having bathed after their return from the bivouac, Isabel tried to remain cool before she dressed for dinner. Wrapped loosely in a silk robe, she lay across the bed, fanning herself as she idly turned the pages of old volumes from Marmaduke's bookcase. Curious as to which authors and literature had comforted the loneliness of his youth, she hoped this would give her some insight into his mind, the cause of his swings of mood and bouts of melancholia.

Distracted by the sounds of Marmaduke washing his hair in the next room, she smiled to herself. It reminded her of bathing a dog. No doubt he would emerge smelling of that distinctive Indian sandalwood soap that she knew had been part of Queenie's ritual when bathing him as a small boy – a touching sense memory linking him to his childhood.

Isabel tried to avoid her own image in the full-length Gothic mirror that Garnet had ordered to be moved to the nursery to await her return. Carved from mahogany, it stood tilted on its intricately carved stand, one of the many luxurious pieces Garnet had imported. She recognised it from an illustration in *The Repository of Arts* which each month had proclaimed its endorsement of the latest English and European fashions in architecture, landscape, interior décor and works of art fit to grace the finest town and country mansions – styles that the Quality in New South Wales copied.

This mirror was certainly regal enough for one of the royal princesses but Isabel's reflection showed an anxious head full of paper-curlers that she hoped would emerge as decent curls to camouflage her half-shorn locks.

Thumbing through books half hidden at the rear of Marmaduke's boyhood bookcase, she came across a curious volume sandwiched between *An English Gentleman's Journey by Elephant Through the Punjab* and *The Memoirs of a Scottish Merchant's Career in the East India Company.*

The mysterious book was wrapped like a gift in gold-threaded Indian silk. Its title page bore the name *Miranda Gamble* in faded copperplate script. Emblazoned in theatrical flourishes she recognised Marmaduke's handwriting in his name, *Marmaduke Garnet Gamble.* There was also a footnote which read, *translated from Hindi by Colonel James McAlpine.*

Intrigued by the discovery of a work by Miranda's father, a Scottish Highlander who evidently had the soul of a Hindophile, Isabel idly turned the pages. At first glance the text contained archaic words and descriptions beyond her understanding. But the volume's naively coloured illustrations soon proved a very different matter. Her shock discovery of the true nature of Vatsayayana's *Kama Sutra* made her sit bolt upright, her cheeks inflamed. The more pages she turned the more amazingly contorted were the positions assumed by the inno-cent-looking little lovers enthusiastically engaged in their execution. Isabel was breathless with amazement.

God in Heaven! Tangled arms and legs everywhere. They might as well be tied in knots. How do they get out of these positions? Is this what Marmaduke does with his sweet ladies? An appalling thought struck her. *Does he perform all of this with them?*

At the sound of Marmaduke's light tap on their adjoining door Isabel thrust the manuscript under her pillow and hastily assumed a cool demeanour.

Marmaduke's half-dried hair flowed freely over the shoulders of a paisley dressing robe loosely knotted across his naked chest. He came armed with a bottle of wine and two wineglasses. Trust Marmaduke never to be loath to try a new vintage, on the excuse that he had bought shares in a new winery in the Hunter Valley and had high hopes their wines would in time rival imported vintages from France and the Rhine.

'There's time for us to sample this new claret before we dress for dinner. Forgive my state of *deshabille* – too damned hot to dress one minute before absolute necessity. Being forced by fashion to wear those infernal stiff collars is as Hellish as seven years under Captain Patrick Logan at Moreton Bay.'

Isabel let the callous remark pass. 'I'll fix it for you if you'll lace me into my gown.'

'Deal,' he said but on the point of handing her a wineglass he hesitated.

'What's wrong, Isabel? Your face is scarlet. Not going down with some fever?'

Isabel realised she had betrayed herself by her involuntary glances at the book protruding from beneath her pillow. He clearly recognised the Indian silk cover.

'Well, well, well, Isabel. Your catholic taste in literature never ceases to surprise me. Most well-bred English ladies would be content with Samuel Richardson's *Pamela, or Virtue Rewarded*, where the heroine is so pure she faints at the mere suggestion of the hero's lust. But then you're a far more adventurous young lady, eh?'

Marmaduke's eyes were laughing in amusement. Isabel decided that attack was the best weapon of defence. She waved a hand airily at her pillow. 'I can't understand why anyone would find that Indian nonsense romantic.'

'I reckon romance is like beauty – in the eyes of the beholder. But in my experience women find some of the *Kama Sutra*'s ideas quite exciting.'

Isabel still harder tried to appear uninterested. 'I suppose men like you need to attend a school for libertines to learn all that stuff?'

'Personally I learnt on the job.' He clinked his glass against hers then stretched out languidly like a leopard across the foot of her bed.

'The truth is, Isabel, I was born clumsy in bedroom matters. It required the patience and expertise of a retired courtesan to teach me the art of pleasing a woman in bed. I discovered that time and a willing partner are all that's needed. Call it by whatever euphemism you will – the connection, consummation, shagging, lust, or the bible's polite 'Cain knew his wife'. Whatever. To me the art of becoming one flesh is God's greatest gift to man.' He added, 'And woman.'

Isabel held her breath. *He's just waiting for me to hang myself.*

She found her voice. 'I must take your word for it. I never intend to find out.'

To cover her confusion she began to unwind her paper curlers.

'So that's how it's done, eh?' Marmaduke watched her progress with interest. He sipped his wine in silence but his lazy eyes never left her face. On impulse Isabel decided to break down the barrier she had created around the forbidden subject.

'You assume that because I conceived a babe it must follow...' She began to flounder. 'I remember full well how I gave birth. But I don't know how I *came by* that babe. I don't even know what a naked man looks like. Greek statues always have fig leaves *down there.*'

To her surprise Marmaduke did not laugh but nodded politely.

'There's nothing to fear, Isabel. Men come in all colours, shapes and sizes but we're all pretty much the same down *there.* Except some of us are circumcised, like those of the Hebrew persuasion. Some of the British nobility and the royals tend to favour the snip but the working class can't afford the additional fee. No doubt Garnet had me tidied up as a babe to follow the fashion set by the upper classes.'

Isabel was stunned by how effortlessly Marmaduke explored taboo subjects. *Even physicians wouldn't discuss this with a female patient. But it is interesting.*

'I may be a rogue in many ways, Isabel, but no woman has ever had cause to fear me or my body. I would hate to think that you were the first.'

Isabel tried not to bite her lips but she knew every twitch of her body betrayed her taut nerves. *Where are these revelations leading? Why can't I simply walk away? He's not holding me prisoner, except with his eyes.*

'Do you remember how you felt learning to swim, Isabel? You conquered your fear of drowning. Didn't that give you a sense of freedom?'

At her nod of agreement he continued. 'If I promise not to touch you and reassure you that you won't even need to *look at me,* will you allow me to banish your fear of a man's body?'

'Is this some kind of cruel joke?'

'Far from it.' Marmaduke seemed intent on studying the bed canopy above him. 'Tell me, what did you think of the old priest's sermon in chapel this morning? The story of Adam and Eve and the snake.'

Isabel's voice sounded breathless with nerves. 'It made me sad. Eve paid a heavy price for her curiosity and disobedience, to be banished forever from that beautiful garden. Adam was a coward to lay the blame on her. It was half his fault.'

'Agreed. Ever since Eve men have blamed women for arousing their lust. Most unfair. If we blokes can't control our God-given lust that's not the fault of the fair sex.'

'The law doesn't agree with you.'

'It seldom does. As Shakespeare said in *Henry IV*, 'The first thing we do, let's kill all the lawyers.' He added quickly, 'Edwin excepted of course.'

He eyed her speculatively. 'Well, my young actress, to put your mind at rest on the subject of fig leaves, let's play a game before we go down to dinner.'

He beckoned her to follow him. 'We're now going to step inside this mirror.'

'But that's physically impossible.'

'Not with *this* mirror. It's magic, an illusion. You know that phrase magicians use to conceal the secrets of their trade from the uninitiated?'

'Yes. They say, "It's all done with mirrors."'

'Right. So now we're going to test the truth of that. But remember you're in complete control of this illusion, Isabel. You can walk away whenever you wish, understand me?'

She nodded, uncertain.

'You once told me you would love to be an actress. Here's your chance. Just imagine that the two people reflected in this mirror are not Isabel and Marmaduke – they're just two actors in a play. We are the audience. You and I must *not* touch or look at each other on this side of the mirror. Look only at *them*. They exist only inside this mirror.'

Marmaduke did not look directly at her as he beckoned her. Tentatively she took a step closer. They both stared straight ahead into the mirror.

'On this side of the mirror the reality is we are Isabel and Marmaduke. Two human creatures locked into matrimony, each for our own mercenary reasons. You dislike me intensely and—'

'Well, not *all* the time.'

'Thank you. The trick is we must now abandon Isabel and Marmaduke on *this* side of the mirror. We will step through the mirror into the Garden of Eden and become Adam and Eve. See their world through their eyes. Step into their shoes.'

'No shoes. They were naked.'

'Precisely. As God made them, naked and unashamed, like two children.' He paused, 'Close your eyes, count to ten. Then you will meet Adam.'

Isabel closed her eyes and counted but trembled as she realised the significance of the game she had agreed to play. She heard the rustle of silk as his robe fell to the floor. *Ten.* She opened her eyes and blinked but kept her gaze fixed on Adam's face in the mirror. He did not look at Eve. He simply waited.

Isabel knew she had the right to break away and end the game. But she chose not to move. Her eyes were drawn sidelong to the strong lines of Adam's body. Not smooth and white like a marble statue, his flesh was light olive in colour. Not classical. There was a matt of dark hair on the chest, the forearms and legs – and even *there. No fig leaf.* Adam's body was slightly flawed with occasional fine scars. Strong and virile though he was, the thought struck her that naked Adam looked surprisingly vulnerable. Imperfect, yet at the same time more perfect than any marble statue she had ever seen.

Isabel suddenly felt as if the actress playing Eve was cheating. Wearing a robe like a suit of armour to protect herself – from what? She felt quite sure Adam would not touch her. Her heart began to beat wildly as on impulse she untied the sash and allowed her robe to slip to the floor.

Adam kept his eyes fixed straight ahead. He said very gently, 'Hello, Eve.'

'Hello, Adam.'

'Thank you for coming to keep me company. Animals are quite fun to play with. But I felt terribly lonely in this beautiful garden with no one to talk to.'

'I had no choice in the matter,' Eve said promptly. 'God took one of your ribs and created me out of it. Like it or not.'

Adam counted his ribs. 'So that's where the missing one got to. Clever of Him to fashion you from just a bit of bone. But I guess if He can make dinosaurs and elephants, He can make just about anything He fancies.'

Adam's eyes remained fixed ahead. 'We're different from all the other animals, Eve.' He gestured casually from his chest to his groin. 'You're the same as me – but not quite.'

'I'd noticed,' Eve said, trying not to blush.

Adam frowned with the effort of thinking. 'I quite like the difference. But I wonder why God didn't make us exactly the same? Did He tell you?'

'No. But all the animals have a female and a male of the species. Why not us?'

'So they do!' Adam said in surprise. 'Eve, you seem to have been born knowing things that I didn't notice. Does that mean Woman is cleverer than Man?'

'No. But you're bigger and stronger than me, so I guess God gave me something to help balance things.'

Adam hesitated. 'Are you happy to share this garden with me, Eve?'

'I don't know. It's quite beautiful. And we'll never go hungry with so many kinds of fruit to eat. Everything seems to grow without help from us. God seems very kind. Do you think He has a special plan for us?'

'Oh, yes,' said Adam. 'Our Creator is *full* of big plans.' He held out his hand sideways but didn't look at her directly. 'Let me show you around the garden.'

Tentatively Eve slipped her hand into his. She felt comforted by the warmth of it.

Adam dropped his voice to a whisper. 'There are only two trees we're forbidden to eat. I suppose God told you that too?'

Eve nodded. 'I wonder why.'

'Never asked him. But He seems pretty determined on that score. He keeps telling me, "Do this, don't do that. And you can live the life of Riley."'

Adam's eyes flicked sideways to Eve. 'Have you ever noticed a snake in our garden?'

Eve looked a bit wary. 'Only one. He seemed quite a friendly fellow.'

'He really knows his way around the Garden of Eden. Slithers up and down trees like he owns the place. What do you think? Maybe *he* has all the answers about the forbidden trees?' Adam sighed. 'I'd give anything to know.'

Eve hesitated, 'What are you suggesting? Do you want *me* to go and ask him?'

'Why not? What have we got to lose?' Adam asked.

Where on earth is this game leading? Isabel suddenly froze and the spell was broken. Marmaduke casually draped her robe across her shoulders then turned his back as he slipped into his own paisley robe.

'You played the scene beautifully, Isabel. Eve never stepped out of character. I think you would make a very fine actress.'

Now the game was ended Isabel was startled to find she was no longer nervous. She tied the sash of her robe and wrapped it like a silken skin around her body.

'It was my dream as a child. To run off with a troupe of strolling players and change my name. Can you imagine a Plantagenet treading the boards – and a woman at that? Uncle Godfrey would have had a pink fit. I wonder why they say that fits are pink?'

'Maybe because people go red in the face.'

'In that case they should be red fits.'

'So they should.' Hands in his pockets, Marmaduke paused in the act of crossing to the door of the adjoining room. 'Time to dress for dinner. By the way, what did you think of Adam? A bit of a clod I thought, but harmless enough without his fig leaf?'

'Quite nice looking. Just a boy at heart. Eve had nothing to fear.'

Marmaduke nodded thoughtfully as if digesting a compliment paid to another man. Gently he closed the door between them.

Isabel sank down on her bed and felt her heart racing, no longer from fear but an oddly excited feeling of self-discovery.

What is happening? Who am I really?

Her impulsive decision to drop her robe and stand naked beside the first naked male she had ever seen had been like plunging into cold water. After the initial shock it had felt almost natural. Not the unforgiveable sin that Silas had made her believe she must have committed to become a fallen woman.

It felt innocent. Is this the way God really intended it to be?

The sound of the dinner gong reverberated through the house as Isabel hurriedly rustled through the new gowns hanging in her wardrobe and chose another of Marmaduke's designs made by Madame Hortense. Isabel slipped the turquoise belled skirt over her head and slid her arms through the fashionable balloon sleeves, ready for Marmaduke to lace up the back placket. She looked at her reflection in the 'magical' mirror, conscious of a second wave of liberation quite unlike any previous emotion she had experienced.

When I stepped into the world on the other side of this mirror I suddenly wasn't afraid any more. I was free! Like a butterfly breaking out of a chrysalis. I felt I was truly inside Eve's skin and Marmaduke was truly Adam. What on earth is happening to me? Is this the way actors feel when they're on stage?

Isabel said the words out loud to the girl in the mirror. 'Does this mean that even the wildest dreams are possible?'

The girl in the mirror smiled knowingly back at her. 'It's all done with mirrors.'

CHAPTER 31

The dinner gong had just sounded its summons to dress for dinner when Garnet strode into the empty dining room. His eagle eye scanned the dining table extended with leaves to its full length. Was any detail contrary to his instructions to Elise? Everything must be perfect.

Tonight's intimate dinner for six was a dress rehearsal for his forthcoming birthday banquet for twenty of the local gentry who had shunned his invitations since Elise's installation as resident mistress after Miranda's death.

Aware that Elise was hovering nervously in the doorway, Garnet gave a snort of amusement at the sight of her, tightly laced to the point of fainting in a Regency-striped affair that some whorehouse madam might wear.

'Look at you, woman. More feathers than a lyrebird.'

'Aren't I fine enough for Isabel's company?' Elise asked plaintively.

'You'll do well enough.' He added grudgingly, 'Colour suits you.'

'Is everything to your liking, Garnet? I wrote the placecards myself – with Rhys's help. He's most pleased with my reading progress.'

Garnet was irritated by her air of superiority, her intended one-upmanship. His own literacy had never progressed beyond the signature he signed with a flourish on the legal documents he was unable to read.

'What's so damned clever about being able to read nursery rhymes and the 23rd Psalm?'

He pointed to the framed gilt-edged Masonic certificate he had ordered to be hung here to impress his guests. This document was the first time he had signed his name, no longer a 'marksman', confined to a humiliating cross.

'Now *that* signature was a real milestone. The third of March 1823 when I – and Sam Terry – were initiated as Freemasons in the Australian Social Lodge 260. Its roots were in Ireland so its bold decision to accept Emancipists as Masons really put the cat amongst the pigeons for Exclusives the selected!' he said triumphantly.

'Sam and I dined with our Masonic Brothers that night at the Free-masons' Tavern in George Street. Drank the health of our sponsor, Francis Greenway. '

'Wasn't he the architect transported for forgery?' Elise asked slyly.

'So what? Governor Macquarie granted him an Absolute Pardon in 1819. And Greenway fulfilled Macquarie's grand architectural vision for Sydney Town.'

Garnet flicked a finger at a wineglass, satisfied by the ringing tone that it was genuine crystal. 'Poor bastard fell from grace. He's doing it tough. Barely able to subsist on his marshy land grant on the Hunter but too proud to accept charity. I must get Powell to commission him to design a house for me somewhere.'

Elise was eyeing him warily. 'Has Dr Bland accepted your invitation to the banquet? It would be good for you to see him, Garnet, yes?'

The inference was clear. Bland was the one physician who might be able to control Garnet's dark 'episodes'. For years Bland had gen-erously provided his professional medical expertise to the Benevolent Society. The bitter irony of this did not escape Garnet. The most wretched lunatics benefitted from Bland's knowledge but it was impossible to keep madness under wraps in Sydney.

'I don't need Bland for medical advice,' he snapped. 'I refuse to be made a public spectacle in lampoons like mad King George III. Or poor old John Macarthur, who no longer has control of his land and fortune.'

He turned on her. 'And don't drink too much wine, tonight. That arsenic cosmetic has turned your skin so white your nose goes red at the smell of a cork.'

Elise's eyes flashed in a way that he had never noticed. Had she grown to hate him more than she loved his money? He threw her a crumb of kindness to mollify her. 'Bright idea of yours ordering this new mirror.'

Elise flushed with pleasure. 'They say it's a larger version of the one that will grace the mansion the Colonial Secretary is building on his Elizabeth Bay grant.'

'That so? Alexander McLeay thinks he's the arbiter of good taste in Sydney.' Garnet eyed the mirror with satisfaction. 'Mine's bigger than his, is it? Just proves anything that a Scots Tory can do, Garnet Gamble can go one better.'

The mirror was not unduly large but had an extraordinary range of vision. Its concave glass gave a fish-eye perspective of the entire room.

Elise slipped her arm through his. 'Once the assigned servants serve each course, they must line up facing the mirror, their backs to the company. I gave them strict instructions to keep their eyes on the mirror to anticipate anything that we or our guests require. Watch!'

Like a mischievous child she ran to the far end of the table and seated herself in Garnet's master chair. 'Look in the mirror. Can you see me? What am I doing now?'

'Touching your glass to show you want more wine,' he said.

'Right! This clever mirror also gives us a measure of protection from servants' gossip. They'll miss out on the conversation of their betters.'

At the second ring of the Chinese dinner gong Garnet crossed to the withdrawing room to welcome his guests. Rhys Powell arrived dead on time, his shock of dark hair and side whiskers groomed to a shine, but as nervous as a colt in his well-worn frockcoat.

Diminutive Queenie sailed into the room with all the dignity of a Maharani, adorned in a midnight blue sari patterned with silver stars. Her collection of exotic Indian jewellery was a painful reminder of Miranda.

The arrival of Isabel on Marmaduke's arm caused Garnet's heart to race with pride. Isabel looked enchanting in a bare-shouldered turquoise gown with huge belled sleeves. Her complexion glowed in the candlelight. He noted there was something unusual about the way her hair was threaded by a rope of pearls, a single lock trailing down her naked shoulder in a way that made her look innocently coquettish.

He welcomed Isabel with a kiss on the cheek and an audible aside. 'Don't hesitate to draw Elise's attention to anything that's amiss. Her knowledge of etiquette is limited.'

He noticed Isabel flush but put that down to upper-class modesty.

Garnet escorted her into the dining room then gestured to Rhys Powell and Queenie to take their seats on either side of Elise at the far end of the table. He directed the newlyweds to be seated at his left and right hand and steered the conversation with gusto.

Garnet noted the unfashionable tan Marmaduke had gained during his bivouac in Ghost Gum Valley. The informant he had paid to ride out and check on the couple had reported back that they were living off the land and Marmaduke had taught his bride bush skills, even how to crack a stock whip like a drover.

Intrigued, Garnet wanted to hear Isabel's account. 'So how was your first bivouac together, young lovers?'

Isabel responded with charm and enthusiasm, praising Marmaduke for giving her 'the most romantic honeymoon adventure any bride ever had'.

Garnet nodded tolerantly but he wasn't fooled. He knew from every nuance of his son's face, every quicksilver change of mood that Marmaduke was hiding his true feelings.

The lad's a fool to try to out-trick me. I'm the puppet master – I pull the strings. Damned if I know what's wrong with him, but I'll dig out the dirt before the moon turns over.

Garnet dominated the conversation but nothing worth noting escaped him. For Isabel's amusement he held forth about the Colony's most powerful men, ignoring Marmaduke's raised eyebrow in response to the impression he was trying to create for Isabel that he was on intimate terms with them.

'Take William Charles Wentworth, a powerful barrister and major landholder. He's the acknowledged son of Dr D'Arcy Wentworth and a convict lass transported on the *Neptune*. WC sees himself as the champion of the rights of Emancipists. Way too radical for my taste.'

Marmaduke rose to the bait. 'You've certainly changed your tune since you stepped ashore from the *Fortune*, Garnet. *The Australian* is the first independent newspaper in the Colony, a desperately needed advocate for many things including trial by jury.' He sent a dangerously quiet challenge to his father. 'Would you dare argue with that, Garnet?'

Garnet quickly turned the conversation back to John Macarthur's mental decline.

'Poor old chap. You'll hear his enemies ridicule him as "John Bodice the Bligh Killer". But mark my words, Isabel, history will remember him as the man who put the Australian Agricultural Company and Australian merino wool on the world stage!'

Elise ventured a sly comment. 'Samuel Terry's certainly earned his title of "The Botany Bay Rothschild". Terry's not only a leading...' She stumbled over the word philanthropist but quickly amended it. '...donor to every Sydney charity. He and his wife Rosetta live most modestly but he's enormously generous to *everyone he loves*.'

That conniving woman's going to push me too far one day. Does she think I don't know what she's up to? Garnet was determined to put her back in her box. 'Terry's *wife* Rosetta deserves their success. That woman's worked at his side in business for their entire marriage. I wouldn't fault his good wife's *loyalty* to him.'

Elise's dead-white face flushed with revenge. 'People say Terry's the largest landholder in the Colony after Wentworth. They say he has ninety thousand rural acres under his control but that can't be right, can it, Garnet? That's more than the size of some English counties.'

Garnet was nettled by the injustice of his rival's greater wealth.

'It sticks in my craw. If you take the 1828 census at face value Terry only declared some twenty-seven thousand acres, but add the eight thousand held by his superintendent at Bathurst plus other estates held in his children's names and God only knows what the true tally is by now. What's more Terry was granted thousands of choice acres by three successive governors. Why not me?'

'You've not done too badly, Garnet,' Marmaduke said, languidly twirling the stem of his wineglass.

'Apart from a small initial grant from Macquarie I've clawed my way up the entrepreneurial ladder by my own efforts!' He glared around the table to defy any argument.

Isabel's words were a balm to his pride. 'Your extraordinary success is all the more to your credit, Garnet. No doubt it springs from your qualities of leadership and determination. You are beholden to no man.'

Garnet laughed out loud. 'You hear that? For all her youth and beauty our bride has sound British common sense.' He struck his wineglass with his spoon and the wine steward came in haste.

'So much for your damned mirror!' he said pointedly to Elise.

When a fresh bottle of Hunter Valley claret was brought for his approval, Garnet examined the label but exchanged a silent coded message with Queenie.

Is the love play between the newlyweds genuine?

Garnet looked across at Marmaduke lounging in his chair, more handsome than any errant son had a right to be. He gritted his teeth at the sight of his son's absurdly luxuriant mane of hair, tied back with a ribbon like some eighteenth-century cavalier – to annoy him.

Garnet continued to direct the flow of conversation, all the while watching how Marmaduke, believing himself unobserved, fixed Isabel with that intense, Byronic expression whenever she gave encouragement to Rhys Powell's shy comments.

Why is Marmaduke so jealous? Rhys Powell wouldn't know what to do with a woman in bed. And he's as poor as a church mouse. No catch for any woman.

Garnet noted Elise's flash of envy in her ambiguous compliment about Isabel's gown. And the way the bride expertly deflected it.

'My dear husband has an acute eye for fashion. I suppose it's all those years he spent in Paris and London.'

Garnet was of two minds, admiration for Isabel's pretty compliment and his irritation towards his son.

What kind of red-blooded man designs ladies' gowns?

But Isabel's dulcet tones reminded him of Miranda – the same high-born accent he had longed to hear grace his house once more.

Leaning towards him, Isabel asked confidentially, 'Garnet, is it true that you've invited musicians and entertainers to perform at your birthday celebration?'

'My dearest girl, I have a number of surprises up my sleeve that I've designed primarily to please *you*, my guest of honour.'

Unwilling to be sidelined, Elise chipped in to the conversation. 'In the atrium there's a *faux* wall that folds back to reveal a charming little stage. Sadly neglected in recent years. '

Garnet was quick to respond in a teasing tone. 'But which will now return to life, eh Marmaduke? I understand you've become quite a lover of Thespians. If you put as much time into being a gentleman as you do hanging about Barnett Levey's theatre I'd be a happy man.'

He realised he had created an uncomfortable silence. Isabel was blushing.

Marmaduke gave a tight smile. 'My love of theatre I share with my bride, Garnet.'

Garnet switched his attention to Isabel. 'I built my own little theatre for the amusement of my beloved wife. Miranda was passionate about amateur theatricals – a traditional pastime of the military, garrisoned in India and elsewhere in the Empire.'

He patted her hand. 'I understand you play beautifully. It may please you to know I've just secured the finest pianoforte in the Colony at Sam Lyons's auction house for you.'

Flushed with wine, Elise suggested brightly they should all plan to show off their talents as singers, musicians, declaimers of poetry, even as dancers.

Marmaduke gestured to Queenie to draw her into the conversation.

'I will always remember, Queenie, how you and Mother performed your wonderfully exotic Indian dances? As a child you allowed me to beat my toy drum to accompany you. Would you please dance for us again one day, Queenie? I swear none of you have ever seen a dancer perform with such grace as this lady.'

Queenie smiled but dismissed the idea with an elegant wave of the hand. 'Too old.'

'Ageless,' Marmaduke said gallantly as he caught her hand and held it to his lips.

Elise clapped her hands together. 'Isabel must play the new pianoforte. And Rhys has a fine Welsh tenor voice. That leaves you, Marmaduke. How do you plan to entertain us?'

'I'll applaud you all with pleasure but count me out, thank you,' Marmaduke said quietly. 'I never perform in public. I was cured of that as a boy at a fancy dress ball.'

Garnet eyed him keenly. *So, he's never got over his humiliation being invited as a guest to a fancy dress ball where that dragon of a hostess made him serve her guests because he was an Emancipist's son.* Even after all these years Garnet felt a wave of anger at the boy's suffering. He felt a helpless sense of guilt.

Isabel knew the story and stretched out her hand to Marmaduke.

'My darling, how I wish I'd met you as a boy and asked you to dance with me.'

Marmaduke's mouth twisted in amusement. 'My sweeting, you forget I'm seven years your senior. You'd have been tucked up asleep in your nursery.'

Marmaduke turned to Garnet. 'Which is my cue to ask you all to excuse us. Isabel is an intrepid traveller but the bivouac was most demanding. We narrowly escaped an accident.'

'Marmaduke is modest. He saved my life,' said Isabel. 'I didn't want to upset you.'

Everyone around the table was ready to hear the full details.

'Oh, do tell all,' Elise demanded.

Marmaduke was firm. 'Some other time. I bid you all good night.'

He cupped Isabel's elbow and steered her to the door. Queenie silently inclined her head to Garnet and Rhys Powell but ignored Elise and took her own leave.

Garnet smouldered with irritation at their abrupt departure. He gave Elise a dismissive wave and ordered his secretary to join him for cigars and brandy in the smoking room. For the first time that evening Rhys Powell was no longer on guard, freed from the strain of circumnavigating his way around conversations fraught with ambiguity. The young Welshman was clearly sensitive to the minefields but lacked the confidence to deal with them. Garnet almost felt sorry for him.

'Here, try this Napoleon brandy. It will put hair on your chest, old chap.'

Rhys Powell gave a sigh of satisfaction. 'A fine dinner, sir. I look forward to implementing your plans for your birthday celebration. It promises to be a memorable occasion for you and your son. A most egalitarian young man, if I may say so, sir.'

'Huh! Egalitarian is a polite way to put it,' said Garnet. 'He's one of the new breed of pig-headed Currency Lads who think they can break down class barriers that have stood the test of time for centuries in Great Britain.'

'Perhaps the world is changing, sir,' Rhys Powell observed. 'But then perhaps I see the British class system differently, given I am a Welshman.'

Garnet gave a short laugh. 'When the wine is in, the truth is out, eh, Powell?'

His secretary's face flushed scarlet. 'I assure you, sir, I am far from being inebriated, I only meant—'

'No matter, lad. Let's just run over the lists before we call it a night. Who is signed, sealed and delivered?'

Rhys Powell ran through the list of invited guests.

Garnet drew on his cigar. 'What of the musicians?'

'I've reserved their accommodation at your Garnet and Rose Inn as you ordered, sir.'

'And what about my star attraction? I can't wait to step onto the stage and announce my coup. What's her name?'

'Madame Josepha St John.'

'Yeah, that's her.'

'The diva will be accompanied by her Italian pianist, Federico. Thomas will transport them from Sydney in your carriage. I presume you wish them to be given the best guest chambers in the east wing, sir?'

'Do they cohabit?' Garnet asked with interest.

Rhys Powell looked deeply discomforted. 'I could not presume to ask, sir.'

'Well, give 'em the option. Bed down Josepha St John and the Eytie in adjoining chambers. I've ordered a canopied bed from Sam Lyons that Boney's Empress Josephine is said to have favoured. Due to arrive here any day. And make sure that new pianoforte is perfectly tuned. Nothing's too much trouble for that Yankee nightingale.'

'Indeed, I will, sir.'

Garnet wagged a warning finger. 'Whatever you do, keep Josepha St John under wraps. I can't wait to see the expression on Marmaduke and Isabel's face.'

CHAPTER 32

Dawn had just broken through a maze of dark clouds that held the promise of an electrical storm before sundown. Already the wind was blowing through the Bloodwood trees as if intent on striping the cloak from Marmaduke's shoulders as he rode down the carriageway towards the wrought-iron gates and the road to Sydney Town.

At the sight of the entwined *GG*, the reverse side of the emblem designed to impress the outside world, Marmaduke was sharply reminded of his feelings that extraordinary evening when he had reversed reality and 'stepped through the mirror' with Isabel into the Garden of Eden.

He tried to convince himself he had invented the game purely to allay her fears about the male body. To break down the barriers between them. It had not been a preliminary move towards seduction. Yet on the other side of the mirror the unexpected had happened and left him shaken. In the guise of young Adam, stripped of his fig leaf, he had discovered his Eve and was now strangely enchanted by her.

What the hell is happening? I've practised every trick in the art of seduction. Bedded voluptuous, sensual women. Why her for God's sake? Why do I feel I'm beginning to melt when she looks at me? Those speaking eyes of hers. What's wrong with me? It's almost enough to make a bloke believe in witchcraft.

Marmaduke was jolted by such an appalling thought that he jerked the stallion to a sudden halt.

God forbid! Am I falling in love?

The wind carried the distant cry of a female voice calling his name. Marmaduke turned in the direction of the house.

And there she was. Isabel. Running awkwardly towards him down the pebbled avenue. One hand clutched the tail end of a shawl flying behind her, the other hand waved a piece of paper. Marmaduke hid a smile at the sight of her, like a runaway schoolgirl, her ragged hair blowing around her angry face. He felt a glow of satisfaction to have broken through her cool good manners. As she drew closer it was obvious she had dressed in such haste the buttons of her bodice were wrongly fastened and her petticoat was at half mast, the folds of her skirt whipped by the wind so they outlined the long slender lines of her legs. She looked as sweet and wanton as some English milkmaid.

But I'm not moving an inch, girl. You will come to me!

She was breathless when she finally drew level with him. When she stabbed a finger in the air at him he saw she was trembling. He was on the point of an apology until she opened her mouth.

'Is this the way an Australian husband treats his bride? You just ride off to Sydney Town without a word and leave me to be humiliated, having to hear it from a servant. What's wrong with you? Why are you leaving me here?'

'Good morning,' Marmaduke said calmly, smothering the smile he knew would antagonise her. 'I see Bridget gave you my message. The fact is I only received Edwin's missive by courier at dawn. No time to brief you. I'll write you from Sydney when I know the full story. Edwin wouldn't waste my time so close to the handover of Mingaletta if it wasn't urgent. It has something to do with your Cousin Martha. Something of value.' He added casually, 'I didn't want to worry you. You know how often couriers and mail coaches get bailed up by bushrangers.'

Marmaduke could see her anger beginning to deflate.

'That's all you know about Martha?' she asked quietly. She lowered her eyes but not quickly enough to disguise her concern.

'I swear on a stack of bibles.'

'Well you might at least have had the courtesy to say goodbye.'

'You were smiling so sweetly in your sleep that I didn't have the heart to kiss you awake.'

At the intimate inflection in his voice Isabel seemed caught off guard. She clutched her shawl around her, wincing as the wind stung her eyes.

'Martha came to me in a dream last night. Wearing her bridal gown. Smiling. She looked younger, in perfect health. Just as I remembered seeing her for the first when I was a child.'

'Perhaps she's sent you a wedding gift.'

She shook her head. 'I think she came to say goodbye.'

He reached out to stroke her cheek but she pulled away and regained her composure.

'I bid you a safe journey.'

He dismounted. 'I'll take you back to the house. You're cold. Here, take my cloak.'

'We *could* share it,' Isabel suggested.

He swirled his cloak like a matador's cape and drew it around her as her arm slipped around his waist. She looked up into his face with *that* expression he could never read. Was it concern for him or mere female curiosity? He was determined not to melt.

'I was wondering...but no, I haven't the right to ask.'

'You have every right,' he said quickly. 'You are my wife. Ask me what you will and I'll always tell you the truth.'

'Well, after you've met with Edwin in Sydney, will you...will you visit your new sweet lady?' Embarrassed, she added quickly, 'I wouldn't try to stop you, of course.'

You're the only girl who could. If only my answer mattered enough to make you care.

Marmaduke gently lifted her chin with one finger and made her meet his eyes.

'The truth is, I *must*,' he said.

Isabel fingered the lapel of his jacket, intent on brushing away non-existent dust.

'I have no right to ask you because of our contract. But will you step through the mirror with her, as you did with me?'

Marmaduke felt a catch in his throat. 'No. Only with you. What I have done with other women in the past was a mutual exchange of pleasure. I regret nothing. No love involved. No one was hurt. But you and I, we have found...something else. It isn't love, of course. Both of us are immune to that mirage, thank God. But it seems to me something has grown outside the bounds of our contract.'

'Oh? So what happens to our contract?' she asked anxiously.

'What say we tear it up?' he suggested. 'Then begin again, very slowly. One step at a time. One simple kiss at a time.'

He whispered the last words in her hair, feeling absurdly desperate to kiss her mouth but knew he must wait for her answer.

'There's no such thing as a simple kiss – they all lead to drowning.'

Oh God. Will she never be free of the spectre of that bloody beloved cousin?

He waited. At least she didn't pull away from him.

'I don't know what to do, Marmaduke. I mean, *like that*. You know everything, I know nothing. All those weird illustrations that claim to be acts of love – they make me feel so awkward. Don't you understand? I can't compete with all your worldly sweet ladies. I promise you, I would disappoint you.'

'Hush, sweetheart. *I'm* the one who should be afraid. You're not like any female I've ever taken to bed. Let's forget about the *Kama Sutra*. We don't need it. If you wish we could explore things together, gently. You don't have to *like* me, Isabel. But if you could bring yourself to trust me just enough to say the words, 'I want you, Marmaduke', that's all I'd need. To take you with me on a journey to Paradise.'

'Does Paradise exist on Earth? You seem so sure of yourself.'

'I am. That isn't just male vanity. Believe me, making love is the one and only gift I possess. That moment when we "cheated death", that was just the beginning. There's so much more I'd like to share with you.'

He traced the curve of her lower lip with his finger. 'You want the truth, Isabel? You have done what no other woman has ever done to me.' Gently he took her hand and slipped it inside his shirt. '*You* have touched my heart.'

Isabel's mouth opened in surprise. He felt his heart beating wildly in the hope she would seek his mouth. Instead, she took a step back and said the words in a rush. 'Perhaps when you return you could show me what it's like to be kissed in four places.'

Marmaduke almost laughed with relief. *Thank God for the* Kama Sutra*!*

He bowed politely. 'My pleasure. The sooner I am gone, the sooner I will be on my way home to you.' He leapt into the saddle and hoisted her up behind him to ride pillion back to the house.

Marmaduke did not kiss her goodbye. They both knew it would not end at one kiss.

'Travel safely,' she called from the porch. 'If you're bailed up, don't play the hero. Give them whatever they ask.'

Marmaduke suddenly backed the stallion to the front steps. With a swift tug he tore his wedding ring from his finger, kissed it and thrust it into Isabel's hand.

'This is the only thing of value I possess. Keep it safe for me.'

This time he galloped away and did not look back. He kept the image of those luminous green eyes before him, sure now that Isabel would remain watching him until he disappeared from sight.

This time I've got you hooked, girl.

The cabbage tree palms seemed to have doubled their height in the months since he had last visited the Bentleigh home at Woolloomooloo. Today everything in the landscape looked bolder, brighter and newborn.

Edwin greeted him warmly, clearly pleased to see him but appearing preoccupied.

'Forgive me, my friend, but the world has been tilted on its axis in recent weeks – both your world and mine. First, allow me to clarify my urgent message. I have received a letter from London from the de Rolland family's lawyers informing us of the death of Isabel's cousin Martha, the deceased wife of our old adversary Silas de Rolland.'

'Isabel loved her. It seems Martha genuinely treated her like a daughter, unlike her husband.'

Edwin handed him a package. 'You will see why I did not dare risk this falling into the hands of bushrangers. Martha de Rolland willed to Isabel a valuable piece of her own family's jewellery that she had evidently managed to hold in trust with Godfrey de Rolland, even when the family fortunes were at their lowest ebb. Or else her husband Silas would no doubt have sold it.'

Marmaduke held the diamond tiara in his hands and marvelled at its delicate beauty.

'This is the genuine article, all right. Cleverly designed by a master craftsman. No hint of ostentation. And, yes, this centrepiece can be detached to wear as a brooch.'

Marmaduke replaced it in the velvet case. 'You were right to keep it here. I'll have it secured in Josiah Mendoza's safe ready for Isabel to wear to the Governor's Ball.' His voice took on an edge. 'But this pretty inheritance comes with an implicit warning. Now the Will is read Silas will be free to sail down here and try to lay claim to Isabel.'

Edwin looked uncomfortable. 'He may well already be on the high seas. Our London lawyers report he planned to sail from England shortly after the Will was read. He had long ago spent his wife's dowry. She had precious little to leave beyond this bequest to Isabel.'

Edwin added quickly, 'But do not concern yourself unduly, my friend. You are legally Isabel's lord and master and I gather your bride is content to remain with you?'

'Happy enough for now. But I've discovered the full extent of Silas de Rolland's manipulation.' He selected his words with care. 'He's even worse than we knew. He abused Isabel's affections as a child. He'll stop at nothing. Keep me informed of his movements.'

'Consider it done.' Edwin gave a discreet cough. 'Now we must face the complex matter of the Gamble financial affairs. Your father's fortunes have taken a sharp turn. Good news and bad. This year has proved extraordinary in terms of finance and speculation. It is difficult to predict how it will all end. But land prices in the heart of Sydney have soared through the roof. Would you believe Wentworth sold one of his George Street properties for forty-five pounds per foot?'

'If that's the bad news. What's the good news?'

'That depends on how seriously your father values the wise counsel of his financial advisors. He certainly wouldn't listen to my advice. I am suspect as your friend. But I hear on good authority your esteemed father's title as a leading entrepreneur is shaky due to risky business ventures.'

Marmaduke knew his friend. Edwin hated to discuss others' finances when his own accounts trembled on the brink of the red. His mother owned this house but Edwin owned nothing outright apart from his horse. Although in great demand as a barrister, he was always short of money because he chose to represent so many prisoners who never paid his modest fees – due to poverty or being sentenced to swing on the scaffold for Green The Finisher.

Marmaduke took the warning seriously. 'Let's not beat about the bush, mate. Are you telling me Garnet is heading for bankruptcy?'

'When he bailed out Godfrey de Rolland from the threat of debtors' prison that alone didn't threaten to bankrupt him, but lately he's begun buying and selling properties wildly as if on a whim. Forgive me if I am totally blunt. Having been party to the intimate details of John Macarthur's tragic decline and the reduction of his merino wool empire, I must ask you if your father is in full command of his mental faculties.'

Marmaduke hesitated. 'I don't actually know, mate. Garnet plays his cards so close to his chest I reckon God doesn't know what he's up to. He chides me for being a wastrel on one hand, yet is appalled at the idea of me engaging in trade which, as you know I am – with good old Mendoza as well as fingers in other pies. Now I'm responsible for supporting a wife I'm even more determined to be financially independent. But Garnet insists we live with him in that mausoleum of a house until the deeds are handed over. I reckon he'll keep stalling, so I won't wait any longer. I've come here to find an architect and a pattern for an Indian-style Colonial bungalow to rebuild on Mother's land.'

Edwin looked faintly surprised. 'Marriage seems to have changed your plans.'

Marmaduke tried to sound off-handed. 'Isabel was an orphan. She's always lived under sufferance in other people's houses. I want to surprise her. Involve her in the planning of the first real home of her own.'

Edwin nodded sagely, saying nothing.

Marmaduke felt uneasy. 'What's that funny wise-owl look in aid of? Don't think I've fallen in love or any of that romantic rot.'

'Of course not, I can see that,' Edwin said carefully. 'But it sounds as if your year-and-a-day contract might well be extended indefinitely, eh?'

Marmaduke back-pedalled quickly. 'That's up to Isabel. I miss the freedom of bachelor life but the poor girl *needs* me now more than ever.'

Maeve stood smiling radiantly in the doorway. Marmaduke rose to his feet and drew her into a brotherly hug.

'I've never seen you look happier. Edwin must be doing something right.'

Maeve's laugh was one part reassuring, one part wicked. Edwin looked pleased but embarrassed.

'Everything would be perfect except that Mother is performing her own three-act melodrama of guilt and recriminations. As you know she is a rigid Anglican and Maeve is a Catholic. Mother throws a fit at the thought of her only son, a Quaker, being married by the Papacy.'

'To a fallen woman,' Maeve supplied cheerfully. 'Mrs B won't have a bar of me in an Anglican wedding ceremony either.'

Edwin gave a weary sigh. 'The drama continues night and day, week in week out. She claims our marriage would be the death of her – and she *is* bedridden and nigh on eighty...'

Marmaduke decided it was time to take charge.

Edwin's a tiger in the courtroom but he's been emotionally black-mailed by his mother all his life. He's trying to keep both women happy and making himself miserable in the process.

'There's a way out of a stalemate like this. Two sets of banns and two weddings on the same day. And as far as any future plans, the English have a neat, equitable solution – raise the boys in their father's religion, the girls in their mother's. When a babe pops out just plonk it in Mrs B's arms and she'll fall in love with it. 'Owzat?'

'Fine with me, dear,' Maeve said hesitantly to Edwin but was startled when Edwin raced out of the room without a word.

Marmaduke sat with her in the ensuing silence that grew increasingly uneasy. *Jesus, surely he hasn't rushed upstairs to tell his mother!*

Edwin returned armed with a bottle of wine and three glasses.

'You,' he said pointing at Marmaduke, 'are booked for best man at both ceremonies.'

They downed the champagne. Marmaduke saw the pair exchange glances awash with tenderness. They seemed to be encased in a private cocoon. Someone had to wrap things up.

'Right, so now that's settled. If you have trouble organising it here, our chapel at Bloodwood is used by every religion in the locality. Garnet's an atheist but he says it keeps our assigned men quiet on Sundays if they're allowed to bow and scrape whichever way they want. What's your next problem?'

'You're an angel!' cried Maeve.

Enveloped in her tearful hug and with his back thumped by a grateful Edwin, Marmaduke felt content.

Shining with happiness Maeve rushed off into the kitchen to bake an Australian cake of her own invention, a mixture of passionfruit, bush apples and berries.

Marmaduke was not sure how to broach the next subject.

'Isabel understands I won't risk fathering kids, but I reckon she needs a child to mother. I've reason to believe there's a child called Rose Alba, about four years old. Maybe in the care of a relative. Born on the wrong side of the blanket. The de Rolland family doesn't know she exists. So your lawyer mate in England needs to be dead careful making enquiries. I'd be glad to bring the kid out to New South Wales to live with us. A surprise for Isabel, understand?'

Edwin eyed him intently. 'Consider it done. My London colleague is the soul of discretion.'

Marmaduke was itching to put his plans into action. 'I'd better be off, mate. Until we meet again in your chambers. I need to make a Will leaving Isabel well provided for in case I come to some sticky end. You never know what's lurking round the corner in this Colony.'

He tried to sound light of heart. 'I haven't the slightest doubt Silas de Rolland is going to lob on our shores. I've only got a short time to turn my whole life around. From being an idle wastrel and woman-iser to being a respectable landholder, a man of substance.'

Marmaduke turned at the front door with a self-deprecating smile. 'I know it sounds crazy, mate, even impossible. But I want to see myself reflected in Isabel's eyes as the man who came to her rescue. Don't laugh. I want to be Isabel's *hero*.'

Before Edwin had time to answer Marmaduke bolted out the door, leapt into the saddle and rode off headlong into the face of the wind.

Book Two
The Mask

Love is always a stranger in the house of avarice
– Andreas Capellanus, late twelfth century

CHAPTER 33

Darkness at Bloodwood Hall had a deeper, darker dimension than Isabel had ever experienced, even in her nightmares. It wasn't the darkness of the night sky, that vast, midnight blue cocoon around the bush in which a myriad of alien stars fought for space – God's creation of darkness.

This other darkness was human and malevolent. Without Marmaduke's presence to protect her, Isabel fought to keep a rein on her imagination, yet was drawn by an invisible undertow into a whirlpool of psychic blackness that seemed to permeate every room of Garnet's mansion. No amount of lighting – oil lamps, candelabra or firelight – could dispel her feeling that unspeakable things had occurred here in the past and more were to come.

The lingering sense of evil was not confined solely to the stone walls of the house. Walking in the bush with Elise in the direction of Ghost Gum Valley, Isabel left Elise to rest her feet for a few minutes while she went on ahead down a track leading to a secluded water-hole. The sun was shining brightly, yet she became uneasy, feeling sure she was being observed.

It was then she saw them. A small group of tribal men stood watching her in silence some twenty feet away on the far side of the waterhole. Their half naked bodies were glistening with sweat and they carried hunting spears, but judging from their stance they did not appear threatening. She glanced over her shoulder in the hope that Elise had caught up with her. She was nowhere in sight. Isabel knew she must handle this encounter alone. Marmaduke had told her Aborigines considered it good manners for strangers to exchange names. And not to look directly into a person's face.

She dropped a curtsey. 'Good morning. My name is Isabel Gamble. You are most welcome.'

She tried to avoid direct eye contact but was aware that the oldest of the warriors was observing her. His deep-set eyes challenged her.

He knelt on one knee and scooped up a handful of water to drink, but his eyes never left her face.

Isabel felt unnerved. At the sound of Elise calling her name she turned to answer her, 'I'm here.'

She spun around, suddenly chilled to the bone. She was completely alone. There was no one else here – nothing except a lingering sense of death that made her flesh creep.

Elise drew level, fanning herself with a switch of gum leaves. 'What's the matter, Isabel, you're as pale as a ghost?'

'Elise! Something terrible happened here – can't you feel it?'

Elise gave her an odd look. 'Nothing important. It was years before Garnet gained title to the land. His convict shepherds ran flocks of his sheep here. Naturally they forbade wandering blacks to hunt kangaroos on Garnet's land. So the blacks speared a sheep for their tucker. Shepherds were punished for losing sheep by having their Government rations cut. So they poisoned the waterhole. Killed off a whole tribe of the poachers.'

Poachers? But it was their tribal land.

Isabel found her voice. 'Did Garnet know of it?'

Elise shrugged. 'Don't look so shocked. It's not like the blacks are human like us.'

Isabel picked up her skirts and turned back to the house, too angry to trust herself to speak. She remembered Marmaduke's warning. All the evil that had occurred here had indeed left its mark.

That night Isabel lay curled up in bed in Marmaduke's old nursery isolated from the rest of the household, reading by candlelight the loved books of his youth in an attempt to form a closer bond with him. Her first impressions of Marmaduke had passed through many stages from arrogant, hated adversary to comrade-at-arms, teacher, friend, protector – to the haunting image of the strangely shy, tender Adam. And he was also the hero who had saved her life.

As the shadows danced with the candlelight she held at bay her fears of the creaking sounds magnified by the darkness she had heard for several nights. Now in the absence of Marmaduke's reassuring sleeping presence in the little dressing-room, Isabel gave in to a child-like impulse. She retrieved his pillow from his cot bed and took it back to her own. Cradling his pillow in her arms she smelt the lingering trace of the sandalwood soap he used to wash his hair. She blew out the last candle and fell asleep, her face on his pillow, knowing that if she woke, the smell of sandalwood would give her a comforting sense of his protection.

In the dark of night she awoke sweating with fear from a vivid dream of that moment in her childhood, the strange expression on Silas's face when she confessed to him she had prayed to the Devil to save her from drowning. She heard his words echo in her mind. 'You are now dead in the eyes of God, *ma petite cousine.* You have no one else to protect you. Pray only to *me.*'

Unable to define any outline in the pitch blackness, Isabel froze when she heard the familiar feathery sounds of footsteps muffled by the carpet runner in the corridor. The footsteps paused outside her door. She clutched the sandalwood pillow to her breast like a shield.

The Other! My God! Did I remember to turn the key in the lock?

She held her breath and waited. Then, just as those other nights, there was a sharp clicking sound before the footsteps faded away down the corridor. Was this the ghost that Queenie and the Irish servants had heard? Isabel was sure of only one thing.

Martha's ghost would never frighten me. And I'd know if Silas was dead.

Isabel trembled at the indelible memory of his blasphemous words, 'Pray only to *me.*'

She buried her face in the sandalwood pillow to draw strength from it.

I'm no longer a child. Silas has no power over me. I will pray to God if I want to. Maybe He hasn't forsaken me. Please God bless everyone I love. Aunt Elisabeth, my little Rose Alba. And protect Marmaduke from all that is evil, especially bushrangers.

At last the sandalwood perfume worked its magic. Isabel fell into a deep sleep.

There were no letters from Marmaduke all that week. The motive behind his continued absence remained a mystery. Each passing day had brought no further word since the hasty note he'd penned on arrival in

Sydney Town, telling her that Edwin and Maeve were to be married. Isabel felt pleased for them but strangely abandoned, as if she were shipwrecked on an island called Bloodwood, cut off from the world by an ocean of bushland.

This isolation was not entirely friendless. Queenie never came to the house except on request but passing Isabel in the rose garden the old nanny had gently touched her arm. 'You know where to find me if you need me, girl.'

Isabel was lavished with attention by her flamboyant father-in-law, a situation Marmaduke warned she must play with care. Isabel prided herself that she had found the perfect solution. How to spend time alone with him, yet hold him at bay. Chess!

Their daily games were played out in the dappled light of the bougainvillea-shaded terrace. She took care to give Garnet the illusion he was teaching her the intricacies of the game that, unknown to him, she had mastered as a little girl alone in Uncle Godfrey's library where she played both sides – the White Rose of York versus the Red Rose of Lancaster.

Living in Garnet Gamble's world I feel like a pawn in a human chess game where there are no known rules. And yet I remember the Italian proverb: 'Life is like a game of chess. At the end of the game the Pawn and the King go back in the same box.'

Seated opposite him in the Indian planter's chair on the terrace, Isabel glanced up from the chessboard, aware of the intense way he studied her. She knew she was also under scrutiny from Bridget each time the girl brought Garnet fresh jugs of cold water from the well. Isabel suspected these jugs, if not the well, were laced with gin.

Through the open French windows Isabel could feel Elise's eyes boring into her back, her sighs audible as she stabbed her needle into her eternally unfinished tapestry. This was a scene in Empress Josephine's garden at *Malmaison,* celebrated for the exotic flora and fauna French scientific teams brought back from their explorations in the Southern Hemisphere as tribute to Napoleon, including species from this mysterious continent known on maps for centuries as *Terra Australis Incognito.*

Isabel felt a flash of pity for Elise. *She's so desperate to appear a lady she apes the Quality and worships all things French. Who can blame her? No doubt the French were designing elegant fashions when we Britons were painting our bodies blue with woad.*

As Isabel mentally toyed with the next chess piece she must move to ensure Garnet's ultimate check mate, she was reminded of the relevance of the exquisitely carved and painted chess pieces. Each day they played chess Isabel chose the white side, miniature replicas of the Duke of Wellington and his army, victors of the 1815 Battle of Waterloo. She chose white being aware that despite his British heritage, Garnet preferred to use his chess strategy on the side of Napoleon, his Empress Josephine and the gallant French officers in their glorious uniforms. Garnet always led the Little Emperor to victory. Isabel suspected this was Garnet's symbolic triumph over what he saw as the British system that had transported him.

No doubt Garnet admires Boney's genius for appropriating whatever he wanted – crowning himself Emperor and spreading his family dynasty across the map of Europe. Given half a chance Garnet would control the entire eastern half of Australia from Cape York to Van Diemen's Land – if he doesn't already!

Garnet's discreet cough prompted her. It was time to make her move. She felt unnerved by the sensuous way he was rolling the Duchess of Wellington between his thumb and finger while eyeing Isabel as if intent on penetrating her most intimate secrets.

Hastily she pushed her knight into the vacant square she knew would lead to her downfall and gave a mock sigh of defeat when Garnet declared, 'Check mate, m'dear!'

'You are most patient, Garnet. I fear you must find me a boring opponent.'

'Utter nonsense. No one else around here has the wit to learn from their mistakes. I'll turn you into my little chess mistress before the year is out!'

Not if I can help it.

Downing his final tumbler of 'lime' juice he proffered his arm.

'Come, bride, let's take tea in the garden. We can talk in private.'

The columns and roof of the summerhouse were entwined with flowering vines that blended two sensuous perfumes. While Garnet gave exacting orders to Bridget for afternoon tea, Isabel chatted to the young Irish ticket-of-leave gardener whose given name had long been lost in the dozens of 'Paddys' – as Garnet called all his Irish Government men.

'I must compliment you on your rose garden, Paddy.' Isabel lowered her voice. 'Do you by chance have my favourite rose in cultivation, the white Rose Alba?'

Paddy grew confidential. 'I do not. But sure it's a strange thing. Your good husband asked me that same question. Himself wants Rose Alba cuttings to be planting at Mingaletta when it comes to him. I advised him to try Thomas Shepherd's Darling Nursery in Sydney – he's the man who sends us our fruit and grapevine cuttings.' Paddy looked stricken. 'By the saints, I trust I've not spoilt the young master's surprise for ye, ma'am?'

Isabel smiled her assurance that she would pretend surprise when the Rose Albas arrived.

At the sight of Bridget and Black Mary heading towards the summerhouse bearing enough paraphernalia for a tea ceremony, Isabel crossed to Garnet's side. After young Black Mary scuttled back to the kitchen, Bridget lingered to pour their tea. Garnet, on his best behaviour to impress Isabel, politely asked Bridget if she minded him calling her 'Irish'?

Isabel noted that the quick flash of anger in the servant's eyes did not fade after she assumed a coquettish smile. 'Sure that's what I'm proud to be, being a daughter of Dublin. Not that I'm likely to see home again or me old Granny before she goes to God. But I'll not be minding for ye to call me Irish, sir, whenever ye have the *need for me to serve ye.*'

Isabel looked away, stunned by the girl's implied intimacy. Yet she also sensed Bridget's sad memories of home were genuine.

Bridget thinks I'm the enemy – British nobility. If only she knew the truth. We were both in a sense forced 'to leave our country for our country's good'.

Garnet did not take offence at Bridget's words. 'You never can tell how the cards will fall in this Colony, Irish. Take me. Transported on a Hell-ship to the farthest corner of the British Empire, but I built an empire of my own!'

'Indeed ye have, sir.' As she departed Bridget cast him a final look. Isabel had seen that same expression on the faces of other assigned servants under Garnet's dominance – cold resignation that was a hair's breadth away from pure hatred.

Isabel was struck by the disparity between Garnet's attitude to assigned females and Marmaduke's remembered words: 'I wouldn't dream of taking an assigned woman to bed. Those poor wretches must do as ordered, not as they please. I do have *some* standards.' How wrongly she had interpreted Marmaduke. She now knew these careless words meant he did not hold convicted women in contempt as his social inferiors. He had refused to exploit their vulnerability, their desperate desire to latch on to any man to be their protector.

The Gamble father and son were both womanisers but poles apart in their code of practice. Garnet, despite his claims of undying love for Miranda and his installation of Elise as resident mistress, behaved like a medieval lord claiming his right to deflower virgins.

I must admit the Droit de seigneur *was abused by my own ancestors.*

Isabel masked her amusement as Garnet made great inroads on the pastries. He ate with the same gusto with which she imagined the Tudor King Henry VIII tackled each meal.

He caught her eye. 'What do you think of the Colony now you've had time to evaluate us?'

Isabel was pleased that he had asked her but would he be offended by her answer? 'It's a whole new world, Garnet. I adore the wildness of the landscape and I'm adjusting to the seasons. But the thing that really excites me is the revolution!'

Garnet looked startled so she pressed on.

'I like the way the English class system here is being turned upside down, not only by the lower orders but by Governor Bourke, *The Australian* and Marmaduke's friend Rupert Grantham. They have really gone out on a limb to champion the Emancipist cause against the Exclusives, demanding for all the same rights enjoyed by British citizens – trial by jury, *Habeas Corpus*, plus a Legislative Council to pass the Colony's new laws, instead of automatic British laws.'

Oh God, have I gone too far? Garnet is both an Emancipist and powerful landowner. So which side of the battle is he on? The opposite camp to Marmaduke, no doubt!

'What it is to have a woman who's not afraid to take a stand. Just like my Miranda!'

Isabel stiffened when Garnet suddenly grabbed hold of her and ignored her instinctive attempt to withdraw her hand. She gasped in recognition at the emerald he slipped on her finger – a ring so magnificent it almost overpowered her gold wedding band.

'Yes,' said Garnet, 'this is the Indian emerald in Miranda's portrait. Always intended to be the betrothal ring for Marmaduke's bride. At last it's found its rightful home.'

'I don't know what to say,' Isabel said, trying to mask her feelings.

That's a bald-faced lie. I know exactly what I'd like to say to his face! How insensitive can a man be? Does he think I don't know that Marmaduke gave this ring to the bride who jilted him? Elise has been wearing it for years! It is tainted with unhappiness.

'Just wear it in good health, dear girl. One day you may care to pass it on to the bride of your first-born son.'

Oh dear, I can see what's coming now. Garnet's dynasty speech!

He folded his arms across his chest in patriarchal mode. 'We are family so I have the right to ask. Marmaduke is kind to you? He's attentive to…all your needs?'

Isabel felt herself stammering in anger but was determined to fight fire with fire. 'If I take your meaning correctly, Garnet, you are either enquiring if I am already *enceinte* or if my husband is the virile man his father is. The answer to both questions is a private matter. But I can tell you that if every female, bond or free, had a husband as romantic and passionate as Marmaduke, there wouldn't be an unhappy woman in this Colony!' She rose to feet and added haughtily, 'Now if you'll excuse me!'

Garnet threw back his head and crowed in delight. 'My God, there's no intimidating you, girl! You are a woman after my own heart.'

He jumped to his feet and blocked Isabel's exit to the archway. 'Forgive an older man his impatience. I simply want to be sure that when you bring my grandchildren into the world they will be conceived in love. Every child deserves that. Few gain it.'

Suddenly weary, he looked into the middle distance. 'Marmaduke was born of a great love. I adored Miranda to distraction but for years I refused to give her another child at the risk of losing her in childbirth. Fate decided otherwise.'

Isabel felt her heart constrict as her thoughts tumbled in confusion. *Garnet really did love Miranda. Is that the true reason he slept with assigned women – to spare her the risks of childbirth? Did he suspect her second child's paternity? But at least Marmaduke was conceived in love. So was I. But I failed to give Rose Alba that same precious gift. What does the future hold for her? Marmaduke vows he'll never father a child and he expects me to lie about this to Garnet to help him claim Mingal- etta. I'm paid good money to be my husband's ally. So why can't I lie to Garnet? He's a bad man and yet, oh God, he looks so terribly sad.*

Isabel placed a tentative hand on his sleeve. 'Forgive my hasty words, Garnet. I assure you I am willing to bear Marmaduke all the children he desires.'

Garnet gave a nod of resignation. 'Yes, that's what I thought you'd say. You are nothing if not honest.' He looked suddenly old and weary as he stepped aside and gestured to Isabel to lead him from the summerhouse.

The tranquility of the afternoon was shattered by the ugly sound of a man's groans piercing a confused meld of noises – horses' hooves, the rattling of iron chains and harsh commands from voices of authority.

Emerging from the dense bush lying to the west of the estate was a band of mounted troopers dragging a prisoner in chains towards the square behind the house. Already a silent stream of convicts had emerged like reluctant shadows from their quarters. At the centre of the square Fordham the Flogger stood in readiness, tapping the coiled whip against his thigh. He was the only man present who had a smile on his face.

Flanked by the troopers' horses the young prisoner stumbled along, his bare feet shackled, his head cowed as he was prodded by the butt of a trooper's musket to keep pace with his captors. This trooper looked more absent-minded than vicious.

Isabel suspected this young prisoner was the bolter who had absconded from Bloodwood Hall and who newspapers claimed had been 'in the bush' for weeks, suspected of bailing up lone travellers on horseback.

The trooper remained in the saddle as he confronted Fordham.

'By rights we should dump him at the Watch House, but Magistrate Summerhayes is away on the Circuit – no knowing when he'll be back. Can't spare a man to guard this bolter until then. Y'know what these bloody Irish are like – so sharp they manage to escape through keyholes. So this one's yours for the keeping, if you want him.'

'My cat is waiting to purr,' Fordham grinned and one trooper barked a laugh of response. The others glanced away, too weary to care.

The cat! Fordham means his cat-o'-nine-tails! He's going to flog the lad!

Isabel wore a house dress covered with a pinafore because she had been washing her hair. But there wasn't time to change. She ran back inside the house in search of Garnet and passed Bridget on the stairs.

'Where's Mr Gamble? Is he up yet?'

Bridget gave her usual surly reply. 'How do I know? I'm not my master's keeper.'

The thought was automatic. *So Garnet's back in Elise's bed. I need to keep my finger on the pulse of this crazy household, but right now I've more important work.*

'Find your master immediately. Tell him the bolter who threatened to assassinate him has been brought back in chains to be flogged.'

'Paddy Whickett?' Bridget turned deathly pale beneath the freckles that bridged her cheeks. Isabel wondered if it was from fear or concern for the bolter.

Isabel hurried outside, combing her fingers through her hair. She gave no thought to her appearance. One image was uppermost in her mind.

The Cat! Garnet forbade that scoundrel Fordham to use it. Marmaduke said it's illegal without a magistrate's sanction but Fordham will stop at nothing.

The sun was already blazing hot. The square between the rows of assigned men's cabins trapped the air like a baker's oven. Fordham ordered the men to stand witness to their fellow convict's punishment.

The sound of the troopers' horses was fading in the distance.

Isabel hurried to the rear of the assembled men, wincing in sunlight so strong she was unable to focus properly on the face of the young prisoner who was being roped to the flogging post by two assigned men. His shirt was ripped open to bare his back. Isabel's gorge rose at the sight of the raw wounds that were the legacy of Fordham's previous flogging.

This lad was transported from Ireland's poorest county. He'd have died of hunger if he'd stayed at home. Now he'll die anyway if he's flogged before his wounds have healed.

Fordham strutted around like a ringmaster in a bear-pit, addressing the circle of slouching figures. Some were clearly unwilling to be spectators; some were patently relieved to be officially free from their assigned work for an hour.

Fordham prodded the prisoner's bare back with the leather-braided handle of his whip. 'Get the message, Whickett? There ain't no road over the Blue Mountains to China. That's a fool myth only an Irish eejit from Tyrone would swallow.'

Fordham taunted his prisoner for the amusement of the spectators.

'Still believe in leprechauns and banshees, do ye, eejit?'

Raucous catcalls came from a few cowards but the Irish element remained silent.

Paddy Whickett turned his head to stare at the overseer in contempt. Isabel was shocked by the startling strength she saw in the lad's eyes. Bright blue – the sole colour in his haggard face. The rest of him was dull grey from head to foot – complexion, dusty red-blonde hair, ragged slop clothing. Bare feet bloodied at the ankles by his iron shackles.

'Your failed escape is gunna cost you heavy, Whickett. I'm adding fifty stripes to what I first thought was a fair thing. But if you start bleating for your mam, like you did last time, I'll be generous and add another score.'

In answer the lad twisted his head and spat full in Fordham's face.

Isabel gasped. *My God, he's forced Fordham to lose face. He's ready to die!*

The overseer wiped his cheek with the back of his hand.

'Stand back all ye miserable bastards, unless you want to be splattered with Irish flesh. I carved out this bloke's shoulderblade last time. Watch me make it a double!'

Isabel looked around her, praying for a sign of Garnet's approach.

Fordham planted his feet wide ready for action and bent his beefy arm back to unleash the Cat.

Isabel felt sick to see his arm was tattooed with two hearts pierced with an arrow.

What a mockery of love!

Isabel found her voice. It sounded high-pitched and cracked with anxiety but it carried across the open space with startling clarity.

'Stop at once! You've no right to go against your master's orders.'

Fordham turned open-mouthed. 'Who said that? Show yourself and I'll have ye locked in the stocks.'

Isabel called back without thinking. 'Lay one hand on me and your master will send you packing, Fordham!' She took a few steps towards him, her knees trembling.

'When did they drag you off the boat?' Fordham demanded.

Isabel was chilled by the way the assigned men stared at her body. She knew she must look as unkempt as a slatternly housemaid – and fair game. She brazened it out.

'I'll have you know I'm the new mistress of Bloodwood Hall!'

Fordham hooted. 'Well, howdy-do. And I'm King William's love child!'

Isabel looked around at the leering faces, the missing teeth, the vacant eyes lit by an unexpected show of amusement as they edged towards her, ready for sport.

Garnet's voice sounded from the rear of the crowd.

'You're a bastard, all right, Fordham. Never doubted that, but this time you're a stupid bastard. This lady is indeed the bride of my son, Marmaduke Gamble.'

The laughter died on every man's lips and the smile froze on Fordham's face.

Garnet Gamble stood in the midst of them, tall, unshaven and robed in a linen sheet like a Roman senator – magnificent in his contempt. Right at that moment Isabel could have thrown her arms around his neck and kissed him but remembered her role just in time.

Garnet took control. 'There'll be no flogging today. Put this bloke in the stocks overnight. Go back to your duties, the pack of you.' He turned to Isabel and said quietly, 'You may return to the house. I'll deal with this.'

Thankful that Paddy Whickett had been reprieved even if only in the short term, she picked up her skirts and hurried back to the house.

Bridget stood motionless in the doorway of the kitchen, her face as white as milk.

'Your friend is all right for now,' Isabel said quietly. 'The Cat is back in the bag.'

Bridget swiftly crossed herself. She turned away then on second thoughts turned back, barely willing to concede a point. 'I saw what ye done. I didn't know the likes of you had it in ye.'

'Neither did I!' Isabel's knees suddenly buckled under her and on the point of fainting she grabbed hold of the back of a chair to break her fall.

Bridget's arms caught her, thrust her into the chair and the next moment Isabel felt the girl's hands sponging the back of her neck with a cold, wet compress. Like an obedient child Isabel took the glass offered to her and thirstily drank down the contents. Her throat was so parched with fear that the glass was empty all too soon. One of Garnet's 'lime' jugs.

'This is good. Is it gin?'

'Sure and it's being Mother's Ruin. But I'm thinking you've earned it, trouncing that rotten swine Fordham.'

Isabel was surprised to see Bridget's hands were trembling as she filled a second glass to the brim with gin and lime juice. On the point of downing the contents herself Bridget hesitated, expecting Isabel's disapproval.

Isabel saw that glance. *She's got a heart in there somewhere after all.*

Isabel clinked her glass against the one in Bridget's hand.

'Here's to your freedom, Irish. One and all of you!'

For the first time ever, Bridget looked her straight in the eye without guile or malice.

'I'll not mind drinking to that with ye – madam.'

They drank together in silence, gradually emptying the jug until the raucous sound of kookaburras' cackling laughter brought an odd tremulous smile to Bridget's lips. But it was the bird's laughter that broke her. She cursed the tears that poured down her cheeks.

'That damned eejit, Paddy Whickett. He wanted me for his woman. To get churched. I turned him down. So wild and angry he was, he disobeyed Fordham's orders. Copped fifty stripes for his trouble. So he bolted. Sure it is he's ruined his last chance of freedom. I didn't want it to end this way, just because I chose to go me own way of it.'

Suddenly conscious that she had betrayed herself Bridget resumed her cold manner.

'All right for some. I've got work to be doing.'

Isabel returned to the nursery, deep in thought.

Bridget turned her back on her man. Chose Garnet's protection. She won't fare better than Elise. But who am I to talk? I can't even tempt my own husband to love me.

Isabel turned side on to look at her reflection in the long cheval mirror.

If only Marmaduke knew what's inside me.

CHAPTER 34

'Stop the carriage in front of the Theatre Royal, thanks, Thomas. I have urgent business with Barnett Levey.'

Thomas's wise sidelong glance reminded Marmaduke that subterfuge was a waste of time with such an old lag, a past master of the game. But it *was* half the truth. Marmaduke welcomed a lively chat with the theatrical entrepreneur whose life was nothing if not colourful. He was often simultaneously involved in public disputes with his business partners and his actors. Barnett Levey's wildly imaginative ventures had included a tontine to raise shares in his hotel and theatre which fizzled out. The string of libel claims he initiated meant his name was seldom out of the court lists or the newspapers.

Marmaduke's hidden agenda in visiting the Theatre Royal was the imminent encounter with his mistress, whose name was writ large on the billboard.

Josepha St John. At the thought of the scene he must soon play out with the tempestuous diva, Marmaduke felt acutely confined by his damnably tight winged collar in Sydney's humidity.

He found Barnett Levey in a high state of anxiety, charging around his office in search of elusive documentation to prove his contention that yet another of his actors had broken his contract by demanding a higher salary than his fellow players.

The office was filled with cigar smoke. A tailored frockcoat was flung carelessly across a chair exposing its London label. Barnett Levey's shirtsleeves and vest were lightly speckled with paint from inspecting a backdrop a scenic artist was painting.

A swarthy, handsome man, Barnett's slim build was more than compensated by the kind of spring-heeled vitality Marmaduke associated with pugilists. His dark eyes seemed fired by a glorious vision that was always just out of reach. Marmaduke was reminded of the extraordinary power of Edmund Kean's eyes.

Barnett has the soul of an actor trapped in the body of an

*entrepreneur with more vision than business acumen. God willing
he'll be spared Kean's self-destructive bent.*

Marmaduke clapped him on the shoulders. 'Good to see you,
mate. You're keeping Sydney Town in a state of high excitement as
always.'

His hand was wrung with enthusiasm. 'What a welcome sight you
are. Where have you been? Are yes! Took yourself a wife. Happily
wedded I trust?'

The words were delivered with genuine concern. Barnett was
one of only two men Marmaduke had entrusted with the details of
Garnet's machinations.

'Marriage is not exactly how I'd planned to live my life. But I've
discovered Isabel is a lady of surprising qualities. I must admit she
never bores me.'

'Admirable! Every man should be married. May you be blessed
with a house full of little Gambles.' He gave a wry shrug of the shoulders. 'Mine keep arriving with great regularity, but what can you do
when you love your wife, eh? I must work longer and longer hours
and trust that the Almighty will continue to provide for us.'

Uneasy about the paternal bent to the conversation, Marmaduke
returned it to the theatre. Although his affair with the diva had been
conducted with discretion, he knew Barnett was no fool.

'I notice Sydney's warring newspapers are in agreement for once –
raving about Madame St John's every appearance. I take it your star
is drawing packed houses?'

'Excellent. She gives you full credit, Marmaduke, for the success
of Portia's "quality of mercy" scene. But on some nights when her
name is not the drawcard...'

Barnett's hands rocked in a gesture of instability. Marmaduke
knew that anxiety was endemic in theatre managers. House Full signs
could be followed by a half-empty theatre.

Marmaduke was determined to raise his spirits. 'I hear your sets
and costumes are greatly admired and that Governor Bourke's patron-
age is proving a magnet for the Quality.'

'May His Excellency be blessed with good health! Bourke is a
cultured Irishman of liberal views. I would never have gained my
theatrical licence without his endorsement.'

It was still mid-morning but Barnett poured wine for them to drink a toast to his forthcoming *Richard III*. His troubled mood returned. 'You're one of the few who appreciate the problems I face in this peculiar Colony, having access to only a small core of actors with professional experience. The rest I must mould from former convicts or at best genteel amateurs – all with delusions of grandeur they rival Mrs Siddons or the Great Kean.'

'You've built our first professional theatre company – you're making history, mate.'

Barnett's eyes shone with gratitude. 'You really think so? Three nights weekly I present Sydney Town with scenes from the genius of Shakespeare – his Shylock, Hamlet, Romeo, Julius Caesar as well as crowd-pleasing pieces like *Black-eyed Susan*. A few of my actors would not disgrace the boards of Drury Lane. Others murder their lines or turn up shickered. You've seen how unpredictable Colonial audiences are. Last week they were so excited by *Othello* that after the scene where he throttled Desdemona they stamped their feet until he agreed to murder her all over again!'

Marmaduke shared his groans of laughter. 'Poor actress, killed twice in one night.'

'Save your pity for me! The cheeky wench has hauled me into court, claiming I should double her fee for two performances on the same night!' Barnett's eyes filled with despair. 'I give Sydney Town culture but it's pearls before swine. Last week in the midst of King Lear's mad scene they started yelling for the entr'acte – a girl in tights dancing the sailor's hornpipe! What can I do? I give the theatre my life's blood! But I am surrounded by Philistines!'

Marmaduke didn't know whether to laugh or cry. 'Courage, my friend. May I suggest my friend Edwin Bentleigh is the right man to sort out your problems with the law?' He went on to enquire about Josepha St John. He must find the right time to talk to the diva, not risk upsetting her before a performance.

Barnett asked pointedly, 'Your wife will accompany you to see Madame St John?'

Marmaduke interpreted his warning glance to mean *you are now a married man*!

'I will on Isabel's return to Sydney. My bride's an ardent

theatre-lover and Edmund Kean's most loyal champion. I suspect she knows all Shakespeare's female roles by heart.'

'Does she indeed? Perhaps we could tempt her to favour us with a scene or two? Heaven knows I need young actresses capable of playing Juliet and Rosalind credibly in the eyes of the Quality. Currency Lasses are best suited to bawdy wenches and broad comedy.'

Marmaduke hesitated before making his request. 'I am in need of a favour myself.'

'Name it, my friend.'

'You know my life has been less than exemplary, Barnett. And that I killed a man in a duel. But I believe a man can change himself, become a better man if he is really serious. I know you are so respected in the world of Freemasonry that two Masonic Lodges attended the laying of the Theatre Royal's foundation stone. I was in the crowd!'

Barnett Levey sighed, 'What a day that was. Everything seemed possible.'

Marmaduke pressed on. 'My father Garnet Gamble is a very proud Mason but I don't wish to ask my father any favours. Would *you* consider nominating me for membership to your lodge?'

'You surprise me, Marmaduke, I thought you had no interest in the craft.'

'I've had a major change of heart on many levels. It may be hard to believe but I've turned over a new leaf. To be accepted as a Freemason confers a public seal of approval. I ask this favour not to please my father. And the Exclusives can go hang. Isabel's opinion of me is all that matters. I'm embarrassed to say it – I want her to look up to me.'

Barnett Levey shook his hand. 'It will be a pleasure, Marmaduke. Consider it done!'

Marmaduke stepped back into the heat and bustle of George Street where a gentleman's carriage was forced to veer from the path of a bullock train. Marmaduke enjoyed the scene. The gentleman was furious, but no man alive could outswear a bullocky.

He climbed back into the landau and mentally ran through the list of things he needed to accomplish before his return home: his interview with the Worshipful Master of Lodge 266; his consultation with an architect about his plans for Mingaletta; Edwin's drafting of his Will; a visit to his bank to set up an account for Isabel's quarterly 'salary'; and special advice from his partner Mendoza.

The most uncertain outcome of all was his meeting tonight with Josepha. Next year she planned to sail for New York and tour the Americas from British Canada as far south as Argentina. He remembered her seductive words whispered on their last night in bed together. 'Darling, come with me as my manager. It will be the adventure of a lifetime.'

Marmaduke felt a momentary loss of buoyancy.

What if Isabel rejects me? Keeps to the terms of our contract, takes the money and sails out of my life? An American tour in the arms of Josepha is tempting compensation.

'Shut up! And put your plans in action!'

Marmaduke had not realised he had said the words out loud until he saw Thomas's startled expression.

'Not you, Thomas. Just thinking out loud. Next stop, Mendoza's Store.'

Through the wrought-iron bars guarding the jewellery store window Marmaduke saw the single light illuminating the corner bench where Josiah sat hunched over his work. Marmaduke ignored the sign on the door that read, 'Closed until Monday.' He repeatedly knocked until the old man looked up in annoyance, squinted in recognition and unbolted enough locks to impress the Bank of England.

'G'day to you, Jos. You make me feel guilty as hell seeing you hard at work on a Friday afternoon, given I haven't pulled my weight for weeks. I reckon that's what honeymoons do to a bloke. No excuses. Sorry I haven't been in contact.'

'No apology needed. I must complete an urgent repair before sundown. So you and your bride have returned from your honeymoon?'

'No, just me. Isabel's keeping Garnet company until he hands over my inheritance.'

Mendoza nodded. 'The land given you by your mother of Blessed Memory. But you are here to discuss something urgent, yes? You wish to check our books?'

'Nah. I'd trust you with my bottom dollar. Tell me, is this as valuable as I think it is?'

Marmaduke handed across the velvet box and watched Josiah's reaction.

Without a word Mendoza lowered the canvas blind to block them from sight of pedestrians. He crossed over to the light at his bench, secured his magnifying eye-glass in place and examined the tiara front and back, link by link, gem by gem, then gently released the section that served independently as a brooch with a perfect pearl at its heart.

He turned to Marmaduke and said sharply, 'Who stole this?'

Marmaduke gave a surprised laugh. 'It's *that* good, is it? It's so old and dusty I wasn't quite sure if some of it was paste.'

'It certainly is not *good*,' Mendoza said firmly. 'It is perfect. Again I ask for the truth? Who stole it for you?'

'Hey, hang on a minute, mate. I might turn a blind eye to a gem's exact provenance from time to time but I'm no jewel thief. I've never seen anything like this except maybe in a portrait of some European monarch. I thought you'd enjoy taking a gander at it, not accuse me of being an underworld fence!'

'I warn you it is most dangerous to possess this rare, beautiful thing. It is so old its value is beyond calculation. Return it to wherever it came from at once. No questions asked.'

'Stop worrying. It was Willed to Isabel by her cousin – their family goes back to Willie the Conqueror. If you don't believe me, ask Edwin Bentleigh, he's got a copy of the Will. But what got you so riled up?'

'A visit by the traps. They are quizzing every jeweller, auctioneer and known fence in the Colony about a tiara stolen from a grand house in England. This fits the exact description. There's a reward for the conviction of the thief. With my record if I come under suspicion I'll be sent to Moreton Bay in chains.'

'Hey, Jos, you must be joking.'

'No man jokes about Moreton Bay! You were born free. I am a convicted thief. Years ago I neglected to check the ownership of a broken clock I bought from a desperate woman. That decision cost me fourteen years in chains in Van Diemen's Land. Do you think I'm such a fool I will invite a second sentence?'

'Righto. I understand. But I'm not going to hand over this tiara for the traps' inspection. Chances are it would disappear without trace.

Isabel won't care about its monetary value but she loved the cousin who left it to her. I'm going to see she gets this.'

Mendoza shook his head. 'And put yourself in danger of carrying stolen goods? No. Your father was transported for the theft of a garnet ring. Imagine what the law would do to you – this is a thousand times more valuable. It is too valuable to secure in our wall safe in the store. I will lock it away in my other secret safe beneath the floor.'

Mendoza jerked his head towards his living quarters behind the store.

'But what if the traps do return? I'd be putting *you* in danger. I won't allow that.'

'I only survived transportation on the *Fortune* because your father protected me. Tonight I pay my debt to him. I will guard this tiara for your wife until Mr Bentleigh establishes your legal ownership with the police.'

As Marmaduke hurried down the cobblestone lane towards the Princess Alexandrina Hotel, his mind kept returning to the question of the tiara and the traps' claim it was stolen. Despite the legality of Martha's Will someone in the de Rolland family must be laying claim to the tiara and the perfect pearl at its heart. Marmaduke was struck by the thought that another piece of jewellery, a garnet ring, had caused Garnet's downfall at the hands of that same family. Was history repeating itself?

He was reassured that the tiara was in safe hands. Right now he must dress for this evening's Benefit Performance at the Theatre Royal before facing his own performance with the tempestuous Josepha St John. He sensed that this evening would be no ordinary farewell.

At the end of the concert, Thomas drove Marmaduke to the elegant new townhouse that had been leased by an admirer of the Yankee Nightingale.

Marmaduke knew he had no right to judge Josepha's decisions but he could not prevent a reaction that was not quite jealousy but seemed to be a twinge of nostalgia. Despite the terms of his contract with Isabel that he would continue his bachelor lifestyle, he had not lain with another woman since the night before his marriage. He had not known then that night was the last time he and Josepha would make love. They had never said goodbye.

Unused to sexual abstinence Marmaduke felt confused by conflicting memories. In the forefront of his mind he saw Isabel's sweet, heart-shaped face, those haunting green eyes. Yet he also remembered every curve of Josepha's generous, voluptuous body – and remembered how very good they had been together.

Ushered into a drawing room furnished in a theatrical style that would have served admirably as the set for a Doge's Palace at the Theatre Royal, he was asked to wait.

Looking across the rooftops to the olive green pattern of bushland that stretched down to the foreshores of the harbour, for the first time in his life Marmaduke felt strangely incomplete. The girl who was an annoying English tomboy on her arrival in the Colony had become oddly indispensable. He smiled at the memory of the day he took her to Mendoza's store and, ever curious, Isabel had asked how pearls were created.

Marmaduke had explained he was no expert on pearls but understood it was a rare chance occurrence in nature. Occasionally a minute grain of sand entered an oyster shell and acted as an irritant, chafing the oyster and causing a perfect pearl to form.

Isabel's eyes had opened wide at the idea. 'Just like us! I'm the grit of sand that has to transform you into a pearl. Perhaps that's why you find me so irritating. That's my job!'

Now as he gazed down into the darkened street where Thomas nodded asleep on the driver's seat, Marmaduke laughed aloud at the idea of Isabel as a grit of sand.

He was startled by the sound of Josepha's voice from the adjacent boudoir. The lady's maid left her mistress and discreetly disappeared from sight down the corridor.

'Was that a laugh I heard from you, Marmaduke? How rare. Come here, darling, I am in great need of amusement after tonight's difficult audience.'

Her voice was rich and velvety with promise and Marmaduke had a fair idea what he would discover when he entered her boudoir. He was right.

On a wide four-poster bed, festooned and draped like a mermaid's cavern with three shades of turquoise green and blue watermarked silks, Josepha St John lay languidly across the bed, her mass of dark auburn hair uncoiled and trickling in waves down her body – her hair a substitute for the filmy nightgown that left one breast exposed and did little else to conceal the lush proportions of her body.

Marmaduke wanted to sound chivalrous. 'Goya knew what he was doing when he painted that lady with one breast exposed. It is far more provocative than total nudity. How Goya would have been inspired to paint you as you are tonight. Any artist would. Oh God, if I were only a poet,' he sighed.

Josepha stretched out a beckoning hand. 'We have no need of words, you and I.'

Marmaduke chose to seat himself casually on a sofa near the bed.

'I have never seen you look more devastatingly desirable, Josepha, which makes me a fool in my own eyes because I am here tonight to be totally honest with you.'

'Honest?' Her peal of laughter was light and caressing but so practised it was difficult to tell if it was genuine. 'Honesty is a bourgeois vice totally outside the boundaries of our relationship, darling. Honesty and pure lust were not designed to be good bedfellows.'

'Nonetheless I must say it. I told you the truth about my arranged marriage. I had every intention and my bride's full consent to continue to take my pleasures freely outside the bonds of wedlock. But something unexpected has occurred.'

Josepha gave an elegant yawn and her body moved sinuously into an even more inviting position. 'Don't tell me, Marmaduke, you have fallen in love. You of all people. How Sydney Town would enjoy spreading that gossip.'

'Love? Far from it,' he said quickly. 'That is totally outside my nature – as it is your own. No, it is simply that I find myself responsible for—' He was shocked to find he had almost said Isabel's name and hurriedly back-tracked. 'I am in a situation I have never before encountered. Despite all natural inclinations to the contrary, I hope to remain your ardent friend,' he paused, 'but abstain from the incredible range of pleasures I have shared with you.'

God, I hope that sounded gallant enough. I do want us to remain friends.

Josepha began to play with the ribbon of the lover's knot that would release the remaining shoulder of her negligee.

'Marmaduke, you are such a romantic at heart. I have been expecting this, my darling. You were gone so long without a word. But I notice you have returned with a hand naked of a wedding ring.'

Marmaduke faltered. *Damnation. Women never miss a trick.*

'A long story. I'll not bore you with the details, Josepha.'

'No matter. You and I are above bourgeois sentimentality. But to please me, walk to the window, sweetheart. Look down in the street and tell me what you see.'

The request was so strange Marmaduke sensed there must be some 'method in her madness'. He did as he was bid.

'The street is quiet. Apart from my own carriage placed some distance away for the sake of discretion, there's only one other stationary carriage. A fine pair of greys. A driver garbed in burgundy livery. I can see the occupant is a man wearing a top hat, an opera cloak and, how odd, his opera glasses are trained in this direction.'

'Ah, that's *him*,' Josepha said.

Marmaduke asked politely, 'I presume he is an admirer intimately known to you?'

'Not yet,' she said lazily. 'A most patient nobleman with a delicious French accent. He wants badly to become my protector. I have accepted the use of this townhouse from him. That is all – as yet.'

'I understand,' Marmaduke said. 'You would prefer me to take my leave of you.'

'On the contrary, darling. He has the traditional Frenchman's jealousy but his manners are perfect. He will not come to me unless I invite him. He will remain there all night, if I wish it. The answer is in your hands.'

Marmaduke felt his pulse quicken.

She's playing a scene but does she care one way or the other how it ends?

'This mysterious Frenchman. He asks nothing of you?'

'Nothing more than to dance for him – in private.' She added softly, 'Salome's Dance of the Seven Veils. Remember how well I performed it for you?'

Marmaduke said lightly, 'How could I forget? You would fill Levey's theatre to overflowing if you gave a public performance.' He fought to banish the memory of that night he had been her sole audience, lying naked in her bed.

'My Gentleman Frog is handsome,' she teased. 'I am attracted to his generosity but not yet to him. He follows my every movement. I find his carriage parked outside the theatre, my milliner, my hairdresser and this villa he has placed at my disposal.'

'The price you must pay for his adoration,' Marmaduke said. 'My sweet lady, I know I will hate myself in the morning for my decision, but I recognise I have been outflanked. The hour has come for me to bid you goodnight.'

Marmaduke bowed deeply with a cavalier's flourish of the hand.

'Only for tonight.' Josepha said softly. 'Our time together is not yet played out. You know it. I know it. A great many exciting changes will reshape our world before my ship sails for New York.' She rolled over to give him a last glimpse of the woman he had been fool enough to put aside.

She added as an afterthought. 'You are welcome to bring your little wife to America with us. As long as she knows her place and understands the demanding needs of a diva.'

Josepha's voice changed key to take on a pleading note that would melt a diamond. 'I ask you to do something for me – as my friend.'

Marmaduke waited, unwilling to commit himself.

'Would you sleep the night here, outside my room? I will feel safer, knowing he is watching my window all night waiting for a sign from me. A sign that I am unwilling to give him – as yet.'

Marmaduke nodded his consent and gently closed the door of her boudoir behind him. He pulled back a velvet drape and looked down into the street. Both carriages were stationary. A faint trace of cigar smoke trailed from the window of the Frenchman's carriage.

Marmaduke removed his boots and stretched out on the bearskin rug – no sofa was long enough to contain his height. Covering himself with his opera cloak he felt a sense of pride that he had been strong enough to pass his own test, to grow into his new role – a man Isabel might one day learn to trust.

I hope I allowed Josepha to believe she played the game beautifully tonight and saved face. She knows me intimately. But she has no idea she's met her match in Isabel.

He smiled at the absurd idea of Isabel meekly 'knowing her place' and playing second fiddle to the legendary Nightingale as the trio trooped around both American continents in a *ménage a trois.*

On the point of sleep he was suddenly sobered by the thought.

But what if I can't even tempt Isabel into a ménage a deux *with me?*

It was half light when Marmaduke stirred and, feeling his duty accomplished, checked his pocket watch. Half five.

Throwing his cloak over his arm, he was in the act of reaching out to claim his top hat when he was suddenly on guard. He and his mistress were not alone. On the console table beside his hat and gloves was an even more fashionable version of his own – and a cane with a gilt head in the shape of a mythical beast. A wyvern.

He grew tense, ready to charge into Josepha's room to protect her, but he was stopped by the tinkling sound of her laughter. And Josepha's American-accented French when she said teasingly, 'Monsieur, you flatter me.'

Her admirer's reply was so soft that Marmaduke was not able to translate the words beyond the odd Gallic endearment but he recognised full well the seductive tone. It drew from Josepha a trill of laughter that Marmaduke had often aroused when sharing her bed. Was her teasing laughter designed to encourage the Frenchman? Or was she giving a performance aimed at her intended audience – Marmaduke?

He retrieved his hat with a wry smile. A woman's revenge was bittersweet in any language. He knew when it was time to take his leave.

Check mate, Josepha. I hope I leave you in good hands, sweet lady.

CHAPTER 35

Marmaduke submerged himself in a hot bath in Garnet Gamble's chambers at the Princess Alexandrina Hotel. He had accomplished most of the things for which he had come to Sydney but his gut instinct told him today would be a day like no other.

In Josepha St John's chambers he had agreed to offer her his protection – a chaste night on her couch. Instead, he had been forced to play gooseberry while she entertained her Gallic lover in her boudoir. For the first time in his adult life Marmaduke had declined a lusty night in a mistress's bed. He was reminded he was approaching the age of twenty-five.

'I must be getting old,' he said under his breath but knew the truth. *Isabel.*

He was warmed by the memory of her half-innocent expression when she requested that he demonstrate on his return the art of being Kissed in Four Places. Had she any idea how erotic this was? Images from his past encounters with voluptuous female bodies flooded his mind then vanished, to be replaced by Isabel's slender, almost boyish naked form – the face, the eyes, the sweet taste of her lips were hers alone.

'Enough!' he warned himself. 'You've chosen to play the role of hero. Get going. You've only got a short time to prove it before Silas de Rolland drops anchor.'

Dressed in one of his 'English gentleman's' suits of clothes, he swore in resignation over his failure, yet again, to perfect his cravat then attacked his French breakfast. Today he would be forced to play the Quality at its own game. It went against the grain but he was determined to do it for Isabel's sake.

His first call was an exhibition of paintings and memorabilia donated by the Colony's artists and the Exclusives to raise funds for the Orphans' Benevolent Asylum. The Quality would no doubt want be seen trying to outbid each other at an auction of paintings, an event to be opened by Governor Bourke's daughter, Mrs Deas

Thompson. He hoped an encounter with her would facilitate Isabel's acceptance into Sydney society.

Marmaduke was aware that Anne Maria Bourke had married her father's most trusted public servant, Edward Deas Thompson, an industrious Scottish-American whom Bourke had inherited from Governor Darling and appointed to the arduous dual role of clerk to the Executive and Legislative Councils. The young man's record was so exemplary none could claim nepotism should Bourke appoint his son-in-law Colonial-Secretary in the event Alexander McLeay agreed to vacate the post.

On Marmaduke's arrival at the Georgian sandstone offices of the Surveyor-General he made a cursory inspection of the items listed for auction, including work by Augustus Earle, the artist who had painted his mother's portrait. But he was more attracted to the adjacent room that held a magnificent Government-owned Australian collection assembled by William Holmes. The young curator had been sent to the Colony at the directive of Westminster but allocated by Lord Bathurst to the limit of a paltry two hundred pounds a year towards the formation of a public museum.

Standing in front of a showcase housing Aboriginal artifacts of great antiquity, Marmaduke felt a distinct sense of Currency pride. He was addressed by a young man with a diffident English accent.

'I trust you find these worthy of your attention, sir?'

'*Worthy?* They're magnificent, mate. Europe would go *nuts* over this exhibition.'

Too late Marmaduke realised his gaff. *Nuts! Shit, I just dropped my English façade.*

He hastily introduced himself. 'So *you're* William Holmes, the genius behind all this. Thank God you're making the Colony wake up that Australia's cultural heritage is unique!'

William Holmes gave a self-deprecating shrug. 'No genius, Mr Gamble, simply a humble but passionate curator.'

'You underestimate yourself. If you hadn't fought to preserve what the *Sydney Gazette* likes to call "Australian curiosities" they'd be lost to posterity. This stuff doesn't just belong to *us*, it belongs to the whole damn world. To the future!'

The curator's face flushed with pleasure. 'I wish politicians and benefactors could see it through your eyes. I've had to pack up this entire collection and move it from pillar to post, literally from the Old Post Office to wherever the Government grants me house room. I trust that our leaders will someday grant the necessary funds to build a permanent home for it.'

Marmaduke spread his arms wide to encompass that vision. 'The first Australian Museum! That's no mere dream, Will. It's gunna be reality, with you as its director!'

Catching Marmaduke's enthusiasm, the curator shepherded him around the room, animatedly confiding the stories behind his discoveries and their tribal significance.

Turning a corner they encountered a lady immaculately dressed in dove-grey silk with a touch of black indicating she was still in mourning. Marmaduke recognised he was face to face with His Excellency's daughter.

William Holmes bowed to her and gestured to Marmaduke. 'Mrs Deas Thomson, may I introduce *my good friend*, Mr Marmaduke Gamble?'

Marmaduke was grateful for the exaggerated introduction.

She blinked at the name Gamble. Garnet's nothing if not notorious. But if Bourke's daughter is a chip off the old block, she won't snub me for being an Emancipist's son.

Marmaduke made her an elegant bow and during their exchange of polite English chit-chat he managed to balance the correct degree of formality with a hint of self-interest. He indicated that his bride was a member of the English de Rolland family.

'Ah yes. Godfrey de Rolland is well known to my father's family. Perhaps it would interest Mrs Gamble to join the ladies' committee of the Orphans' Asylum?'

'I can guarantee it, ma'am. Isabel is dead keen about the welfare of orphan kiddies,' Marmaduke said firmly. He was rewarded with a smile.

On the point of departure the Governor's daughter inclined her head to him. 'I shall have my secretary send you and Mrs Gamble an invitation. I look forward to welcoming her to the Colony.'

When the auctioneer's gravel sounded in the next room Marmaduke warmly shook William Holmes by the hand.

I must get Garnet to make a handsome donation towards this bloke's museum.

Determined to make his presence felt, Marmaduke raised his hand to bid for a number of paintings that he did not really want. He was not disappointed when he was outbid.

I've got to put a roof over Isabel's head and stock Mingaletta with a mob of sheep and cattle before I go nuts buying paintings.

Before sundown Marmaduke had discussed his house plans for Mingaletta with a gifted young architect who was not yet fashionable and therefore affordable. He had also drafted his first ever Last Will and Testament and bought a thoroughbred mare with a bloodline almost as impressive as Isabel's.

He penned a letter to be delivered by messenger to Waratah Waters, Rupert Grantham's vast estate that fronted the Cook's River a few miles west of Sydney.

Dear Rupert,

My warm thanks for your Invitation to ride out with you this coming Sunday to see your new white Stallion. I really regret I must decline. I gave my word to Isabel I'd return home. You know how nervous young Brides are about the Bushranger plague.

It suddenly occurred to Marmaduke that Rupert being a worldly bachelor who had been devoted to his late mother, probably had little experience of nervous young brides.

Aware that the messenger was waiting downstairs in the tap room ready to ride off to deliver this letter, Marmaduke dipped his quill in the inkwell.

P.S. I trust you will invite me to Waratah Waters on my return to Sydney. I can't wait to hear more of your outrageous stories about what's really happening Behind the Scenes in this scandalous Colony.

Until we meet again,
Your sincere Friend,
Marmaduke Gamble

*

That Saturday night Marmaduke dined with Edwin at the Princess Alexandrina. Maeve had declined on the pretext of sewing her gown for both their forthcoming weddings.

Edwin had had a bad week in court. Marmaduke refilled his wineglass, concerned by his friend's haggard appearance due to what he considered his failure to his client.

'Hell, Edwin, you aren't God. The bloke was a twice-convicted thief. What was he up for this time?'

'The lad was caught red-handed in the Point Piper mansion of a man of Quality. The young fool had ample time to make his escape with his loot. But the police found him in the cellar, his pockets lined with stolen goods, roaring drunk and singing anti-British songs.'

Marmaduke tried to keep a straight face. 'He's lucky you saved his neck from Green the Finisher's rope.'

'Not so lucky. The magistrate's an Orangeman. He sentenced the lad to seven years at Moreton Bay.'

Marmaduke was determined to end on a positive note. 'Well, it's gorgeous country and at least the notorious Commandant Patrick Logan who they say got himself murdered by his convicts.'

Edwin was beyond consolation. 'I don't like his chances under Logan's successor.'

Marmaduke insisted on booking Edwin a room overnight to allow them to breakfast together before their visit to reassure Josiah Mendoza that Isabel's tiara was perfectly legal.

'Tonight's melodrama is just what the doctor ordered to lift your spirits. *A Tale of Mystery* is a hoot. It's Holcroft's translation of *Coelina, ou L'Enfant du mystere*, the work of René Guilbert de Pixérécourt, who cleverly aimed it at an audience who could not read. That will apply to more than half of tonight's audience.'

Marmaduke was delighted to see how quickly Edwin caught the mood of the crowd that packed every layer of the theatre from the pit to 'the gods'. The most volatile members of the audience pelted the arch villain with oranges each time he dared lay a hand on the 'poor but virtuous' heroine. The hero, incorruptible to the point of stupidity, was often outwitted by the villain. The heroine remained painfully virtuous. The audience was both sympathetic to and frustrated by the mute, Francisco, who repeatedly witnessed the villain's attempted outrages but could only communicate via pantomime, despite shouted warnings from the audience.

Fuelled by Hunter Valley wine, Marmaduke and Edwin cheered the heroine and hooted the villain along with the rest of the boisterous crowd.

At interval Marmaduke expressed his bemusement. 'Colonial audiences are morally outraged in defence of female characters on stage. Yet in real life they ignore women's human rights and turn a blind eye to the sport of wife-beating.'

Edwin was philosophical. 'Melodramas give them the illusion they can deliver justice in a Penal Colony where most of them, bond or free, are pawns in the transportation system.'

Following the melodrama Josepha St John's performance drew waves of excitement. She crossed the stage wearing a revealing red gown with a flowing train that she deliberately kicked behind her at each turn to give the excited audience a glimpse of her shapely ankles.

Following Josepha's return after a change of costume, Edwin commented that her diamonds looked real to the uninitiated.

'But no doubt you can pick the genuine from the paste at a glance, eh?'

Marmaduke leant forwards, stunned to see that as well as the 'legendary' necklace she wore which he knew to be paste, pinned between her breasts was a large diamond brooch in the unusual shape of a peacock.

'Jesus Christ, Edwin. That diamond brooch is real. I'm damned sure because Josiah Mendoza's been keeping it in his safe for me to give to Isabel for her birthday!'

Marmaduke was instantly on his feet, propelling Edwin out of the box.

'Jos would never give up that brooch except by force. God willing he's still alive!'

They hurtled down the stairs and out into George Street where rain was pelting down on the line of waiting carriages. Marmaduke put two fingers in his mouth and produced such an ear-splitting whistle that Thomas, huddled under his oilskin cape, almost fell off his perch.

'Mendoza's Store, Thomas! And don't give way to anything!'

The store window was plastered with a notice that read 'Closed by Order of His Excellency the Governor Sir Richard Bourke'.

Marmaduke fished around for his key to the door, knowing how futile that would be if his partner had bolted the padlocks. To his surprise the door swung open without resistance – there was no evidence of disorder. He charged up the narrow stairs to the attic with Edwin at his heels. When he saw the scene before him he called out to Thomas.

'Fetch my whisky flask, then go for a doctor!'

Josiah Mendoza lay shivering violently on a cot bed covered only by an old blanket. The flesh between his gray side whiskers and beard was chalk-white and he was sweating profusely. One eye was bloodshot, the other badly swollen within a sea of bruises. His lips and teeth were edged with dried blood. His teeth chattered as he attempted to speak. Marmaduke cut across the broken phrases.

'It's all right, mate. A doctor's on his way.' Marmaduke grabbed the whisky flask and was about to hold it to his lips when Josiah stayed his hand, demanding to know the contents.

'Medicine, distilled in Scotland. It'll stop the shakes if nothing else, mate.'

Josiah drank thirstily from the flask, nodding in relief.

'I knew you would come – so I did not bolt door. The tiara—' Josiah began coughing.

'Forget all that for now. What mongrel did this to you? The traps?'

'No. Yes. I do not know. I suspect a thief in another man's pay.'

'Try to tell us, slowly, what happened. Whoever did this won't get away with it.'

The old man's account was laboured but coherent. Marmaduke and Edwin pieced together the story. Only minutes after Marmaduke's departure on Friday evening when he handed over the tiara to Mendoza's safe-keeping, a fine carriage had drawn up, bearing a gentleman who sat watching the store. His servant, a big, tattooed man, knocked on the door, demanding to collect a watch he said his master had left for repairs.

'I could not recall it but as it seemed the gentleman was waiting in the carriage. Like a fool I unbolted the door and let the servant enter.'

'Damn it all he must have just seen me leaving. Did he do this to you?'

Josiah nodded. 'He tied me to a chair. Demanded to know where I had hidden a stolen diamond tiara. I played dumb.' He gave a self-deprecating shrug. 'I have a lifetime of experience at that.'

Josiah pointed a trembling finger at the wall safe covered by a small curtain. 'I let him beat me before I revealed to him the combination of this safe – to see for himself that it contained no such tiara.' He confided in a whisper, 'I had hidden your wife's tiara in my other secret safe beneath the floor of my kitchen as I told you I would.'

'Jesus, Josiah, you've got guts. What happened next?'

'The thief opened the wall safe and took a tray of wedding rings, uncut diamonds and I'm sorry to say that peacock diamond brooch you wanted for Isabel and—'

Marmaduke exchanged a meaningful glance with Edwin before reassuring Josiah.

'Look, mate, don't worry about the full inventory. Stick to the story. You gave him the combination and he stole some valuable pieces. So why did he bash you up like this?'

'He was angry there was no tiara. The gentleman gave the order to beat me.'

'The so-called gentleman! Did you get a good look at him? Did he have an accent? English? Colonial?'

Josiah shook his head. 'His face was in shadow. He never spoke but each time he gestured with his cane it was a signal for the thief to beat me, again and again, to make me reveal the whereabouts of the tiara. The last thing I remember was the ruffian's boot aiming at my head. I passed out with the pain. Later I found myself alone. A constable pasted that sign on the window and he told the crowd in the street, "This Hebrew has been disturbing the peace." It was *my* fault I got beaten up?' He let out a hacking cough. 'So now I am the crook? I am to be charged!'

Edwin was firm. 'An idle threat. You have no case to answer, Mr Mendoza.'

Marmaduke reassured him. 'Edwin brought the Will to show to you and the police. We promise you the charge will be dropped.'

Josiah smiled through his broken teeth. 'I knew you would come, my boy. You are Wine Son from Vinegar!'

Edwin looked startled. 'He's hallucinating?'

'No. That's just Jos's way of saying I'm a decent bloke. A cut above Garnet.'

Marmaduke tried to convince his partner he would take him to Garnet's hotel where he'd receive the best of care but Josiah was adamant he must protect their business interests. He had orders to complete. He whispered the position of the hidden safe.

It contained the velvet box holding Isabel's tiara. Marmaduke knew that no matter how Josepha St John had come by the diamond peacock brooch he did not have the heart to ask her to relinquish it or tell her the true story. His former sweet lady deserved something genuine after being reduced to a jewel box full of paste diamonds. He would reimburse his partner for the brooch. The tiara was safe. That was the important thing.

Edwin tried to draw from Josiah details about his attackers.

The old man was exhausted. 'The hands that beat me had letters tattooed on the knuckles.' He gave an apologetic shrug. '*Jesus Saves*.'

'Could you identify the gentleman if you saw him?'

Josiah looked a bleak. 'He stood in the shadows. But I remember his walking stick. The gold knob was a wyvern with ruby eyes. I am a jeweller. I notice these things.'

'Jesus!' Marmaduke said softly under his breath, but at that moment the surgeon arrived so he took the situation in hand and arranged to pay for a sober woman to cook and care for the old man as long as needed.

Back in the carriage Marmaduke directed Thomas to halt at the hotel where he secured the velvet box in Garnet's safe overnight before taking it to the bank vault next day. When they resumed their journey both men were preoccupied until Marmaduke finally spoke.

'Sorry, mate, I intended to take you to *see* a melodrama, not end up being *in* one.'

Edwin agreed. 'The plot certainly thickens. But I suspect you know more than you care to admit. I saw your start of recognition when Mendoza described the cane.'

Marmaduke looked serious. 'A cane of that description belongs to a jealous Frenchman determined to be Josepha St John's protector. He sounded a bit dodgy but I hoped I was wrong for Josepha's sake. But why would a wealthy Frog who already has Josepha in keeping in a villa hire a thug to beat up Mendoza?'

'If he knows you're Mendoza's silent partner, perhaps he's jealous of your intimate friendship with the actress?' Edwin offered tentatively.

Marmaduke looked startled. 'My business in Sydney was almost finished. But now I must try to warn Josepha discreetly about the Frog. My God, Edwin, life gets complicated when a bloke's married!'

CHAPTER 36

Seated together in the 'ladies' drawing room, Elise was working away on her dog-eared tapestry as Isabel read her way through the latest newspapers, torn between hunger for news of Home and Europe and her growing fascination with Colonial events.

The Colony's many newspapers ranged from the reliable, informative, pompous, partisan or libellous to muckraking. But she soon discovered even the most polarised Colonial editors were agreed on one point. The convict bolters 'in the bush' who had become bushrangers now threatened the foundation of law and order.

Isabel felt an angry rush of blood to her face reading the English newspaper that had just arrived on a mail vessel at Port Jackson.

'This is an outrage!' she cried out so forcefully that Elise jumped in her seat with fright.

Breathless with rage Isabel burst into Garnet's office waving the newspaper like a baton, suddenly aware she had interrupted his business with Rhys Powell.

Garnet looked concerned. 'Isabel m'dear, what on earth's wrong?'

'It's here in black and white. Those five brave men were sentenced to be transported for seven years, just for taking an oath! Those union lads from Dorset. The Tolpuddle Martyrs!'

'Ah, *them*,' Garnet said knowingly.

Isabel sank thankfully into the chair Rhys offered her.

If I can't shed a tear for those heroic Tolpuddle Martyrs, I'll never be able to cry, but Garnet acts as if they are of no importance.

'Yes, *them*! No doubt you haven't had time to read it,' she added tactfully, remembering Garnet habit of mislaying his glasses when presented with the written word.

'Five of the six. They're heroes. Agricultural labourers found guilty of administering unlawful oaths, violating an Act that was only intended to prevent sedition. But what they did wasn't seditious, Garnet. They just swore to stick together and establish a farm labourers' union. And unions are legal in England now, aren't they?'

'Indeed, since 1824,' Rhys Powell said quickly, earning Garnet's glare of disapproval. Clearly Garnet saw unionists as rabble-rousers.

Isabel again remembered Agnes's advice to her as a child when she lost her temper: 'Honey attracts more flies than vinegar!' She fixed her gaze on Garnet and tried to appear on the verge of tears.

'Garnet, I appeal to your sense of justice. These labourers were only attempting to raise their wages above starvation level, from seven shillings a week to ten. Some landowners agreed. But their own masters retaliated by cutting their wages to *six* shillings. *Six*! To feed a whole family. It's a travesty of justice! I'm ashamed to call myself British!'

Garnet said quietly. 'I've been known to think the same, from time to time.'

'You have so much influence in the Colony, people will listen to *you*!' Isabel said, handing the newspaper for Rhys to read.

'It's true, Mr Gamble. It lists their names. The sixth man, their leader, George Loveless, was too ill to be transported. He isn't just a simple ploughman; he's also a respected Wesleyan preacher. His written court statement is quite moving, sir. May I?'

'Read it, read it!' Garnet snapped.

Rhys cleared his throat and delivered Loveless the martyr's words in a Welsh-accented voice rich with feeling. '*We were uniting to preserve ourselves, our wives and our children from utter degradation and starvation. We have injured no man's reputation, character, person or property…*'

The room was silent. Isabel became aware that Elise was standing immobile in the doorway, no doubt drawn by curiosity to the reason for Isabel's dramatic exit.

Isabel hoped her final plea would hit home. 'Garnet, I've often heard you say that wrongs can be righted. Pardons can be granted.'

But her heart sank at the sight of Garnet's flushed face.

Garnet doesn't want to be seen to be siding with union men who are fighting for increased wages. But is it more than that? His eyes have taken on a strangely remote, glassy quality. Elise seems nervous, as if she's afraid Garnet will have one of his manic episodes.

Isabel longed to see Marmaduke swagger through the door, no matter which of his complex moods he was in – kindly, teasing, angry, melancholic – just so long as he was *here.*

She saw the warning glance Rhys exchanged with Elise in silent confirmation that all was not well with his master. He turned politely to Garnet.

'May I draft for your approval a respectful letter to Governor Bourke? His Excellency is said to be related to the great parliamentary crusader Edmund Burke and he's also proving himself to be a champion of British justice, whatever opinion the Exclusives hold. May I suggest that a letter applauding his initiatives and enquiring about the welfare of the Tolpuddle Martyrs would not go amiss and bring you merit in his eyes, sir?'

Isabel felt a growing sense of unease when Garnet looked distracted.

'A letter to Bourke. Whatever for? Oh well, invite him to my banquet by all means. He won't come but he might send his son-in-law Deas Thompson.'

His secretary bowed. 'As you wish, sir.'

Garnet seemed suddenly mindful of Isabel's presence. 'Forgive me, dear girl, if I don't keep you company at dinner tonight. I'm not feeling quite myself.'

Giving Isabel a small dazed smile he left the room arm in arm with Elise.

Rhys Powell seemed intent on shuffling papers to cover his embarrassment.

'You know Mr Gamble's state of health better than I do, Rhys. Should we write to Marmaduke and advise him to return home at the first instant, do you think?'

'It is not for me to say, Mrs Gamble,' he said, bowing formally as he departed.

Isabel was left to contemplate the empty room. Her eye fell on a set of duelling pistols in the glass cabinet.

Is this the pistol Marmaduke used to kill Klaus von Starbold? Men are so difficult to understand. They value the appearance of honour above everything that's important.

She gently patted the nose of the sad-eyed lion whose head was a trophy on the wall.

'Leo, I think you have more true human emotion than anyone else in this house.'

Changing into her outdoor shoes in the nursery she decided to go for a walk, feeling in need of fresh air to clarify her thoughts.

In the picture gallery she paused in front of Miranda's portrait to study the woman whose expression subtly altered depending on the time of day, the quality of the light – and perhaps Isabel's own mood. For some odd reason this end of the gallery always seemed colder than the other end. Today it was completely silent, so Isabel was in no danger of providing servants with gossip about 'Marmaduke's strange bride' if she spoke out loud.

'The more I learn about you, the less I know you, Miranda Gamble. I wish I could confront you face to face. You are like a chameleon, your character changes colour when seen through different eyes. To Garnet, you are an obsession – a lost love that haunts him because of his guilt. To Queenie, you're the excuse to fuel her hatred of Garnet to avenge your death.'

Isabel stepped sideways to study the hauntingly beautiful face from the opposite angle, aware of the illusion that Miranda's eyes followed her movements. Was her expression today teasing, amused or did it even hold a glint of malice?

'To Marmaduke, you're an adored but remote mother, filtered through his youthful need, loss, guilt and now his growing confusion about your true nature. No doubt you loved Marmaduke but did you really love *anyone* without manipulating them?'

Just then a shadow passed across the face of the sun and Miranda's face darkened. But the eyes remained unnaturally bright – almost alive.

She won't rest until Marmaduke lays claim to Mingaletta. But there's something else. Isabel felt her heartbeat accelerate uncomfortably as a vivid thought came to her.

'My God! She doesn't want me here!'

As always, when faced with her fear of the creatures from the other side, Isabel fought to overcome her terror with bravado.

'Well, I have news for you, Miranda Gamble. You are no longer the mistress of Bloodwood Hall. I am! You may still have the power to manipulate everyone else who loved you. But you can't control *me*. I'll live my life *my* way! I'm alive!'

But Isabel was still shivering from that unnatural pocket of cold as she hurried down the cantilevered staircase and out into the heavily perfumed sunlight of the garden.

Queenie's little cabin seemed to bask in the sun, a small oasis of normality that welcomed Isabel.

Today the old nanny was in full European garb, a floral print morning dress covered by her Mother Hubbard apron. Her dark hair with its white tiger stripes was coiled on top of her head. Her one concession to her Indian heritage, the silver earrings shaped like lozenges, swung in rhythm with her movements. She was so busy straining blueberries, strawberries and raspberries into measuring bowls on the kitchen table that she did not even look up at Isabel's entrance. But her words were kindly.

'We didn't get off on the right foot but you know you're always welcome. Don't stand on ceremony, girl, sit yourself down and I'll make tea for us.'

'May I help you?' Isabel asked.

'I'm not so decrepit I can't boil a kettle,' she said tartly, then gave Isabel a reluctant smile. 'But you can take the teacups from the dresser and set them on the table.'

I want her to help me understand Marmaduke. I suspect she was more a real mother to him than Miranda was.

The tea and Queenie's exquisite lemon cake were an antidote to Isabel's ever-present hunger. Her genuine enthusiasm for the nanny's cooking brought a smile of satisfaction to Queenie's eyes.

'What's that I'm making? Good Heavens, girl, and you call yourself English? Never heard of English Summer Pudding? It is the essence of summer – courtesy of our glasshouse. I made it for Marmaduke from the time he was old enough to walk down here on his own. With Summer Pudding you'll find your way to Marmaduke's heart, if you're brave enough to try it.'

The glittering black eyes warned Isabel that no living soul could fool her.

Isabel decided truth was the only way to go with Queenie. 'I have much to learn about life in general. And Marmaduke is a complex man whose moods change like a weathercock. I don't really know who he is. He's always doing things to please me, so I would like to surprise him by learning the secret of this pudding.'

Satisfied with Isabel's answer Queenie wrapped a pinafore over her dress. She impressed on Isabel she must use three kinds of berries in season, slices of stale bread and sugar. That it was a cold dish best made a day or two in advance so that the flavour of the simmered berries when crushed together seeped through the layers of white bread that lined the bottom and sides of the baking dish and then formed the covering lid of bread.

'Top the bowl with a plate and weigh that down with something heavy. I use my heaviest iron. Keep the pudding in a cool place under a net safe from blowflies for a day or two. Now you make one!'

Isabel impulsively kissed the wrinkled brown cheek. 'You don't know what it means to me to be able to do something special for Marmaduke.'

Queenie's quicksilver mood became serious. 'I am beginning to think you really care for my boy after all.'

'I do, but don't tell him that. He's vain enough as it is.' *Oh damn my careless tongue. Now I've insulted her boy she'll never forgive me.*

To her surprise Queenie chuckled like a fellow conspirator. 'You're learning fast, girl. Marmaduke plays many roles to protect his true feelings. Maybe one day he'll discover that it takes courage to love – and pay the price. There's always a price to pay. Will you be the one to teach him, I wonder?'

Isabel didn't know how to give an honest response.

'Will you dine with me tonight, Queenie? I would really like that. Garnet seems strangely unwell and taking to his bed so we may well be alone.'

'Garnet out of sight? That's an invitation hard to resist,' Queenie said, 'but tonight's the full moon and the anniversary of Miranda's death. If Marmaduke didn't warn you then I must. Sleep here tonight, child. I could make up a bed for myself by the fire.'

'Thank you but there's no need. I've witnessed Garnet's wild fits of temper before and survived. I intend to go to bed with one of Marmaduke's old books. A volume of eighth-century Indian poetry, *Amarushakata*, I think. Do you know of it?'

'How could I ever forget? Miranda quoted from it as if it were her bible.' Queenie held Isabel's arm with such intensity her fingernails dug into her flesh. 'Promise me you'll go straight to bed and lock the nursery door. Remember, no matter what you hear or *think* you hear tonight, don't unlock your door until morning.'

Isabel gave an involuntary shiver but tried to lighten the mood. 'Dear Queenie. I'm eighteen now. A married woman. Why does everyone treat me like a child?'

'Because you *are*. Pure of heart. I fear for you. Old houses have memories. That house has a soul in torment. Don't be tempted to explore the dark side – only the strong can survive. Stand warned!'

'Don't worry. I'll lock my door just to put your mind at rest.'

As Isabel hurried back down the path towards the house she was unable to shake herself free of Queenie's ominous words: *what you hear or think you hear*. The dark side – was she referring to the Other? Or Garnet?

It was her duty to remain by Garnet's side in Marmaduke's absence but she could not dismiss the growing sensation that invisible walls encompassed Bloodwood Hall and were closing around her, isolating her from the real world. Tomorrow she must ride out in the bush to regain a sense of freedom.

In sight of the stables she decided to check on the mare that Marmaduke had assigned for her special use. A bay stallion stood with its reins looped to the hitching post, nervously pawing the cobblestones. The horse used by Rhys Powell.

Isabel found her own mare in her stall. Her saddle hung on the wall. Everything was in place ready for tomorrow's ride. Slipping inside the stall she stroked the velvety nose and whispered sweet words as much for the mare's benefit as her own. Instinctively she drew back into the shadows at the unexpected entrance of Rhys with Elise. Isabel realised it was too late to announce her presence.

Rhys gripped hold of Elise's shoulders and Elise did not struggle to break free.

I'm trapped here as an eavesdropper. I don't want to see this.

Rhys's whisper was urgent. 'You can't allow him to do this to you. You must leave him.'

Elise's voice had a bitter edge. 'How can I? I am well paid for my services.'

'Don't talk like that. You're not a whore! You don't need him any more. I'll take care of you. Come away with me, Elise. Now. Tonight!'

'It's impossible. You can barely support yourself.'

'Money! Is that all you care about? You love me, I know you do, *say* it!'

He kissed her awkwardly but ardently, until she broke free.

'Poor boy, you're so naive. You don't understand.' Her voice sounded weary, old.

'You're wrong – I understand you only too well. If you refuse to leave Garnet to begin a new life with me as my wife, then you *are* his whore!'

Elise slapped his face with such force that Rhys rocked back on his heels. Isabel saw the red imprint on his cheek as he pushed past Elise, mounted the horse and rode away.

Isabel watched the woman return to the house. She remained in the stables until her heartbeat returned to a steady rhythm and she felt it was safe to emerge. Her head ached with the problem of the night ahead.

I could almost feel sorry for Garnet. All his wealth has failed to protect him from disloyalty. What on earth do I do? If I remain silent I am party to their betrayal. Yet I am Marmaduke's paid ally. I must wait for his return.

Isabel went to the kitchen to inform Bridget she planned to retire early and would take a simple cold meal on a tray in her room. She feigned surprise when Bridget informed her that Rhys Powell had ridden off to the village on business.

'Oh really? That means no one will be present at dinner tonight. Please feel free to share all the food with the servants – or what you will. I won't be needing anything more tonight, Bridget.'

Alone in the nursery the light from three candlesticks gave her a much-needed feeling of calm and companionship. She drew the curtains, locked the door to the corridor and sat cross-legged on the bed, eating cold mutton sandwiches, drinking cider, and absorbed in the reading of a well-thumbed manuscript yellowed with age. The cover of the collection of hand-written poems was entitled *One Hundred Poems of Amaru and Other Poets.*

Isabel was intrigued by the inscription on the flyleaf:

To his precious daughter, Miranda. Legend has it many of these poems, compiled in the 8th century, are the work of the poet-king Amaru of Kashmir. Translated from Sanskrit by her father in honour of his grandson Marmaduke.

It was dated the year of Marmaduke's birth.

Each poem was a little gem, meticulously translated into English on a page facing the original Sanskrit script. Asterisks offered alternative phrases in the footnotes, proving the translator's determination to do justice to the archaic language.

The Colonel must have had a romantic soul and a deep love of India to teach himself Sanskrit. No wonder Marmaduke treasured his grandfather's gift.

She continued reading in awe the distilled essence of the many facets of love – romantic, erotic, passionate, tender, heart-rending, teasing, even bitter and cynical. Poets dead for centuries had left this legacy of exotic imagery that resonated in her heart and fired her imagination with Marmaduke's face, voice, his naked body.

Struck by a poem that gave voice to her own thoughts, she read the lines aloud, her emotions a mirror of the young bride who had shied away from her beloved's kisses, his touch, unable to meet his eyes. Yet in his absence she aches with regret for those precious lost moments. Isabel trembled in recognition.

This poet is speaking for me! Marmaduke has aroused me, made me blossom with the sweet love arts of the bedchamber. Please God it is not too late!

She cradled in her arms the pillow that gave up the lingering perfume of sandalwood as strongly as if Marmaduke had just that moment left the room and would soon return to her. He was all that stood between her and her fear. What if Cousin Silas should reappear before Marmaduke's return? She tried to control a rising sense of panic at the rush of forbidden memories of Silas.

Turning a page she was startled to find fresh solace in the poet's words.

Yes! I must never again allow that evil man to cast his malignant shadow across my life – or Marmaduke's.

She reverently kissed the cover of the manuscript. 'Thank you, Your Majesty King Amaru! Your words speak across the centuries from your soul to mine!'

Overcome by weariness she closed the book and placed it by her bedside.

'The true test of my courage – or cowardice – comes when I blow out these candles.'

Prolonging the light she blew out the candles one by one. In the darkness that was now only filtered by cracks of moonlight, she snuggled under the blanket, clutching the sandalwood pillow to shield her through the night ahead.

CHAPTER 37

Isabel knew she was trapped in the nightmare and with a great effort of will she could force herself to wake up. Invisible, distorted voices filled her with fear. A woman's cries. The broken, guttural sounds of a man's voice – his words strung together, unintelligible. The darkness in the dream world merged with the darkness of the room. Isabel felt her mind was pinioned between two night terrors, unwilling to break free from one fear only to be trapped by the other, greater fear. Reality.

Were these sounds distant or present in this very room, filtered but close by?

With trembling hands she fumbled with the box of waxed matches. Striking one on her third attempt she lit a candle to form a tiny, flickering ball of light.

The room was empty but the sounds that had penetrated her dream were true – even if they came from the Other. She repeated the words like a mantra.

'I'm not dreaming. I'm not walking in my sleep. This is real. I'm real. Somewhere in this house a woman is crying out for help. Do I lie here and protect myself by my silence and leave her in pain? Is this what Queenie meant when she said, *what you think you hear?*

Isabel tried to swallow the fear that formed a hard lump choking her throat. 'I'm a coward at heart but not *that* much of a coward. If she's a ghost then she sounds even more terrified than I am.'

Trembling violently Isabel placed the soft kid slippers on her feet, wrapped a shawl around her shoulders. Candle in hand, she unlocked the bedroom door and padded along the corridor of the picture gallery, unsure if she was being drawn in the right direction.

Just before she reached the portrait of Miranda, she heard the muffled cries again. *Closer.* They seemed to be coming from behind the oak panelling of the wall.

She remembered the wainscotted half-timber wall lining the picture gallery of the de Rolland ancestral house. *Garnet built replicas of so many things, maybe he built a priest's hole as well.*

Holding the candlestick close to the wall she traced her fingers along each panel, searching for a hidden spring. Chilled by her fear and on the point of conceding defeat, she heard a faint click and a panel slid beneath her fingers. Through the filtered darkness she saw a narrow staircase leading up to a closed door. Beneath it was a thin sliver of light.

The ugly cacophony of sound was unmistakeable. Two voices. Elise's shrill cries. Garnet's rasping voice. The sound of a whip.

That bastard is taking pleasure beating her.

Elise's voice. 'Garnet! Please. No! I can't take this any more.'

His voice grated in answer. 'You can and you will. It's the only thing you're good for. I haven't had enough! Learn to like it!'

Isabel felt the sweat running down her body, soaking her nightgown. Blindly she removed her slippers and ascended the stairs. Kneeling on the top step she looked through the keyhole.

Fragments of ghastly images flashed past the tiny eye of light. Flesh. Traces of blood. The knotted leather thongs of a whip cut across her line of vision. Sick to her stomach, Isabel's mouth was dry and her lips parched as she was overcome by a second wave of shock.

For a moment she caught the barest glimpse of the hand that held the whip. It was not possible – it's not Garnet! The hand was soft, white. A woman's hand.

The hand withdrew from sight. Then Isabel saw the whip fly through space to find its target. Garnet's back, scored with long-healed scars and the welt of a fresh wound. His guttural cries were forced between clenched teeth.

When the lash ceased and the room fell silent, he commanded Elise: 'Don't stop. Not enough pain!'

Isabel gasped at the terrible words that seemed ripped from his throat.

'Miranda! God in Heaven, will you – never – *forgive* – me?'

Isabel felt so sick she panicked at the thought that she was on the verge of fainting. *They must not find me here.*

Driven by the need to flee she tried not to stumble down the stairs. Willing herself to conserve her remaining energy she slid the panel shut behind her. The candle was now almost melted into a pool of wax.

For a moment she held up the flickering light and looked up at Miranda's portrait, the face of beauty smiling mysteriously in the darkness. 'Are you satisfied *now*?'

As if in answer, a strange gust of wind blew out the candle.

Isabel fled in the darkness down the length of the corridor to the only safe refuge she knew. Marmaduke's nursery. And bolted the door behind her.

Sleep was impossible even given her state of exhaustion. She lay under the covers, unable to block out the brutal sounds and images she had just witnessed.

How long had this pact of self-torture been going on? Since Miranda's death? Or since Marmaduke's aborted wedding day when Elise was enthroned as Garnet's mistress and Garnet realised he had lost his son? What did time matter? This terrible pact had become a savage ritual of dependency. But Isabel was at a loss to understand how any woman could continue for years to be Garnet's accomplice. Was Elise so hungry for Garnet's money there was no end to her degradation? Or did she feel some twisted element of responsibility for his guilt – and her own?

Although Isabel felt contempt for the way Elise had publicly humiliated Marmaduke at the altar, she was confronted by contrary thoughts that demanded exploration. Could a woman who had been transported along with the dregs of humanity be so desperate to gain a wealthy protector and the hope of respectability that she would not only sell her body for a man's pleasure, but her services as his personal scourger?

Isabel half dreaded, half welcomed the approach of that preliminary invitation to the day, the fragile pink reflection on the horizon Marmaduke called 'the picaninny dawn'.

Now that she knew one of the darkest secrets trapped in this benighted house, what must she do? If she had proved that Elise was the victim of Garnet's brutality, Isabel would not have hesitated to expose him to Marmaduke. She could not suffer in silence the abomination that most of the world accepted as the natural order of things – men who beat women.

But now, knowing the reverse was true, that the punishment was Garnet's unquenchable need to assuage his guilt, she was at a loss to know how to confront it.

Damn Marmaduke. He's left me here to handle this alone but I can't believe he's so callous he'd allow any woman, even Elise, to be flogged without his intervention. He must know the truth about their arrangement. So there's no point in my waiting for his return – whenever he can tear himself away from the Theatre Royal and his mistress.

Isabel resolutely pushed from her mind a stab of envy at the thought of the lush beauty of Josepha St John. Determined to put her plan into action at day break she blew out the last candle.

The water for her bath was tepid but she lathered her body with Marmaduke's sandalwood soap and washed her hair. She glanced outside to check the weather, which seemed to be so quixotic in this part of the world it could span all four seasons in as many days. Deciding that the day promised to be hot, she dressed carefully in her prettiest sprigged muslin morning dress and hesitated before adding the miniature house pendant to complete her toilette. She thoughtfully fingered the gold wedding band that hung in tandem with the gold house on the delicate chain – Marmaduke's ring left with her for safekeeping.

Well, it's an odd order for an ally but I gave my word so I'll wear it until his return.

A quick glance in the three-faceted Gothic mirror drew a grimace of distaste. There were mauve crescent shadows under her eyes, evidence of a sleepless night. She pinched her cheeks and bit her lips to give them instant colour. She had no desire to copy Elise's unnatural arsenic-induced pallor.

Hurrying down the picture gallery she gave a quick salute to Miranda's portrait in passing, uneasy at the reminder of the inexplicable draft that had blown out her candle at this point last night. However, this morning Miranda looked serene.

'I'm glad one of us slept last night!'

Isabel took her accustomed seat in the breakfast room, surprised to find Elise busy loading her plate with an English breakfast of sausages, scrambled and poached eggs, baked tomatoes, black pudding and French toast from the sideboard. Breakfast was the one meal of the day that Garnet insisted they serve themselves, free from the inevitable servants' gossip.

How strange life is. No doubt Garnet observed this tradition when he was a servant at de Rolland Park.

Isabel had expected to find Elise looking haggard and sleepless after her duties in the priest's hole. Not so. She gave Isabel a short but cheerful morning greeting and tucked into her food as if famished.

'What plans have you for today, Isabel? Would you show me how to do that embroidery stitch that's said to be in favour with gentle-women at Home? I'm bored with Empress Josephine's garden and cross-stitches. I'd like to make a cushion cover for Garnet's birthday. His initials framed by a Greek Olympic coronet. Will you show me how to do it?'

Isabel was bewildered by the normal tone of the request. Had last night been a dream? 'Of course I will, but first I must play a game of chess with Garnet.'

Isabel moved her Knight with the necessary degree of hesitation needed to convince Garnet she was learning but was still well out of his league as a chess player.

'Good girl, good move,' he said encouragingly.

It astonished her that today he had not cancelled their game. Despite the heat of the day he wore a winter-weight jacket and the line of the back appeared to be padded. The only clue to any pain or discomfort was his tendency to shift in his seat and his increased reliance on the inevitable jugs of lime juice. He had long since dropped the pretence that it was free of a heavy quota of gin.

His jubilant 'Check mate!' on the side of Napoleon, was caused by the move that Isabel had designed to end their game earlier than usual.

'Garnet, may I speak with you in private about a matter that concerns me?'

'Of course. Let us go to our trysting place,' he said with a chuckle, in reference to the summerhouse that was also free from servants' eavesdropping. Amaru seemed to be sulking from lack of attention and hardly spoke as he marched up and down on Garnet's shoulder.

As they passed the aviary Garnet took her arm. His breathing seemed slightly more laboured than usual, which was hardly surpris-ing given last night's punishment.

'My dear, it touches me to see your interest in Miranda's beloved budgerigars. Pretty little creatures but few around here show 'em much interest, perhaps because they're native to this land. Arrant snobbery if you ask me.'

Isabel nodded in agreement while concentrating on sorting out phrases in her head as they took their seats in the summerhouse.

'What's troubling you, m'dear? Nothing I can't fix, I'm sure.'

Isabel inhaled deeply to begin. 'How I wish that were true, Garnet. No, please allow me to continue. It isn't easy for me to say this but it must be said. You have shown me all the concern and affection a true father shows his daughter. And this has now become a burden. I feel guilty. I have been less than honest with you. I have a confession to make.'

Garnet interrupted firmly. 'Nonsense. You owe me nothing but to continue as you have begun. To grace this family with your beauty and kindness – and to put up with my son's temperamental moods and love him anyway. There's good stuff inside that lad, somewhere. It only needed a good woman to bring it out. Let's have no more talk of confessions. You have brought honour to my house and the Gamble name.'

Isabel reached out and took hold of his hand. 'The truth is, Garnet, I am not exactly sure what my family led you to believe.'

'You are a true de Rolland by birth?' he asked quickly. 'Then that's all that matters.'

'I am a legitimate de Rolland but my guardian did not disclose to your lawyers details of my life – my childhood. If he had done so no one would have blamed you for seeking a bride from some other aristocratic family in need of your assistance.'

'Then I would have been a fool to have lost *you*. I've been called many unflattering names in my day but no one has ever called Garnet Gamble a fool.' He held up his hand in a gesture of command. 'Enough. I know what I see. No revelations of any past little indiscretions are necessary.'

Past little indiscretions are one thing. If only he knew the web of lies I have woven. My false confession of infanticide to protect Rose Alba from discovery. How much dare I tell him?

'Garnet, I must speak plainly if I am to remain under your roof

– as I so dearly wish to do. I believe you and I have more in common than you realise. I know what it is like to carry a burden of guilt so heavy that you feel you can never be free of it – no matter how hard you try to set things right.'

Garnet leant forwards intently and gripped her hand. 'Go on.'

'I want you to know you are not alone. If there is any way I can help lighten – any painful memories you carry—' She took a deep breath, knowing the fine line she was treading. 'Please remember that Marmaduke's wife is your friend. My first duty is to my husband, but I see no division in my loyalty to the Gambles, father and son.'

Garnet turned away as if searching for something that was out of sight. When she saw him blink she realised she had struck a deep chord. He was fighting for control.

The sound of the dinner gong gave her an excuse to jump to her feet. 'Are you as hungry as I am? I do hope so. Cook showed me how to make a special pudding that I understand is a favourite with you. Spotted Dick. Please tell me what you think of it.'

Isabel took his arm and shepherded him towards the house, chattering about the roses, the aviary of budgerigars, Amaru's vocabulary, the wallaby that crossed their path. Anything and everything she could seize on to lighten Garnet's mood.

I don't know whether I've just betrayed Marmaduke or brought him three steps closer to Mingaletta. Only time will tell.

CHAPTER 38

Random images of Isabel flashed before Marmaduke's eyes as he lingered over breakfast in the Gamble suite at the Princess Alexandrina Hotel. Bittersweet memories of Isabel in a wild variety of moods since his first encounter with 'the boy' with the black eye in the Watch House. Her fighting spirit at the Sign of the Lame Dog, her wistful wedding vow, her sleepwalking revelation, her fists beating him when she discovered Elise's role in his life, her eyes staring at him underwater, knowing she was drowning, the way she kissed him when he saved her, as if she was offering him her soul...

Marmaduke felt hot at the thought of her. He was more than ready to return home to her; his work in Sydney Town was near completion. The architect's blueprint for his new Indian bungalow was being drawn up and Marmaduke decided he would begin to oversee the building of it whether or not Garnet signed over the deeds to Mingaletta. Possession was indeed nine-tenths of the law. He was reminded of the parallel with the way Garnet had squatted on Crown land and succeeded in building up his rural holdings piece by piece.

In the weeks following the attack on Mendoza's store, Josiah's injuries had healed and his business continued to flourish once his mind was at rest that the tiara had been established as legally belonging to Isabel. The law declined to state the source of the false claim but Marmaduke had little doubt. He felt an involuntary stab of rage at the thought of Silas de Rolland. When that man arrived in the Colony it would be for one reason only. *Isabel.*

Marmaduke had manged to resolve the matter of Josepha and the diamond peacock brooch. Expecting a temperamental outburst from her he had tactfully escorted her to Mendoza's store to have the brooch evaluated, after briefing Josiah he would pay for it to prevent the embarrassment of her having received stolen goods. In the process Marmaduke established what he had suspected – the brooch had been a gift from an admirer who wished to remain anonymous. Was her Frenchman still 'stalking' her? He was.

This morning as Marmaduke tried Emile's latest gourmet breakfast dish, he kept glancing with a sense of pride at the ornate certificate that proclaimed he was now a Master Mason. Last night at Barnett Levey's Royal Hotel at the meeting of Freemasons he had passed the Third Degree of his initiation into his lodge. Barnett Levey had been an eloquent sponsor but Marmaduke had also been greatly assisted in his Masonic studies by Dr William Bland, who had been transported for killing a man in a duel in England and had dismissed Marmaduke's confession of his youthful duel.

'You are in good company, young man. Quite a collection of scandalous duellists in this Colony, including Rupert Grantham and old John Macarthur. Even our recent British Prime Minister, the Duke of Wellington, fought a duel with an earl who opposed a bill he wanted to pass! But there are better ways to settle scores. We Masons learn to keep passions and prejudices within due bounds,' Dr Bland had said.

Passions and prejudices within due bounds. An interesting choice of words. It doesn't say a man must not have those qualities – only that he learns to control them.

Although his desire to become Isabel's hero had been Marmaduke's prime motivation, on being initiated into the Masonic brotherhood he had been drawn to the craft's marked egalitarianism.

These past months had changed his view of the world. All the Masonic regalia, the painted aprons and symbols used in Freemasonry, which Marmaduke had previously dismissed as meaningless when Garnet had pressured him to join his own Lodge, now represented a new dimension in his life.

As soon as the house plans were completed, he would return home to present it as a gift to Isabel.

For some unaccountable reason his head ached as he drank his second cup of coffee. He was pleased but surprised by Edwin's unexpected arrival, looking sombre, dressed in black. He handed across a copy of the *Sydney Herald*.

'I come bearing bad news, my friend.'

The front page was crammed with the usual columns of advertisements and the arrivals and departures of sailing ships. Marmaduke was jolted by the sight of the black-bordered notice in the centre of the page. The funeral of Rupert Grantham.

Marmaduke shook his head in disbelief. 'Jesus, it can't be true. Rupert dead? I saw him only a few weeks ago. We dined together. He was full of vitality, ranting at the Exclusives, challenging Governor Bourke to take action to change our laws! What happened to him?'

Edwin gestured wearily at the newspaper. 'I'm as stunned as you are. I only just read it myself. Our friend was murdered.'

'Murdered? Who the Hell by?'

'Assailants unknown. There's a full account on the next page. I haven't read all the details. I came here straight away to tell you.'

Marmaduke scanned the coverage of the murder. 'It's all here. The police report. Dr Bland's autopsy, everything. Rupert went missing on Sunday. Searchers found his body later that day. Shot dead at point-blank range. Bloody cowards! The man had simply been riding around his own estate as he did every Sunday afternoon. I've been there. Waratah Waters covers several thousand acres around Cooks River. Wild country bordering on the marshes.'

'Are there any clues as to who murdered him?'

'Marmaduke stabbed his finger at a paragraph. 'Yeah. It says, *Several refractory characters had been sent to iron-gangs for offences committed in Mr Grantham's service...one had been heard to vow revenge. Some of these men are said to have absconded from the Government iron-gangs and are now in the bush.* Bolters!' Marmaduke put down the newspaper. 'It was murder all right. Poor bastard!'

'That strongly suggests it was no random killing,' Edwin said cautiously.

'The odds are against it, mate. Everyone knew where to find him. Rupert was brilliant and powerful but we know he attracted enemies as well as friends in high places. Maybe his murderers aren't just absconders "in the bush" who wanted to take revenge on him. Maybe he was set up by powerful men who wanted him dead. They could have manipulated bolters to assassinate him. To do the job for them!'

Edwin paused to examine the idea. 'You could well be right. But if there was a mastermind behind his murder I trust it will come out at the trial. How many men are they searching for?'

'It says three sets of footprints were traced to George's River where they appeared to cross over to that known haunt of bushrangers, the

Seven Mile Brush. They also found two trees with marks of shot. It sounds as if the mongrels used it for target practice – planning to kill the poor bastard.'

Edwin reminded him that they must soon depart.

Marmaduke pulled a dark suit from the wardrobe and began changing. 'I hate to say this, Edwin, but it seems a real paradox. In public Rupert fought brilliantly for the rights of Emancipists yet it's said he was responsible for some of his own convicts being flogged and sent to iron-gangs.'

Edwin eyed him speculatively. 'Human beings are complex creatures, Marmaduke. Perhaps we didn't know Rupert Grantham as well as we thought.'

'I dined with him at Waratah Waters. He sent Isabel a wedding present. He was great company, had a fund of wild stories and seemed to keep tabs on everyone in the Colony. Knew where all the Colonial bodies were buried.' Marmaduke winced. 'Dammit, I could have phrased that better.'

'It's true there are many powerful men who had cause to want him silenced. But I believe in judging people as I find them. You liked Rupert Grantham and he liked you.'

'Yeah. We had a fair bit in common. Wine, horses, raving on about the inequalities under the law. Both of us determined bachelors. Both with a history of duelling scandals.'

'Rupert boasted that was *one* reason he wasn't welcome at Government House.'

Marmaduke was stopped by a thought. 'Hell. Only last week Rupert sent me a note, inviting me to visit his estate. *Last Sunday.* If I'd been free that day I'd have been riding with him in the bush when he was murdered!' Marmaduke thumped the table in frustration. 'Christ! If only I had been there. At least there'd have been two of us to fight the cowardly mongrels who killed him. Rupert wasn't armed. I'm *always* armed!'

Edwin rose. 'Well, you can't go to a funeral bearing firearms. We can do nothing for our friend now, except honour his memory. It's near nine o'clock. We must depart now if we want to escort his funeral cortege to the burial ground.'

Marmaduke was already out the door to organise their horses.

Dressed in black, crepe armbands on the sleeves of their frock-coats and crepe streamers tied around their top hats, Marmaduke and Edwin set out to join the carriages that were headed for Rupert Grantham's estate to accompany his body to its final resting place.

They passed a bank that was closed for the day out of respect for his funeral.

Among the mourners they recognised judges, politicians, members of the legal fraternity and newspaper editors.

Edwin said quietly. 'I wonder how many of these men were Rupert's friends?'

'Yeah. And how many of them were his enemies?'

CHAPTER 39

Spring had come early, flooding Bloodwood Hall's garden, orchard and glasshouse with a cornucopia of fruit and flowers. In Isabel's eyes they were a virile marriage between exotic natives and traditional English species that bloomed larger and more abundantly in Garnet Gamble's Eden than she had seen them growing at home. The isolated world of the estate looked tranquil but Isabel knew it was an illusion. Nothing would ever be the same again.

During Marmaduke's absence there had only been a second short message. Written in his wildly flamboyant hand and dated three days earlier, it said more about Barnett Levey's production of *Richard III* than any of the developments in Marmaduke's life but he promised all would be revealed on his return. The tone was lighthearted except for the postscript written in black ink indicating it was dashed off a day later.

Our whole world has changed forever. Do not under any conditions leave Bloodwood Hall. That's an order, soldier!

For two days those words had lingered in Isabel's mind, her growing sense of alarm fuelled by wild rumours fanning out from the village that a prominent Sydney landowner had gone missing under mysterious circumstances.

Isabel was sitting on the terrace re-reading Marmaduke's note when she saw the assigned lad galloping up the carriageway and hurried down the steps to meet him. His face was shining with perspiration and his eyes signalled the importance of the news he brought. Davey was illiterate but, unlike others, his word could be relied upon.

'They done him in, missus,' he said as he handed across his swag of mail and newspapers. 'It's all in here.'

Isabel felt her knees buckle. 'Who, for God's sake?'

She seized the copy of the *Sydney Herald* dated two days earlier. It confirmed the truth of Marmaduke's warning in columns full of lurid detail. The unthinkable had happened. One of the most powerful men in the Colony had been assassinated.

She ran to the library, where Garnet was seated alone at his desk.

'Forgive me, Garnet, I know you prefer Rhys to cull the newspapers before you read them but this can't wait.'

She read out the news to Garnet in the absence of his secretary, trying to gauge his reaction. There was none in evidence. At the end she faltered, out of breath.

'Do you see, Garnet? If a powerful man like Rupert Grantham can be assassinated on his own estate, none of us are safe any more!'

Garnet patted her hand in reassurance. 'No reason to concern yourself, m'dear. That Grantham bloke had many enemies in high places. No one was safe from his pen. He even went to prison for libel. But no man would dare lay hands on me or mine on *my* estate. Unthinkable!'

He rose and inclined his head to signify the subject was closed.

'Would you be a dear and ask Elise to make sure cook includes Spotted Dick on the menu at dinner? The Quality can eat French pastries 'til the cows come home. Can't beat traditional English puddings, eh?'

Isabel nodded and left the room but was overcome by a wave of frustration. She had totally failed to get the truth across. Garnet was in a state of denial.

Rhys Powell joined them all at midday in the dining room. Isabel was not surprised that he looking haggard.

He's young, a moral Wesleyan and a gentleman of honour yet he's turned his employer into a cuckold. What do I do? Expose the lovers? No, I must wait and take my orders from Marmaduke.

Isabel was stunned that Rhys's manner towards his employer combined his usual respect, civility and commitment to perform his duties to the high standard he had set for himself and which Garnet demanded. During a lull in the conversation Rhys raised the subject of the Grantham murder.

'May I suggest, sir, it would be wise to put additional security measures in place?'

'Why, for God's sake?' Garnet demanded.

'Landholders throughout the Colony will be on high alert, in the wake of Mr Grantham's murder at the hands of what the mounted police believe is a trio of bolters. True or false, there's wild talk he had previously ordered the illegal flogging of convicts. It is not unreasonable to suspect an act of revenge – assassination.'

'Assassination? What melodrama!' Garnet hooted in derision. 'That's a term reserved for royalty, warriors and politicians.'

He turned to smile reassuringly at Isabel. 'And your chap Shakespeare. Who was that old Roman who came to a sticky end at the hands of a pack of his senators?'

'Julius Caesar,' Isabel said politely but felt shocked by Garnet's nonchalance.

What does it take to get through to the man? Does an armed bolter need to march into the room and interrupt his dinner?

Garnet tried to sound reasonable. 'Grantham didn't deserve to be cut down, but as a landowner he was just a minor player compared to me – and Samuel Terry. Two-and-a-half thousand acres and a handful of assigned men? A mere bagatelle. His demise was due to being the wrong man in the wrong place at the wrong time. We'll say no more of it.'

At the end of the meal Garnet and Rhys removed themselves to the office. Isabel was surprised to overhear Garnet say, 'How many of our men can be trusted as guards, eh?'

Elise pleaded a headache and took to her day bed. Isabel noticed she had been eating double portions, no doubt as a remedy for her unhappiness.

In an effort to keep her own emotions under control, Isabel gently banished the servants from the kitchen and resumed making a fresh dish of Summer Pudding. Her hands were stained with berry juice and, as she had tasted it several times to ensure the right balance between sweetness and the natural flavours of the fruit, she suspected her face must bear tell-tale smears like some hungry child's.

Singing snatches of old songs in an attempt to keep her mind off her fears for Marmaduke's safety, she had just put the white bread lid on the dish when she reached the words of *Scarborough Fair*, '*once there was a true love of mine*'.

'I thought you didn't believe in true love.'

Marmaduke stood leaning back against the closed door. His head cocked to one side, a cynical half smile playing at the corners of his mouth. His dark hooded eyes were watching her in a way that made her blush with pleasure. His face was touched by the sun, his clothes looked as crumpled as if he had slept in them and his hair hung freely around his shoulders, dripping wet as if he had just emerged from a billabong.

God, he's so handsome, even when he looks like a vagabond. How could those 'sweet ladies' in Sydney manage to resist him?

She felt the words dry in her mouth. What on earth was it safe to say?

'You're all wet,' she said. 'Is it raining?'

Marmaduke threw back his head and laughed in disbelief. 'I ride through the night to race home to my bride. I bathe in the creek so I won't be sweaty when I kiss her and all she can ask about is the weather!'

She took a step closer to him, trying to rub her face clean with the back of her hand. 'I'm glad you're home safe. I was afraid for you. We know about the assassination and what that means to all of us. Why didn't you write properly? Too busy entertaining your mistress?' She faltered. 'I'm sorry, I forgot Mr Grantham was your friend. You were at his funeral?'

'Yeah. I rode with Edwin behind the cortege to the old burial ground. Every judge, magistrate, politician, newspaper editor and Uncle Tom Cobley *et al* were there, most of 'em mouthing platitudes. We could have been standing cheek to jowl with Rupert's murderers, who knows?' For a moment Marmaduke's eyes were serious then unexpectedly his attitude became nervy as he rattled off a list.

'I've been busy. Got myself initiated as a Freemason. Nailed down the plans for the house I'm gunna build you on Mingaletta. Wrote a Will to see you right in the event some villain sends me to meet God in a hurry. Oh yeah,' he added, 'and I set up an account with the Bank of New South Wales in your name, no questions asked, so you can be financially independent of me. Money's what it's all about, the reason you married me, right?'

'It was,' she admitted, 'but I didn't know you then.'

She noticed Marmaduke register a faint flicker of surprise before he asked the question softly, 'So what's my little shrew been up to?'

Isabel could feel the power in his half-closed eyes drawing her towards him.

'A lot has happened in your absence. Ugly things you need to know, but I decided it was best to wait for your return to discuss Garnet. I'm sorry for the loss of your friend, but you might have written to put my mind at rest – about things that matter.'

He took a step towards her. 'The only thing that matters to me is us. The outside world can go hang.'

Marmaduke beckoned her with a theatrical gesture as he quoted Petrucchio's command, 'Come. Kiss me, Kate.'

He reached out and held her face in his hands. Isabel met his lips and drank deeply from a kiss that was gentle but very much on his terms. She knew they were both playing a scene. Yet she also felt her body was dissolving into his. Never to be free again – if she didn't fight it. The desire to surrender completely struggled with her sense of panic.

She broke free of the kiss but kept her fingers entwined in the wet coils of his hair.

Marmaduke's voice sounded as parched as a man in the desert. 'Do you want what I want?'

I don't really know what that means. Isabel shrugged. 'All right. I'm willing, that is – just get it over with.'

Marmaduke pushed her away from him to hold her at arms' length but his fingers dug into her shoulders. Despite his laughter she knew he was very angry.

'You're unbelievable. I invite you to share a night of ecstasy with me, to take you with me to paradise. And all you can say is, "just get it over with!"' Marmaduke emphasised each word individually. 'Just – get – it – over – with? Jesus, woman, you sure know how to quench a man's fire.'

He brushed her aside and moved to the kitchen table. 'So what's this then? Summer Pudding. Queenie's welcome home present. I'm glad *someone* missed me.'

Humiliated by her awkwardness, Isabel gestured to the dish. 'I was Queenie's apprentice. I've made one of your puddings every day for weeks, to make sure one would be perfect on whatever day you decided to grace us with your presence. It's easy for you to be generous. I didn't have any money of my own to buy you a present. It's the only thing I could think of to please you. Why did I bother?'

'To please me, huh?'

He picked up the carving knife and was about to slash at the pie when Isabel swiftly stayed his hand.

'No! This one must rest a day or two. There's one in the pantry that's ready to eat.'

He shook his head. 'Can't wait, I'm hungry *now.*' He picked up her berry-stained hand and sucked gently at each finger in turn, murmuring satisfaction like a hungry child. 'Are you game?' he asked. 'To borrow Lord Byron's words, "You should have a softer pillow than my heart".'

Isabel pulled her lips from his kiss long enough to say, 'Byron also said, "All tragedies are finish'd by a death. All comedies are ended by a marriage." So are *you* game?'

'John Donne was right! "For God's sake hold your tongue, and let me love!"'

Before Isabel had time to retaliate in their duel of poets, in one fell swoop Marmaduke hoisted her over his shoulder and ran with her down the length of the house, while Isabel, struggled, yelled to be released and thumped his back with her fists.

She felt mortified at the sight of two giggling housemaids running after them, not to come to her aid but for their own amusement. 'Put me down immediately, Marmaduke,' she hissed. 'I did not consent to this!'

'Too late,' he yelled back. 'I'm out of control. You've driven me nuts.'

From her upside down view of the world she saw the black-and-white checked tiles of the entrance hall and, when Marmaduke paused at the foot of the stairs, she raised her head to see a tableau of amazed faces watching them. Garnet, Elise, Rhys and every house servant under the roof.

Garnet bellowed out, 'What the hell do you think you're doing, Marmaduke?'

'What does it look like, Garnet? I'm demanding my marital rights!'

Isabel called back to reassure him. 'Don't worry, Garnet. We're just rehearsing a scene from *The Taming of the Shrew.*'

Marmaduke took the stairs two at a time, pausing only to deliver a heavy thump on Isabel's backside.

''Owzat for realism, eh? Yell louder, Katherina, you're not convincing enough!'

Isabel's voice rose an octave. 'Just you wait until we're alone! I'll give you realism. You Currency wife-beater!'

'That doesn't sound like a line from Shakespeare!' Elise said petulantly.

Garnet was cheering the scene as enthusiastically as a member of a Colonial audience.

The final words Isabel heard bouncing off the walls of the vestibule were delivered by Garnet's booming voice as he watched their progress from the foot of the stairs.

'I never thought I'd live to see this day. Marmaduke should kiss my boots. Isabel Gamble has brought light and laughter back into my house!'

As Marmaduke ran with her past Miranda's portrait he said politely, 'Excuse us, Mother, I'll explain later.'

Isabel gave an uncertain smile as she watched Miranda's portrait diminish in size to a sliver at the far end of the gallery. *If God is willing I'll make Garnet's words come true. I'll do my damnedest to bring light and laughter back into this tragic house.*

Marmaduke lowered Isabel to her feet with a theatrical flourish in front of the door to their chambers. His eyes, his face, the lines of his body and the inflections in his voice were subtly transformed. Another Marmaduke stood before her. She saw the uncertainty in his eyes as if this night would be different from all others. When Marmaduke entered the nursery that had become their private world, he would be an explorer in unfamiliar territory.

She broke the silence. 'What's wrong? Is it locked?'

'I never carried you over the threshold as a bride. That's bad luck, isn't it?'

'It's not too late. I'm officially a bride for a year.'

'So you are.' Marmaduke swept her up in his arms and, humming *The Wedding March,* he kicked open the door and carried her to the bed.

Isabel shed the bodice of her dress but hesitated and remained in her petticoat.

Lying on her belly on the bed, she bit her lip, unable to restrain a giggle that sounded just like a nervous housemaids as Marmaduke struggled to remove a stubborn boot.

'Shit! I can see why the Duchess of Marlborough wrote in her diary, "Last night my Lord returned from the wars and pleasured me twice with his boots on." Sensible bloke, that Duke.'

Isabel watched him as he divested himself of his clothes with such deft grace it was almost as if the clothes were washed free from his body.

He's so beautiful he'd put ancient Greek athletes to shame.

But she tried to sound worldly to cover her confusion. 'I can see you've had plenty of practice. Lesson one in the libertine's manual I expect? Always prepared for some irate husband to burst in, I imagine.'

Marmaduke looked almost wistful. 'Must you always drag up my past follies? I've turned a new leaf. To prove I'm worthy to be the man you can trust to take care of you.'

Isabel felt the pulse on her temple jump at the joy of hearing those words, but she drew her knees up under her petticoat and cradled a pillow in her arms, needing to talk to forestall what was to come. She was now in the room alone with Adam, his body tanned lightly by the sun. No fig leaf. No bravado. Marmaduke stretched out across the foot of the bed and rested his head on the triangle of his bent arm. His body was relaxed but his hooded eyes watched her as if ready to spring.

Please God, don't let me be clumsy. Let the room be dark. Let me seem beautiful in his eyes. How can I win his heart?

She searched desperately for a question. 'What do Masons do, exactly? Do they really have secret handshakes, wear funny clothes and make you swear never to tell your wife?'

Startled, Marmaduke's laugh was cut short by an intake of breath. 'You know I've taken an oath. I can't tell you everything, soldier. Do you really need to know about Freemasonry *tonight*? I had other plans.'

Isabel nodded quickly – anything to postpone the moment.

'Right. Well, in a nutshell, for years I rebelled against Garnet's pressure on me to follow in his footsteps. I made up my mind it was an absurd, antiquated tradition designed to suck up to royalty and men in high places. I see now how wrong I was. My initiation really meant something to me. I can see why great men of many nationalities, like Mozart, Sir Joseph Banks, George Washington, the French tragedian Talma and other great minds past and present were drawn to it. And no doubt your father, too. The craft embodies the highest egalitarian principles – tolerance of all religions that practise the brotherhood of man. Open to all decent men, Catholics, Protestants, Hebrews and Emancipists like Sam Terry, Francis Greenway, Dr Bland. There's no stigma on them or on the sons of Emancipists. I'm proud to call fellow Masons my brothers. Just think, Isabel, it's the Masons here in this penal colony who've set a new example for Britain and the rest of the world to emulate.'

Isabel heard the excitement in his voice and she gazed at him with love. *Is this the same young man I considered rough and uncouth when first we met?* 'Thank you. I understand now. You must think me a fool asking questions at a time like this. It's laughable. Me! A fallen woman.'

Marmaduke moved with such swift, naked grace she was only belatedly aware he had tilted her face to meet his eyes. 'Isabel! I forbid you to describe yourself as fallen. Unless one day you tell me that you have fallen in love.' He took a deep breath and added quickly, 'Almost as deeply as I love you.'

Isabel felt her heart was ready to burst. She opened her mouth to speak those very words but Marmaduke trapped her lips in a kiss that banished her confession. She found herself trembling violently in fear that her memories of the terrible acts she had obliterated from her mind would flood back while she was in Marmaduke's arms.

'Hush, my love, there's nothing to fear.'

Marmaduke gently drew her clothes from her body, smiling in discovery as he caressed and kissed each part of her. He tossed the last delicate item of silk underclothing over his shoulder and said lightly, 'No more fig leaves between us, Eve.'

The candles flickered in some undetected current of air. A sliver of silver light stretched across the carpet through a gap in the curtains.

When he slipped his finger through the wedding ring that hung on the chain around her neck his eyes were serious.

'The day we went through our Quaker wedding ritual, despite the beautiful words I had no intention of honouring the promises I made.'

'Neither did I,' she agreed quickly, but knew that wasn't quite true.

'But now I want to say things *my* way.' He placed her hand in his upturned palm and kissed her wedding ring. 'Isabel Alizon, with this ring I thee wed. With my body I thee worship and with all my worldly goods I thee endow. And from this day forward, the past is dead – mine and thine. I shall forsake all other and keep myself only unto thee...' He studied her intently. 'On one condition. Tell me you *want* me.'

Isabel felt the words on her tongue but she could not force herself to say them.

'Perhaps not yet, eh?' Marmaduke gave a shrug of acceptance. 'What is your pleasure, my love? Shall we blow out the candles and invite moonlight to watch over us?' He stroked her hair. 'You're trembling. It's warm tonight but you're cold. Please tell me you're not afraid of me.'

'Not of you. *For* you. I can't dismiss the power of that witch's curse that I will destroy everyone I love.'

Marmaduke shook his head in adamant denial. 'That is an evil lie. Your cousin abused you as a child. Tried to bind you to him body and soul. The past is dead. I promise you, my love, tonight we will create wondrous new memories you will never *want* to forget.'

The room was lit by ribbon threads of moonlight that filtered through the shadows of the trees, bringing the delicate perfume of eucalyptus blossoms into the room.

Moonbeams transformed the nursery into a magical fairy bower worthy of *A Midsummer Night's Dream*. She lay cradled in Marmaduke's arms listening to the pattern of his breathing, careful not to wake him. She wanted to relive every moment of the hours of the journey that had, as promised led her to Paradise. She had followed him, growing in confidence and hunger as he fuelled her passion in a series of escalating peaks that left her almost satiated – yet crying out because she felt cheated and did not know why. This Marmaduke was lover, master, friend. Unwilling to deny him she had followed wherever his imagination beckoned. She was conscious of the way he watched her, murmuring sounds of encouragement, guiding her hands to explore his body, gauging the right time to increase the heat that burnt her or to allow her respite, exhausted in the circle of his arms. Time and time again he granted her a brief reprieve before he rolled her above him, below him, astride him, enticing her onwards to the next, even higher peak.

'Now I know the truth. Paradise is a secret place right here in his nursery,' she whispered under her breath, startled to find Marmaduke had been awake all the time.

'There are many roads to Paradise. Give me time and I'll take you along all of them.'

'Tonight?' she asked hopefully.

Marmaduke buried his mouth in her hair to smother his laughter. 'How wonderful. My bride is cut from the same cloth as I am. We're insatiable.' He tenderly nuzzled her throat. 'But this time will be different. Forgive me. You'll understand why when it happens.'

Isabel felt her whole body tense. *This time? What does he mean? He promised he would never hurt me, never do anything I did not want. Oh God, what's going to happen?*

Isabel soon realised that this time was indeed different. His kisses and caresses were even more urgent, demanding. Marmaduke did not pause to allow her to rest. He observed her, waiting for something. She began to fight him. Not from fear, but frustration. Enraged, she became the aggressor, digging her fingernails into his back, wrapping her limbs around him, demanding that he stop then instantly forbidding him to stop. Wild anger consumed her because despite her fatigue she never wanted to let him go.

Finally she cried out, 'You bastard. You *know* I want you. Why are you doing this?'

He pinned her down, his kisses teasing yet urgent. 'Yes! You can do it, my darling.'

Isabel gave a cry of rage. Then a cry that had no name. It came from her throat, a primordial sound like some trapped animal that had broken free from its prison. She felt her heart break inside her and the pain gushed out in wordless agony.

She was shocked by the power of it. Her face was wet with tears and she was sobbing violently, her body soaked with a flood of tears that washed over his chest and hair.

Marmaduke rocked her in his arms. 'At last. Thank God,' he said softly.

She gave in to the grief that poured out of her body. She felt as if a secret dam inside her had shattered the walls that had confined it. All the pain and rejection of her childhood, the night terrors, the fear of darkness, the whirlpool of her feelings for Silas, love, fear, hatred. Everything evil was being washed away forever – powerless to hurt her again.

Isabel felt a sudden surge of energy that reminded her of the rare moments in her childhood of shared laughter, a clear memory of running in the sunlight of a beautiful garden with a woman's voice behind her, laughing as she chased her.

My mother! I can't see her face but I know she was there. I can remember her voice!

She wriggled around within the safe circle of Marmaduke's arms and looked down into the face of a friend. He was tired and his chin was covered with dark stubble but he was smiling like a cat satiated by a bowl of stolen cream.

'I hope you're satisfied now?' Isabel asked after a final sniff. 'I need a handkerchief.'

He stretched out a weary arm to take a crumpled ball of linen from the bedside table. 'Use mine. You might as well. You steal everything, even my soap. Here, blow.'

Isabel obeyed. As embarrassed as a small child she tried to regain her dignity. 'Do you make all your mistresses cry like that?'

Marmaduke raised an eyebrow. 'No. I've never seen anything quite like your performance, soldier.'

'But you did it deliberately. You wanted to make me cry.'

Marmaduke rolled her over and ran his finger gently along the curve of her nose.

'To prove you can trust me. And to prove to you that your cousin Silas was a lying bastard. Witches *never cry*!'

Isabel gasped at the truth that had escaped her. She snuggled down into Marmaduke's arms and kissed his neck.

'Now that my tears have proved I'm not a witch, you're in no danger I'll destroy you.'

'That's a relief,' he said lazily.

'So now it's my turn to teach *you* something you won't find in the *Kama Sutra*.' She knelt beside him and gently drew her leg across his thighs as if carefully testing the waters before diving into a creek.

'Close your eyes. Lie back. And learn what it means to be made love to by a lover who *wants* you more than any woman you have ever known.'

Marmaduke closed his eyes and smiled. 'I'm game if you are, sweetheart.'

CHAPTER 40

The early dawn light was wan and watery, coating the walls of Bloodwood Hall's farm buildings like a weak solution of whitewash. Garnet strode in the direction of the stables, glad to be free of the household tension. Fear was running rampant throughout the whole Colony since the news of the murder of Rupert Grantham.

Four weeks after their killing spree the three faceless bolters who had cut him down when he was alone and unarmed continued to be hunted by a small army of mounted police.

Garnet was furious that despite his orders for calm the tension at Bloodwood Hall was at fever pitch. No one was immune.

Elise reached for her smelling salts at every sound of horses' hooves on the gravelled carriageway and even refused to walk in the garden unattended. The servants were quick to escalate petty quarrels into warring factions. Even Bridget's usual cocksure manner was replaced by wariness. The three Marys, Red, Black and Spotty, genuflected at the drop of a hat. The young manservant had become increasingly sloppy in his livery and Garnet suspected the lad rubbed his teeth with cinnamon in a vain attempt to disguise the moonshine whisky on his breath. Their anxiety was palpable.

Garnet considered the tide of fear was nothing short of cowardice.

Rhys Powell was preoccupied with a bout of unspoken depression that Garnet recognised as the national trait known as 'the Welsh hour'. Queenie's mind was, as always, locked into avenging the wrongs of the past rather than concern about today's villains and bolters.

Not all at Bloodwood Hall had lost their heads. Garnet was satisfied that at least two others under his roof had kept their heads – only to lose their hearts.

Marmaduke and Isabel walked together in the garden as if they had been joined at the hip. It was clear to Garnet the nights were never long enough for them.

As he threw open the stable doors he gave a wry smile.

What a fool Marmaduke was to think he could hoodwink me. Does he think I'm so old I can't remember what it is to be in love? God willing that girl will soon translate my son's lust into an heir while I'm still spry enough to teach the little chap how to ride a horse and be a man. To grow up to be Wine Son from Vinegar, as old Mendoza used to say.

Garnet yelled out to the ostler sleeping in the hayloft above the stables. Davey wore his slop clothing day and night. He peered over the edge of the loft, his tousled head threaded with hay then stumbled down the ladder begging Garnet's pardon.

'I'd have been having your horse saddled and waiting for ye, sir, if I'd known ye had a mind to be riding out early this morning.'

Feverishly saddling Garnet's choice of stallion, Davey asked, 'Is it wise to be riding out alone, sir? To be sure it's dangerous times we live in, what with the villains who murdered that fine Mr Grantham still being at large in the bush.'

Garnet was not sure if the lad's expression was sly, disrespectful or genuinely concerned. How many of his assigned labourers would consider the murderers to be heroes and turn feral themselves?

'No need to feel concern on my behalf, lad. I'm always armed to the hilt,' Garnet said, patting his hip to underline his reference to firearms.

He rode the stallion at walking pace past the aviary; the large domed bird house was covered with fine wire netting to contain the swirling kaleidoscopic patterns of brilliantly coloured budgerigars, the tiny descendants of those long ago captured in the bush for Miranda's pleasure.

He pictured Miranda in his mind, seated at the heart of the aviary on a wrought-iron garden bench, dressed in a filmy white Empire gown, her dark hair tumbling over her shoulders, her outstretched arms holding lines of the tiny creatures that she had tamed to come to her in the way she attracted everyone to her. The bird she loved most, an emerald green and turquoise one more adventurous than his companions, attached its tiny claws to the crown of her head, gently rubbing his minute beak in her hair and repeatedly chirping the words she had patiently taught him when she had separated him from his brothers.

'Love me, love me not,' Garnet echoed softly, reminded of the ironic contrast between a romantic female like Miranda who was enchanted by these clever birds and the practical attitude of Aborigines who lived off the land. He remembered how Miranda had taken a tribal elder to admire her aviary and to her horror the old man had cheerfully confided, 'Budgerigar plenty good tucker, missus.'

Now as these tiny caged beauties played and flirted together inside the aviary, flying from miniature swings to the branches of potted shrubs, they were a living reminder of the first year of his marriage when Miranda was radiant, blossoming with child. The whole Colony had then seemed to him like a trunk full of freshly minted golden sovereigns.

Everything seemed possible. Now I'm growing older and my time is running out.

The screeching laughter of kookaburras high in the treetops heralded daybreak as Garnet rode unhurriedly along a bush track, screened from sight of the estate's farm buildings and the fading voices of the Government men Fordham was assigning to their labour.

Riding past the graveyard Garnet averted his eyes from the corner where a slab of stone pinned down the last remains of Klaus von Starbold. He knew the inscription by heart as he had ordered the stonemason to write it for two reasons. To give the whole locality the illusion that the lavish public funeral paid full tribute to his son's tutor, who was well liked in the village. Secondly, he chose the words written in stone specifically to conceal from posterity the fact the scoundrel met a violent death at Marmaduke's hands. The words were weathered but the memory was as sharp as hell.

KLAUS VON STARBOLD. BORN HESSE – DARMSTADT.
1788 – 1825
REMEMBERED WITH RESPECT BY GARNET GAMBLE AND FAMILY.
A WELCOME STRANGER FAR FROM HIS NATIVE LAND.

A welcome stranger. Garnet remembered how that phrase had nearly choked him and caused young Marmaduke to charge through the house in uncontrollable rage. It had taken all Miranda's powers of persuasion to calm her son and convince him this lie was necessary to shield her reputation, part of her desperate attempt to prevent Marmaduke being convicted on the grounds of 'wilful murder' in the guise of a duel.

The fact that Garnet had been forced to bury von Starbold's body in the Gamble family cemetery was the reason Garnet had insisted that Miranda be buried on her own land.

No way on earth I'd let her lie in the same graveyard as that Hessian scoundrel.

Now overlooking the mouth of the Ghost Gum Valley beyond Mingaletta, Garnet paused to take stock of the land that he had been loath to visit for years.

Through the dense frieze of eucalypts of many species, tall thin stragglers soared to the sky between the trunks of giants that had taken scores of years to expand their girth. At their feet, a thick undergrowth of ferns and shrubs had sprung up, freed from the controlled fire-farming methods he knew had been practised by tribal blacks who had hunted here for untold centuries, before the British came and claimed the whole country as a gaol.

For criminals like me. Now I'm buying it back from the Crown block by block. But the time has come to let go of Mingaletta – Marmaduke's rightful inheritance.

Garnet heard their voices before he saw them. The quicksilver ripples of Isabel's laughter sounded in response to the dark, rich voice of his son.

He wanted to join them, to be accepted on the fringe of that warm circle that surrounded all young lovers in a private cocoon of their own making. But even more Garnet wanted the truth. Knowledge was power. What exactly were these two hiding from him?

Looping his horse's reins to the limb of a gum tree, he took care to remain out of sight as he manoeuvred himself closer to hear their conversation.

Isabel and Marmaduke stood with their backs to him, their heads bent over the blueprint of the house that covered the circular stump of a tree, serving as a drawing board. Before them lay a cleared section marked out with pegs to define the dimensions of future rooms.

Marmaduke's voice was confident. The sun was shining on the coil of hair that cascaded down his back. His sleeves were rolled up, the arms tanned and muscular. His head was close to Isabel's honey-brown hair as he pointed out details in the plans.

'It isn't grand, I admit. But it's as close as I could get to the drawing of the Indian Colonial bungalow that the Colonel built here for Mother. The verandahs are covered except for this central section. It's larger than the original homestead. See? Here's the plan for the additional rooms.'

Like a boy he sprang inside the pegged spaces to demonstrate the layout and beckoned her to join him.

'Here's the library to hold all our books. Here's the music room and this is your own little sitting room to do your sewing.' He pointed to the open area beyond the house. 'That's where I'll build the stables and a cabin for however many assigned men the authorities allow me. Only a few to begin with and I'll be working like a dog myself. But I'll build a successful life for us – just you watch me, soldier.'

Garnet felt moved by the natural way Isabel slid her arm around her husband's waist in a gesture of possession. The sweet expression on her face, the soft, rounded lines of her body belonged to a girl who had begun to blossom in the hands of her lover.

'No counterfeit love this time,' Garnet said the words under his breath and fervently hoped it was the truth.

Isabel's voice was teasing. 'Marmaduke, it's perfect. But haven't you forgotten something? One day, maybe a little nursery?'

Marmaduke stiffened. Quickly recovering his composure he took hold of her upturned face between his hands. 'My darling girl, we have each other. That's enough for you, isn't it? I never lied to you. The Gamble line must die out with me.'

'But we're both healthy. You could well take after your mother.' Her eyes were pleading. 'Just one babe? I'm willing to take the chance all will be well.'

'But I'm not!' Marmaduke drew her into his arms and kissed her hard as if by the sheer force of his physical passion he could put an end to the forbidden question. Recognising the sad resignation in her eyes, he appeared to capitulate.

'You deserve to be a mother and I'm the man to give you what you want. I intended to surprise you but I can see you need to know what the future holds. I've already sent a letter inviting your Aunt Elisabeth to join us in the Colony. And to bring out the babe who is your family responsibility. They could live here with us at Mingaletta.'

'Rose Alba! What have you done?' Isabel pulled away in distress but Marmaduke turned her to face him.

'What's wrong? I thought this is what you'd want. They must be close to your heart, I know you send your aunt the allowance I give you.'

'Of course they're dear to me, but how ever will I explain the truth to Garnet?'

'Simple. Call the child your little sister or cousin. What the hell does it matter? I'll adopt Rose Alba. Give her the Gamble name if you'll allow me.' He gave a wry laugh. 'I haven't a clue how to be a good father. My parents fought over me like I was their personal War of the Roses. But I can learn, can't I? Rose Alba is part of you, darling, so I'll love her as I would my own child.'

Murmuring soft reassuring words, Marmaduke drew her down to lie in his arms in the shade of a tree. Garnet watched how quickly his son's kisses aroused the girl. His hand caressed her naked foot and moved gently up under the folds of her skirt. Isabel's hungry cry of surrender forced Garnet to acknowledge it was time to leave them in their own private world. Marmaduke's pistol belt lay abandoned on the grass, his normal sense of caution lost in the moment. Garnet withdrew a short distance away, averting his eyes from the lovers as he kept guard, hearing Isabel's cries of ecstasy.

When he finally rode away he was in no hurry to return home. His eavesdropping had delivered more truth than he had bargained on hearing. His thoughts were tangled threads of pleasure and pain. He replayed in his mind the words Marmaduke had said lightly, for once without any deliberate desire to hurt him. Words spoken from his son's heart were all the more painful...*to be a good father...my parents fought over me...their own personal War of the Roses...the child is part of you...so I'll love her...as I would my own child...*

Suddenly profoundly weary, Garnet admonished himself. 'You fool. You wanted the truth and you bloody well got it served up in spades. Marmaduke won't risk the possibility of passing on my malady to future generations to avoid a replica of me. Who could blame him?'

Garnet dug his heels into his horse's flank to break into a gallop. He had no intention of returning home without a thorough exploration of the past hour's revelations.

Isabel's shocked response to her aunt's future arrival triggered Garnet's memories of the pale, romantic young Elisabeth de Rolland, the unwitting cause of his transportation. The babe was unlikely to have been born to Elisabeth, who was his own vintage. Rose Alba: a pretty name for whoever she was. A white rose of York. He considered what the advent of a toddler at Bloodwood Hall would mean.

I built it in the hope Miranda and I would fill the rooms with little tykes. This child is welcome to my name. Rose Alba Gamble. It has a good ring to it.

He thought about the significance of Isabel's likely sufferings as the impoverished ward of Godfrey de Rolland's whose family motto should have been 'Honour For Sale to Highest Bidder'.

It's London to a brick that Rose Alba was born on the wrong side of the blanket. No wonder the de Rollands were keen to trade Isabel. But I played the winning hand. Isabel has made a man of my son. The only problem is Marmaduke. He's not shy of servicing her, just Hell-bent on avoiding progeny.

Night was fast falling when Garnet approached the rear of Bloodwood Hall from the opposite direction to the one he had taken to ride out. For the past hour he had felt a discomfiting sense he was being observed. Yet each time he checked the lay of the land nothing was visible except a mob of grazing wallabies or some red-bellied black snake slithering through the yellowed native grass.

It wasn't until Garnet arrived at the aviary that he understood the unnatural silence. Budgerigars were never less than excited. The metal door of the aviary was wide open.

Garnet gave a bellow of rage. 'I'll have the balls of the bloody fool who forgot to close it! I've bred Miranda's birds for years. Now all of them are lost in the bush.'

He leapt down from the saddle, slammed the door on its hinges in a vain attempt to release his frustration. Then struck by the thought the fault might have been Isabel's carelessness, he swung open the door and stepped inside.

The truth turned him ice-cold. The entire floor of the aviary was covered with the tiny corpses of budgerigars – blue, gold, green, speckled white, all lying with their tiny beaks wide open, their eyes glassy in death.

Breathing heavily he looked around him. Found the cause lying in the corner. An empty bottle printed with a single word. Laudanum. He knew by the smell of it the seed bowls were covered with the same deathly liquid.

Garnet knew this was the handiwork of a sick, vengeful mind. These tiny helpless creatures had paid the price in a cowardly act of terrorism aimed directly at him and those he loved. Marmaduke and Isabel.

The shadow of death had returned to blight Bloodwood Hall again, but this time Garnet knew the game was lethal. Personal. No one in his Gamble empire would ever be safe again.

Garnet hurried to the stables. He confronted Davey quietly.

'You want to gain your ticket-of-leave? Earn wages like a free man?'

The boy blanched and nodded.

'Then fetch a shovel and hessian bags. Remove every dead bird and feather from the aviary. Bury 'em so deep the Devil couldn't find them. Spread the word they escaped. I don't want my womenfolk to panic on the heels of that Grantham business. Hear me?'

The boy nodded mutely.

'If no one finds out the truth I'll get Magistrate Summerhayes to grant your ticket. But if the panic spreads I'll see you're chained in the stocks for the magpies to peck your eyes out!'

The boy sucked in his breath. 'Be Jasus!'

Garnet did not wait to see his order carried out but returned to the house. The aviary would be cleared and, by the time the lovers returned from Mingaletta, the birds would be buried for eternity.

CHAPTER 41

Each day the rider collected the post from Bloodwood village the tally grew of handwritten or formally printed cards from those on Garnet's invitation list, stating their regrets that they must decline his invitation to the banquet at Bloodwood Hall. Some used the euphemism 'due to unavoidable circumstances', the loophole that fooled no one. Most of them feared that they might be the next target of the still unidentified trio of assassins. It was widely believed that Aboriginal trackers working for the mounted police had given descriptions of the wanted men's height, weight and gait from the evidence of their footprints.

None doubted all three were bolters in the bush. Since Grantham's murder there had been a pattern of robberies fanning out across the far side of the marshland south of George's River, cowardly attacks by two or three young men. Their leader always threatened death.

Marmaduke raised the subject during dinner. 'The police expect to announce the names of Rupert's murderers at any moment. No doubt the fear through the Colony has affected your plans, Garnet. Rhys tells me the guest list has shrunk to a few local bravehearts, Magistrate Summerhayes, the local quack and maybe one member of the Quality – the gentleman who has leased Penkivil Park while the colonel's stationed in India.'

'What would Rhys Powell know?' Elise snapped and everyone looked at her in surprise.

'Everything, I should hope, given he's Father's right hand.' Marmaduke said dismissively then turned to Garnet. 'Isabel's friends and mine seem to be made of sterner stuff. Edwin has promised to be here and Isabel's shipmate, the Scotsman, Murray...?'

'Robertson,' Isabel supplied quickly. 'He'll be here. Once a Highlander gives you his word you can count on him for life.'

Garnet was uncharacteristically silent so Marmaduke pressed his advantage. Mingaletta was everything. The date of the handover must not be postponed.

'Well, we'll celebrate your birthday on the right day, no matter what. But I presume you've cut your cloth accordingly and cancelled the musicians and entertainers?'

Garnet beckoned the young manservant in livery to refill his glass.

'The entertainers were prepared to risk the journey, more guts than most of the Quality, but I wasn't prepared to risk their lives. Naturally I paid 'em and Madame St John their full fee in lieu.'

Startled, Marmaduke and Isabel reacted in unison. '*Madame St John?*'

'Yes, the Yankee Nightingale. No doubt you know of her?'

Marmaduke and Isabel stumbled over themselves to assure Garnet his choice had been perfect but it was a wise decision to cancel all entertainment for the sake of the performers' safety.

Garnet appeared to grow increasingly edgy. 'Where *is* Rhys Powell? Overnight in the village again? Been gone for two days, hasn't he? What the Hell's he up to?'

'Who cares?' Elise said petulantly. 'If you ask me, he's disloyal – a turncoat.'

Marmaduke exchanged a swift glance with Isabel. Surely Elise had heard village gossip. The usually abstemious Wesleyan had been on such a belligerent drunken bender for two days that the local police constable had been forced to put him in the lock-up. No formal charges had been laid due to Garnet's friendship with Magistrate Summerhayes.

"You've certainly changed your tune, Elise. Only last week you were singing your teacher's praises.'

Elise chose to ignore Marmaduke and turned her full attention on Garnet, leaning forwards so that her large bosom rested revealingly in a sea of coffee-coloured lace.

Marmaduke was amused by the lack of subtlety in her performance. Elise's eyes were on the brink of tears and her pouted lips quivered.

'Garnet, dear, it hurts me to have to say this when you have been so kind to your Welsh secretary, but you should know in all honesty I can no longer bear to be seen in his company. If you were not blinded by his servility and fawning manner you'd have sent the man packing months past. There's much truth in that saying, "Taffy was a Welshman, Taffy was a thief". If you'd been able to read the fine print in your contracts no doubt you'd have discovered the truth.'

Marmaduke felt strangely resentful of her barbed reference to Garnet's illiteracy.

'Ah, so *you* can read contracts now, can you, Elise? What wonderful progress,' Marmaduke said smoothly.

Elise looked distressed to be caught out in her lie. 'Rhys told me,' she snapped.

Garnet eyed her keenly. 'Strong words of condemnation, Elise. I've fired many secretaries, managers and overseers but never without just cause. Do you have proof of Powell's betrayal? Or would you like to tell us the true reason you are so upset with him?'

Garnet's words were delivered quietly but Marmaduke knew his father well enough to realise there was a hidden agenda.

Elise burst into a noisy flood of tears and fumbled for her napkin to blot her face. Isabel quickly offered her own handkerchief, a flimsy square of lawn that would serve no purpose beyond token empathy.

Marmaduke failed to be moved by the flood. He noticed Garnet's face was impassive.

'You are unwell, Elise?' Marmaduke asked politely but more to impress Isabel that he was not a callous brute.

'I should think I am,' Elise said. 'And I am hardly done by. Garnet knows why!'

Elise turned to Garnet, her tragic dark eyes shedding rivulets of tears down her chalk-white face. She looked suddenly tired as if she had aged overnight and Marmaduke felt irritated by a twinge of pity despite everything he remembered he had once loved and now despised.

Fluttering her pale, be-ringed hands in a helpless gesture, Elise was desperately seeking support from whoever would rally to her aid. Intuitively turning to a female ally, she gestured imploringly to Isabel. 'During all these long years I have been Garnet's faithful companion, he promised me he would take me in marriage on one condition. Well, if Garnet is loath to announce the news today, it seems I must. I am at last with child!'

Marmaduke decided to count to ten before he ventured a comment. *If what Isabel told me is true, Rhys Powell may have done the deed. Does Garnet suspect he's a cuckold?*

Everyone appeared too stunned to respond so Marmaduke at last broke the silence. 'So Garnet, I take it congratulations are in order. I am to have a young brother or sister. That *is* a surprise.'

Garnet's face was a mask of indifference. 'Congratulate Elise. More to the point, you should congratulate Rhys Powell. None of my doing. I've been fully occupied elsewhere,' he said with insulting emphasis, openly glancing in Bridget's direction.

'That's a dastardly lie and you know it,' wailed Elise. She knocked over her wineglass as she stumbled to Garnet's side, grasped the lapels of his coat and shook him.

'You can't do this to me. After all I've done for you, all I've suffered at your hands, forced to fulfil *your needs* in that ghastly attic. Tell them the truth, I beg you. I am having your child, Garnet. I am! I am!'

While she shook him, Garnet's hands hung limply by his sides as though incapable of touching her. Finally his lack of resistance forced her to stop.

'If only that was the truth,' Garnet said quietly. He shook himself free of her and walked from the room.

In Marmaduke's eyes his father seemed suddenly transformed into a tired but dignified older man. One look at Isabel and he knew they were of the same mind.

Thank God for my girl. She keeps a cool head in a crisis. Perhaps that is the quality that helped her survive her own childhood trauma.

He drew Isabel aside and placed a hand gently on her shoulder.

'Take Elise to her room. Stay with her until I come to you. I must go to Garnet and get this sorted out. I don't want to be guilty of shoving a woman who's with child out into the snow, so to speak. Especially as the babe she's carrying might be my brother.'

He watched Isabel shepherd the weeping Elise towards the stairs, gently assuring her all would end well but that she must think of the babe and not to overtax her strength.

Marmaduke felt saddened by this evidence of Isabel's motherly instincts. God willing little Rose Alba would in time arrive safely and fulfil the one need that Marmaduke would never be able to satisfy.

Distracted by the sound of a horse approaching at a gallop he went outside to greet the courier. The letter from Edwin was urgent. Two men had been charged with Rupert Grantham's murder. The date had been set for the trial. He must act at once.

He dismissed the servants and, left alone, fortified himself with a glass of wine before confronting his father on the delicate subject of the paternity of Elise's babe.

Marmaduke's thorough search of the house proved that Garnet was not in his usual bolthole, his library or anywhere else. Marmaduke questioned all the servants who had been on duty all evening. None had seen or heard Garnet exit the house. That left no place to try except one. The priest's hole.

He took a candlestick, touched the secret panel and sprang up the stairs. The priest's hole was empty. But Marmaduke fancied he could feel the residue of pain that was trapped in this tiny dark space. A hole indeed. Not used as in past centuries in England to escape from religious persecution, this priest's hole served for Garnet's vain attempts to escape from his guilt by suffering self-inflicted physical torment.

Marmaduke closed his mind to a brief flash of pity and closed off the priest's hole.

Hurrying down the picture gallery he paused by his mother's portrait.

'Where the hell is he? He's crazy enough to top himself.'

Marmaduke blinked. Was it an illusion caused by the flickering candlelight or had the dark eyes in the portrait for one split second glanced upwards? Marmaduke had the sudden thought of the one place he had not thought to look. *The parapet walkway.*

He backtracked to the seldom-used spiral staircase that led to the roof.

The night air was chilly when he stepped out onto the castellated parapet that ran between the gothic gables of the roof. The sky was filled with that extraordinary map of the Southern Hemisphere's stars that always convinced him that Creation was no mere accident. He stopped short when he saw the figure standing at the far end of the parapet so close to the edge that Marmaduke was uneasy.

The breeze was blowing Garnet's mane of white hair and the eyes that turned to him held a wild, bewildered sadness that made Marmaduke remember Edmund Kean's portrayal of King Lear.

'Mind if I join you, Garnet?' he asked and took a few tentative steps towards him, watching him intently for any sudden movement and prepared to hurl himself across the space between them.

Garnet looked surprised. 'Leave me alone. What are you doing here? You should be in bed with your bride.'

Marmaduke tried to sound casual. He had despised this man for most of his adult life, but he had no wish to see him leap to his death. Not even Mingaletta was worth that price. He decided not to raise the question of Elise's revelation in case that was what had disturbed the balance of Garnet's mind. He had no idea what on earth to say until the words came out of his mouth in a desperate, inspired improvisation.

'I wanted to have a private word with you away from the women. Man to man. I came to ask your help, Garnet.'

'Did you indeed? That's a turn up for the books,' Garnet said, but despite the sarcastic edge to his voice, Marmaduke saw that his back straightened and he seemed to be trying to resume his mantle of authority.

Marmaduke took another step closer and leant an arm casually on the edge of the parapet.

'I didn't want to discuss it with Isabel without first asking *your* advice. You know how emotional young girls tend to be about bolters and all that stuff.'

'Indeed. What's wrong?' Garnet seemed suddenly alert and cooperative.

'Nothing really. A courier just delivered an urgent message from Edwin. Advising me that some cargo from England that I've been expecting has just arrived in port. And that the date has been set for the trial of James Leech and Will Barrenwood, the two young bolters accused of murdering my friend Rupert.'

'So they've caught 'em at last. Let's hope the jury makes short work of the trial and the villains swing for Green the Finisher.'

'My feelings exactly, Garnet. But the problem is I've been asked to go to Sydney Town to serve on the jury.'

'Why's that a problem? Do your duty and hang the bastards!'

'Naturally I want to honour Rupert's memory by serving on that jury. It's the last thing I can do for him, but it means leaving Isabel behind. It would put my mind at rest if I knew that Isabel was safe in your hands.'

'Do you think I'm too old and infirm to protect the girl in your absence? What kind of a Miss Molly do you take me for?'

Marmaduke laughed and casually placed his arm around Garnet's shoulder. He began to steer him towards the spiral staircase. 'I knew I could count on you, Garnet. Isabel could not be in safer hands than yours. I can leave her in your care with a clear conscience.'

'Of course you can, m'boy. We'll play chess together and Isabel can play the pianoforte for me. I'll keep the girl happy and free from worry, you can be sure of that.'

Garnet seemed unconcerned about Elise's revelation. Marmaduke wondered if it was another of her phantom pregnancies or if it was a deliberate ploy to force Garnet's hand.

Marmaduke gestured for his father to precede him down the staircase and with a sense of relief bolted the door securely behind him in case Garnet was tempted to return to the roof alone. He would order Bridget and the servants that the door must be kept locked.

He must warn Isabel to play the game and give Garnet the illusion he was protecting her.

CHAPTER 42

Garnet and Marmaduke were like two raging bulls with their horns locked in a duel to the death. It had all begun at the breakfast table with the question of firearms. Isabel had hoped that, as this was the morning of Marmaduke's departure for Sydney Town to sit on the jury of the Grantham murder trial, for once father and son could part company in a state of peace.

'Don't tell *me* how to run Bloodwood Hall. I've been managing this estate since you cut your milk teeth, boyo!' Garnet roared. Clearly he found Marmaduke's opinion an affront to his manhood.

Marmaduke kept his anger under control although the edge in his voice was sharp enough to cut glass. 'I'm simply confirming what every landholder in the county knows. You need men to guard this place night and day. Men who carry arms.'

'Are you blind? I've had that in place for months past.'

'Yeah, *assigned* men. But who knows where their sympathies would lie if bushrangers front up here to avenge Fordham the Flogger's brutal treatment of your Government men? You, their assigned master, are legally and morally responsible, but for years you've appeared to tolerate Fordham's methods.'

'I'm a far better Master than any landowner around here, damn you! I've stopped Fordham cutting their rations. And Paddy Whickett was the last man flogged here. I leave it up to Magistrate Summerhayes to pass sentence.'

'Yeah, but all this has come years too late to whiten your *reputation*.'

Isabel leapt into the fray. 'Please stop, both of you. We can't change the past, but we can all pull together to change the future. Please don't part in anger. If something happened to either of you – you'd never forgive yourself.'

'Isabel's right,' Marmaduke said coolly. He offered his hand to his father, who shook it for the sake of appearances.

Isabel managed a final word alone with Marmaduke. 'I'm anxious about you travelling alone, armed or not, but I know you have no choice. Rupert was your friend and being on that jury is the last thing you can do to honour the memory of a great crusader. His murderers must not be allowed to go free.'

'That's if these two bolters did the deed. That's not proven yet. I suspect it's going to be a volatile trial. Anyone can walk off the street and enter the courtroom. James Leech had escaped from an iron-gang just before Rupert's murder and the other one had bolted from his assigned master, so no doubt the court will be packed with these blokes' sympathisers. I might find my fellow jurymen biased in their favour or ready to hang them because they *are* bolters.'

'There could be no better man than you to sit on that jury. Rupert Grantham will be counting on you to fight to see that British justice is seen to be done!'

Marmaduke gave a short laugh and called across to Garnet, who was observing them. 'What did I tell you, Garnet? Forget about all that de Rolland blue-blooded crap. This is one gutsy Currency Lass!'

Isabel remained on the terrace watching Marmaduke's retreating figure gallop through the avenue of Bloodwood eucalypts to the iron gates, where he turned and gave her a mock military salute in final farewell.

My God, what have I done? What if I've sent him to his death?

Banishing that fear, she smiled wistfully at the memory of his parting words. 'Being a gutsy Currency Lass must be Marmaduke's idea of a high compliment. I'd better try to live up to it.'

The track was bordered by bush wildflowers; Isabel rode astride her mare in the direction of the Gamble graveyard the following after-noon. The tiny, sunny faces of these native flowers were a world away in nature and geography from the English bluebells and daffodils she had gathered as a child from the fields beyond the de Rolland country manor.

Isabel's destination was her weekly visit to Miranda's grave, a duty of care she had taken on in the knowledge that the ribbon-tied bouquets of flowers she took from the garden to honour Miranda's memory were a tribute that also pleased Marmaduke, Garnet and Queenie.

Honouring her promise to Marmaduke, she carried a lady's muff pistol in the purse attached to her belt. But today it was difficult to be afraid. The sun was shining so brightly her shady straw hat was little protection. Heat penetrated the layers of fine cotton that already clung to her skin. She was reminded of the ever-so-correct English maxim: 'Only men sweat, ladies *perspire*.'

Isabel grinned. 'Whoever said that had never lived in Australia. When it runs down your back and chest and soaks you to the skin, it's *sweat* not perspiration!'

Miranda's grave was in an isolated spot on the edge of Mingaletta some distance beyond the white picket fence that bordered the graveyard so Isabel dismounted, tied her mare's reins to the trunk of a sapling and walked on foot to the grave.

She removed last week's wilted flowers from the stone urn and filled it from the water bottle she had brought. She addressed a few words to Miranda's soul as she always did. This time she was quite firm.

'It is not for me to judge you, Miranda. My own past is far from spotless. But the man who loved you most is suffering terribly. If you have the power to haunt his house, as Queenie and the servants say you do, I ask your soul to show some compassion to Garnet.'

Isabel pulled out the weeds that had grown since her last visit and arranged the fresh flowers in the stone urn.

Ever since that extraordinary act of love with Marmaduke when she had cried for the first time in her life, Isabel had lost her fear of many things. She now felt it was quite possible that God might be listening to her, so she decided to pray as an act of faith.

'Please God, let Miranda's soul rest in peace. And bring peace to the living souls in the house. Comfort Garnet so that he will no longer feel the need to punish himself. Thy will be done, Lord, not mine. And bring Marmaduke safely home to me.'

On her return to where her mare was tethered she passed the public right of way that cut across the Gamble estate, granting access to any villagers who wanted to tend the graves of the pioneers buried in Garnet's family graveyard.

At the far end of this lane where it joined the road to the village, Isabel noticed a stationary carriage. Even at that distance the elegant lines proclaimed it was a fashionable carriage; it was drawn by a pair of greys. The livery-clad driver had alighted to stretch his legs and smoke a pipe. Who in that backwater village owned a carriage as fine as this?

The graveyard was empty except for its staggered rows of tombstones but Isabel's throat constricted with fear at the sight of a gentleman's top hat resting on a raised marble tombstone. A hat tied with a black chiffon streamer of mourning. Beside it lay a gold and ebony walking stick.

Her heart raced with sickening speed. From behind the wall of Garnet's mausoleum emerged the tall figure of a gentleman of rank dressed in mourning regalia, a black armband on the sleeve of his tailcoat.

The sun shone on his light brown hair and his smiling face but Isabel gave a shudder of dread.

'What are you doing here, Silas?' she demanded.

'Waiting for you, *ma petite cousine*. I was told in the village it is your custom to visit here each Friday. What else would I be doing in this God-forsaken hole?' His laugh was light and careless. 'I promised I would come to rescue you. Did you doubt it?'

Rescue me. Isabel took a step backwards, relieved that her horse was tethered only a few feet away ready for her to take flight. The mare gave a whinny as if to reassure her of its presence.

'You have no right to come here, Silas. This is private property,' she stammered.

'Not so, cousin. Even local rustics have right of way to honour their dead. Why are you so surprised to see me? The letter I placed in your cabin trunk made it clear—'

'I chose not to open it. I have no wish to see you again. Ever.'

There was an expression of hurt on Silas's face that might have convinced a stranger.

'But Isabel, I have travelled thirteen thousand miles on an appallingly uncomfortable vessel to honour my promise to you. And bring you Uncle Godfrey's sad news.'

'Uncle Godfrey? Tell me, what's wrong. Now!'

'Not so hasty, cousin. What became of the fine de Rolland manners you were taught? Tut, tut. Don't tell me that Emancipist's son has reduced you to the level of a Colonial wench in less than a year?'

Isabel clenched her damp palms, determined not to play by the rules of his game.

Silas is toying with me, confident that his charm is his birthright. What people said is true. He does look like a taller male version of me – enough to be mistaken for my brother. I must avoid looking directly at his eyes. Marmaduke, why aren't you here when I need you?

Despite her panic she managed to answer coolly. 'I see you are in full mourning. For Martha? Not for Uncle Godfrey? He was well when I left London. Be so good as to deliver his message – then leave.'

Silas flipped the tails of his tailcoat and seated himself beside his hat on the tombstone as casually as if he were an invited guest at a tea party. His eyes were laughing, their power momentarily softened. Silas looked able to live outside of time. He never seemed to have aged beyond his early thirties, except for the fine pencil-thin lines on either side of his mouth.

Don't look at his mouth, don't remember his kisses.

Silas was sure of himself. 'Impetuous as ever, sweet girl, a rush of questions before a man has time to answer them. It indicates the confused mind of a little English schoolgirl. You have not yet learnt, Isabel. *Ce qui n'est pas clair n'est pas français.*'

'What is not clear, is not French,' she translated. 'Your French accent always was appalling, Silas. That quotation is amusing but doesn't apply to me. I see things very clearly now. As Heraclitus said, "You can't step twice into the same river." I'm no longer your little creature, Silas. I am my own woman. My husband has changed me. Genuine love can do that. That's a joy you're never likely to experience.'

Silas gave a wistful smile. 'You choose to forget, Isabel. The joy of arousing your love was mine. But my desire to take you in marriage was denied me by your guardian.'

'I now understand why Uncle Godfrey sent me here. To protect me from you. Deliver his news or I'll leave you to your own company to deliver a graveyard elegy to Martha.'

'How sharp your tongue has grown. I quite like the change in you, cousin. Docility in a woman becomes cloying over time. As poor Martha proved.' Silas gestured to his mourning weeds and sighed. 'I must wear this public tribute to her dear memory for a year. Society demands it.'

Martha loved you with her whole heart. I must refuse to take the bait in her defence – that's just what he wants me to do.

'I don't believe Uncle Godfrey would use you as a courier when he could write to me directly,' she challenged.

'That's physically impossible, alas. He has suffered a stroke. Mentally he's quite recovered but his hands are crippled, unable to hold a pen. Your guardian is quite dependent on me.'

'No longer my legal guardian. I am a married woman. I owe obedience to none but my husband.'

'Why be faithful to a philandering husband?' Silas looked startled. 'Forgive me, I see you don't know.'

'You know nothing of him!'

'On the contrary, I encountered him recently early one morning in the villa of the actress Josepha St John, where he slept the night with her. I understand from her that you two have a most accommodating marriage. If you don't believe me, ask your husband.'

'My marriage is no concern of yours. Give me Uncle Godfrey's message or leave!'

Silas's tone was languid. 'Godfrey wants you to understand that when you wish to end this sham marriage he will welcome you home to resume your rightful place in English Society. He will arrange a divorce. It takes some time, of course, an act of parliament. But what impediment is that to a de Rolland? All is in readiness. Our berths are booked on the first available vessel bound for home. I have only to confirm the date of our departure. On our return to England, when my period of mourning has passed, we will marry. As it was always meant to be.'

'No! None of that will ever happen, but I will write to Uncle Godfrey myself to thank him for his concern for my welfare.'

Isabel turned away to avoid direct contact with those green eyes that seemed to be a mirror image of her own – except that in Silas's eyes she could find no trace of a soul.

'I'll save you the trouble, *ma petite cousine*.'

Isabel was quick to regain control. 'No. I have no need of you to mistranslate my feelings, Silas. You've already done enough harm in the past as a witness. Garnet Gamble is forever banished from England due to your fabricated evidence at his trial.'

The smile was gone, his tone dangerously polite. 'Ah, so you've turned your coat, Isabel. You prefer to take the word of a thieving agricultural labourer and convicted felon against the word of your de Rolland kinsman.'

'Garnet Gamble has never lied to me. *You* have never told me the truth.'

Silas rose with outstretched arms, his palms open in supplication. 'The truth is I love you. You are my blood. Flesh of my flesh. You were always destined to be with me. Only me.'

'Don't dare take one step closer.'

Isabel's hands were shaking as she warded him off, determined to divert his attention. 'Tell me the *whole* truth for once. How did Martha die?'

Silas removed the ebony cane from the top of the grave and idly fingered the gilt knob, fashioned in the shape of a mythical winged creature. There was something about the way he stroked the dragon-like bird's head that made Isabel shudder.

'Martha. Ah, now thereby hangs a tale. I am afraid it will break your heart.'

'My heart was broken as a child. I survived. My husband made me whole again.' There was a catch in her voice. 'Did Martha die at peace? I must at least know that.'

His words were soft but hit their target. 'Of course, you share my guilt.'

Damn him. He knows exactly how to stab his finger in old wounds that never heal.

'Carry your own guilt. Just tell me she did not die alone?'

Silas hesitated. As if it was a habit of his he began turning the head of the gold wyvern knob that screwed into the cane. The flesh across his cheekbones was taut, the lines around his mouth deepened. Isabel was afraid that at any moment she would be looking into the eyes of a stranger, the transformation she had learned to fear as a child.

'Martha knew she was dying before you sailed from England. The leeches could do nothing for her. We all knew it. You alone refused to face the truth, Isabel. Martha wanted you to sail away happy in the false hope she would recover.' Silas gave her a glance of great sadness. 'My wife trusted you – the truth would have destroyed her.'

Isabel felt a wave of panic as splintered images of the past flickered before her eyes. *Please God, don't let me remember what I did. I must hang on to Marmaduke's words. Whatever happened, I was only a child – Silas was an adult. I must keep Marmaduke's face in front of me. Marmaduke is real!*

'Go on,' she managed to say coldly.

'You remember our last night together in London? When Edmund Kean gave us *Othello*?'

'What has that to do with Martha?' she snapped.

'I was haunted by the scene Kean never managed to play that night. The scene where Othello smothers Desdemona with a pillow.'

Isabel felt herself rock on the balls of her feet. Her hand reached out but there was nothing on which to steady herself. Unable to move, she dug her fingernails into her hands. As long as she could feel pain she could cling to reality.

Silas's voice was sad as he unscrewed the knob of the cane and held it in the palm of his hand. 'You have no idea how Martha suffered, Isabel. It was painful for those who loved her to watch her fight for each breath. Believe me I did what I could to relieve her suffering.'

From the top of the cane he removed a small phial.

'Do you recall this smell, cousin? A little like frankincense, they tell me, an ancient, aromatic aroma laced with spices to make it palatable. Wonderfully effective for a thousand remedies is laudanum.'

Oh God, this isn't happening. Marmaduke – your eyes, your mouth, your words. Don't leave me!

To Isabel is seemed Silas spoke in the protective, comforting voice of a loving husband Martha had deserved but never known. 'This gentle white powder took away Martha's pain, enough to keep her calm and still. I swear she understood. She watched me, her eyes wide open as I held the pillow. I said, "Goodbye, Martha." And I ended her suffering.'

Silas raised the cane to his nose and inhaled the laudanum as another man would smell a rose.

'This little device served me well. The fresh bottle of laudanum by her bedside was discovered next morning untouched. The doctor's verdict was that the night nurse had accidentally given Martha an overly strong dose of laudanum, causing Martha to roll over in her sleep and smother in her pillow.'

Isabel felt the rising nausea that she remembered was a prelude to fainting. She stepped backwards, edging towards the waiting mare.

Silas was instantly at her side, his arm around her waist pressing her body against him. She felt the heat of his breath as he whispered the words in her ear.

'It was the right thing to do. From now on we need never feel another moment of guilt. Don't you see? We ended Martha's suffering. It was a kindness. We are free from all impediments. The de Rolland debts are wiped out. Once again we live in luxury. The world is ours, Isabel. We will never be parted again!'

Silas's kiss covered her mouth. Isabel closed her eyes to break contact with those green eyes. She had a vivid image of herself as a young child.

Alone in the darkness of her bedchamber she stirred from sleep. Aware of Silas's face in the shadows. He looked strangely excited as he bent over her, she felt his cool hand slip beneath her nightgown... caressing her body, between her thighs as if it was his right.

Isabel found herself drowning beneath this new kind of kiss – a terrible but exciting kiss that sucked air from her body, blocking her words. She had no power in her body except to move her eyes, searching the wall, the pattern of wallpaper in desperation, trying to escape into the curlicues of the wallpaper, to lose herself so completely that no one would ever find her again.

Isabel was screaming silently inside her head now – as she had as a child. She tried desperately to free herself from Silas's kiss by an act of will.

In her mind she saw Marmaduke's dark eyes watching her. Heard the echo of his words: 'You had no choice as a child. Now you have. Say you want *me*, my darling!'

Isabel's felt her body flooded with white-hot energy. Her hand clawed Silas's face, drawing deep rivulets of blood down his cheek. As she broke free and ran to the mare she felt sickened by the thought that fragments of his skin must lie beneath her fingernails.

Overwhelmed by the horror of the way Silas had extinguished Martha's life, she did not doubt that Martha had died in terror, aware that Silas was about to smother her and unable to call for help. The long-buried memory of what Silas had done to her as a child triggered an even greater fear. What would happen should Silas ever discover Rose Alba's existence?

It took moments for Isabel to register reality – Silas's face, shocked by her violence. As she hoisted herself into the saddle he lunged towards her. His eyes were the eyes of *that stranger*. Her mare was so nervous it reared in fright. Isabel clung to its neck to prevent herself being thrown down at Silas's feet.

'You stole my innocence. Blighted my childhood, cousin. I will not allow you to ruin the rest of my life. It's mine, do you hear me? *Mine*!'

It chilled her to see Silas smile. She had left four thin scars on his cheek – her own personal brand on him. He did not seem to feel any pain, only excitement.

Silas shook his head in denial. 'No! Our lives will run parallel for the moment, Isabel. I have taken a lease on Penkivil Park, only a few miles away. I am your neighbour. Next time we meet, Isabel, *you* will come to *me*.'

Those strange green eyes were so sure of their power over her.

Isabel clung to the horse's mane and dug her heels into its flanks. She prayed that her mare knew the way home to Bloodwood Hall because right now she was blind to everything around her, her mind filled with the terrifying images her memory had suppressed for years.

...as a child lying naked in the priest's hole...drowsy...unable to move...the crucifix upside down on the altar...a man wearing the mask of the Horned god...its green eyes...the eyes of Silas...

Isabel ran through the house, ignoring the open-mouthed expressions of the servant girls she passed. She found Garnet sitting alone on the terrace, a half empty jug of gin and lime juice on a table beside him. His brooding expression quickly changed to welcome as she burst out onto the terrace.

'Garnet, something terrible and yet wonderful has happened.

I have just recovered lost memories from my childhood. I know it makes no sense but yes, terrible, yet wonderful. For the first time in my life I am truly free.'

Unable to control her joy, she flung her arms wide and whirled in the circle of an impromptu dance before she sank into the planter's chair facing him.

'Free, m'dear? Not from Marmaduke, I trust?'

She gave in to a peal of laughter. 'Not Marmaduke! He is the one I must thank for my freedom. I'm broken away from the sins of the past, Garnet. Do you know what that means? I feel light-headed. Young in the way I never felt as a child. For the first time in my life, I truly belong to myself!'

Garnet poured two glasses of gin and lime juice and handed one to her.

'Here drink this, it'll steady your nerves, girl. And mine!'

Isabel accepted the glass trying to contain her laughter. She knew she was on the verge of hysteria and couldn't control the pitch of her voice, but she did not care.

'Let's drink to the future. To Marmaduke's safe return and to all of us, freedom from the past!'

And then she began laughing and crying at the same time.

Garnet needed no second invitation. They clinked glasses and downed their drinks in one unbroken measure.

Isabel leapt to her feet and brought the chessboard to the table, brushing aside his bundle of business papers as if they were as unimportant as old confetti.

'Today I choose to be on the Duke of Wellington's side. But stand warned, Garnet, at long last I am going to beat Napoleon Bonaparte.'

Garnet's eyes were brimming with merriment. 'And about time too. Do you think I don't know when a clever young lady is allowing an older man to win?'

Isabel gasped in surprise until, recognising Garnet's true delight, she joined his laughter and the wonderful new feeling of closeness that she felt must be the bond a daughter shared with a loved father.

CHAPTER 43

Arriving in Sydney Town Marmaduke felt a surge of conflicting emotions. After the past weeks of sharing with Isabel an oasis of romantic, idyllic serenity, mentally shielded from the outside world, he felt he had been catapulted back into the brutal reality of the Colony – a world of crime, murder, executions. Within days he must give his full attention to hearing the evidence at a murder trial in which the victim was Rupert Grantham, the man whose company he had enjoyed and although he did not know him intimately, he had been glad to call friend.

But Marmaduke's immediate concern was the 'special cargo' Edwin had advised him had arrived – the two people whom he had invited to share his life with Isabel but who had arrived independently under unusual circumstances. He was now responsible for Isabel's widowed aunt, Elisabeth Ogden née de Rolland, and Rose Alba, a small child reared by her aunt but who Marmaduke was sure was the unacknowledged child of Isabel and her 'double cousin' Silas.

I told myself I wanted to become Isabel's hero but I didn't realise just how complicated that role would become. I must now simultaneously take responsibility for the lives of two men who may or may not have butchered my friend. Take on the role of de facto stepfather with absolutely no experience of kids. And be prepared to confront Silas de Rolland when he lobs in the Colony.

Soon after Marmaduke's arrival at the Princess Alexandrina, travel-stained and weary, Edwin came straight from court, in his robes and barrister's wig, to brief him.

'I thought it unwise to go into details in my letter to Bloodwood, knowing Garnet's penchant for reading your mail. And your wish to keep under wraps your plans to bring Isabel's aunt and the child Rose Alba to the Colony. The true story is rather complex.'

Edwin explained that Elisabeth Ogden had sailed prior to Marmaduke's invitation on her own initiative. She had paid their ship's passages to the Colony but their voyage had been broken at Cape

Town when they contracted a severe fever. On their arrival at Port Jackson, Edwin had installed the woman and child in a suite at the hotel. As they were both suffering from effects of the fever, he had placed them in the care of Dr William Bland and two hired nurses who cared for them in alternate shifts night and day. The hotel staff had strict instructions that until Marmaduke's arrival they were to receive no visitors with the exception of the surgeon and Edwin.

'I trust I have done as you would have wished, Marmaduke. Both patients are quite debilitated from the fever. Dr Bland assures me they are expected to make a full recovery but must not be moved or indeed travel to the country for some time.'

'Edwin, you are a gem of a man. Not only are you fighting to save prisoners from the gallows, balancing the needs of your own family – your mother against your bride – but you've taken on the responsibility of Isabel's family of invalids as well.'

Marmaduke enveloped him in an extravagant hug then was startled by a sudden thought. 'But if you found their names on the ship's passenger lists that means Silas de Rolland would also be able to find them when he arrives in the Colony.'

'No. Mrs Ogden had the foresight to book their passage under the assumed name of Jones, and I continued that practice here at the hotel. I gained the impression that the lady regards her nephew Silas with the same degree of contempt that we do.'

'Does she realise her connection with me – the son of the man who was transported for the so-called theft of her garnet ring?'

Edwin looked embarrassed. 'I did not feel it I my place to do so. However, Mrs Ogden is aware this hotel is owned by a wealthy entrepreneur named Gamble but she doesn't appear to have connected him to the young servant called George who served her family nearly three decades ago. I thought I'd best leave you to sort out the delicate web of de Rolland and Gamble family history.'

'Thanks, Edwin, I look forward to that,' Marmaduke said dryly.

Edwin returned to what to him was more comfortable legal territory by summarising the known facts of the murder case. The police had only been able to bring James Leech and Will Barrenwood to trial because nineteen-year-old Paul Brown, had turned King's Evidence.

'Hell, Edwin, when one of a trio of murderers rats on the other two, their trial promises to have more fireworks than the King's celebration of Guy Fawkes' Night.'

Edwin reminded him. 'All men are innocent until proven guilty under British law. I trust no impediment will be placed in your way of serving on the jury. Despite your bias in being Rupert's friend, or indeed because of it, you of all jurymen can be counted on to ensure that the prisoners accused of his murder are indeed innocent until proven guilty.'

'I hear you loud and clear, Edwin. I'm the last bloke who'd want to see innocent men hanged – and know that the true villains got off scot-free.'

Marmaduke immediately arranged for Mrs Jones and child to be moved into the commodious Gamble family chambers as soon as Dr Bland gave his approval. Meanwhile they were in rooms adjacent to his and, after changing his clothes in an attempt to make a decent impression on Isabel's aunt, he received permission to visit her.

A young housemaid advised him. 'They are both very fragile, sir. The doctor said one of us assigned girls must sit by their bedside night and day, we must.'

Marmaduke thanked her. One look at the two figures lying together in the large four-poster bed and Marmaduke was confronted by two projections of Isabel past and future. The woman Isabel might grow to resemble in her later years; the child an image of how Isabel must have looked as a little girl. The family resemblance was unmistakeable in facial structure and colouring. Each pale, drained face bore the stamp of what he now realised was the legacy of generations of aristocratic de Rollands. The woman in her late forties had a natural beauty that poverty and illness had diminished but failed to destroy. When Marmaduke's eyes rested on the small pinched face of the sleeping Rose Alba, he felt an odd sensation that reminded him of the florid language in romantic novels – 'his heart turned over at the sight of her'.

Rose Alba. No doubting she's Isabel's child. She's exquisite. But as fragile as china. God willing she hasn't travelled this far only to be lost to us! No, I won't allow that to happen. She's the only child Isabel and I will ever have.

Remembering his manners, Marmaduke bowed to the lady and tentatively addressed her by her widow's surname. Instantly charmed by the gentle smile in her green eyes and her outstretched hand, when she corrected him and established herself as Aunt Elisabeth, he kissed her hand and sat by her bedside.

'Aunt Elisabeth, you are so dear to Isabel's heart. I'm terribly sorry I wasn't here to welcome you to New South Wales. I've just learnt of your broken voyage and the fever you both suffered. The child is she...will she...?' He could not bring himself to ask her fate.

'Rose Alba is exhausted and weakened by fever but she is a healthy little soul. The kindly surgeon, your friend Dr Bland, is confident she will make a full recovery given time. However,' she added with a faint smile of resignation, 'my old bones will take a little longer, Cousin Marmaduke – if I may call you that?'

Despite her ordeal Elisabeth's English county accent and calm manner reminded him of the duchess he had witnessed opening a charity fete in Sussex on the same day that her husband the duke had been carted off to debtors' prison.

You've got to admire the Brits – it takes a lot to knock 'em off their perch.

'Call me Marmaduke, please. Let's dispense with the word *cousin*. In my book it has unfortunate connotations.'

Elisabeth watched him intently. 'Ah, I see Isabel has told you about our de Rolland black sheep. Even the most illustrious family tree harbours a villain in one of its branches. Ours is...Silas...I can hardly bear to say his name.'

Marmaduke held her hand. 'Put all that behind you. You're safe with us now. I'll take care of you both.'

'How kind. But I'm afraid that's not possible.' Her breathing became laboured and Marmaduke could see her effort was emotional as well as physical. 'Something extraordinary happened before I left England. My older brother Godfrey, who had chosen to ignore my existence for the past twenty-seven years, paid me a visit. It was quite moving to see such a proud man bearing an olive branch. He had discovered that one of the orphaned children I've had in my care was Rose Alba – Isabel's *half sister*.'

Marmaduke nodded. 'Don't worry. Isabel told me everything.'

He noticed Elisabeth Ogden had a guarded look on her face. *Shit, don't tell me there's another skeleton in the de Rolland closet.*

'My niece must really trust you. There's more you need to know. Godfrey paid our passages to New South Wales to visit Isabel. He warned me that Silas's wife Martha had died under suspicious circumstances and he feared that Silas's obsession with Isabel was so strong it would even drive him to sail down here to claim her.'

Marmaduke couldn't prevent a mental flinch. *Even down here! Seems like even the nicest Pommies think of New South Wales as the cesspool of the South Pacific.*

Despite this thought, his words were firm and reassuring. 'You and the kid are perfectly safe in my care, Aunty. But I have to tell you we are fully prepared for Silas's arrive. He's been in correspondence with Governor Bourke, but don't worry, he wouldn't have the nerve to contact Isabel. If he did it'd be over my dead body!'

This lady probably reckons my threat is just a heap of Colonial bravado. No need to tell her I've already killed one man in a duel.

Elisabeth made an effort to squeeze his hand. 'Now that I have met you, I am no longer afraid for Isabel. God surely chose her the right husband.'

Marmaduke felt uncomfortable about her graceful compliment.

God? With a bit of help from Garnet Gamble's manipulations.

'I've got to play fair and square with you, Aunty. That's our Currency way of doing things. From where you de Rollands stand, Isabel married beneath her. In the Colony you'll hear some folks claim she married a villain. I'd have to second that. It's true Isabel couldn't stand a bar of me when we married. We fought like cat and dog. But I finally won her heart. I promise you one thing. I'd die before I'd give Isabel cause to regret being my wife.'

Elisabeth Ogden smiled. 'I knew that the moment you swaggered into the room. There's something about you Currency Lads. Cut like rough diamonds you're as genuine as the Crown Jewels.'

Pleased by her heartfelt compliment Marmaduke assured her that as soon as Dr Bland gave them both a clean bill of health he would reunite them with Isabel.

Elisabeth nodded. 'I prayed I'd live to see the day Isabel would be free to share her life with Rose Alba. When we're strong enough to travel I hope to see the child settled in her new family before I return home to England.'

Marmaduke made a swift mental adjustment to the blueprint of Mingaletta.

'You're most welcome to live with us. I'm building a house big enough for all of us.'

Her smile was philosophical. 'If I were twenty years younger I would leap at the chance of beginning a new life in this strange new land. You and Isabel are young, but my time is running out. My roots are in England now that my brother Godfrey has taken me back into the fold and put my disgrace behind us.'

High time he did, for God's sake. All she did was run off and marry an honest sailor.

'Listen, Aunty, if I told you the full story of my own history of shame we'd be here until next Christmas.'

'Is it your family shame? Or the eternal shame of the de Rolland family?' she asked enigmatically.

'I'm not sure I follow you, Aunty,' he said carefully.

'Before we set sail my brother Godfrey told me about the connection between our two families. That our young family servant George was the same Garnet Gamble who saved him from debtors' prison – and is the father of Isabel's husband.'

She reached out and grasped Marmaduke's hand. 'I was banished after my elopement so I never knew that my gift to your father of a little garnet ring had caused him to be tried as a thief. I assure you if I had known I would have given evidence on his behalf – to counteract Silas's evidence against him. And he would never have been transported. How on earth can I ever face your father?'

Marmaduke couldn't stop laughing until he saw Aunt Elisabeth's shocked expression. 'If Garnet hadn't been transported he'd probably still be Godfrey's badly paid house servant. What that garnet ring did was turn him into the second wealthiest man in New South Wales!'

As exhausted as she was, Elisabeth Ogden found the energy to laugh until her eyes filled with tears.

Mindful of the sleeping child, Marmaduke had tried to keep his voice muted but after this revelation, little Rose Alba opened her eyes and looked directly at him.

Green eyes. Isabel's eyes. God, I wish she was mine.

The little girl studied him without the slightest trace of fear until, as if she had made the decision to trust him, she smiled.

At that precise moment Marmaduke knew what it felt like to be a father – he was ready to lay down his life to protect his little girl.

CHAPTER 44

Amaru's grey-speckled claws kneaded the cloth of Garnet's jacket like the hands of a tailor testing the quality of the fabric. His sulphur crest fanned out in excitement as he chanted his favourite phrase from *Punch and Judy*: 'That's the way to do it! That's the way to do it!'

Garnet felt an unaccustomed mood of contentment as he returned to the house with Isabel's hand resting in the crook of his arm.

Isabel had been especially sunny and attentive during the days since the double departure from Bloodwood Hall – Marmaduke to Sydney for the Grantham murder trial, Elise to the Garnet and Rose Inn in the village. His informants had told him Elise locked herself in her room refusing all visitors. Garnet interpreted her avoidance of any medical examination to mean she was attempting to hide the fact she was *not* with child. He felt strangely relieved that Elise had chosen to flee the coop. It saved him making a decision about her fate that at best would be a double-edged sword.

Garnet hid a wry smile at the sound of Isabel's rendition of *Strawberry Fair* in a voice more noticeable for its chirpiness than talent. Suddenly breaking off in mid-verse she switched to singing the praises of her Scottish friend, her shipmate on the *Susan*'s voyage to New South Wales.

Isabel had clearly armed herself with the facts. Drawing from her pocket Murray Robertson's recent letter she quoted his plans to leave his rural employment and seek further 'Colonial experience'.

I'm nay afraid of hard work. It's happy I am to Labour from dawn to dusk. But in all the months I've been here I have not seen my Master crack a smile. You'd think every day was the Sabbath. No Music, no joshing, not even the whiff of a dram of Whisky. I came 'Down Under' hoping for a wee bit of Adventure. But I might as well be six feet under. I would welcome any suggestions as to how I could better my station, Lass.

Isabel was quick to reassure Garnet. 'Murray is as honest as the day is long, quick to learn and has an adventurous spirit. He's a Highlander but loyal to the Crown, though I don't doubt he would prefer a Stuart on the throne. Would you be interested in meeting him on the chance you might have an opening for him on one of your rural estates?'

Garnet shied away from the question of 'one of his estates'. He had been forced to sell more property than he had intended in order to honour his contract with Godfrey de Rolland.

He remembered the warning given him by Rhys Powell before the secretary had gone on a bender in the village, fighting all comers until the constable had been forced to lock him up in the Watch House. When sober, Rhys had laid before Garnet the unpalatable facts that he now trailed so far behind Sam Terry in wealth he had not only forfeited his title as the second wealthiest man in the Colony, he was sailing fairly close to the wind financially.

Garnet was determined to keep face in front of Isabel.

'If your mate Robertson is as good a man as you say, Isabel, I'll give the matter some thought, but right now I have my full quota of Government men and hired ticket-of-leavers. Whether or not I approve of Fordham's methods, it takes a tough overseer to keep a rabble of convicts working productively.'

With Amaru's eerie instinct for picking up a cue from his master's tone of voice, the cockatoo ruffled his crest to gain Isabel's attention and spliced an interjection into the conversation with, 'What a heap of rot!'

Isabel was so weak with laughter she clung limply to Garnet's arm for support.

'Amaru! What a cheeky cocky!'

Garnet's tone to the bird was mock serious. 'You might find your seed rations cut if you don't mind your manners, old fella!'

Amaru's smooth rounded beak pecked at Garnet's ear and snapped a few words.

Isabel gasped. 'I could have sworn he said, "You old reprobate!"'

'He *did*.' Garnet chortled despite himself. 'This old bird even captures the teasing inflection in Miranda's voice. She spent hours teaching him phrases designed to take a rise out of me. She had a wicked sense of humour.'

Isabel struggled to keep a straight face as she patted his arm. 'Amaru must be a great comfort to you. How long do these cocka-toos live?'

'God only knows. I caught him in the bush for Miranda when he was a little squirt. Some claim that tamed sulphur-crested cockies might live from fifty to a hundred plus years, so this one will probably outlive me.' He suddenly grew serious. 'If he does, could I count on you to give him house room? Despite his foul mouth, Amaru is faithful – a quality rare in the human race.'

Before Isabel had a chance to respond, Amaru squawked, 'I'm a Currency Lad, mate!' Returning to his favourite *Punch and Judy* routine he began his lively little dance on Garnet's shoulder chanting, 'That's the way to do it!'

Inside the vestibule Garnet felt the blessed relief of the cool marble interior but was disconcerted when the wide-eyed Aboriginal maid, Black Mary, bobbed in front of him and confided in a nervous whisper.

'Him is waiting for you in your office, Mister Garnet.'

'Who's that?'

'*Him*! Man that bolted.'

Isabel kissed his cheek. 'I'll leave you to your mystery visitor, Garnet. I'd welcome an afternoon nap – the heat is really getting to me,' she said and hurried up the stairs.

It was Garnet's policy never to reveal his hand so he registered no emotion when he entered the library. Looking haggard and shop-soiled young Rhys Powell sprang to his feet hat in hand and began to stammer out an excuse.

Garnet cut him short. 'So the constable finally released you from the Watch House did he? I imagine the Wesleyans drummed you out of their ranks for being the town drunk?'

'Indeed they did not. But *you* have every right to reject me, Mr Gamble. I ask your indulgence to hear me out first.'

Garnet eyed him coolly as he took his accustomed seat behind the desk.

'You've got a lot of gall showing your Welsh face around here, I'll say that for you.'

'Your opinion of my conduct cannot be any lower than my own. You were a decent employer and I betrayed your trust in me, Mr

Gamble. Nothing can change that. I am here to set one thing to rights. A theft.'

Garnet was quick to pounce. 'So you did steal my money? Did you also fiddle my account books? Out with it!'

'I have not touched one penny of your money, sir. I am guilty of attempting to steal the affections of your woman but never your wealth.'

'Then what are you belly-aching about? You got her, didn't you? I'm told she's at the Garnet and Rose living free off me, while you went off cap in hand to the new tenant of Penkivil Park in search of work. Not so easy without a character from me, eh? Especially when your new woman's carrying your child.'

Rhys Powell's eyes were bleak and his words sounded painful. 'There is no babe. It was only a ploy to get you to the church. I am not without sin, sir, but even if the babe had existed it could never have been mine. I did not *know* Elise in the biblical sense.'

Garnet gave him a penetrating look and decided to believe him. 'So what do you want from me?'

Rhys lifted his chin in a desperate attempt to salvage his pride.

'I did not come to ask for *your* help. I'll find work of some kind somewhere. I'll work as a jackeroo, shepherd, anything. It's a big country. I'm told the West Coast and the Moreton Bay district up north are wide open to men who aren't afraid to work.'

'The best of British luck to you,' Garnet said sarcastically. 'But I can't quite see my former mistress traipsing after you.' He rubbed his thumb and forefinger together in the traditional gesture indicating money. 'Elise loves the stuff.'

'I'll be going it alone, I will.'

Garnet roared in triumph. 'So she's ditched you already has she? Thinks she's going to wear me down, does she? You can tell her I don't pay blackmail. Never have, never will!'

'I broke off all connection with her when I discovered this. The woman claims it was a gift. No doubt another of her untruths.'

Rhys opened a chamois bag and the contents spilled out on the desk.

Garnet kept his face blank at the sight of the *navratan,* Miranda's glorious nine-gem Indian necklace she had worn for Augustus Earle's portrait of her. It shimmered in the light, lying there as carelessly as if Miranda had just discarded it. For a moment he imagined her standing in the doorway, watching him with that teasing smile of hers.

Garnet found his voice. 'It took courage to return this. It rightfully belongs to Marmaduke's wife. I posted a reward for it with the constable. Claim it. It's yours.'

'I must refuse it,' Rhys Powell said quickly. 'To have remained silent would have made me an accessory to the theft. Despite the wrong I have done you I wanted you to know that this Welsh Taffy is no thief.' He rose and bowed. 'I bid you good day, sir.'

Garnet allowed him to reach the door before he called him back. 'Not so fast. How far do you think you can get with no money and no reference from me?'

'It's not lazy, I am. And I'm no coward. I'll take my chances.'

'Do you think I can't recognise a man who is hungry and on his uppers?'

Rhys glanced in embarrassment at his battered boots. 'Mine were stolen.'

'Sit down and don't be a bigger fool than Elise made us both. We're in the same boat.'

Rhys Powell guardedly resumed his seat. Garnet stared at him with narrowed eyes. 'I'm offering you two choices to get yourself out of this mess.'

'I want no favours.'

'I never give 'em. You'll pay in kind. My first offer is this. You can write yourself an excellent character and I'll sign it. And I'll pay your ship's passage to the Swan River Colony in Western Australia on condition you take Elise with you and guarantee she never returns to Bloodwood Hall.'

'Even if Elise agreed, I would refuse. I will not marry a thief and a liar.'

'Then you've only got one choice left – or starve. I will arrange to pay that conniving woman to leave town and never return. And as from today you will resume your duties and handle my financial affairs at the increased salary I promised you when you started. You've worked better for me than the dishonest buggers who preceded you.

So think it through. *Fast.* If you return to work here it will put a gag on all the gossip in the locality. What do you say?'

Rhys shook his head in bewilderment. 'I can't believe you're willing to give me another chance, sir.'

'Neither can I. I must be touched in the head. There's no need to go back to the inn; I'll send Davey for your things and pay your tab.'

'Nothing to pay, sir. I was sleeping in the bush – when I wasn't in *custody.*'

'Then it's all settled. Back to work with you before I change my mind.'

Rhys Powell seemed to have grown perceptibly taller on his exit than when he arrived.

Garnet held the stolen *navratan* necklace so that the gems sparkled in the light. He was moved by the unexpected manner of its return. The memory of the night he had given it to Miranda came vividly to mind – that night early in their marriage when he believed Miranda was growing to love him.

The evening was hot and languid, the house silent as he had dismissed the servants on their return from the ball at neighbouring Penkivil Park. Miranda sat opposite him and they drank a final glass of champagne. Garnet felt a surge of jealousy mixed with pride of possession.

'You were the belle of the ball but you know that full well. You had that arrogant American ship's captain eating out of your hand.'

'Arrogant? I thought the captain was charming in that courtly way of Southern gentlemen. So few men in the Colony have mastered the art of flirting.' She cast him a teasing glance over the rim of her goblet. 'Are you tired, Garnet?'

He made no answer, just watched her gloriously wanton smile as she unfastened the clasp of his gift, the Indian navratan *necklace. She entwined the gems between her fingers in a delicate, snake-like movement.*

'This must have cost a small fortune, Garnet. You do spoil me.'

Garnet felt his muscles tighten as Miranda slipped her gown from her shoulders, allowing it to fall in a flimsy white pool at her feet, arching her foot to step free of it. She dangled the necklace from one hand as she crossed to the door, covered only by the sheer film of the slip that clung to her body, damp with the heat.

Pausing in the doorway she said the words softly as if on an after-thought. 'I love this necklace so much that I'm willing to pay the price. Anything you want...'

For once Garnet hesitated as he noted the growing curve of her belly. 'Are you sure it's safe? I don't want to hurt the little one.'

Her answer was a beckoning of the hand. 'You won't. He was conceived in love.'

Garnet followed her up the stairs and took her at her word.

The nine-gem necklace was cool to the touch in his hand. He could sense Miranda's presence in the room.

'I know you're here, my love. Are you happy now? Thanks to that sad young Welshman your beloved necklace has found its way home again – for Marmaduke's bride.'

There was no sound but the ticking of the clock, but he caught the lingering trace of Miranda's rose perfume as if she had just that moment left the room.

Was this a further sign of his growing madness? Garnet did not care.

CHAPTER 45

Marmaduke had barely managed five hours sleep since his arrival at the Princess Alexandrina to prepare for his jury service at the trial of Rex versus Leech and Barrenwood.

He had transferred Aunt Elisabeth and Rose Alba to Garnet's family suite and made sure they had every aid necessary to speed their recovery. His most enjoyable hours were those he spent at the child's bedside, amusing her with stories of his own invention about bush animals and birds, telling her about Amaru, the talking sulphur-crested cockatoo who mimicked the puppets in *Punch and Judy* shows. He spoke lovingly about Isabel, the new family member Rose Alba was eager to meet, but he avoided defining the child's exact relationship to her. Aunt Elisabeth had been cloudy on that subject.

This morning when describing Isabel and Bloodwood Hall, the big country house where she was going to live, the wide-eyed little girl asked wistfully, 'Do you think the lady Isabel will like me?'

'*Like* you? Sweetheart, you're just what the doctor ordered,' Marmaduke said reassuringly but saw that he had only increased her concern.

'Oh dear, does she have a bad fever like us? Will she get better?'

'Don't worry, Isabel's as healthy as a horse. I just meant that Isabel has wanted you to live with her for a long, long time.'

That anxious exchange brought home to Marmaduke that he was totally unused to the company of children. From now on he must always be on guard in her presence, not only to eliminate his swearing but to be mindful that small children interpreted everything adults say quite literally.

Shit! What a responsibility. I'll have to watch every damned word that comes out of my mouth.

Visiting Mendoza's store he was relieved to find his silent partner was returned to full health and vigour and cautiously pleased by the recent upturn in their business.

Josiah handed him a brooch he had saved for Marmaduke's inspection before putting it for sale in the window.

'This just arrived on the transport *Blenheim* in a parcel sent to me from a pawnbroker in Cork.' Josiah added carefully, 'It has no known provenance but I have no specific reason to believe it was stolen.'

Marmaduke examined the exquisite cameo and instantly recognised it was inspired by the profile of the celebrated beauty, the notorious Lady Emma Hamilton, who was the great love of Lord Horatio Nelson's life.

'Jos! It's perfect for Isabel! She's so damned sensitive about her nose. I told her Emma Hamilton made the retroussé nose fashionable. Thanks, mate, if it's all right by you I'll take this in lieu of my share of the profits.'

Josiah gestured his approval but betrayed a sense of relief that this item would not be placed on sale in the window. Marmaduke knew that although the old man had recovered physically from the violent attack on him, he had remained wary of harassment from the traps ever since the false claim about Isabel's 'stolen' tiara.

Josiah nodded. 'The Neapolitan artist who modelled this cameo was a contemporary of Lady Hamilton. It seems the lady won all men's hearts.'

'Yeah. Except for damned British politicians.' Marmaduke's mood suddenly darkened. 'I'll never forgive Whitehall. Nelson was a national hero. They give him a splendid state funeral, erected statues and named towns after him all over the British Empire, but the bastards never honoured the one thing Horatio asked when he lay dying after the Battle of Trafalgar. He Willed the care of Emma and their babe to the nation. The nation refused to pay her a pension. Emma Hamilton never got so much as a penny. She died destitute. So much for honouring a hero's dying words.'

Marmaduke pocketed the cameo, Isabel's face vividly in his mind.

On his return to his hotel suite for a belated meal, Marmaduke checked *The Sydney Herald* for details of tomorrow's murder trial. His eye was caught by the announcement of the forthcoming Theatre Royal's Benefit Night for Josepha St John, stating that *the Colony is saddened by the news that the American Nightingale will soon sail to Rio de Janeiro for a theatrical tour of South America.*

Caught off guard, Marmaduke decided to arrange for a bouquet of flowers to be delivered with a note expressing his hope she would allow him to call on her. He was aware it was often the custom for actors to have a number of 'final' benefit nights before they retired or left town, but he could not take the risk of Josepha departing from his life without seeing her again. They had never formally said goodbye.

His mood brightened when Edwin called in to discuss the imminent trial.

Marmaduke had heard the rumours. 'It's said James Leech has a history of violence – gaoled for attacking a previous assigned master. It seems he's fast becoming a hero in the eyes of the convict population. That's hard to stomach when Rupert publicly championed Emancipist causes in the *Australian* and any other newspaper that would give him space.'

Edwin nodded. 'That's a prime example of Colonial sympathy for the underdog taken too far. Leech escaped from a George's River iron-gang just days before Grantham's death.' He hesitated. 'The talk in legal circles is that certain aspects of this trial may have been *arranged*. But I am sure you appreciate that for ethical reasons I am unable to elaborate further. I have no proof.'

'But you'll be there in court to see British justice is seen to be done?'

Edwin looked bleak. 'I'd planned to attend as a private citizen but I have received an invitation I cannot refuse. The public hanging of a lad whose case I defended – and lost.'

Marmaduke spoke without thinking. 'And he wants *you* to see him drop?'

Edwin sighed. 'I offered him my abject apology. My failure to gain him a stay of execution weighs heavily on me. He's barely twenty.'

'Forgive me. Poor little bugger. What was he up for?'

'He escaped from irons at Moreton Bay. He was a second offender. As I departed his cell last night the lad told me, "Cheer up, Mr Bentleigh. Hanging's more fun than serving seven years on Norfolk Island."'

Marmaduke felt sobered by the gallows humour that was not uncommon from prisoners facing the scaffold. Norfolk Island's penal system was notorious for its cruelty. Death was often seen as a preferred alterative to transportation there. Marmaduke understood how depressed his friend was whenever he lost a client to the Finisher.

Edwin seemed relieved to answer questions about tomorrow's trial.

'The case is to be heard before Francis Forbes, our first Chief Justice. In my opinion he's the perfect choice. But his attitude has shocked some of the legal fraternity. He believes the law here shouldn't be hidebound by British tradition. So he refuses to wear the full-bottomed wig – he sits on the bench bare-headed. He's derided by some as "the Roundhead", a reference to Oliver Cromwell's Republicans.'

Marmaduke grinned. 'Sounds like a decent bloke – for a judge.'

Edwin let that pass. 'British justice ultimately lies in the hands of the jury. Twelve men will decide the fate of Leech and Barrenwood. Whether those two young men live or die. And you, my friend, are one of the twelve.'

Marmaduke arrived at the Supreme Court dressed in sober black in respect of his civic duty. He had barely taken his seat in the jury box when he began to feel trapped. Sweat trickled down his forehead and under his stiff collar. All the windows were closed and the air was stifling. The courtroom was filled to overflowing with spectators and it was clear Leech and Barrenwood had attracted a vocal faction of once-and-future convicts. The majority were so rough and belligerent they looked as if they had just been landed from a convict transport. The smell in the room was rank, like a soup of beer, tobacco, garlic and unwashed bodies.

Marmaduke glanced around at his fellow jurors. Twelve Good Men and True. All apparently sober and upstanding citizens. Whether they were Old Lags or Came Free, they had one thing in common. All were substantial landowners. Land was the ultimate stamp of respectability. Marmaduke had joined their ranks thanks to Mingaletta, but how ironical for him to be sitting here in judgement – a killer who had been found Not Guilty of murder.

As he studied the two prisoners standing in the dock Marmaduke tried to banish the gut reaction to the lurid newspaper accounts of Rupert Grantham's murder. Both looked like ordinary young boys. James Leech, a former London mariner, was a head taller than the pale and weedy Will Barrenwood, a former chimney-sweep. The pair had been transported on the same convict ship.

Marmaduke's eye was repeatedly drawn to Leech's handsome face, flawed by a heavy jaw and fleshy sensual mouth. He radiated an aura of leadership – yet also a sense of suppressed rage.

The opening words were read out. 'James Leech and Will Barrenwood stand indicted for that they, not having the fear of God before their eyes, but being moved and instigated by the Devil...did shoot one Rupert Grantham, inflicting on his left breast a mortal wound, of which he then and there died.'

Both prisoners pleaded Not Guilty, Leech in a voice of authority.

Marmaduke remembered Edwin's covert warning that some aspects of the case might have been 'arranged'. His suspicions were aroused when the legal status of the prisoners' barrister was challenged. The court was told his name would be erased from the list of Barristers of the Court – *after* the trial.

Surely all prisoners are entitled to proper counsel. The charge is murder – not picking pockets. This isn't a kangaroo court.

Marmaduke listened intently to each witness, determined to divorce himself from an emotional response to graphic details of the autopsy and his friend's corpse.

If only I'd ridden out with Rupert that Sunday, he might well be alive today.

Marmaduke was conscious of his dilemma. Weighing against his instinct to avenge Rupert's death was the reminder that he was now a Mason.

I vowed to see justice done and to uphold the law of the land. So what if these blokes aren't guilty? What if those wild conspiracy rumors are true and Rupert's assassination was a plot engineered by powerful enemies?

The Prosecution's star witness was an eighteen-year-old bolter, Paul Brown, who had accompanied the accused pair but escaped a murder charge by turning King's Evidence. His nervous testimony drew raucous, angry catcalls from the large sector of partisans supporting their hero James Leech.

Brown described how the trio had been 'in the bush', a colloquial term for bushranging. Armed with musket, powder and cutlass, Leech was clearly the trio's ringleader. Brown was the organ-grinder's monkey.

Marmaduke grew tense at Brown's description of the morning of Rupert's murder. How the trio had 'amused themselves' firing at a target on a Red Gum tree.

The court was hushed as Brown recounted his first sighting of Grantham. 'A gentleman on a white horse rode up to us and dismounted. He asked Leech his name. Leech answered, "I am a man!"'

Leech basked in pride at the murmurs of approval from the rabble faction.

Paul Brown was intent on playing the innocent. 'Leech told Will Barrenwood to fetch the musket. I tried to talk them out of it. It would be better to receive a Bob, fifty lashes, than risk our lives. The gentleman's horse was prancing back, terrified. Leech walked up to the gentleman, presented the piece and fired. The gentleman said, "Oh God, I'm killed". The white horse bolted.'

Marmaduke envisaged the whole murder scene in his mind. He felt icy cold, stunned when Paul Brown continued his litany as if nothing untoward had happened.

'We were on the run from the traps for five weeks. Crossing a river Barrenwood nearly drowned but Leech swam after him and saved him.'

Leech's partisans cheered their hero.

Crucial evidence was given by the mounted police constable who had been confronted by Will Barrenwood. 'I told him to consider himself my prisoner. I then began bouncing him.'

Marmaduke knew the term bouncing could mean either advised, hustled, tricked, scolded or bullied. He was convinced only half the story was being revealed.

'Barrenwood pointed to the two men in the bush and warned me Leech would shoot the first man to try to arrest him. When I apprehended Leech and Brown they readily surrendered. Later Barrenwood admitted he knew all about Mr Grantham's murder and if he had a chance to turn King's Evidence he would tell all.'

James Leech gave a bellow of rage at this proof his shipmate had betrayed him. Leech's supporters booed and threw missiles at Barrenwood.

Marmaduke sensed all Hell was about to erupt when James Leech dismissed his barrister. His eyes were feverishly bright as he began to conduct his own defense. Leech stated he had four witnesses willing to testify that he was elsewhere on the day of the murder. His agitation escalated when three of his witnesses failed to appear. His mood grew confident once more when his fourth witness, Patrick Finlay, took the stand.

Finlay avoided all eye contact. His replies to Leech's questions were tight-lipped. 'I disremember anything of that day.'

Leech's eyes narrowed but his tone was determined. 'Come now, Paddy, you have nothing to fear from your master, Morden. Speak up like a man. No harm can come to you. Were not I and Paul Brown in your company that day?"

Finlay was adamant. 'I never in my life saw you and Brown together. You were *never in my company.*'

Leech had a violent change of mood. He whirled around to face the Chief Justice, jury and spectators in turn.

'You see? He's afraid to speak the truth on my behalf. No witnesses present in court. No one willing to come forward for me!'

The court was in an uproar. Marmaduke kept his eyes fixed on Leech, trying to gain the key to the young man's psyche. *One of these two is lying. And I wouldn't trust the King's Evidence rat as far as I could throw him. I can't condemn Leech to hang unless I'm bloody sure he's guilty.*

Leech was inciting the spectators to fever pitch. The guards looked ready to spring as the Prosecutor began his emotive summary.

'This act of assassination against Mr Rupert Grantham, one of the most celebrated and respected men in the Colony, has set a terrible precedent. No landholder can ever again feel safe from the threat of assassination at the hands of vengeful bolters.' The barrister gestured directly at the jury. 'Without a shadow of a doubt James Leech and Will Barrenwood murdered Rupert Grantham in cold blood. Do your duty, gentlemen. Bring in a verdict of Guilty.

Marmaduke led his fellow jurors as they filed into the cramped jury room. He placed his open watch on the table, ready to debate aspects of the case. The other jurymen dismissed the idea and took an instant vote with a show of hands – guilty.

'Gentlemen, I feel this warrants further discussion. It seems an act of indecent haste to return a verdict involving the death penalty,' he glanced at his watch, 'in less than four minutes.'

'Do you reckon they both murdered Grantham?' the elderly foreman asked.

Marmaduke hesitated. 'Yes, but—'

'Then we're all agreed. No time to waste. I've got a business to run.'

The verdict of Guilty was delivered. Marmaduke felt no sense of elation that justice had been done by Rupert. He felt hollow. Three lives wasted.

Called upon to give his statement, Leech's eyes were blazing like a zealot.

'I demand a fair trial!' He pointed at the barrister he had dismissed. 'That bloody old woman was shoved in on us to lead us to our destruction!' He spun around and pointed directly at Marmaduke. 'This jury was biased against me. If I had my gun in hand I'd shoot the pack of you with the greatest of pleasure!'

Leech repeatedly struck the dock with his fists in a violent outpouring of rage.

Marmaduke was now convinced. *James Leech doesn't belong in this court – or on the scaffold. He belongs in a lunatic asylum.*

Chief Justice Forbes was visibly shaken as he placed the black cloth on the crown of his head and pronounced the sentence of Death.

The ruffians who had cheered Leech were on the brink of mutiny. A voice shrieked, 'That bastard landowner Grantham was a tyrant! Leech did us all a favour!'

James Leech broke free and, with the speed of a panther, hurled himself bodily at Will Barrenwood, hammering him with ferocious blows to the head.

It took six policemen to restrain Leech, who was bucking like a wild animal.

Marmaduke watched as Leech was dragged through the dense crowd that choked Hunter Street. Halfway along the short route to the gaol Leech went berserk at sight of the approaching Chief Magistrate.

'Stand warned, you bastard. I'll take my vengeance on you before I die!'

Standing alone in the wind-blown street Marmaduke watched the mob milling around the condemned youths on their final walk to the prison, cheering Leech and chanting his name as if he was their leader.

He was forced to face the truth. Rupert's murder proved that now no man, no matter how powerful, was safe. The underbelly of the Colony was taking its revenge.

CHAPTER 46

In a quiet room at the Princess Alexandrina Hotel Marmaduke sat drinking with Edwin, exchanging their strangely parallel experiences of the day – both had ended in an execution.

Marmaduke was unable to erase the face of James Leech from his mind and Paul Brown's testimony of Leech's strangely disturbing words – '*I am a man!*' – uttered just before he murdered Rupert.

'There's no shadow of a doubt in my mind that Leech fired the shot that killed Rupert. But I've no way of knowing if a surgeon would diagnose James Leech as clinically mad – or mentally unbalanced. Although illiterate he's far from unintelligent. He made a better fist of his defence than his half-baked barrister. Sorry to criticise one of your fraternity, Edwin.'

'Feel free. You were there. I was not.'

'Leech has the kind of animal magnetism that attracts weaker lads to follow him. I can't escape the feeling there's far more to this crime than came out in court.'

'Some men are born with blood-lust,' said Edwin. 'Leech has a history of violence. Since he was transported here he's been found guilty of two counts of violent assault. The second attack, on a wealthy landowner, Morden, landed him in an iron-gang for twelve months. He escaped a week prior to Rupert's murder.'

Marmaduke was stunned. 'Morden! That name was raised in court. A convict assigned to Morden was called by James Leech to provide him with an alibi at the time of Rupert's murder. But the witness flatly denied it.'

Edwin nodded. 'Witnesses often renege due to fear, coercion or a bribe. But it might have been the truth and he refused to provide Leech with a false alibi. '

'What do you think, Edwin? This was no random murder. Either Leech harboured a personal grudge against Rupert. Or his desire for revenge was fuelled by Rupert's enemies, who wanted him dead. Maybe men in high places promised Leech an alibi if he did the deed, then betrayed him.'

'We're never likely to know. The law is taking no chances of the rabble engineering his escape. Leech and Barrenwood are to be executed by midnight.'

Marmaduke pulled the pocket watch from his waistcoat. 'Half of seven. Not long for a man to make his peace with God. Chief Justice Forbes refused them a stay of execution.'

His voice was bleak. 'It's only taken us forty-five years to turn this God-given land into a penal colony where scaffolds and flogging posts spread across the landscape like the plague.'

Edwin refilled their glasses. 'I wonder if future generations will condemn us?'

'God only knows, mate. But I reckon I've got my time cut out trying to deal with *my* generation. This trial really bounced home the truth. James Leech did far more than escape from an iron-gang and murder a powerful man. He declared war on the whole rotten System. No landholder is safe from some escapee who sees himself as an avenging angel – ready to forfeit his own life to send a member of the Ruling Class to Hell ahead of him.'

Edwin nodded. 'I take it you are concerned about your father's reputation for turning a blind eye to his overseer's brutality?'

'Yeah. Garnet's a rogue and I've been at war with him since the cradle but that doesn't mean I'd stand by and see him butchered. At first light I'm heading back to Bloodwood to put security measures in place. I've got Isabel to protect – and very soon little Rose Alba. Have you found a record of her birth?'

'Nothing in the English parish records, I'm told. Legally she doesn't exist. But don't worry, old chap. I'll make her adoption watertight.'

Marmaduke hesitated before raising the question he had tried to avoid for weeks, the threat to his pride and independence. Money. 'You know how I hate banks, Edwin,' he began. 'I'd rather swim across the Tasman to New Zealand than borrow money from Garnet. Well, the thing is, I'm beginning to wonder if I can get Mingaletta up and running without a loan.'

'I'm not surprised. It's a big enterprise, old chap.'

'Yeah, I've toted up the costs of building a homestead, putting in dams, felling timber and stocking a property that Garnet ran into the ground after Mother died. There's nothing there but kangaroos and wild brumbies. Don't get me wrong. I know I can make a real go of it. I'll work my guts out to give Isabel and the kid a good life. But I'm going to be cutting it fine. I want you to sell my shares in everything except Mendoza's Store. Jos is like family and I wouldn't risk selling my partnership to some bloke who'd rip him off. It's not dead urgent, mate, but if push *does* come to shove, what's the safest short-term loan?'

Edwin nodded. 'Understood. I'll look into the question of a private loan at a reasonable rate of interest. Sometimes a new settler has money to invest.'

'Just as long as his name isn't Silas de Rolland, right?' Marmaduke said lightly but both understood the threat beneath their laughter.

The last high C of Josepha St John's final encore was greeted by an emotional round of applause and thunderous stamping of feet from an audience that believed this was the American Nightingale's swansong in the Colony and was unwilling for her to leave the stage.

Marmaduke reluctantly decided to forego the pleasure of watching two knockabout comedians bring the house down. He slipped out of his dress-circle box and made his way past Barnett Levey's office to the dressing-rooms backstage.

Despite Josepha's earlier note of acquiescence, Marmaduke felt uncertain about his reception when he knocked on her door. He was admitted by Josepha's dresser, Bessie. The shy little Aboriginal girl silently took her cue from her mistress, bobbed and departed.

Josepha was ready for him, posed before the dressing-table mirror. Her bare shoulders were bathed in candlelight and swathed in gold-coloured tulle. He saw in her eyes that familiar mixture of elation, bravado and childlike uncertainty he had seen in actors immediately after their exit off stage, when despite the lingering sound of rousing applause they are again vulnerable about their performance and hungry for praise.

The air in the tiny room was a war between two heady perfumes – the basket of flowers he had sent her and the exotic fragrance of Egyptian jasmine that was Josepha's signature perfume. The scent rising from the coiled nest of her hair and the warmth of her flesh aroused vivid memories of the torrid nights they had spent in bed.

Despite his good intentions Marmaduke felt his pulse racing. Nostalgia did not have the same driving power as lust, but Josepha was not a woman easily forgotten and Marmaduke was not a man to forget.

He bent and kissed her hand. 'Your performance tonight was riveting, Josepha. A superb memory to be treasured by your audience. They couldn't bear to let you go. The Colony's loss is Argentina's gain. But why didn't you tell *me* your change of plans?'

Joseph smiled enigmatically. 'Would it have changed your mind about coming with me? Marriage to your little blue-blooded bride has clipped your wings, *n'est-ce pas?*'

Both were aware that Josepha's fluency in the French language was confined to a handful of song lyrics she had learnt by heart. This gentle pretence was a game that Marmaduke continued to play – but honesty was also an intrinsic part of their relationship.

'I told you the truth, Josepha. I had no intention of falling in love with any woman. Heaven forbid not with my own wife! It took me by surprise to find an artless young girl who hated all men – needed *me*. Like a prize fool I lost my heart to her.'

Josepha's romantic sigh was purely theatrical. 'You should set those words to music. A lyrical love song like that would no doubt appeal to the masses.'

Marmaduke knew she was hurt and wanted them to part as friends. He must allow her to save face by playing the leading role in their final scene together.

'If I wrote any song it would be for you, Josepha. A tribute to a beautiful woman of a certain age who gave a Currency Lad more pleasure than he had any right to deserve.'

'Write *that* and I promise to sing it!' she said with the infectious note in her voice that always drew them together in shared laughter.

Josepha ran her hands playfully along the collar of his coat and as he bent to kiss her cheek she turned her head quickly and took his mouth in a kiss that lingered.

Finally she drew back and sank onto the cushioned sofa. 'Oh dear. That resembled the kiss of a faithful husband caught by surprise.'

He could not deny it. 'But I'm never less than your faithful friend, Josepha. I really want you to reassure me that when you depart these shores you'll be happy under the protection of your mysterious

Frenchman. Surely by now he can reveal himself? Unless he's some claimant to the French throne?'

'Mysterious, indeed. You are the one lover in my life who has always been honest with me. You deserve no less from me. That gentleman is very generous, but he's not quite what he portrayed himself to be. His name, his title – he was travelling incognito. He isn't even French.'

She waved her hand gracefully to draw attention to her large ruby ring.

'Whereas the ring you gave me was, like you, totally genuine.' She paused for effect. 'I must warn you Marmaduke that my protector has long been unusually interested in you. Now I know why.'

Marmaduke stiffened, suddenly sure he knew the answer before he asked the question. 'His real name?'

Josepha's luminous dark eyes studied him over the rim of her ostrich feather fan.

'Silas de Rolland. I presume he is a member of your bride's family, but why his elaborate subterfuge?'

'It is the nature of the beast.' Marmaduke said equally casually, 'Is he going to accompany you to South America?'

'Not for some time. He has persuaded me to remain in the Colony a little longer. He has leased a grand house in the country from some military officer who's transferred to India. I am going there to enter-tain his guests. No doubt Penkivil Park is miles from you?'

'Ten,' Marmaduke said promptly. *Hell. Penkivil Park! I don't know how to warn her about Silas without putting Isabel in danger.*

'Then we will meet again, I trust. Tell me, Marmaduke, why has your wife's kinsman not contacted you directly?'

'It's a long story, Josepha. It goes back to the War of the Roses. But if you are staying at Penkivil Park, I guarantee you and I will meet again.'

Josepha's sigh came with a gentle, self-deprecating laugh. 'If only I had been born closer to your age, Marmaduke, what a life we would have shared.'

Marmaduke tried to conceal the fact he was desperate to depart and return to Isabel. But Josepha had obliquely warned him about Silas de Rolland and he was grateful. 'I am only thankful that we did meet and make love, Josepha. John Donne spoke for me when he wrote: *No spring nor summer beauty hath such grace, As I have seen in one Autumnal face.*'

Josepha tapped him on the shoulder with her fan. 'Go, sweetheart,' she commanded, 'before I regret my warning about Silas. And tell my little black dresser I must change my gown. Barnett's giving a farewell supper for me with the whole cast.'

Marmaduke paused in the doorway. He must pay her a final tribute in words that were his own, not borrowed from a poet. 'We had something special. There will never be another Josepha St John in my life.'

'And only one Currency Lad in mine, darling,' she said softly.

The last glimpse Marmaduke had of the actress she was studying her image in the mirror, dabbing a powder puff under her eyes. Was this to camouflage dark shadows or her tears?

CHAPTER 47

The midday sun seemed, to Isabel, to be draining the air of oxygen and replacing it with a pall of humidity that made breathing difficult.

Seated beside Queenie on the front terrace, she felt rivulets of sweat coursing down her back, between her breasts and making her petticoats stick to her thighs. Her hair curled in a mass of wet tendrils on her forehead and at the nape of her neck. Isabel abandoned the use of her fan because it demanded more effort than relief.

'Tell me, Queenie, how long did it take you to get used to this heat?'

'You call this heat? Coming from India, I'm not the person to ask, girl. But when you stop expecting snow to fall at Christmas, you'll be on the road to adjustment. You had best grow to like what you can't change, Isabel.'

Isabel nodded agreement. She put aside her sewing, the embroidered cushion for Garnet's birthday that had been abandoned by Elise before she bolted. She bunched her skirt and petticoats to fan her nether limbs – a most unladylike gesture unthinkable at home.

She caught Queenie's eye and said defensively, 'Who cares? No one can see me!'

'I didn't say a word,' Queenie said but there was wicked gleam in her eye when Amaru chortled, 'That's the way to do it, that's the way to do it!'

'You're a pretty clever bird, Amaru, I just *love* the way you choose appropriate phrases. I can't believe it's an accident.'

'Love is blind, love is blind!' he squawked and broke into a cackle of laughter that sounded almost human.

'That's Miranda's doing. She spent hours each day teaching Amaru to speak when she was bored, forced to remain in bed to avoid a premature birth during the last months before Marmaduke was born. Miranda looked very voluptuous but she had great trouble giving birth.' Queenie looked over her spectacles and said pointedly, 'She didn't have child-bearing hips. *You* won't have much trouble.'

Isabel was quick to change the conversation to Mingaletta and how frustrated she was at not being able to monitor the building progress because Marmaduke had vetoed her visits to the site until his return.

'All I can do is study the blueprint and try to decipher what all the arrows and scrawled numbers and adjustments mean. It's very frustrating, Queenie. Couldn't we slip down one day and look at it when the men have returned to their cabins?'

Queenie gave her a severe look. 'You're supposed to be Marmaduke's ally. Not going behind his back, girl.'

Isabel felt chastened and, as always when nervous, her appetite increased. When she had eaten a second slice of Summer Pudding, she felt Queenie eyeing her knowingly.

'All right, I know I'm putting on weight. But Rubens's nudes are Marmaduke's idea of the perfect woman so if I keep on like this I soon will be too.'

Queenie was watching her speculatively and Isabel decided it was wise to change the subject yet again. In Marmaduke's absence the threat of Silas's near residence had heightened her anxiety. The line was blurred between reality, imagination and memory.

She wondered if the strain of hiding two secrets from Marmaduke and everyone else had triggered the return of the element that had been dormant for many months. The invisible presence of the Other.

She wasn't sure if it was safe ground to discuss with Queenie so she began tentatively. 'I've been meaning to ask you, Queenie. Marmaduke said this house used to be haunted. And I understand you have the gift of seeing...ghosts. Several times in recent nights I'm sure I heard footsteps in the corridor outside the nursery. And an odd clicking sound before the footsteps faded away down the gallery in the direction of Miranda's portrait and the priest hole. But there was no one there.'

Queenie gave a sage nod. 'So they've come to you, too. I'm not surprised. Presences have been seen or heard here over the years. Irish and Aboriginal servant girls are particularly sensitive. Some say they've seen a man as well as a woman. Garnet's the one person who's desperate to see Miranda but never will if she has her way.' She added, matter of factly, 'But Miranda comes to me quite often, warns me what's going to happen.'

Isabel shivered at those words but decided to press on. 'Is there any pattern to their visits? Any reason?'

'Ghosts are said to be attracted to heightened emotion. Fear, grief, anger, passion, which means they are hardly ever allowed to rest in peace at Bloodwood Hall, this house is such a whirlpool of negative emotions. They're also drawn to special currents of energy given out by a small child, a stormy adolescent or a pregnant woman.'

'I see,' Isabel said carefully. 'I've noticed the energy has been reactivated since Elise's stormy departure. I hear she's the thorn in Garnet's side, refusing to leave the Garnet and Rose public house until he agrees to pay her off as his rejected mistress.'

Queenie put her sewing aside and said frankly, 'I wouldn't blame Elise for attracting ghosts. It's more likely to be *you*.'

Isabel deliberately pricked her finger to avoid a response.

Oh dear God, has she guessed the secret I've hidden from Marmaduke? That Silas contacted me?

Village gossip abounded about the mysterious, handsome English aristocrat who was said to have taken the lease on Penkivil Park and was planning to entertain the Quality there at balls, kangaroo hunts and duck shooting. Isabel had heard that he had the famous Yankee Nightingale 'in keeping'. Newspapers confirmed Josepha St John was performing a series of 'final' benefit nights.

Silas had made no further attempt to contact Isabel since their encounter in the graveyard but the knowledge that he could be in residence only ten miles distant cast a malignant shadow over her happiness.

Silas is stalking me mentally, like a living ghost. What is he waiting for? Why doesn't he return to England where he belongs?

The cause of another anxiety lay in the pocket of her skirt, the envelope addressed to her in Aunt Elisabeth's elegant hand. Written in haste the letter advised her that she was ready to depart with Rose Alba for Southampton. The letter was undated and the vessel unnamed so she had no idea when they might be arriving.

Isabel tried to imagine how the child might have changed since she last saw her asleep in Aunt Elisabeth's cottage on the eve of her departure, earlier. Desperate as she was to see Rose Alba the idea terrified her.

I've never even held her in my arms since the hour of her birth. Aunt Elisabeth's love is all she's ever known. I don't know how to be a real mother and I can only acknowledge Rose Alba as my half-sister. What if she doesn't like me?

Isabel's anxiety came in tandem with the bitter realisation that no matter how many thousands of miles she had travelled from the land of her birth, she could never escape her past while Silas was alive.

Queenie was relentless. 'Tell me the truth. You're suffering from nausea, aren't you?'

Isabel was startled by the intensity in the old lady's expression. Her eyes were as dark as night and twice as enigmatic. She began to stammer a denial but Queenie ignored her.

'I've brought you some herbal tea. The Romanies swear by it. Drink it three times a day until your time comes.'

Isabel jumped with fright. 'I beg your pardon?'

'Enough of this secretive business, Isabel.'

Isabel was so confused she pricked her finger again and caused a drop of blood to fall on the white rose tapestry. 'Shit!' she exclaimed then flushed with acute embarrassment. 'A bad habit I acquired from Marmaduke.'

'Clearly not the only thing you acquired from Marmaduke. How far gone are you?'

'I'm not sure what you mean.'

'Come, come. No use trying to hide secrets from me, girl. Tall, skinny girls often carry well – you aren't showing yet. But your body is blossoming like a rose. No doubt Marmaduke thinks that's his doing – making you happy in bed. Men!' She gave a deep chortle. 'But I recognise the signs. Those fine blue veins on your breast, preparing them to carry milk. Your nausea. Sudden tears and laughter without warning. How far gone are you?'

'I don't know!'

'Well, we'll find out soon enough.'

Isabel stifled a sob.

Queenie sighed. 'Don't tell me you haven't told Marmaduke? Ah, so that's it!'

Isabel burst into tears, suddenly as insecure as a child facing her first day at school.

'I tried to tell him before he left for Sydney but I couldn't get the words out. Please, Queenie, don't tell him. He's forbidden me to have his child – ever!'

Queenie's laugh was mocking but not unkind. 'Famous last words. So what are you planning to do? Find the baby under a cabbage?'

Isabel began to teeter on the edge of hysteria. 'It isn't funny, Queenie. It's not that Marmaduke doesn't *like* children. He'd make a wonderful father, but we married on the clear understanding that the Gamble line must die out with him because – just because.'

'Because Garnet may well end up in a lunatic asylum, which is probably the best place for him,' Queenie said crisply. 'Well, there's no proof it's hereditary. Could be the legacy of Cape Fever, like John Macarthur. The reality is Marmaduke's besotted with you. Love and a good helping of lust made him careless. It happens to women all the time, but now you're left worrying yourself sick about telling him. Huh! Talk about truth and consequences!'

Isabel stroked her belly and said plaintively, 'So what do I do now?'

Queenie became serious and patted her hand. 'Garnet and I have been hoping for this pleasant little problem for some time. There's a solution for everything and we're prepared for it. I warn you it's not going to be easy. Your role is to stay very calm and don't abandon Marmaduke no matter how badly he behaves. He's just a boy at heart. We must all give him time to grow up.'

Isabel felt suddenly tired and confused. 'I'm sure you're right. Marmaduke has an appalling temper but I assure you he'd never lay a finger on me. He's very protective – in an odd Currency kind of way.'

'You don't have to sing my boy's praises to *me,* girl. I brought him into the world and had to spank his backside to make him take his first breath.'

Isabel felt her spirits soar. 'That means you'll be able to help deliver this babe?'

Queenie nodded. 'First things first. Marmaduke has a tough adjustment to make. Remember one thing. What's going to happen isn't *your* fault. The future was written long ago!'

Isabel wondered if this referred to some Eastern philosophy or poetry but she felt too tired to question it. When Queenie accompanied her to the nursery and gently undressed her in preparation for a *siesta* Isabel felt as comforted as a small child. On the brink of sleep she kissed Queenie's hand.

'I now know why Marmaduke loves you so much. As a boy everyone around him was driven by passion, love and hate. Pulling him every which way. You were the sole lodestar that guided him through his painful childhood.'

The last thing Isabel remembered before she fell asleep was a faint feeling of surprise. It was the first time ever she had seen tough old Queenie's eyes fill with tears.

CHAPTER 48

The sound of galloping horses caused Isabel to run down the staircase and out onto the terrace. The wheels of the carriage sent showers of pebbles in its wake.

She instantly recognised the driver by his hat. Thomas's battered old tricorn was pressed against the wind and even from this distance his wide grin promised the pleasure he was bringing her. *Marmaduke.*

Isabel was so excited she skipped like a child at the sight of the beloved head jutting through the window, the wild hair whipping around his face as he repeatedly called her name. Isabel melted at the sound of his voice.

Thomas swerved the pair of greys to a halt in front of the front steps and Isabel ran to the open carriage door. Marmaduke pulled her inside and there were no words that mattered, only Marmaduke's laughter and soft grunts of pleasure between their kisses and his longed-for hands urgently caressing her body.

Isabel felt hot, cold and hungry for his touch, desperate to be alone with him. To possess him. At last he broke his mouth free. Ruefully running his hand over his jaw he apologised for not wasting time to stop and shave.

'I didn't know what real hunger was until these past weeks away from you. I couldn't sleep – hungry to see you, touch you, arouse you, take you – love you!'

Isabel tenderly stroked the stubble on his chin. 'Our bed is ready and waiting, my love,' she whispered.

'We must wait just a little longer. The world has changed overnight. There are plans I need to put in place to keep you safe. Come, I must make Garnet understand the urgency. If he refuses I must take full control myself.'

He lifted her down from the carriage and signalled Thomas to drive on to the stables.

Marmaduke's mood was suddenly serious. 'But first I must know the truth. You've not had any unwanted visitors at the house in my absence?'

'No,' she said, believing that to be close to the truth. Marmaduke was such a hothead he would see the encounter with Silas in the graveyard as an invasion of his territory and be likely to front him at Penkivil Park and challenge him to a duel. She must choose the right moment to assure him she had banished Silas from their lives forever.

'But I'm happy to say my shipmate Murray Robertson has just arrived here at my invitation. Garnet has agreed to interview him for a position on one of his properties. Do you think you could put in a good word for him to Garnet?'

Marmaduke frowned. The teasing note in his voice was a thin veneer to camouflage jealousy. 'He's the bloke whose clothes you wore to masquerade as a boy, right? Anything else I need to know about your relationship? He's nutty about you, isn't he?'

'Good Heavens, nothing like that. Murray's like a protective brother.' Isabel seized her cue to ease her way into difficult subjects. 'Marmaduke, during your absence our world here has changed dramatically. I have many things to tell you. To begin with Elise has—'

'Father's mistress is of no consequence. Come!'

Drawing her by the hand in the direction of Garnet's study Marmaduke took long strides that forced her to double her steps to keep apace. Outside the door he kissed her hurriedly, his mind already working on the scene ahead of him.

'I must beard the old lion in his den. Alone. Wait for me. I want you by my side when I put my plans into action. It's a matter of politics and survival.' The door closed leaving Isabel sitting on a hall chair alone in the corridor. She felt a slight wave of nausea from the heat that managed to penetrate even the darkest recesses of the house in summer. Straining to hear their conversation she was rewarded with nothing but the familiar rising pitch of insults and the tattoo of fists banging on Garnet's desk. She knew this confrontation must be urgent for Marmaduke to put politics ahead of taking her to bed.

Why did God in his wisdom create us women to wait in suspense while our men duel with words? Heaven knows what this argument's about. But I'll wager women could resolve it in a civilised manner over tea and scones without resorting to foul language.

The grand Georgian clock in the corridor chimed the hour, a sound instantly echoed by timepieces throughout the house as if taking their cue from patriarchal authority.

Frustrated by the waiting game Isabel was on the brink of knocking on Garnet's door when Marmaduke burst from the room and bowled into her.

He steadied her on her feet then called back to Garnet. 'Wake up, Garnet. Your methods are as dead as the dodo. I'm doing things my way!'

Isabel knew what to expect from Marmaduke's anger. Her heart raced as she hurried down the corridor beside him. Without missing a step he shed his coat, ripped off his neck linen and thrust the bundle into her arms.

'Good Heavens, what *is* the matter? Tell me. I'm your wife, not your servant.'

'What I expected. Garnet's in denial. Round up all the servants, fetch Queenie. I want you all assembled in the convicts' courtyard in half an hour – with Garnet. I need the master of Bloodwood Hall, my wife, our whole household to be seen to be in solidarity! I'm going to address our Government men.'

'Dressed like that? Unshaven, in your shirtsleeves?'

Marmaduke paused to lay his hands on her shoulders. 'This isn't England, Isabel. The lower orders in this Colony don't respect their betters or tug the forelock to the master. I've just witnessed the full story of Rupert's murder. When he confronted an escaped convict and demanded his name, the bolter answered, "*I am a man!*" then shot him dead. Those words will reverberate around the Colony and they're likely to trigger a convict insurrection if we're not careful.'

Striding ahead of her Marmaduke called back over his shoulder. 'Half an hour!' Then registering her concern he added, 'Don't worry, I know what I'm doing.'

Isabel was left cradling his coat.

I've never seen him like this. He's a changed man. But I feel he's in grave danger. Our assigned men hold Garnet in contempt and would be happy to see Fordham dead. Marmaduke will be outnumbered ninety to one.

Isabel looked around the convicts' courtyard where every Government man assigned to Garnet Gamble had been assembled, except for a few shepherds and boundary riders stationed in remote back-blocks of the estate. These men looked like a hostile, defeated army of soldiers. Dressed in drab versions of the convict 'uniform' of slop clothing, sun-bleached shirts and trousers, their handkerchiefs were tied around their necks to soak up sweat or knotted around shaven skulls to ward off sunstroke.

Isabel met their eyes and exchanged a slight nod with a few she knew by name, like Davey the ostler and Paddy the gardener. It seemed odd that Fordham was nowhere in sight.

The sun was intense and despite her shady straw hat her eyes watered from the glare. Her hand was securely looped through Garnet's arm as they stood positioned at the apex of the body of house servants. Flanking her side was Queenie, who had sensed the unusual nature of Marmaduke's meeting and had exchanged her house dress for her Sunday best. Her eyes were shaded by a leghorn hat as she watched Marmaduke's every move.

He stood like an actor holding centre stage, the focus of all, bare-headed, unarmed. His white shirt was open at the neck, his sleeves rolled up ready for action. Isabel noticed the slight twitch of fingers that betrayed his nerves and longed to stand at his side. She had never felt more pride in him – or more afraid.

A young lion. Strong, alert. Fully aware of the danger. Challenging Garnet while keeping up the front of solidarity. All these men must know the details of James Leech's crime – and the price he paid on the scaffold. This confrontation could end in bloodshed.

Marmaduke began quietly, choosing down-to-earth language in typical Currency style to hold his audience, his voice projecting clearly to engage their attention.

'I've called you here together to inform you of changes that affect every man Jack of you and every woman – whether bond, free or holding a ticket.

'I don't have to tell any of you the Colonial grapevine spreads wild rumours as well as the odd grain of truth, so it won't come as a surprise that with Garnet Gamble's blessing I've inherited my mother's land. I'll be working Mingaletta myself.' He paused to add significantly, 'without an overseer.'

Isabel glanced furtively at Garnet's impassive face.

Marmaduke's gone mad! He's waving a red rag at a bull. Garnet hasn't even handed over the deeds yet. Or is that what just occurred in the library?

As Marmaduke continued talking up the crowd he moved deeper into their midst, turning to focus on different faces, an actor intent on involving his whole audience. But the circle around him seemed to be shrinking as men edged closer. Isabel grew tense, reminded of that dramatic scene in *Julius Caesar,* when the Roman senators surrounded Caesar and plunged their knives into him.

Marmaduke seemed oblivious to danger. 'I return on the wings of change. I doubt if any man, bond or free, would argue that radical improvements to the System are long overdue.'

His gesture invited their response. Their murmured comments were not aggressive but Isabel knew it only needed one violent mind to turn the mood of the crowd.

'The question is which changes are possible? A wise old Greek once said, "Even God cannot change the past."'

Isabel rolled her eyes to heaven. *Aristotle! Even in a crisis Marmaduke can't resist quoting from the classics. Now I know just how nervous he is.*

'The past is history,' he said. 'But every man and woman in this Colony, bond or free, can help alter the future. Begin to build a new life.'

An Irish voice belonging to a wild giant of a man broke through the crowd in open mockery.

'Easy for him to say. Master's son is not having to serve fourteen years or life!'

Marmaduke seized on the open challenge. 'Spoken like a true Irishman. You hit the nail on the head. I was born free, the son of an Emancipist – a Currency Lad just like your own sons will be. But at nineteen I left my father's house to do it *my* way. I travelled the land we live in. Learnt to work it, respect its challenges. I've done time on the West Coast as a drover, a stockman. Been a carpenter's mate, built bush huts from the mighty Murray River to the Swan. I learnt bushcraft from old lags in Moreton Bay and Van Diemen's Land, who weren't above teaching a greenhorn like me. I can brand cattle with the best of them. No shearer would call me a top gun, but I can hold my own in a shearing shed. I drove a bullock team from beyond the Black Stump to South Australia – where else do you think I learnt to swear like a bullocky?'

There was a rumble of reluctant laughter and Isabel sensed the tension was draining from the crowd. Some men were eyeing him as if for the first time.

'Now you know *my* record. Most men here are serving seven or fourteen years. Whether you copped it guilty or innocent – I can't change that. I don't have to tell you blokes about British law. Grand in theory, rotten at worst and dodgy in practice if you don't have the price of a decent lawyer. But British democracy is all we've got until we Australians invent something better for ourselves, eh?'

He paused to let that idea sink in. 'Meanwhile you have my word and I speak for Garnet Gamble. From this day onwards every man here who chooses to stay and work Bloodwood Hall and Mingaletta will earn his ticket of leave and be free to work for wages long before his sentence expires.'

Angry voices called from the rear of the crowd. '*Choose* to stay?' 'Fat chance of that!'

'Three choices! You can bolt. Have a brief taste of freedom before the traps or the Finisher cops you.' Marmaduke looked around him. 'Yeah. Like James Leech and Will Barrenwood.'

There was an ugly silence. Isabel's knees buckled when she saw the same Irish giant was cradling an axe. Had Marmaduke seen him?

He pressed on. 'Or you can return to Hyde Park convict barracks in Sydney Town and take your chances on being assigned to a master who's better or worse. Or you can choose to remain with us.'

Marmaduke gestured in the direction of the avenue of Bloodwoods. 'The gates are open. Your choice.'

The red-headed Irish giant had appointed himself spokesman.

'Ye would be suggesting we stick with the devil we know, Fordham the Flogger? What rum choice is *that*?'

Marmaduke quickly agreed. 'No choice at all. That's why I called you here to witness *this*.'

At his signal the crowd divided to allow young Davey the ostler to cross to Marmaduke's side leading a stallion loaded with two saddlebags.

An incredulous voice called out, 'Saints preserve us, that is being Fordham's nag.'

Marmaduke stroked the horse's nose. 'Right. Fordham is in Bloodwood village. Your overseer has ended his tenure at Bloodwood Hall,' he gestured to his father, 'on the orders of Garnet Gamble.'

Alarmed, Isabel tightened her grip on Garnet's arm. *Marmaduke's really rubbing salt in the wound.*

At a nod from Marmaduke, Davey swung himself up into the saddle.

'Davey is delivering Fordham's horse to the village. The Flogger's quitting this locality forever. We're got a good bloke ready to step into his shoes.'

Necks craned as Marmaduke beckoned to a figure at the back of the crowd. Isabel smiled with real pleasure when she saw the young man step forwards wearing a cabbage tree straw hat, striped shirt, moleskin trousers and riding boots. He was suntanned and carried himself with confidence but there was no mistaking the old Murray Robertson.

Marmaduke introduced him. 'Don't let this bloke's youth fool you. He's as tough as they come, descended from a clan of Highland Jacobites – they don't come much tougher than his mob. Murray Robertson's dead straight and gives every man his due. He's in Fordham's shoes as from tomorrow. It's Davey's job to make sure the Flogger hits the road tonight.'

Davey was clearly elated to be entrusted with the task. He directed a question at the crowd. 'Any farewell messages ye want me to deliver to the Flogger?'

A sea of hands was instantly raised in the insulting two-fingered salute, followed by a wave of comments so ribald Isabel bit her lip to conceal her laughter.

Davey rode off to the sound of cheering. Marmaduke took back control of the crowd and spun around with a dramatic sweep of his arms.

'Fordham's methods of punishment are dead and gone. Murray and I will investigate all claims of abuse – of *any* nature. No woman or lad on this estate will be molested or harassed by *any* man. All of you have the right under the law to go before a magistrate if you have a grievance.' He turned to Garnet. 'Right, Father?'

Isabel saw from Garnet's clenched jaw that he was inwardly seething, but his voice still had the ring of authority.

'You heard him! You have the word of the Gambles. Father and son.'

Isabel searched the faces in the crowd trying to assess the range of feelings from guarded disbelief, confusion to a bewildered sense of triumph. She froze when she saw the Irishman cradling the axe move forwards again.

Marmaduke held up his hand for silence. 'I want every man on this estate to be vigilant about unwelcome guests. That includes a gentleman named Silas de Rolland, who's leased Penkivil Park. He has no business here.'

Isabel's flood of relief came in tandem with her guilt that she had not told Marmaduke of Silas's visit. Too late now. Marmaduke drew her to his side.

What on earth is he going to say now?

'I understand my wife is well known to you,' he announced on a note of pride.

A young lad was quick to respond. 'Yeah, it was her what stopped Fordham from flogging Paddy Whickett. She put an end to the lash. No more "red shirts".'

Marmaduke's question caught them off guard. 'Which man is our top timber-cutter?'

The crowd pushed forwards the giant, whose arms were tattooed with hearts and anchors.

'I reckon that'd be me,' he said, nursing his axe.

'Right,' said Marmaduke. 'I see you've come ready for work. So you'd be the right bloke to make short work of hacking *that* down for firewood.'

All heads swivelled in the direction of the hated wooden stocks that had been used to punish and humiliate prisoners for years.

'No time like the present,' Marmaduke said.

The woodcutter gave a beatific grin, exposing broken teeth, and turned to cut a swathe through the crowd. He swung his axe over his head. His first blow cut deep into the stocks' framework and drew a unanimous cheer that was repeated with each successive blow until the structure lay like splintered firewood.

Marmaduke slipped his arm around Isabel's shoulder. 'Before you return to your assigned places, next Friday is free from all work. We'll be turning a few sheep on the spit and draining a few kegs of ale to celebrate the new era on Mingaletta and to welcome Murray Robertson as the new overseer of Bloodwood Hall.'

Isabel knew that no man present was going to respect an overseer until he proved himself to be decent, but as the men filed back to their tasks she was relieved to see most of them appeared to be relaxed. She was suffering a wave of aftershock from the realisation how close Marmaduke had been to an armed convict – and a riot.

When Murray bowed to her, hat in hand, she impulsively embraced him then quickly explained to the Gamble men. 'This man was a protective brother to me on the voyage out. I'd not have survived without him.'

'I trust I'll live up to your son's confidence in me, sir,' Murray said to Garnet.

The response was polite but Isabel knew the older Gamble was furious his son had gone behind his back and usurped his power to interview, hire and fire men in his empire.

When Murray was escorted to his new quarters in Fordham's former cabin, Isabel fell into step between the two Gamble men, linking her arms with them to return to the house.

'I'm so proud of you both. Like father like son. Today is a shining moment in Bloodwood history, isn't it? A fine example for neighbouring estates. I think this calls for our own celebration tonight, don't you, Garnet?'

'Of course, m'dear.'

Marmaduke's smile now reflected genuine relief. Isabel saw he needed no reminder of the danger of his impromptu performance. He had walked unarmed into mass of hostile felons in whose eyes the executed James Leech was a martyred hero. No doubt a legend had already begun to grow around his name.

Isabel sent up a fervent prayer that Marmaduke's courage had begun to establish his own reputation as a landowner who played fair.

Invited by Garnet to join him for a dram of whisky in his office, Marmaduke hesitated but Isabel quickly included herself in the invitation, sensing her father-in-law was all geared to challenge his son but would not do so in her presence.

Isabel longed to share Marmaduke's urgent bedroom plans but she was determined to prevent Garnet's post mortem about his son's revolutionary tactics.

Father and son drank a toast 'To the Land, boys, We Live in'. Then as Isabel expected, Garnet began to probe Marmaduke under the thin guise of praise.

'How industrious of you to fund your Grand Tour of Europe by the sweat of your hands, Marmaduke. I'd no idea you'd led such a colourful working life in the Australian Colonies – from the Swan River to Moreton Bay. Bullocky, shearer, jackeroo and, no doubt, card sharp?'

'That just goes to show, Garnet, a man can't rely on the accuracy of his spies.'

Garnet's complexion turned puce. 'Spying on you? No such thing. It was my only way to keep track whether you were alive.' He softened his tone to Isabel, to justify himself. 'When I first arrived in the Colony it was a rum currency, a monopoly run by the military. Dog eat dog. I don't deny my own business dealings were shady. I took advantage of human weakness – paid men to inform on each other.' He paused. 'Marmaduke ridicules the whole idea of Freemasonry, but I was inspired by my brother Masons. I strove to become a better man – in the hope of making Miranda proud of me.'

The note of resignation in his voice caused a subtle change in Marmaduke's expression. 'I reckon your informants have fallen down on the job this time, Garnet. I'm already a Master Mason – in another lodge.'

Garnet looked pleasantly surprised. 'Are you indeed, m'boy? Well Lodge 260 was good enough for me and Sam Terry, but I hear that new lodge has a number of fine members. Dr Bland and your mate Barnett Levey shifted over to its ranks with Sir John Jamieson.'

Garnet raised his glass and said pointedly, 'So my son's a Mason at long last. That's the first good news you've given me today! Apart from knowing Leech and Barrenwood danced on the scaffold.'

Marmaduke downed his whisky and on behalf of Isabel took their leave on the excuse he needed to bathe and shave after his journey. He ignored Garnet's innuendo.

'Of course. *Shaving's* the first priority after a long absence from a bride. We dine at seven. Don't be late.'

'I make no promises, Garnet.'

The moment they were alone in the corridor Marmaduke gripped her hand and quickened his pace to take the stairs. Passing Miranda's portrait on the way to the nursery he gave a perfunctory nod.

Isabel was overcome by curiosity. 'I must congratulate you on becoming a Master Mason, Marmaduke, but like Garnet I was surprised by the range of your experiences in the Outback. I understood you'd spent most of those absent years in London and on the Continent.'

Catching his subtle shift of expression, she broke free and stood, arms akimbo.

'Did you *really* have all those adventurous around Australia?'

Marmaduke looked like a hurt puppy. 'Would I lie to you, Isabel?'

'You certainly would if you could get away with it! The truth and nothing but!'

'Well, I did *visit* those places. And one day I hitched a ride on a bullock train. That's how I learnt to swear like a bullocky.'

'So how *did* you earn your ship's passage to England?'

'This and that. Mostly cards. That's how I financed my half of Mendoza's store.'

Isabel shook her head in amused disbelief. 'You're unbelievable. So most of what you said to the Government men was a Colonial tall tale?'

'Yeah. Went down pretty well, eh? Had you and Garnet fooled. You see, being Mingaletta's new master, I had to win the men's respect fast.'

They had reached the nursery and Marmaduke was shedding his clothes with more speed than seduction. Isabel refused to allow the subject to drop.

'I'll bet you don't even know where to begin to shear a sheep, do you?'

'Well, I can tell the head from the daggy end. Don't worry, I'll pay a top shearer to give me lessons on the quiet. That's what makes us Currency Lads different from your British gentlemen. We excel at bullshit. You'll soon get the hang of it, Isabel.'

'I never know when you're telling the truth or lying through your teeth.'

Isabel had kicked off her shoes and was stripped down to her petticoats but Marmaduke was miles ahead of her. He sponged his body, rubbed himself dry and tossed the towel to the far side of the room. His dark, lazy voice sent shivers down her spine.

'I don't want to be guilty of grazing that creamy English flesh of yours. I'll shave – if you're willing to wait for me.'

Isabel tried to sound equally careless. 'Tomorrow morning will do.'

She lit the candle in the darkening room and felt herself flush with anticipation as Marmaduke stretched his body to its full height in a pretense of weariness then flipped back the bedcovers. Lying naked on his back he was more than ready for her. He beckoned her imperiously like a sultan bestowing his royal body on a harem favourite.

Isabel decided it was time to bite the bullet. Now or never. Share two secrets.

'Marmaduke, first there's something I need to tell you. While you were away... '

But it was too late. Marmaduke borrowed the lines she recognised John Milton had written in a religious context but which Marmaduke now made his own to seduce her.

'Take me to you, Isabel. Imprison me, for I, except you enthrall me, never shall be free, nor chaste – except you ravish me...'

Isabel finally fell asleep wondering if making love to Marmaduke was a case of mutual conquest – or mutual surrender?

Isabel had hoped day would dawn like every other day before the weeks of Marmaduke's absence in Sydney Town. The first trace of the pink picaninny dawn and the infectious sound of kookaburras' laughter was their cue to begin the day with a pattern of lovemaking that was fresh and frantic. They snatched time against the clock as if Marmaduke was a mariner whose vessel was scheduled to sail on the tide. The reality was he needed to depart early to rally his team of carpenters on the house he was building at Mingaletta.

This morning the moment she opened her eyes she sensed her world had changed.

Marmaduke stood leaning in the open French doorway, dressed in work clothes, observing her with that familiar expression that made her guilty before she knew the cause.

'What's wrong, Marmaduke? Were you going to leave without waking me?'

'As a matter of interest when were you intending to tell me?'

Does he mean Silas? Elise? Or the other secret?

'There's so much to tell you, darling, I hardly know were to begin.'

'Let me help you.' His eyes were cold. 'It slipped your mind to tell me you are with child. Did you truly think I wouldn't notice the shape of a naked woman's belly?'

'I forgot you were a connoisseur of the female body,' she snapped, clutching at anger like a shield to prevent her tears flowing.

'You forgot something else. The only thing I asked of you. To be my ally. And never lie to me.'

He strode towards her, gesticulating in anger.

'Don't you know I love every inch of your body? And haven't I always given you everything you asked of me? But I have damned good reason to avoid fathering children. Why do you think I wanted to bring Rose Alba to live here with us? So at least *you* wouldn't be deprived of a child. Why the hell didn't you tell me earlier? Now it's too late.'

Her eyes filled with angry tears. 'That's *why* I didn't tell you. I wanted it to live!'

'Well, there's nothing for it but to wait and get through this somehow. You're my only concern. I insist you rest each day. Eat healthily and have someone to attend you night and day. I'll send for a physician to examine you. And tell Queenie.'

'She knows.' Isabel instantly regretted her careless words.

'And Garnet too?'

'He guessed.'

Marmaduke laughed at himself but without humour. 'It seems I'm the last to know! Very well, as my role in your life is no more than provider I'll spend most days and nights at Mingaletta to see the house is made ready for you. Send Davey to fetch me if you need anything.' He hesitated, observing her tears. 'No doubt you think I'm heartless because I don't want this child. I blame myself for its conception – not you. But you *lied* to me.'

He paused in the doorway. 'What a fool I was. I trusted you to be my ally. Yet you never told me Cousin Silas had contacted you. I had to hear it from a servant.'

Shocked by his cold manner Isabel watched him through her tears…as he turned away from her and strode from the room. The door closed with a note of finality. Waves of sorrow, anger and despair struggled for dominance.

What's wrong with me? Why won't God ever allow me to be like other women? To bring a babe into the world with joy!

CHAPTER 49

Marmaduke worked alone on the building site, occasionally conscious of the sounds of church bells, the distant drunken laughter of revelry among the felons, to whom Rhys Powell had issued Christmas cheer in the way of traditional food and drink on the Gambles' instructions.

Since his confrontation with Isabel, Marmaduke had chosen to work and sleep in the shell of the new house for days at a time. Rhys Powell visited him daily and kept him informed of Isabel's progress but Marmaduke continued to banish her from the site. He could not so easily break free from the waves of melancholia that came with the unwanted thoughts of his impending fatherhood.

On the occasions he returned in the dark of night to Bloodwood Hall he showed concern about every detail of Isabel's health, saw to her comfort and joined her for supper in her room, but he chose to sleep in the room adjacent to the nursery, which Queenie always occupied on the nights he was absent.

He presented Isabel with the cameo brooch inspired by Lady Emma Hamilton but he politely countered her protests that she would welcome his company in bed with the excuse that she needed her sleep undisturbed. In truth, he often lay awake listening to the sound of her breathing, forced to remember the trauma of watching his mother die in childbirth.

At dawn he made a hasty departure before she awoke.

Only once was there a slight chink in his dark mood. He frowned at the sight of an envelope addressed only to him. An anonymous invitation deliberately delivered too late for him to attend the Roman Catholic christening of Patrick Sean Cagney – three days after his birth.

Marmaduke hastily calculated the interval between this date and his own final performance in the Cagney glasshouse. *Thank God! that's proof even to Cagney the child is his. How thoughtful of that sweet lady to put my mind at rest.*

*

The black stallion showed unmistakeable signs of restlessness and anxiety as Marmaduke rode from Mingaletta past the graveyard towards Bloodwood Hall, where he had agreed to share a meal with Isabel. The crescent moon seemed placed for artistic effect in a dark blue sky peppered with stars, reminding him of the backdrops painted by Barnett Levey's scene painter William Winstanley whose daughter Eliza Barrett was said to be grooming to play Juliet.

The thought of the creative world of the Theatre Royal aroused bittersweet memories. One half of Marmaduke longed to be involved in theatrical life, touring the world and living the life of a vagabond player. The other half of him was committed to reclaiming his birthright, Mingaletta. Ever since his youth these parallel desires had struggled in an internal duel. He knew it was not feasible to follow one demanding life path without abandoning the other. Building a home for Isabel, Rose Alba and the coming babe was the price of freedom. He tried not to envisage his child, depressed at the idea of what its future might hold.

Aware that Dangar, his new black stallion, kept tossing his head and breaking the rhythm of his gait as if warning him something was wrong, Marmaduke drew rein to scan the silent graveyard and the track that lead to Bloodwood village. Visits by the villagers were rare by day and unlikely at this time of night. His sweeping glance encompassed his father's ornate mausoleum and in the far corner the raised granite plinth ironically dedicated to 'the welcome stranger' – Klaus von Starbold.

The stallion neighed restlessly, the whites of his eyes rolling.

A sudden thought occurred to Marmaduke. 'I reckon it's the brumby blood in your veins. You want to run free with the rest of the mob, eh, Dangar? Righto, that's your belated Christmas present.'

Young Davey, the Irish ostler whose freckles multiplied every summer, was waiting for him at the stables, his youthful forehead knotted in a frown befitting an old lag. But unlike other assigned lads, entrenched in their old ways, Davey was eager to learn new tricks.

'You said to be informing you of unwelcome visitors, Marmaduke. I dunno if this fits the bill, but this morning when I was exercising a new colt I saw a flash carriage stationed at the end of the public right of way. At my approach the driver seemed to be taking his instructions from a gentleman passenger. He drove off at high speed. Not like a regular mourner from the village.'

'Did you see their faces?'

'I did. To be sure it's not likely I'd forget the servant. He had a metal shield on his nose. I didn't get a proper look at the gentleman except he was dressed flash and held a fancy cane. I am believing it was the new resident of Penkivil Park.'

Marmaduke masked his reaction to the descriptions. They tallied with those of Josiah Mendoza and his own memory of that morning in Josepha's villa when she was visited by the protector who had posed as a Frenchman. Marmaduke's frustration lay in his lack of proof. He was itching for Silas to make one false move out in the open.

'You did right to tell me, Davey. Spread the word among the lads to keep a sharp eye out for him. Tell me the minute you spot either of them.'

On reaching the house Marmaduke checked his pocket watch. The hands were frozen at half past midday.

'Hell and damnation, it's finally died on me.'

He told himself only fools believed in omens but he was reminded that the clocks of William Shakespeare and Edmund Kean had each stopped at the hour of their death.

'Well, this watch didn't stop when von Starbold died, so why now? Is it a warning of my death?'

Having laboured bareheaded out of doors all day installing Mingaletta's new water tank and a windmill to pump water for his future stock, it came as no surprise to find he had copped a heavy dose of the sun. His head ached, he was bad-tempered and hungry for a decent meal. He had built his mounting anger into a reason to avoid Isabel for days, yet felt an irrational sense of irritation when she was not in the nursery on his return.

If I can't trust her, who can I trust?

After shedding working clobber that was rank with mud and sweat, he washed and changed into a clean shirt and trousers then sat at the nursery desk to examine the watch, trying to recall Josiah Mendoza's exact instructions on how to repair different timepieces.

Marmaduke had never needed to open this watch. It had never faltered. The back cover of the gold case was blank but he was surprised to find the inside contained layers of small circles of paper. Each one was printed with the name and date of the watchmaker who had serviced or repaired it, making it a virtual history of the watch's travels. Marmaduke felt curious as he pieced the sequence in order. The most recent receipt was from a known watchmaker in George Street, Sydney and dated 1825.

The year of our duel – and von Starbold's death.

Traced backwards in chronological order the receipts indicated watchmakers who had examined the watch in London in 1821, the same year von Starbold had sailed to Van Diemen's Land. The previous one was dated 1818, Belfast.

Was he stationed there as a soldier attached to a British regiment?

A receipt written in what Marmaduke recognised was Dutch, showed it had been repaired in the Cape Colony in 1808. The earliest, written in German and dated 1805, was signed by a watchmaker in a Hessian village.

I remember him talking nostalgically about that place, maybe his family home.

The removal of this final receipt revealed the heart of the lid. It was engraved with a miniature coat of arms bearing the unmistakeable outline of an eagle. Marmaduke turned the watch full circle to read the engraved inscription written around the internal rim. Inscribed in High German script, the words ran into each other so there was no clear beginning or end, just two minute leaves linking the two phrases to form a continuous circle.

He read it as written, inscribed words that were instantly translated in his head. On the other half of the circle was his name.

Klaus von Starbold. For my son in all but name...

The spoken words seemed to hang suspended in the air, waiting for confirmation. 'That suggests at least one of von Starbold's colourful tales was true. He told me his father was a nobleman who fell in love with a struggling young actress but because of his arranged marriage to a woman of his own rank, he never acknowledged his lover's child as his own son – Klaus von Starbold, or whatever his actress mother's true name was.'

Marmaduke gripped the watch as he realised its significance.

'No wonder this watch was important to the bastard. Yeah, *bastard*'s literally true. This watch was von Starbold's only proof of paternity, the gift from the father who never publicly acknowledged him.'

Despite his long-held hatred of the man, Marmaduke felt moved by the discovery, a feeling soon overtaken by a blinding headache. He saw in his mind the circle of German words whirling faster and faster until they merged together and lost all meaning. In urgent need of fresh air he found himself staggering along the portrait gallery and down the servants' stairs, the watch gripped in his hand.

His head ached so badly that when he passed Isabel in the hallway he looked straight through her until jolted by her words.

'Marmaduke, what's the matter? You look ill.'

'Tired, nothing more. I need to be by myself.'

Marmaduke headed straight for Queenie's cottage, instinctively reaching out for his old nanny to cure the inexplicable pain in his head in the same way he had done as a child when he was hurt or troubled.

It seemed as if Queenie had been expecting him. The kettle was on the hob, freshly baked buttered scones and biscuits on a plate.

He sat beside her and gripped the long-fingered brown hands that had tenderly cared for him since the hour of his birth.

'Queenie, I need you to tell me the truth. Have I been burnt up with hatred all my life for the wrong reasons? I don't know where to begin. I've discovered information about von Starbold's family in his watch that doesn't quite make sense.'

'Where's Isabel? She should be here,' Queenie said.

'I'm the one who killed him. I have a right to know.'

Queenie opened her mouth to answer but a rap on the door cut across her words.

Marmaduke looked up in frustration at the sight of Isabel framed in the doorway, her face pale and strained. She clasped a shawl around her shoulders like a shield against the cold though the night air was warm. Marmaduke knew she was there as a gesture of defiance against his rejection of her.

'I told you I wanted to be alone, girl.' His voice sounded sharper than he intended. 'Please go.'

Isabel shook her head. 'I can't leave you, Marmaduke.'

'God damn it, will you never do as I tell you?'

'No! You need me now more than ever!'

Queenie's hand sliced through the air to sever their argument.

'Hush! This is my house, you are my guests. Sit over there, Isabel. Don't say another word – either of you! But what I have to say concerns you both, Marmaduke.'

He held his aching head in his hands but watched her intently, recording in his mind every nuance in Queenie's voice, every subtle change of expression in her eyes, every gesture of those fine hands. He trusted Queenie as he had never trusted any other woman.

'I'm counting on you to tell me the truth and nothing but the truth.'

'You deserve that.' She began softly, 'Miranda left Mingaletta as your inheritance. But she also left in my care a box and charged me not to hand it over to you until such time as you loved a woman and had won her love in full measure. Is that now the truth for both of you?'

Marmaduke felt himself subjected to that piercing stare that had seen through all his childish lies.

'I speak for myself. You know how I feel, Queenie. I don't need to spell it out.'

He felt the chill in Isabel's voice as she ignored him and spoke directly to Queenie.

'It seems Marmaduke has run out of dead poets to quote. Well, I'm not afraid to speak my *own* words. I never knew what love was until this man used every trick in the book to worm his way into my heart, but right now I wish I'd never set eyes on him!'

'I guess both your statements will have to pass muster for love,' Queenie said wryly.

She stretched out her hand and stroked the lid of a plain ebony box that was like a travelling writing case but was not as ornate as the one he remembered his mother using.

'Will that box tell me what I need to know? Did I kill my mother's rapist or her lover?'

Queenie folded her hands in her lap and spoke in the serious voice of a storyteller.

'Marmaduke, your memories of that terrible night you found your mother in the cellar of Mingaletta are accurate – as much as truth could be understood by a boy of sixteen. But truth, like a prism, has many faces. I ask you to look at the truth through my eyes. Don't interrupt me. It is painful for me to re-live it.'

Queenie took a deep breath. 'All her life I was your mother's shadow. As a child I had every reason to be jealous of the younger half-sister whose Irish mother had died giving birth to her. Miranda was unlike me in every way. White, beautiful, loved, spoilt by her father – and legitimate, but from the moment baby Miranda curled her hand around my finger I had no room in my heart for envy. We grew up like twin souls. We shared lessons with governesses. I shared all your mother's secrets. Her love for you, Marmaduke. Her years of unhappiness because of Garnet's obsessive passion.

'One day, as was our custom, Miranda asked me to accompany her to the ruins of Mingaletta. The only room intact, the cellar, was her sanctuary. But this time was different. She needed to be alone to make an important decision. "No need to keep guard, Queenie," she said. "I'm perfectly safe here. It would please me if you'd gather some bush flowers and place them on our father's grave. I'll call you when I'm ready to return to the house."

'I tended the Colonel's grave then waited, concealed in the bush for her to call me. It was a hot day. I fell asleep. I woke up, shocked by the sound of a woman's cries. Miranda!

'I ran to the cellar door and was about to fling it open when I heard a man's deep voice. The Hessian tutor! His anger was controlled but Miranda's cries grew wilder.

'I remember every word they said. Miranda cried out, "No! You can't do this to me. I forbid it!"

'"You have no choice, Miranda. The die is cast," he said.

'"You have a contract to teach Marmaduke – on my terms!"

'He told her, "I have done so to the best of my ability. I shall leave tonight. I shall leave Marmaduke a note of explanation, some kindly lie. He is a young man of honour."

'I heard von Starbold say, "*Gott in Himmel!* I refuse to spend another day under Garnet Gamble's roof. I depart tonight. Leave him! Come with me!"

'"You know I can't. Not now!" Miranda said.

'"Then this is to remember me when I am gone!"' There was no mistaking the sounds of what was happening between them,' Queenie said.

'I was unable to think, unable to act. I ran away when I saw you riding up, Marmaduke. I saw the confusion on your face when you saw the open padlock...and you entered the cellar...'

Queenie's fingers fluttered like the wings of a bird then dropped into her lap.

'You were just a boy, Marmaduke. You had no way of understanding what you saw.'

Marmaduke leapt to his feet in denial. 'It was rape! I heard Mother scream, "No, No!"'

Queenie gave a deep sigh. 'I also heard that. But moments before you rode up in search of her I heard Miranda cry out, "No, no! Klaus, *don't leave me!*"'

The silence in the cabin hung so heavily that Marmaduke had trouble breathing. Inside his head he had been once again sixteen years old, shocked by the carnal images before him. His mother, his tutor – naked. He finally found the courage to say the words that would alter the past forever.

'So, I didn't kill her rapist – I murdered her lover. How she must have hated me!'

Queenie grabbed hold of him. 'No, my boy, Miranda understood you were trying to protect her. So did Klaus.'

Marmaduke gripped hold of Queenie's shoulders. 'The moment I shot him we both knew he was mortally wounded. I brought him here to your cabin to die. Mother told me you prepared his body for burial. Don't spare me, Queenie. Was he delirious? Did he say anything before he died? Was it in German or English? I must know!'

Queenie nodded. 'Miranda never left his side the final hours of his life. His last words were, "You must live for the babe!" He died in Miranda's arms.'

Marmaduke warded off Isabel's attempts to touch him. He was beyond all comfort.

'You mean von Starbold knew Mother was with child – *his* child?'

Queenie gave a reluctant nod. 'He was desperate for her to run away with him.'

Marmaduke's laugh was cynical, a shield for his pain. 'But content to leave me a *kindly note of explanation*. How noble of him. But Mother chose to stay. Why? For my sake? Or for the sake of the coming babe?'

'I must leave Miranda to explain the rest of the story. Here is her diary. *Read* it. The box? It holds something that was precious to her. She begged me to make it for you. In the hope that one day you'd understand – and not condemn her.'

Like a dreamer trapped in a bizarre nightmare, Marmaduke opened the lid and felt sickened by the contents. A man's face that was totally lifelike except it was pure white. The eyes were closed.

Marmaduke stared at the death mask of Klaus von Starbold. The face seemed to smile back at him.

Marmaduke flashed along the track towards the house propelled by an invisible force.

He was aware of Isabel at his heels. The distance between them increased as he cut across the convicts' courtyard, blind and deaf to all but his objective. Garnet Gamble.

He gripped the diary. He had just read random extracts. Some were passionate, playful or ambiguous – all vividly evoked his mother's voice. The dates of her diary entries shuffled in his mind as he tried to form a cohesive sequence linked to the dates inside the gold watch. Dates that clearly intersected in Sydney Town in 1821.

That was the year Garnet hired him as my tutor. Did he suspect they became lovers? Will he refuse to destroy the myth of the love he shared with my mother?

Garnet was seated in the smoking room when Marmaduke burst into the room and flung down the diary like a gauntlet.

'Isn't it high time to face the truth? We've been living a lie all my life.'

Garnet seemed to be prepared for the confrontation. He answered with a degree of calm that belied the fact the colour had drained from his ruddy complexion.

'The truth is you are Marmaduke Gamble, my only son and heir. And your mother was the only woman I have ever loved. If that isn't the truth, what is?'

Marmaduke turned to see Isabel enter the room. Although trembling she stood defiantly with her back pressed against the wall of books.

Garnet said quietly, 'Sit down, m'dear, this family conference involves you.'

Garnet's attempt to diffuse Marmaduke's anger only increased it. He studied his father's face, trying to evaluate the man he had loved and feared as a small child but who had become as much his enemy as the villain he had murdered. That macabre death mask was such an uncanny replica Marmaduke felt as if Klaus von Starbold had returned from the grave.

Mother ordered Queenie to make that death mask from his corpse but her diary doesn't mention it. How much does Garnet know? How much will he admit?

Marmaduke made a conscious effort to control his anger, aware he must not antagonise Garnet until he had extracted the truth. Piece by piece.

'Let's begin with my grandfather, Colonel McAlpine. Why did he commit suicide?'

Garnet glanced at him then at Isabel. 'To a military man like Colonel McAlpine, Honour is next to Godliness. To him it was a terrible social stigma for Miranda, the jewel in his crown, to marry me, an illiterate ticket-of-leaver squatting on a few hundred acres.'

'So why did he give his consent and attend your wedding?'

'He discovered we were lovers and Miranda was with child. You!'

'So I'm to blame for your shotgun wedding. Her diary states my actual birth date was four months earlier than the date I've been told. Her diary describes you as young and nutty about her – and you'd already begun to amass your fortune. You built this mansion before the ink had dried on the parish register. Yet the Colonel killed himself two years later. Why *then*?'

Marmaduke realised he'd at last asked the important question. *Damn it all. I'll kill Garnet if he fobs me off with another pack of lies.*

Garnet looked cornered. 'Two years after your birth Miranda discovered her father had intercepted letters written to her and destroyed them without her knowledge. Miranda swore that because her father had manipulated her life he would never see his grandson again. That was the price he must pay for burning her letters.'

Garnet's hand curled into the shape of a pistol. He inserted the index finger in his mouth and fired it.

Marmaduke snapped, 'What letters?' He knew the answer before Garnet said the words. '*Love* letters, written by another man before our marriage.'

Garnet's voice rasped out in his defense. 'The scoundrel had abandoned her!'

Marmaduke's voice was soft, without mercy. 'Not quite. It's all here in Mother's diary. The young soldier she met on the voyage out. That they intended to marry, but when their ship reached Cape Town the Colonel contrived to have the soldier imprisoned on a trumped-up charge that led to his court-martial. Miranda was forced to continue the voyage to Port Jackson, heartbroken in the belief her lover had abandoned her – unaware the Colonel had destroyed the soldier's letters begging her to wait for him.'

Marmaduke tapped the diary cover. 'Mother only married you in desperation to give her fiancé's unborn babe a name – Marmaduke Gamble.'

Garnet's lips turned white with rage. 'I didn't damn well care! I would have married Miranda at any price. And I loved you like my own son.'

Marmaduke leant across and said softly. 'Mother was too much the born lady to name her child's true father in her diary. But we both know him, don't we, Garnet? And then, she describes twelve years later, their accidental reunion in Sydney. How she tricked you into hiring Klaus von Starbold as my tutor.'

'That's a lie, pure coincidence!' Garnet roared.

In answer Marmaduke opened his watch. 'Klaus von Starbold gave me this before he died. I read the inscription to mean it was his father's gift to him. Now I know the truth. *For my son in all but name – Klaus von Starbold.* This was *my father's* gift to *me.*'

Garnet's eyes were glassy. Marmaduke jumped to his feet, unable to restrain his anger.

'You used me as a hostage to bind mother to you.' He stabbed his finger at the diary. 'Read it! Mother's lover might have been a scoundrel but he was no coward. He confronted you with the truth. You told him he was welcome to take Mother with him but you refused to relinquish me. You were the second wealthiest man in the Colony. You knew when a woman commits adultery the law grants custody to the *legal* father.'

'Why not? That was the only time the law was ever on *my* side,' Garnet said acidly. 'When I discovered von Starbold's identity I knew I'd lost Miranda's love forever. But I was damned if I was going to let them drag my son around the world, living like a pack of gypsies. Playing in barns when he couldn't find work in a theatre.'

Marmaduke was stunned. 'You mean Klaus von Starbold was an *actor*?'

'An *actor*?' Isabel gasped in admiration.

'An actor!' Garnet said contemptuously. 'What else but an actor? Von Starbold – or whatever his true name was – probably gave the best performance of his life in the role of your tutor. Had *me* fooled. All I ever knew about Miranda's first love was he was some *soldier* who ended up in gaol. When I advertised for a tutor for you, a German turned up who spoke four languages and quoted Shakespeare and that Goethe bloke at the drop of a hat. I had no reason to suspect who he was. Why should I? He came armed with a glowing letter from some Weimar court claiming he'd tutored some duke or prince's sons. No doubt the cunning bastard wrote the damned reference himself.'

Marmaduke had a sudden painful flash of memory of an afternoon in the garden, reading aloud to his tutor Goethe's *Wilhelm Meister* in the original German. Marmaduke had finished the passage and asked anxiously, 'Is my accent all right, sir?'

His tutor nodded approvingly then asked, 'But do you understand what Goethe is telling us? I had the great good fortune to meet the genius when he was producing a play. I was overcome with nerves but Herr von Goethe kindly discussed with me the answer to my question, "What does a man do if he does *not* die when his love is unrequited?"'

Von Starbold's words were now alive with fresh significance. Marmaduke turned his anger on Garnet.

'So my foolish duel of honour solved your problem of Mother's love triangle. By then you knew the truth. Why in hell didn't you stop the duel?'

'Because you needed to believe in your mother's honour! Von Starbold was a trained soldier, you a raw novice he'd given a few duelling lessons. He'd never have fired at *you*. The shot that killed him was a fluke.'

'Fluke! It was murder! I meant to kill him.' Marmaduke lost control, grabbed hold of Garnet's shoulders and shook him like a terrier with a rag doll.

Isabel cried out, begging them to stop but Marmaduke was beyond all reason.

'You manipulative bastard! I'm twenty-five years old and I only found out tonight I'm the cuckoo in Mother's love nest. For my whole life, you, Mother, Queenie, you all knew the truth – yet you trapped me in a conspiracy of silence.'

Garnet offered no resistance. 'What else could I do? You were a miserable little sod who wanted to be a hero. Would it have made you happy to grow up knowing you'd murdered *your own father*?'

Confronted by the truth Marmaduke was shocked into silence.

Garnet combed his fingers through his hair, his eyes wild with despair. 'Don't you understand? I never stopped loving Miranda but after I knew I'd never win her love I rogered every piece of skirt I could lay my hands on. In all these years I never managed to plant one of them with child, except your mother. Even you were courtesy of that Hessian bastard's seed!'

Marmaduke stared into space, his mind flooded with fragmented memories of the two men he had hated for years but until this moment had never really known.

Garnet's ragged words rasped out breaking the silence. 'You've always hated my guts, Marmaduke, but I'm the man who loved your mother. I'm the man who gave *you* your name. You are...the only son...I will ever have!'

Marmaduke's voice was cold. 'So that's why you refused to send for a physician and let Mother die. To punish her for bearing a second bastard to Klaus von Starbold.'

Garnet was defeated. 'Believe what you will. You can't hate me more than I hate myself.'

'No? Just watch me, Garnet, I haven't even *begun* to hate you!'

Marmaduke brushed past Isabel and stormed out, hoping to lose himself in the anonymity of the darkness of night.

He ran blindly through the bush, only halting when he reached the graveyard.

Moonlight etched the outlines of the tombstones. Marmaduke made straight for the stone slab in the far corner where he rested his hand on the name Klaus von Starbold.

Forgive me, my Father, I didn't understand what I was doing.

He spoke the words in anguish, in German. '*Verzeih mir, mein Vater, ich verstand nicht, was ich tat!*'

The terrible, guttural cry that seemed to be ripped from his throat echoed across Mingaletta to the Ghost Gum Valley.

CHAPTER 50

The end of her first long Australian summer brought Isabel conflicting feelings of elation and acute anxiety. She knew this imbalance was partly a symptom of her condition as she was only a few months away from giving birth.

The world around her was a thing of beauty. The eternal blue of the sky, the golden orb of the sun, the hot sunlight that drenched the terraced gardens and filtered through the canopies of eucalypts. The blend of perfumes of the native plants with those from English gardens. Her ears had sung with the high-pitched buzz of cicadas and the choirs of excited birdsong that seemed to Isabel to be the epitome of the bush's voice in summer – heat translated into sound waves.

Though its beauty comforted her it could not wipe out the anxiety that stemmed from Marmaduke. Not once had he returned to the house since that shattering night he had discovered his true identity. He had totally withdrawn to work on the final stages of Mingaletta. She knew he was too proud to admit he was fast running out of money to finance it, so he worked seven days a week, alone when no assigned men were available.

Although Isabel's sleepwalking pattern had not returned, the Other was again making its presence felt. She tried to dismiss her fear of it as an irrational symptom of pre-natal imagination, that it was the babe kicking inside her that was causing her emotions to swing like a metronome, but she sensed it was far more than that. Signs of the Other increased to become a daily occurrence. She remembered how Silas had frightened her when she was a child, telling her that because they were so close in blood as double cousins they shared a strange gift – they attracted dark beings that ordinary mortals could not see or hear. Silas was in residence barely ten miles distant. Was this the reason the dead were drawing psychic energy from her body?

Silas had not openly contacted her since his appearance in the graveyard but every week she received another of the anonymous 'letters' that made her shiver with dread: a blank page wrapped around a pressed rose. The white Rose Alba, the white rose of York.

Today as she hurried down the staircase en route to the kitchen in search of Bridget, she faltered at the sight of the plain white envelope lying on the console, addressed simply to 'Isabel'. It was identical to all the others. She did not need to open it to know what it contained. Who brought these letters here? They never came by mail. She always found them lying around, on a table, once in the summerhouse. The servants when questioned looked blank and she had no right to accuse anyone. The letters unnerved her. Silas was mentally stalking her.

Take hold of yourself, girl. How can anonymous white roses hurt you? Don't allow Silas to get inside your mind again.

Isabel hurriedly retraced her steps to the nursery, opened the drawer and placed the pressed rose with the others beneath her undergarments. She wanted to destroy them but felt if she did it would attract bad luck to her own little Rose Alba.

As she took the servants' back stairs to the kitchen her thoughts returned to Marmaduke.

Although Davey rode to Mingaletta daily to deliver stores and Murray Robertson in his new role as overseer kept Marmaduke informed, Isabel was forbidden to go to the site.

Marmaduke has cut himself off from us all like an animal licking its wounds. Queenie warned me this would happen but it's time I broke through the barrier.

In the kitchen she found Bridget packing up the boxes of stores for Davey to deliver.

Since Elise's dramatic exit Isabel was on alert for signs of the return of Garnet's mood swings, suspecting that Bridget had inherited the role of his scourger.

Although her father-in-law remained unfailingly kind in his dealings with her, Isabel was afraid that since the break with Marmaduke, his burden of guilt was building towards a peak of self-loathing that only physical pain could alleviate.

Isabel tackled the problem head on. 'I'll deliver the stores today with Davey.'

Bridget resisted the idea. 'I have strict instructions you are not to visit the site.'

'Rules need to be bent when occasion demands, Bridget. I need you to tell me if my father-in-law orders you to go to the priest hole with him. You know what happens there?'

'I do. Sure and I can be delivering what Elise did,' Bridget said coldly. 'So what if the Master does take pleasure from pain? I know when to stop. I won't be killing him.'

Although the words were said with contempt Isabel sensed the underlying anxiety.

'I understand it's difficult for you to defy your master's orders and reject money—'

'It is not being the money! I'm not a common whore, ye know! The master promised he'd be recommending me for my ticket. Free to choose me own boss and earn wages. That's one step closer to joining me Mam in Van Diemen's Land – if she's still alive when she's finished her fourteen years.'

Isabel knew Bridget and her mother had been transported for the same crime, rolling a drunk in her grandmother's shanty in Dublin, but she was stunned by the pain in Bridget's voice.

'I promise I'll do what I can to help you win your ticket, but you must warn me about the priest hole.'

She searched for words to soften Bridget's resolve. 'Long ago he made a terrible mistake that caused his wife's death. Your master has lost his way to God. No priest can give him absolution. He punishes himself for his guilt.'

Isabel saw Bridget begin to waver and pressed her advantage.

'Garnet Gamble's pardon didn't make him a free man. For all his wealth he's never been free in his mind. Yet freedom is what lies at the heart of this country. If it doesn't break your spirit or kill you, it gives you a second chance.'

'A pretty speech coming from a lady of Quality who came free.'

Isabel chose to ignore the insolence. 'You think I don't know what guilt is? This is *my* second chance.' She stopped herself in time.

The girl's face was blank. Isabel finally lost her temper.

'For pity's sake, Bridget, you don't have to *like* Garnet Gamble, but can't you find it in your heart to help me set the poor man free from his demons?'

Bridget finally gave a nod of assent. 'I will,' she said.

Isabel rode in single file behind Davey towards Mingaletta, seated on the gentle mare that Davey had saddled for her despite his unease about defying Marmaduke's explicit orders.

In her pocket was the letter from Aunt Elisabeth from Sydney Town.

As they drew closer to the orchestrated sounds of hammers, sawing timber, pick-axes and the different accents of male voices, Isabel was reminded of the tangled plot of *A Servant to Two Masters*. Like the play's wily servant, Trufaldino, Isabel felt trapped in the similar role she had agreed to play – being the ally to two masters – though in her case both her masters were Marmaduke. One Marmaduke was kind, patient, warm and loving. The other was obstinate, demanding, melancholic and had a foul temper. God only knew which mood she would find him in today when she confronted him about Aunt Elisabeth's letter.

I can't allow the threat of bushrangers stop me joining Rose Alba and Aunt Elisabeth. Bolters will be part of this landscape as long as The System is in force. Marmaduke wants to protect me but I can't live life marooned in a safe house afraid to travel the highway to Sydney Town.

When Isabel caught sight of Marmaduke before he saw her, she dismounted and led the mare to the building site on foot.

'I'm a Greek bearing gifts!' she called out, counting on her husband's pride to conceal his annoyance at her forbidden arrival.

Marmaduke stood outlined against the sun, balanced precariously on a half-timbered section of roof. He made no response, so Isabel turned the full force of her nervous smile on the only other person in sight, a young lad whose head rose like a mushroom from a hole between the floorboards.

'Could you help Davey unpack the saddlebags, lad? Bridget and the three Marys have cooked a large amount of fine food to heat up in your camp oven.'

Murmurs of approval followed when a number of bodies swung easily down from the rafters. The men were so busy unloading

Davey's saddlebags and getting the campfire going for their meal that they were well out of earshot.

Isabel squinted up at Marmaduke and tried to sound playful.

'If Queenie's special Summer Puddings won't tempt you down off your high horse, Marmaduke, what will?'

In two moves he swung down effortlessly to her side. If the glance he gave her body held any trace of desire it was well concealed. Isabel felt deflated.

It's not fair. The puffier and pudgier I grow the leaner and browner he is. He hasn't shaved for days but he's so handsome I could race him off to bed as soon as look at him. Oh dear, this babe's making me so lusty, I'm dangerous.

Marmaduke took a swig of water, wiped his sweaty face with the back of his hand and tried to sound casual. 'You all right?'

'Never better. I've also brought you clean clothes, towels and your special sandalwood soap. And Garnet sent you a couple of bottles of Hunter Valley red wine from a new vintner he says is the best yet.'

'Tell Garnet to bounce 'em right back in his cellar. I'm not here to party. Time enough to celebrate when the roof's finished and the building is ready to be locked.'

'Marmaduke, there are serious things I need to tell you face to face.'

'I made it clear all visits from you were *verboten*. Your reason for defying me had better be good.' He added quickly, 'You haven't been bleeding?'

'I'm fine. Queenie says she's never seen an expectant mother in a ruder state of health. I'm eating like a horse, sleeping like a babe, full of energy. And if I hold my breath I can still fit into most of my clothes. But there's one thing I can't control. I laugh or cry at the most unpredictable moments. And...and I miss you like crazy.'

There was no one else close enough to overhear but Isabel whispered it anyway. 'Our bed is far too big without you, darling.'

The response she was counting on was not forthcoming so she added, 'My temper flares like a rocket, so stand warned.'

'Tell me something new,' he said mildly.

Isabel handed him a wicker basket and drew him to a secluded corner of the bush where she quickly spread out a picnic.

Sprawled in the shade of a Bloodwood tree, Marmaduke tilted his hat to shield his eyes from the sun. Or was it to disguise his thoughts?

At last, overcome by hunger and curiosity he began to poke around in the bundles of food wrapped in fine cotton squares. He ate and drank without comment until Isabel snapped.

'Have you taken a vow of silence?'

'You want to tell me why you're really here, soldier? A tour of inspection? Or a report back to Garnet from his latest informer?'

She was stung by the word used contemptuously about those who betrayed bolters.

'That's unfair. I wanted to find out what was taking so long to build my new home. Why you are still sulking?'

Let's hope that draws blood...oh my God, Vesuvius is going to blow its top!

He sat bolt upright. 'Sulking! You haven't the remotest idea, have you? In the space of one day I discovered my whole existence is a flaming lie. Nothing is real. Not my name, my age, my birth. Everyone I loved or hated is the reverse of what I believed. My mother wasn't exactly the perfect lady. The rapist I killed in a duel wasn't a villain but my true father who lived and died by his own code of honour. And I'm not Garnet Gamble's son and heir. So who am I? A cuckoo in the nest who's forced to share Garnet's name and the boundary line of Mingaletta with a manipulative bastard I never want to set eyes on again!'

Marmaduke had run out of steam but not of anger. 'I thought *you*'d understand what it feels like to have your whole childhood gutted.'

Marmaduke lay back and jammed this hat back over his eyes. Isabel sat with her arms wrapped around her knees to disguise her trembling limbs.

Well, that certainly did the trick. The boil is lanced. What do I say now?

'Thank you for sharing your feelings. I'm sorry I inferred you were a sulky little boy. I can imagine your shock. But now you've had time to think it through you must see there's a big difference between us.'

'Yeah,' he said, 'you're the one who's pregnant.'

I know you're hurting but you're not going to deflect me. I'm not leaving without saying what I came to say.

'You hated being Garnet's son but now you're shocked to find he isn't your father by blood. I'm truly sorry you had a miserable childhood and that you were caught in the middle of a family war. So was I. But there's a big difference between us. You had four people – your mother, Queenie and two fathers – who all loved you and wanted you. I was an orphan taken in under sufferance. I'd have felt blessed to have just *one* person I could count on to love and protect me.'

Marmaduke took his time to answer. 'Well, you do now, soldier.'

Her heart leapt. His words sounded tender but his rage was far from exhausted.

She tried again. 'One positive thing came out of all this. You were afraid to become a father in case Garnet's illness was hereditary. That's one fear removed. But I believe Garnet will be a devoted grandfather and—'

'Hey! Don't think you can sweet talk me into waving an olive branch. Garnet's years of manipulation are over. I'll never enter his damned mansion again as long as I live!'

'Manipulation? What a hypocrite you are! Rose Alba arrived in Port Jackson weeks ago, yet I'm the last to know! What gave you the right to keep us apart?'

Isabel was breathless with anger. Marmaduke waited for her to cool down.

'Quarantine. The kid's been out of bounds, that's why. Next question?'

Isabel gasped in fright. '*Quarantine?* What's wrong with Rose Alba, is she all right? She's so fragile. And my aunt? Why didn't you tell me? I would have rushed to Sydney!'

'That's why I didn't tell you! Quarantine laws are strict. All you could do was wave your handkerchief from across the street. I've had them both under the care of Dr Bland and paid women to nurse them at the Princess Alexandrina. If you'd come within coo-ee of their sick room you'd have copped their fever and dropped your foal too early for it to survive. Then you'd have blamed me for my not wanting it!'

He eyed the curve of her belly. 'Well, you're half right. I didn't want it to begin with, but I'm not taking any chances of losing *you*. It's taken me a whole flaming year to break you in as a wife. I wouldn't be caught dead marrying you again for all the diamonds in King Solomon's mines!'

That said, Marmaduke lay back and jerked the brim of his hat back over his eyes.

Isabel digested his words. 'I suspect there was a Currency compliment buried in there somewhere. You still haven't told me how soon I can go to Sydney to see them.'

'You can't!' he said firmly. 'When I tried to take you to Sydney to put you under Doc Bland's care until the birth, you went off like a firecracker! Wanted Queenie to deliver the goods here at Mingaletta. Now you've gone and put paid to the surprise I'd planned for you.'

'What surprise?'

'I've been breaking my neck to finish this place so Thomas can drive them down here with Edwin. If you behave yourself you'll see Rose Alba and your Aunty by sundown Friday.'

'In a week? Oh, darling, I'm truly sorry I misjudged you.' Isabel raised his hand to her lips and covered it with kisses.

Marmaduke gave a half-cocked smile. 'Hey, fair crack of the whip. Most of these blokes haven't had their paws on a woman in years. Don't want to get them too excited.'

Isabel looked at him with love, his image shimmering through the film of her tears.

Marmaduke shook his head. 'There are times I really regret teaching you how to cry.'

'Don't. That was the most wonderful night of my life.'

'Yeah?' Marmaduke ruefully rubbed the stubble on his chin and his voice was as soft and dark as if they were in bed. 'Lady, that was just for starters. I've got a lot more tricks up my sleeve.'

He pulled her to her feet. 'Come on. Seeing as you're here I'd better give you a quick look at the place. It's bigger than the original plans.'

Isabel followed him through the skeleton of the house, exclaiming with admiration over those rooms which had four walls, and the remaining shells that only had windows anchored in place between the beams. She responded to his plans with eager questions, feeling moved by his offhand pride and his anxiety to please her.

'Of course, it's as rough as hell at the moment, but you won't know the place in a couple of weeks. Once it's painted and papered. There'll be plenty of room for your aunt,' he added casually, 'and both the kiddies.'

'It's a wonderful house, Marmaduke. I'm so proud of you. Didn't I tell you that you could do anything you set your mind to? At last you really will be the master of Mingaletta – doesn't that have a grand ring to it?'

'Yeah. Not half bad.'

'You know why I want to give birth to our babe in this house? To replace all the sad, bad memories of things that happened here. I want to bring joy into your home.'

Marmaduke drew her into the crook of his arm and Isabel had no doubt that their truce was signed in his hungry kiss. She also knew her other mission had failed. There was no chance of his making peace with Garnet Gamble.

CHAPTER 51

Marmaduke climbed back onto the roof of the house and watched Isabel ride away. She turned in the saddle and waved to him like a child. Marmaduke felt a longing to call her back to his side and never let her out of his sight again.

Working all afternoon, unmindful of the sun, he hardly felt the hot wind burning his face. His mind replayed the words of Isabel's arguments. His pride rejected some of them his love retained others to warm him. '*Our bed is far too big without you, darling.*'

Despite his ironclad refusal to return to Bloodwood Hall and see Garnet, Marmaduke began to feel a reluctant touch of pity for any man whose beloved wife made him the cuckold in a triangle.

As he began to see himself in a new light, a child caught at the heart of three passionate adults Hell-bent on messing up their lives, he was reminded of one of the key tenets in the wisdom of Freemasonry.

A Mason must keep his passions and prejudices within due bounds. I reckon for me that's gunna be a lifelong occupation!

He gave a wry smile at the thought that since Isabel had crept into his heart and taken up residence there, the unthinkable had happened. He now had no trouble focusing all his sexual drive on one woman. He was afraid to touch her now she was with child, but tried to content himself with fantasies of making love to her.

Isabel had not mentioned Silas de Rolland but Marmaduke's anxiety was aggravated by Davey's sighting of his carriage and the ever present knowledge that Penkivil Park was only a few miles away. The man's lack of contact didn't align with what Marmaduke knew of the nature of the beast.

His mind kept revolving around his desire for revenge, to meet Silas de Rolland face to face and challenge him. Legally he had no recourse by which to bring Silas to justice for his abuse of Isabel as a child. Marmaduke knew that the acts which in his eyes were clearly sexual abuse of a minor were not covered by British law. The age of consent was twelve and it was not uncommon for rape cases in the

Colony involving adult men and girls of eight or nine to be dropped because females, even children, were considered guilty of enticing men to have intercourse.

Was a second murder disguised as a duel the only way to stop Silas stalking Isabel? Fate had tricked him into killing Klaus von Starbold, an act he must live with for the rest of his life. He was ready to kill Silas but what would happen to Isabel and his babe if *he* should be the one to die? Silas would claim them!

'Never!' he cried out aloud.

I refuse to die. Silas doesn't deserve to live, but does that give me the right to play God? Shit, I'm beginning to feel like Hamlet! Life was a Hell of a lot easier when I was young and stupid and didn't stop to weigh the consequences.

At sundown Marmaduke watched Garnet's assigned men troop back to their cabins at Bloodwood Hall. As usual he cooked a meal over the campfire but his eye was repeatedly drawn to the section of the ruined house beneath the foundations of the new building. For the first time Marmaduke saw the scene vividly in his mind as if from the other side of the mirror. His mother lying naked in the arms of her lover – his true father.

Marmaduke crossed to the door where the padlock hung open on the sprocket. The cellar was in darkness. In the doorway he struck a match and lit the stub of a candle, causing a fragile web of shadows to bounce off the walls.

The open door allowed a cool draft of air inside as Marmaduke re-entered the past, seeking to free himself as a man from a boy's memories.

He now knew this was not the scene of his mother's rape but her final desperate act of love with her lover – their farewell.

Marmaduke lost all sense of time but finally he knew he had found it – a sense of peace with the past.

They were young, consumed by passion. No matter how badly it all went wrong, I should be grateful to them. They gave me my life.

With a sense of shock he realised the dual significance of Klaus von Starbold's dying words, *'You do not take my life – I give you yours.'*

Marmaduke wiped his eyes with the back of his hand and was about to leave when he heard the sound of an approaching horse.

Heavy footsteps were followed by something that caused the hairs on the back of his neck to stiffen – the unmistakeable pungent smell of kerosene.

He charged towards the door ready to hurl himself at the man and foil his plan. He glimpsed a thick-set torso. A battered face. The flash of moonlight on a metal triangle shielding the nose. Silas de Rolland's henchman!

The man lit a match that threw his face into sharp relief, scowling to find he was not alone. Seconds before Marmaduke reached the door a beefy arm slammed the door shut. Marmaduke let out a bellow of rage at the metallic sound of the padlock being locked in place.

Marmaduke threw his full body weight against the door in a series of violent blows that rattled the door and would eventually break it down, but there wasn't time enough. He heard the man's laboured grunts and the crackling of flames.

Now there were two men's voices. The rough Cockney voice called out, 'We got company, sir, in there!'

From a distance came the languid, mildly amused accent of an English gentleman. 'How very convenient. You take care of things, Cooper. Must return to my guests...'

The voice faded as a horse rode away.

Just like that mongrel to leave his henchman to do his dirty work for him.

Only minutes remained to act. Flames would leap hungrily from room to room and burn the house to the ground. A thin trail of smoke filtered through the slit beneath the door. His lungs would soon fill with acrid smoke and choke the life out of him.

The plan was so bizarre he almost laughed. *Death by suffocation. Jesus, I came to this cellar to lay the family ghosts. Instead it's gunna be my tomb!*

Wracked by a fit of coughing, Marmaduke tried to control his panic. In a desperate attempt to drag air into his lungs, he sank to his knees, every instinct of survival fighting against the knowledge he was done for. It was then he saw it – or did he?

The thing outlined by the flickering light of the candle was a dark shadow on the wall, the outline of a man's outstretched hand pointing to the floor in the corner – a small patch of grey. He crawled towards the light and felt a draught of air through a hole at ground level, perhaps just big enough to force his body through...

Mustering a final burst of energy Marmaduke dragged himself towards it. As he hunched his shoulders and began to thrust his body through the opening, he was almost sure he heard it. A familiar, oddly comforting sound he remembered – the sharp click of heeled boots, von Starbold's mark of approval when he bowed to his young student in tribute to his success.

The face of the moon was clouded by smoke. Flames leapt and crackled like spears pointed at the night sky, showering the air with burning fragments like pollen blowing on the wind. Fire devoured the timber, raging in control, no longer in need of the arsonist's fuel.

Marmaduke knew it was all over. Mingaletta was lost. By dawn it would be a smouldering black ruin. Two dreams were dead: his mother's and his own. He had wanted to create a safe refuge for Isabel. Failure tasted as bitter as gall.

Torn and bruised, struggling from the cellar, Marmaduke shielded his eyes from the flames as he ran to the *gunyah* to arm himself. His weapon was gone.

The click of a cocked pistol caused him to spin around, face to face with the man with the tin nose. Cooper pointed his gun at him. The irony wasn't wasted on Marmaduke – he realised he was the target of his own pistol. His was conscious how cold his hands were. The same icy chill he had felt minutes before the duel.

He looked Cooper in the eye. Unarmed and faced with death Marmaduke had little choice. He took a gamble on wounding the older man's ego.

'I'd rather fight the puppeteer who pulls your strings, Cooper, but seeing as you're the bloke who struck the match for the bonfire – you'll do!'

Cooper hesitated before jerking his head towards the burning house.

'That's me master's business. I ain't got no personal grudge against you. No call to kill you unless you force me hand.'

'I'm not armed.' Marmaduke raised his hands to confirm it. 'If you're a *real* man and not just the organ grinder's monkey, you'll give me satisfaction. Chance it! Fight me man to man. Or have you turned coward in your *old age?*'

Cooper grunted. 'Want to be a dead hero, do you?'

'Let's find out!'

Marmaduke seized the moment. He lunged at lightning speed, dislodged the pistol from Cooper's fist and sent it flying sky-high to land somewhere in the bush.

'Now we're even, mate. Come and get me!' Marmaduke beckoned him with both hands, shifting his weight from foot to foot, shaping up to fight him.

Cooper was furious but confident. 'You want to put money on that?'

The Cockney grunted and began to feint and spring on the balls of his feet. Surprise registered in his eyes when Marmaduke's first blow caught him off guard, dislodging the metal nose guard from his face and sending it flying with a metallic ring onto the ground.

Marmaduke gave an involuntary flinch at the gaping hole where the nose had been eaten away by disease. The wound was repugnant but sympathy was misplaced. This brute had savaged Josiah Mendoza, an elderly man so gentle he even said a Hebrew prayer before he killed a Redback spider.

Marmaduke sized up his opponent's fighting style while careful to dance out of range of the first jabs that came his way.

Shit! He's no spring chicken but he's built as tough as a British man-o'-war.

Marmaduke taunted him. 'You sure picked a rum boss cocky. Didn't Silas de Rolland warn you? In this Colony arson's a crime on a par with murder. Burn a bloke's house down, you end up dancing on the scaffold.'

Marmaduke's next telling punch was to Cooper's belly and drew a barrage of blows that signalled to Marmaduke exactly what he was up against – a trained pugilist.

Knowing he was outclassed, Marmaduke fought on, driven by rage and frustration. He imagined the faceless de Rolland kinsman who had stolen Isabel's childhood and now, piece by piece, was demolishing every facet of Marmaduke's world.

Cheated of fighting the true villain, Marmaduke slugged it out with his henchman.

Chance gave Marmaduke a freak punch that landed in the hole in the ex-prize fighter's face and drew a howl of outrage. But Marmaduke paid a heavy price for it. Cooper rained a storm of blows to every part of his head and torso. When Marmaduke in exhaustion allowed his defences to slip, Cooper's dirty streetfighter tactics came into action.

He delivered his *coup de grâce* – a series of savage blows below the belt.

Marmaduke fell to his knees doubled up in agony. His opponent seized the moment to put the boot in. Marmaduke lost count of them, overcome by excruciating pain.

He realised he must have passed out for a few minutes when he discovered his hands were bound behind his back, his feet shackled like a convict in an iron-gang.

Shit, I'm trussed up like a Christmas turkey. From the looks of it Cooper's gunna tie me to that tree.

Moonlight glinted on the metal nose guard that was back in place. As Cooper tied a rope around Marmaduke's chest he kept up a cheerful running commentary.

'Tomorrow one of your felons will come here and cut you down – dead or alive. You're no coward so I'll give you an even break. I'll rope you to a tree that's out of range of the wind – so you won't catch fire.'

'You're all heart, Cooper, giving me a front row seat to watch my house burn down!'

Cooper shrugged. 'Nothing personal, cobber.'

Marmaduke recognised Cooper was a walking example of Newgate prison's code of ethics.

Marmaduke felt the taste of blood in his mouth but was determined to have the final word. As Cooper rode off he called after him.

'Tell your master Marmaduke Gamble sent him a warning. "It's not over until he's six feet under an Australian tombstone."'

A grunt sounded in the darkness then the horse galloped off in the direction of Penkivil Park.

Marmaduke felt crushed by a wave of melancholia as he watched the fire raging. The metal roof of Mingaletta collapsed into the ruins of the house with an almighty crash.

My whole life has been wasted. I never told Isabel she did the impossible – taught me how to love. I never got to see my babe born at Mingaletta. Never fulfilled my mother's dream. Never reunited Rose Alba with Isabel. Never told Klaus von Starbold he was my hero. And I never got the chance to say to Garnet...what?

It was then Marmaduke realised the wind had changed direction and was directing the flames of the fire towards him. This was it. He was a sitting duck.

CHAPTER 52

Isabel entered the empty dining room alone, feeling deeply in need of Marmaduke's company but resigned to the fact that was impossible.

Although Isabel longed to begin a joyous new era in her new home, now that her days were numbered at Bloodwood Hall she felt strangely sad that Garnet had failed to have his long-awaited banquet. Every detail had been planned. The light from the candelabras caused the crystal and silver to glisten. Under Bridget's direction the servants had lifted their game. Even the scruffy manservant's livery looked spruce. The dinner originally planned for this evening would have been perfect. Instead a pall of gloom hung over the whole house.

During the past few days all the dinner guests who had accepted Garnet's invitation, even Magistrate Summerhayes, had sent their regrets on the grounds of a 'previous' engagement that Isabel knew was the first of a series of musical soirées at Penkivil Park. Silas de Rolland had successfully attracted all the residents in the locality who were eager to be seen on the fringe of the Quality. Garnet's banquet was no match for three days of concerts by the legendary Josepha St John, who was to sing in English, Italian, French and German and on an undisclosed date would perform a biblical dance for the first time in Australia. Curiosity was aroused to a pitch of fever that had infected even the priests and clergymen of every denomination in the locality.

As Isabel took her seat alone at the table her emotions were in conflict. Relieved that the cancellation of the banquet meant that the possibility of one of Garnet's manic 'peaks' would now pass unnoticed by the neighbouring landowners, she was also infuriated that Silas had deliberately sabotaged his banquet.

That predatory woman has had one 'final' appearance after another. She was supposed to be sailing to Argentina. But as Silas has her 'in keeping' I suppose she has no choice but to perform for his guests.

Garnet had handled the obvious social rebuff with quiet dignity, more wounded by Marmaduke's rejection than he cared to admit.

Tonight he had sent Isabel his own apologies via Bridget, that he was 'not quite himself'.

Rhys Powell was secluded in darkness in his chambers attempting to combat a severe migraine attack. Queenie had returned to her cabin at Isabel's request to sew a party dress and dollies' clothes in readiness for the imminent arrival of Rose Alba, who was to be introduced as Isabel's half-sister.

Isabel had assured Queenie she would be fine sleeping alone in Marmaduke's absence but she had an ulterior motive in declining the offer. Isabel recognised the signs. She had no doubt Garnet was building towards another peak of anguish. Although Queenie expressed sympathy for the madness of poor old King George, the popular late father of the reigning monarch, she was scathing about Garnet's mental imbalance.

Garnet is family. I must be close at hand if he needs me.

That morning Isabel had followed Garnet covertly as he strode around the estate delivering random orders to assigned men in the stables, cool room and forge that left a trail of confusion in his wake. Only Murray Robertson had been equal to the situation, responding patiently to Garnet's inarticulate raving with calm assurances.

'Aye, I will carry out your instructions to the letter, Mr Gamble.'

Thank you, God, for sending Murray to us in place of Fordham the Flogger. Murray's already won the grudging respect of even the toughest felons.

Isabel had asked Murray to dine with her but he had excused himself on the grounds of Marmaduke's absence.

'A young bride canna be too careful. Government servants thrive on gossip. A wee smile between old friends would be seen as proof of dalliance. Aye, and spread like wildfire by sundown.'

Isabel had to admit the truth of that. When Rhys Powell entered the dining room and apologised for his belated appearance Isabel saw immediately that his migraine had come in tandem with his latest 'Welsh Hour'.

'I'm pleased you could join me, Rhys. Pray don't overtax yourself. You've been closeted for hours with Garnet ever since the messenger brought that urgent correspondence from Edwin Bentleigh's legal chambers.' She pushed her curiosity as far as she dared. 'I trust all is well?'

Rhys's dark eyes were shadowed from sleepless nights.

'Forgive me. Mr Gamble gave me strict instructions you are to be shielded from all unpleasantness in your delicate condition.'

Why does everyone handle me with kid gloves? I'm with child not in my dotage.

'I appreciate your loyalty to your employer but *not* knowing is worse than facing the truth no matter how unsavoury.' Isabel lost all patience. 'For pity's sake, Rhys, give me a clue!'

'The empire is crumbling,' he said.'

'Nonsense, you can't believe everything you read in Colonial newspapers. Just because we lost the American Colonies doesn't mean the British Empire is falling apart!'

He replied in a whisper. 'Not Britain's Empire, ma'am. Mr Gamble's empire.'

'I see,' Isabel aid evenly, aware they were both under the servants' scrutiny albeit via the fisheye lens of Elise's mirror.

She continued to eat in silence, covertly watching Bridget.

Marmaduke says everything in the Colony has its price. I know Bridget's been paid for past services, but it's not my imagination that she is now casting wistful glances at Rhys. Poor Rhys was so wounded in love by Elise he's probably blind to any admiration.

When Rhys later pleaded ill health and asked to be excused, Isabel was left alone.

'Bridget, please take Mr Powell something to ease his migraine.' She added, as if an afterthought, 'I'll go up to my room now, but don't hesitate to call me if any problem should arise. I plan to read Miss Austen's last novel, so I may well be awake all night.'

Bridget gave a knowing nod.

If nothing else I may have helped Bridget's case in being granted her ticket. She's a better prospect as a wife than Elise would be for any man. Oh dear, if only I could control my own life as cleverly as Miss Austen does her characters?

Isabel was jolted awake by agitated tapping on her door, shocked to find she had nodded off to sleep over her book, leaving the candle alight.

The floorboards were cold under her feet as she raced to open the door.

Bridget stood wide-eyed, gripping a candlestick in trembling hands. Her nightgown was covered by an old Irish plaid shawl, her long red hair hung in a plait over her shoulder. Normally pale, her complexion was chalk white, throwing into relief the freckles that bridged her nose. She looked as vulnerable as a child.

'Ye had best come right away, ma'am. The master has taken an odd turn, he has. I have not been seeing him act as strange as this before.'

'Garnet's in the priest's hole? You took him there?'

'Only to calm him down. I had no choice – he banged on my door fit to be waking the dead – but when we got to the priest's hole, he was telling me he wanted to be left alone tonight. He closed the door on me. I swear by all the saints it was *two* voices I heard inside it. It made my flesh creep. That other voice is *herself* I am telling ye. His dead wife. He called her Miranda!'

There was no doubting Bridget's distress or her conviction that she spoke the truth.

Isabel grabbed hold of her own shawl, a candlestick and a fresh candle. It might well be a long night.

Padding barefoot down the carpeted gallery shoulder to shoulder they both froze at the foot of the narrow stairs that led up to the priest's hole.

Bridget touched her arm. 'You hear them? It's not me that's also being demented, is it?'

Isabel felt the hair stand up on the back of her neck. The words from the priest's hole were indistinct but there were indeed two voices.

'Thank you, Bridget, I'll take care of my father-in-law now, but Rhys Powell is ill so I need you to go for help. Murray Robertson is a man to be trusted. Tell him to ride to Mingaletta immediately and not to return without my husband, you hear?'

Bridget nodded and shielding her candle flame walked swiftly towards the servants' stairs. Left alone, Isabel took deep breaths in an attempt to control her fear before ascending the stairs to face Garnet and whatever manifestation of the Other was waiting for her.

She cautioned herself. 'Take a hold of yourself. Your fear is nothing compared to the fear inside poor Garnet. He's afraid of dying and afraid of living. Right now Garnet needs Marmaduke even more than he needs God.' She rolled her eyes. 'No disrespect intended, Lord, but you know what I mean – the poor man is lost. Grant Garnet peace *on Earth* – don't wait until he's dead and buried.'

On the point of ascending the stairs Isabel was distracted by the sound of raised voices carried on the night air; they seemed to come from the direction of the assigned men's cabins. She was reminded that the full moon was said to be a time of imbalance for those who were mentally disturbed, drunk or angry.

That covers almost everyone at Bloodwood Hall! If there's a convict riot brewing I'll just have to leave Murray to handle it. My first duty is to my family.

Isabel hurried up the stairs. She had only seen the priest hole through the keyhole so she had no idea of what to expect apart from blood-splattered images in her imagination.

When she entered the shadowy room her candle revealed the bleak, whitewashed walls had cobwebbed corners. There were no windows but a small aperture in the sloping roof revealed a square of starry sky. A thin shaft of moonlight fell like a spotlight on a stage waiting for an actor to deliver his soliloquy. She glanced quickly about her. No sign of a whip or ropes. It did not look like her feared image of a torture chamber. Then she saw him.

Garnet sat on a chair in the darkest corner, the whites of his eyes glistening as he stared unseeingly into space. There was clearly no one else in the room – except for Amaru. The cockatoo flew across the room and began muttering, his sulphur crest fanned out in extreme agitation.

The reason became chillingly clear. The light from her candle outlined the metal object in Garnet's hand. A duelling pistol.

Isabel's hand instinctively splayed across her belly to calm the babe kicking in her womb.

Don't be afraid, little one, I'll take care of you.

Afraid to make a move that might startle Garnet, she gave him time to adjust to her presence then carefully lowered the candle to the floor and knelt at his feet. There was a long silence before he spoke.

'Why are you here, girl? I wanted to spare you being involved in my problem.'

'I am your family, Garnet. My place is with you. I cannot bear to see you so unhappy. There is no need for this,' she said with a slight gesture towards the pistol.

'No need?' He waved the pistol and gave such a painful laugh that Amaru began squawking in agitation, dancing on Garnet's shoulder. The bird seemed so afraid he had lost his power of speech.

As if suddenly reminded of the weapon, Garnet rested it on his thigh under his hand. His eyes were now focused on Isabel, his voice bleak – but calm. Once he began he did not falter. At times Isabel wanted to deny his words but he was so lucid she decided to hold her tongue and hear him to the end. It was impossible not to be reminded of *King Lear*.

Poor Garnet is haunted by guilt and the fear of madness. I don't know how but somehow I'm going to give his life a happy ending.

'The truth will out, Isabel, any day now. I not only destroyed my Miranda's last chance of happiness. Now I'm going to ruin Marmaduke's life and yours. It's all over. Everything I did to build my empire, every sharp trick, was to try to win Miranda's love and the boy I wanted to respect me as much as I loved him. I failed all of you.'

Isabel was struck by the pale blue eyes of youth trapped inside an older man's face.

'I had no gift for love. I only have one gift – attracting money. I became the second richest man in the whole of New South Wales.'

Amaru picked up on the note of pride in his voice. 'That's the way to do! That's the way to do it!'

Garnet absently stroked the cockatoo's back. 'But now my Midas touch has deserted me. I mortgaged my rural estates, my George Street properties and shanties. Edwin Bentleigh has just discovered my bank betrayed me. Sold off my mortgages on the cheap.' His voice rose in outrage. 'Damn their greedy hides. To think I used to be a board member of that blasted bank! They could have done the decent thing, warned me they were going to foreclose on me!'

Isabel was thinking rapidly. *The Sydney Herald said Silas is on the board of that same bank! No doubt he holds sway – the scion of a noble English family. My God, is there no end to Silas's infamy?*

She watched his fingers tighten around the pistol.

'My prized Princess Alexandrina Hotel is lost. I'm no threat to Samuel Terry now. I'm not stone, motherless broke but all I've got left is Bloodwood Hall and even this place has a mortgage over it.'

Isabel wanted to comfort him but she was afraid to make a sudden move. She felt sure he would never hurt her but was equally certain suicide was in his mind.

She smiled and gave a shrug of acceptance. 'So what? You faced far greater odds when you arrived in the Colony. You'll re-build your empire with Marmaduke by your side – and me too. And a child to begin the Gamble dynasty. Isn't that worth living for?'

It was then that Isabel felt her heart would break. Garnet was staring past her at the door, his mouth half open, unaware that tears were rolling down his cheeks.

'You came back to me!' he said softly.

Isabel shivered, too scared to turn and face Miranda's ghost. Until a voice said softly, 'Did you ever doubt I would, Garnet?'

Marmaduke was standing in the doorway. She had no idea how long he had witnessed the scene. She was shocked by his transformation, his clothing torn and filthy, his shirt stained with blood, his eyes and mouth bruised and swollen.

She jumped to her feet without thinking. 'My God, what happened to you?'

'Nothing I couldn't handle,' Marmaduke said casually. 'Some runaway lout from Penkivil Park tried to best me. I sent him packing.'

Isabel watched in admiration the way he swaggered across the room. She knew every inch of his body so intimately she was aware that despite his cavalier attitude he was in acute pain. He knelt on one knee and put his arm around Garnet's shoulders.

'Now what's all this crap about losing the Gamble empire? Isn't that what Australia's all about? We make a fortune, lose a fortune, pick ourselves up and start again. You've already proved The System can't keep a Gamble down. Now there's *two* of us. You and I are gunna take on the whole Colony together, Garnet.'

Isabel saw what Garnet had failed to notice while he hung on his son's words. Marmaduke had surreptitiously removed the pistol and placed it out of sight. Gently he drew Garnet to his feet, slung his arm around his shoulder and steered him to the door, then nodded for Isabel to dispose of the pistol.

Her eyes filled with tears of admiration. She followed behind them as Marmaduke walked the broken man down the gallery towards his chambers, the cockatoo flying haphazardly to guide them.

Amaru flew up to perch on the frame of Miranda's portrait chanting, 'Love is blind, love is blind!'

Father and son paused in front of the portrait. Marmaduke looked thoughtful.

'Mother looks proud of you. You finally succeeded in making a man of me, Father.'

Garnet flashed Marmaduke a suspicious look. 'Are you sick or something? That's the first time ever – you called me Father.'

'Behave yourself or it might be the last,' Marmaduke said gently. 'Now, let's get you tucked up in bed. We've got a heap of plans to discuss tomorrow. Rose Alba is coming to live with us. And the new babe is on its way. Isabel and I plan on raising a heap of kids. So I want your advice about the blueprint for Mingaletta. I reckon I've gone off on the wrong track. It might be better to build it *your* way – with a double storey. What do you reckon, Father?'

'I *told* you my plan was far better...!'

Isabel watched the two men in her life arguing amiably as Marmaduke steered Garnet inside the bedroom and closed the door behind them. Isabel was left holding the candle and the duelling pistol, her face wet with tears of happiness.

CHAPTER 53

That autumn had the lingering feeling of an endless summer. Marmaduke rode Dangar towards Bloodwood village to await the arrival of the Gamble carriage from Sydney Town.

Edwin would be travelling with Rose Alba and Marmaduke hoped his friend was coming armed with her adoption papers. As far as Marmaduke knew Silas was still not aware of the existence of the child Isabel had hidden from him since her birth so he would be unlikely to lay claim to her. But Marmaduke was taking no chances. Above all Isabel must be kept calm during the remaining weeks before the birth.

The possibility of the travellers' encounter with bushrangers worried Marmaduke less than the escalation of Silas's violent acts of subterfuge. Since the destruction of Mingaletta all had been quiet until Marmaduke discovered the pressed white roses that had become his weekly ritual. Marmaduke knew this was Silas's unspoken message to Isabel that he would never cease his stalking, never relinquish the power he had held over her mind since she was a child.

En route to Bloodwood village Marmaduke was determined to put the first stage of his plan into action.

I refuse to stand by and have my girl living in fear of a coward who hasn't got the guts to show his hand. Silas de Rolland is going to come face to face with me. I'm gunna put an end to his long reign of terror one way or another.

He turned off the road that led to Bloodwood village and rode through the gates of Penkivil Park. At the sight of the mansion at the end of the avenue of Dutch elm trees he was reminded of the dramatic irony of this moment – the contrast between past and present.

Miranda Gamble, the socially acceptable daughter of Colonel McAlpine, had attended Captain Dench's balls and assemblies in this grand house accompanied by Garnet, her socially tolerated husband. As a boy Marmaduke had attended the Dench son's birthday party. But following his mother's death and Elise's installation as mistress of Bloodwood Hall, Garnet's name had been eliminated from the captain's invitation list. The scandal of Marmaduke's duel and the death of his tutor von Starbold (rumoured in the village to be a German aristocrat) had put the seal on the Gambles being socially ostracised throughout the locality.

Marmaduke was grimly amused to think that it had taken Captain Dench's departure for India with his battalion and the consequent leasing of his estate to Silas de Rolland (known to be an English aristocrat), for Marmaduke to be able to return to Penkivil Park albeit as an unwelcome guest.

The Penkivil Park mansion was not architecturally as ostentatious as Bloodwood Hall but grand enough in the English Georgian tradition to be a showpiece in the county. Silas de Rolland had wasted no time in putting his own stamp on the estate and was already known for the lavish hospitality of his balls, banquets, assemblies and the kangaroo hunts that replaced traditional English fox hunts.

The star performer of this evening's assembly of the Quality would be Josepha St John.

At the front portico finely dressed gentlemen and their ladies were in the process of alighting from their carriages and being ushered inside by servants in silver-trimmed livery. It was known that de Rolland had refused to allow assigned men and women under his roof. All in his service were bona fide English servants who came free – and knew their place.

In the entrance hall Marmaduke placed his card on the silver salver to ensure Silas knew he had called. Then he handed his letter to the tall, cadaverous English butler.

'I'm a friend of Madame St John's. This letter's dead urgent. I'm sure the lady will appreciate its safe delivery.'

With not so much as a flicker of an eyelid at the marked contrast between the elegantly dressed guests and Marmaduke's long hair, moleskin trousers and riding boots, the butler inclined his head and politely assured him of the letter's immediate delivery.

No doubt about Pommie butlers. Their manners run rings around the jumped-up gentry in this colony.

On the point of making his exit Marmaduke's step faltered at the sight of a lady standing apart from the crowd. She wore a low-cut black satin gown, a shawl of black ostrich feathers and the moment she caught his eye she assumed a haughty demeanour. Elise was doing her damnedest to look like a lady.

Marmaduke was divided between ignoring her and bowing in her direction, but decided Elise would be appalled to have people notice she was acquainted with a disreputable Currency Lad. So he enjoyed her shocked expression when he openly gave her a thumbs-up sign of approval. Just then Garnet's friend Magistrate Summerhayes crossed to Elise and offered her his arm to escort her to the assembly room. The flirtatious way she lowered her eyes and clung to Summerhayes's arm gave Marmaduke a sense of grim satisfaction.

Up to her old tricks again. Thank God she's hooked another fish. That's one problem less for Garnet to worry about.

As Marmaduke turned to take his leave he was alerted by the sound of a man's voice behind him. Who could forget the arrogant accent that had ordered Cooper the pugilist to burn his house down?

Marmaduke turned around in the hope of confronting Silas de Rolland but the milling guests concealed him. Marmaduke sauntered down the steps and remounted his horse.

That bastard's as slippery as a Parramatta eel. He's damaged every part of my life yet I still haven't set eyes on the mongrel.

Marmaduke took the horse at a gallop in the direction of Bloodwood village. A few hundred yards before the bridge at Scavengers Creek he caught sight of the Gamble carriage on the opposite bank. Beside the wooden pylons of the bridge that spanned the creek, Thomas stood in front of the carriage, waving his arms as if in warning.

Thomas looks agitated. Shit! The bridge has gone!

Scavengers Creek was a scene of carnage. A giant Bloodwood eucalypt had fallen, smashing the narrow single-carriage bridge into a heap of kindling.

'G'day, Thomas,' Marmaduke called out against the noise of the rushing waters.

Thomas pulled off his tricorn hat and slapped it against his thigh in frustration.

'So what the bloody hell do I do with your guests? Mr Bentleigh checked the Garnet and Rose, but that bloodhouse ain't fit for a little kiddie.'

Edwin emerged from the carriage carrying the sleeping child.

Peering down at the rapid current he looked extremely anxious. Rural life was not Edwin's forte.

'Any bright ideas, Marmaduke? I'm here to deliver this child and sort out your father's *problems*, but I absolutely must be back in court on Monday – or some inept fool will get my client hanged!'

'Hold your horses, mate. I'll get you across, just you watch.'

Shit! I hope that sounded convincing. What the hell do I do now?'

Marmaduke stripped off down to his trousers, removed his boots and tied them together with the cord that he used to tie back his hair. Boots in hand he backed away from the creek and then like a demon bowler at a cricket match made a flying run towards the creek. Pulling up inches from the edge, he swung his arm in an over-arm throw that sent his boots hurling across the creek to be fielded by Thomas.

'Jolly good show!' Edwin shouted in admiration. 'I've always said you'd be good enough to play for the England team at Lords.'

'Over my dead body,' said Marmaduke, 'I'd only bowl *against* you Pommies, mate.'

Marmaduke evaluated the potential force of the creek, aware of the danger of rocks and the unknown degree of submerged debris. He decided he needed a good head start to be able to swim against the current. So he walked Dangar upstream about thirty yards then slipped into the water, drew the horse in and swam beside him, forced by the strong current downstream, so that they finally emerged on the opposite bank almost level with the carriage.

'Nice day for a swim, Thomas,' he said.

Marmaduke went straight to Rose Alba, who was staring at him and the horse wide-eyed in awe.

Marmaduke felt his heart turn over again at the sight of her sweet, vulnerable little face – so like a miniature Isabel it was uncanny.

He said the words gently. 'Remember me, Rose Alba? I'm your Uncle Marmaduke.'

She nodded. 'You told me the story of the little black boy and his friend the kangaroo.'

'Plenty more stories where that came from, sweetheart.'

He took her hand and showed her how Dangar liked to have his nose patted. Standing back, watching the little girl learn to trust the horse before they made the crossing together, he had a quiet exchange with Edwin.

'I take it you have all the legal stuff in hand? I don't want the traps to pick me up on a charge of kidnapping Rose Alba. And I can't guarantee Silas won't wake up to her real identity. The crazy bastard's obsessed with his so-called royal Plantagenet bloodline. So I want the law on my side – for once.'

'The adoption papers are signed, sealed and delivered by Isabel's aunt. She was adamant the child must be reunited with Isabel now but the lady herself is not yet fit to travel. Don't worry. Maeve said to assure you she is taking good care of Elisabeth Ogden at our Woolloomooloo house.' Edwin looked discomfited. 'You understand why your family could no longer stay in the Gamble family suite at the Princess Alexandrina Hotel?'

'The Bank of New South Wales foreclosed on it. Yeah, I heard. Garnet got done like a dinner – thanks to Silas de Rolland's *recommendations* to his board.'

Edwin apologised profusely that Garnet had mortgaged his properties against his advice and without his knowledge.

'Not your fault, mate. But is Bloodwood Hall safe? It would kill Garnet if he lost that. He built the place to impress Mother.'

'Safe for the time being. And Mingaletta's deeds are now in your hands so at least you and Isabel will have a roof over your heads.'

Marmaduke gave a forced laugh. 'Burnt to the ground, mate. Thanks again to Silas de Rolland. But don't worry, I've just delivered a letter to Penkivil Park that's likely to force a confrontation.'

Edwin closed his eyes. 'Oh God, not another duel?'

'I would if I could, mate, but there's no way that so-called gentleman would lower himself to accept a challenge from *me*. In his eyes I'm not only his social inferior. I'm the son of the convict transported on Silas's crooked evidence. I'm beyond the pale, mate.'

'I'll advise you of the legal measures you can take, Marmaduke, limited as they are without proof of de Rolland's crimes. But promise me you will stop short of murder.'

Marmaduke looked at him levelly. 'No promises, mate. I'll do whatever needs to be done. I won't have my wife living in fear of what he'll do next. My problem is to find a way to remove the scoundrel from

Isabel's life without losing everything that matters to me – Isabel, my kids, my liberty. If I got killed, Silas would claim her and Rose Alba.'

Both were aware that Rose Alba was happily talking to the horse. Edwin told him of their encounter with a bolter during the journey and Rose Alba's plucky response.

'That child seems to see everything, good or bad, as high adventure.'

Marmaduke was suddenly serious. 'I'll give that little kid the best life I can afford. But the fire was a real setback. By the way, mate, Isabel doesn't know Mingaletta was burnt to the ground. I gave her the impression we lost a couple of rooms in a blaze from a campfire that got out of control. No hint there was any connection to Silas bloody de Rolland. But it means I've got to go like the clappers to rebuild it – Isabel's determined to give birth there!'

Edwin said quietly, 'I've found you a safe loan. An English settler newly arrived in the Colony is willing to put up the money on a two-year loan at rock-bottom interest rates.'

'Jesus! Who is he? Santa Claus?'

'You've always claimed the English are an eccentric race and for once I'd have to agree. I would suggest you don't argue with good luck. Just sign your name beside The Far Horizon Agricultural Company and the loan is yours.'

Marmaduke clapped him on the shoulder. 'Edwin, your blood is worth bottling!'

Suddenly light of heart Marmaduke crossed to Dangar and talked to him as he would to a mate, briefing the horse and Rose Alba about what was now expected of him. Then he turned to the men.

'Righto, who's Dangar's first passenger?'

Thomas quickly backed down. 'I can't swim. Besides there's only one horse to ride on the other side.'

Edwin tentatively suggested he would stay overnight at the inn and try his luck in the morning.

'Pikers, both of you!' Marmaduke said amiably. 'I'm not letting you off the hook, Edwin. You mightn't be too hot as a swimmer, but you can hold on to Dangar and he'll do the swimming for you.'

Edwin nodded unhappily but Marmaduke turned to find Rose Alba had put her hand trustingly in his.

'May I have a ride on Dangar, please, Uncle?'

Marmaduke bent down on one knee and stroked her hair. 'Rose Alba, you're a girl after my own heart. You're as brave as your big sister Isabel. She can't wait to meet you. So over you go! I'll swim beside you – we'll be across the creek in two shakes of a lamb's tail.'

He hoisted Rose Alba onto the horse's back and walked with them some yards upstream where it was possible to enter the water.

'Can you sing me a song, Rose Alba? Dangar loves music. Right. Now hang on tight, I'll be beside you all the way.'

They entered the water and, although buffeted by the current, they swam across the creek with Rose Alba singing 'God Save the King'.

Safe on the opposite bank, Rose Alba called to Edwin who was standing nervously awaiting his cue.

'It's easy, Mr Edwin.'

Thomas released one of the carriage horses from the harness and walked him upstream to the safest place to cross with Edwin on his back. Marmaduke was amused to see his friend's eyes were closed all the way.

He's a tiger in the courtroom, but as nervy as a kitten in the bush.

When Edwin was safely deposited at their side, his suit dripping and his face blanched, Rose Alba clapped her hands in delight.

'Isn't this fun, Uncle Marmaduke? Can we do this again?'

Marmaduke rocked with laughter. 'Rose Alba, you were born to be a Currency Lass! And sweetheart, there's no higher compliment than that in my book.'

Edwin, shivering with cold, changed into Marmaduke's dry shirt and Rose Alba's wet dress was covered by Marmaduke's jacket as she rode pillion behind him. Marmaduke enjoyed the feeling of being her shield from the wind, her little hands clasped around his waist.

Rose Alba kept up a string of curious questions about everything they passed. When a kangaroo hopped to the side of the track and cocked its head to one side as they rode past, the child was enchanted.

'I saw a drawing of a kangaroo in a book. I didn't know they were *real*!'

Despite his pleasure in her company Marmaduke grew tense as they rode past the gates of Penkivil Park. Every window in the mansion was alight and the sound of chatter was suddenly hushed, followed by the beautiful strains of a woman singing. There was no mistaking the quality of Josepha St John's voice and Marmaduke's seductive memories of her lush body came unbidden.

Rose Alba's piping tones jerked him back to the present. 'What a lovely house. Who lives there, Uncle?'

'Nice enough house, but the man who lives there isn't nice at all. Don't worry, we'll have plenty of parties of our own now you're here, sweetheart.'

Edwin tried to sound casual. 'That sounded like Josepha St John's voice.'

'It was. I've invited her to come over and sing for us at Bloodwood Hall in between her concerts at Penkivil Park.'

Edwin blinked. 'Good God, that's opening the door to trouble!'

'There's no saying she'll come, but I told her I'd invite her. Don't worry, Silas de Rolland's too much of a coward to front up at Bloodwood. He only gets pleasure from manipulating others to carry out his dirty work.'

Edwin was clearly not convinced and remained silent for the remaining few miles.

On their arrival Rose Alba was in awe of the size and grandeur of Bloodwood Hall and Marmaduke was reminded it must seem like a palace to her in contrast with the only house she had ever known, a two-room tumbledown cottage in a rural English hamlet.

When he lifted her down from the horse, Rose Alba looked anxious.

'Oh dear, look at my dress. The red has run from my petticoat!'

'Don't worry, you look just perfect! Come on, Isabel's dying to meet you.'

Marmaduke left Bridget to show Edwin to his room. He carried Rose Alba up to the nursery were Isabel was preparing Queenie's old bedroom.

The moment Isabel saw them Marmaduke recognised the flash of panic in her eyes. He knew this long-awaited moment of reunion was something his wife must handle alone. He should withdraw as soon as possible.

Isabel stared at them. She only managed to stammer out, 'You're both wet. Is it raining?'

'It's a long story, it'll keep for later,' he said quickly.

Bedraggled as she was, Rose Alba made Isabel a deep curtsey. Her polite speech sounded as if it had been drilled into her as carefully as a catechism.

'I am so very pleased to meet you. Aunt Elisabeth sends you her fondest wishes. I will be no trouble at all. I'm four years old but tall for my age. And I'm very quiet – well most of the time.'

Isabel nodded and smiled but she was nervously fingering her throat as if trying to free the words trapped inside her. Marmaduke decided he must break the ice.

'Rose Alba told me about her exciting journey along the highway with Edwin. *A toll man* stopped their carriage and everyone had to give him their money,' he said significantly.

Isabel looked bewildered. 'But there isn't any toll house.'

'Yes, there *is* dear,' Marmaduke corrected politely. 'You know the toll man, *Mr Bolter*. He wears a handkerchief across his face!'

Isabel turned pale. 'Oh, my goodness, *that* Mr Bolter!'

'Yes,' the child said helpfully, 'and Mr Edwin even had to hand over his gold watch to pay the toll!'

'Yeah,' Marmaduke added firmly. 'But all's well that end's well.'

Rose Alba explored the other room where she was to sleep. Isabel was trembling, so Marmaduke crossed to her and folded her in his arms.

'You've nothing to be afraid of – the kid loves you already.'

'But I don't know what to say to her! I've rehearsed the words for years but I can't remember them.'

Marmaduke cupped her face in his hands. 'I taught you how to overcome your fear of water. I taught you how to make love – even how to cry. You don't need me to teach you this. It's all inside you, Isabel. Just open your heart to her – that's how you won *me*.'

He spun around at the door and gave her the thumbs-up sign of total confidence. 'You can do it, girl. I know you can.'

Out in the corridor Marmaduke pressed himself against the wall and listened for the words he hoped would come.

He heard Isabel say softly, 'I have been waiting to meet you again. I do hope you will be happy here, Rose Alba.'

'Oh yes, I will, Sister. I saw a kangaroo in your garden. Can I play with him?'

'Yes, of course. But it's a mama kangaroo. The baby in her pouch is called a joey.'

There was a little silence. 'What would you like me to call *you*? Are you *really* my sister? My aunt? Or my cousin? Aunt Elisabeth said you would tell me one day.'

There was no reply so Rose Alba covered the silence. 'When I was a little girl Aunt Elisabeth told me when I grew bigger you might ask me to live with you. I'm four and a half now. Is that big enough?'

Marmaduke heard the cry in Isabel's voice.

'Rose Alba, I want you to live with us for ever and ever. Please, may I have a hug?'

Marmaduke sighed with relief when he heard Rose Alba's whisper.

'Are they happy tears? I'd give you my handkerchief, but I lost it when I swam across the creek on Dangar's back.'

'What happened?!'

'The bridge fell down. Uncle Marmaduke swam beside me all the way so I was quite safe.'

'Yes,' said Isabel, 'he's rather good at that!'

Marmaduke finally knew it was safe to leave when he heard the lovely sound of two little girls laughing together.

CHAPTER 54

Isabel had one overwhelming fear that she refused to express in words in case she gave it energy and made it reality. This was the safety of those she loved deeply, Marmaduke, Rose Alba and the little one who was the constant companion inside her body.

Starved for years of the opportunity to release her maternal instincts, in the two days since Rose Alba's arrival at Bloodwood Hall she had watched the child with hungry eyes, trying to store in her mind every word, every expression and gesture as the little girl explored with wonder the new world of the mansion, the garden full of exotic plants, birds and animals.

Isabel understood her enchantment. From an isolated hamlet Rose Alba had been set down in the Garden of Eden.

Isabel knew that Marmaduke's air of secrecy involved measures for their protection. He had been careful to define the child's boundaries. Rose Alba was free to wander anywhere in the house but must not go outside into the garden without him or Isabel to accompany her. Isabel knew that Marmaduke had alerted every house servant about the need to guard the child's safety and had instructed Murray Robertson to brief their assigned men to be on the look out for the appearance of strangers on the estate. All were given descriptions of Silas de Rolland and the pugilist Cooper, the man with the metal nose.

But Isabel knew these measures were not foolproof. The anonymous envelopes containing the white roses had increased but no one admitted seeing them delivered. Someone at Bloodwood Hall must be in the pay of Silas.

Isabel was touched to see that the child had instantly adopted her new grandfather and fetched Garnet anything he wanted, placed a footstool at his feet unprompted, and sat beside him, wide-eyed at the cleverness of Amaru, the magical cockatoo who talked with a human voice.

Now as she trailed through the house behind Rose Alba, Isabel felt oddly uneasy when the child stopped at the far end of the picture gallery in front of the portrait that most fascinated her. Miranda.

'She's very beautiful, isn't she?' Isabel said. 'That's Uncle Marmaduke's mother.'

'Indeed yes, Sister.' Rose Alba cocked her head on one side. 'But not quite as lovely as she *really* is. Her eyes are kinder. A bit sad. Why doesn't she eat with us?'

'Eat with us?' Isabel felt conscious of the chilly aura that was almost tangible at this end of the galley. 'What do you mean? Marmaduke's mother isn't with us anymore.'

My God, what does she know about death?

'Yes, she is. I met her yesterday in the garden. When you sat in the summerhouse and fell asleep. This lady told me she taught Amaru to speak.'

'Garnet must have told you that, dear. You're mistaken.'

Rose Alba politely shook her head. 'She showed me the birdcage. She said a bad man poisoned all her little birds. He lives at Penkivil Park and I must never speak to him.'

Isabel felt faint and steadied herself against the wall. No one had ever linked Silas's name to the disappearance of those budgerigars. Garnet had only said someone had forgotten to close the aviary door. She distracted the child from Miranda and suggested they hurry downstairs and join everyone for breakfast. But her thoughts were in turmoil.

Rose Alba can see the Other! She's inherited it from me – and, God forbid, from Silas.

'Today is a day you'll never forget, Rose Alba. We've planned a special surprise for you,' Marmaduke told the child at the breakfast table where the whole family was gathered in company with Edwin and Rhys. As usual they were was serving themselves breakfast from the dishes on the sideboard, so the conversation was relaxed, free from the eavesdropping of servants.

'Do you know what the surprise is?' Rose Alba whispered to Isabel.

Isabel nodded. 'Yes, but my lips are sealed, darling.'

Rose Alba looked in turn at Garnet, Edwin, Queenie and Rhys Powell but realised by their expressions they were all sworn to secrecy.

'I will tell you one thing,' Isabel confided, 'it begins at noon – that's when both hands on the clock are together at the top. And it would please Queenie if you wore that lovely new party frock that she made for you.'

Rose Alba nodded happily and Isabel had no doubt that as soon as breakfast was over she would seek out Bridget and the three Marys and try to learn the secret.

But she also suspected Marmaduke's surprise was a blind for something else. His air of innocence was so convincing Isabel knew he must be lying.

Marmaduke felt edgy as he surveyed the scene. He had initiated an idea to welcome the child to her new home – a garden party at which everyone, including the house servants, would be dressed in make-shift fancy dress. He had taken out of storage the small theatre and puppets for the Punch and Judy shows Miranda had performed for him and which he had loved as a child.

The puppets' faces and limbs were in good condition but the clothes were moth-eaten and dusty so he had co-opted Queenie and Bridget to sew fresh costumes for them.

No other children lived on the estate but for the past two days Rose Alba had introduced herself to all the servants, the gardeners, blacksmiths and carpenters. Her questions about their work had been so genuinely interested that she had won a coterie of admirers among the transportees, who had either been forced to leave families behind them, or knew they had little chance of having children of their own in a colony that was so short of women.

Marmaduke knew how much the child loved to sing so he had planned for the Punch and Judy performance to be followed by a concert. He strode around the garden where the new pianoforte had been placed beside a small raised terrace that would serve as a stage.

He listened anxiously as Rhys Powell tuned the instrument. Isabel, albeit a gifted actress, was not noted for her singing so she would accompany the performers.

'I know you have perfect pitch, Rhys, but this instrument must be tuned to top professional standard worthy of the world famous guest artiste I've invited to perform here. No doubt you've read about the celebrated Josepha St John, who Barnett Levey brought to the Colony?

Rhys looked flustered when Marmaduke announced the name.

'Indeed I have, sir. I shall do my level best, I will. But are you quite certain the lady shall be performing here today? The village has it that the lady has been engaged to entertain Mr de Rolland's guests at Penkivil Park tonight.'

'Yeah. So I heard. As a special favour to a friend, I reckon she'll be here to entertain my new daughter this afternoon.'

Marmaduke's show of confidence was fast deflating. There had been no word from Josepha since he delivered his invitation that offered to send the Gamble carriage to wait for her at the gates of Penkivil Park at half eleven this morning in the hope she would be free to honour him with a farewell performance.

For the child and for me. And to show Isabel she has no need to be jealous. Maybe Josepha never got my note. Or else it's her idea of payback. Or Silas is manipulating her, too. What the hell, I'll send Thomas as arranged just in case.

He glanced up at the French windows of the nursery, where Queenie had been asked to read to Rose Alba as a ploy to keep her occupied and unaware of the preparations for the entertainment.

I now know how nervous Barnett Levey feels before every performance.

Marmaduke glanced at his watch, feeling a sense of panic. Only half an hour remained before the scheduled overture for beginners. Virtually every portable chair in the house had been brought into the garden and arranged on three sides of the oval-shaped terrace that would serve as the stage. He had had the carpenters build a light timber proscenium arch from which hung the elaborate green velvet, gold tasseled drapes he had commandeered from a set of dining-room windows. These curtains were so lavish in size that they also acted as wings to conceal the entertainers who were ready to take their cue.

His final touches were the pots of blooming shrubs that were aligned on either side of the stage and a well-padded piano stool for Isabel's comfort beside the pianoforte in front of the stage. And although the sun was shining brightly, as a tribute to the theatrical profession he had arranged little oil lamps around the apron of the stage.

Marmaduke was pleased to see that all the servants who were racing around setting up platters of food and drinks on the trestle table had entered into the mood of the day and wore begged or borrowed finery. Even some of the assigned men, who were already loitering on the edge of the garden, wore paper hats or masks. Some had drawn moustaches and beards on their faces with charcoal. Rhys Powell sported the outfit of a Welsh bard, Murray Robertson was striding about in his full Highland regalia. Edwin, the most conservative member of the party and whose luggage was still in Bloodwood village, appeared wearing a borrowed striped mariner's jersey, a scarf knotted around his head, and one of Queenie's hoop earrings – a most unwilling pirate.

'I feel a damned fool, Marmaduke,' he hissed.

'We all do, Edwin, but Rose Alba will be tickled pink and that's all that matters.'

Marmaduke wore the simple, romantic garb of a seventeenth-century Shakespearean actor, his full-sleeved white shirt unlaced at the chest, legs covered by tight breeches, silk stockings and silver-buckled shoes, a velvet cloak folded back over his shoulders, his hair tied back and topped by a velvet cap.

Edwin stood at this side. Despite his piratical appearance his manner was subtly transformed as if ready to go into court to fight a difficult case.

'This is a lovely way for a father to introduce his newly adopted daughter, but as a matter of interest, is Isabel aware Madame St John is the star of the show?'

'Not exactly,' Marmaduke admitted as he checked the time by his pocket watch. 'I'm not even sure Josepha will come. But I wanted to give Isabel the chance to hear the greatest singer I've ever heard in my life before she leaves New South Wales forever. And for Isabel to see that Josepha's my friend, nothing more.'

Edwin sighed in resignation. 'You might know everything about women, old chap, but I suspect you still have a fair bit to learn about wives.'

'I feel like a dog trying to learn new tricks, mate.'

Marmaduke was preoccupied as he glanced again at his watch. At the thought of Josepha he plucked a quotation that jumped to mind.

'*What's done cannot be undone.*'

The moment he said the words he froze. 'Shit! I can't believe I said that! It's bad luck to quote from The Scottish Play.'

'*Macbeth*? But surely that's merely a superstition for actors.'

Marmaduke was already outdoors as the antidote to the superstition demanded and he spun around three times on the spot then spat into the garden.

Edwin looked astounded. 'Have you gone stark, raving mad?'

'No, mate, that's what actors do to counteract the bad luck. Klaus von Starbold was an actor. So I'm not taking any chances!'

'Klaus von Starbold? What on earth has he got to do with this?'

Marmaduke had forgotten Edwin was unaware of his biological discovery.

'Everything, mate. But it's a long story so I'll fill you in some other time.'

Marmaduke was now resigned that Josepha was not going to appear. Everyone was assembled in their seats and the assigned men sprawled on the special tarpaulin for their use when Garnet Gamble made his grand entrance swathed in a linen sheet toga, a wreath of gum leaves around his head like some eccentric Roman senator with Amaru perched on his shoulder. At his side Isabel looked amazingly beautiful in a loose flowing robe, Queenie in a silver-threaded sari and Rose Alba was dressed like a little princess in a muslin dress embroidered with white roses.

The child led Garnet to the special seat reserved for him in the front row.

Platters of food were passed around among the assigned men and each was given a mug of ale for the toast to His Majesty, though Marmaduke did not doubt they would need to be refilled at the stage of the toast.

Isabel's conclusion of the overture at the pianoforte drew

encouraging applause and the curtains were drawn back enough to allow Marmaduke to take centre stage, making a sweeping bow that encompassed his audience as he asked everyone to raise their glasses in a toast to the memory of George Barrington.

There was an audible murmur of, 'Who the hell's Barrington?'

Marmaduke responded with a smile. 'An Irishman none of us should ever forget. Barrington is said to have written and spoken the prologue for the first ever theatrical play performed on Australian soil, only one year after the arrival of the First Fleet. The play was Farquhar's comedy, *The Recruiting Officer,* performed on the Fourth of June 1789 to celebrate His Majesty King George III's birthday,' he said as he looked across at the rows of assigned men, 'by a cast of *convict actors* to an audience of marines and assigned men, and attended by Governor Arthur Phillip.

'To quote a couple of lines from what is known as Barrington's speech: *True patriots, all, for be it understood, We left our country for our country's good.'*

There was a rousing cheer and all mugs of ale were soon emptied.

After the cheering subsided, Marmaduke bowed deeply to Rose Alba before addressing the whole audience.

'Ladies and gentleman, today is a special Command Performance to welcome to these shores Miss Rose Alba.' After the applause he continued. 'This young lady is my wife Isabel's *half-sister*. She has graciously consented to make her home with us at Mingaletta as soon as the carpenters have completed the building repairs.'

'Very soon I hope – I can't hold on much longer,' Isabel said intending the words for Marmaduke's ears but the natural projection of her voice carried it to all present.

The assigned carpenters, already fuelled by ale, called back, 'Don't you worry, Mrs Gamble!'

Marmaduke continued, 'Rose Alba, the white rose of York, is now our legally adopted daughter and from this day onwards will by law bear the name of Gamble!'

'Hear, hear!' roared Garnet Gamble.

On his shoulder Amaru squawked in excitement, 'That's the way to do it!'

The applause was punctuated by cheers. Rose Alba had already won all hearts.

Marmaduke gestured to the closed curtains behind him, 'And now for the delight of everyone, including those of us who rejoice in Celtic ancestry – which is half the population of New South Wales – may I present "Miss Bridget and Friend".'

The curtains parted to a fiddler's rendition of a lively Irish air to which Bridget danced an Irish jig with great dexterity, her feet tapping furiously, her arms hanging straight to her sides in the style of the dance, and a flash of her ankles and buckled heeled shoes drawing roars of approval from the predominantly Irish male audience as well as a look of surprised admiration from Rhys Powell.

Next the curtains drew back to reveal a Punch and Judy box theatre on stage, just large enough to hold Marmaduke and Murray Robertson, who had rehearsed the traditional play. The rogue Punch was cheered by the convict element even when he beat up his puppet wife, Judy, and the puppet policeman was booed by the partisan crowd.

Queenie performed an Indian dance and Marmaduke felt himself transported to the past. When she danced Queenie looked as young as he first remembered her.

Marmaduke then faced the moment he must apologise for the inability of his star entertainer to appear.

From the stage Marmaduke paid a glowing tribute to the gifts of the American Nightingale. He was just about to fabricate an excuse for her non arrival when his eye caught a flash of scarlet moving through the garden towards him.

'I am now proud to present to you an artiste whose magical voice will be remembered by all who hear her. The American Nightingale, my dear friend, Madame Josepha St John!'

And as all faces turned in the direction in which he gestured, on perfect cue a heavenly voice broke into a thrillingly sustained high note. And there, walking through the garden towards them, her arms outstretched as if to hold them all in her embrace, was the magnificent Josepha St John, swathed in gold-striped red velvet that generously revealed enough of her pale arms and generous bosom to showcase the legendary 'diamonds'.

What a woman! Trust Josepha to make an unforgettable entrance.

Isabel's place at the pianoforte was smoothly taken by Federico and the enthralling performance held the audience spellbound.

Isabel was now free to sit back and enjoy the performance but Marmaduke froze when he saw the expression on her face.

Isabel was exhausted. Marmaduke's idea for them all to entertain Rose Alba was lovely in theory but this concert needed a week's rehearsal. What did Marmaduke expect of her as an accompanist with no one to turn the pages? *I'm not Mozart or Beethoven! I'm a woman only weeks away from giving birth. And trying to pretend I don't know that my house burnt down. Nobody tells me anything! And now I'm face to face with the gorgeous Josepha St John and I look like a dumpling!*

Her eyes filled with tears of frustration that turned to anger when Josepha drew Marmaduke on stage to sing a passionate aria to him. He looked as lithe and boyish as Romeo. When Josepha plucked the scarlet flower from her bosom and gave it to Marmaduke – he kissed the flower! It didn't matter to Isabel that the lyrics of Josepha's song involved two lovers whom fate had forced to part forever.

Isabel felt white-hot with fury.

That's my husband you're making love to – you female predator!

She was just about to gather up her skirts and cross to Garnet's side to sit with Rose Alba when she felt taken over by a sudden, inexplicable change of mood. The frightening drop in temperature she had known all her life was a warning of the appearance of the Other.

Rose Alba was not in her place but she had seen Marmaduke lead her to the wings to watch Josepha's act and be ready to lead the audience in singing, 'God Save the King' at the conclusion of the concert.

Logic told her that Rose Alba was safe under Marmaduke's eye, but Isabel's instincts were stronger than logic. All the sounds around her seemed to fade. Her senses acutely attuned like a deer that smells danger. Something was terribly wrong – and it wasn't in the little theatre. It was something out of sight. *In the garden.*

Unable to cry out Isabel picked up her skirts and ran towards the rose garden.

Garnet looked around his domain. He felt sure that if it weren't for his curiosity to hold the coming babe in his arms, he could die a happy man at that moment. *Everything I have ever wanted is within easy reach – thanks to iIabel. Even an uneasy truce with Marmaduke.*

All in his world, bond and free, were riveted by the diva's performance on stage. Garnet returned Rose Alba's excited wave as she hurried from the wings, headed for the house hand in hand with Black Mary.

Garnet was not surprised. *The little poppet's been beating a track to the water closet all morning. Obedient child. Remembering not to go anywhere unaccompanied.*

Rose Alba had only taken a few days to steal his heart. Her engaging mind and sunny smile had brought love and laughter into the house he had built in the vain hope of raising a family of Miranda's children. The house that had attracted nothing but recriminations, anger, betrayal, tragedy and years of bitter estrangement from the son he loved more than his own life. Isabel had made a man of Marmaduke.

Garnet was startled to find himself sending up a begrudging, sideways prayer for the first time in years.

There must be a God up there somewhere. Just when I decided He didn't give a damn about me, He brought Isabel into my life, the babe she and Marmaduke created and that little girl I will love as my own kin. I hate to admit it after all the bad cards you've thrown at me, God – this day was worth waiting for.

But the thought was no sooner in his head than he had a premonition that everything was about to change. Why? Everyone seemed to be in place. Isabel was intently watching Marmaduke on stage – revelling in his role as the focus of the diva's love song. *Damn it all, I suppose it's not unreasonable that he has inherited a theatrical gene or two from that damned Klaus von Starbold.*

Garnet told himself that the Hessian who had stolen Miranda's heart was dead. And he was alive.

He was just about to join the audience's wild applause when his eye was caught by the distant figure in the garden. He froze. *That face.* He strained his eyes to focus on it. And then with slow certainty he knew that the past had come back to haunt him.

Garnet was outraged that God had created a man who was so handsome, so noble in bearing that it gave no hint to the evil of his mind. The man who had given false evidence at his trial.

Blinded by fury and gasping for breath, Garnet rose and broke into a run. Silas de Rolland was in his rose garden! Bold as you please. Not a moment to lose. The villain was walking away from him, smiling down into the eyes of a little girl he held by the hand...Rose Alba Gamble.

Isabel was confused to find the rose garden deserted. She stumbled along the path towards the house. At the sight of Black Mary returning with a platter of food for the guests, Isabel grabbed hold of her with shaking hands.

'Where is she, where's Rose Alba? I saw her leave with you.'

The Aboriginal girl was wide-eyed with fear at Isabel's unexplained rage. She mumbled something inaudible about 'the gentleman'.

'What gentleman? What did he look like?"

'Like *you*, ma'am. He asked the child to show him the white rose garden. The gentleman told the child you wouldn't mind – he was her cousin.'

Silas! Isabel ran towards the white rose garden feeling she was trapped in one of her own nightmares. If she concentrated hard enough she could make herself wake up. Until she saw the carriage in the turning circle in front of the house and knew the truth. Nothing could ever wake her.

The man waiting in the driver's seat. The same man who had driven her to the London docks and made sure she boarded the *Susan*. Cooper, Silas's henchman. The pugilist forced to work for him because Silas held the evidence he was wanted for murder. He now wore a metal shield over his nose.

Isabel screamed out to him. 'Cooper, for pity's sake, tell me what Silas has done with my daughter!'

Cooper frowned but turned his head away.

It was then she saw a movement inside the carriage. Silas sat with Rose Alba beside him, his gloved hand covered the child's whole face except for her terrified eyes.

Silas's voice was silky, gentle. Were his words an echo of the past inside her head? Or were they alive and happening right now?

Silas looked at Isabel then stroked the child's hair. 'What a pretty little girl you are, sweetheart.'

Isabel's mind went blank with horror. She froze, locked in a space between her childhood memories and the present. For a moment she stood transfixed, sick in the stomach as Silas gently tilted Rose Alba's face to make her look into his eyes.

'When you grow up, *I will ask you to marry me.*'

Isabel saw her fear reflected in Rose Alba's eyes and knew exactly what the child was thinking, feeling.

Rose Alba broke the spell. She twisted her face away from his hands.

'Let me go!'

A wave of cold rage drove Isabel. She hurled herself at the carriage, her foot on the step, her hands gripping the open windowframe of the door, unable to open it.

'Let go of her! I won't let you ruin her life as you did mine.'

Silas smiled at her through the window and gave her a look of appraisal.

'I don't need you any more, Isabel,' he said softly, 'you have grown too old.'

He wrapped his cane against the side of the carriage. 'Drive on, Cooper!'

Isabel screamed out Marmaduke's name then yelled at Rose Alba.

'I won't ever leave you!'

They all turned at the roar of a man's voice. Garnet Gamble was racing towards them brandishing a duelling pistol. He stopped short, saw the whole situation so aimed his pistol at Cooper.

'One move and you're a dead man!'

Rose Alba's clear voice screamed Marmaduke's name in a high-pitched chant of desperation. Isabel clung to the door, one foot still on the step as the horses pawed the ground in agitation. She didn't know how long she could manage to cling to the carriage but when Cooper pulled the horses to a sharp halt despite Silas's orders, she seized the moment and managed to climb inside. She clawed Silas's face with both hands.

'Run, little one, run home!'

When Rose Alba jumped free from the carriage Isabel smiled despite the pain when Silas's cane struck her face.

Rose Alba ran past Garnet screaming Marmaduke's name.

Marmaduke leapt down from the stage the moment he saw Isabel leave and realised that Garnet was running in the same direction. Then he heard Rose Alba calling his name. He ran to the carriage where Garnet was yelling blue murder and waving a pistol in frustration, afraid to fire at Silas in case he hit Isabel.

Marmaduke lifted Isabel free from the carriage and held her in his arms but his eyes were fixed on the face of the man inside the carriage, who was banging his cane on the roof and ordering Cooper to drive on.

Cooper sat with folded arms, refusing to budge.

'Changed sides have you?' Marmaduke asked.

Cooper looked at Marmaduke fearlessly and jerked his head at his master. 'I'm armed. He's not. I've done all his dirty work. I can kill a man and sleep nights. But I don't hurt no little girls.'

'I believe you.' Marmaduke said. *Thank Christ for Newgate "thieves' honour"*.

People were running around like a disturbed hornet's nest but keeping a healthy distance from the carriage. Only Edwin, Murray and Rhys drew closer.

Marmaduke glanced back at Rose Alba, who was the calm in the eye of the storm beside Queenie. Garnet waved a pistol, almost incoherent with rage but threatening to fight Silas de Rolland. Bridget shouted at him not to be a fool and Amaru screeched his head off.

Josepha St John stood a little apart from all of them, staring at Silas, her face a white mask of fury.

Marmaduke knew this was the moment he must sublimate his rage until the time he needed to let it rip.

As Silas de Rolland made a languid gesture to Josepha to enter the carriage, Marmaduke saw the hands of his enemy were finely shaped, elegant. He felt sickened to think these same hands had caressed and abused the child Isabel. That the mouth now curled in faint amusement was the mouth that had kissed the child Isabel and seduced her with adult passion and lies that had destroyed her innocence – and was now ready to corrupt Rose Alba.

Edwin hurried to Marmaduke's side ahead of Rhys Powell and Murray Robertson. Marmaduke wanted his family safe and to shield them from what was to come.

'Queenie, take Isabel and the child upstairs. I leave them in your hands. They could be suffering from shock.'

If Isabel loses the babe I'll have Silas hanged, drawn and quartered and his head on a pike at the front gate.

With Federico at her heels Josepha moved towards him with intent. Marmaduke was not sure where her loyalties lay. Her luminous dark eyes searched his face, as if memorising it feature by feature. She said the words in a throaty stage whisper.

'Do whatever you have to do, my darling. But handle yourself with care. They don't make men like you any more.'

Marmaduke held her eyes as he kissed her hand then beckoned to Cooper, who had turned his back on his master.

'If you see Madame St John safely wherever she chooses to go – I'll give you a job. No questions asked.'

Cooper hesitated. 'I believe you.'

Marmaduke pulled Silas from the carriage then helped the diva inside it with Federico and nodded when she gave the order, 'To Sydney Town!'

Everyone had dispersed except for Edwin, Rhys and Murray. Marmaduke knew the moment had arrived.

'Silas de Rolland, this day has been a long time coming. The man who lives to see the end of it is never going to forget it.'

The handsome face was the epitome of arrogance. But Marmaduke saw that the pupils of his eyes were strangely cloudy. There was a musty, spice-like smell about him that reminded him of an Eastern bazaar. Laudanum.

'Silas eyed him with contempt. 'You must be as insane as your criminal father if you think you can challenge a de Rolland. Who do you think you are?'

'I'm the man who's going to kill you, mate.'

'Afraid to face me in court, eh? Afraid the law would never convict me on the word of Colonial scum?'

Edwin stepped forwards, his voice cold with authority. 'I'm the Gambles' barrister. I have enough evidence of the crimes you've committed in this Colony to send you to Norfolk Island for the term of your natural – correction *un*-natural – life!'

Marmaduke knew the words were a bluff. Murray kept his pistol trained on Silas as Edwin drew Marmaduke aside.

'We are all witnesses to what de Rolland did tonight. I beg you, Marmaduke, for once allow British law to deliver justice.'

Marmaduke was adamant. 'Too many men of Quality get away with blue murder in this Colony. The crimes this bastard committed against Mendoza, Mingaletta – and *little girls* is only our word against his. If we claimed attempted abduction of a Rose Alba he'd say he was just taking his little *cousin* for a drive – no law against that. You know the mongrel would get off with a slap on the wrist!'

'Let me shoot the bugger,' Garnet demanded. 'I've done time before. I can survive.'

Silas de Rolland looked amused. 'By all means try, Gamble. You're only fit for Bedlam anyway.'

Before Edwin could calm Garnet, Marmaduke saw Silas's smug expression and lost control of his pent-up rage.

'Bugger the law! You're on my property. I make the rules here! Cop this!'

Marmaduke struck him forcibly across the mouth then delivered a backhander that drew blood.

'I've publicly insulted you in front of three witnesses, including a barrister. I'm giving you three choices, de Rolland.

'One. A voyage. A Greek sea captain who hates paedophiles as much as I do can dump you on a desert island for life. Two. If you're too much of a gentleman to fight me, I'll just have to shoot you down like a mad dog with rabies. Three. We can play this out on the duelling field. That gives us both an even chance to kill each other. It's your choice.'

Silas de Rolland shrugged. 'Very well, pistols. I've nothing better to do this afternoon. But before I attend your funeral I'll give you a lesson in how a gentleman conducts himself in a duel. Spare me one of your raggle-taggle Colonial duels. Like the one you fought in vain defence of your mother's *dishonour.*'

Marmaduke was thrown off guard but Garnet gave a bull-like roar as he hurled himself at Silas. It took all four of them to restrain him bodily.

'Trust me, Father. I'll take care of this cur.' He turned to Silas. 'You may have noble ancestors, de Rolland, but for all your pretensions you're the daggy end of the line. You're free to leave amuse yourself with laudanum. And make your Will. At ten tomorrow morning Rhys Powell will escort you to the place we'll meet.'

Marmaduke added, 'Don't even think about bolting. If you're yellow enough to try, I'll hunt you down wherever you go. You'll be the laughing stock of the Colony.' He turned to Murray. 'Get the man a horse,' he said and turned his back on Silas de Roland and walked away.

Inside the house Marmaduke had Edwin draw up a fresh Will that included his children and had it witnessed and signed.

Edwin gave a sigh of resignation. 'You realise, Marmaduke, what will happen if you kill a second man in a duel, albeit under great provocation?'

'Yeah, mate, I'll be socially ostracised. Never get invited to dine at Government House. What a crying shame that'd be, eh?'

They exchanged a grim smile. Both knew it was bravado.

CHAPTER 55

Isabel woke with fright, her body damp with sweat. The sound of kookaburras' laughter mocked the night terrors she had just escaped. The image was so vivid that she was still uncertain whether she had been dreaming or actually visited by the Other. The figure of a man wearing a long black hooded cloak had stood at the foot of her bed. It was the same face she had seen watching her that day on the bank of the river. *Klaus von Starbold.*

Queenie woke up in the chair in which she had been guarding Isabel all night. When Isabel described her dream, she felt chilled by Queenie's calm acceptance.

'Yes. Klaus *was* here last night. I heard his heels click together as he bowed to you. Don't worry, Isabel. He was a man of honour in life. His shade would not hurt you,' Queenie said firmly. 'It isn't their way. Ghosts only return when they have unfinished business.'

'Is that why Miranda comes back to you?'

Queenie sighed. 'Perhaps I'm selfish. I don't *want* her to leave me.'

Isabel crossed to the open door and felt her throat constrict at the sight of the sleeping child. 'Even after everything that happened to her yesterday she looks so peaceful.'

'That child is most resilient. She was born to be happy.'

Isabel insisted on dressing, determined to go downstairs to find Marmaduke, but she made Queenie promise to remain at Rose Alba's side until the child woke.

The house appeared to be deserted but when Isabel saw Garnet stride out the front door to where Davey held the reins of a saddled horse, she hurried after him.

'Where's Marmaduke? What's wrong, Garnet?

'You must rest, m'dear. This is men's business. All will be well.'

Placing his boot in Davey's cupped hands, Garnet hoisted himself into the saddle and rode off at a gallop.

Isabel grabbed hold of Davey and demanded he tell her where the men had gone.

'To the cricket ground, ma'am.'

Oh God, that means Marmaduke's going to fight a duel with Silas!

When Isabel halted the mare at the edge of the oval there was no sign of the duellists or their seconds. From the sunburnt grass around the cricket pitch little eddies of dust were caught by the breeze. The miniature grandstand was empty. There would be no spectators at this match – except for Garnet. He was standing in the shade of a RedGum, his hands flexing at his sides.

Cold with fear, Isabel rode up to him.

'I'm not leaving,' she said defensively. 'Garnet! We must stop this!'

'It's already too late,' he said quietly.

Dear God I'll promise you anything if you'll just keep Marmaduke alive! Silas tried to destroy Rose Alba's innocence as he did mine. But better he should go free than risk Marmaduke's life. What price revenge if Marmaduke dies?

Isabel screamed silently with frustration when she saw all five men ride up, tethering their horses at the far end of the oval in the shade of giant eucalypts.

They sauntered on to the field almost as if they were preparing for a game of cricket. Marmaduke bent his head to listen to Edwin's directions. He was dressed in a plain white shirt open at the throat and moleskin trousers and bare-headed, his hair tied back against the breeze. He looked serious and strained as if he had slept little that night.

Isabel kept saying his name like a prayer, hoping God was listening.

She forced herself to look at Silas. Flanked by Murray Robertson and Rhys Powell, he looked as nonchalant as if a duel were an everyday occurrence. He was dressed in an immaculate morning suit and casually draped his jacket across a bench, balancing his top hat beside them.

Isabel saw his hand linger on the gold knob of the ebony cane, the source of his laudanum.

The four men assembled around Edwin to discuss details of the duel and check the pistols to everyone's satisfaction.

Isabel wanted to charge her horse into the middle of the pitch and force them to put an end to the manly posturing that could end in tragedy just as had happened nine years earlier on this same ground. But she knew that any distraction could be dangerous to Marmaduke's concentration.

Refusing to obey Garnet by leaving, she dismounted and only agreed to conceal herself from sight in the bush.

Seen from this distance Silas looked as handsome as her first childhood memory of him, 'the brave soldier returned from the wars'. Now the wind ruffled his hair, the same colour as hers. Her de Rolland 'double cousin' appeared so youthful she found it difficult to accept that he was close in age to Garnet.

The illusion of gallantry was shattered by Silas's outburst of hostility.

'For God's sake, Bentleigh, what do you think you're playing at? Do hurry along. I've better things to do than give you lessons...No no, that's not how it's done! Don't you Colonials even know how to conduct a proper duel...? Never heard of the Code Duello?'

Edwin's reply was quiet but in no way intimidated. 'If you're such a stickler for the duelling code, de Rolland, why did you fail to appoint your own second?'

'What?' Silas gave a contemptuous laugh. 'And allow another gentleman to witness this farce? A duel must only be fought between men of equal rank.' He flicked his wrist in Marmaduke's direction. 'There's no man more inferior than a convict's spawn.'

Isabel was outraged. She felt the babe kicking in her womb in empathy.

I'm *cursed in being your equal, Silas! If only I were a man I'd kill you.*

Her eyes hungrily followed Marmaduke's every movement, the line of his head, his limbs, the gestures of his fine hands. This man was the centre of her world. He had taught her how to love and created within her body the gift of life. Sunlight highlighted the coil of long dark hair hanging down his back as he walked away from her. He was so virile, so wonderfully alive. Yet seconds from now he could be dead. His name was her prayer.

Marmaduke and Silas stood back to back. She held her breath as they began the measured walk away from each other.

Time was stretched to breaking point as Edwin counted the twenty paces...eighteen, nineteen...

Then it happened. Silas whirled around, aimed his pistol at Marmaduke's back – and fired. Marmaduke staggered. Voices shouted in outrage. Isabel tried to run to him, but Garnet, white in the face, held her back.

'It's not over, lass!'

Edwin and Rhys ran to Marmaduke's side as he rose unsteadily to his feet. His right arm had been hit. Blood stained his sleeve. He tried to steady his pistol with both hands.

Garnet held Isabel against his chest but his eyes never left his son's face and his voice was unnaturally calm.

'Marmaduke has the right to return fire.' He added under his breath, 'Shoot him down like a dog, son!'

Silas stood transfixed, his face contorted with an expression Isabel had never seen before – a look of sheer terror.

It was then Isabel saw that Silas was staring at the thing that she had feared all her life. The Other.

The figure stood behind Marmaduke's right shoulder. All eyes were fixed on Marmaduke as he tried to remain upright and take aim at Silas. No one on the field seemed to be aware of the man in the black cloak as he walked steadily towards Silas. The Other slowly pulled his hood back to reveal his face.

But Isabel saw it wasn't a face at all. In its place was the white death mask of Klaus von Starbold.

Isabel swayed against Garnet. 'Can't you see what I see? That other man in the black cloak?'

Garnet looked confused. 'What other man? You're as pale as a ghost!'

Isabel pointed at Silas. 'Look, Garnet. Look at Silas's face. He can see it too!'

Sweat poured down Marmaduke's forehead and stung his eyes, blurring his vision. His hands shook as he tried to grasp the pistol with both hands. Pain seared along his right arm and he felt oddly surprised to see blood running in rivulets between the fingers of his right hand.

He had a vivid memory of his German father lying at the other end of the pitch – in the exact place where Silas de Rolland now stood rigid, staring at him.

He's afraid. Jesus, he looks like Isabel. What's preventing me from returning his fire? My hands seem frozen – why the Hell can't I fire this bloody pistol?

Silas de Rolland gave a broken cry and staggered back a pace. His face took on an expression of indescribable horror. His eyes bulged as he stared in front of him, his hands raised as if warding off some unseen adversary. He grappled the air a few inches in front of his face then began clawing at his throat.

Silas was choking, desperate to gasp out the words, 'Who – are – you?'

Thrust backwards as if by an unseen force, he lay writhing on the ground.

All four men on the field moved towards him. Murray Robertson bent over him.

Marmaduke staggered up to the prone body, bewildered.

What the Hell do I do now?

Silas's eyes were wide open, his mouth twisted in a ghastly leer.

'I thought I was immortal but he's come for me. The Angel – of Death!

Marmaduke watched in silence as his enemy died with his eyes wide open.

Isabel leant against the trunk of a tree, watching the men circle around Silas de Rolland, arguing about what to do with his body. Garnet hesitated about joining them.

'Go to Marmaduke. I'm all right, Garnet, but I need to be alone for a few minutes.'

Isabel's first instinct had been to thank God for the death of the kinsman who had blighted her life. Instead she chanted a mantra of gratitude that her beloved Marmaduke, though torn and bleeding, was alive.

Aware of the rapidly overlapping voices that fired questions at Edwin as they all stood around the corpse, Isabel was relieved when Garnet whipped off his cravat and tied it around Marmaduke's arm to staunch the flow of blood.

Isabel knew it was her role to go to her husband's side to take care of him but she was suddenly so drained of energy she could not move. She knew she was in shock.

It seemed each man present had the perfect solution about disposing of the body, but no two of them agreed as to what that was.

Ever practical Murray Robertson was closest to Edwin's line of thinking.

'A duel has been fought. A man of Quality canna be made to disappear into thin air. De Rolland took a year's lease on Penkivil Park, his house is full of Exclusives and he's heir to a wee fortune in England. He needs to be given a proper funeral or else the Colonial newspapers will suggest there's been foul play. Ye know how they love to dig their teeth into a juicy scandal.'

Marmaduke's voice was weary. 'Maybe I'm biased because I've already killed one man here, but why hand the Colony a scandal on a plate? No one but us ever needs to know that this duel took place.'

'Quite correct,' said Edwin. 'Silas de Rolland did not die as a direct result of a duel. Any autopsy would show there's not a mark on him. And we are all witnesses to the fact that Marmaduke's pistol never fired a shot.'

There was a pause until Murray asked, 'Exactly *what* did kill him? Heart failure? Laudanum? Fear?'

Rhys said quickly, 'Indeed, fear it was. I saw de Rolland's face full on. I swear to you it was as if the man really was looking into the face of the Angel of Death.'

Isabel was about to go to Rhys's side to confirm her sighting of the apparition but Marmaduke, light-headed from shock, dismissed the idea.

'I reckon we should dump his body miles away in the bush. Then spread some rumour around the village about how he disappeared.'

Garnet Gamble had been silent. He looked coldly down at the body of his enemy from the house of de Rolland.

'Get a crowbar. I've got the perfect place for him to spend eternity.' He paused for dramatic effect. 'Where's the last place the traps would think to look for an English nobleman who's disappeared?'

Marmaduke looked at him in admiration. 'Father, are you suggesting what I think you are?'

'You're damned right I am, son. All you need to do is gemmy off the top of the tomb in my mausoleum.'

Isabel covered her mouth to stop herself laughing at the macabre idea. For a man who was half crazy, Garnet had come up with a better, more devious solution than the combination of three sane men and a barrister.

Garnet was adamant. 'No trap would think of looking for the bastard in *my* grave!'

Isabel felt disoriented as she watched them. They were like senior schoolboys, exhilarated by the solution as they slung Silas de Rolland's body over the back of Garnet Gamble's horse and tried to make a suitably solemn procession, their hats over their hearts, as they wended their way downhill to the Gamble graveyard.

Pale and exhausted, Marmaduke guided Isabel's mare along the track, concerned that she might be suffering from a double dose of shock.

'You all right, love? I'll take you home right now if you're not up to it.'

'I'm fine,' she said crisply. 'I want to make sure Silas really is dead and buried.'

In truth Isabel felt as if she was observing the scene from outside her own body. She kept looking at Silas's limp hands swinging over the horse's side and felt confused by the conflicting childhood memories of those hands. Stroking her hair tenderly. Holding her under the water of the lake until she lost consciousness. Touching her in the dark of night in her bed as a child. Determined to block the images from her mind she nodded approval when Marmaduke leant on his father's shoulder for support.

'This is a generous gesture, Garnet. I know what that mausoleum cost you and what it meant to you to have a grand funeral.'

'Aye, lad, but I don't intend to fall off the twig for years yet. I've got a grandson on the way and this time I don't intend to fail. It will take me a few years to make a real man of *him*.'

Marmaduke gave a hoot of laughter and sought support from his ally.

'Hey, Isabel, are you just going to sit there and not defend your husband's honour?'

Isabel shook her head in irritation. 'What honour? I've got bigger things on my mind right now.'

Murray arrived with a crowbar and the men removed the body from the horse, carried it inside the mausoleum ready to open the sarcophagus.

Isabel waited outside, feeling strangely restless as she listened to them urging each other how to hoist the top off the sarcophagus.

Garnet was giving directions. 'Come on you lads, pull together, that's the style.'

'Jesus, he's as heavy as a dead weight,' said a voice, followed by smothered, embarrassed laughter.

'Shouldn't we say a prayer or something?' Rhys asked.

Marmaduke said, 'Feel free to say whatever makes you happy, but don't ask me to say Amen.'

Murray agreed, 'Aye, but we'd best ask Isabel what faith her kinsman professed. I can do it if he was a Catholic.'

Isabel was so eager to depart the scene she yelled back at them, 'My cousin didn't believe in God. He only believed in the power of the Devil – and himself!'

This was followed by an uneasy silence. The men filed sheepishly out of the mausoleum, advising Rhys to offer up whatever prayer came to mind. And lock up after him.

Marmaduke rejoined her. 'I'd best get you home, sweetheart. Hey, what's wrong?'

Isabel pointed a trembling finger in the direction of the valley. 'What on earth have you done to Mingaletta? I thought it was almost finished. I'd arranged with Queenie to give birth to the babe in our new home! Now you've ruined everything!'

She was crying like a tired child throwing a tantrum, unwilling to stem the flow of her tears.

Marmaduke was ready to promise her the world. 'I'll finish the house in plenty of time, I promise.'

'No, you won't! It's coming right now!'

Marmaduke looked blank. 'It can't be. It's too early.'

'Try telling that to the babe. It's coming, ready or not!'

'Right, I'll get you home to Queenie.'

'No! I'm not going to let Silas de Rolland manipulate my life from the grave. I'm going to give birth to my baby my way – at Mingaletta!'

Before Marmaduke could prevent her, Isabel dug her heels into the mare's flanks and rode off towards the ruins of Mingaletta.

She looked back Marmaduke. He threw up his hands in frustration and winced at the pain in his injured arm.

'You heard the lady. Send for Queenie and bring everything she tells you. We've got a babe to deliver!'

The scene around the new skeletal timber frame of the Mingaletta homestead was chaotic. It looked to Marmaduke like some makeshift hospital on a battlefield with everyone giving each other orders. Only Queenie was calm and in control, directing Marmaduke, Garnet and Bridget to bring her whatever she needed. Garnet for once was subservient to Queenie's orders. The cauldron was bubbling with boiling water over an open fire. Figures were running back and forth with buckets, drawing still more water from the well.

Marmaduke hurried back to Isabel's side. Inside the wine cellar a padded calico palliase had been spread out on the floor for her to lie on and the room was well lit by candles and hurricane lamps hanging from the rafters.

'How are feeling, my love?' he asked gently.

'What a fool question is that?' Isabel snapped, engulfed by the onslaught of another contraction.

Queenie gave him a nod to reassure him this was perfectly normal behaviour at this late stage of labour. She signalled she would return in a moment then slipped outside.

Marmaduke remained calm and soothing in the face of Isabel's demands, smiling despite the savage bite of her fingernails in his flesh as she rode out each contraction. He was oddly comforted by the sight of Klaus von Starbold's gold watch lying open on a makeshift table to register the frequency of Isabel's contractions.

The time between them grew shorter, the contractions more violent. Isabel screamed out words he didn't realise she knew existed. Marmaduke cracked.

He took her face between his hands and fervently assured her.

'I swear by all that is holy, my darling, I will never put you through this hell again. I shall never *ever* lay a hand on you. We will live as brother and sister. I am a swine for making you go through this!'

Isabel caught her breath. 'Oh shut up, Marmaduke. Spare me the melodrama. This is my big scene – not yours!' Her eyes widened. 'Oh God, there's another one coming!'

She gave a deep moan and dug her fingernails into his back.

Standing outside the cellar door, Garnet was deathly pale, shaken by the sound of Isabel's cries and forced to remember the terrible images of Miranda's deathbed and the child trapped in her womb. He felt a glimmer of relief when Queenie's head appeared around the door.

'Whisky, and plenty of it. Pronto!'

Garnet raced for the box of liquor he had brought and delivered it to her.

'Not for me,' Queenie said tartly, 'fill those two big bowls, one of cold water, one hot but not boiling. Towels, and set them up on that trestle table over there.'

She was gone. Garnet followed her instructions, hearing Isabel's deep, guttural cries of labour and Marmaduke's reassuring voice. But there was no sound of a baby's cry.

Isabel's moans suddenly ceased – followed by an ominous silence.

Marmaduke came from the cellar ashen-faced, holding a bundle in his arms. He thrust it in Garnet's arms.

'Queenie says you're to deal with this. It's blue. Never cried. Still-born.' His voice broke. 'Not a bloody sound. Here take it away for God's sake. Isabel needs me.'

A moment later Queenie emerged from the cellar and ran to join Garnet at the trestle table. They massaged the mottled blue chest and limbs of the tiny babe, coating its lifeless little body with whisky before plunging it back and forth between the cold and hot water. Garnet blindly followed Queenie's directions.

Time had ceased to exist. Queenie was exhausted but Garnet refused to give up.

'This is not acceptable to me! I won't allow it.' He yelled at the tiny body. 'Breathe! You can do it!'

His hands were rough and desperate, his heart crying out to hear the wail that never came.

There was no one else in sight, everyone was in the cellar, focused on Isabel, who was sobbing out in denial.

'No! no! Why won't you let me see it?'

Suddenly Garnet froze. Queenie touched his arm. They turned and watched in silence as it moved towards them. The thin stream of mist had no form but seemed to have a life-force of its own.

The filmy outline wrapped around the babe. And then Garnet heard the God-given sound – the cry of life. The babe turned pink and took its first breath.

Garnet picked up the bundle and held it over his head, naked, squirming and wailing. The babe's tiny penis sent a gentle shower down into Garnet's face.

Garnet roared with laughter. 'Angel's piss!'

Queenie sank to her knees, laughing and crying and thanking God, Jesus, the Buddha and all the gods in the Hindu pantheon.

With shaking hands Garnet wrapped the babe in a towel. He raced back to the cellar yelling in triumph and laid his grandson in the arms of his rightful owners.

Marmaduke fingered the miniature gold house on the pendant around Isabel's throat. She lay there exhausted, pale and drenched with sweat. But he had never in his life seen a more beautiful, desirable woman.

'I reckon Josiah Mendoza was dead right. He said something about a man's true home being his wife.'

Isabel's words were slurred with weariness. 'Just as well. You keep burning our house down.'

Marmaduke stroked her hair. 'I know this isn't the perfect time to say this, Isabel. But I need to retract my promise. What I said about never touching you again – to spare you the agony of childbirth. I panicked. The truth is I think I handled the whole performance pretty damned well. I was as cool as a cucumber. So just to put your mind at rest, I'll be more than happy to make a new babe for you – every year.'

When Isabel's mouth hung open in disbelief, he added, 'How about we start trying for a brother for Rufus later tonight, if you're not doing anything?'

Isabel stared at him. 'I can't believe you said that, Marmaduke. I only gave birth an hour ago. You're insatiable!'

'Well, you can't hang a man for his thoughts,' he said with that twist at the corner of his mouth that always gave him away. 'But I'm happy to take a kiss on account.'

He took her sweaty face between his hands and tenderly kissed the tip of her nose. 'Who was it said something like, "Was ever woman so wooed, was ever *man* so won?" Oh yeah, I remember. It was Romeo to Juliet.'

'It was *not*. You're misquoting again to suit yourself. And it was Richard III.'

'I'll lay you five guineas it was Romeo.'

'I haven't *got* five guineas. We're broke, remember? You can't even afford to pay me my contract wages.'

'That's all right, sweetheart. I'll let you work off the debt – in bed.'

Garnet listened to the sound of their mock fight and gave a weary smile of satisfaction. He looked across at Queenie boiling the billy for tea and they exchanged a nod of mutual respect. The whisky had all been used up in a good cause.

Garnet knew in his heart that Miranda would never again return to him in this lifetime. But to sustain him he had the wonder of that moment when she bent over the stillborn baby and gave it the kiss of life. Then she had turned to Garnet and smiled at him.

Garnet looked through the doorway of the cellar at the make-shift birthing room. On Marmaduke's prompting he had sent Murray Robertson back to the house to bring Rose Alba to see her new baby brother. The little girl now lay asleep, curled up like a kitten in a rug at her mother's feet. Marmaduke lay beside Isabel, loving her passionately with his eyes as she held the babe to her breast.

Garnet said the words in his heart. *This is the happiest day of my entire life, Miranda. What we began – you, me and that damned Klaus – the unholy mess we made of our lives. Well, it's all come right in the end. It took the three of us to create Marmaduke – and my dynasty. Now all I've got to do is build another fortune.*

Struck by a thought that came in a sudden shaft of light, Garnet's laughter was wild and long.

Queenie stood over him arms akimbo and demanded, 'Don't tell me you've chosen *tonight* to throw another one of your crazy turns!'

Garnet tried to quell his mirth. 'Mother England did me a big favour when she chucked me out. But it just hit me – my sweetest revenge is yet to come! Silas de Rolland has "disappeared" forever. Isabel is now the last of that Plantagenet line to bear the de Rolland name. That means all Godfrey de Rolland's future generations will bear *my* name – thanks to Rufus *Gamble*!'

Isabel lay awake looking around the cellar, the tragic trysting place where Marmaduke's mother and her lover had conceived a babe in one of their last desperate acts of love. Now this room was a place of joy where Marmaduke's son had been born.

Everything close to Isabel's heart lay within reach. Marmaduke was asleep on her shoulder and Rose Alba at her feet. Baby Rufus lay wide-eyed in the crook of her arm, his fuzzy hair shining like a little red halo.

Isabel kissed his hand and whispered, 'Thank you for coming to us, little one.'

Only one thing remained to be set right.

'Marmaduke, are you awake?'

'I am now,' he said, his voice ragged with fatigue.

'There's something I need to tell you. A sort of confession.'

Marmaduke looked at her warily, suddenly wide awake. 'Yeah? What is it?'

'I found out about the loan you needed to rebuild the house and stock Mingaletta.'

'Don't worry, love, I'll pay it all back in a year or two. Edwin says The Far Horizon Agricultural Company is safe. The new English settler who put up the loan is decent – even if a bit eccentric.' He was suddenly alert. 'Hang on a minute, what's your confession?'

'Don't be cross, Marmaduke. That eccentric new English settler and The Far Horizon Agricultural Company – well, that's me.'

'*You*?! How in Hell could you put up a loan? I haven't paid you in months.'

'Well,' she said nonchalantly, 'what do I need with a tiara? I sold it to Uncle Godfrey at a very reasonable price.'

'Hell! I'd never have allowed you to do that. Your tiara was your inheritance.'

'No. You and the children are my true inheritance.'

Marmaduke drew her into his arms, searching for words. 'Isabel, you are one gutsy English Rose...and my Currency Lass.'

Isabel drifted off to sleep smiling in the circle of her lover's arms.

Beyond the ruins of Mingaletta, from the ghostly eucalypts at the heart of Ghost Gum Valley, came the sound of kookaburras' laughter at the break of a brand new day.

AUTHOR'S NOTES

Ghost Gum Valley is a work of fiction, a marriage between imagination and history. I am indebted to the scores of historians and biographers whose work I read or who I consulted personally. The final choices and interpretations are mine and so of course are any errors of judgement. The opinions expressed by my characters about people and events in their era do not necessarily reflect my own.

All the characters involved in the contrasting worlds of the Gamble and de Rolland families are fictional although I have borrowed some names and reputations (for better and worse) from my own ancestors. Their lives straddle the complex caste system of Penal Colony society of the era, described by Governor Sir Richard Bourke as 'a most peculiar colony', in which they intercept with historical characters who played public, even notorious, roles in the snakes-and-ladders pattern of colonial life. These include Barnett Levey, Father of Australian Theatre; Alexander Green, 'The Finisher', hated public hangman; Quaker social reformer James Backhouse; artist Augustus Earle; William Holmes, an early curator of Aboriginal artefacts; Emancipist Freemasons Samuel Terry, Francis Greenway and Dr William Bland.

Samuel Terry is seen solely through the eyes of the fictional Garnet Gamble, who is obsessed with toppling his rival from his status as the wealthiest man in NSW. Samuel Terry's remarkable career as entrepreneur, philanthropist, respected family man and high-ranking Freemason, is meticulously documented in Gwynetth M. Dow's fascinating biography, *Samuel Terry: The Botany Bay Rothschild.*

Marmaduke Gamble's ambiguous social status was experienced by many free-born first generation Australians who were the offspring of wealthy Emancipists. Although often widely travelled and well educated as hybrid 'English gentlemen', their inherited 'convict strain' made many of them social outcasts among the Colony's Top Thirteen families (who no doubt would have been impressed by Isabel de Rolland's blue-blooded ancestry).

Rupert Grantham's murder and the trial scenes of his assassins

are a fictional interpretation of the real-life murder of firebrand barrister and newspaper owner Dr Robert Wardell. I acknowledge with
gratitude the detailed accounts in the *Sydney Herald* and *Australian* newspapers of the era. This rich archival material gave me the
freedom to dramatize Marmaduke's role in a trial that triggered the
threat of convict insurrection and spread wild rumours that the ringleader was manipulated by men in high places. One of these executed
youths became the convicts' hero, later idealized by Frank the Poet.

Whenever I was faced with contradictory accounts by respected
historians I chose the version best suited to the story. For example the
famous so-called 'Barrington Prologue'. Reputable theatre historians
are divided about the true identity of the author and/or actor (I have
read six candidates to date) and exactly when the first version was
performed. Marmaduke is a lover of theatre, *not* a contemporary
historian with hindsight knowledge. Marmaduke never allows strict
adherence to facts to get in the way of a good story. Therefore on
stage he quotes with authority *one* of the theories circulating about
the Prologue in order to inspire the illiterate convicts in his audience
with the idea that they too are making Australian history.

For the creation of Garnet Gamble's empire and Bloodwood Hall
I owe special thanks to Matthew Stephens, Reference Librarian of the
splendid Caroline Simpson Library and Research Collection, Historic
Houses Trust NSW. He guided me to a cornucopia of richly illustrated material, including Rudolph Ackermann's journal published
monthly in Britain from 1809–1828. *The Repository of Arts* covers
the arts, literature, commerce, manufacturing, and fashion and gives
a vivid insight into how the wealthy in the Colony kept abreast of the
Georgian era's designs and lifestyle.

My fictional world of Bloodwood, Mingaletta, Ghost Gum Valley
and Penkivil Park was drawn from colonial estates built by free
convict labour some of which have survived thanks to the dedica-
tion of private families, historical trusts and societies. I was inspired
by visits to Parramatta's Old Government House, Vaucluse House,
John Macarthur's Camden Park, architect Francis Greenway's Hyde
Park Barracks, St James's Church and South Head Lighthouse, and
Tasmania's wonderful colonial heritage. On a personal tour of Alexander Macleay's Elizabeth Bay House, Curator Scott Carlin gave me

fascinating insight into the Colonial master-servant relationship. The contrast between lavish assembly and family rooms with the assigned servant girls' cramped quarters in attics hidden behind the parapets, and the 'fish eye' lens of the servants' mirror in the dining-room, inspired dramatic scenes at Bloodwood Hall.

My addiction to the BBC series *Antiques Roadshow* was a rich source of antiques and architecture of Britain's grand country mansions, many of which found their way into Bloodwood Hall, including the 'priest hole' and the secret at the heart of Marmaduke's watch.

Ghost Gum Valley is my fictional name for a remarkable Aboriginal site I was privileged to visit but out of respect for the traditional custodians of the land I have not identified the location. Isabel's awe and respect for Aboriginal culture is a direct reflection of my own. Garnet Gamble's treatment of the Aboriginal tribes whose land he usurped is a matter of bleak historical record but does not of course reflect all landowners of the era. Marmaduke's lost opportunity to explore Aboriginal culture and to sustain the friendship with tribal men he shared as a child, are a reflection of some members of his generation. But his use of the term 'blacks', common to the period, is used by him in a non-derogatory sense. While it is important to avoid political correctness, it must be acknowledged that many attitudes and language used in an historical context are unacceptable and offensive in contemporary Australia.

I am greatly indebted to many people and research sources for their help, including:

REBECCA EDMUNDS, Assistant Curator of the Justice and Police Museum, Sydney. Her expertise and tireless enthusiasm in accessing legal, police and courtroom archival material made my work a research adventure.

FABIAN LOSCHIAVO and LINDSAY ALLEN, Archivists of State Records NSW, for guiding me to a treasure trove of historical material including convict indents, shipping records, maps and census records.

PROFESSOR JOHN PEARN, Department of Paediatrics and Child Health, Royal Children's Hospital, Brisbane, Queensland, author of many fascinating books on colonial medicine which proved invaluable in my research for both *Ghost Gum Valley* and *Ironbark*. I owe him special thanks for drawing my attention to colourful stories about duelling, the cause of transportation of a number of well-known 'Gentlemen Convicts'. Colonial duels were often rough and ready events far outside the duelling rules of the era's Code Duello.

DR ANDREA BANDHAUER, Senior Lecturer, Director of International and Comparative Literature Germanic Studies, School of Languages and Cultures, University of Sydney for her interest and advice about aspects of German language.

RABBI DR RAYMOND APPLE, AO, RFD, celebrated author on many subjects including Masonic history, was Chief Rabbi of The Great Synagogue for 32 years, Senior Rabbi to the Australian Defence Force, and Past Deputy Grand Master of the United Grand Lodge of NSW and the ACT. I am enormously grateful for his speedy e-mail responses from Israel to my questions, his Masonic contacts, insight into the influential role played by Masons in Penal Colony society and the impact of their acceptance of Emancipists into their ranks.

GRAHAME H. CUMMING, OAM, author, historian of The United Grand Lodge of NSW and ACT. My warmest thanks for steering me through complex Australian Masonic history via interviews, access to books, documents and memorabilia in the Masonic museum, his research of historical Masons. And not least helping me create credible Masonic backgrounds for the Gambles. To MICHAEL GOOT, Past Master of Lodge Mark Owen my thanks for his long support of my work and his introduction to historians of the United Grand Lodge.

JENNY MADELINE of the Society of Friends provided me with fascinating historical material, family documents concerning the beautiful Quaker Commitment ceremony, and understood my need to blend history with fiction when portraying Quaker missionary James Backhouse – renowned for his work in hospitals, prisons and the conditions of Aborigines and for establishing the first Quaker meeting houses in Tasmania (VDL) and mainland Australia.

ELSPETH BROWNE of ISAA (Independent Scholars Association of Australia) for her long-term interest and generous advice on historical questions.

The AUSTRALIAN JEWISH HISTORICAL SOCIETY's archival team for their valuable suggestions about Jewish convicts of the era from which I drew the fictional Josiah Mendoza. I am particularly grateful to the society's volunteer NOELA SYMONDS for her research help that included her ancestor Barnett Levey.

MARION MCCABE kindly gave me permission to use the extraordinary true story, told to me by her late mother, my friend Anne Goldie Cousland, that is the essence of the birth scene in *Ghost Gum Valley*.

UTA HERZOG, psychologist, for her valued expertise concerning the repercussions of childhood trauma suffered by adults. My friend SUSAN ARBOUW's sensitive professional exploration of the repressed memories of child abuse. REV. DAVID HILTON for his remarkable insight and help to JAN D., a victim who willingly shared her childhood experiences for the benefit of this book.

DAVID SCOTT MITCHELL (1836–1907), legendary bibliophile and philanthropist whose vast legacy to Australia of his collection of books, art and historical memorabilia created the Mitchell Wing in the State Library NSW. In the reading room he endowed for historians and writers, where I read biographies of Edmund Kean, Governor Sir Richard Bourke, Thomas De Quincey's *The Confessions of an Opium Eater*, it was a thrill to find his hand-written inscription DSM in the flyleaf and realize I was sharing loved books from the personal library of this great man.

My particular thanks to Librarians in the State Libraries of NSW, Victoria, Tasmania, Queensland, the National Library of Canberra and rural historical societies.

Finally I am grateful to my father, FRED PARSONS, TV and radio comedy writer, playwright and biographer of *A Man called Mo* (Roy Rene, 'Mo McCackie'). He bequeathed to me his love of Shakespeare, comedy, the treasures in his theatrical library and a fund of anecdotes about actors, playwrights, and comedians dating from the strolling players of Shakespeare's time.

AUTHOR'S ACKNOWLEDGEMENTS

My journey along the road to *Ghost Gum Valley* could not have been accomplished without generous personal and professional help from a number of very special people, not all of whom I have met face to face, but to all I offer my heartfelt thanks.

I am most fortunate in having *Ghost Gum Valley* in the hands of Simon and Schuster's exceptionally gifted Australian publishers, Managing Director LOU JOHNSON, Head of Publishing LARISSA EDWARDS and their wonderfully supportive team who work together to make publication a memorable adventure. Every author needs fine editors and I was delighted to be reunited with two who had worked with me on *Ironbark*. My heartfelt thanks to JODY LEE for her sensitive insight into my characters, their era, and not least for her buoyant sense of humour.

Equally to KATE O'DONNELL for her fresh, meticulous eye, for gently challenging perceptions and stimulating further exploration. And to Larissa Edwards for her guiding light throughout the editing journey.

To SELWA ANTHONY, my Australian agent since the development of *Ironbark,* I pay full tribute to her remarkable combination of nurturing, straight talking, wisdom and the mutual trust enjoyed by all in her 'family' of authors; to my German agent BASTIAN SCHLÜCK of the Thomas Schlück Agency, my champion in Europe.

Author BRIAN NICHOLLS, the first person to read *Ghost Gum Valley* at a late stage of development, gave it the benefit of his experience as documentary writer, producer, director and editor. His support during marathon races towards deadlines is a gift every author deserves.

My family and friends were generous and forgiving when I was so locked into the 1830s time zone of *Ghost Gum Valley* I overlooked social milestones. EADIE CASSIM, 5, and GUS CASSIM, 2, keep me grounded and revitalized. Their joyous celebration of life is a gift shared with their actor parents, my son NICHOLAS CASSIM and his beloved Niki Owen. As always I am indebted to my sister and friend Donna for her uniquely Australian sense of humour and wisdom.

I hope to acknowledge face to face the long-term encouragement of many friends but especially those separated by distance and who took 'May Day!' phone calls, including: Anne Robinson (W.A.); Bill and Penny Owen, 'Wydidya', North Star, NSW; Dr Stephen Shumach; Anne Austin; Philip Bray; Catherine Taylor, Michael and Toni Cassim, Olivia Nelson (Q'ld); Sister Mary Constable; Mick Djekovic; Lionel and Delys Dunk, Keira and Graham Lockyer, Lois Radeski (Vic); Rosalind Ihaka in Bali; John Arbouw; Peter Nicolaidis; John Allard; the family of Dr Tom Selby and 'all the Melton mob'; John and Judy Barry in Switzerland; Ulrike Bauer in Germany; Fennie Pos in Holland; the Muldoon, Nicholls and Kinney families; Jean and David Trevor; Janette Boot; Peter Dunne; Wendy Borchers; Richard and Helen Walker; Kevin and Joanne Schluter; Earle Cross, Philip Thorniley and Harry (Cop This Young Harry) Griffiths. And not least the great support given me by Philip Brady, Denise Drysdale, Richard Stubbs and Roger Lupton.

Two special friends who Always Believed, have been around 'for the long haul'. Enid Isabel Morrison, my journalist 'friend for all seasons' since our teenage copy-girl era, mastered the gentle art of keeping me buoyant during crises.

And legendary TV comedy writer and author Mike McColl Jones whose friendship and guidance I was blessed to inherit from his mentor, my father Fred Parsons.

To all the readers of *Ironbark* who took the time and trouble to write to me c/o Simon and Schuster, and warmly encouraged me to write this novel. I cannot measure all your support.

Ghost Gum Valley is for you.

ABOUT THE AUTHOR

Johanna Nicholls comes from a theatrical family. She was a journalist and magazine feature writer in Sydney, Melbourne and London. In television she worked as a researcher/writer and Head Script Editor of TV Drama at the Australian Broadcasting Corporation.

Johanna has lived in England, Italy and Greece. Her home is an 1830s convict-built sandstone cottage in Birchgrove, Sydney, where she is currently writing her third Australian historical novel and researching her fourth. Her first saga, *Ironbark*, was published by Simon and Schuster Australia in Australia and New Zealand in 2009 and 2010. *Ghost Gum Valley* was first published in 2012. Both books have been translated into German and published in Germany, Austria and Switzerland.

LOOKING FOR ANOTHER GREAT READ?

Well you've come to the right place! Before you start wondering what to read next visit our website for more great reads. We just know there's going to be something you love there.

www.simonandschuster.com.au

Visit www.simonandschuster.com.au for great book recommendations, free chapters, author interviews and competitions.

And don't forget to follow us on Facebook, Twitter and Youtube.